Co A

WITHDRAWN

Swan

Swan

Frances Mayes

Thorndike Press • Chivers Press
Waterville, Maine USA Bath, England

This Large Print edition is published by Thorndike Press, USA and by Chivers Press, England.

Published in 2002 in the U.S. by arrangement with Broadway Books, a division of the Doubleday Broadway Publishing Group, a division of Random House, Inc.

Published in 2003 in the U.K. by arrangement with Transworld Publishers Ltd.

U.S. Hardcover 0-7862-4853-X (Americana Series)
U.K. Hardcover 0-7540-1885-7 (Windsor Large Print)

The text of this Large Print edition is unabridged.
Other aspects of the book may vary from the original edition.

Set in 16 pt. Plantin by Elena Picard.

Printed in the United States on permanent paper.

British Library Cataloguing-in-Publication Data available

Library of Congress Cataloging-in-Publication Data

Mayes, Frances.
    Swan / Frances Mayes.
        p. cm.
    ISBN 0-7862-4853-X (lg. print : hc : alk. paper)
    1. Mothers — Death — Fiction. 2. Exhumation — Fiction. 3. Georgia — Fiction. 4. Large type books.
    I. Title.
PS3563.A956 S93 2002b
    813'.54—dc21   2002032100

For Ashley

Acknowledgments

During the writing of this book, I received generous help from Toni Mirosevich, Shotsy Faust, and Josephine Carson. My editor, Charlie Conrad, and the entire staff at Broadway Books are an exemplary publishing team. My luck with being a part of Broadway is due to Peter Ginsberg, my agent and friend. I would like to thank Dr. Robert Mayes Jackson and Dr. Bruce Bonger for their counsel.

I am more than grateful to Edward, my husband, for ten thousand acts of kindness, and to Ashley and Stuart, my daughter and her husband.

My last thanks begin a long way back and go to my family in the South, to my sisters Barbara Mayes Jackson and Nancy Mayes Willcoxon.

But in you, from
birth
foamed the other spring,
up the black
ray memory
you climbed to the day.

PAUL CELAN
BREATHTURN
[TRANS. BY PIERRE JORIS]

Peaches and fireworks and red ants.
Now do you know where you are.

C. D. WRIGHT
DEEPSTEP COME SHINING

Of those so close beside me, which are you?

"THE WAKING"
THEODORE ROETHKE

Swan, pop. 7,000, county seat of J. E. B. Stuart County. An attractive town with broad avenues and well-preserved late-nineteenth-century architecture, Swan is situated on a forested rise between the Altamaha and Ocmulgee rivers. Origins are unrecorded, but the area formerly was held by Creek and Seminole Indians and later was populated by Scotch-Irish and English settlers, who farmed and engaged in timber clearing for northern companies. During the early unincorporated years, it was known as Garbert, but in 1875 it was chartered as Swan by the Town Council and Mayor John Repton Mason. The name change recognized the migratory whistling swans once common in the swampy environs. The first industry was a cotton mill established by Mason, who engaged the Washington architect Ransom Gray to design an elliptical town plan inspired by Bath, England, Mr. Mason's original home. The chief crop today continues to be cotton, but local farmers have diversified and now raise pimentos, tobacco, corn, and sugarcane. Other industries include poultry ranches, a trouser factory, turpentine and fertilizer plants. Population has declined from a high of 11,000 to 7,000 due to the closing of J. R. Mason Mills. An active Chamber of Commerce is engaged in attracting new light industry to the area. The Cottonmouth Countdown is a colorful annual festival every July. The Jeff Davis Museum exhibits memorabilia from local combatants in the War Between the States. The Ogelthorpe Hotel is an outstanding example of late plantation architecture in the Georgia vernacular. Other attractions include Sassahoochie Springs, with ancient oaks surrounding a large spring believed to be bottomless.

FROM *A GUIDE TO GEORGIA PLACES*
BY ADAM LUMPKIN ADAIR

July 7, 1975

J.J. stood on the end of the dock, feeling as if the four pilings might rip loose in the current and send him rafting. But the dock held. He loved the smell of rivers. In July heat, in wavy air, in the throbbing of cicadas, in the first light on the river, he was what he would call happy. A full moon angled down between pines, casting a spiraling silver rope across the curve of the water. He watched the light, flicking through his mind for words to describe it. *Luminous, flashing.* Ordinary. The light seemed liquid, alive, annealed to the water, too changeable for any word. The river rode high after two storms. A cloud of gnats swarmed his foot, then moved as a single body over a swirl in the current. He stepped out of his faded red bathing suit — automatically he pulled on this suit every morning when he got out of bed — and climbed down the ladder into the water. His morning libations, he called this routine. In all the good months, and sometimes in the cold ones just for sheer cussedness, he dipped himself in the river early in the morning. Near the dock he could stand on the bottom, feeling the swiftness or languidness of the current, sometimes jumping as a fish nipped at the hairs on his legs and chest. He floated for a minute, listening to water whirl around his head, letting himself be carried, then turned his body sharply and swam over to the crescent of washed-sand beach his parents had cleared years ago. From there he could walk out of the river and follow a trace covered in pine needles back to the dock. He noticed a fallen sourwood sapling, tangled with muscadine vines, and leaned to pull it out of the water. As he jerked loose the roots, a wedge of earth cleaved from the bank, spilling dirt onto his wet legs. At his feet he saw something white — a bone, a stick bleached by the sun? He waded back into the river and rinsed off.

Maybe what he glimpsed was an arrowhead. J.J. had found hundreds. He turned over the earth with his foot. There — he picked it up, blew off the dirt, and washed it. Never had he found one of these. He held a perfect bone fish spear, three inches long, with exquisitely carved barbs like a cat's claws on each side. He admired the skill — the delicate hooked end of each barb would bite into flesh while the fisherman dragged in the fish. At one end he saw slight ridges where the line was tied over and over by the Creek Indian who once fished these waters. Ginger, he thought, Ginger should see this. But his sister's green eyes were light-years away. He pawed through the dirt and pulled out other roots from the bank, but found only a smashed can. What a beauty, this small spear in the palm of his hand. He took in a breath of pine air as far as he could, the air driving out of his head the familiar surge of what felt similar to hunger and thirst. Ginger was not there, so to whom could he show his treasure? He regarded it intently for himself. He had no talent for needing someone else. He shook his hair and banged the side of his head to knock the water out of his ear. Rainy night in Georgia, he mocked himself. Last train to Clarksville.

He dressed in khaki shorts, not bothering with underwear. Six-thirty and already hot, heavily hot, steamy hot, the best weather. Nothing to eat in the refrigerator but some rice and a piece of left-over venison from a week ago, when he'd brought Julianne, the new schoolteacher from

15

Osceola, out here. She'd said it was so interesting that he lived way in the woods all alone. As down-to-earth as she looked, she turned out to be afraid for her feet to touch the bottom of the river. She'd hung on to his back, her laugh verging toward a squeal, and he felt her soft thighs on his. She was hot to the touch, even under water. But then she couldn't eat venison because she thought of Bambi. She cooked the rice, which, as he remembered, had hard kernels at the center of the grain. Then she looked at his wild salad as though it were a cow pie. J.J. often went for days eating only greens he picked and fish he caught. He chewed slowly, watching her. If she was beautiful, as Liman MacCrea had promised, why did he think her skin looked so stretched tight across her face that it might split like a blown-up pork bladder? And eyes that close together made a person look downright miserly.

Then he'd rubbed his temples and looked again. A pleasant face, kind and expectant. Warm. What is she wanting? he wondered as she smiled. Then he noticed her teeth, which were ground down, like an old deer's.

"Pokeweed and lamb's-quarters? I've heard of dandelion greens before. Can you

16

eat these? That's so interesting." She pushed the fresh, pungent greens around with her fork. With the one bite she took, grit crunched between her teeth. Something she saw in his eyes appealed to her, some waiting quality. Not just a flirt or the good ol' boy he sometimes appeared to be, he was someone to solve, she told herself as she changed into her bathing suit in his room. She looked carefully at his things, comparing her own box bedroom to his, her pink chenille spread and the prints of Degas dancers on the wall, the lace curtains and view out onto an empty street, to his crammed bookcases, twenty or more ink pens, mounted fish and deer heads, his rough Indian blanket on the bed. I have no way to reach him, she thought, and would I want to? She felt suddenly tired but practiced a big smile in the mirror, lifting her thick chestnut hair off her neck. Her teeth gleamed white and even. The new red maillot certainly showed off her Scarlett O'Hara waist. "Cherry Bomb," she whispered. Cherry Bomb had been her nickname at Sparta High, when she was Homecoming queen. But that was twelve years ago. She wished she had washed the lovely greens because she was not about to eat grit.

17

J.J. thought if she said "so interesting" again, he'd drive the fork through her eyes. He poured glasses of bourbon. "Let's toast your seventh-grade class who gets to spend all that time with you." She lowered her eyes with pleasure, which shamed him. Was he becoming a God damned hermit? He wondered how he would feel with her legs wrapped around him. Lost in outer space? He knew he'd find fault with Christ Almighty. She played the flute, had a degree in music education. So what if she turned freaky in the woods? Still, he had felt a tidal wave of boredom flood through him, a craving to be alone so intense that he shuddered. Although he'd expected to be driving her home at one or two in the morning, top down, a little night music, he was burning up the road at nine-thirty.

He made a pot of coffee and heated Julianne's leftover clump of bad rice with some butter. The kitchen table was littered with chert, flint, a flat stone, and two antlers. Lately, he'd tried to teach himself flintnapping, using only tools the Indians had used. He'd ordered *A Guide to Flintworking* and driven over to a rock shop in Dannon to buy pieces big enough to work. He wanted to make a stone knife for gutting fish, but so far he'd split a lot of stones and created a pile of waste flakes and chips. One try, by accident, actually resembled a scraper.

He held up the fish spear to the sunlight at the window, admiring the fine symmetry. Balancing coffee, bowl, and notebook, the spear held lightly between his teeth, he pushed open the kitchen door with his elbow. Yellow jackets worked the scuppernongs, and bees burrowed into the rose that sprawled among the vines, his mother's yellow rose, still blooming and her gone an eon, a suicide. He did not want to think about that. She had loved the cabin as much as he did. Her rose had long since climbed from the arbor and bolted into the trees. He placed the fish spear on a piece of white paper and opened his notebook to record his find. July 7, he wrote. The early sun through the grape arbor cast mottled light onto the table. He might love the light at the cabin even more than the water, but no, they were inseparable. The emerald longleaf pines tinted the light at all hours, casting a blue aura early and late, and in full sun softened the hard edges of objects. He moved the paper into a splotch of sun. The bone looked like ivory. First he measured the length, then in light pencil carefully he started to draw.

What kind of bone, he wondered, maybe boar, maybe beaver. How long would it have taken the Indian to carve it?

He quickly went over his lines in black with his Rapidograph. Drawing, he thought, never captures the thing itself. At least mine doesn't. Maybe Leonardo da Vinci could get this right. But Leonardo never heard of the Creeks, or of the belly of the beast, south Georgia. Easy to get the *likeness*. The unlikeness is what's hard. Where the object ends and everything around it begins, that's the impossible part to negotiate. He held up the spear and turned it around. He decided to look at it under his father's microscope. He might find a speck of blood from the fish that swam away with the spear in its side. Too bad Ginger's not here, he thought. She ought to see this.

Ginger crouched in the hip bath, running the nozzle over her dusty body. Her damp field trousers and shirt heaped on the floor seemed to exude more dust. She bathed fast. This far into the Tuscan summer, the well might go dry, leaving her to cook and sponge off with bottled water until a rain came, raising the water table again. She slipped into the hot cerise dress with straps she'd bought at the Saturday market in Monte Sant'Egidio, thinking, I'm thin again. Marco will like this dress. She allowed herself to think of the pleasure of his hand on her back, guiding her across the piazza. His *Italian* hand. She loved his foreignness. She sucked in her breath. Lithe, she thought. Amazing what miracles a few months of digging and hauling can accomplish. She changed the sheets, boxed the pillows, stacked her books neatly on the bedside table. Stuffing her nightgown and robe in a drawer, she stopped in midgesture. A memory hit her of Mitchell, whom she'd married at twenty-four. Mitchell in bed, reading *Time*, all scrubbed and expectant in pressed boxers. For most of their three years together, he spent his nights waiting while Ginger out-waited him downstairs, reading or listening to music until he dozed off and she crept to bed, carefully lifting the magazine off his chest and turning out his light. What was it? she asked herself. Not him. When they dated, she'd thought she would fall into *his* love, his certainty; she would begin to feel something. She would sit, crawl, walk. She would be like everyone else with a silver pattern, a honeymoon in Nassau, a foil card of birth control pills, curtains to choose, recipes. Mitchell was so fine, she thought, patient. Anytime he walked in a door, she'd been happy to see him. What a disaster.

Her hometown, Swan, would talk for years, and still, about Ginger not coming downstairs on her wedding day. At first she'd been just late, then Jeannie Boardman sat down at the organ they'd trucked in for the day and began to play "Clair de Lune" and "Moonlight Sonata." Finally, Aunt Lily, after throwing a hissy fit outside Ginger's locked bedroom door, had served the champagne, puffs filled with crab salad, cheese straws, platters of macaroons and ladyfingers. The guests had eaten with appetites piqued by the shock of Lily announcing that Ginger was not feeling well and we should all enjoy ourselves.

Secretly, Ginger had looked down on the garden through the veil of curtains at all of them, whispering and laughing. The ice swan centerpiece with rose petals frozen inside, a local tradition, melted and lurched against the side of the punch bowl. She wished she could touch her tongue to its cold beak. She'd wanted to be radiant, a laughing bride stepping out of her grandfather's house into a bright future. She'd wanted to climb onto the roof and fly down on them. Wanted this not to be happening. She wanted her mother undead, her father restored to himself. She wanted Mitchell not to feel misery and humiliation. She could not go. She could not *have*. It had not been a decision but a state of being.

Later, J.J. had reported that their cook, Tessie, washing glasses in the kitchen, hummed "I Come to the Garden Alone" to herself as a way to keep calm but every few minutes muttered, "Those chillin, those chillin." Tessie had worked for

Catherine and Wills Mason ever since Ginger was a baby, then for Lily ever since the children moved to the House. When J.J. had made a foray into the kitchen for a shot of bourbon, he'd heard her low singing — *and he walks with me and he talks with me and he tells me I am his own* — as she held up each glass to the window, checking for lip prints. The lowering afternoon sun reflected bright rainbow circles onto her black uniform and her dark face.

"Hail, Tessie," J.J. had toasted her. "Another memorable afternoon at the Mason patch." He'd left his dinner jacket somewhere and had pulled open his collar. She watched him pour the shot of bourbon straight down his throat, just like his daddy used to after their mama died. The corners of her lips pulled down and she turned on the hot water full force.

Mitchell and his parents had secluded themselves in the living room, where his mother quietly cursed the day he'd ever brought Ginger into their home, and didn't he know Pattie Martin, who'd always been crazy about him, would not have pulled a stunt like this in a million years?

Caroline Culpepper, Ginger's maid of honor, had talked softly at the door, but Ginger had only said, "I'm sorry, Caroline, but you might as well go on home." Not even J.J. could get Ginger to unlock her door until the last guests drove away. When she did, her dress lay in a jumble on the floor, and the satin shoes, akimbo in different corners of the room, evidently had been tossed at the wall. She looked splotched and ugly sitting on the floor with her knees drawn up. She'd gotten only as far as putting on her underwear and the garter that was supposed to have been tossed to the groomsmen. She stretched out her leg and ripped off the puckered blue elastic. J.J. just stood in the doorway, shaking his head. "Well, now you've done it," he said.

He barely could hear her. "I woke up this morning from a dream that Mother had come to the door. I was getting ready to go out, spraying perfume in my hair. And she looked at me with a smile and said *you are pathetic*. My will just keeps withering, J.J." Then she'd cried, wouldn't speak until the next day. He'd brought her a robe and sat with her, not even having to ask anything else.

Three days later she and Mitchell were married in the garden, where the wicker baskets of flowers had drooped. His parents had refused to come, then refused to speak to her for seven months, his mother having said to Mitchell that he would rue the day he married her. Oh, wasn't she right? Ginger had worn a pale suit and J.J., standing with his arms crossed, had stared at the run in her stocking, alert to the possibility that she would bolt. But she was as pallid as the ivory linen she wore, and she swayed as if she were just up after a spell of malaria. J.J. told her later that she looked like a dog staring in a mirror without seeing the reflected dog.

Lily and Tessie had warmed up the limp leftover cheese straws to crisp them, and the dozen guests they'd called back wouldn't have missed it for the world. J.J., who gave her away, had felt that she was not really going anywhere.

"Sugar, you just got a case of jitters. Everyone gets them, you just got them *bad*," the guests repeated as the cake was cut. Mitchell would have been raving mad if he were anyone else. Instead, he stayed close, his arm always protectively around her.

Ginger heard Marco's car door slam. She had not thought of Mitchell in weeks. She wished now that she'd been able, even once, to make up their bed with the pleasure of anticipation. Now, four years since she'd seen him, and still the idea of his body, his perfect body, made her shoulders tense and rise.

From the upstairs window she saw Marco kick the car door closed because his hands were full. He never arrived empty-handed. Striding up the path to the house — there was something of the faun or satyr about him — he was smiling. Ginger smiled to think of him with hairy haunch and goat feet. She loved his black, black curls and tanned skin. ("Is he olive-com-plected?" Aunt Lily had asked her, trying to be tactful.) Ginger had never known anyone whose natural facial expression was a smile. He must have been born laughing.

The candle she placed on the bedside table, meant to be lighted before a saint, would burn quickly. She smoothed the bed and scattered across the pillows wild mint and yellow sunflower petals from the basket she'd filled earlier. A tremor of joy ran through her. Like a prisoner, she ex-plained to herself, who digs a tunnel with a spoon and finally breaks out in the woods — I'm free, I will be happy. While most women would look on the fulfillment of sex as a deep pleasure, her first emotion was pride, as though she'd broken the rec-ord for the hundred-yard dash, or accomplished a high pole vault. Her bare soles on the cool tiles made her want to dance.

Climbing down the ladder stairs to the kitchen, she saw the terrace doors opened to the early evening air and the slope downhill to the river Nesse. What they call a river in Italy hardly qualified as a stream back home in Georgia, but she loved the chuckle of water in the night. She'd rented the farmhouse because it faced the Nesse. All winter she'd slept with the window cracked just to hear the sibilant slide of cascades pouring over rocks, the sweet gurgle where water surged over a dam built by children in summer. Now the flow had slowed to a faint trickle.

Marco, handing her yellow and apricot roses from his mother's garden, embraced her at the same time. "You've transformed! Your neck doesn't have any more rings of dirt." Her eyebrows flew up, two circumflexes, two bent wings. He touched her face with his palm: she felt as smooth as a holy-water font. He thought she sometimes hid behind her cameo-perfect face, but tonight, no, she looked vibrantly *here*. His sister-in-law criticized Ginger's nose — bony, she said — but Marco thought it must be like an English queen's nose. His lips brushed her ear, her raucous hair — a

28

blaze he'd warm himself by anytime.

She felt his compact, muscular body as a jolt (the prisoner, now up and running for the woods), breathed in his soapy shaving scents. He smelled good always; even after hours of work in the sun he smelled horsey, like wet earth and oats. After making love, his underarms let out an acidic, lair odor. What a good animal, she thought, submitting to his arms. Good, she thought. I didn't shy away.

He held a box up, almost out of reach. "Don't open! This is for later."

She grabbed and shook the box.

"No! Give it back. You're terrible!" He took the box inside.

Ginger clipped sprigs of rosemary. "We're having roast chicken with potatoes — surprise, surprise!" Ginger had a limited interest in cooking, though she loved to eat. Roast chicken with herbs was her idea of triumph in the kitchen.

"I could smell it from the car." On the table, a millstone set on top of a thick stone column, she crisscrossed two grape-vine cuttings and placed the plates and glasses. His feet up on the low terrace wall, Marco sipped the Campari she brought him and watched the swallows dip and glide, devouring, he knew, thousands of bugs. *"Rondini,"* he told her, "those birds — swallows. We watch for them because they are graceful. They fly high when it is dry, low after rain." He only seemed to teach her nouns.

He watched Ginger against the darkening cobalt sky, where a mellow moon like a worn gold watch hung suspended over the mountains. As she moved back and forth from the kitchen to the table, he observed that she had an odd quality of just having landed, something like an annunciation angel, with coral robes barely settling as she pointed her lily toward the Virgin Mary. Other American women he'd met were solid and demanding; they knew what they wanted. Ginger was slippery. She seemed usually vivid at times, like now, whistling "There's No Business Like Show Business." He loved her legs, which he considered wholly American. (The one thing that irritated Ginger about Marco was his habit of stamping certain things generically American.) When he'd studied in Virginia for two years, he'd found the southerners exotic. Ginger had joined his Etruscan research group as an intern after her first year and a half of graduate work at Georgia, while she decided whether or not to continue. Some fear he didn't understand seized her when she contemplated writing a dissertation. To him she seemed a born archaeologist, took in at a glance what other associates hardly saw after it was pointed out to them.

As they excavated the site side by side all day, he had his eyes on her — squatting in the dust as she brushed off an artifact, stepping over the rivulets that sprang from underground springs and ruined their work. American, he thought. It's because she's foreign that she's familiar and unfamiliar — sometimes far from him, with her lower lip bitten and her chin angled up as if she were viewing him from the long end of a telescope. He loved her, but thinking of building a life together confused him. Maybe she was too different from his old girlfriends, from Lucia and Cinzia, his brothers' wives, who moved into Bella Bella, his parents' house, without a murmur and fell into the family as though they'd always been there. He could not see Ginger moving into the other side of the top floor — not that he would want that himself — blending into the rhythm that everyone in the house seemed to find. If Lucia shopped, Cinzia shelled the peas and did the laundry, while his mother presided over the kitchen. They all told the two children what to do, usually contradicting each other, so the children learned to choose among the instructions, essentially doing as they pleased.

As the only unmarried son, he was exempt from all operations of the house, though he helped his father in the vegetable garden more than his brothers did. The house, alive with smells of ironing and stewing, the boys' sweaty hair, an array of boots in the cantina, various colognes and cleansers — the collective odor of family — would it admit the stoic posture, the diffident, aloof Miss America? He summoned a picture of Ginger standing in a doorway having to ask how she could help. No, that would not ever be the scene. They would have their own house, like this one, in the country, and make trips once a year to the States, where her family operated like the labyrinthine, plotless Faulkner novels, and trees grew out of dank swamps. When Cinzia watched TV on the divan, her head sometimes lobbed onto his mother's shoulder. He'd seen Ginger step back from contact, but when the two *baci* on the cheek were unavoidable, she smiled afterward, touching her fingertips to her face.

After the chicken, Ginger brought out the salad. He stretched his arms and

pounded his chest with his fists. *"Lu*
luna," he shouted. "Moon, moon." :
hurry, he remembered, let it play. Let
loop and rewind and play again.

Tonight they were celebrating th
team's find — an intact Etruscan six-st
stone staircase with a mythological he;
carved into the base. Gaetano, a classma
of Marco's and a palynologist, had drive
up in the afternoon from his work site ;
Pompeii to consult with him on the fair
imprints of plants they'd also discovered
He brought Marco vials containing scent
he had re-created from remains he'd dis
covered in a recently unearthed apothecary
shop.

Ginger and Marco lingered at the table
She brought out a bowl of the season's las
cherries and a paisley bedspread so the}
could lie down and look as long at the star
as they wanted. "See that constellation.
She pointed. "That's one of Hannibal's el
ephants coming over the Alps."

"That, *amore,* is Orion." He dangled ;
cherry above her lips and she snapped at it.

"And that — you see up there to the lef
the Model T Ford? And there — the tilt-a
whirl."

"What is tilt-a-whirl?"

"A tilt-a-whirl you ride at a carnival. I

slings you round and round." He doesn't even know what a tilt-a-whirl is, she thought, and I'm so glad for all he doesn't know. The vacant eyes of her father flashed through her. She could see the horizon in those eyes.

"Are you as good at anything else as you are at astronomy?" Marco rolled on his side and kissed her arm. She threw her other arm around him and moved closer. "Oh, wait a minute." He ran into the house and returned with the box. "Gaetano brought these when he drove up from Pompeii this afternoon. You'd just left — too bad."

He unwrapped tissue paper from around a vial, which she recognized as the cloudy aqua blue of ancient glass. She'd heard that Gaetano had found a cache of dried unguents, oils, and perfumes last year. He'd spent months analyzing and reproducing them. Marco unwrapped two more. "Let's go upstairs."

Behind her on the ladder stairs, he ran his hand up her leg, his fingers brushing the edge of her panties. She lighted the candle and pulled off her dress in one motion. He had no way of knowing what that action meant to her, but caught a flash of her pleasure. As Marco slowly unbuttoned

his shirt, she thrust her arms under his arms, her head against his chest. "Let me hear your heart."

"Let me *show* you my heart." They lay crossways on the bed, which dipped in the middle where light from the moon pooled. Marco reached over for one of the vials and twisted the wax-sealed stopper. He held the opening to her nose. She inhaled the fresh scent of lemon with a smoky, burned edge behind the fragrance. He poured the gold oil into his palm. "Wait for me," he said. He slid down and rubbed his hands together. She closed her eyes, her arms folded behind her head, and felt his hands around her foot, rubbing in the warmed oil. He pushed against each toe, pressed the ball and heel, and gently worked his palm against her instep. The other foot. Her feet stung with pleasure. She looked at Marco at the side of the bed, intent, as she sometimes saw him concentrating at work, but his body had a sheen of silver outline from the candle, and his mouth was parted like that of a small boy sleeping. *Mitchell, we never,* flitted across her mind.

He opened the second wax seal and waved the vial under her nose. She touched her finger to the mouth of the vial and he tipped it. "Grass and cloves." They were kissing deeply, but he moved away, straddled her legs, and began lightly to brush the ancient scent onto her breasts, circling his hand over her nipples, then in larger concentric motions. The oil sent an electrical charge into her blood. Slowly, even the part of her she always held in reserve ignited. *So this is what they mean.* In the last instant of unyielding, she thought fleetingly, *there must be life after death.* She moistened her hands on her breasts and reached down to caress him. "I can't take much more," he said.

Ginger pushed him over on his back, opened the smaller third vial, and emptied the contents on his chest, quickly spreading the oil. The fecund, grapy heart of the wild iris steeped into her hands, running along his sides and down his body. *Water falling over rocks.* He heard the small cries that came from his throat. Startled by the new sound, he laughed, said "Bless Gaetano," wrapped his arms around her back and up through her hair, and they had their love.

July 8

Cass Deal turned his pickup into the gates of
Magnolia Cemetery. He stopped at his caretaker's shack for a cup of instant coffee. A
scorcher coming up, he thought. The magnolias over in the Confederate Corner were
heavily in bloom, sending out their sweet
stench. He hated the smell. So many of the
coffins that rolled out of the Ireland Funeral
Home hearses held a single magnolia on the
polished mahogany. Elegant, he'd been told,
but he figured it was just cheap. Sure made
cleanup easier. He poured hot water over the
acrid granules. Not many of the grand fu-
nerals anymore. Just get them in the ground
and go. People live too long these days, out-
stay their welcome. Cass, at seventy, did not
put himself into this category.

He threw his rake and bucket into the
pickup bed and drove toward the new part
of the cemetery. Funeral Friday at two. He
had a grave to dig and prepare before the

funeral home people came out to set up their tent and rows of chairs, which tended to sink into the soft earth under especially heavy mourners. He rolled slowly along the grassy lanes, hardly glancing at the granite angel in the Williams plot, the jar of yellow glads on old man Conrad's grave, and the diamondback stretched on the grave of the Adams child, who died of infantile paralysis. Collapsed lung, wasn't it? The new part of the cemetery sloped toward a swamp. Snakes often came up to warm themselves on a convenient stone. He passed the Mason plot, the only one with a fence. The iron gate long since had rusted open, and the tangled roses that Wills Mason planted for his shameful wife always drooped in the heat. A mess and Cass was not paid extra for cleaning up, even though extra work was required here. They did sometimes send their own help out to prune. Just beyond the Mason's, he spotted trash on the ground and stopped to pick it up. A smashed Dr Pepper can and a white handkerchief. Dirty, too. He threw them in his bucket and gunned the truck. He caught the flicker of ribbons from four standing wreaths. Raw red hump of dirt and Merrilee Gooding lying under it. Who'd ever think someone that pretty could up and die? They say Dr. Strickman took out a tumor the size of a football. Her blanket of red roses looked like dried blood. Just goes to show how quick it is from can to can't.

Morning sun exploded through the slash pines at the edge of his domain. Rain two days ago. The ground would give easily. He'd long ago lost count of the number of graves he'd dug, but he knew to the minute how long it used to take before he got the Bobcat a few years back — five hours and ten minutes steady unless he encountered a limestone shelf. That was trouble. The Bobcat saved his back. Quicker now. Rake, level, drive the backhoe to the site, make sure the dirt lands in a neat clump. Then he'd get Aldo out to pour the cement liner. He knew everything about his job after forty years at it. That's what he liked about the dead, he often said; you always know what to expect from them. Once he found two skeletons and some beads and broken pots about four feet under. A professor from the college over in Douglas had taken them away and no one ever heard any more about them. Creek Indians, he'd told Cass. He'd hit water sometimes. The Ireland people just hoped the bereaved didn't see the coffin float for a second before the dearly beloved settled into the ground.

Lily Mason aimed rather than drove her Lincoln out Lemon Street toward Magnolia Cemetery around nine o'clock. After Tessie had called and said she'd be late to work on account of a sick neighbor, Lily had bathed, dressed, and then put together her own breakfast of black tea and two chocolate cookies, a vice she permitted herself, along with a cordial in the afternoon before her nap and a strong gin martini before supper. Gin, she thought, tasted pure and clean, the way water ought to taste and didn't. By quarter of nine, she had fed CoCo, her green parrot, and wandered in her garden among the larkspur, lemon lilies, invasive verbena, and rusty camellia bushes. She needed to tend to the irises on the slope down to the pond. The spent flowers had dried to ash blue on their muscular stems. CoCo squawked at her from his wicker cage. He had spent his early birdhood in a machinist's shop, so instead of words he made car sounds, a metallic clattering and shrieking that amused Lily but no one else. The jessamine, she saw without any intention to do anything about it, tangled into the spirea's drooping arcs of white blooms. This summer everything wants to escape its boundaries, she thought. Bridal bouquet, they called spirea, but no bride ever carried it down the aisle — too common. If she'd ever been a bride, she would have carried blue delphiniums, white roses, and trailing ivy. Ginger's bouquet — but she didn't remember. It must have been half-dead by the time she stood right here clutching it in the garden.

Lily snapped off two flowers to take out to her parents' graves, imagining that she could show them to her mother as she used to. "Look at the white star inside this morning glory. Isn't that something?" she might say, or "That daylily — it looks freshly dipped in yellow paint." But she was not fool enough to speak to them aloud. She slipped her clippers into the glove compartment and laid a newspaper on the back seat. Her closest friend, Eleanor, was meeting her at Magnolia Cemetery to pick roses, then they were going to the Three Sisters Café for coffee and a chat.

Eleanor laid a bunch of purple foxgloves across her husband's name carved in north Georgia granite, Holt Ames Whitefield. Four years ago, after his death, she'd fallen into the habit of visiting at his graveside every morning except Thursday, her beauty parlor day. She'd had a marble bench erected and she sat there a few minutes, sometimes reading to herself a daily meditation from *The Upper Room*, sometimes just remembering the trips they took to Haiti, Jamaica, California, and Alaska. Those frozen aqua waters and the ship cracking through ice, the sudden looming icebergs against a pure blue sky — she couldn't help but think death must feel like that. It was still impossible to think Holt — Holt! — would not return. Sometimes when she took in the mail, she thumbed through the junk, half expecting a letter from him. The sudden red arterial hemorrhage from his throat after the surgery and he was gone. "His time was up," Father Tyson had said, a remark that caused Eleanor to cut the contents of her donation envelope in half. She and Lily agreed on the subject of Father Tyson. Eleanor smiled to remember her friend's dismissal of him as "neither useful nor ornamental." But poor Holt. Who's to say his time was up? When she was a fresh widow, she used to curl into the fetal position every morning when she woke to realize that he was not there. Finally, after four years, the sharp edge of pain subsided. Now she was at ease in the mornings and liked to look downhill toward the cypress trees standing in black water and the white floating hyacinths.

She was irritated to hear Cass Deal's motor and to see his red machine charging at a grave site in the distance, lifting and dumping forkfuls of earth. Where is Lily? she wondered. She said aloud a few lines from a poem Holt liked — he had been the high school English teacher and she had been the math teacher — remembering as she said them that she used to be annoyed when he shifted to his oration voice and quoted verse.

> *Some say the world will end in fire,*
> *Some say in ice.*
> *From what I've tasted of desire*
> *I hold with those . . .*

She could not remember the rest. Would desire lead one to favor fire or ice? She wasn't sure; Holt would have to finish it for himself. Not that for an instant she thought she was communing with him. Dead is dead. Father Tyson can hold forth all day and dead is still dead. She just liked seeing his name and dates so solidly present. 1906–1971. *Q.E.D.*: Existence proven for as long as granite lasts.

She shaded her eyes and spotted Lily's car speeding around the curve before the cemetery gate. Good. Plenty of time. Eleanor's bridge group was coming to her house for lunch. Hattie at this moment must be stewing the hen for the chicken salad, she thought, and taking out the starched pink linen place mats she brought back from the Jamaica trip. The bridge club met every Tuesday for lunch and a few rubbers. Over the years two tables had dwindled to one, and, frankly, Eleanor was not sure how much longer she would be willing to listen to her friends discuss their phobias and aches. Lily had become exasperated and quit three years ago. Now the others enjoyed being able to win. Lily had remembered every bid, every card, and was prone to trump brilliantly. When partnered with Eleanor, no one else had had a chance.

Eleanor intended to fill her house with bunches of the lovely Lady Godiva roses that just went to waste clambering all over the fence of the Mason plot, a double waste, really, those scented perfume clouds — blackberry, melon, lime water — floating over the dead. They flourished almost all May and June, and even now into July, a profusion of rambling pink double-bloomers, their canes twisting between the iron fence spikes. Of course by August, everything gave up and wilted. She and Lily had gathered them before, although Lily never wanted to take any home. Eleanor already envisioned them on her sideboard in the silver pitcher. She should have left Hattie a note to polish it.

She slung open the car door, making sure it caught and would not slam back on her ankle. She felt as strong as she had at sixty-five, though less agile since the left hip replacement she'd had over in Tipton two years ago. They'd installed a new metal hip to replace the bone that crumpled as she jumped over a ditch to pick black-eyed Susans. She'd had to sit in the ditch until a passing tobacco farmer saw her, hauled her out, and took her all the way to the hospital. A nice man, he was. After she'd recovered, she sent Holt, Junior out to his house with several jars of her peach pickles and plum chutney.

Eleanor drove over to the Mason graves just as Lily swung the cream puff, as her nephew J.J. called it, inside the gate. Eleanor watched her run over the edge of Annie Ruth Steepleheart's grave. Lily swerved and lurched back onto the path toward the Mason plot. Eleanor closed her eyes. Lily was such a wild card in the deck.

With both feet on the ground, Eleanor hoisted herself out of the car and felt inside her bag for the scissors.

"Am I late?" Lily slammed her door. She pecked the air near Eleanor's cheek. She'd known her all her life. Eleanor, a few years older, had taken Lily in when she was a new teacher at the mill school, but all her good advice came to nothing: Lily hated teaching. After Lily's daddy, Big Jim, died, she resigned and devoted herself to gardening. She and Eleanor were the founding members of the Robert E. Lee Garden Club and had talked on the phone and swapped a cutting, recipe, or magazine article almost every day since. As Lily saw Eleanor flicking open her clippers and rolling up her sleeves, she flashed on her, radiant and capable, presiding over a long table at Christmas dinner when Holt, Junior was a baby, at the beginning of their close friendship.

"No more than usual. How are you, sugar?" She saw that Lily had hennaed her own hair again. The orangy cast of the dye shone like cheap mahogany furniture. Otherwise, Lily's coiled chignon pinned high looked the way it had at fifteen when they'd run into each other at club dances at Carrie's Island and boys swarmed around Eleanor. Eleanor had glimpsed Big Jim holding forth at a table where Lily bit her lip and sipped lemonade and her mother, Florence, looked supremely bored. Lily would have been a fine wife for someone, Eleanor thought loyally, if she hadn't been overshadowed by her parents when she was young. She had remained a daughter rather than making that necessary transition into her own woman. Later, she was raising Ginger and J.J., for which, surely, she would have stars in her crown.

They scanned the voluptuous roses hanging in bunches like ready-made bouquets. "I like that blouse. Is it new?" Lily was prone to wear old clothes, so anytime she appeared in something decent Eleanor praised it. "Yellow is a good color for you."

"Ginger sent it for my birthday last year." Lily muzzled her nose into a full bloom. "If Paris could get that scent into a bottle, women would pay any price." She would not, of course. A dusting of talcum was fine for her. She snipped stems and handed an armful of roses to Eleanor, who took them to the car. As Lily clipped, something caught her eye, a quick glimmer

49

— a blue jay wing? She leaned down and squinted. Through the cascades of bloom, she glimpsed a pile of clay on the other side of the fence near the graves. What on earth? She pushed through the gate and stopped.

Immediately, she reeled away, suddenly unable to see. She looked up at the sky and tried to focus. The early morning buffed blue was turning to the bleached midday paleness, which would stay that way until twilight, when farm dust turned the lower horizon a streaked rose and orange. Harmon Dunn, the druggist, said he saw blue and gold confetti when his retina detached; maybe hers had come undone. She blinked several times, then opened her eyes slowly and turned back to the sight she always would see incised on her eyeballs. A surge of rejection pushed through her. "Eleanor," she managed to say, but Eleanor was spreading roses on the back seat of her car. Blue dress, black hair. "No," she whispered. A gash in the ground, stone smashed, bronze coffin turned upside down. Catherine. Preserved, darker but preserved, lying on the side of her own grave.

Then Eleanor was beside her. "My stars above!" Eleanor heard her own burble as though her throat were filled with water, then she tried to regain herself so she'd know she had not simply flipped, as her older sister, Rebecca, had when she walked out of the dentist's office and had no idea where she was. Rebecca ended up in a crib in a rest home in Crossaway, curled up like a baby. Eleanor had to faint or scream, but she only stood steadily, taking in the inconceivable sight of Catherine Mason, dead and buried for years, tumped out of her grave.

Lily grabbed the gate. No sound came from her except for a stopped moan, as though she'd had her breath knocked out. A memory rushed through her. *How do you like to go up in the swing, up in the sky so blue? I'm soaring through the pecan tree, my hands grasping the ropes, feet out straight, but my mother pushes my swing too high, I'm falling through the air. Falling and falling.* She grabbed Eleanor's arm. From the swamp, a breeze blew up, just enough to scatter rose petals across the graves of the other Masons. A bank of them had gathered under Catherine's feet.

Eleanor's brain began to tick. She must help Lily. Oh Lord, Catherine's feet, her feet, her bare feet splayed out with red polish still on the toes. Eleanor remembered Alan Ireland handing back Holt's polished wing tips when she took in his burial suit. "We won't be needing shoes," he'd said dryly. Catherine lay perfectly composed, as she had in the coffin, her hands crossed over her stomach. Rigid as stone, Eleanor expected. The light caught Catherine's hair and it still shone. But her skin had turned leathery, almost gold, like the worn-out suede jacket in the back of her closet. Holt. He, too, would still be recognizable, thanks to all the chemicals the Ireland boy pumped into him. Eleanor would not want to be seen like that.

"Oh no, Eleanor, look, Daddy's . . ." Lily gestured to the other side of the plot. Eleanor took in at a glance Big Jim Mason's grave sloshed with black paint. She put her arm around Lily and firmly steered her to the car.

Cass admired the precision of the hole he'd dug. He sat down for a smoke before he rode back to the shack. He saw the two ladies clipping roses over in the Mason grounds, then a few seconds later watched them both get in Eleanor's car, leaving Lily's Lincoln blocking a crossroad. Eleanor was about the only regular morning visitor. Most of the locals came on Sundays, if at all. That old maid Lily Mason shouldn't just leave her car wherever she pleased. But that's the Masons for you, he thought. He watched Eleanor tear up the path as she pressed the accelerator too quickly and spun gravel behind her. The pair of them, Cass thought. One of them a speed demon; the other old biddy will uproot a telephone pole one of these days — her son ought to stop her from driving. Matter of time. But that Holt, Junior wore his pants hiked up around his waist. Pansy, some said. It would be a cold day in hell before he could stop his mama from doing anything she pleased.

Lily feared for her heart, which gonged against her chest. She slumped over, her face in her hands. Eleanor scratched off, tossing the roses she still held to the floor.

"Stop, Eleanor, I'm going to throw up." Lily opened the door and leaned out as her stomach wrenched. When she pulled the door shut, she closed it on the tip of her little finger. Eleanor leaned over, shoved down the handle, and jerked Lily's arm inside. The flattened fingertip and pushed-in nail turned purple. Lily began to whimper. Eleanor drove the entire mile into town — swerved once to avoid a cat and almost hit a child on a bicycle — before she thought of what she should do.

Tessie came running out of the House when she saw Eleanor leading Lily from the car. The bright yellow blouse was spotted with blood. "We'll talk in a minute, Tessie. Let's get her into her room."

Eleanor turned back the bed. Tessie got a bag of ice to put on Lily's finger. "You just lie down," Eleanor said. "I'll go to the sheriff's office. Don't get up, now. You stay right here. I'll ask Tessie to make you a soothing cup of tea. Where's J.J.?"

"J.J.'s off fishing. Eleanor, how can we bear this?"

"They'll catch the animal who did it and put him *under* the jail. I'm going to call Deanie Robart and have him come out and look at that finger, too. And I'll find J.J. You just rest." Eleanor picked up the phone beside Lily's bed and dialed the doctor. Deanie himself answered and promised to stop by Lily's before noon.

"I'm so sorry, Eleanor, but I'm glad you were with me. You know that my feelings about Catherine are mixed-up. I can't help that, but even so, she didn't deserve this." Lily felt about to throw up again.

"No. No one deserves this." Eleanor well knew that Lily always had had an unac-

knowledged jealousy of monumental pro-
portions toward her sister-in-law. Lily's
younger brother, Wills, had seemed to shift
all his devotion to Catherine when he married her. Then when he came home exhausted from war, he treated Lily in a fond
but distracted way. Since Lily never married, her brother's desertion had wounded
her. After the war, he never quite seemed
to hear what she said.

As soon as Sheriff Ralph Hunnicutt
helped Eleanor out to her car, he took the
steps back up to his office three at a time,
flipped fast through his Rolodex, and dialed. A secretary answered, "Ireland Funeral Home."

"Let me have Alan, please, ma'am."

"He's counseling right now," she answered. "May I have him call you?"

Counseling, my ass, Ralph thought. He's
showing some sad sucker around that
gloomy room of coffins, advising them to
buy the one with the hand-stitched satin
lining. "Tell him it's an emergency. This is
Sheriff Hunnicutt and he'll need to meet
me right fast at the cemetery. He'll see my
car at the Mason plot in the old section.
I'm leaving right now." With the phone
wedged between his ear and shoulder, he

buckled on his gun while he talked. He'd only been the county sheriff for three months and he hadn't faced anything other than car wrecks and fistfights.

"Well, Sheriff, what is this in regards to? He's very busy with a client just now."

"Just tell him to come. I'll talk to him there." He grabbed his notebook.

At the entrance to Magnolia, he stopped where Cass Deal was raking pine needles. He looked like a child's stick figure drawing. "How ya doing, Cass? I got a pretty strange visit from Eleanor Whitefield. Have you noticed anything odd this morning?"

"No, what's her gripe?"

"Get in." He repeated what Eleanor had told him.

"That's crazy. She's losing her marbles — you should have seen her drive out here. And look — the two of them left Lily's car just parked haphazardly."

"She always drove like a bat. You know she's sharp as a razorback hog."

Ralph parked behind Lily's car. Everything was exactly as Eleanor had described.

They stood silently, staring. Ralph's ears rang. He thought something had gone wrong with his hearing. He wiped his neck with his handkerchief. Finally, Cass said, "Holy, holy shit. Jesus H. Christ, if this isn't the damndest . . ." He faltered and grabbed onto Ralph's sleeve while the plain of the flat earth tilted upward then steadied. "Sumabitch. Those ladies came upon this."

The two men stood still until Ralph forced himself forward. *He* would have to handle this, he realized. A few bees plied the roses and one buzzed around the face of Catherine Mason. Ralph was not close enough to her to shoo it away but waved his hand in the air anyway. "Have you seen anything, Cass — that is, anything else . . ." He gestured toward the body on the ground. He touched the dry black paint on Big Jim's grave. "Any cars stopping, any people at all?" Any vampires, he wanted to say, but he couldn't bring himself to joke. Cass shook his head no. "That dirt has been rained on," Ralph went on, "and look here, the side of her dress is muddy. She's been lying here at least since that thunderstorm we had two days ago."

"Well, I can't check every damn grave every day."

Evidently, Mrs. Wills Mason had been out in the rain. Ralph looked at her hands and throat for jewelry; there was none.

"The only motive I can imagine is grave robbing. Do people get buried with their rings?"

Cass thought not, though come to think of it, he hadn't seen an actual dead person in years, just their sealed coffins.

Her mouth was firmly shut, a faint smile on her lips. Odd, given the way she died. Ralph figured the grave robbers hadn't looked for gold in her tight mouth. Her tongue — was it still shaped around her last word, whatever that was? He stepped nearer. Holy Christ. His stomach flipped as he noticed the fringe of her eyelashes in the sunken sockets. He'd seen worse in Vietnam but this was different. He'd heard that nails keep growing after death but hers were still neat ovals on her dried-up fingers.

The men saw the Ireland limousine approaching and stepped out to warn Alan what he was about to see.

Even he, who handled corpses all the time, lunged backward, then forward, with his arms out as though balancing on a floating log. Crazily, he started to laugh. Ralph noticed that his eyes were odder than Catherine's, like a partially submerged hippo's looking out of the murk. His black suit hung on him as though from a hook. Why is it that morticians look the part? Ralph himself, or so he imagined, could be a lawyer or manager. He had planned to study pharmacology at Georgia State but instead had gone into the army at nineteen, after a year of bad grades from too much partying. His grandfather was sheriff for thirty years, and when he died, the torch passed to Ralph, home after ten years in the army and already sick of working the counter at Walgreen's. He'd been easily elected last year, with an uppity black candidate as his opponent.

"Have you notified the GBI, or are you planning on investigating this yourself?" Alan asked.

Ralph hadn't thought of calling the state Bureau of Investigation yet but quickly covered himself. "Cass, you stay here until I can get back with a guard. I'm going in town to call this in right now. Alan, would you see if you can come up with a tarp to cover her up tonight? I guess we better not touch anything until I get in touch with the GBI fellows." He was sorry he'd said "guess"; he should be more decisive. "I'll call the paper, too. They can send out a photographer for my records."

Cass leaned against a tall headstone in

the plot opposite the Masons. What was he supposed to do if the crazy came back to view his handiwork? The stone cast no shade but felt cool against his back. He was trying to think. What day was it? It was Friday — the rain came on Saturday. He'd arrived in the morning and thought that the Bobcat was not parked exactly in the usual place but closer to the shed wall. He remembered having to sidle to it, but he'd assumed he'd just parked funny. The key was in the ignition, where he always left it. He should have told Ralph but he didn't want any blame for this. I'll remember later, he thought, if I have to.

Hattie heard Eleanor pull into the driveway, then softly thud into the back wall of the garage. She came in looking wild-eyed, her hair sticking up. "What on earth's the matter, Miz Eleanor? Have you done been in an accident?" That she hadn't so far, Hattie considered a miracle. She and Miss Lily both drove like maniacs. Eleanor walked straight through the kitchen and cranked up the living room and dining room air conditioners. Hattie already had set up the card table. Eleanor thought she never would calm down again or ever shake the image of Catherine from her head. Worse, she felt a new kind of horror over Holt's death. Everybody died, death is a part of life, of course, but she felt hot rage at the thought of how we're squished out like bugs even after — she knew she was being irrational — all the times we've washed our hair, tended to the insurance, wiped grease off the counters, taken in the paper. Daily life was what she passionately loved. It's so easily assumed while we're living it — running downtown when shrimp come in from the coast, taking up a hem, dreaming of floating in a warm pond. She saw the bright blood from Holt's mouth, spurting red on white tile. She was barking mad. She ran her finger over her lower lip, the gesture that calmed her.

"Hattie, pour us a cup of coffee, please, and sit down. I have something to tell you."

Hattie's son, Scott, was the hunting companion of Catherine's son, J.J. Because Scott was black, no one ever would say simply that he and J. J. Mason were friends. J.J. was peculiar, everyone knew. He had few friends of any color, and if seen with any woman, she was bound to be someone beneath him. Since J.J. was notoriously hard to find, Eleanor had told the sheriff that Hattie might know if the two men were fishing. Hattie had shown her a Polaroid last week of J.J. holding up a rockfish he caught — a thirty-five-pound monster, prehistoric-looking with barnacles around its mouth. J.J. had one foot up on a stump. His glistening chest, Eleanor thought, looked barbarian in the sun, and although he was not actually smiling, he had a pleased look. He wore his hair combed straight back, black as a burnt match, just like Catherine's. Just like Catherine's still looked. Eleanor wondered how he could be all that pleased when he had not amounted to much. With all his gifts of superb intelligence and money, all he did was roam around the woods, an outcast. And charm — he could turn the charm off or on. She'd seen him many times looking stormy. Lily had plenty to put up with.

The kitchen table sat under a row of uncurtained, small-paned windows. The air-conditioning tamed the sun pouring through the thin limbs of the mimosa. Eleanor sat down and concentrated on the face-sized blue hydrangeas pushing against the glass. She treated them with sulfur every year to get them to bloom the exact shade her own mother's always had; otherwise, they reverted to the common pink. As she concentrated on Catherine, her vision blurred with tears. It seemed that infant faces, deprived of oxygen, drifted against the glass. She wondered if she should check on Lily. No, later, when Lily — and I — calm down. Lily, she supposed, will have to tell her brother, Wills. Heaven knows what she'll say.

Hattie looked at her expectantly. Eleanor recounted her morning with Lily. "A shame and a disgrace," Eleanor concluded, "Catherine Mason lying out in the rain."

Hattie said, "Lord, Lord," and shook her head. She hadn't talked to Scott since Sunday dinner. As far as she knew, he was out at the grocery store he managed for J.J.

When Eleanor had told her everything, she suddenly remembered the roses. "Hattie, would you mind getting those roses? I think they slid to the floor of my car. I'm too pooped."

"You mean you still intending to have them ladies over? After what you've been through?"

"Yes, I might as well. I might need some company." It never occurred to Eleanor that she could cancel the bridge club, that she could lie flat on her big bed with a washcloth over her eyes until she calmed down.

"Every time you look toward them roses it's going to all come rushing back on you."

"Well, it's a pity for them to go to waste. Life goes on, or should," she finished uncertainly. She suddenly had no idea what to do with herself. She went into the bathroom to change the guest towels and replace the bar of Ivory with a soap shaped like a scallop shell.

She then filled the pitcher, took the roses to the sideboard, and carefully began to arrange them. Her breath still came in shallow puffs. Breathe normally, she told herself, breathe in the fragrance, calm down, be normal, go slowly. But images of Catherine flashed like fast slides. Lily never mentioned her, and Eleanor had not thought of her in months, years. Now she saw her coming down the church steps in a fur coat that dragged, her right eyebrow raised as she made peanut brittle for the Christmas bazaar, her picture in the paper when she caught a blue marlin down in Apalachicola, with Wills holding up forked fingers over her head and looking goony over her shoulder. She brushed her face across the pink rose petals, trying to take in their quietude. Oh, Catherine in her coffin at the funeral home. Eleanor had filed by during visitation, as had everyone in town. She was surprised that there was a viewing, given the circumstances. The room was crowded with wreaths. Little Ginger stood off to the side looking like Orphan Annie. Wills sat on a folding chair with his hands in his hair and wouldn't look up at anyone. Lily fluttered around him, not that he noticed. Not only was Catherine on view — no sign of damage — but she was half propped up. Eleanor stripped leaves off the fleshy roses. She paused, eyes closed, and the image unlocked. She saw Catherine in the coffin at Ireland's, looking not at all as though she were asleep but looking uncomfortable and seriously dead in a bright blue dress.

Irritated with the floppy blossoms, Eleanor haphazardly plopped the Lady Godivas in the gleaming pitcher and they fell perfectly into place. "God damn, what a morning," she murmured.

When Ralph came in from the cemetery, Carol, his two-mornings-a-week secretary, was typing carbons on the two arrests from Saturday night's fight at the Gulf station. Her blond hair, teased out a foot this morning, looked more like the explosion of a mushroom cloud than a beehive.

"I've already heard," she announced. "Alan Ireland called to tell you he has a tarp pinned down and told me all about it. Bizarre is not the word! This is going to shake the town to its bare little roots!" She pounded both fists on the typewriter and laughed. "It's like a horror movie that you turn on at three in the morning: matron of prominent family assaulted by ghouls after exhumation."

Ralph didn't know what "exhumation" meant, but he assumed it meant she'd been dug up. Carol was studying to be a court reporter, commuting three mornings a week all the way to Macon. Her wild laugh startled him. He was sickened by the sight he'd seen, but his own impulse had been to joke about vampires. He could still hear Alan's strangled laugh. To outsiders this whole thing would have a grisly humor. "We'll be the laughingstock of south Georgia. It's not six months since all the papers had a big time with that nut out at the mill who was found dead in his garage with eighty birdcages full of squirrels. And no doubt some old-timers who remember way back will say the Masons had something coming."

"Meaning?" She was from Savannah and didn't know the Masons from borscht.

"Old man Mason — Big Jim — was a character of the first order. He organized voting the dead, acted like he'd invented this world. I don't know — you used to hear stories. People danced to his tune around here. And his daddy before him. Then they're some who think Big Jim hung the moon and stars." His own grandfather, for one. Big Jim had given Ralph's grandfather the money to buy the large house, where Ralph grew up with his parents, an aunt, his grandparents, and a cousin. Why Big Jim came up with the cash, Ralph never knew. Other relatives came and went over the years. Now Ralph lived there alone.

"Sounds charming, this Big Jim."

He sat at his desk for a few moments, trying to take notes before he dialed the GBI. Was this even in their jurisdiction? He hoped to hell it was. He dreaded the calls he would have to make. He'd pass on as many as he could to Carol. He would have to call J. J. Mason immediately and, he guessed, then go out to talk to Lily. He'd just as soon Lily go out to the Columns Rest Home to tell Wills Mason.

He rehearsed what he would say. "I have some bad news . . ." "Something you need to know about has come up . . ." "Your mother has been found . . ." For some situations there just are not any words; at those times you just have to make them up on the spot.

"Jesus H., Carol, she's lying out there sprawled in the mud. What the hell is going on? She's been dead forever. A suicide."

"Ugly, ugly. I don't know. The buck stops with you, soldier."

"Hey, lay off." Screw you, he wanted to say. He always blushed when she called him "soldier," a reference to his Vietnam medals and maybe not a flattering one. He would have to look into the stored files later. He swiveled his chair right then left.

When Catherine Mason did herself in, her daughter, Ginger, was in Ralph's seventh-grade class; J.J. was in junior high, two years ahead. When Ginger finally came back to school, they'd all looked at her in awe. Everyone had heard that she discovered her mother dead on the kitchen floor with a hunting rifle beside her. He'd heard endless whispered stories: about Mrs. Mason pulling the trigger with her toe to shoot herself in the heart; about Ginger walking in with her plaid book satchel, expecting the aroma of brownies, and finding her own mother's blood splattered all over the floor; about J.J. disappearing into the woods for days after he heard; and then a couple of years later Dr. Wills Mason having a stroke that left him gaga for good. After that, Ralph wasn't as able to think of his own family as nuts, with their ordinary drinking and shouting in the night, a mother who believed that the end of the world was at hand. He still had dish towels around the house that she'd embroidered with the red word *repent*.

Back in school, Ginger didn't cut up like she used to. Before, she'd been a smart-ass. Now she'd stay in at recess and read at her desk. Everyone was shy around her. Once he and several others had tried to drag her out to play softball — she had been the top choice among the girls before — and she fiercely shook them off and said, "Leave me alone!," emphasizing each word through gritted teeth. Ralph's memory of her after that was fuzzy. When Dr. Mason later took his nosedive, she and J.J. went to live with their daddy's sister, Lily, on Palmetto Road in their old family place. In high school, Ginger became one of the pretty, popular girls, the model-student type. But no running onto the football field to embrace a hero; not much backseat fun with her. Ralph was, at that time, pre-occupied with baseball and working at the Sacred Pig. They'd had the prom on the lawn at old man Mason's. It was a smear of memory. All the beautiful girls, and what stuck for Ralph was the sight of Ginger's Aunt Lily serving punch in a green evening dress. He'd looked down and noticed she had on grass-stained tennis shoes. He remembered making out like crazy with skinny, hot Connie Sims, even though his date was Judith Ann Krasner, privately called Big Dinners among the football team.

She looked toward the top of the hill at the Etruscan wall made from stones as big as Fiats. Under the shade of a linden tree, Ginger spread out her work. Planks across the sawhorses so engagingly called *capretti* (little goats) made a good surface for her two boxes of stones from the Melone III site, numbered according to where they were found. These she had selected to look at over the leisurely weekend. She took her coffee out, too, with slices of the unsalted Tuscan bread she was finally used to, piled with tomatoes and chopped basil. She couldn't get enough tomatoes and bought a cascade still attached to the stalk every day. She sat down at the table. Here a breeze stirred even on inferno days like this one.

These pale gold stones all bore some distinctive evidence of carving, perhaps only a ridge or curve that showed the use of a tool against it. They'd come to light next to a long flat stone incised with a spiral. They could be something or nothing. Several smaller stones seemed to have similar flourishes.

She separated those, then began to look at various pieces, turning them from side to side. The damp one-thousand-piece jigsaw puzzles of the White House and the pyramids that she and J.J. used to put together at the cabin always ended up with something the shape of Florida or Montana missing — the crucial tip of the pyramid or the edge of the roof — never just a piece of sky or grass. The puzzles took days; they'd become obsessed to finish, and when she fell asleep in the cot next to J.J.'s, she'd see pieces of the puzzle all night. Somehow the incidents and people in her dreams would also be puzzle pieces. She'd get up the next morning and wander in her shorties back to the card table, where she'd find J.J. already trying a piece, absently eating cereal.

She rubbed the edges of the tufa, consciously pushing out of her mind any thought of J.J. The Philandering Hermit, she'd begun to call him. Although she understood why he kept on treading water, she wished he would change. Unformed, too, was the instinct that if he didn't change, she couldn't either. Together they'd been Romulus and Remus, exposed on the hillside. But Lily was no she-wolf. Lily was a calm, benign presence who allowed them to bring up each other.

After Wills's stroke, their own house in Swan had been sold. A dentist had installed his office in the sunroom and lived with his wife and three bucktoothed children in the rest of the house. They didn't know what happened to the wicker porch furniture, their old toys, the curvy white radio their mother used to play when she made chocolate jetties on the marble-topped kitchen table, or even what happened to the kitchen table. When Wills was taken to the hospital, Lily had driven them to Atlanta to the Ice Follies; they'd stayed in a hotel and ordered ginger ale and hamburgers sent up by room service; they saw the Battle of Atlanta at the Cyclorama. Lily let them order ice cream at midnight. Lily said Wills was going to need a very long rest at the Columns and they should stay with her; after all, the House was their daddy's home and their home, too, and always would be.

Ginger and J.J. had tried not to look when they rode by their old house on their bicycles, not wanting to see the swing still hanging in the pecan tree, their mother's rose garden looking scrawny. They'd survived and each of them began to develop the clever barricades against memory that would become their personalities and characters. They didn't know if Lily loved them. Silently, they had only the knowledge of the solidity of each other. They didn't talk about that either.

The C-shapes on the Etruscan stones could be curls of hair. A head, or maybe the whole body, formed on the lid of a sarcophagus. That's not what she hoped, though she loved the carved likenesses of the departed on Etruscan coffin lids. The museums were full of them, all attesting to the life of the person so long dead. Her favorite was a double statue, a man and a woman raised from reclining, looking off at something in the distance. Ginger found it impossible to see them without almost overhearing their conversation. *Look,* he is saying, *do you see that* . . . They both had those ancient, sweet, archaic smiles of mystery and intimacy, their physical bond clear from the harmonious folds of their gowns, their ease with each other — not easy to find that in this life or the next. She imagined them, not on a sarcophagus, but on a boat, floating toward a large happiness.

Something whispered, a secret between them, lasting all these centuries. Her own marriage never hinted toward a voyage into eternity together.

At the site she was working, Marco's team of Italian archaeologists found the first tomb last summer, perhaps seventh century B.C., and of the characteristic half-cantaloupe shape they called *melone*. In the past two decades, several of those had been uncovered outside the town wall. She looked at her photos — the stairway they'd found and a small sphinx. They'd also located another broken section of stairway, after digging through several strata of carbonized sheep dung, the remains of a stone wall, sherd, and ash as hard as lava. One of the old Italian workers was disgusted: "The whole town is a museum. This land is prime for olives."

She sipped her coffee, glancing up at her fragment of wall, as she thought of it. For four months, she had logged the time that every dawn and noon struck the stones. It was easy enough to wake up because the house, six or seven olive terraces below the wall, had the exact same southern orientation, and the sun came blaring into the bedroom as soon as it cleared the low, undulating foothill of the Apennines across the valley. By six in the afternoon, the sun moved over the hill behind her house. She had a theory. The texts said that the wall was part of Monte Sant'Egidio's original town wall. But the angle seemed off, even after studying all the ancient maps. Oddly, not much site work had been done since 1885.

Since college, since divorce, since a stint in San Francisco, where she found the hippie movement revolting, then a dismal year in New York working for an insurance company, she had found nothing to stick to for long. Her attempts to move *out* all ended with several despondent months back at the House, with Lily suggesting various impossible men around Swan. During the last siege, she'd ordered a course catalogue from the University of Georgia. Partly because it was listed first, she read the offerings in archaeology. Immediately, she decided to go. Typical of Ginger. To everyone's astonishment, including her own, she loved her courses. Although everyone in Swan expected her to become bored and drop this work, she had sustained her interest for over three years now. If she could get a Steimleicher grant, she could start to solidify her speculations on the possibility that the wall was a portion of a sun temple. But she would have to go back to graduate school first. She could almost imagine heading her own team.

Privately, she'd had it with how the Etruscans went to their deaths. Her two previous intern digs took place in dank underground tombs tunneled into hillsides, with a director who farted when he walked fast and left all the scut work to the interns. Marco's project was all in the light.

She ran inside to answer the phone. An unmistakable southern voice said, "May I please speak to Ginger Mason? Is that you, Ginger?"

"Yes, I'm here." The drawn-out *Gin-jah* suddenly sounded exotic; she was used to the strain of speaking and understanding in another language. No one from Swan would be casually calling — how's Italy, how's the research, are you travelling, how's what's-his-name, Marco? Negative. She held the phone out from her head as static jagged through the line.

A strange voice but familiar, too, said, "Ginger, hello, I'm sorry to disturb you on your vacation . . ." Long pause. When would they ever accept that she was not on vacation, that she was living here, working?

"This is Ralph Hunnicutt — you remember me?"

"Yes, of course, Ralph. How are you? Is something wrong?"

"I'm afraid so. I'm the new sheriff in Swan, guess you've heard that." He paused. Ginger could imagine him looking across the bare courthouse lawn and down at Sister Sissy's Barbecue Shack below. "Ginger —" He stopped, then plunged on. "I'm so sorry . . ."

Ginger wandered to the front door and looked out. The heavy spring rains had sprouted every summer wildflower possible. Her gaze followed splotches of late red poppies along the edges of the terraces and clumps of irises, long since naturalized, moving in drifts across the long grass. The apples were plumping up, the hard knotted pears still looked bitter green, and a row of plum trees along the edge of the first terrace was breaking into what looked like a bumper crop. What does the *bumper* in bumper crop mean? she wondered, and turned to go look it up in the dictionary. Instead, she ran back to the phone and dialed J.J.'s number.

She tried to imagine the shrill series of rings beginning under her finger ending in that cabin on the river four thousand and some odd miles away, the sound waves hitting the arrowhead collection beside the fireplace, the blue sofa exiled there since her mother bought the curvy Duncan Phyfe one with ivory Napoleonic wreaths woven into the yellow satin. No answer. She held the cool phone against her temple. "Where are you, J.J.?" she said aloud.

She thought of dialing Aunt Lily or the Columns and asking to speak to Daddy, but why waste thirty dollars? He would be hopeless. Lily might be sleeping and right now she couldn't comfort *her*. How horrible that she smashed her finger.

"Two o'clock," she said aloud. What is that white rime on the plums? Seven, eight, nine, must be fifteen trees. Yellow finches darted among the branches. She stared until her eyes teared, and the trees smeared and shifted. She felt jarred, unable to take in what Ralph had told her. Is this what shock feels like? she wondered. Like looking through a twirling kaleidoscope? She loved the ovoid purple plums, known locally as nun's thighs. What will I do with so many plums? Already birds are diving at the green ones. But now I may not be here for the ripe plums. Now I must accomplish thirty things and get myself on a train to Rome, on a plane to Atlanta, in a car to Swan.

For whole weeks she forgot that Swan existed. She was far enough, finally, far in miles but, better, farther in those latitudinal spaces that arc mysteriously and blot out memories of other places and people, as if they have dropped off the flat horizon of the world.

Bumper: unusually full or abundant, a drinking vessel filled to the brim. From *bump, lump,* hence something large. That hardly explains the usage, she thought, slamming the dictionary shut. She circled the yard, and finally her mind wheeled in, coming to rest on the actual, brutal fact she heard from Ralph Hunnicutt, the back of whose white-blond buzz cut she'd stared at in Eleanor Whitefield's math class.

Her mother, exposed. Mother, Mother, Mother. Her stone broken in half. *Mother, Mother, I feel sick.* The jump-rope rhyme whirred by her ear, double-time. *Call for the doctor, quick, quick, quick.* Ginger remembered her red shoes rhythmically striking the gravel playground in fifth grade, the sweep of fear that her mother would die and she would be left to count cars at the funeral. But the rhyme said

Mother, Mother, will I die? and she had concentrated hard not to trip on the terrible
turn of the line *Yes, my child, but do not cry,*
each one-syllable word accented with a
jump.

Exhumed, he'd said, pronouncing the *h*.
Exposed to death. No: exposed *in* death.
And what did he say — Lily and Eleanor
found her. And the body? Stained with
mud. Lily must be shattered. He said her
mother was lying in the rain. Something
about grave robbers, and did she have on
jewelry when she was buried? How could
this happen? "No," Ginger had said,
looking at the lapis and pearl ring on her
own right hand, "no, and the wedding ring
is in Daddy's cuff link box in his top
drawer." No, no, no, the words had separated from her mouth, risen like smoke
rings and faded into space. She saw suddenly how young her mother was, then she
saw her open eyes, that blinding yellow
kitchen. "No," she repeated.

She knew the rest of her mother's jewelry was locked in a safe-deposit box.
Three or four pins, a coral pendant, a
square emerald Daddy gave her on their
tenth anniversary. Ginger had the string of
good pearls from her mother's mother, a
few pairs of earrings. She felt the familiar

sliver-thin knife cut through her mind —
Mother. Mother in the rain. *Mother,
Mother, quick quick quick.* And where the
hell is J.J.? She dialed again; no answer.
She wished he would walk up the path
from the road right now. She would like to
lie down in the weeds and just cry, but she
had not cried in years. Ralph Hunnicutt
had been gentle. She knew this news
would fly around Swan; he'd be in the eye
of a hurricane. "An investigation is under
way," he'd said like someone in a play.

Ginger would get the six o'clock train to
Rome, spend the night, catch the flight out
in the morning. He'd said he would tell
Lily she was coming. Ralph Hunnicutt, in
his flannel shirts from Sears, his haircuts
always razored up the back of his head.
Washington, Atlanta, a rented car, hideous
trip. Hell.

To get through the night. She must. To
get hoisted into the air and flung across the
sky in a silver bullet and to come down in
another world. To find her father uncom-
prehending. Sitting in a pressed white shirt
as though about to go see patients again.
To find Lily crying, her makeup badly applied and her housecoat spotted with cigarette burns. Her mother, exhumed, oh,
sickening. Why? She never walked around

Swan dripping with jewels — why would anyone think to unearth her after nineteen years? No sense at all. Nothing ever has made any sense. *Life was just starting to make sense.* A box of golden stones. Marco, tanned in his cutoff jeans, pulling out sixth-century B.C. glass beads from a heap of rubble. "Ginger, these would look magnificent on you." Waking with him this morning, his body still so seriously asleep. Touching the black arc of his eyebrows. His eyes the color of the dust-rimed blue plums you clean with your thumb. Tracking the sun across the hills. The long-cooled stones of the Etruscans lay in the fields waiting, the intact jug still with a residue of wine, the bronze votive animals, a coil of rope in the sand. Oh crap, she thought, I haven't even done the laundry.

She packed almost nothing but her cosmetics, some underwear, and her photos of the site to show J.J. She'd wear her navy linen just back from the cleaners, then, at home, go into her old closet and wear what she'd left. She knew she had shorts and good pants and blouses there, hanging in the closet year after year. At home, she'd thought. Was it always to be home? The place that if you go there, blah, blah, blah, they have to take you in, as her father used to say. Swan. She could not imagine Marco there. Her past was a long blank to him, punctuated with occasional pictures she created in the siesta afternoons after they made love. "The land used to be a sea and the rivers still have white sandbars that emerge when the water is low," she'd tell him. "In the summer, the heat makes you feel as though you're walking under water, the heat engulfs you, and as you can in water, you feel currents of heavier and lighter heat when you walk, moving streams and rivulets of coolness in the air. Way in the country, we know — J.J. and I know — deep springs that gush thousands of gallons a minute of the purest water. You can dive straight down and feel icy water pushing up from the bottom."

She had told Marco about her mother's immense rose garden, how they visited country relatives who gave them cuttings of heirloom roses, about the camellia hedge under her window when she was a child, about the bed of pine needles she made for herself in a back corner of the yard, where she took her box of colored pencils and drawing paper. She'd told him little about J.J. and only the briefest information about her mother's suicide and her father's strange history afterward.

"America, America," he'd say, and Ginger would think, No, he doesn't get it, but I don't care. He listened as though she were telling him about someone else. She'd seen him take the photo of J.J. on her dresser over to the window and turn it to the light. He'd only said, "He looks like Montgomery Clift in that old movie where the big girl drowned so he could have Elizabeth Taylor." What was important to Marco was the present. Now, today, and the specialized worlds of archaemetallurgy and paleobotany — the work they were doing — and along with it the easy joy between them that seemed to be expanding. He could not even work up a little jealousy when she told him about her college romances, her marriage to Mitchell. Sometimes she felt that her life was a fan she only partially had unfolded for him, but she was willing to let her past go. So what if he saw everything about her family as emblematic of America? She didn't want to think of them. Shed that skin — there's no more to learn from home, she thought, and nothing at all to *do* with it. She loved living in a foreign country where everything was *other*.

Better to lay bare the glass phial, the eroded foundations of a temple, an earring that dangled gently from an ear eight thousand years ago. Much better to go on Sunday to Marco's parents', where ten, fourteen, sometimes twenty gathered around that endless table, and even she felt gently folded into the rhythms of the family. She was kissed and called "bella," she was seated in the middle, urged to eat, eat. Whatever nasty secrets they had, nothing showed. They laughed, laughter rippling around the table with the platters of roast rabbit and potatoes. How would it be to grow up like that? Hence, Marco, she thought, hence Marco.

She wrote a note to him and left it on the kitchen table. He and an archaeologist on the staff of the University of Georgia team had taken the interns to Bologna, a trip she wanted to make because Etruscan remains outside town indicated a sun temple with the same orientation as the one she suspected once crowned Monte Sant'Egidio. If she had gone, instead of plugging away here, this ludicrous news would not have reached her. Ralph Hunnicutt in his sweltering office over the jail could have worn the skin off his finger dialing her number and she would have been happily sketching foundations, having pasta at a trattoria, talking nonstop with Marco.

*Dear Marco, I have to go to Georgia imme-
diately — a family emergency. I don't know
the details but will call you tomorrow. Back as
soon as possible! Don't forget me. Cold tomato
soup in fridge.* She tore it up and rewrote it
without the pathetic *Don't forget me* and
the wifely soup part. He'd find the soup or,
more likely, he'd just go to the pizza place
on the hill with friends.

As an Italian, she reflected, he might not
be as shocked as she at this news. Weren't
they always digging up saints, whose un-
corrupted bodies filled the towns with
mysterious fragrance? Ralph Hunnicutt
had said cryptically that her mother didn't
look that different. Perhaps she was a saint.
But saints didn't blast themselves into
oblivion. Suicide — had she ever looked up
that word? No need. *Sui* — of oneself —
and the ancient suffix -*cide*, appearing in so
many awful words. More than a word, to
her it was a powerful, hidden, primitive action always forming in her mother's life
from the moment of birth. The word itself
was totally inadequate to the finger on the
trigger.

Ginger found her passport and the envelope of dollars she kept at the bottom of
her underwear drawer. Seven or eight
months back, she'd had to fly home be-

cause her father was taken to the hospital with pneumonia, and the doctor gravely said he probably couldn't survive. By the time she arrived twenty hours later, her father was trying to maneuver a smoke under the oxygen tent. J.J. had not been found until the next morning. He had been miles into the wiregrass over near Retter, hunting bobwhites with Scott. She'd crossed the ocean and driven two hundred miles, while they strung quail on a pine spit and grilled them, lying back in the dry grass drinking awful moonshine out of Mason jars. She was furious. She had not spoken to J.J. for the rest of the week she was there.

Although she had not given up on him, she had trouble imagining J.J. living a normal life, whatever that meant, outside the woods. She held on to the old image of him from a weekend she'd visited him at Emory back in her sophomore, his senior, year of college. He actually invited her down from Virginia to the Spring Ball. He arranged a blind date with his roommate, Mitchell Sloane, and he took Lisa Bowen from Augusta. Ginger remembered the stiff, old-fashioned way he held Lisa, and the slight upward turn of his profile. He'd bought the tuxedo instead of renting it, which was a good sign, Ginger thought. He looked totally natural, as if he'd been born in it. His hair curled over the collar, and as he danced by her he swept his green eyes over her as though she were a stranger, and she felt how wonderful it would be to meet him if he were. They'd learned to dance together at the cabin, awkwardly counting steps out loud and practicing dips in the kitchen. Neither of them seemed to have any innate feel for the music. But that night, she saw his controlled, expressive turns. The sureness of his moves left no room for awkwardness from his partner; Lisa melded into him and they danced under the immense chandelier of the ballroom, twirling, Ginger saw, until the thousands of lights must have streaked into one. She would never forget watching J.J. that night. She had sat at a table with Mitchell, sipping her rum and Coke, probably the third drink of her life, and heard little of what he told her about his contracts class. J.J. was new to her. He would go to med school, marry Lisa, have four children, live in Swan. Maybe she would marry Mitchell. They would have a little girl in a smocked dress, a boy who liked horses. She made the rim of her glass ring, leaned to Mitchell, and gave him her brightest look. The powerful trajectory of their futures — all four together — carried her closer. They would have big family parties at the cabin, cut down a Christmas tree, barbecue ribs, and float on rafts.

Now J.J. disappeared down the river for days, as he always had since their mother's suicide, or he left word with Lily that he was driving down to the Okefenokee, or as far as the Everglades. At the cabin, where he spent four or five days a week, he lavished an inordinate amount of time on cleaning guns and fishing gear, writing in notebooks, reading, or just stalking through the woods looking for arrowheads and bits of pottery.

As children, on a morning after pelting rain, he and Ginger had once found what must have been a Creek target practice area on a sharp incline of new-growth slash pine. Gullies running downhill left dozens of arrowheads perched on alluvial peaks of dissolving red clay. She had picked up two large, crudely cut triangles, which must have been for deer or bear, then they found in one spot a cache of flint bird arrowheads, perfect, smaller than her little fingernail. They'd stuffed their pockets, then J.J. stripped off his shirt and they gathered more, tying them into a bundle. They loved the arrowheads and spent hours lining them up on the coffee table, admiring the ivory and rose veins of the flint and imagining half-naked Indians around a campfire, chipping them expertly with a sharpened stone. They checked out all the books on Indians from the Swan library and spent the winter nights cross-legged on the sofa, passing them back and forth and reading aloud to each other. J.J.'s collection now covered the entire wall around the fireplace.

But Ginger had shifted her allegiance to the Etruscans, far from Swan.

Lily aired Ginger's room and dusted the tops of the picture frames, which Tessie always missed. Deanie Robart had bandaged her finger. She might lose the nail, but with two aspirins the pain had subsided. That Hunnicutt boy had turned out just fine, she thought, despite that awful mother raving about Judgement Day, polite as he could be, and with such terrible news to discuss. Wasn't one of his eyes a little cocked? A war injury, but he was too young for the war. Then she remembered Vietnam was also a war, later and farther away. How thoughtful of him to call Ginger. Lily had told him she'd tell Wills, as best she could. Tessie had tried to keep her in bed, but as soon as Ralph called back and said Ginger would be coming home, she'd jumped up. CoCo rode her shoulder as she moved around Ginger's room.

Most of the dead stay gone, she thought. Yes, her own mother stayed dead. The time of year when they went to White Springs came and went every year and still her mother stayed dead. She remembered when they would sit on the piered porch built around the spring and sip Dixie cups of sulfur water. "This is good for what ails you," her mother always said. They'd worn white spectators, polished every morning, and print voile dresses. In the evenings they'd sat in rockers on the porch of the White Springs Hotel, after suppers of fried chicken and platters of sliced tomatoes.

Lily's mind was still swarming. As if from a distance she watched herself skidding fluidly through the past. She got on her knees and gave a swipe to the feet of the bed with a dust rag. The old days were best. Even tomatoes aren't that good anymore, she thought. Everything had more taste when it was Mama's house and the maid pressed the flounces on their cotton slips. She remembered her mother's lavender ways, her cologne, her hats trimmed with silk flowers, Mama's blue Packard, the drive along the Swanee. And the blowout when that Negro had been kind enough to change the tire. Charleston, too, was very nice on their visit, and once Bermuda, with sunrise-colored bungalows and blooming poinciana, when Lily wrote postcards to her friends Agnes and Eleanor on the balcony and Mama was old and floated her bridge in a glass of water by the bed at night, moonlight combing through the shutter, hitting the three white teeth and the ridge of pink gum. Nothing pointed toward horrible events.

Lily scuffed into the kitchen and poured herself a glass of ice water. Catherine, found again. She noticed that the cigarette she'd been smoking when the sheriff visited had burned into the edge of the table. She blew the ashes onto the floor. Maybe Catherine never died when they thought. Maybe she was alive all the time, yes, teaching school over in Willacoochee. Once Lily thought she'd seen Catherine's face in a train window. The woman waved and suddenly was not Catherine. Or maybe she ran away with a soldier years ago, back in 1945, a crazy time with the Japs and the Germans, and oh, yes, the Italians, though Ginger did not want to hear a word of that. Why Ginger wanted to go live in a foreign country where she has no people, Lily didn't know. Divorced, carrying on with some Italian mackerel-snapper, Marco Polo or some such. She realized her hands were shaking. Get control, she told herself.

She took down the flour and lard, imagining Ginger's big smile tomorrow when she'd open the cookie jar on the counter and reach in for a biscuit. She would be tired after the long trip. Biscuits and gravy. Tessie would bring a fresh hen tomorrow. Lily decided to order the groceries over the telephone. She looked in the refrigerator. A toasted biscuit would be good. What should she do now? There was a little left-over potato salad. Catherine had nothing valuable, those thieves got nothing but the shock of looking at a dead person. And a shock that was. What is in that mouldy bowl? She peeled back the plastic wrap. Squash casserole. Serves them right, the savages, she thought, but why couldn't they just cover her up, at least, and spare us this final humiliation?

She uncovered a plate of cold ladyfinger peas, her favorite summer vegetable, and ate some at the sink. She'd snapped a ton of those peas in her day. My day, she realized, has passed, and what was the meaning of *this* day if a day, all the days, any day, could come to this horror. As if the unforgivable death were not enough, as if leaving those children were not enough, as if causing Wills to have a stroke tragically young were not enough. Lily slipped into her habit of blaming Catherine for everything. As if my life were hers to hand over to raising Ginger and J.J., she thought. As if I had no choice — and I didn't. I had no choice. Now this, Catherine, and how could you? Lily poked out her bottom lip, a gesture since childhood when Mama would say, "I could ride to town on that lip." Fortunately, Mama did not live to see any of this. How quietly Mama left this world, unlike Catherine. Mama would agree that Catherine was still the troublemaker.

Big Jim, her father, all at once loomed in her mind, as though in the doorway wanting his rice pudding. Loose pants held up by sprung black suspenders and hair like boar bristles coming out of his ears. He ruled the roost, ruled many roosts, too many, at least one too many, that house on the edge of the mill village where that floozie Aileen Boyd stood on the porch, her hip jutting out, and Mama wouldn't look right or left when she drove the Packard down Mason Road to the mill office to take a potted plant or a cake to someone sick. Lily remembered once going in her parents' bedroom to say good night. Big Jim was out. At the door she saw her mother lean over the pillow and pick up a long blond hair. Lily had quietly turned and gone back to her room. The next day she and her mother drove to South Carolina to visit Mama's people. Lily felt a wave of rage that her mother had died so soon. She was simply eaten up and no one knew she'd had those pains for years. She and Mama should have had years of freedom. Mama had liked to travel and Lily could go, too, since she'd never married, though she had a few beaux who sat on the front porch in her day. My day, she thought again. She supposed her day was raising those children after their mother . . .

Her mind stopped at the subject of suicide, and as it did she saw a picture of Catherine Phillips when she first came to Swan for Thanksgiving. That was Wills's final year in medical school. As he brought Catherine in the front door, Lily saw her through the glass panels of the foyer and stepped back into the hall to watch until the introductions were over. Catherine — oh, Lily could see her — wore red, which Lily never liked, a red suit with a red print silk blouse under it. Oh, we're very bold, Lily had thought to herself. We have wavy black hair, do we, and surprised-looking blue eyes. A funny blue. Wills never looked away from Catherine. He hovered over her,

97

gawky and smitten, reminding Lily of a heron with folded wings. They were sorry to rush, they said, but the annual Tipton-Swan football game started at two. Mama and Big Jim had greeted Catherine and taken her straight into the dining room, where Lily also slipped into a chair and said how they'd all heard so much from Wills, and how did she like Georgia State College for Women? She herself had gone to Agnes Scott. Catherine did not seem to see the distinction. She'd looked young, young, young. Lily, thirty then, already had a sense that her youth was gone. On trips with Mama she would stock up on henna rinses to cover alarming premature gray hairs. Certainly she would not buy hair dye in Swan. She had been teaching at the mill school for eight years. One by one the local boys had married other girls. She hated the school, especially the children's dirty feet and the days they had to return the specimen canisters for the hookworm tests. Big Jack said she should damn well quit and sit home if the children got on her nerves all that much, but what else would she do while waiting for her life to begin?

"How did y'all meet — I don't think Wills has told us that," Lily had asked, and Catherine's young face seemed now to

98

come close to her own. Those eyes, like looking down into the springs at Glass Lake — the pale aquamarine, blind-looking eyes with irises ringed with a darker blue. Unpleasant to look into, Lily found. But she could find no other fault. Anyone would have to admire her skin, creamy and luminous without a speck of powder. When she turned on that 150-watt smile, you couldn't help but feel pulled toward her. Lily noticed that Catherine's right eyebrow flew up when someone asked her a question.

In the image that rushed over Lily, she experienced a sudden warmth for Catherine that she had not felt that day when Catherine had not particularly noticed Lily's special cornbread dressing and instead talked about the dorm mother who patrolled the date parlors, about deciding to major in design, and asked Big Jim questions about the fabrics produced at the mill. We're confident, too, Lily had thought. The few girls her brother ever brought home usually spoke when spoken to, leaving Wills to do all the talking, while they gulped iced tea and hardly ate at all. None had the gall to address Big Jim familiarly. From this distance, Lily felt the hum of Catherine's energy run through her. Then Wills wrapped Catherine's camel hair coat around her. They had to hurry for the kickoff promptly at two; he wouldn't miss it. His red number 35 jersey still lay folded in a chest in his upstairs bedroom. Big Jim, who usually didn't notice anyone unless they could do something for him, fetched her pocketbook and feigned kissing her hand. Wills kissed his mama but forgot to say good-bye to Lily. The first warning of what was to come. Catherine, however, took her hand and squeezed it. "Wills says you're the real thing. I'm really looking forward to getting to know you better." That megawatt flash.

Lily saw that she had, ever so slightly, a gap between her front teeth. She was so charmed that she forgot to withhold her approval and said, "Do come soon."

The door had barely closed when Big Jim whooped, "That one's a firecracker! Wills will have his hands full there." He snapped his fingers and clapped his hands. "I like her." I do, too, Lily had thought. No, I don't.

Lily jumped, as though her father's clap still jarred the room. Old age has its moments, Lily mused. When she was younger, only dreams gave back faces and sometimes retrieved memories. Now, all of a sudden, full-blown pictures came back whole, with devastating clarity. The memory trailed off with Big Jim sinking into his cracked leather chair. The newspaper rattled and he switched on the radio. Lily and Mama went to Lily's room to take out her winter clothes and adjust hems. They had no interest in the game or in breathing the fumes of the Cuban cigar Big Jim was about to light.

Looking that far back, who could have guessed that she would be called on to raise Catherine's children? She'd never liked children, but their powerful needs, when they came to her, by far outweighed her reluctance to meet them. They were her own kin. Where else could they go? Her life had shaped and continued to shape around what befell her.

Lily opened a drawer and stared for a full minute at the green handle of the biscuit cutter before she recognized it as what she wanted. Wanting company, she rolled CoCo's cage just inside the door. He bit his nails and fixed his yellow eyes on the window. Without having to think, she cut lard into the flour with a fork, rolled out the dough on a board, and cut it expertly into perfect circles. Yes, Ginger would be hungry after such a long trip. CoCo cracked seeds and made a low, purring motor sound. She'd make more biscuits if J.J. stopped by today. J.J. would eat the whole pan.

When the bridge club — Margaret Alice, Billie, and Ellen — parked out front, Eleanor was regretting her decision, but if she had canceled, later they would have heard she was the one who discovered Catherine with Lily and would have been incensed because she had not confided in them. A part of Eleanor looked forward to the telling; she was ashamed of that. She abhorred small-town gossip. Still, she knew any one of them would have been on the horn immediately, and isn't gossip speculation, whereas this was fact?

Eleanor seated Ellen closest to the air conditioner so her smoke would blow away. Margaret Alice announced right away that storms were expected, so she was a little distracted. The other three dreaded stormy bridge club days. Margaret Alice had a phobia and screamed at each thunderclap. When forked lightning and thunder closed in until they occurred almost simultaneously, she'd weep and have to be led to the sofa and covered with a throw. Eleanor waited for the right time to tell them what happened, but for now, it was too pleasant, just dealing the cards, writing "we" and "they" on the tally, falling into the orderly progression of the game. She was annoyed at how Margaret Alice kept looking out the window as though a burglar were outside. Ellen had never been quite the same after the shock treatments she'd had up in Atlanta years ago. Strange, she was fine with the cards but a bit whiffy on past events, and she lost the French language entirely after two years of study in college. Distant thunder mumbled and she saw Margaret Alice's hand tremble. "Don't worry, it's miles away. There's not a cloud."

After the first rubber, Eleanor asked, "Are you girls ready for lunch?"

As they moved into the dining room, Eleanor was faced with the cascade of roses on the sideboard. "How lovely!" Ellen walked over to the flowers and put her face close. "Lemony scent. Gorgeous. Where did you get them?"

Eleanor motioned everyone to a chair. The table looked fine. She could see that

Hattie even had polished the salt cellars. Hattie came in with her ring of tomato aspic and served, carefully including a sprig of parsley for each chilled plate. Only Eleanor noticed the jiggle of the aspic and Hattie's set lips. Eleanor sipped her iced tea and leaned back. "I might as well get this over with. I had a terrible thing happen this morning and I'm still spinning from it. A tragic thing."

Ellen crushed out the cigarette she'd brought to the table and leaned forward, frowning. Margaret Alice was craned around looking out the window. Billie, forty pounds overweight, was eyeing her food. "You know I always go out to visit a spell with Holt every morning," Eleanor began. "This morning I met Lily out there so we could cut some roses." She glanced at the roses and rushed on, describing Lily's glimpse of something blue, then their full view of Catherine tilted out of her coffin and lying in the mud.

"Eleanor, you have lost your mind," Billie shrieked.

"This is impossible. Where was Cass Deal? Why would anyone do such a thing?"

"Obviously, there's a madman at large."

"Nothing like this has ever happened in

105

Swan. The worst thing this year was the sawmill burning down back in October. Remember, it had been a dry month and the fire lit up the night for four hours."

"Ellen, that's beside the point now," Eleanor reminded her. "A macabre event like this is entirely different." Hattie brought in the cold pressed chicken and a basket of rolls, even though no one had eaten their aspic. "Just leave it, Hattie, thank you, we'll serve ourselves."

For the next hour, the four women ate with good appetite and talked. The Masons were one of the old families, after all, and everything was known about them, back to Big Jim's father, John, who had started the cotton mill a hundred years ago, in 1875, when Swan was a railroad crossing, four stores, and a scattering of sad frame houses.

Eleanor and Margaret Alice, both born in Swan, remembered the most. Ellen and Billie had lived there only as adults, about forty years. The Reconstruction years were brutal most places, but Big Jim's father was from England, Eleanor recalled, and didn't particularly hold notions of white superiority, at least in the mill.

"It's a wonder the Klan didn't go after him," Billie remarked.

"This part of Georgia was so empty there wasn't even a Klan back then," Eleanor reminded her. "Besides, he pretty much bought the place. He hired men and women, black and white, if he thought they would work like mules."

"He drove my uncle into the ground my family always claimed," Margaret Alice said.

John's own father, who lived in England, had mills in North Carolina. John worked his youth away learning the business, and when his daddy offered to set him up with a mill of his own, he scoured the South for the right location. Swan not only had two railroad lines, it was close to the steamboat lines on the Altamaha and Ocmulgee rivers. Old John bought land, built square pine houses for tenants, and planted cotton. Margaret Alice said her daddy always remembered John calling cotton his white gold. The second year, he built the mill and started on the mill village. His wife, Mary, from Charlotte finally arrived with the boy, Jim.

"She was said to be horrified, but whether she was or not, she died three years after Calhoun was born," Eleanor recalled.

"That Calhoun . . ." Margaret Alice trailed off.

Twenty workers from North Carolina came when Mary did, lured by John's offer of decent wages. By then, he'd hired an Englishman to lay out the town. In three months, they built the four-chimneyed house out on a low rise of land overlooking the cotton fields. Mary chose the site because of the wild palmettos, two spreading oaks, and the pond choked with water lilies at the base of the slope. "Still the prettiest house in town, especially since Lily took over the garden."

Their conversation started far back in time, not because any answer was located there, not because some clue lay along the hundred-year history of the Masons in Swan — clearly, some nut had escaped from an asylum and had done this horrible thing — but because a suicide reverberates forever and the garish reappearance of the suicide unearthed all they had thought about in the days after Catherine died, leaving no note, no clue at all as to why she would turn violently on herself and leave a legacy of violence to Wills and the two children. How could any mother do that? And how could she just leave everyone in Swan? They moved on through Big Jim's time. "Old coot," Billie pronounced. "No wonder Florence left town all the time."

"What a piece of work is man," Ellen quoted.

They talked about Lily giving up her teaching to raise the children.

"Not that she gave up much. She always thought the mill children were lazy and dumb," Margaret Alice said.

"Well, they probably had pinworms, rickets, a diet of grits. Lily was just not suited for teaching," Eleanor replied. She knew no class of students was lazy and dumb on its own.

"How Lily stuck it out for as long as she did was the wonder," Margaret Alice pitched in. "She was such a spoiled brat herself. Taking over Catherine's children was the best thing that ever happened to her. She had to think of someone other than herself for once." Margaret Alice had forgotten the storm warnings, but now serious thunderheads gathered outside the windows and pine branches scratched the panes. Her husband once had courted Lily briefly, but said he couldn't look at those bug eyes even if she was the daughter of the richest man in town.

"I wouldn't say spoiled. Imagine growing up under the roof of Big Jim. It wasn't that she didn't care . . ." Eleanor knew that Lily privately had contributed substantial sums to the high school for mill village students' lunches and fees.

Billie said, "When I moved here, Wills was in high school. The golden boy, but I remember there was some problem. He got in trouble for slamming a teacher up against a wall. What was that all about?"

"Who knows."

"Big Jim sent him off to Beauregard Military Academy to teach him some discipline. First thing anyone knew he was the star student in his class at Emory, then got a free ride to medical school." Margaret Alice gazed out the window.

"He was so good-looking before the war." Eleanor was remembering Holt, working his way through school by waiting on tables in the fraternity house.

"He drank, though. I heard he, excuse me, urinated over the stairwell onto his fraternity brothers one night." Billie laughed raucously and reached for another roll.

The women were ready to move into the subject of Wills and Catherine, but a bolt hit nearby and powerful thunder exploded near the house. Margaret Alice felt it in her backbone. The entire sky lighted white. "Sheet lightning," she said. She started to cry a little bit. "Think of Catherine out there in the rain. She was an unusual girl.

Who would have thought she had it in her to purely murder herself? They say it runs in families. Thank goodness no one in my family ever did that to me. Those poor children — babes in the woods."

Ellen was dying for a smoke but did not dare light up while Billie was still eating. "It's not raining, so it probably will blow over. The forecast is for continued heat and a hundred percent humidity."

Hattie brought in coffee on a tray, and Eleanor sliced the pound cake. "Hattie, would you please take those roses out of here? I can't stand to look at them another minute."

No one could concentrate on the second rubber. Eleanor decided they could all use a little sherry. She opened Holt's liquor cabinet and poured out generous glasses. Ellen offered cigarettes, and even though the others had stopped smoking, they lit up. Margaret Alice blew a ring toward the ceiling. "They say Big Jim died in a Tipton motel. Second heart attack. Whomever he was with had the good sense to call the sheriff and get him to move the body home so he could be discovered dead properly, in his own bed. Old goat."

"I never heard that. How crude," Eleanor said.

"Yes, honey, they say Florence never

knew, just drove herself home with Lily from her people in the Carolinas and put on a state funeral. After that, we didn't see much of her in Swan for weeks. They say she took up with a musician from home, although he was purely doddering. Then she got sick, so quickly, poor thing."

"Well, she didn't live long after that." Eleanor remembered Lily's call on a Thursday, saying she'd just quit teaching at the mill. "I told the children it was a two-day holiday and to go home," she'd told Eleanor. "I figured by Sunday they'd find someone else."

When the girls finally left at five-thirty, Eleanor took the glasses to the kitchen. Hattie had left a note: *I found Scott and asked him to find J.J. This is a bad day.* A bad day, indeed. Eleanor felt ancient. She was dizzy from the sherry and smoke. Her entire hip had gone to sleep around the artificial joint and she could barely move her leg. She realized she had not told Holt Junior what had happened. She dialed her son's number but no one answered.

Hattie had very thoughtfully turned down her covers. Eleanor took a bath with a scoop of mineral salts and went to bed, even though it was too early for sleep and far too late for a nap.

J.J. kept one fishing boat downriver from the cabin. He took the Jeep along the sandy trail and set off from there when he wanted to fish beyond the sandbars, down where the river started to slow and widen. He'd caught some perch and planned to cook a couple for dinner with some boiled potatoes. As he came around the sandbar with the motor on low, a clean breeze skimmed the water and rose to his face. He loved the sudden silky glide of the river as it straightened out downstream from the cabin.

He cut the motor and bumped into a gnarled cypress knee, the one with his chain on it. The cypress trees growing in the shallows, with long gray moss and their knobby knees protruding, seemed half-human to him, haunting, silent presences in the swampy margin. Some trees have as much being as a person, he thought. The boat nudged the bank and J.J. secured the rope around some roots. No cottonmouth here today. Last week one fell into the boat as he tied up just at nightfall — a right fine specimen, about as big around as a leg. Whose leg, he'd thought, and smiled as he pictured the legs of several women, most recently the strapping gal he'd entertained on his St. Clare fishing trip. Legs like a damn Amazon. The snake had flopped in the end of the boat, quickly straightened out full length, and had given J.J. the benefit of looking into its white, white mouth. J.J. resisted the impulse to step out in the shin-deep water, where for all he knew umpteen relatives swam, and instead scooped his oar underneath its belly and dangled the moccasin in the air — a mean-looking s.o.b. — before tossing it back in the river.

He looked around just to be sure the old boy was not sprawling along an overhead branch today, and hauled his gear up the slippery bank, landing the string of perch on the grass. Ginger had once followed her first impulse and jumped out of the boat when a moccasin fell in. Their father had rammed the moccasin with the oar and jerked Ginger back in the boat all at once. She'd screamed enough to scare every living creature in the vicinity. Of course, it *had* landed on her foot; she usually was not squeamish and squealing. Wills had taught them to respect snakes but not to fear them. "They're more afraid of you than you are of them," he'd always told them. As a child, J.J. wasn't too sure about that old saw. It paralleled "This hurts me more than it does you," which Wills always had barked out when he picked a thorny stick to switch their legs.

J.J.'s first memory of his father was the day his daddy tied two truck inner tubes together and he and J.J. flopped across them and went sweeping downstream. It seemed to J.J. they were almost flying, skimming the surface of the wide river. He had dropped his face in the water to drink because it was the color of Coca-Cola. The taste was plain water. The current fumed and surged. J.J. had felt terrified, exhilarated. His father had held his hand and kept shouting, "Hey, how about it, big buddy!" At Buck's Landing, they picked up some bait and got a ride back to the cabin with Buck. Although Wills at that time often drove the ten miles out of town to the cabin to eat supper, then had to turn around and go back to deliver a baby or fish a button out of someone's throat, leaving Catherine, Ginger, and J.J. alone,

J.J.'s memories of the cabin always starred Wills — coming in from duck hunting, fastening cotton bolls to the screens to keep out bugs, unloading a deer from the back of a pickup, building shelves in the pantry. Easier to imagine him back then. The old husk sitting out at the Columns didn't seem like the same human who cooked smothered duck on the outdoor fireplace. As a child, J.J. had been fascinated at how his father could spit out the buckshot while still chewing the duck. He still couldn't do it himself.

He drove slowly. The pines fringed the bottom of the sun, which later would sink toward the river, bending light through the understory scrub oaks and glazing the water. The river, sometimes brown, looked green today, green, he recognized, like the river in his recurrent dream where the water felt like his own element and he was carried — buoyed, tumbled, and lifted — by a swift current. He swam, totally at home in the water, an exultant dream he woke from feeling suddenly beached and abandoned.

The Jeep dipped in and out of low, swampy puddles. With one hand on the wheel, he maneuvered around stumps and fallen logs. This road was as familiar as the lines on the palm of his hand; he could drive it blind.

The trail followed the bluff for about a hundred yards, then swung inland through dryer, higher ground of forest and palmettos for a mile, curving back toward the river near the cabin. He came around the back of the cabin. Scott's VW Bug was parked close to the scuppernong arbor, and as J.J. jumped out, he saw Scott sitting out on the dock sloshing his feet in the river.

Scott had been waiting almost two hours. His mother, Hattie, had told him to find J.J. if it took him all night. He'd left the store in charge of the new clerk, Mindy, who seemed one brick shy of a load. He didn't know why J.J. hired her and hoped he wasn't banging her, but you never could tell with J.J.

Scott stood up, shaking his wet feet, as J.J. took his gear up on the porch, tossed the fish in the sink, then walked down to the dock. "Hey, Scottie, good buddy, what's up?"

"Man oh man. I don't even know how to begin with this one." He was shaking the water off his feet and rolling down his pant leg.

J.J. assumed something had gone wrong

at the market. He left all decisions to Scott, except for a few hires. Now and then he'd meet with the salesmen, when Scott had business at the other Mason market on the east side of Swan to tend to. Some people in Swan had fits when J.J. hired Scott to manage a store in the white part of town. Gradually, the convenient location overcame their hidebound prejudice. Business had even picked up. Scott's friendliness put them at ease and now they thought he was doing fine.

"Let's have a beer, ol' hoss. It can't be all that bad." J.J. could be counted on to take little interest in the stores, or in any of the real estate and other small businesses his grandfather Mason had left. "I plain wore a hole in the river pulling out fish today," he bragged.

"This is serious bidness." Scott sat on the porch swing and J.J. brought out cold Budweisers.

Scott stared at the floor. "My mama was at Miz Eleanor's this morning when she come back from visiting at the cemetery. This is unbelievable but it's true because the sheriff and the undertaker have been out there and seen it, too."

"What the hell are you talking about?"

"Miz Eleanor was taking some roses

from your family's graves."

"And they're going to arrest her for that?"

"No sirree, that's not it," Scott almost shouted. "She was with your auntie and they done found your mama lying by side her own grave. Dug up by somebody."

"Hey, wait, wait, stop — is this your crummy new idea of a joke?"

"Hell no, it's the Lord's truth. She's out there right now in the open." He told J.J. everything Hattie had said. "You gotta go on home and see about Miss Lily. You want me to drive you in?" He watched J.J. drain the beer. They both looked out at the green river. A fish leapt out of the water, paused in midair, arched, and neatly disappeared in the water. J.J.'s mouth puckered like a pouting child.

"Nah, no, Scott. You go on back home. I'll head in and call Eleanor and the sheriff, then I'll see about Lily. Thanks for coming out here with the glad tidings."

"You sure you're all right?" Scott knew J.J.'s habit of duck, cover, and hold.

"Peachy." J.J. rubbed his clenched fist against his other hand. He wanted to ram it into the porch post.

He watched the brake lights of Scott's car disappear down the sand road.

★ ★ ★

Eleanor's phone rang eighteen times. No answer. Maybe the shock had killed her. J.J. reached Ralph Hunnicutt right away and told him he'd heard the news. Ralph had just put down the phone with the GBI, who couldn't come until the next morning. He was going to have to take a turn himself sitting out at Magnolia; his deputy was scheduled to fry catfish at the Rotary celebration and, besides, just plain refused to stand guard at the grave site. Said he wouldn't go near the place. Ralph assured J.J. that he would do everything possible to locate the crazy criminal who had done this. "Right now, we have no idea, not one. The State Patrol has no report of anyone missing from the prison farm or the nuthouse. I've never heard of anything like this in my life. If you come up with a theory, let me know. We assume the motive here must be grave robbing. There had to be at least two involved. No one person could pry off that granite stone."

Sherlock Holmes, J.J. thought.

Personally, Ralph wanted to believe but instinctively doubted the grave-robbing theory. Why wouldn't the thief go for Mrs. Coleman Swift? The Swifts had even more money than the Masons, and so did the

Pearlmans, who owned a chain of clothing stores all over south Georgia.

"My mother was never ostentatious. A lot of women lying out there wore big shiny rocks on their hands. This doesn't make sense on any level. Where is she now? Was she — ah, fuck, was she damaged at all?"

Ralph had an uneasy hunch that something even screwier than grave robbing was involved and was disappointed to hear J.J. bring up the same doubt. "No, she's . . . She's . . . Shit, she's, she's lying there like the day she died, more or less." The color of her face flashed yellow through his vision. "I've closed the gates of the cemetery. We can't move anything until the site has been thoroughly inspected. I'm as sorry as I can be about this and I hope you'll convey this to your family. I talked to Ginger over in Italy. She'll be coming in tomorrow. And I'll call you later if anything comes up."

J.J. sat on the porch step, closed his eyes, and imagined himself in his canoe, floating through the Okefenokee. He rubbed his temples, concentrating on skinny palms reflected in water black with rot, a yellow-headed heron in a catalpa tree, and moody cypresses with strands of gray moss lifting

121

like hair. If you were still for a long time, you could see the slow drift of a palm which grew out of an unmoored mound of humus. Land of Trembling Earth. Maybe all the earth is trembling, he thought. We just can't see it. The swamp at dawn with a passel of white egrets rising out of the trees, the floating leaf-mould pillows of pitcher plant, those green vortexes for luring insects. He tried to sense the fecund smell — sometimes he thought he breathed in a touch of the ancient salt sea as his yellow canoe parted the shallow water just over the lowest point of the sea that covered lower Georgia eons before it was Georgia.

If Scott had not come, J.J. would have fried his perch in cornmeal, had a glass of bourbon, spent a serene evening reading the book that had just arrived in the mail and making notes in the margins.

Fight or flight impulses pumped first through the backs of his legs, then all the way through him. What if he disappeared? He'd done it before. Only Ginger had guessed that he'd be in the hut that only the two of them knew about. He'd walked by it recently, hacked branches still leaning sideways, still furnished with the two stumps that had been their seats. The river deepened right there because of a spring, and they could swing out on vines and drop into icy water. She finally told on him before the funeral, and his daddy came to get him. He found J.J. awake, curled in a damp sleeping bag, the remains of a pork-and-beans dinner still in the can. "You have me," his father had said gently, "and Ginger. And Lily. We'll be all right. You've got to trust me on that right now." J.J. had sworn never to enter Swan again, but he crawled out of the bag and walked back to the car behind his father. Whenever the funeral came to mind, he willed it to blur in memory. He moved his mind so fast he could not stop for any detail.

No doubt Ginger is on her way, he thought. What a stinking mess. Seven-thirty in Swan, one-thirty in the morning there. Planes bound for Washington and the Atlanta connection only flew out in the morning. He had all day tomorrow to see about this. She'll roll in around five or six tomorrow, he calculated, if she makes it, if the plane doesn't spiral into the ocean — no, that's stupid — if she has no delays. He picked up his notebook and turned back to the pages on the swamp in April, where he'd sketched a newly hatched alligator sleeping on its mama's back, the finest thing he saw on that trip, except for *Jesus Saves* spelled out in hubcaps on a hillside. He would like to fry his perch, spend the evening with his notebooks, lulled by the chorus of tree frogs outside.

J.J. threw a tarp over his open Jeep and took the Jaguar to town. The cabin was four miles off the main road. He turned toward Swan at the fish hatchery, passing Hunter's Mill, then nothing. He pressed the accelerator. With one curve in ten miles and no human habitation in sight, he let the speedometer needle touch 100, wishing the car would take off into the sky and fly away. He slowed at the black cemetery beside a peeling, boarded-up church. He and Ginger used to shout for their parents to stop there and let them pick wild blackberries. They'd gather handfuls, unmindful that the rampant bushes rooted in graves. The sunken wooden crosses headed each hump of clay and some graves were decorated with jugs and bits of broken, colored glass. Voodoo, their mother said, spirits live in the jugs.

With the top down, J.J. breathed the swells of honeysuckle scent he drove through. He made an effort to relax his grip on the wheel. The sun had finished its raging for the day and no trace remained of the storm that had started brewing in the afternoon. Swan in the dusk he hardly noticed. In the woods not a bird feather or a leaf moved without his attention. Lily thought she raised him but he had raised himself as close to a Creek Indian as he could come. In town he drove over the brick streets, turned at the Four-Story Building, passing the Surprise Store, passing the small unlighted storefronts, where he knew every owner and clerk whether he wanted to or not, and on down Center Avenue with its oval islands planted by the three garden clubs. Clumps of red amaryllis his mother had planted a quarter-century ago still bloomed on cue.

Swan's original layout survived in the broad elliptical road, Whistling Swan Boulevard, circling the town, and in the four inner concentric drives. Other than these curved roads, all planted in 1875 with moss oaks, Swan's streets conformed to the usual American grid, but even streets no wider than pig tracks were lined with dogwood and crape myrtle. Some dreamer, must have been his great-grandmother, named three of the four drives for faraway islands — Minorca, Corsica, Corfu — then in a moment of grim reality, named the fourth for a bloody Civil War battle in the

Mississippi River, Island 10.

J.J. swung into Island 10, then took the unpaved road which led to Palmetto House. To all the Masons, it always had been just "the House." The marble block with *Palmetto House*, 1877 carved on its face lay hidden under a bramble of Cherokee roses. When the rutted clay road was built, it cut through an old-growth long-leaf-pine forest. A wooden bridge crossed Land's End Creek. Through the years, the Masons sold off pieces of property and now people were moving out of the old houses in town to build squat brick ranch-style houses along the road. J.J. glanced at the waterlogged lot he'd just sold to the Covenant Pentecostal Church. A worthless piece of Mason land J.J. never expected to sell. The church members were battling over drinking and dancing, and some loud-mouths intended to split off and build their own church where no one could have a lick of fun. May the mosquitoes lift them by the seat of the pants.

From the end of the road he could see Lily standing on the porch looking off into nothing.

J.J. gave her a hug and she began to search her pockets for a tissue. She cried into his shoulder. "I can't stand this. I'm

not made of iron. This is beyond the call."
He felt her shaking.

"You look bushed." J.J. closed his nose
against her bandaged hand's scent of io-
dine and her sour apron left too long in the
washing machine. He led her into the
kitchen and poured iced tea. She looked
lost in her housedress. Her cowlick poked
up and wisps of hair had escaped her twist.
J.J. looked at the yellowed whites of her
eyes and three layers of circles drooping
beneath. He thought, not unkindly, that
she looked like an old horse.

She was exhausted, beyond exhausted,
depleted after her trip out to the Columns
to see Wills. She told J.J. that he had just
stared at her with his starved look when
she told him the ghastly thing that had
happened, then he said, "Catherine, Cat,
Cat, how wonderful it will be to see her
again." He'd smiled and become agitated
trying to stand up. "Get me a comb, Lily.
I'm going down to the train." He raised his
chin, as though adjusting his tie, showing
her his lithic profile.

"There is no train. The train doesn't
even run through here anymore. Don't you
remember we used to take the train but
now we can't? The train station is the Jeff
Davis Museum, full of tarnished old uni-

form buttons and canteens. We can't even take a bus, not that we'd want to."

"Has she had a good trip?"

"Who?"

"That woman you were telling me about."

"Wills, my dear, it was Catherine I was talking about. There was no trip. I'm sorry I had to tell you this, and I know it's hard to understand, but you were going to hear it from somebody. I do not understand how anyone could do this to us."

He shifted in his chair and groaned. His left side was paralyzed except for his huge, twisted hand. She thought his blue veins looked like needlepoint thread. "Turn on the TV. I'd like a Co-Cola and would be much obliged if you'd ask for one. This hotel doesn't have a liquor license, and I've told them they're never going to make it. I've stayed at the finest hotels and they all have room service."

Lily smiled. Sometimes she almost thought he was being ironic. "Wills, you know you're at the Columns. They take good care of you here."

"I'm checking out at noon tomorrow. It hurts right here." He waved his right hand from his shoulder to his knee. "I hurt all over." Usually, he forgot that he'd been a doctor. He complained like a child but seemed to have no expectation that anything could be done for him.

She didn't tell J.J. that she had walked down to the nurses' station. Doors into the rooms along the hall were open and she tried, as usual, not to look at the shriveled bodies with diaper bulge propped in chairs looking out into the hall for some sign of activity. She avoided looking at the woman with fist-sized tumors all over her face and neck, but stopped to speak to Besta Warren, who was from a nice family and had simply fallen apart at fifty and had been making hideous turquoise and blue afghans here ever since. By the time she got to the nurses' station, she had forgotten what her brother wanted.

Now she remembered. "Wills wants so little; it was too bad he didn't get his Co-Cola."

"He'll get over it. He gets over everything else, doesn't he?" J.J. was alarmed at Lily's leaps. She's on the brink, he thought. He'd seen her like this before, when they'd lived through a hurricane warning and she'd feared the House would blow off its foundation and lift into the sky. "I'm going to shower, then let's fix some dinner." In his old room, he flopped backward on the

129

bed. Christ, J.J. thought, I left those perch in the sink.

Lily jumped when J.J. came back downstairs. He looked like a pure apparition of Wills when he'd come home from medical school at Emory. J.J.'s hair was too long. Wet from the shower and slicked back, his hair shone blue-black under the kitchen light. He was tan and barefoot. "Too pretty to be a boy," they'd teased him as a child. He had Wills's speckled green eyes, but his eyelashes were curled and thick. He didn't quite have Wills's height, but he was built solidly, while Wills was lanky and more elegant, Lily thought. He'd changed from what had appeared to be a torn undershirt into a proper white shirt with short sleeves. He never wore anything but white shirts, never cared about clothes a bit, and, on the two or three nights a week he slept at the House, he always put on a spotless one, leaving his fishing or hunting clothes in a heap on the floor for Tessie to pick up. A grown man stepping out of his pants like a four-year-old.

Lily felt like something carved of wax that had started to melt. J.J. heated leftover butterbeans and ham and she sat at the kitchen table. "The day your mama died,"

Lily began. He popped open a jar of bread-and-butter pickles and fished out some for each plate.

"Lily, we're not going to talk about any of that now. You've had a hell of a day — the worst day of your life. *I've* had a hell of a day. Let's just eat and then you go straight on to bed." He could not take even the idea of any histrionics.

She picked at her beans. This was not the worst day of her life. "Where's Catherine?"

J.J. lowered his fork and shook his head. "Lying on the ground, I guess."

"When's Ginger coming? Where's Ginger now? I made her biscuits."

J.J. went to the biscuit box. "So you did. Let's just have some samples of that major talent of yours. Ginger won't get here until late tomorrow. Maybe you can whip up a fresh batch in the mañana." My God, if she were not so worked up, maybe I could be allowed to be just a tad thrown myself, he thought. "You know it's a long flight, then she has to drive two hundred miles. I wish she'd waited before flying off like that. This may be completely over with to-morrow. Aunt Lily, you've got to keep calm, try not to get overwrought." Hysterical, more like it. J.J. spread a biscuit with butter that had softened in the heat. "They'll catch those idiots. That'll be the end of it. I hope to God, anyway."

Lily burrowed into the concept of traveling and time. "You're right, I'm just spinning. I'm sure Ginger's sound asleep right now — where is she? I've heard they're kidnaping people in Italy or shooting them in the knees."

"Rome. I'm sure she's in a nice hotel. Nobody's going to bother her knees. She flies out of Rome early." And she's probably wide awake, wondering what in God's name is going on here. He lifted his glass. "Whoop-de-do, Ginger, the divine Lily and I are feasting on cracked crab and champagne, discussing the fine points of thoroughbreds. Come on home, down to the heart of Dixie, summertime and the living is easy, fish are jumpin', root hog or die."

"Hush, J.J." Lily smiled even though she didn't want to. With J.J., she sometimes felt that she and Wills were young again, sitting together while their mother snapped the wilted flowers off the centerpiece and their father wandered into the living room to listen to the radio. "She drives too fast. She'll be here for supper. Maybe she'll bring some of that cheese she brought last time. She's thrilled to pieces over this work, digging around in the dirt pulling up little things nobody would want. She had this eentsie clay foot she thought was the prettiest thing."

Lily stared at the back door. "Everyone saw her spirit. You could tell right away that she was somebody. She always lifted her chin when she turned away from you. Like that." Lily looked at him, then at the wall, slowly raising her chin as she turned.

"Who're you talking about?" But he knew.

"Oh, that Catherine — but I was talking about Ginger, too. She has always been the sweetest thing. She used to bring me a tussie-mussie on May Day. But Catherine — hair black as yours, that's where you got it. Wills's hair was a rich brown, like mine, before he went snow white. They stole the show wherever they went. She could be tart-tongued."

"You're talking about Ginger or Mother?" Irritated, he followed her drifting even if he didn't want to. The tall dining room windows opened to the night sounds, the wild chorus not so different from the voice of Lily.

"That Ginger almost won the state debate when she was in high school. The segregation mess, I think they were arguing about even then. Lucky they didn't have guns, those demonstrators. Guns go off. That's what guns are for, to go off." She paused. "And they will keep going off for the rest of our born days. Catherine always wanted her way."

J.J. kept quiet and ate. She was on a tear. Deep shock, probably. Let her river run.

"I'll never forget that day. I felt so sorry for her. Little Gin-Gin shivering and crying like she'd never stop. Holding on to that doll she'd outgrown and yanking at her own hair. That hair's her glory. Like a house afire. You ran off and no one knew where you were, adding to the worry. The mystery I'll never fathom — Catherine was supposed to go to Macon the next day — that red Jaguar she wanted had come in, of course Wills gave her everything she could ever want. I never will understand that; if you'd ordered a car, would you . . ." She trailed off as she dropped three beans in her lap.

"You want a cup of coffee? I'll be glad to make it. I'm going out for a while."

Lily dropped her meandering reverie. "J.J., we must remember to ask the sheriff if she still had the envelope."

"Look, I'm going on out. Let's leave

these dishes." Let's sail them out the back door. Hit the fence hard.

"Sugar, there was a note in Catherine's hands before they buried her. I wonder if it was stolen."

"What did it say?" He barely could bring himself to ask, from his long habit of cutting off any memory, any fact, any speculation about his mother.

"I don't know. Maybe it was a good-bye letter, maybe a love letter from Wills. It would be awful if they took it, whatever it was." He didn't ask her who put the letter in Catherine's hand.

"I'll ask the sheriff tomorrow." He always tried not to think about his mother lying in the funeral home in the dress she'd worn on vacation. On Carrie's Island she wore white sandals, which she would kick off in sandy places and dangle from her fingers. When she leaned forward in her bathing suit, he could see a rim of white sand on her breasts and the sheen of suntan oil, which smelled like coconut and sunlight. Her charm bracelet jangled, and holding his and Ginger's hands, sometimes she'd do a little dance step and pull them along. All summer they'd played canasta, Monopoly, Chinese checkers, and Parcheesi. In the hottest part of the day, she made pimento cheese sandwiches, opened big bags of potato chips, and the three of them sat in the breezeway drinking lemonade and playing penny ante poker. He could still hear the waves breaking, then the quick sluicing back into the sea through banks of coquina shells, a sound like breathing in through clenched teeth.

J.J. drove out to the mill village to have a drink with Mindy. Water sprayed as his car crossed the almost-submerged wooden bridge over Cherokee Creek, which marked the entrance to the village. Rains had swollen the creek where he and Ginger used to play when they went to the office with Big Jim. Beyond the creek the rows of workers' houses began. He'd seen Mindy a few times since her divorce. Her husband drove an oil truck and last summer had taken hard to the Holy Rollers, which Mindy thought was all crap. His religious fervor supplied a lot of rules but somehow did not now leave him with the moral obligation to pay child support for Letitia, who was now five. J.J. hired Mindy to work at the store, right now stocking shelves and checking in orders.

Although Big Jim's mill closed ten years back, half the workers' houses were still lived in. J.J. collected the forty-dollar-a-month rent from each whenever he got around to it. He glanced at one house where he never collected rent, just beyond the creek. Ever since he'd heard from Scott that Aileen Boyd, the woman who lived there, had been Big Jim's mistress, he'd figured he would just let her be. And maybe it wasn't true. Scott had heard it through the maids' grapevine when he was a boy. A cat slept on her front steps. Farther on stood three empty houses he had boarded up after the Adventists complained that teenagers were using them to have sex and drink beer. The square street around the mill was lined with board houses set up on blocks, with slanting front porches and generous yards. Lard cans of geraniums, hollyhocks, so tall they arced, cornflowers and weedy larkspurs ornamented some yards. Most were packed dirt with holes where dogs curled. A few big chinaberry trees along the road provided what shade there was.

Mindy had painted her place sea-foam green, as she called it, and grew a potato vine up strings on either side of the porch. He saw her sitting on the steps polishing her toenails, even though it was almost dark. A patch of gold sky remained over the sprawling brick building where his great-grandfather and his grandfather had for decades manufactured cotton drapery material. Mindy's father had been a foreman and her mother worked at the looms, but they were now living in Florida and had moved up. He ran a gas station and she worked inside, selling cold drinks and her own fudge. People came from miles to buy her pecan-studded fudge. They were able to send Mindy a little money, always with a note encouraging her to leave this backwater and move to Denton, where she and Letitia could live in their spare room. They could expand the fudge business easily with an extra pair of hands.

J.J. opened the trunk and took out a bottle of gin. Mindy waved the silver-tipped brush at him and wiggled her toes in the air. "Hey, J.J., I didn't expect to see you. I heard Scott on the phone with his mama and I made him tell me what happened. This just gives me the willies. Are y'all right? You poor thing!"

J.J. realized this was exactly what he'd come to hear. She brought out ice in tall glasses and a bottle of tonic. Letitia was asleep in the front room. J.J. heard the whirr of a fan blowing back and forth over her. He sat down on the steps and poured. Mindy's toes were the color of dimes. "Silver Fantasy" — she waved the bottle of polish — "that's me." Now that her husband was gone, she spent hours on her skin, hair, nails, clothes. Even after six hours at the store — she couldn't get to work until ten, when she could take Letitia to play at her sister's — there were hours and hours to fill, hours when she'd shell peas, iron, and she didn't know what all. She brought home TV dinners from the store and Letitia loved the sectioned foil trays. She'd boil some corn, maybe, or cook some rice, but dinner now took minutes and then the day still continued. Only around nine-thirty, when dark finally fell, did she feel like the day might actually end. She had rinsed her hair in lemon juice tonight and rolled it on orange juice cans. She could see J.J. looking at her springy blond curls. He handed her a drink and sat down beside her on the steps. She pressed the glass to either cheek for the coolness. She stretched out her legs to admire her shiny toes.

Great legs, he noticed. Nice feet, too. Long and thin like a rabbit's. "My aunt is falling apart. You can imagine. Well, maybe you can't — I can't get a handle on any of this. My sister's flying in tomorrow. They've called in someone from the GBI. I hope they'll solve it soon — tomorrow — and take care of my mother. I'd like to forget this ever happened." He paused. "Fat chance." Bad hair, he thought. Looked like she'd run smack into a tornado. But as she turned her head, he caught the fresh, lemony scent and felt a shock of coolness from the strong drink he'd mixed. She was plain but he liked looking at her. She had a straightforward face with pale freckles, a pert nose, and large dark eyes that always looked sleepy. Her thin-lipped smile almost covered her overlapping bottom teeth. She was stacked. Her breasts looked pointed and full, but somehow she missed being sexy. Or maybe he missed, or something. He wanted company, wanted to feel a grand rush of desire that would land them in the middle of her ugly iron bed. It was not going to happen. Maybe the nest was still too warm. "For God's sake, let's talk about something else."

"Okay. Have you seen *Jaws*?"

"No."

"Okay. Let's see, we had a delivery today of tomato paste and barbecue sauces. And a little brat kicked loose the electrical plug

140

of the ice cream box and all the Popsicles melted. Letitia colored in the alphabet without going out of the lines. She talked back to me twice today."

J.J. laughed, leaned back against the railing, and watched the stars come out. There, his old friend, the Corona Borealis, pointed out to him by his mother from the porch of the cabin on a summer night like this when she was sitting on the log railing and he and Ginger barely swayed in the swing. Catherine's white hydrangeas grew just up to the porch, moons in wet, shadowy leaves. His mother had taken astronomy in college in order to avoid the math requirement. She remembered the Pleiades, Orion, the Dippers, the Bear. Others she made up. "Look, there's the Anthill, and there's the Train Wreck, and over there's the North Star, just above the Wandering Jew."

He and Ginger had protested. "The Wandering Jew is a plant at Lily's," they'd yelled. "There's no Wandering Jew in the sky." Still, they weren't sure.

"Look, there's his beard, and just follow the imaginary line — his knees, his feet. Of course there's a Wandering Jew constellation. There has to be . . ." Below them, the river plunged through the night. They heard the water surging over a clot of logs along the bank. Their father sat by himself out on the dock. J.J. closed his eyes around the image of his father barely touched by the porch light.

Mindy brought out two peaches. She ate hers, skin and all, letting the juice drip. J.J. leaned over and touched the point of her chin with his tongue. She pressed her breasts forward, then laughed and put her arms around his neck. He felt her hard lips against his, then her driving little tongue parted his mouth and he tasted the juicy sweetness of the fruit when she opened her mouth wider, breathing out into his mouth and deeply in, with his hands in her hair, her hand under his shirt. He knew where this would lead. He was willing now, but something stood apart from him, watching him go into action, and would not go. He leaned back, pulling her head down onto his chest. "You're hard to leave but I've got to get back to the House. This day has gone on into eternity. I'm pretty bushed. Lily's probably wandering the hallowed halls."

She didn't answer. He'd done this once before. The night they danced at Lake T the temperature hovered in the mid-nineties even at ten o'clock. Some guy from

Osceola who was dancing alone stumbled and whooped and poured a cold beer over his own head. They'd walked outside, where it was fresh and damp, though not any cooler. He kissed her neck, tickled her bare shoulders with a weed, teased her about stepping on his feet. He was a fine dancer and she thought that men who could dance were good in the sack, at least that's what she'd thought before her marriage. She'd been three years behind J.J. in school and always thought he was gorgeous, nothing like his big old bull of a granddaddy, who'd stand on the back of a truck handing out Thanksgiving turkeys to the millworkers. Like they were peons. She remembered how thrilled her mother was to cook a bird for the holidays. J.J. didn't have any of the boss man in him. When Scott asked his opinion about a new meat case, he just shrugged and said, "Whatever you think, big chief."

Mindy was just out of a marriage with a taskmaster. Carleton had wanted his undershorts pressed. He straightened the refrigerator every morning. He flew into a devil-minded fit when he came home and found baby Letitia wandering the yard with a dirty diaper. He had sharp yellow incisors which he bared when he ate. He ate dinner with his fork clutched in his right hand and his left hand on the table curled around his plate in a fist. She liked J.J.'s roll-with-the-punches lifestyle, but the taskmaster, at least, had wanted sex almost every night. "Take that thang off," he'd say. "You get on me first." The iron bed had creaked and banged against the wall. She smiled to remember Letitia waking up and calling out, "Mommy, are you all right?" Quick, unromantic, yes, but she was used to the big O on a regular basis. She didn't understand this holding back. She'd heard plenty over the years about J.J. and various women. She was prettier than a lot of them. Much prettier than Wynette Sykes, whose ears stuck out like Dumbo's.

"Why didn't you ever marry?" she'd asked J.J. that night at the lake. Faintly, they heard Jimi Hendrix singing "Purple Haze."

"Darlin', my life's not over. Don't say 'ever' yet."

"Well, why haven't you yet? How could you *avoid* it?"

"You ask a hard question."

"You've been out with so many women."

"You want a long or a short answer?"

"Have you ever had a long relationship?"

"Now, who's counting? No, I guess not.

In college once, maybe nine months."

"What happened?"

"What happened to your marriage — things go to hell." He did not say he quickly lost whatever it took to sustain a relationship, would turn viciously critical no matter how lovely, intelligent, suitable the woman. "Maybe I was born in the wrong era."

He knew that she would now say, "Maybe you just haven't met the right person," and she did.

"Could be. Let's exchange life stories some other time. Let's go back and dance." They'd danced and had a couple of beers. She had her car and he had not asked if he could follow her home. He stayed on after she left, waving good-bye with both hands. Her friend who tended bar told her later that J.J. danced with a short skinny girl and finally staggered out alone about two.

Mindy rested her head against his chest. His white shirt looked blue as thin milk in the moonlight. He stared up at the stars and they heard the splash of the creek where the sewage used to be emptied in Big Jim's time. She listened for his heartbeat. Bang. Bang.

On her dark front porch, Aileen Boyd
rocked and knitted. No need to see. She had
a feel for the rhythm of the needles, and the
pattern was simple, a white baby blanket for
her niece who was expecting in September.
Since the mill closed, Aileen had supported
herself by knitting and sewing baby clothes
for people in town. A twist of fate, since
she'd never had any children of her own. She
saw J. J. Mason's car pass, saw him glance
her way, but she was screened by a piece of
lattice.

She liked her work, edging little gowns
in lace and threading ribbon through crib
sheets. It beat the bejesus out of her old
job, sitting at a loom all day. So J.J. was
seeing a mill girl. Chip off the old block,
although he'd seemed obliging enough the
times he'd come for the rent. Then he'd
stopped coming and she didn't inquire.
People said J.J. didn't care about money.

Only those who've got buckets of it can afford not to care. Big Jim would not have wanted her rent. She wondered if J.J. had heard she had been Big Jim's fancy woman, mistress, lover, which was the word she preferred — *lover* made her think of satin sheets. Not likely, they were always careful. In Swan you had to be. And not so fancy, she thought, not a real mistress, but lover, yes, for four years. Dead for twenty years, Big Jim didn't seem as lost as other dead people; even his memory was magnified.

She was nineteen, married to Sonny for two years, when Big Jim first noticed her walking to work. He offered her a ride and she didn't refuse. He was the boss. Suddenly, she was transferred to the office and taught to send out bills and orders and sometimes make fabric sample deliveries in the mill car to nearby towns. Sonny didn't like it from the start, but Aileen was awestruck by her promotion. That first week Sonny shook her by the shoulders, demanding to know if Big Jim pawed her, and she'd screamed that not everyone was as sex mad as he was. Sonny went sour fast for her. She couldn't remember why she'd married him, though he'd dazzled her at sixteen, stopping in front of her house in his pickup. She'd run out when he blew the horn. Elbow out the window, hair blond as hers, he smiled and cracked his gum. He kept a pack of Camels tucked into his rolled-up T-shirt sleeve. They went bowling and to the bush-league ball games. He parked on country roads and rolled out a thin mattress in the bed of the pickup. Aileen had been with enough boys by then to know they weren't supposed to fire off immediately, but Sonny didn't seem to mind twenty-second sex. They hadn't been dating three weeks when he started getting mad if she even talked to another man. Fool that she was, she took his jealousy for love.

She was dying to escape her violent father, the smells and fights of seven people crammed into four small rooms, her mother's hacking and spitting. They were just as glad to see her go. She married Sonny at the Justice of the Peace because it cost only ten dollars. He slapped her on their wedding night because she was too friendly to his own brother. Soon they moved into a mill house. Sonny operated the big machinery at the mill, while she sat at a loom for nine hours a day, wondering what she had *thought* would happen.

When she transferred to the office, Big

Jim paid her an extra ten a week in cash, which she instinctively hid for herself in a coffee can under the house at the back of the storage bin. At first she only felt his hard eyes on her, but later that changed. By then, Big Jim told her she was not like other women; he said she was supple like a young peach tree and her long braid was the color of wheat with the sun shining on it. They met at a motel on the other side of Tipton after her deliveries. Sometimes he gave her money, but money was not the point. She had to admit sex was the point for both of them. Sonny's jealousy festered, but he had no proof she was fooling around, and she became a smooth liar. Even though Big Jim was old enough to be her father, he had a vigor and drive Sonny never had. Under Big Jim's body, her own felt shocked and ravished. But she learned to please them both and Big Jim grew to love her. She knew he did, though he never said so. They had a big time together. He was powerful, and when he surrendered to her, she was powerful. His wife had tight, no-color curls. Aileen would unbraid her hair and drag it loose over his body. She'd sass him, too. He liked that.

Sometimes when his wife and daughter were gone, she'd slip into the office at night when Sonny was on late shift at the mill. Big Jim always parked in the portecochère on the woods side of the office, so it was easy enough for him to turn out the light and open the car door to let her in without anyone seeing. With her crouched on the floor, they'd drive to the House, where they'd go at it right in the marital bed. Aileen smiled to remember his gratitude. He'd take her foot and press it to his cheek. He'd get on his knees and cover her with kisses, his large hands on her back. And he could go twice. Sonny couldn't; he'd fall dead asleep. She liked the second time better and Big Jim roared his pleasure. She'd be home by eleven. She wouldn't take chances like that now, for anyone. But at forty-three, she wasn't in as much demand for amorous risks.

So J.J. was leaving his calling card in the village. That lynx-faced Mindy no doubt. Well, Mindy need not get her hopes up. J.J. might be his own man, as people said, but he was not going to be waltzing down the aisle with a mill girl. It did not work that way.

Rome never quits, Ginger thought. Her hotel window opened above a street too narrow for cars but filled with strolling people even at two, three, four in the morning. As the numbers decreased with the hours, the voices of those remaining seemed to grow louder. Because of the heat, she had to leave the window open. She'd taken off her shirt and lay on top of the sheet in her panties, arms and legs stretched out so no part of her body came in contact with any other.

Marco didn't answer at nine-thirty when she came in from the trattoria down the street. She was surprised to find herself starving and for a whole hour didn't think of what had happened or why she was going, only enjoyed the pasta and wine at a table on a small piazza, where what looked like twelve-year-old boys zipped around on their Vespas and a cat curled in the chair

151

opposite her. Back at the hotel, she showered. At ten he still didn't answer so she gave up. At eleven he called. They were late getting back and he'd just seen her note. Ginger found that she couldn't tell him what had happened. Later, face-to-face, not now. Instead, she said, "There is some crisis and Aunt Lily can't handle it. No one knows where J.J. is at the moment. He must be off fishing somewhere. He's very unpredictable."

"Someone always unpredictable is therefore predictable, no? You will then count on him not to be around when you want him to be."

"You have a point," she conceded, although she didn't like him disparaging J.J. when he didn't even know him.

"I am sorry you have to go — I will be longing for you and I will miss your face."

Ginger fell asleep reading, then woke up suddenly after an hour and couldn't go back to sleep. She practiced emptying her mind by imagining herself to be a bride doll lying in a long box of green tissue paper, imagining herself on a fast horse galloping across Andalusia, imagining she had levitated from bed and was floating near the ceiling, bumping into corners gently like a helium balloon. Since childhood, she had found dozens of "trips" to take her away. A yellow helium balloon . . .

This is crazy and I'm going to get back to Marco as soon as I can, she told herself. One more flat-out disaster in the family. Hold on, just go through it. How do the Indian mystics walk over a bed of burning coals — empty your mind and just go fast. She imagined her mind as a primitive abacus, like one in Peru she'd read about, a network of knotted strings, with each knot holding a memory. She willed all the knots to be happy ones. While people shouted and laughed below her window, Ginger imagined knot after knot, almost feeling the coarsely-knotted rough twine: the armful of bounding, joyful, curly Tish, a mixture of all the good dogs in the neighborhood, leaping out of a basket on her seventh birthday; walking the beach at Fernandina just at sunrise with her father, picking up sand dollars; riding on the back of a sea turtle scuttling back to the ocean after laying eggs in warm sand. Ginger again let herself balance, arms out all the way to the edge of the water, then leapt off and watched her turtle swim out. For a long time, she followed the turtle into the tide. Then she shifted to her cot at the cabin, with the shelf of orange Twins

books beside her bed — *The Polish Twins,*
The French Twins, The Swedish Twins — and
on the shelf above, her mother's jars of tomatoes and peach and watermelon pickles,
their jewel colors crimson, icy green, and
the peaches like little rising suns. Ginger
went back to herself reading by kerosene
lantern, loving the exotic places in the
Twins books and realizing, at ten, reading
while snuggled under quilts, that she could
have that pleasure all her life. No matter
what. The knots of memory, so many of
them in, she loved the word, a *quipu.* Many
cultures had mnemonic systems with
beads, ribbons, knots, or pebbles. The
word *calculate,* she remembered, comes
from the Latin for pebble. She slipped toward the present, Marco's tanned back,
her mouth on the hollow of his neck while
he slept, the nightingale singing. When she
woke him to hear it, he turned and said,
"Let's do the nightingale, let's do the
moon in the valley, let's do the fox." She
had no choice but to love a man who
thought like that. Marco — always laughter
even in the middle of the night. Laughter
— the polar opposite of her expectations.
The knots of the present felt small and
slippery, while the old ones seemed heavy;
maybe they were pebbles after all, or

stones, the golden stones she piled into boxes at the Etruscan temple. I'll take those stones into my mind, she thought, and discover something new.

Finally, she slept.

In his old room, which was also his father's old room, J.J. ended the endless day by looking through one of his father's medical textbooks. Oddly, the section on strokes was all marked up with a pen. Other sections were underlined here and there, but J.J. scanned "then obstruction in the artery cuts off oxygen to cells," and "when toxins are released, cells start to die quickly," and "oxygen depletion will cause the molecular pumps to fade, disrupting the regulation of sodium, potassium, and . . ." He slammed the book shut. His father, not many years after studiously noting those passages, had a stroke himself. He leafed through Wills's senior yearbook, also abandoned along with old *Life* magazines, then shoved it back in the bookcase. The short story of his father, downed at forty-four. J.J. thought of the duck blind at dawn, aiming at a duck flying against the splintered light. The shot, the shock — how the airborne bird would turn instantly to dead weight and thud heavily onto the water.

J.J. had come to this room when he was sixteen. Lily never had wanted to change the stiff curtains printed with sailboats or the table set up with his father's HO model trains permanently stalled outside a village, with miniature frosted Christmas trees and a little red post office. J.J.'s old fishing baskets, rods, and archery equipment hung on racks around the big square room, which was identical to Ginger's, except his looked out toward the woods behind the house, and hers on the front faced the pond, where Lily's two fierce white swans glided on their reflections in the black water.

Lily slept in her parents' old room downstairs, in the bed so high you had to use a step stool to climb in. If she left her door open, J.J. could hear her snore when he came in late and went back to the kitchen for something to eat. The snores were lighter when he was a boy, but often he'd crept out of bed to listen for them, just to assure himself that at least she was still alive, even though she drove him mad with her senseless rules: you can't cut paper on Sunday, it's bad luck to leave a hat on a bed, so-and-so's beneath you, so-and-so's from a nice family, on and on. Fussbox, he and Ginger had called her. Willy-Nilly Lily.

The House itself was a comfort then; he'd had a sense of its immense stability. His grandmother's amber wax grapes still sat on the dining room table, and he always opened the door to the smell of lemon beeswax polish, faint cigar smoke, and something good frying in the kitchen. He found his great-grandmother's yellowed sheet music inside the piano bench. Tomorrow Ginger would be in the room beside his, the head of her bed separated from the head of his by a wall. As he tried to sleep, he kept cycling on Ralph Hunnicutt parked in the county's Ford, slapping mosquitoes, dozing, and jerking awake every time a frog croaked, his mother with a bullet hole in her heart, lying under a tarp. Ginger, yes, three, four, five, six, seven, eight hours, already in the air. Heading out over Europe, coming home, the Atlantic glittering below like hammered pewter. He hated flying over water. The Atlantic, a powerful magnet pulling her plane. No. He would keep that plane up by the force of his will. He only slept by thinking of her already there in her room, her left hand under her head the way she always slept, there, just opposite him but close, the way she'd always been.

July 9

Eleanor spent the early morning reading magazines on her terrace, the only time of the summer day she could enjoy being in the garden. She told Hattie to stay home because there was plenty of food left over from the bridge party, and the day was going to be too sultry to move. She did not visit Holt, had not even considered going, but had surprised herself by considering the possibility of never going again. She'd come out of sleep this morning already thinking. "Catherine would be, let's see, she and Holt Junior were about the same age, she'd be around fifty-five," she'd said aloud. Holt Junior by now had developed a spongy paunch and a bald spot you couldn't miss when he walked down steps in front of you, even though he tried to comb a pale strand of hair over it.

If Ralph or the GBI thought this was a grave robbing, they were whistling "Dixie."

Why would a common thief go into a grave after so long? She turned the pages of *House Beautiful*. A woman with a castle in England planted an all-white garden. How dull; did she have dresses all the same color, too? Eleanor ripped out a recipe for turkey with tarragon and bacon. She'd make it when Holt Junior next came to Sunday dinner. Holt Junior — too bad he never married, never found the right girl. She thought of Catherine. What secrets would this drive out? What blessèd thing can we ever know? What if Catherine had lived? She wondered how Lily would have lived her life.

Catherine would have aged well, Eleanor thought, and Wills, if he had not had the stroke, would be at the height of his powers as a doctor. They would have transformed Palmetto House. Ginger would have shown up on her wedding day instead of locking herself in her room. That poor Mitchell forgave her, although it still didn't work out. She imagined Palmetto House lit up like the *Titanic* at night, music spilling from all the open windows. *When all the things you are, are mine . . .* Holt Junior might have met one of Catherine's friends from Macon. Even J.J. might have been different — put that good

162

brain to use. Lily didn't fit in that picture. Lily would have been forced to invent a different life, but Eleanor could not imagine a life for Lily away from the House.

Eleanor reached for *Holiday*. She'd been nowhere since Holt died. Maybe she and Lily should take a trip together in the fall. It would do Lily good. A cruise to the Caribbean — what a grand idea. They could find bridge partners and stay on board if natives in the ports of call looked unpleasant. On one of her trips with Holt, a lovely lady from upper New York had been hit with a tomato in Barbados.

Lily called Eleanor but no one answered. She knew Eleanor liked the early morning outside, as she did, and must be out pinching back marigolds or having her coffee in the backyard glider. She knew for sure Eleanor would not be paying her visit to Holt's grave today. Lily was restless. She freed CoCo from his cage and let him fly around the porch. He lighted on her shoulder, fluttering his green wings, and gently pecked her ear. She wished Eleanor would come over for a game of Scrabble while she waited for Ginger. The house was ready. She decided to ride over to visit her other close friend in Swan, Agnes Burkhart. Lily had a raincoat to shorten. Since she wouldn't be long, she let CoCo go in the car with her.

As she drove up Palmetto Road, she passed Wills and Catherine's old house but did not glance in that direction. Catherine had kept Agnes's Singer whirring ninety miles an hour. Once Lily had been at Agnes's getting a linen duster hemmed when Catherine came in with a sketch of a dotted-swiss dress with a fluffy skirt. Agnes, mouth half full of pins, kept squeezing a rubber bulb, marking Lily's hem with a puff of chalk while she mumbled to Catherine about covered buttons and French seams. Lily had greeted Catherine coolly. It was just like her to breeze in wanting what she wanted right then. Catherine wanted Ginger to have the dress for Easter, three weeks away, and Agnes already had a pile of alterations to do for Maggie Everett, who had lost fifty-two pounds on a meat and martini diet. There were complicated inserts of narrow lace on the bodice. Agnes hauled herself off the floor and promised Catherine she'd get the dress made. They say Agnes Burkhart almost went blind from all the hand-sewing she did. She loved

Catherine's clothes the most. And Lily, too, had admired Catherine at church with the two children, Ginger in hand-smocked dresses, J.J. in just-pressed sailor suits, and Catherine, oh, she remembered a good-looking navy dress with big buttons, and one winter a lavender-gray cashmere suit with a rolled collar. Lily had combed *Harper's Bazaar* looking for beautiful dresses and skirts, wanting Catherine to envy *her.* Her bond with Agnes came from childhood. They'd gone all through school together; their mutual passion for fabric began with dressing dolls. Often Lily would forget her rivalry with Catherine and buy yardage because she knew Agnes would love it.

"Well, Lily, I Swan, come in out of the heat." Agnes flung open the double door. Lily entered Agnes's airless hall fanning herself with a newspaper. This was the house children avoided at Halloween because of Agnes's sister, Evelyn, who hung her hair over the upstairs balcony. Children thought roaches fell from it. Actually, she was only drying it in the sun. Once the sister had called to a child, *"step on a crack break your mother's back,"* and since then children crossed the street and walked on Lard Bascom's side, even though he had a biting dog. Well-dressed women never had compunctions about crossing the broken sidewalk, bringing Agnes a handful of daylilies and plopping down a piece of material bought in Macon. Agnes sewed like an angel.

In what could have been Agnes's living room, Lily found the one chair not covered with clothes and bolts of cloth. Agnes took a seat behind her sewing machine, as though she were about to press the pedal and run the needle down a seam. Lily wondered where Evelyn might be. She used to give foot treatments, trimming yellow corns and scrolling off waxy crescents from calluses. Many times Lily had watched her massage customers' bunions. She worked with a tub of scalding water in the kitchen while Agnes held forth in the living room. It was said that she had her own coffin ready in her bedroom, but who'd ever seen upstairs? The two maiden sisters had lived together their whole lives, inheriting the two-story house, the only stone one in Swan, and so very damp inside. Their father, an electrician, a native of Germany, could not pronounce his *w*'s and *th*'s. Evelyn, who never had cut her hair, was subject to fits, and Agnes often had to rush to her with a spoon so that she did not bite her tongue in two.

Agnes no longer copied dresses. The most anyone could get her to do was a hem or a tuck in a jacket. Her hair, harshly cut like a monk's, shone white under the bare bulb dangling over her machine, and her plucked-to-nothing eyebrows gave her a look of permanent foreignness. In the center of the room stood a worktable stacked with thousands of patterns, spools, pinking shears, scissors, pincushions, and bobbins.

The place was a veritable archive of the dress habits of Swan ladies, if anyone were interested, which, of course, no one ever would be. There was a peculiar, heavy odor. Had a mouse died among the folded tissue-paper coats and prom dresses?

Agnes had not heard about Catherine. She made a little whickering cry and balled her fists to rub her eyes. "My dear, you poor thing. Sometimes I think we are in our last days. These beasts among us . . ." While she recovered from the shock, Lily waited. She cast a glance at the window to see if the jar of Agnes's gallstones still rested on the sill. It did.

"Agnes, I thought of you later yesterday when I kept seeing that blue silk dress,"

Lily began. "I just wanted to talk to you. I've had quite a setback from all this. You can't imagine. You must have made that dress for Catherine? Doesn't that seem so strange, the dress . . ." Lily couldn't quite articulate what she felt, "that the dress was made for an occasion, no doubt," she continued, "but it played a part in something unbearable later . . ." She shivered.

"Rabbit jump over your grave? I know what you mean." Agnes thoughtfully rubbed the small hump emerging just below her neck. "Catherine's favorite color was blue. Of course, with those eyes. What a shame." She scraped back her chair and turned to take down a ragbag sewn from a U.S. Navy bedspread. "My brother Hugo brought this back from the war. I've kept it for scraps, in case I ever got the desire to make a quilt. I kept a piece of everything pretty." She emptied the contents on the floor. "Hugo's been gone almost as long as Catherine. What shade of blue?"

"Bright blue, marine — with a dollop of turquoise."

Agnes picked through the remnants, passing each one to Lily for the pleasure of the textures. "Here's a burgundy mohair. Little Sarah George wore that suit for seven winters straight." Little Sarah George

Godwin, named for her mother's father, was at seventy-something still called Little Sarah George. Agnes stuffed plaid wool and printed cottons back in the bag, then found a scarf of tangerine silk. "This was the prettiest material, so soft it'd tear if you looked at it."

Lily remembered Catherine rising from a table, a sparkling swish of sound like tissue paper crumpling. She'd held a drawstring evening bag in both hands. "Wasn't that Catherine's?"

"Yes, went over one shoulder, cut on the bias, and not everybody can carry that off, believe you me. Catherine out of all the people I ever sewed for had a style — she just knew how cloth would drape."

"You know she studied design those two years she went to college."

"Yes, she could draw just what she wanted. All those notebooks she kept were full of pictures. Not just clothes, which she brought over to me, but I'd see columns drawn out, and notes on how the shadows angled off them, and all that. She drew floor plans like an architect, gates and porches, that sort of thing."

Lily didn't want to discuss Catherine's notebooks. The last thing on earth she wanted to hear about was Catherine's notebooks. A crash — a bed collapsing? — came from upstairs but Agnes ignored it. She fingered dimity stripes of watermelon and sage, rough cotton scrim, and ebony velvet. She rubbed a Scottish tweed between her fingers. "Tsshhh, Libby looked like a strutting peahen in that tweed getup, don't tell her I said so. That was a crying shame about Catherine. I never would have thought she'd do anything like that. After all these years, here's a piece of her pedal pushers, navy denim laced up the side. She wore them with red shoes and a white blouse. I remember as though it were yesterday."

Lily suddenly pictured Catherine on the side of the grave, her face the shade of tea. She buried her own face in the tangerine silk. "I'm sorry, Agnes. I'm upset."

"Of course you are." She brought Lily a cup of coffee with a lot of sugar, the way she knew Lily liked it. "This is good and hot." Agnes sifted through balls of lace the color of clotted cream, a swatch of green-and-yellow-checked taffeta, russet flannel, then she jerked up a piece of blue silk in the shape of a short sleeve. She nodded. "That's from the dress she's buried in."

Lily recognized the intense blue immediately.

"She changed her mind and wanted three-quarter-length sleeves." Agnes held it up to the lightbulb. "She wore a ring of lapis lazuli in those days. Said it was to go with that."

"Remember the funeral, that tragic day?" Lily suddenly realized why she'd come to Agnes. It was to ask that question.

"Yes, who could forget. Ah! I remember her crossed hands. She was not wearing the ring but she was holding an envelope. I wondered if it were her suicide note — you know they say there's always a note left behind. That's how they get back at the living."

So others had noticed it. "No, that was a personal good-bye." Lily did not explain.

In the car Lily saw that the raincoat was still folded on the front seat; she'd forgotten to take it in. CoCo imitated the sound of the car engine. Lily laughed for the first time since her sight had been seared by the vision of Catherine. As she left Agnes's driveway, she scraped her fender against the crape myrtle. She did not see Evelyn on the upstairs porch, hair down and one breast hanging out of her robe. CoCo squawked his best hundred-crashing-hubcaps song.

A maniacal antlike hurry started at the end of the skyway. The strap of Ginger's carry-on bag dug into her shoulder until she thought her collarbone would snap. Flights delayed by thunderstorms in the Midwest had left hundreds of people lounging in the waiting areas and foraging the bars and food stands.

The arc from Europe to America always disrupted what Ginger thought of as *long time*. To fly across the Atlantic, she felt, was more drastic than simply crossing over miles of ocean. She came down into a present tense where she stepped lightly on the surface, while in the other world, she felt the strata of time below her feet. Even the light came from a more ancient, softened sun.

Outside, the sky looked hazy, whether from pollution or from temperature and humidity, she didn't know. As she headed the rented Pontiac out on I-75 South, she immediately saw the familiar watery, wavering heat lines rising from the highway, just at the far point of her vision. As she came closer, they receded so that where she was going appeared in an agitated state of semi-mirage. The cancerous odor of melting tar flowed up through the vents. She snapped on the air.

Noon, one hour late because of head winds. She'd slept badly in Rome and not at all on the flight. She'd forgotten to bring anything to read and had been able to find only the in-flight magazine and a golf club newsletter someone left in the seat pocket. She'd stared at pictures of an up-and-coming woman golfer for several minutes until the submerged knowledge that her mother had at some point become interested in golf slowly rose in her mind. Ginger remembered red and white socks that fitted over the clubs. She'd wanted them for hats for her dolls. In the returned memory, she saw her mother tee off. Her mother leaned down and pushed the yellow tee in the ground, balancing the shiny ball on top. She hunched forward, poised, and the cutting swoosh of her swing startled Ginger. The ball did not come down on the fairway but hooked in midair and landed in or near a dank little swamp. Then Ginger saw only herself, legs pumping as she ran down the slope to the water, where mud turtles plopped off their logs as she scanned the perimeter for the ball, spotting it, not in the water, but too far out in slimy ooze. Who else was there? Memory shaded a part of the scene. A long-legged crane stepped warily, as though despising to get its feet wet, but did not fly. A man appeared but far away, and by the time Ginger reached her mother again, he was gone. Ginger stared at the beautiful bird, then looked back toward her mother waving to her as she pulled her cart along the grass.

End of glimpse, but Ginger felt a rush of exhilaration. Her mother was young, younger than Ginger now, playing golf alone in her brown tweeds and neat brown and white cleated shoes. The memory widened: Ginger turning flips, sometimes landing wrong and skidding her knees on the frost-burned grass. Frost-burned grass — it must have been late fall.

She was glad to have recaptured this memory and lingered on her mother striding toward the next hole.

Ginger flipped the air dial up another

notch and stepped on the accelerator, passing three and four straining trucks at a time. The fumes, stale air, and crush of the airport fell away. She felt herself unfurl after the cramped last-row seat on the plane. I-75 cut through the heart of Georgia, running by towns which prospered by its proximity. Millions of transport trucks, plus carloads of Yankees heading for Florida, tanked up at gas stations, pecan candy stores, and Wagon Wheel restaurants, or paused to shop at the cotton mills' outlet stores. The towns I-75 missed languished, their formerly tortured two-lane state roads reverted to country lanes, and most of their downtown Purple Duck and Blue Willow cafés had been boarded up. Who went that way, unless they had to?

At Perry, she turned off and took the slow road through orchards and small towns spared the ugliness of haphazard development. Kudzu-covered tenant farms bordered fields abandoned in the sixties. She slowed, let down the window for the scent of peach and the dusty smell of the pecan groves and corn rows breaking into tassel. One night she'd told Marco the names of towns she liked: Unadilla, Hahira, Osierfield, Lax, Omega, Mystic,

Enigma, Headlight, Friendship, Calvary, Lordamercy Cave, Milksick Cove, a litany he countered with Italian places.

Marco always maintained that America must constantly reinvent itself, and she supposed that was true, but maybe not here. The straight road turned dreamy blue in the early afternoon heat. If no oblivious farmer or pulpwood truck pulled out of a side road, she could safely exceed the speed limit, go faster than on I-75, whizzing through rising and falling land soon to be dotted white with cotton bolls, and across all the creeks named by the Indians. The Pontiac moved so quietly on the surface of the road that she might be sailing.

Her earlier thought about the ancient sun in Italy and the present-tenseness of America felt wrong, she realized. She was tunneling through luxuriant blue air in a place profoundly old because it *was* empty. This low dip, this slow hill, were formed by the tides and currents in the warm shallow sea that once rolled over these fields. I'll have to talk about this with J.J., she thought. He'll understand geological time. She and J.J. loved the white sand beaches they found near the cabin. Since a sea flowed, she mused, those who were born here must have a knowledge, a sub-aqueous, preliterate intelligence. Or maybe it is just the damn heat that makes people look as though they're walking underwater, dreaming with their eyes open. On the windowsill of her room at the cabin, she'd kept her proof of the sea, a line of bleached seashells she and J.J. had found in dried creekbeds, lying there for eons until she'd scooped them up and crammed them in her shorts pockets.

From the crests of the rises, she looked down as she drove into a green sea of expansive longleaf-pine forests. As far as the eye, as if she did not exist. The smell blew through her hair, deeply fresh, one of the scents most basic to her memory. Even public bathrooms scrubbed with harsh, pine-scented disinfectant could make her stop and inhale. The wind in pines, the sound of the human soul, J.J. once said, if the human soul had a sound. No one would say that but J.J. No one has his hot brightness.

Where there's such emptiness, Ginger thought, I feel my mind expand. Italy is everywhere shaped by the human touch — that's why I feel warmed there. But those who worked this land left almost nothing. Unpainted board houses lean for a few decades, turn silvery, then collapse into heaps quickly covered by vines. Even graves with their crude crosses are swallowed by the land itself, which resumes its own contours. All because they built with wood, she thought, like the Etruscans, whose towns have been completely erased by time, except for graves, stone foundations, and mammoth walls.

She stopped to eat at a diner in Hakinston and decided to have coffee with a piece of the lemon pie, even though a fly was trapped under the plastic dome. It seemed more intent on getting out than on burrowing into the meringue. The waitress called her "honey," and Ginger smiled to remember her struggles with the Italian formal "you." In Italy, never in a thousand years would someone address a stranger familiarly. She had heard *"Buon giorno, Contessa"* to a slow old remnant of the nobility making her way to the piazza, and in the bread store, *"Buon giorno, architetto,"* an impossible-in-America greeting — "good morning, architect" — that happened every day in Italy. Life is untranslatable, she thought; suddenly I'm "honey," but why not, I'm almost home.

Forty miles down the road, she passed the turnoff to the cabin but kept going —

J.J. better not be off on some fishing trip. When the profile of Swan appeared in the distance, she finally began to think of what, exactly, she faced. She dreaded, more than the stupid crime and its stupid solution, the fight to keep memories away. She already had felt the thrill of imagining her mother swinging a golf club. The sorrow of her father's life, harder to ignore than her mother's because he still lived, lodged against this hideous event. A push of memories seemed to be pressing somewhere between her shoulder blades, between her breasts. Just in the exact place, she realized, where her mother shot herself.

Glancing east, across the knee-high cotton, she saw slats of gray rain in the distance, moving toward her, racing the car toward some intersection up ahead. Her father used to call it *the walking rain* and she loved the figure of speech. Rain walking across the ground, a change in the weather visible and stalking. Around Swan you always must be alert to nature. Porous limestone suddenly can collapse in a perfect circle, leaving a green sinkhole pond of infinite depth. A tornado can appear on the horizon, a clear conical image imprinted against the vast sky. Or a hurricane, with a secret eye trained on who knows what or where.

After hurtling herself across the ocean, she suddenly was in no hurry to get to Swan. She drummed the steering wheel with her fingers. Let the GBI settle this before I get there, she thought. I can have a quick visit with J.J., cheer up Lily, who must be devastated, and check on Daddy. J.J. and I can go out to the cabin; I'll lie on the dock and listen to the river. She would not get to see Caroline Culpepper, her best friend since nursery school. She'd be at the beach with her children and her sister's family all of July. A wave of affection for Caroline rolled over her. Growing up, they'd played bridge thousands of afternoons. All through high school Ginger slept over at Caroline's on Saturday nights. If only J.J. had married her! Caroline finally gave up on that idea and married Peter Banks, balding even in his late teens, but sweet and number four in his law school class at Florida. During the chaos of Ginger's life the past few years, she always looked forward to seeing Caroline and Peter when she limped back to Swan. Her other close friend from childhood, Braxton Riddell, now bored her. Once she'd thought his azure-blue eyes looked like a Greek statue's. Now he just looked

180

preternaturally blank. I'll see no one, she thought. Only J.J. and Lily and Tessie. I can go back to Rome early next week.

On impulse, she turned toward Magnolia Cemetery. The gates were open. She turned left, then right at the Bryon plot and down the grassy road to her family's graves. The roses, she saw, were innocently abundant, as though nothing had happened. She had expected someone standing guard, but there was only Cass Deal in the distance, working on a new grave. She got out of the car and stepped cautiously toward the gate. The hole in the ground looked newly dug. The broken stones were stacked in a corner and the clay-stained gravel had been hosed clean. Her mother's body and the coffin had been removed. Ginger rubbed her stiff neck. "Once again we failed her," she said out loud. Great-grandparents, Daddy's Uncle Calhoun, Big Jim, and Mama Fan all remained in their appointed places, their Georgia granite markers leached to white by the strong sun, except for Big Jim's, which was smeared black.

Glittering trails left by snails zigzagged across Big Jim's stone. Who would disturb a grave? On the top of the pile of broken stone, she saw her mother's name incised.

A clump of clay obscured the letters. Ginger brushed it away and with a marble pebble gouged each letter. *Catherine Phillips Mason.* She went back to the car to get a tissue from her bag and rubbed the name clean. She looked up and saw Cass coming toward her.

"Well, Ginger, I wondered who was snooping here. You haven't changed a bit, pretty as a picture. I cain't tell you how sorry we all are about this crazy nonsense. We got your aunt's car back to her. Never had a thing like this happen before. Over there in Europe, aren't you? When'd you get in?"

"Just now. I haven't even been out to the House yet. I just came here . . ." She stood with her arms folded, as though she were cold. Could he have done this? Of course not.

"Ralph was here all night, him and his dog. Slept in the car and the mosquitoes about carried him off. The boy from the GBI came out with Ralph a while ago and the officer ordered the remains to be taken to the funeral home for a look. He found some paint scrapes on the gravestone, found out the fellow who did this even used my Bobcat. I remembered when I got here the other day, I noticed it had been moved." He did not add that he had with-held that information until confronted. "So they think a man operating alone could have done it. I'll get Big Jim all cleaned up and I'm hoping we can end this whole thing before long. A shame, a cryin' shame."

"Thank you, Cass, we appreciate that. Everyone has been so kind," she said auto-matically. "This must have been hard on you, too."

The rain came, immediately pelting hard. Clay rivulets ran red. Cass dashed for his truck. Ginger stood for a moment. Out of old habit, she tipped back her head and opened her mouth for the taste of the warm rain. Then she slid into the Pontiac and headed home.

Ginger found Lily and Tessie in the kitchen, Tessie rolling out shortcake crust and Lily swatting flies with a rolled-up newspaper. "Lord, Lord, we didn't hear you come in, sugar baby, how are you?" Lily dropped the paper. Tessie's hands were up to her wrists in flour. The room smelled like old honey in a hive. They both embraced her, sat her down, and plopped a glass of pineapple tea in front of her. Tessie stuck in a sprig of mint.

"Oh, Lily . . ." Ginger began.

"Let's don't say a thing about what happened. That can wait. I just want to look at you — a sight for sore eyes, sugar, I'm just so glad you're *home*."

Tessie quickly cut the circles of dough with the top of a glass and placed them in a pan. "Yes, sir, strawberry shortcake — I know what you like, and J.J., too."

"Where is J.J.?"

"He's down at the sheriff's office signing some papers. He's been gone about an hour so he should be back soon." Lily opened the screen door and futilely motioned flies out, while others flew inside. Ginger was alarmed at how wild she looked with her hair falling around her face and a dollop of strawberry jam on the front of her blouse. Lily asked her how the flight had been, and how was the drive from Atlanta. Ginger and J.J. always feared they would lose her, too. Ginger drank the cold tea, comforted by the familiar kitchen, with its round table and tall cabinets, whose doors inside were completely papered with handwritten recipes on index cards. Behind the table stood glass-fronted cabinets full of sets of dishes. Her grandmother Fan's collection of glass lemon squeezers still lined the top shelves, and a set of Depression-era ice cream dishes was stacked below. How could green dishes sit there all those years — not one of the twelve broken — and her mother be dumped out of her grave? The flower-sprigged Limoges and the gold-rimmed good dishes occupied the lower shelves. "I think I'll bathe and get ready . . ." Get ready for what? she wondered.

Both Tessie and Lily followed her upstairs, switching on the attic fan in the upstairs hall and opening the door to her high yellow room, where the curtains billowed out with the humid gusts drawn in by the fan. Earlier, they'd turned down the linen spread and placed a handful of zinnias and snaps in a vase by her bed. Ginger very much wanted to lie back in the tub, to be clean, to fall into her own bed, with the whirr of the fan, wanted nothing to be wrong. "Is it painful?" She saw Lily holding her bandaged finger away from her body.

"It smarts. Yesterday it throbbed so I guess it's on the mend." Lily had a gift for closing off the unpleasant and moving on.

Ginger slept easily. She woke as she had many times in her life — with J.J. tickling the end of her nose with one of CoCo's feathers. His green eyes startled her. "J.J., you rat!" She sat up and gave him smacking kisses on both cheeks.

"Italian laziness!" He grabbed her foot hard and began to tickle the sole. She kicked loose, pushing him back and digging her nails into his ribs, where she knew he couldn't take it. They rolled around, shouting laughter. On the stairs with an armful of fresh towels, Lily thought they'd gone mad. Those two. What could be funny? Under the circumstances.

J.J. kicked off the espadrilles she'd once brought him. "Are you okay, gal baby? A loaded question, given the conditions of your triumphal return to the bosom of the family. How's the old country?" J.J. sat in the window seat and Ginger pushed the pillows behind her in bed. So many talks began this way, J.J. looking out the window, her with her arms around her knees.

"My work was going well and Italy *was* heaven for me — I'll tell you about it — but I already feel like I've come a million miles." She tried to picture Marco's dense curls, his movie-star look when he wore sunglasses, and his jacket tossed over his shoulders. "I was all right until I stopped by Magnolia before I came home . . ."

"Oh God, why, Jesus, Ginger, why would

you do such a fool thing?"

"It didn't seem real. Now it does but I feel numb, kind of sucked dry. Is it the heat — somebody gone crazy with the heat?"

"Maybe somebody Big Jim suckered. Some fool with something against the Masons or Mama, at least. Some lunatic after a diamond or gold."

"What if he has something else in mind — torturing Lily with cigarette burns or setting the house on fire . . ."

J.J. smiled. "Or it's our old friend the devil. Pops up, bored with diddling Persephone in the underworld, and thinks, let's see, it's been a long time since I really performed on those Masons. They're always good for a laugh. What little twist can I dream up to knock them into a cocked hat." He threw his baseball cap in the air and socked it.

"No, be serious." At least he was not in his redneck mode, which, as he once explained, he often used for protective coloring.

"All right. Calm down. Think with me. What is this saying? Aside from the jewel-heist theory. Maybe someone wanted to damage her, even after she's been dead such a long time. A crude articulation, but he certainly got my attention."

"This is more and more grisly; I just can't absorb it. Do you suppose someone in love with her for all these years has squirreled away his feelings? But there's rage in this. And that black paint, a primitive marking." Ginger knew of cultures that marked the houses of sinners — maybe this was a throwback to that practice.

"Maybe the whole thing is random craziness. We're forcing an explanation so that it begins to look rational." J.J. bit his knuckle, an old habit. "Our ol' buddy Ralph says the GBI loaded her into a hearse and sent her to Ireland's to examine the body, in case of necrophilia, or God knows what. He said we'll hear something from them tomorrow. The only evidence he's discovered is a dirty handkerchief that Cass Deal found. The GBI took it, too, as part of what they hilariously called suspicious circumstances. How suspicious can we get here? But this suspicious handkerchief was wadded-up nice linen, not a cheap three-to-a-package number. This fruitcake apparently had wiped his hands, hadn't even jacked off. No, Miss Nancy Drew, no monogram and no store label. A zero. No chance for *The Case of the Dropped Handkerchief*."

"J.J., stop, stop. When she died . . ."

"Let's don't put each other through a conversation about her. Lily said that Dad probably left a letter in her hand, but Ralph said nothing like that turned up. I have no memory of any letter."

"Me neither."

J.J. stood up. "Let's zip out to the cabin. We can pick up some beer and take a swim."

"Lily has planned dinner. They were making shortcake when I got here and I could smell Tessie's pepper chicken." Her chicken always was known as pepper chicken because she tipped the pepper jar generously when she smothered the pieces in cream. "I hope she fixes mashed potatoes." Ginger was suddenly famished. "I wonder what he wrote. And if he possibly could remember? Do I have a suit at the cabin?"

"Lily seemed vague, said maybe he wrote a love letter, who knows? Your chest of drawers hasn't been touched, except once when a winsome young thang needed to borrow a sweater."

"Who was it? I bet it doesn't bear repeating."

"No one you know."

"I can well imagine."

Two years ago Alan Ireland had outfitted the two-car garage behind his funeral home with a drain in the concrete floor, a sink, and a long table. He did not want to taint his main mortuary when a grisly murder occurred in Swan, or to crowd it when he had an overflow from a collision or a flu epidemic that snuffed out three or four old folks. Most of the embalming took place inside the house, which for fifty years was his family's home, a grand, columned brick house rising out of banks of azaleas, a place of pride for the Irelands. Then his father had started the mortuary, exiling the family forever afterward to living upstairs. Even now, Alan often was startled as he entered his grandmother's front parlors, the now heavily draped rooms choked with fragrances of the standing sprays and wreaths surrounding the viewing alcoves, where the mourners and the curious came to pay their last respects.

No one ever had mentioned it, not even his wife, but he thought he smelled something beneath the cloying gardenias and roses. The smell of iron lingered, the ferrous red smell of blood. Perhaps it was his imagination. He didn't mind his eight-year-old daughter, Janie Belle, playing hide-and-seek in the coffin-selection room or seeing the peaceful dead laid out in the front parlor. She'd even seen him arranging hair and brushing makeup on corpses. She had not witnessed other preparations, or so he thought.

Janie Belle called from the back steps of the house, "Daddy, Mama made coffee." She carried a paper sack trepidly down the steep steps and handed Alan the thermos and cups.

"You go play, angel. Daddy's got business to do." He called her "angel" because she looked like one, a plump dumpling with pale corkscrew curls and a face so little occupied by its features that it gave the impression of a painted egg. He feared she'd inherited the Irelands' physical neutrality. Strangers always forgot they'd met him. Only in old age, when the skin became etched with lines, did Irelands acquire character.

Janie Belle posted herself on the back

porch and watched the arrival of a man she didn't know in a black car. She gouged her fingernail under the last chicken pox scab on her cheek. Janie Belle wouldn't stop scratching even though her mama told her she'd have ugly pox scars on her face and no one would want to marry her. Her mama even threatened Janie Belle by saying she was going to call the police on her if she didn't stop scratching. Her heart quickened as she saw the sheriff's car turn in behind the stranger. She swung over the rail and hid under the porch.

GBI investigator Gray Hinckle, who'd followed from the cemetery into Swan behind Alan, stepped out of his car. He and Ralph wheeled out the stretcher and Alan jerked down the cord on the garage door, which fell hard on the concrete floor. "Alan, you tryin'to wake the dead?" Ralph asked. The air conditioner near the ceiling churned and dripped.

Gray pulled off the tarp from Catherine's body. "Let's whip through this. She's not exactly my idea of a party girl," he said.

"It just makes you wonder at human nature. Who could want a ring or necklace enough to face this in the dead of night?" Alan passed around rubber gloves, tied on an apron, stepped aside. Gray cut the dress up the right side, then the left. He sliced through her stiff slip and partially disintegrated underwear. The folded-back fabric revealed the bony torso, the navel like an olive pit, the blackened edges of the rib cage, and a delta of hair like a matted rat nest. "No recent discoloration or foreign substance such as urine or semen," Gray said. "No evidence indicates necrophilic activities."

Ralph, standing by with a Styrofoam cup of coffee, tried to control the expression on his face. He'd seen plenty of dead bodies. The soldiers he'd dragged to medic stations still had looked like themselves, like they could resume their lives, if the doctors somehow could have saved them. Mrs. Mason's skin looked like the punching bag swinging from the rafters in his attic.

Because the wound almost in the center of her chest was covered by gauze and tape, she had not been buried in a bra. When Ralph saw the wing-shaped brown stain, a last seepage of heart blood on the gauze, his throat seized, and he coughed as he swallowed, spraying coffee drops onto the white shirtsleeve of Gray Hinckle. "I am so sorry."

Gray was irritated. This shirt was made

of Sea Island cotton. He laid the scissors on Catherine's stomach, went to the sink, and delicately dabbed at his sleeve with a wet paper towel.

Not from a sense of thoroughness, but out of embarrassment at snorting coffee and fear of losing face with Gray, Ralph pulled on gloves, picked up the scissors, and cut away the yellowed bandage. Bull's-eye, he thought. He pulled the sheet, rolling her over. The exit wound was small, too, indicating a low-caliber rifle.

"She shot herself with a .22?" Gray asked.

"Yeah, must have been a shorter barrel." Ralph backed up, away from her ancient young breasts with blackened nipples and the hole that had ended her life. Alan clutched the end of the table. He felt woozy. He didn't remember whether or not he'd had chicken pox as a child. Could this be the start? Would his face cover over with pustules? Mesmerized by the sight of this body his father must have embalmed, he did not see openmouthed shock on the ovate face of Janie Belle at the side window, where she stood tiptoe on an upside-down flower pot for a full view.

"No sign of any recent interference anywhere. Our work is finished. She can go back to where she came from. She's all yours, Alan." Gray looked as if he were about to say more. Ralph thought he almost made a joke, but did not want to appear tasteless.

Ralph squeezed the bridge of his nose. He was going to sneeze. Gray unfolded a large muslin sheet, slid it under the body, and wrapped her like a swaddling baby. Alan turned up the air conditioner. At least he would make the sale of another coffin, and the Masons always went for the bronze.

Ralph excused himself for a moment and went inside the house to check in with Carol at the office. After he hung up, he stood by the window looking out into a cement pond with a fountain oozing a trickle of water through moss. Janie Belle kneeled in the crotch of a hog-pear tree, about to jump. Goldfish hung in the green slime without moving. A young tom jumped up onto the stone side and peered intently at the fish. Ralph, fingering the Vietnam medal he always carried in his pocket, felt his mind trawling, but for what?

The cat pawed the water and still the fish did not move. Balanced on the side of the fishpond, the cat extended his skinny front legs, arched his back, and looked down with disinterest at the swollen fish, then nimbly leapt into the azaleas. The perfectly round, cat-sized hole he made in the leaves remained open a moment, then closed.

Ralph stared after him and shook his head. *Suicide.* Oh boy, oh boy, how could we not have seen that? he thought. He rushed back to the garage, where Gray was writing in a notebook. "Hey, we missed something. If she pulled the trigger herself, that exit wound wouldn't be even with the front wound. It would be higher because of the way she had to hold the gun. There's something rotten in the state of Denmark."

"We're looking into necrophilia here — diddling with the dead — not into the intricacies of a suicide that happened years ago," Gray said. But he frowned hard at Ralph. "You know, you are right, son of a bitch! Let's take another look-see."

"I'm sorry as I can be, boys, but I've got to get back to the house." Alan felt ill. Surely this was beyond his services as a mortician. He stood at the door. His shirt clung to his chest and back.

Shoulders round like a girl's, Gray thought. "That's fine, Alan, my boy, we sure do appreciate you taking the time to help us out. We'll just add this as an addendum. It'll probably turn out to be nothing." They shook hands. "We'll close up. And she's sure as hell not going anywhere. Just hold her in your deepfreeze until Monday."

With Gray's calipers, they measured the wound. "We'll be able to determine range, I believe. Given that skin has shrunken away from the original hole, given that she would have had to pull the trigger with her toe from a sitting position, with the gun barrel against her chest, given all this, we can't tell shit for sure right now. Ralph, if you hadn't got coffee all over my shirt, we might never have noticed this."

What Ralph noticed was Gray's "we." "If I'm not mistaken, it was an 'I' what noticed this." When he was nervous, he sometimes lapsed into grammar he'd struggled to overcome.

"Okay, okay, just keeping up the teamwork, pal. I'll get an exact angle on that exit wound. If she did pull the trigger, it sure wouldn't be dead level with the front wound." Gray rolled the body over again. "It would be, say, three or four inches higher, right? I'll take a roll of film and meet you at your office to go over the records."

"I'm starving. Let's meet at the Three Sisters right in the middle of town."

"Now we're cookin' with gas, coach."

Catherine is coming today. The thought was clear in his head, but he wanted to tell the woman with the food on the tray. "Sss . . ."

"What is it, Dr. Mason? Do you want something else?" Mary June was on double shift, trying to save enough money to take her boys to the beach for a week. She had run from one bed to another for nine hours. Flu going around in the heat of summer.

He shook his head, disgusted. "I want . . ." She waited. "If you see her, I want . . ."

He seemed to doze, he jumped from a plane, the checkered, war-ravaged German countryside rose toward him, then his head snapped up with a myclonic jerk.

"Who? Ginger? I heard she's coming to see you. Won't that be nice? She's coming from a long way."

Something roared, the silk parachute

collapsing in his ears. "I don't care about that . . ." Who is coming? Catherine — what was Lily saying about Catherine?

"Now, you don't mean that, I know." She wondered if he'd suffered another small stroke. His language abilities seemed more impaired today. "How are you feeling?" She usually paid less attention to him than to other patients. He looked perfectly all right, maybe a little vacant like some old god left out in the rain. After all, he was only sixty-one years old. She remembered him from childhood, pressing her tongue down to look in her throat, then giving her the wooden depressor, which she took home and painted with a face and glued to it a paper evening gown with a hem of sparkles. Later, he took the Brownies on an overnight camping trip when she and Ginger were in the same troop. He'd cooked hot dogs over a campfire, taught them to sing in rounds, "There was a desperado from the wild and woolly West . . ." She had wished he were her daddy, instead of the mean hired-out drunk who twisted her mother's wrist until the bone popped in two.

"Take two aspirin, drink plenty of liquids, and go to bed," he answered. She had once teased him about doctors always prescribing that, and it was one of the few things he remembered about her. His brain worked peculiarly, as though water started down the chute, then shunted off into a side trough. He recognized everyone, knew who they were to him, sister, son, friend — it just didn't seem to matter. She guessed his neocortex was plain fried. Sometimes tears would well up when J.J. or Ginger started to leave, but the instant they were gone, he forgot. He could go from one to two, but when three came he was lost, like he'd say he wanted a newspaper, and if you said okay, you'll go get it, he'd say go get what? His recurrent demand, "Give those starving people something to eat," she never followed. Mary June knew that the occasional eruptions of some trace of his former self were devastating for his children. She'd seen Ginger leaning against her car door with her face in her hands after he'd suddenly come out with some ripple of vitality she recognized as his. "It's the first of the month. Did you say rabbit first thing? You could use the good luck." How did he know the time of day, much less the day of the month? Another time he said, "Give me some sugar before you go," which Ginger said was his old way for asking for a good-night kiss before she went to bed. He'd never inquired about his health, or why he was sitting at the Columns these many years instead of living at home. "The lights are on but no one's home," Mary June would explain to people in Swan who asked after him.

"Dr. Mason, I was sorry to hear about what happened." She half wanted to say so and half wanted to see what he'd say.

He poked at the fried ham on his plate. He sighed. "What is this crispy critter? Dada doesn't like this one bit."

Ginger imagined the river on nights when she couldn't sleep. She hadn't been there in a year and a half — during her daddy's last emergency she was home so briefly — but even thousands of miles away she could picture driving herself down the sandy white road through the woods, taking the turn at the big oak, glimpsing the stone chimney through the trees, then emerging into the sudden light of the clearing. J.J. pulled up beside his muddy Jeep. "Backy-home-againy," she said, repeating J.J.'s baby phrase.

The river in the twentieth century never rose more than fifteen feet above its banks, but the year before the cabin was built in 1898, it flooded the entire palmetto plain for two weeks. Because of that, John Mason was able to buy five hundred acres, sixty of them fronting the river, for fifteen dollars an acre. On the high point of the land, he built this pine log cabin that always had been, at metabolic level, home to Ginger and J.J.

Ginger thought of the cabin as a way their lives were manifest in another form. "Here we are," Ginger said quietly, biting in her bottom lip. "Isn't this close to heaven?"

"Maybe not at the moment. You might want to walk down to the dock until the place airs out for a few minutes. After Scott told me, I left in a hurry yesterday and forgot to take a string of perch out of the sink. I'm sure they're high."

Ginger went inside anyway, holding her nose. "Not too bad."

J.J. threw open the back door and ran to the woods with the fish. Ginger walked from room to room. Even though J.J. lived here most of the time, little had changed. When they were children, Catherine had cleared out the canvas cots and rusted fishing tackle of the previous two generations. Big Jim never used the cabin after his children were grown because Mama Fan hated the place. One mouse jumping out of the flour bin, leaving tiny white tracks across the floor, was enough, but then a snake was found coiled at the foot of little Lily's bed while she slept. Mama Fan drove home in the middle of the night and never returned. Her old rotted chairs and mildewed tick mattresses had made a lovely bonfire one Saturday, when Catherine had three men help her empty the place. The cabin then became Catherine's retreat, a place she made for Wills to escape constant calls, a place where the children could "run wild," and a place where she turned up the music, read, worked in her sketch books, and wandered in the woods looking for wild azaleas, Cherokee roses, and violets to transplant around the house. Ginger and J.J. loved, and their parents had loved, the long porch stretching all across the front of the house, the double screen doors opening into an enormous, almost-two-story log room with a stone fireplace. The kitchen and three bedrooms opened off the main room. Catherine had found a country man to make beds from pine logs and branches. She scoured the countryside for Wedding Ring and Tree of Life quilts — no one in her family or Wills's knew how to sew a stitch — and rustic local furniture, her prize find being two walnut eighteenth-century huntboards, still standing on either side of the door.

Ginger peered into what she still thought of as her parents' room, although J.J. had moved in long ago. From his desk in front of the window, she looked down at the C-curve of the river. J.J.'s journals — twenty or twenty-five identical black-and-white-mottled school notebooks — stood along the back of the desk, the recent one, pen beside it, opened facedown. Ginger always had wanted to read J.J.'s journals but had caught only glimpses, even though she used to grab one from him and run until he caught her and snatched it back. She hadn't wanted to pry, merely to understand the hidden brother behind the wise-cracking, womanizing, hunter-gatherer man of the woods. But her quick stolen looks yielded only notes on Indian initiation rites, birdcalls, lists of books read, and precisely written descriptions of things he'd seen in nature, with colored-pencil drawings of a dogwood blooming in a tenant farmer's yard, a ragged blue heron posed on one leg in Yellow Jacket Creek, a flimsy mint-green moth that landed on his hand, a bluish stone on its shadow. Even this glimpse — such delicacy and exactness — made her scared of reading further. He'd had a bookcase built in the corner by the bed and had moved the leather chair from their daddy's old office into the angle. The books were all history, mythology, books on birds, fish, geology. She imagined J.J. there, reading and writing through the morning, while she was thousands of miles away. The flip side, the other world.

Otherwise, the room remained the same. Ginger looked at her mother's clunky marble-topped chest of drawers, taken from Catherine's childhood room. She moved a book to see an oval scar on top. Long ago, her mother had marred the marble with a wet bottle of fingernail polish remover. Ginger ran her finger around the faint ring. Her mother had let her polish her nails when she was very small, even though Mama Fan said it was quite tacky for children to wear polish.

The door to Ginger's room was stuck. She pushed it open with her shoulder and pulled apart the blue-and-white-striped curtains. The room looked out on the scuppernong arbor, the stone grill beside it, where her family used to have almost all their summer dinners. Tomorrow, she told herself, tomorrow I will lie on my back in this bed and listen to the bees in the grapes. I'll put on some old records and make brownies. I'll walk all the way to the hideout — there will be perfect arrowheads on the path. She put on her suit and ran past J.J. washing his hands in the kitchen.

"I'm coming," he yelled after her. She paused at the end of the dock, bracing herself for the cold. Holding her nose and shouting, she jumped in. She swam upstream for the pleasure of floating back. Beyond the cleared banks near the cabin began dense growths of gallberry, palmetto, and vine-draped pines. Where the river narrowed, oak branches from either bank intertwined overhead. Through half-closed eyes Ginger saw bolts of light through leaves; she drifted, then turned and kicked her way back upstream toward the boils. J.J. cannonballed off the dock and swam up to her. They crawled out on a sand crescent and, hoisting themselves up by tree roots, climbed up a slick clay bank to a ledge of grassy land.

"All right, O Hisagita Immisee." Ginger ran up the slope to the springs. The rope was yellow, made of some kind of plastic. They used to swing into the water on vines, later a hemp rope, but now J.J. had attached this new thing, which probably was guaranteed not to break. "You first — I'm not sure I can take the cold."

As children they had elaborate rituals improvised from their reading about the Creeks. Hisagita Immisee, the god of the tribe, translated as "Breath Holder." They thought the name must have come from a great swimmer who could hold his breath long enough to swim down into the roiling water at the bottom of the spring. When J.J. first made it to the bottom and stuck his fist into the blue source, he became O Great Hisagita Immisee.

J.J. took the rope back for a running start, swung out, and dropped. He surfaced and flipped downward. She watched his clear body, stippled with light, turn mazarine as he propelled downward through colder and colder levels of water until near the bottom he became a fishy shadow. Down there, she knew, the cold sensation turned hot, because to feel any colder you'd turn to ice. Her own lungs felt the pressure of his held breath. She grabbed the rope with a stick, swung out, her feet on the big knot, once, twice, finally letting go. She came up gasping from the hard shock of cold. As she flipped down and swam with open eyes, she passed J.J. shooting upward and their eyes met, his starved or scared wide, his torso white marble, legs working like some primitive amphibian, but the eyes, suddenly unknowable, someone in a dream, a statue hauled up from an ancient shipwreck. She thought she could not go all the way, but she pulled at the water as though opening heavy velvet curtains, kicking with deliberate strength and *there,* she was at the cleft of white sand and the three dark blue openings they had longed to enter as children, imagining a kingdom where the furniture was made of driftwood, pearls, and shells, where the real Hisagita Immisee lived with fabulous extinct river creatures with no eyes, where the fiery cold water spurted pure and sacred out of the earth. They'd heard, too, that dead slaves lived in a realm under rivers. She held the palms of her hands against the surging water for the push of energy she used to feel move into her arms and down her spine, a thrill then and now, even as the hard bulbs of her lungs tightened and she pushed up and climbed toward the bend of light, the surface of the spring.

Lying in the grass breathing hard, J.J. felt a pain rip through his head, a sharp letter opener through a thin envelope. Migraine. An aura of jagged light appeared to the left in his peripheral vision. Ginger was over him, shaking drops of water from her hair onto his chest. He sat up. "Whoa," he said, "we'd better get moving. The sun's going down." She looked restored to herself, her normal self, jumping on one foot and hitting her head to force the ringing water out of her ear, running her fingers through her hair their mother always had called lucky strawberry blond. Underwater, she had looked as though she could swim forever, like a nymph who returned to earth once a year, her trailing hair coral in the sun-pierced water, mouth an O, as though water ran through her, her eyes flashing flat and quick, all that as they passed, him swimming up, emerging, so much easier than her descent, her parting the waters with the small arrows of her hands, tiny bubbles flowing from her nose, the albuminous spray of her hard kicking, then she was past, and he burst into air. He squinted up at her as a large silence swelled in his head.

Ralph and Gray washed their faces, soaped their hands and all the way up to their elbows in the bathroom at the Three Sisters. It was late, but Martha still had plenty of meat loaf in the oven.

The three sisters who owned the café looked alike and always dressed identically, although in different colors. Angela wore yellow and ran the cash register; Emily wore red and waited tables; Martha wore green and cooked. They all had caps of curls, a color called Bronze Aura, and wore blue eyeliner that made them look round-eyed like dolls. They'd grown up in Swan with a widowed father. As far as anyone knew, not one of them ever had seen the need for any relationship beyond their own tight circle.

Ralph opened his granddaddy's report on Catherine Mason's death while they ate. The report was typed on the old

Remington still sitting on a desk in the office.

CASE 802
SEPTEMBER 3, 1956
Catherine Phillips Mason, dead of self-inflicted gunshot wound to the heart. No attempt to resuscitate. She was discovered at the home address by her daughter, Virginia, 12, at 3:30 p.m. She died at approximately 1:00 p.m., according to Dr. Dare. She was found on the kitchen floor, beside a turned-over chair (Exhibit 1).

Ralph glanced at the small photo, a snapshot attached to the page with cracked tape, of Catherine in a pool of black blood. She was barefoot, indicating that she pulled the trigger with her toe. She was wearing a white sundress with black dots on it. God, what a sight for Ginger. ("She was expecting warm gingerbread and that's what she found," he remembered hearing over and over through the years.) The gun lay beside her, almost cradled in her arm.

Emily brought a basket of cornsticks. She glanced at the page in front of Ralph. "God in heaven," she said. Even a glimpse and she recognized the noble forehead and unforgettable eyes of Catherine Mason. The report continued:

This office was notified by Carla Rowen, the nearest neighbor, who found Virginia (Ginger) Mason in the middle of Palmetto Road near her house. According to the statement made by Dr. Wills Mason, his wife had occasional spells of depression, but no previous signs of self-destruction. He recalled that before the birth of their daughter, Virginia, she had been withdrawn, but in recent years there were no known aggravating circumstances. Weapon was a .22-caliber automatic Savage rifle owned by Dr. Mason. The bullet was recovered from the wall. He stated that he kept the gun in an unlocked cabinet, along with three other more powerful deer-hunting guns. He was not sure if the gun in question had been loaded. The maid, Tessie Mae Cartwright, was at her own residence on West Orange. She stated that on her day off she shopped at Dixie Market and McMillan's Five-and-Ten between 11:00 and 12:00, then visited her cousins Sally and Precious Cartwright on East Oconee for the noon meal. This was verified by the Cartwright cousins. The Mason children were in school. Dr. Mason left his office at 10:00 a.m., made rounds at the hospital until 11:00, then stated that he drove out to the cabin, where he expected to meet his family in the afternoon. Mrs. Mason had no known enemies. No sign of forced entry or struggle. She left no suicide note.

Ralph handed the page to Gray. He read on:

SEPTEMBER 4, 1956
Further interviews with the nearest neighbors and with friends and relatives of the Mason family produced no further cause for investigation. The entire town is shocked and repelled by this act against God.

Two of the last entries in the file were handwritten. His grandfather seldom wrote letters, even when Ralph was in Vietnam on his last assignment before he resigned. He recognized the hand mainly from his grandfather's old-fashioned flourishing signature on birthday cards.

SEPTEMBER 6, 1956
This sad case ended at the funeral yesterday (clipping from *The Swan Flyover* enclosed). A fine family broken up, resulting from a selfish act. How someone could do that to her children, I don't understand. The minister said a troubled soul is at peace, but she left some troubled souls behind her.

SEPTEMBER 7, 1956
Telephone call from Mrs. Mayhew (Charlotte Anne) Crowder, Macon, Georgia. She demanded further investigation. Stated that as a former college roommate and friend she knew without a doubt that Mrs. Mason would not commit suicide. I explained that there was no evidence to the contrary. She became hysterical and said to find some. She insisted that Catherine must have been trying to defend herself with the weapon. She demanded that I look at notebooks kept by Mrs. Mason. My search of the house on the morning after the death revealed four boxes of bullets and ten of shotgun shells in the gun cabinet. One of the remaining three guns, a Winchester .30-06, was loaded. I saw no notebooks. After Mrs.

Crowder's call, I called Dr. Mason with great reluctance. He said his wife sometimes wrote in diaries, but he had not seen them.

Gray held up the photo. "Look, would you, that gun — she's still holding it after dropping out of a chair? Is that the position of someone who just sent themselves to hell? She looks like she's taking a nap — except for the mess. Whatever happened to the two children?"

"They're around Swan. They must have pleasant dreams." Ralph read the last entry:

SEPTEMBER 16, 1956
Fingerprint analysis shows the prints of Catherine Mason. Smeared prints reveal that others handled the gun but these are deemed inconclusive. All evidence points to death by suicide. Case closed.

As Ralph handed the last sheet to Gray, he noticed the back of the folder. A doodle. And in his grandfather's hand, scrawled along the edge, he read, — — *Big Jim, R.I.P.* Under that he made out the scratched-out initials *S* and what could have been a *D* or a *B*. Then *Rotary Club 12:30.*

Gray pounced on each page. He rather relished the turn this case had taken. Ralph felt a wave of defensiveness for his grandfather, who probably simply could not imagine that a Mason could murder, or be murdered, for no reason, although searching the house the day *after* the suicide seemed dumb. He and Gray had figured out in one morning what seemed to have escaped his grandfather, who was on the scene. He felt a blaze of pride. "Hotshot," Granddaddy had called him when he was a child.

An early scene zigzagged up into his consciousness. When Ralph was very young, his granddaddy used to take Big Jim quail and dove hunting near Tallahassee. His granddaddy in his uniform hauling and totin', and Big Jim, with his gleaming shotguns, outfitted in a suede hunting jacket with dozens of pockets inside. From somewhere, somehow, Ralph remembered Big Jim expansively opening the jacket. The pockets held doves with their heads poked out, looking as if they'd nodded off briefly and might wake and fly.

Ralph's grandmother would be mad the whole time her husband was gone. As she washed up, she clattered the plates so hard Ralph thought they'd break. "That old rooster. If I told your granddaddy once, I've told him a hundred times that Big Jim gave him the mill vote, got us this house, and now he owns him. Big Jim says *jump*, and your granddaddy says *how high?* He'll drop everything! And bring home doves for me to pluck." Even then Ralph knew his grandfather usually operated a speed trap on Sundays out on the road to Osceola, stopping Yankee snowbirds' cars and charging them twenty-five dollars on the spot. This wasn't graft; every southern sheriff was entitled to that little bonus. His grandmother didn't like him losing out on this part of his income.

Ralph scooped up the red gravy with a cornstick, while Gray finished reading. He hoped Gray didn't ridicule the investigation of the house taking place the day after the death.

Gray put down the file and concentrated on his plate. Without them ordering dessert, Emily brought over two generous slices of devil's food cake. "Last customers of the day get a prize."

"You are beautiful." Gray flashed a smile.

Ralph felt obliged to point out the note

on the back sheet of the file. "My granddaddy was the sheriff," he confessed.

"Well, don't be too hard on him. Back then they couldn't access range with the exactitude we can now. I'm ninety percent sure she didn't pull the trigger. I'll check everything with my boss. Easiest crime on God's green, husband shoots wife and either he says he didn't know the gun was loaded or he arranges a suicide scene, which he 'discovers' and is all torn up over. Oh, yeah, there's usually a lover boy in the wings. Hard to prove, even now. The husbands will jump all over the place with lie detectors and not a court will look at them because these aren't your hardened criminals. Or" — he pointed his finger at Ralph — "or *maybe* it was disappointed lover boy who stepped in. And who wants to open that can? Suicide becomes the easy way out of the investigation. And then there's the third choice — someone out of the blue."

But why would his granddaddy not follow up? Ralph wondered. Even if he owed his sheriff's election and his home to Big Jim, he was dead by then. The small-town rich man. Did his power triumph over death? And yet his granddaddy had not pushed, had in fact botched the case.

"My granddaddy probably thought too much of the family ever to think in those directions. The Masons planned the whole town." Lame, he knew. He knew, too, that his granddaddy was loyal as a dog.

"Maybe he was protecting someone. Look, we're not looking to understand it at this point," Gray said. "What we'll have to go on is who dug up the grave. By the way, since that red paint residue on some of the stones matches that old coot's Bobcat, our man obviously knew how to operate it. What about that gravedigger, Deal — any chance he's a weird one? I had the feeling he knew his machine had been moved."

"Jesus, no. He's old. He just forgot. Long as I've known, he's worked there."

"Talk to the children, see what they remember, and any other individuals you can think of. If the doctor's really cuckoo, no use in going after him at this point." Gray picked up the check. "You got some cases in Swan, coach. I remember that codger who lived over a garage and saved his urine in jugs. We were called in after an explosion . . ." Gray slapped his leg and whooped. "He was — he was all cut up. Even in the hospital the nurses found out he was peeing in the bedside pitcher." He socked Ralph softly on the shoulder.

"What'chall got in the water over here in Swan?"

Back at his office, Ralph called the House. He told Lily he needed to meet with J.J. and Ginger in the morning, that he had some news of possible interest from the GBI.

"What is it — did they find the criminals?" she asked.

"No, ma'am, I'm afraid not. They've got an alert out to all the counties though, and they'll probably solve this pretty fast. I'd like to go over a few things tomorrow morning with J.J. and Ginger."

"I'm expecting them any minute. I'll tell them."

Lily snapped down the cards. She was in her third try against Old Sol. Tessie's smothered pepper chicken waited on the stove, the table was all set, and she even had filled the fireplace with saucer magnolias after her Scrabble game with Eleanor.

Lily didn't care if Ginger and J.J. were late coming home from the cabin; they always were, and she needed a while to calm down. She sipped a tall, iced Dubonnet. The phone had been ringing all day; now the tree frogs were starting their annoying yammering. People were calling just like they did when someone died. The Rowens from down the road had even brought over a lime Jell-O and cream cheese salad, which she knew those children wouldn't touch. They were picky, both of them, prince and princess from the day they were born, and she supposed she had contributed to that. J.J. wouldn't eat the white of the fried egg and Ginger wouldn't eat the yellow. She wouldn't eat dark meat; he wouldn't eat the light, though they fought over the wishbone without ever, as far as she knew, making a single wish. Never knowing exactly how to be a mother, she just tried to please them with food and whatever she thought they wanted. She gathered up the cards. What didn't sit right was Ralph Hunnicutt's call. He'd held something back from her.

Lily saw the lights bumping along the driveway illuminating the trees. She could tell from the way Ginger slouched her shoulders that she was low. J.J. came up the steps like a sleepwalker. When he kept his mouth open like a panting dog, it meant one thing: headache. "What have y'all gone and done, just worn yourselves out?"

"We stopped by to see Daddy. It was no fun. He looked through us like somebody looking in a store window. I said, 'Daddy, it's me, Ginger,' and he said, 'I know that. It's disgraceful that you haven't been to see me.' I said, 'Daddy, I've been thousands of miles away, but I'm home now,' and he said, 'Blood is thicker than blood.' "

"He made a list of things he wanted, totally ignoring Ginger. He wrote down eyedrops, chocolate wafers, socks — stuff

223

he doesn't need. I got the same things for him not two weeks ago." J.J. brought out ice water, which he felt like dipping his face into. "Let's eat and get it over with. I'm not going to last."

"I'm going to find you one of your pills right now," Lily insisted. "You just sit here in the cool and rest for a few minutes and let it take effect. That sheriff wants to see you both first thing in the morning."

"What for? Did they find out who did it?" Ginger kicked off her shoes.

"No, something about the GBI. He didn't say. Acted real vague, I thought."

You should know vague, J.J. thought.

What Ginger and J.J. both wanted to do was go to their rooms and close the doors. The jagged light still flashed at the edge of J.J.'s vision. Ginger began to feel disoriented. The connection with her work and Marco had been too easily broken. A few hours home and she always felt this way — her real life sloughed off and the old life asserted itself. No one ever asked about what she did. She picked up *their* tempo, *their* concerns, fell into the stream of living that went on here, with or without her. "When are you coming home, chile?" she was asked over and over. Too polite to say, "Never," she al-

224

ways demurred with "I'm home right now."

The air conditioner in the corner window of the dining room labored like a crop duster about to take off. Lily heated the dinner Tessie had left, and opened a jar of watermelon pickles. The familiar starched linen mats monogrammed with Mama Fan's scrolling *FML,* the sedating scent of magnolias in the fireplace, and the impossible smells of the House merged — how could Mama Fan's Fleur de Rocaille perfume and Big Jim's leaden cigar smoke linger this long? Ginger felt suddenly exhausted beyond exhaustion. Nightmare. How could she have forgotten and fallen into the spring with joy this afternoon?

Lily served the plates and passed them. J.J. thought he should help; Lily must be dead about now, but his own head was pounding to the rhythm of "Take Me Out to the Ball Game." The idiotic lyrics cycled with each surge of blood in his temples. "Thanks, Lily, for going to all this trouble. I'm sorry we're not in top form, either of us." As Lily passed the sauceboat, Ginger and J.J. exchanged a smile. Lily's flotsam and jetsam gravy, they recognized.

"Tell me if the potatoes are not hot

enough. These pickles Tessie put up last summer are absolutely delicious. It is too bad Wills is not here with his family. I know he would want to be. It breaks my heart to have him sitting out there year in and year out. If your mother hadn't . . ." It was a sentence she never finished. "I don't think this would have happened to him."

J.J. put down his fork. He pressed his temples, where the pain seesawed. Everything that ever happened was his mother's fault. Ginger wouldn't have choked at the finals of the state debate tournament; he would have gone to medical school in his father's footsteps; his father never would have taken a drink. Stroke they called it, and stroke it was, but massive quantities of alcohol and a fall in the bathroom with a clunk of the skull on porcelain hadn't ever come up in Lily's equations. Was it Mother's fault, too, J.J. thought, that someone has broken into her death? Her fault that the potatoes aren't hot? All he said was, "We're all real tired."

Ginger and J.J. never crossed Lily. For one thing, it just wasn't worth it. For another, she was all they'd had for so many years. She was who she was, and they felt protective toward her no matter what. That no real conversation would occur, they seemed to sense from childhood and never had attempted one. "Don't talk in front of the help" blurred into don't talk about anything that matters at all. As if Tessie didn't know everything about them anyway. Lily had opinions but refused to examine them. In her thinking, ambiguity did not exist; the first conclusion drawn remained conclusive. During their early years with her, all they wanted to do was forget what their mother had done, forget the months after that when their father came home from the office and poured large glasses of bourbon, forget his "accident." Landing at the house with Lily had delivered them. They were safe with Lily in their daddy's childhood home, Big Jim's place. Instead of dying right after Big Jim, Mama Fan seemed more to have faded away. Big Jim they remembered as someone in rough brown who swooped them in the air and then gave them gumdrops. J.J. remembered that Big Jim ate the licorice ones himself. When they were older, he'd let them select pads, red pencils, and staple guns from the office supply cabinet. They remembered his toenails curved down like an owl's beak as he clicked across the floor. And his funeral in the rain when Lily had hysterics after finding a twine-bound bouquet with a card that said *Always and all ways* near the grave.

"Food on the table," Lily mused. "Always food on the table. Not everybody can say that. No matter what, you must eat. You might as well eat well." She herself pushed back from the table, lighting a cigarette. "Our president promised that the national nightmare was over when they locked up half the government last year. And all those boys looked so nice — not Nixon, of course; he looked like he was carved out of a potato."

"What does that have to do with the price of tea in China?" J.J. asked.

"Oh, I just wish *our* nightmare would end. It reminds me that the criminal could be someone in a nice suit, someone you'd never imagine."

Only Ginger fell onto the food, helping herself to more mashed potatoes, a second piece of chicken, another biscuit. "Peach cobbler — just tell me Tessie will make peach cobbler for dessert tomorrow." She was remembering the shortcakes that were under way when she arrived.

"You know Tessie — she's bringing white peaches tomorrow morning."

"I cannot wait." Ginger, buttering the

biscuit, felt her words cut off in the air, her hand disconnected from the knife she held. "This is surreal," she added. "Mother is back in the funeral home. *Impossible.*"

"Sugar, just enjoy your dinner."

"Daddy could at least unzip himself from that fake Daddy suit, step out as real and *do* something." An old fantasy. A black-faced doll she once had became a blond doll when you turned her upside down. Another doll unscrewed, revealing smaller and smaller dolls inside each other. A panda unbuttoned and inside were pajamas and a robe. He was *in there* somewhere.

J.J. knew he had about five minutes left in him. He poured a shot of bourbon to help his head. It scorched right through his stomach. He swayed to the bathroom and threw up. Usually his head felt better after that. He sipped ice water while Ginger ate a revolting mound of whipped cream and red, red strawberries. "I'm gone, you girls. Would you excuse me? Thank you for an enchanting day, another of many enchanting days in the annals of the Mason family."

Ginger helped Lily stack the dishes in the sink and rinse them so Tessie wouldn't face a huge mess in the morning. She made a cup of coffee for Lily, as she had every night when she lived there, and brought it to Lily's room. Lily undid her hair, changed into her nightgown, and propped up in her parents' bed with her coffee. The day had lasted a week. She wanted to say something to Ginger about how none of them deserved this, but she felt emptied. Ginger sat at the foot of the bed. Lily remembered her hanging on the end of the tester like a monkey until Lily thought the wood would break. Ginger loved her grandparents' room, the organdy canopy over the bed, the dressing table's pretty silver combs and mirrors and crystal perfume bottles, even the closed-off fireplace with pictures of the dead great-aunts, uncles, and great-grandparents on the mantel. Rogues' gallery, Mama Fan had called it. Lily had replaced her parents' heavy green damask with a yellow-flowered chintz, replaced their musty Oriental rug with yellow wall-to-wall, but the ornate gold mirror and the blue velvet slipper chair, worn on the arms, were the same. "Take your brother a pitcher of water. He suffers when those migraines hit him. You don't know how often he comes in just flattened. I think they're caused by chocolate. They say chocolate and cheese bring them on. But Catherine had them, too. Maybe he inherited them from her." She wished she hadn't said that.

Ginger did not answer.

Even the wedge of hall light was a fist in the eye. Swallowing hurt and he had the sensation of riding a horse under a constantly expanding and contracting tent of gauze. He willed the two pills to dissolve in his bloodstream and flow up into the bony faults and branching rivers in his head. Canaliculus, canaliculi, streaming with fire. He tasted blood. Always, he was afraid of his father's stroke. A bubble of blood breaks — you're lost. Peace, he said to himself. Peace, let it go, let it be. The distant clinks of cutlery and dishes amplified in his ears, then bathwater running seemed to roar through him. Ginger used to sing "Blue Hawaii" in the bathtub. Tonight she was silent, although J.J. imagined he could hear the soap fall into the water, then slip through him. He felt the glare of the overhead light flash in the steamed mirror in the back of his skull. Pressure in his throat, spine, the backs of his heels.

232

He vomited again, into the pan he'd brought up, then he fell back into what he knew as the blackout, the unendurable crest of pain, the electrical sawing, buzzing, drilling pain that must come from outside himself because it would be impossible for the mere cranium to erupt with such force. For an hour he lay without opening his eyes to the pain of light, unable to call out for Ginger to close the door, unable to kick off his shoes. The feathers in the pillow bothered him with their rustling, as though they wanted to fly again. His own heartbeat, too loud, a tom-tom on a high mesa.

He lost himself, to sleep, to a hard wash of watery tide, and he thought or dreamed he was going in for brain surgery, dingy hospital walls, iron beds like a malaria ward in the tropics, and then he knew it was the Swan hospital before his father transformed it; he saw it at three and four years old and recognized it now, where he was about to go under the big light, big as a sun, his father striding down the long hall with sunlight at the end of it, blinding, his father in his early manhood — maybe thirty-three, the age of perfection, J.J.'s age, the age Ginger was approaching — when he was the angular man in the photo, leaning against the curved hood of his convertible with a horn that played the first few notes of "Darktown Strutters' Ball," *I'll be down to get you in a taxi, honey . . .*, but Swan never had a taxi. J.J. felt a rise of happiness at seeing his father, all power and energy, even coming toward him for surgery. He had no memory of moving from the Emory apartment, when Wills finished his residency, to one of Big Jim's houses in Swan, which Catherine always referred to as the honeymoon cottage. Now he saw his father, restored to himself. A glorious man. Brain surgery, but why? "What is wrong?" he asked the nurse. "Stunted pineal gland," she said, and J.J. wanted to laugh but his stomach wrenched. "What's that?" he shouted to her myopic eyes. "That's the little pine tree in your head, son." Who said that? He was being rolled fast down a wide hallway, the way it was before Daddy went up against old Dr. Dare and had the ward turned into private rooms. Big Jim was mayor and he had seen to that. Anything his son wanted he got. "You can have anything in the world you want," Big Jim was fond of telling his children and grandchildren. When Daddy had just started his practice and was about to deliver his first baby in

Swan, he'd rushed into the operating room to find Dr. Dare repairing the fractured leg of his dog. Wills was brushing dog hair off the operating table as the completely dilated woman was wheeled in. The dream slid away fast. J.J. felt as though he were sinking through layers of rain, of sifted earth, but there was no bottom. Only the sight of his father stayed, moving toward him, that rangy body, now listless by a window at the Columns, energy prolapsed from the hopeless waste of two lives, his mother's high-wire act throwing his father into a spiral of anguish. Was there anguish before? From where, the war? Wills never would discuss the war. And none of them spoke of Catherine afterward, shame folded them inward, too tender a spot, her love that must now be invalid forever.

They referred to "before the accident," when Wills beelined to the sunroom after work, letting down the matchstick blinds and opening the liquor cupboard. From the door, J.J. had seen him drink straight out of the bottle before he even put down his bag. Tessie was left to feed them. Kindly she said, "Just don't pay him no mind," the only point of view that made sense. When Wills dropped them at Sunday School, afterward they waited on the sidewalk until he came for them. Sometimes he forgot. The Bible lessons were about a woman who looked back and turned to salt, about a father who would sacrifice his son, a brother who killed his only brother. They were sent in summer to a long session of camp in North Carolina, then for a visit to Mema, their Phillips grandmother in Vidalia. She was blind and a hypochondriac, who raved alternately about how spoiled Catherine was by her father and about how Catherine would never have done this if she hadn't married into the shameless Mason clan. She'd railed against Wills's breakdown, calling him selfish. J.J. and Ginger had fled and played all day in the limestone caves behind her house. They were old for it by then, but they fashioned horses from the red clay floor and baked them in the sun. The last of the dream switched into the creek behind Mema's and they went searching again for treasure until J.J. scooped his hands into a pool and brought up a cache of perfect quartz crystals, clear as the water dripping through his cupped hands. The dream made another shift, and he was still as a trout in clear water. Still.

He appeared to be sleeping. Ginger

came in quietly with a pitcher of water and a glass. "Are you okay? I brought a wet washcloth." As she had in high school, she wrapped the cloth around ice cubes and placed it across his forehead. She rinsed out the pan in the bathroom. Gently, she pulled off his shoes.

"God, I'm on the slope of it now. Cut the light . . ." His fingers gestured toward the hall.

"Call me if you need anything. I'll leave the doors open." Ginger turned off all the lights and felt her way to her room. Big Jim's clock struck eleven. Westminster bells, Lily once had explained, and Ginger as a child always thought of foggy London, with concentric circles of chimes spreading over the rooftops. She knew the striking chimes hit J.J. like stones. You *had* to count with them every hour of the day — the little dings at the quarter and half hour, marking how hours grow and accumulate and then diminish and start over again. The big hours sounded so solemn, counting off in the dark. The sad *one,* the clipped *two,* the tic-tac-toe of *three,* the neat and hopeful *four,* the swelling insistence of *five,* the alarming now-now-now of *six,* the heavy import of *seven,* the rising hour for school, worker-bee *eight, nine,* somehow magic, *ten* like jackstones thrown, *eleven,* a growing confusion, too many, then *twelve* hard gongs, transformation time, the glass slipper turns to wood. In the dark, Ginger felt the wide board floors, spread her hand for the spool bed just as she reached it, and flung off the bedspread.

Number games, number dreams, how many nights had she used them — they must have come from her first years at the House, falling asleep to Big Ben chimes, waking in the night with the fear that she was the last person left alive on the planet. Relentlessly, she used to multiply — any number, the cost of a candy bar or a sweater or a friend's father's car, she'd multiply by 2, 4, 6, 8, 10, on and on, then start back with 1, 3, 5. Eleanor Whitehead, her math teacher, had been startled by her ability to calculate almost automatically. Everybody knew Big Jim could add a column of three-digit numbers in his head; the skill must have cropped up in the granddaughter. Ginger learned to fall asleep with numbers filling her mind. They spilled into dreams, burgeoning and speeding beyond her ability to fix them. What was 582993 x 93886? Crazily, she would start to count on her fingers, but the numbers receded in space, and she woke up anguishing after them. She hated the number nightmares, and it was then that she trained herself in other ways, the happy memories recalled, the animals she'd loved, the most beautiful places, and, most recently, the favorite Etruscan paintings and votives.

She wanted to think of her project and of Marco, to somehow find him in all this. The scents of orange, grass, and iris would not be summoned. Lately, she'd felt more peaceful and often had not depended on her rituals to sleep. Her mind felt bright and fixed on her work. She'd not had to fight the irrational sense of hopelessness that dogged her, or the moments of shyness, almost shame, that few would suspect she felt. Marco. She tried to bring his face into her vision but kept seeing the joyous flute player painted in the dim Etruscan tomb at Tarquinia, his happy step and curly hair. She let herself imagine the song he played. Reedy, shrill, otherworldly. How very strange, just as she was beginning — at last — to taste the freedom of being adult, her mother violently rising from the ground. Ginger knew that her elaborate games began when she could not, could not think of her mother, when her anger and helplessness had nowhere to go. She knew she had to get through, she knew that at twelve years old, even then on the road, thrashing and crying after finding her mother, her face untouched, blood Ginger skidded into, blood, the scream Ginger still heard in her entire body, bits of her mother's burned raw flesh on her dress, the sharp slam of the door, running, heat pouring over her, flailing, dust, then Mrs. Rowen saying, "Honey, honey, what's wrong?" and holding her, Ginger crazy, fighting, finally saying someone had shot her mother and she was dead. She knew in many small moments since, such as in a restaurant bathroom, when she felt a surge of panic that she'd been left on the road-side, her friends driving off, and when her brain sometimes just locked and she couldn't think at all — she knew she must get through.

She started to relive it. Her usual gymnastic maneuvers could not keep it away. The same strobe-beating colors, the scream in her head, was this J.J.'s migraine in another form?

She tried to see the box of Etruscan stones, what about the golden stones, some with spiral designs broken in fragments? Twenty-five centuries under the ground and now brought into the light by her own hands. The excitement of brushing away the dirt. Marco beside her in a stringed-off area, the other interns, Cynthia and Jessica, in their lanes, all coming up with these fragments. But her mind veered to cleaning her mother's name on the dirty stone that morning. She had to force herself to search her memory, which required thinking of her mother. Her entire training was against that. The question she cycled around was why, why hadn't they known? To kill yourself must take planning, perhaps months of options considered and discarded. That her mother could pick up any gun was unimaginable.

As though it were recorded, she replayed, in the weeks after her mother's death, over and over to the last conversation they'd had. School had just started.

She was in the seventh grade. Her mother had made waffles for breakfast and Ginger didn't want any. She wanted cinnamon toast and orange juice. Tessie always made toast the way she liked it, but Tessie had the day off. Ginger had sat on the kitchen counter beating her heels into the cabinet door.

"Don't do that. You'll chip the paint. Get down and have some breakfast so you won't be late. Daddy has to go." Her mother was slicing the skin off cucumbers at the sink. She wrapped them with carrots and celery in waxed paper and put them in Ginger's lunch sack with her sandwich. Her daddy came in and poured himself coffee. He glanced at the front page of the newspaper, which was already unfolded on the table, and sat down beside J.J.

"Hey, buddyboy, got your report?" He'd helped J.J. with research on the Seminoles for Georgia history class.

J.J. nodded. "Can I have your waffle, Gin?" J.J. asked. His hair was wet. He looked like a little otter. He was wearing a new plaid shirt and had made neat covers from brown bags for his schoolbooks. He was in the ninth grade. Already, girls were looking at him, even sophomore girls.

"Y'all be good! We're going to the cabin tonight." Her mother handed her two pieces of cinnamon toast to eat on the way to school. Her daddy held the door and the three of them walked out. It still felt like summer. A white clematis vine threaded around the columns at the end of the porch. From the driveway, Ginger looked back. Her mother in a yellow dress with dots of blue and green leaned in the doorway as they got in the car and drove away. Her hand on the screen door handle.

They drove away. They drove away and left her. Her hand on the door handle. Ginger could recall the exact feel of that door, its black iron latch. Then she lifted her hand in an ordinary wave good-bye. The door swung shut; her mother a shape, disappearing. They drove away and left her and she shot herself. No, she went back inside the cool kitchen for several hours and then she shot. What did she do for those hours, what did she think? Did she think of the days when J.J. and Ginger were born, the heads with soft fuzz cradled in her arms? Eyelids like moonflowers. Or of her own father, lifting her on his shoulders. Ginger had the old photo, Catherine with scrolling curls pulled up in a ribbon, holding her little spotted dog named Pansy, its wet button nose against her cheek. Did she think of the lace bow around the dog's neck?

Ginger leapt out of bed. She wanted to enter that kitchen with a different role, one that stopped the action, made it run another way. The utter ordinariness and banality of the scene made no sense. Why would you peel cucumbers and read the paper if you planned to kill yourself? Her mother was bright and funny. After so much time, Ginger barely could remember her being funny, just remembered that she was. She remembered more clearly the peeling paint on the kitchen door, the rotation of the latch, the two-note screech as she pulled it open, all those more clearly than she remembered her mother's wit. How barbarian memory is.

J.J. flicked on the bathroom light and reached in to close the door on Ginger's side. "Are you back among the living?" Ginger asked. He emerged in a few minutes.

"It's an empty freight train now, just the cars jangling." He'd brushed his teeth and washed his face and neck, run the wet washcloth all over him.

"I was just thinking about the morning Mother died."

"Well, let me not interrupt a stroll down memory lane."

"If we could understand it . . ."

"We had a pair of doozies for parents, that's all." J.J. took his usual post in the window seat.

"You don't think that."

"I don't? Suicide for a mother? Drooler for a father? Poor Lily as force-fed model adult in the tender years?"

"It's the happiness when we were little

244

that seems so brutal. If we'd always been miserable, it would have been easier. At least we'd have known what to expect."

"Good solid misery. It came soon enough."

"You've never told me. How did you feel when you found out? Somebody came to football practice and told you, and then I didn't see you for a long time. Why didn't you take me to the hideout? I was left with the Rowens. Mrs. Rowen kept trying to give me oatmeal." How to say, she wondered, that it was as if life broke off that day and I balanced, moving fast, on the smallest piece?

"No guilt, now, please. But oddly enough, guilt was what I felt then. We hadn't made her happy. We were trouble. Afterward, when Tessie would take us out to the cabin for the day before I could drive, I'd go to the rack and see what it was like to touch the triggers on all the guns. When I was about fifteen, I used to sleep with that little Beretta pistol of Big Jim's under my pillow. It wasn't loaded but I liked to run my hand under the pillow and find that cold trigger. Mama hated the sound of a gun going off. You couldn't drag her on a duck hunt."

Ginger was quiet, hoping he'd continue

talking, but he didn't say anything more. She couldn't remember when she'd last talked to J.J. without his sarcastic or ironic remarks keeping her away from him. And she hated when he assumed his redneck pose. "I think we've never trusted a human since then. Well, Lily, as far as that goes, and friends" — she thought of Marco — "but that down-deep, intimate, everything kind of trust is hard for me to come by."

No response. Then J.J. said, "Mitchell, for prime example. I thought with Mitchell you'd stumble into happiness. A good man."

"I developed an allergy toward him. I couldn't help it. He was like feverweed to me. I think I always felt close to you because you were the only one who could know. I just can't help but wonder how it would have been different, a plain old normal life. I'm off digging up sherds thousands of miles away and you're out there in the woods — you're almost a hermit — reading about reptiles and Indians. If you think about it, we're just magnified children." I *was* like that, she told herself. I'm not as stunted as he is. Now I'm starting to live like anyone else.

"Yeah, well, this reappearance doesn't do much for my interrupted joie de vivre."

246

There he goes again.

"I always thought you'd be a writer. Faulkner, Eudora Welty, Carson Mc-Cullers, Flannery O'Connor, James Agee, like them."

"I write all the time. Just not books. No 'Song of the South' ambitions. No 'I-don't-hate-it-I-don't' monologue in a Yankee dormitory. No one's ever explained the South — you *know* that? But too many have died trying."

"The South is like the ancient Greek plays. Things happen in Idaho and Michigan but they don't happen the way they do here. It's different."

"Ah, yes. All that old murky stuff, the archetypal swamp mud abides, abides. Something affects little-bitty babies when they are born — the shadow of the hanging tree, Robert E. Lee on Traveler, riding off into the gauzy air. And all of us narcotized by the scent of magnolia."

"Don't mock, it's true. What about Mother? Do we remotely think this is just a gruesome mess without a trail of tears?" She couldn't explain how when she left Swan each time it was more than leaving.

J.J. didn't answer, so she continued. "Even the Jews who escaped from Hitler and, God knows how, came here — before long they're adding columns to the front porch and standing up for 'Dixie' at the football games. The place moves inside you. Even that New Jersey science teacher who came here was yes-ma'aming and talking at half-speed after a year. Really, J.J., admit!"

"Okay. This is the truth. See, I don't really think the first cause of that is the War Between the States or slavery or the lure of the old plantation. The first cause lies closer to that narcotizing scent of magnolia. In a way it's stronger than anything, stronger than evolution. Foreskins persist in covering the penis despite generations of circumcision. Nature's not swayed a bit. But the Feldenkreisses naming their daughter Lee Ann, calling her 'Missy,' and pouring juleps, that's just what they do with the spell they fell into. What we *think* of as South is only what is culturally available. But the land itself holds us in a thrall — the forests, the heat, the waters. I'm waiting to catch one of those eyeless fish we know are down there. If I were to write, a big *if*, I'd like to write something plain and real about the land. But you have to have a story, too. All the ones I know, I don't want."

Ginger wanted to throw her arms

around him or a big Mary-blue cloak to shelter him. She waited to see if he would continue. "Unfortunately, all I know about, other than nature, is freaks and fundamentalists and a family that can't win for losing, and signs for Judgement Day. I wouldn't touch it."

"But *I* would like to read what you could write. No one has seen anything from your notebooks. Forget the old writers, our family, nooses swinging from the hanging tree, or fanatics wrapping barbed wire around themselves. Thoreau is beautiful — you've lived in the woods a lot longer than he did." They loved *Walden* in high school, used to sprawl in front of the fireplace at the cabin in winter, Ginger under a blanket on the sofa, him with his legs slung over the armchair, each with a copy, reading aloud and eating pickles. "You could go travelling in the Amazon and find unknown medicinal plants, or orchids they think are extinct. Maybe you're the Bartram or Darwin of our time."

"Maybe not." He couldn't explain why he didn't write. It was not just his instinct that living in south Georgia trumped fiction any day — more doodley-squat events, violence, and craziness than any square mile in the world. There was more — the feeling of immense silence that words pulled out of, and the lack, the big white space around words once they were written down. He loved Ginger; she was the person he would face all his life. He decided to try to explain himself to her. "You know how a fish sounds when it leaps out of water? If I could write that in a word, I'd know how to be a writer. Or like the bee, that sizzling sound when it goes back to the swarm. Words are all you have to write with and most things don't go into words."

She had an inkling of what he meant. "You mean you can't spell an owl's call or a watermelon splitting open?"

"Yes. They teach you that the alphabet covers all the sounds but it just covers *words*. And words . . ." He floundered now. "The body, how we live in the body. Migraine. Sex. Fear. Power. Can you write the sound of a gunshot that you didn't even hear but fires off in your body every day?" *There*. He felt weak, the God damned migraine had left him empty. He leaned toward the window, his hand on the screen, listening to all the night sounds together, tree frogs and night birds and bullfrogs and mosquitoes and the grace notes of the spring falling into the pond, a nocturne he knew by heart. "Listen." He saw the faint blur of Lily's two swans at the edge of the pond.

"J.J., just try. Write what you want. No one can transcribe a blue jay or that water sound — but isn't that what music is for? Because we can't? You have to make substitutions."

"Ginger, my good girl, always winding in the kite. I could sail off if you didn't keep that string taut."

"You'd better not, mister. How can you even say that?"

They both feared suicide was catching. Now she knew J.J.'s spiraling mistrust of the work she thought he was born to do. She would have to think about what he said. Was it true? In Italy, she often thought something similar. The land, beautifully tamed by eons of farmers, seemed so human in scale, so friendly. Perhaps even the rampaging Visigoths someday found themselves turning Italian. "J.J., you're the best brother. Of all the brothers I could have had, you are the best."

From the dark window, J.J. saw headlights and switched off the lamp to get a better view. A car drove slowly by the house, seemed to stop, then turned around down the road at the dead end. As it passed a second time, the headlights were off. J.J. could see only a black form moving by.

"What was that?"

"Probably someone wanting to see the house where the bizarre Masons roost."

"I'm gone, J.J. Call me when you get up."

July 10

Tessie's kitchen filled with the fragrance of ripe peaches. She squeezed each one in the row above her sink for firmness. Her uncle had brought over a bushel basket from his grove near Perry because she liked to put up peach pickles every year. She picked out six perfect ones for the cobbler she intended to make. Ginger even liked it for breakfast. Those children, as she still thought of them, had downright peculiar eating habits; she reckoned that came from having no mother. Sometimes she had arrived at work and found them eating bowls of ice cream for breakfast, their daddy too, so what could she say but "Mercy on us, wouldn't you rather have biscuits and syrup or some ham and eggs?" Later, Lily couldn't do a thing with them either. They just did what they pleased, but they were always polite about it.

Tessie sat down at the kitchen table and drank her mug of coffee. The house was quiet. She thought she'd miss her two children, who'd moved up North, and Robert, her husband, who'd died, but in truth, she enjoyed the house that stayed clean. She liked the small pile of laundry she gathered on Saturday. Wash it, dry it on the line, iron by nightfall. Her rows of pole beans and a dozen tomato plants she found easy to manage. She liked her cold suppers on a tray on the back porch, with the gospel station turned on low so it wouldn't bother the neighbors, not that much could bother Miss Jetta next door, crazy as a loon. When Ginger drove Tessie home from the House, she'd park across the street just to watch Miss Jetta obsessively sweeping her dirt yard and calling on the devil. Tessie steered clear of Miss Jetta; maybe she really was possessed by a devil. She wore a bracelet of dimes, old conjure, Tessie knew. How she stayed that crazy and alive no one understood. At night when her house was quiet, neighbors left sacks of sweet potatoes and onions, or a wrapped-up piece of cake, on her porch. From her few frizzle chickens running around, she had sense enough to gather eggs. Catherine used to bring her a handful of roses. Everyone else was afraid to go into the yard because Jetta waved her broom like a witch, but when Catherine put down the

dog roses or sunflowers on her step, Jetta
would stand behind the chinaberry tree and
peer around like a shy child.

Tessie walked to work in the mornings
before it was too hot. Late in the afternoons, after she got dinner together, Lily
would drive her home. From the branch off
the paved road onto the road to the House,
Tessie walked slowly. She passed the dentist's, Catherine and Wills's old place,
where she used to turn in to find Ginger
and J.J. already playing in the sandbox or
making a mess in the kitchen, Catherine
clipping the dead roses, Dr. Mason already
gone for the day. Now as she passed, she always closed one eye and said a prayer because the house still was marked by the evil
eye, an electrical force she could feel along
her spine. She passed the Rowens' house,
then down the road, almost to the end.
Rain had done its work on the clay road
and she walked the shoulder, brushing
through the purple vetch to avoid squishing
in red mud. At the turn into the driveway,
the mailbox door was open and she pulled
out a small parcel wrapped in crumpled
white tissue paper and tied with twine.
Didn't look like much of a present. She carried it up to the house and put it down on
the back porch with the sack of peaches.

After a migraine, J.J. often woke with a sense of immense well-being. He was not sure whether a real chemical effect swept through with the cessation of pain, or if it was the body simply feeling the psyche's complementary afterimage of pain. Ginger, too, revived overnight. They dipped doughnuts into their coffees at the Three Sisters Café and Ginger read the paper, not commenting on the small article about their mother on page one.

They'd stopped in early to see their father while he ate cereal and toast from a tray. "Don't come in," they'd been greeted.

"Fine, Daddy, that's fine, you just enjoy your breakfast and we'll stop by later."

"No, that won't be convenient."

Ginger had brought a jar of Tessie's blackberry preserves. "Would you like some of this on your toast?" She spread the jam while he watched sullenly. He caught sight of his own face in the mirror and gestured with the toast. "Who is that and why doesn't he ever say anything?"

J.J. and Ginger had stared at each other. "Who?" J.J. finally asked. But Wills had forgotten his question. "That will be all," he said imperiously.

"Sure thing, Your Majesty, the least your nearest and dearest can do." J.J. was not inclined to humor him when he got in these moods. "Old stuffed goat," he'd muttered. "Old bastard."

Ginger had tried again. "Would you like these pillows fluffed?" His reflection in the mirror suddenly looked spooky to her.

"Where have you been? What took you so long? I've waited and waited." Wills looked up at Ginger. Through the blinds, soft morning light raked across his bony knees protruding from his robe like stunted skulls. His sad, stringy calves looked withered, his feet . . . But she stopped, concentrated on his knife-edge nose, his cocked head where she could see a shade of him as he was when he was her father; she even saw the twelve-year-old boy holding a fish on a string in the photograph on Lily's dresser.

"We got up early and came right out."

"Well, you can tote yourselves back

where you came from. You've made your bed, now lie in it."

Ginger refilled their cups. She loved the blue tables and the crazy collection of salt and peppers. Their table's were a puss and a boot. Martha, the sister who cooked, made the best doughnuts in the world, lightly fried and dusted with powdered sugar. Ginger had three. J.J. never had more than two. "If your butterfly metabolism ever leaves you, you are going to be one fat pig."

"Ah, sugar and grease — that's what I like about the South. I feel my arteries hardening with every bite."

Cy Berkhalter sat in one of the booths along the wall. He nodded gravely and stared into his coffee. His son, also his law partner, was another suicide. Gun in the mouth in the back storeroom. The Masons always recoiled from him, and he from them. Ginger went back to the kitchen. "Martha, it was worth the trip home just to taste your doughnuts."

"Hey, sugar." Martha scooped up two handfuls from a mound of fried holes and put them in a bag. "We're just so sorry to hear about your family's trouble. You let us know if there's anything we can do."

"Just let us know if you decide to make some Brunswick stew."

"We don't make that in the dead of summer. We'd die ourselves." Martha regretted her word choice. "But I could make you some fried catfish with hush puppies, that's good anytime of year." Ginger would have liked to rest her head on Martha's big broody bosom and weep. She would like to be fed by the sisters and listen all day to Emily's banter and jokes with customers.

The screen door of Three Sisters banged behind them. The Jaguar seats were already hot. J.J. made a U-turn on Corsica Street and swung around Oasis Park in the middle of the street, which was the exact center of town. A red Lab, paws on the marble side of the fountain, lapped at the water, and a small boy — looked like Ray Evans's youngest — splashed water at the dog. The Oasis centered on a tall broken column ringed with marigolds, zinnias, and yellowing grass. The falling notes of water gave the illusion of coolness to the tiny park. Marianne Shustoff got out of her car at the cleaners with an armful of laundry. Someone yelled, "Six o'clock, Edna Kay. Don't forget." J.J. took a right on Magnolia, passing Mrs. Woods, who managed the insurance office, slowly walking along the sidewalk with Wilton, her grown son whose tongue lolled and feet dragged. Over the street, sycamore branches met and intertwined. Ginger and J.J. tunneled through the watery green shade where only jagged swatches of sunlight shone, hitting a windshield here, a patch of brick street there. In the Nifty Shop window, Gladys draped a naked mannequin with butcher paper while she unbuttoned a crinkly yellow dress. Maud Richards knocked on the glass and pointed to a handbag Gladys had already arranged with matching scarf near the front. Neither one noticed Aileen Boyd's hip-length braid of blond hair swaying as she jaywalked toward the Nifty Shop carrying a shopping bag of baby clothes to sell on consignment.

"Oh, there's Skeeter Brooks, sexiest boy who ever went to Swan High." Ginger waved but Skeeter was loading croker sacks into the back of a pickup. "Too bad he knocked up that girl from the county and had to get married."

The small shops slipped by the window, the feedstore that smelled of alfalfa and dusty seeds, Uncle Remus Hardware, Hellman's grocery where Jackie Hellman hoisted a dripping side of beef into the front door, Grossman's Mercantile with bins of cheap shoes piled outside. She glimpsed Ann-Scott Williams putting the diamonds and watches back on display in Teebow's Jewelry. Ginger's own wedding ring had come from there. Inside it was engraved one word: *forever.*

Charlotte Crowder poured tea from on high. She liked to watch the steamy stream splash into her flowered cup. She slipped off the rubber band from the morning paper. Jasmine jumped down from the windowsill and twined between her feet. Charlotte pulled her up by the tail, which Jasmine liked, into her lap. "Wild thing." She ran her hand through the cat's mottled fur — she must have inherited the coats of a hundred strays — then rubbed her head with her knuckles, and Jasmine turned and gently bit her wrist. "You bad cat," she admonished, tapping her on the nose, but she liked it that the kitten she'd found at the dump never had become truly domesticated. When she'd finally trimmed back the Confederate jasmine ruling the back garden last spring, the cuttings piled over her head. Rather than waiting for the yardman, she loaded the car and took them to the Macon city dump herself. Typical, of course: Charlotte liked instant results. The kitten had come pouncing over to her from smoking pits of garbage. She could not just leave it for wharf rats to attack. She pulled out the woody, dusty jasmine branches from her trunk, flinging them toward a mound of tires. The kitten began to lunge at the flowers. Hence the name Jasmine, for a kitten who already had done battle with enough rodents that she was formed for combat — affectionate but likely to turn fierce at the slightest provocation, rather like Charlotte herself, so they got along fine. On the way back from the dump, Jasmine leapt from the back seat onto the top of Charlotte's head, digging in just enough to stay perched all the way home.

Charlotte's husband, Mayhew, had felt Jasmine's claws one time too many and steered clear of her. Secretly, he feared Jasmine would jump on his face in the night and scratch his eyes out. He made sure she was closed in the kitchen when they went to bed.

Mayhew surprised Charlotte with two pieces of toasted pound cake, her favorite breakfast. He felt buoyant with a fat contract in his briefcase, ready to be signed at the bank at 10:00 a.m. "Oh, you angel brains." Charlotte broke a slice in two and offered him a bite.

"No, I'm off to see the wizard, my love." He liked Charlotte in the mornings, calm before the day seized her. He drove away thinking of her as a ship in full sail, carving a spuming wake as she moved forward, driven by whatever wind was blowing. Charlotte always *trailed* things, nickels, lipsticks, Kleenex, postcards, sunglasses. Mayhew himself was compact and neat. When he came home from his real estate deals, laden with details of listings and the minutiae of pest inspections, she found him picking up, one by one, all the leaves that had fallen that day from the rubber plant onto the patio. As she emerged from her painting studio every afternoon, she threw her arms around him, her fingernails rimmed with paints, hair practically on end with, he thought, excitement. Or maybe she'd just cut her own hair again. Shot with gray now, she still wore her cropped blond curls as they looked in the photo of her at five years old, when she stood on a dining room chair and blew out the candles on her cake. "To be out of there! Away from that sour household!" she shrieked when he asked what she had wished. She smelled of linseed oil, tossed her head back and forth as she sang *Let's twist again like we did last summer,* scuffed into the house on mules she decorated with fake flowers and sequins. Mayhew, wary by habit, awed by her life force, would follow her into the kitchen, bracing himself for whatever she might be concocting for their dinner. She was fond of coconut and might use it in unsuspected ways.

He smiled to himself as he turned into the opening in the boxwood hedge surrounding Macon Properties. He was crazy about her. She'd never bored him once, though he'd wished many times that she would not always, exhaustingly, surprise him. Charlotte had the biggest laugh he'd ever heard, raucous, unfeminine, making him uncomfortable in a group of his friends, but simply to be in the room with that laugh compensated for whatever he had to put up with from spoiled clients of Macon Properties, who thought they should all inhabit plantations draped in moss dripping she-oaks.

At the most rudimentary level, when you heard a laugh like that, you were pulled in, you rolled into laughter that rocked you in the joy you lost and found and looked for throughout your life but mostly lost.

Charlotte let Jasmine lick butter off her fingers. She read the first page last because that's where all the bad news began. She preferred the recipe page, and the wedding write-ups were good for a laugh. She usually just skipped the news, but today she looked to see if Mayhew's deal for the golf course land was mentioned. She gasped, "No!" as she recognized the photograph on the far right side of the page. Catherine! Those dead-level eyes sizing you up, the tender mouth.

SPECIAL FROM *THE SWAN FLYOVER*
BY RAINEY GROVER

DECEASED WOMAN EXPOSED IN SWAN
The body of Catherine Phillips Mason was found unearthed in the family plot at Magnolia Cemetery on July 8. The grave of another family member, James J. (Big Jim) Mason, was defaced with black paint. Officials are investigating motives for this bizarre crime. Sheriff Ralph Hunnicutt of Swan stated that grave robbery was the likely motive. The body was discovered at 9:00 a.m. by the victim's sister-in-law, Miss Lillian Elizabeth Mason, who was visiting the family plot, and Mrs. Eleanor Whitefield, former mathematics teacher at Swan High, when she visited the grave of her husband, the late Holt Whitefield. Cass Deal, cemetery caretaker, stated that he

had seen no unusual activity. Mrs. Mason died in 1956 by her own hand. Formerly of Vidalia, she was married to Dr. Wills Mason, whose ancestors were early settlers of Swan. She is survived by Dr. Mason, who resides at the Columns Rest Home, and by two grown children.

Catherine! Charlotte banged her cup on the saucer. How impossible. How loathsome, poor Catherine. As she stood up, the paper slipped down, and Jasmine spilled to the floor. Shock rushed down her back. The sleeve of Charlotte's robe caught the teaspoon, which splattered rusty tea spots onto the chair cushion.

Charlotte's robe fell open. Underneath she wore a pair of Mayhew's striped boxer shorts. She walked barefoot on the herringbone walk around the side of the house. She turned on the hose full force, blasting the drooping cosmos she'd seen from the kitchen window, then sprayed the yellow dahlias, forgetting that their leaves do not like to be wet and in this humidity would surely mildew. Crossing the lawn, her memory swerved back to Catherine — yes, she'd suggested the arbor leading down to the creek. In another life, it seemed. Since Catherine's death, there'd been trumpet vine, wisteria, what else? Now Mayhew had planted that pink pea vine she hoped would die. Though they were in their twenties by then, she and Catherine turned cartwheels on the lawn when Mayhew bought her the brick house right in the middle of two acres of dogwoods and camellias.

Now Catherine, brought back into the light of day. In life, she'd belonged in the light. All that passion and fun, all that sharp beauty and tenderness, snuffed out. Charlotte had missed her with a cold fury. She missed the lips peaked like the towers of the Golden Gate Bridge. Missed the way Catherine stepped like a deer through brush. Out of everyone she'd ever met, only Catherine's sense of life lived up to her own expectations. Most people are so tamped down. Catherine was, how to put it, ready. She missed the years they would have had renting beach houses together and going crabbing with the children, turning up Bobby Short tinkling at the faraway Carlyle Hotel in the kitchen, while they made huge pots of shrimp Creole, or, who knows, taking off to Paris, saturating themselves in art and writing postcards at a little iron table. She never tasted my recipe for chicken, coconut, and lime soup, she thought. She imagined Catherine taking a sip, closing her eyes in order to taste more privately. "Hey, Mambo, what is the secret?" she'd ask. The secret was that Charlotte had lived, had been to the Yucatán peninsula and tasted spicy soup, while Catherine lay in the ground.

Charlotte no longer recalled why Catherine called her Mambo; the name came from their first days at Georgia State College for Women, where they'd been assigned to the corner room of Fall Hall. She and Catherine simply linked. They'd painted the beige room lavender, without permission, with clusters of grapes at the corners. Even so small a rebellion marked them. Of course there was precious little acting-up back then. Both girls had studied art. Charlotte loved oil painting then, though she'd since turned to watercolors, which suited her spontaneous, some would say slapdash, style. When they took art history, Catherine went mad for Matisse and decided she wanted to make pottery with bold colors, then she wanted to design patterns on silk, influenced by his blues and yellows. All year they'd lived for art. Charlotte must have drawn the blue-rimmed plate with two oranges a hundred times. Catherine wanted to make things with her hands. She embroidered bees and lizards on their pillowcases, she knitted big wool scarves with chevron designs. Pad after pad she filled with sketches of architectural details taken from photographs of French cathedrals — arches, gargoyles, tracery. Then early sophomore year she met Austin, then right away, she met Wills. Charlotte became active in theatrical productions, then interested in dance, and although she loved Catherine as a friend for life, she was not much interested in the late night discussions about whether it was possible to love two men. Often she fell asleep while Catherine held forth about Wills's brilliance and Austin's daredevil personality. Suddenly, too suddenly, when Catherine came back from Swan after Thanksgiving, she was engaged to Wills.

Charlotte lost touch with Catherine's children after her death. That idiot sheriff acted like she committed some breach of etiquette when she called. "Listen, sheriff man," she'd shouted, "Catherine Phillips would not *do* this, do you understand me? I know, I know she never, ever would kill herself." Until she read the article, she had forgotten that when she asked, he said no notebooks had been found at the scene, and she shouted, "Do you think they'd be laid out for you on the kitchen counter?" She remembered that she'd called him a "donkey turd" for his poor investigation. Where the archaic *donkey turd* had come from, she couldn't imagine. Her letter to the county judge demanding an investigation was not even answered. Wills refused to talk to anyone. The grief he plunged into was harrowing. Even after weeks of notes and messages, he did not respond. She had driven to Swan several afternoons, hoping to see the children, but Tessie said they were at the cabin. Intrepid as she was, she wouldn't intrude on Wills when he so obviously did not want to see her. Perhaps she just reminded him too much of Catherine. After Wills's grand-slam failure, she'd never seen him again. For a few years, she sent birthday and Christmas presents to Ginger and J.J., for which they wrote short notes of thanks, then the tumult of her own three adolescents took over and she stopped.

Now this many years later, watching the play of rainbows in the spray, she wondered about Catherine's death. She suspected that Catherine had a — she wouldn't say lover because she did not think Catherine actually would betray Wills — an affair, probably platonic, going on in Macon. Or maybe she would. Those were war years. Her college love, Austin, lived outside town then. There was a time, she couldn't remember exactly when, that Catherine suddenly had started to visit Charlotte in Macon more but she wouldn't stay long. A coffee, a quick lunch at Davison's, then she'd fly off. Once Wills called — oh yes, it was during the war because he was on leave — and asked to speak to her when Charlotte hadn't seen her. Out of instinct, she said, "She ran out to do a little shopping for the children." Catherine never mentioned the call.

Charlotte waved the hose, wondering what had happened to Austin, driving Mayhew's new alyssum plants into the dirt.

"Have you seen the paper?" Aileen's customer, Mrs. Shad Williams, called to order a set of yellow bootees for a baby shower. "The most awful thing happened."

She related the news about Catherine.

"How sick." Aileen felt her stomach lurch.

"Black paint on ol' man Mason's grave. Sounds like an ancient curse or something." Mrs. Williams read the article. "Honey, take your time with those bootees. The shower is August the first. Now, come see me soon."

Since Big Jim's death, Aileen didn't want to hear about the Masons. She'd been transferred back to the looms immediately when new management took over. Gradually, she'd built up her own business, and by the time the mill went under, she was already supporting herself. Big Jim would have taken care of her, if he'd lived. With her income and the money she'd stashed over the four years of their affair, she lived comfortably.

She still went all over funny every time she thought of the night at the motel when she'd gone back in the bedroom after taking a shower — a shower was a luxury since she only had a small tub with intermittent hot water at home — and Big Jim in his undershirt and shorts was toppled sideways on the bed. She thought he was joking and poked him in the ribs. Then she saw pink spittle running out of his mouth. She felt for his pulse, calling to him *wake up, wake up, no, no, no.* He'd had a previous heart attack, she knew, but he'd always boasted that his mended heart was stronger where it had broken. She'd shoved on his pants and shirt. She called Sheriff Hunnicutt and in a lowered voice told him to come get Big Jim and take him home. She fled. Before leaving the room, she saw his wallet on the bedside table and took all the cash in it, almost nine hundred dollars. She'd read later that Big Jim was found at the House, dead in his bed, by the maid when she went to work at seven the next morning. Apparently, the paper said, he'd died of a heart attack in his sleep. Hunnicutt always had nodded to her whenever she saw him, but never said a word. She knew his loyalty to Big Jim was unswerving but she didn't know why. Big Jim would only say that he'd been able to do Hunnicutt some favors.

Aileen frowned as she stared out her kitchen window. Black paint. Plenty of people hated the Masons, mostly out of jealousy. No one ever hated them as much as her former husband, Sonny, had years ago. But years and years had passed. Good thing he was living out in Arizona now. Even his mama had moved out there. Aileen hoped they were baking. Ever since the day he'd discovered her affair, she had prayed never to see his ugly face in this lifetime or the next.

She had never known whether Big Jim had arranged for Sonny to be drafted or if it happened by chance. Shortly after he was called up, Sonny came home — unexpectedly — on a weekend pass from Fort Benning before being transferred overseas. She'd hated the idea of going with him to Germany, although she'd told him out of fear that she'd follow in a couple of months. As soon as he left the country, Big Jim was going to tell her how to get a divorce. Then Sonny would be stuck overseas. Big Jim laughed about that. Aileen had hoped that by the time he was discharged he would have found someone else. Or maybe, she'd dreamed, she and Big Jim could run away together, and even marry. Big Jim often spoke of Bath, England, where his ancestors had lived.

Aileen was at the mill office when Sonny arrived that weekend. Since she had not known he was coming, she'd left an aqua peignoir on the bed. Big Jim had brought it back from New York. Next time, he'd said, he would take her. She'd left a wad of cash in her jewelry box, which Sonny found, along with an amethyst pendant she only wore inside her blouse because it was too fine and would call attention.

She'd gone to work to catch up on bills, and fortunately Big Jim was at the House. She sorted papers, feeling proud to be there. Maybe she could take secretarial courses over at the ag college in Tipton; she could be promoted again. As she sat at a desk in her corner of the anteroom to Big Jim's office, Sonny's face, dripping with sweat, appeared in the glass of the side door. Before she could get up, he stormed in shouting *whore, bitch*.

"Get out, you're going to get me fired," she'd shouted back. He pushed her to the floor and kicked her in the stomach. Then he went wild and turned over Big Jim's desk in the next room. Said he was going to kill that piss-ant if it was the last thing he ever did. "Screwing that bastard, you low-down slut." He kicked the desk chair, tore papers and piled them in the waste-basket, then set them on fire with a ciga-rette lighter. The blaze shot up, scorching the ceiling, then burned out as Aileen crawled into the outer office, slammed the door, and locked it. Through the wall she shouted that she wanted out of the mar-riage, it was no marriage anyway. She di-aled the sheriff. Big Jim had told her if she ever needed anything, to call Hunnicutt. Sonny battered the door with a chair and broke through. He grabbed the phone and hit her on the head. As she fell, she saw him running out.

Sheriff Hunnicutt, sensing ugly gossip for Big Jim, had driven out to the mill vil-lage in his wife's inconspicuous old Ford. He'd found Sonny back at their house and locked him up overnight, though he wrote no report. The next day he'd taken him in the county car back to Fort Benning.

Aileen assumed Big Jim had pulled strings, because Sonny was shipped over-seas the next week. "The little freak is gone." Big Jim had laughed. "I threw him to the alligators." You can't say that, she'd thought. If you do, the Lord will punish you. Fear had flushed her entire body, fear for Sonny, who, when they were first married, would sing doo-wop in the bathtub when she ladled pots of warm water over his scrawny body. He was only nineteen, a hothead. Then fear for herself had swamped her first fear. Sonny might come back and strangle her or set the house on fire. He might go after Big Jim. Like in the Old Testament, some prideful person was always getting back in spades what they'd caused to start in the first place. The fear had settled into her bone marrow. There was no one to tell, of course, or her affair would be discovered. Big Jim bought her a living room set and said, "Good riddance." His delight in her seemed to increase. She and Big Jim had three more good years. Aileen had begun to enjoy the rest of her life — her work, sewing, a church Bible study group.

While Sonny was overseas, she divorced him and dumped all his things on his mama's porch in Osceola. His mama probably didn't want him back there either. He'd been a hellion growing up.

Aileen checked her basket to see if she

had enough silky cotton yarn for the yellow bootees. She would have to fill this day. She opened her Bible to the lesson for Sunday, but her eyes fell upon the words *sin, iniquity, wicked, wrath.* She put on an old record by the Soul Searchers. She would make a pan of brownies from scratch.

Carol was already at her desk when Ralph arrived. "Mrs. Whitefield called before I could unlock the door. She said to tell you that Catherine Mason was buried holding a letter. She said she remembered it and had asked Lily, who remembered it, too."

"And the letter reveals the naked truth?" A letter, he'd seen no letter but maybe it blew away. He'd have to comb the cemetery. In the school yard across the street, boys were gathering for a baseball game, oblivious to everything except the crack of the ball against the bat. They knew nothing of broken-into graves or burned villages in Vietnam. We should play more ball, he thought. He would organize two teams this summer, when all this blew over. He saw J.J. pull up and park in the jail loading spot.

Ginger gave Ralph a quick hug and pulled the doughnut holes out of her bag.

"From the Sisters. Have some." Ralph grabbed a chair from Carol's office and they sat down. "Well, how grown-up — the sheriff. How does it feel to sit at your granddaddy's desk?"

Ralph grinned at Ginger. "You're sure looking good. Long time no see." J.J. stood behind her chair. Ginger was capable of all the niceties; he wasn't.

"Take a load off." Ralph gestured to the empty chair, but J.J. said he'd stand.

Ralph asked about the fishing at the river. "I heard Ralph Rogers got a forty-pound rockfish out of Resurrection Creek last Friday."

J.J. nodded. "Must of been there since the Stone Age. I hate seeing those suckers come up. They do look like something that oughta be extinct. Kinda pretty though, those jaws, some of them with four or five pieces of line hanging off." Ginger rolled her eyes at his ol'-boy role coming on this early in the day.

They fell silent and Ralph pulled out the folder marked *Catherine Phillips Mason*. "I know you've had a shock and y'all know I'm mighty sorry this has happened. I don't understand it yet and I wonder if we ever will. It falls to me to tell you something else. Something entirely unforeseen.

I don't know what the verdict will be, but we performed an examination — Gray Hinckle from the GBI and I — and we've gone over the evidence — this record here and, well, of course" — his voice dropped — "the body. It's beginning to look like . . . because of various measurements we've made and all . . ." He looked down at the floor because Ginger and J.J. were both staring at him as if a tidal wave were about to break over them. "This is preliminary. All the evidence has to be rechecked." Ginger and J.J. watched his mouth form words, expecting to hear that their mother's body had been violated, watched his mouth while he said, "But we think that your mother did not kill herself. That is, she herself did not pull the trigger . . ." He stopped.

He had no idea of the import of his words. The words seemed to sift through the air from a great distance.

Neither of them said anything. J.J. moved his hand to Ginger's shoulder and she covered his hand with hers.

"Because the exit angle of the wound" — he looked down at the notes he took from Gray's call — "is incommensurate with what would result from a gun held by the victim. I hate to burden you with details, but sometimes the .22 doesn't go all the way through a body. You know, it's basically a rabbit gun. But Mrs. Mason — your mother — must have been thin. I've read the report written back when it happened. That was when my granddaddy was sheriff, I guess you know. They didn't have the fancy equipment we have now. Those GBI boys have other tricks of the trade these days. She's been checked for gunpowder residue in her nose and on her hands. They've got some kind of dust that picks up microscopic particles."

"What are you saying?" Ginger pressed her elbows into her knees and stared at the floor. J.J. shielded his eyes as though he were looking into the sun.

Ralph's words formed a distant hum. "The size and angle of the wound point toward the conclusion that she couldn't have aimed at herself." Ralph thought even back then somebody could have noticed that, but maybe that was because he'd been in Vietnam, where men were shot every which-a-way, whereas his granddaddy mostly saw blacks cut up on Saturday night. "I'm going to ask you to read the report and see if there's anything you can add, from your memory of the event. I know this is damn strange for y'all. In

Gray's call, he'd said his boss, the expert, thought she'd had the rifle put in her hand after she'd been shot. Maybe someone had taken it away from her as she tried to defend herself. She might have first grabbed the gun in self-defense. They'll try to test for powder burn, but after this long they might not come up with anything definitive. Looked to Gray and his boss like she'd been shot from six to eight feet away."

I'll think this through later, Ginger thought. She was the first to speak. "When will they know for sure? How can they tell after so long? She was shot by someone? But that can't be. Who? Who?"

Ralph shrugged and shook his head. "About that letter, do you know the contents?"

"No. Lily doesn't know. She thought it might be a note of love from Daddy."

Ralph said nothing, stared at her, unable to admit his suspicion that it might have been a confession and apology. Now it was lost or taken. What a sheriff. What was that old verse, *the fathers have tasted bitter grapes and the sons' teeth are set on edge.* That about said it. Damnation.

J.J. picked up the file. A surge of elation pushed against his skin. The post-migraine delight — or was it that what Ralph just said was what he'd wanted to hear ever since he first heard the word *suicide?* He read quickly. He did not look at the photograph of his mother sprawled on the floor, but he saw it anyway, saw what he'd seen over and over although he did not in actuality ever see her, only Ginger had. Only Ginger had taken the full impact into her body.

Ginger reached for the report. The photo must have been taken an hour or so after Mrs. Rowen found Ginger on the road. Ginger stared. She heard again her own strangled cry. But if her mother did not pull the trigger, she must look at the picture again. Cabinet door ajar, her legs splayed, one shoe off, the peeling screen door in the background. Surely, something showed that Catherine did not do it. The *something,* if someone had noticed, that would have changed their lives. She forced her memory: Again, she reaches for the screen door and slowly it swings open, the sight of her mother blasts her out again, the indelible, searing blood, the bang of the door. She looked at every detail. She was feeling her way, the way she felt her way to bed in the dark. She had the impulse to drive to their old house, the dentist's, ask to see the kitchen. She'd heard they ripped it out, replaced everything, even extended the kitchen and added a patio so that the hideous event would be obliterated.

She tried to re-create it exactly: the round table by the windows, the shelf of cookbooks, the glass cabinet for hunting guns, the curvy white appliances. Her memory and the photo were the same.

"See anything new to you?" Ralph let them read. He wondered if they'd thought yet that Wills could have pulled the trigger.

J.J. spotted the gun cabinet part in an instant. He kept his own cabinet locked. Back then, no one did. He and Ginger were raised around guns and knew not to touch them. He read the report to Ginger, who was tearing off her thumbnail in her teeth. "Hell, there's some explanation." He looked at Ralph's quizzical expression. Son of a bitch, he thinks Daddy did it. "My dad couldn't have raised a hand against her. Is that what that fuckup said? You don't believe that. That's crap. All these years we've had a suicide. Now we have a father who's a murderer? Do we get to choose?"

As he spoke, J.J. knew without hesitation which he would choose. Nothing could be worse than his mother shooting her heart out.

"Nobody's saying that. Nobody's accusing anyone. Yeah, the agent brought it up as a possibility. He doesn't know your daddy from Adam. We don't have a lot to go on, do we? Can I get you some coffee? Carol always makes a strong pot."

Neither answered. "Also, Daddy is like a big baby now. He's slumped over in a stupor half the time. He certainly doesn't have the I.Q. at this point to break into her grave. It's preposterous even to think of that. If there were any conceivable reason anyway." She dismissed the question of Wills's guilt from her mind as soon as J.J. raised it. Odd to think of Daddy's I.Q. Once he was an idealistic young doctor, who'd refused to step into the family business. For as long as he'd been gone, Ginger had felt an irritated knot of anger toward him. He brought this on himself. But what happened to him went way beyond the bounds of just deserts. Other people had bouts of madness or drunkenness, recovered and went on with normal lives. It shouldn't have happened to a dog. Ginger felt the same stunned glimmer of elation as J.J. A random crime was a whole different grief.

In the folded memory, Ginger still has her hand out, the immense calm of childhood about to be ended, she's about to open the door but the memory cracks — she always called first, "Mama, hey, I'm home, let me in."

Let me in! Always, always, her mother kept the screen door latched, ever since gypsies came through town and stole her underwear off the line. Almost everyone in Swan left their doors unlocked, even at night. Catherine locked hers. But the door swung open in Ginger's hand. Her mother had unlatched the door for someone, a friend, a repairman, a neighbor. She blurted this out.

"Someone she knew. Or maybe she just left the door open this time." Ralph was taking notes. Good. He would have some things to tell Gray.

"J.J., how could I not have remembered this?"

"Because of what was on the other side of the door."

She could never remember her walk home from school that day. In memory, she left the playground, and then she was hit by the sight of her mother. She ran, she's running still down the white road, Mrs. Rowen's floury hands around her, then nothing else until the funeral. When she remembered the dark circle of blood, she was always twelve, wanting to bang her head on the floor.

J.J. kept reading. "Look here, Charlotte Crowder, Mama's old friend, called up," he read on, his finger following the words, "but there's no follow-through here? What did she know?" Wills had cut off everyone after Catherine's death, J.J. remembered. Charlotte sent notes and called at first, then she stopped. J.J. hadn't thought of her in years. "I wonder if she confronted Dad, if Lily knew she'd called the sheriff."

Ginger wandered into the outer office and came back with a mug of coffee. J.J. stared at the doodle in Ralph's grandfather's hand, something scratched over — he made out an *S*.

"We can speculate all day. Sorry to say so, but it's the easiest crime in the world," Ralph smoothly echoed Gray. "Husband goes after the wife and it's your word against his. Nobody can prove a thing."

"But how could he have *thought* Daddy could do such a thing?" Ginger became outraged. "Oh, Ralph, I know you can't speak for him, but do you have any idea?"

Ralph didn't want to continue Gray's speculation about a lover in the wings, or

to go into how his grandfather was indebted to Big Jim for swinging the sheriff's
election. "I'll just be blunt. Your dad's the
only lead out there — it's based on statistics, not on anything real. Why didn't my
granddad do a better investigation? I think
he was in Big Jim's pocket his whole life.
He might have been grateful for certain
things. There's the possibility that he was
protecting your family. Women, you know,
they get unhappy, don't see any way out —
they kill themselves. A murder might have
stirred up some old shame. God only
knows." Could his grandfather have been
lame enough to think it just wasn't *polite* to
inquire too closely?

He shook his head. "We can go two ways
— start investigating a murder or depend
on solving this by finding out who, uh, violated the grave. From my point of view,
I've got to follow up on the latter. I'm sure
you'd want to pursue both," or maybe not,
he thought, "but the GBI agent says
there's no way to trace the killer, short of a
confession, after this long. He said when a
trail is this cold, finding the killer usually
happens only if a surprise confession pops
up, some old guilt working its way out.
That may be years from now. Maybe never.
Let's just get her back in the ground, when

she's finally released on Monday, and hope to close the case."

Ginger looked at the obituary from the local paper, with her mother's photograph above it. She recognized it as her mother's engagement picture, which used to sit on Wills's desk at his office. She had an impressive forehead and direct eyes. Her lips formed the perfect cupid's bow of her era. Around her neck was the flat gold necklace her father gave her when she was eighteen, against her mother's wishes. Ginger could hear Mema, *He spoiled her. She wants too much.* Her mother always loved that necklace. Her gaze was serene; nothing ever could go wrong. She looked out from thirty-five years ago into a future that did not include her two puzzled children huddled in the sheriff's office going over her file, her husband propped into a chair by a window overlooking the weedy tennis court of a nursing home.

Holt Whitefield usually visited the cemetery with his mother on Thursday mornings. It was something for them to do together. Today she refused to go and considering the shock she'd had out there, he was relieved. Instead, he took her to the Three Sisters, so crowded this morning that they had to sit by the door. He read the Macon paper while she chatted with everyone coming and going. Catherine Mason was in the news, page one, a small article about the exhumation, but what, really, was there to say? No one had a single clue. Emily brought a platter of bacon and grits with a side order of limp toast that not even the homemade pear preserves could redeem. "Eleanor, bless your heart, what an *awful* thing to happen to you and Lily. Those children were in here this morning, J.J. scowling as usual and Ginger sweet as she can be." On his way out, Father Tim Tyson leaned over to pat Eleanor's back, and Holt saw his mother straighten her shoulders as though shrugging him off. The priest worked a toothpick between his molars, and a gray food fleck landed on the table.

Holt lowered the paper and stared at it, his top lip rising in disgust. Holt was no friend of the Episcopal church anyway, and he barely nodded to Father Tyson as he passed on by, with "Don't be a stranger."

"I double-dog-dare you to give him the finger, Mama."

"Oh, Holt." Then Eleanor was clasping hands with Rainey Grover, whose bulbous buttocks in pink stuck out so far you could rest a glass on them.

"I don't know how you'll ever sleep again." Journalist or not, Rainey wouldn't think of asking questions that might upset Eleanor. Rainey in her belle-hood had men from three counties swarming around her, a regular Duchess Hotspur. She worked for her husband's Swan newspaper now; who would have guessed she'd end up with Johnny Grover? But who'd have guessed that Holt, with his I.Q. off the charts, would end up as local high school principal? Rainey's small face, polished like a just-dried bowl, rose out of the body of an ancient fertility goddess. Holt remembered hearing years ago Buddy Perrin say a night with her would kill the weak and cripple the mighty.

Rainey looked down at Holt with God-given blue eyes. Holt had helped her boy get a scholarship to Mercer College. He's not *that* old, she thought, and just look at those old-man suspenders and the way he combs that lick of hair over his pate. She smiled good-bye to Eleanor, showing wide white Chiclets, Holt noticed, smiling a tight smile to cover his own slightly back-sloping teeth.

"Would you like to ride around?"

Eleanor thought she would. "Ride by Billie's. Let's see the row of pines she planted down her driveway. Then we'll stop in to check on Lily."

"Mama, what do you think is going on with this Mason mess?"

"If they find the letter out there, then I think it's probably a random piece of work by someone crazy. If they don't, maybe someone wanted it — or something. We'll just have to wait and see."

"What if Wills isn't as damaged as he seems?"

"Lily would know if that were true, and even if it were, I doubt if he could have engineered this from the Columns. And why on earth would he?"

She did not ask what he thought. Just as well. Holt, after years and years, still was not about to erode Catherine's trust. She never had betrayed his secret.

Father Tim Tyson drove the three blocks from the Three Sisters to the post office to mail his request for a new parish. Swan was a constant ordeal, especially after the two years in Newman over in Meacham County, where the people were more gracious and the rectory considerably nicer for his wife, Rosemary. Every month she complained when the Circle met for New Testament study. At least two members had to sit on straight chairs in the hall, barely able to hear, because the living room was too small. Five years here and he still didn't feel accepted. Just now Eleanor Whitefield pure snubbed him and ditto that queer son of hers; everybody said he defied the teachings of Jesus and practiced sodomy. For a moment, he concentrated on what sodomy might be, exactly. Buggering, yes, he knew that, but he saw only biblical hordes led by Charlton Heston, pillaging and looting. Now he had to think about this disgrace with the Masons. He'd been told that Big Jim donated the chandeliers in the church years back and had his men build the pierced-brick serpentine wall around the Memory Garden, but the current clan donated a few hundred dollars a year, if they remembered at all. Lily still brought flowers for the altar on her parents' birthdays, enormous sloppy bunches from her garden. J.J. never darkened the door, and when, as the new priest, he'd made his rounds, calling on the members, J.J. had offered him a drink of whiskey and told him not to expect him, as Sunday was sacred fishing time. Tim Tyson's lips twitched in anger as he recalled J.J.'s cruel little smile. Had his own way of praying, he had said; that old excuse. As if we were meant to be solitary. As if the church were not about holding the community together, as this sinful one needed.

He stopped at the Pappas fruit stand and surveyed the bushels of corn and baskets of plums and peaches lined up along the sidewalk outside the shop.

"Mighty fine peaches, Father Tyson. Would you like a sample?" Tony Pappas seemed to smile all over his face. His large black eyes made him look like an icon painting from centuries ago. Everyone in

Swan came to Tony. He lavished his attention on mounds of lemons and polished apples on his green apron.

"I'll take your word. Give me a sack of those, please, Tony." He pointed to the yellow plums Tony had picked earlier from along the roadside toward Osceola. Father Tyson had other things on his mind besides fruit for Rosemary's pie and stared off into the middle distance as Tony examined each plum for bugs or bruises. The letter had dropped to the bottom of the mailbox with a thin *plink*. Maybe the bishop would send a young man just out of seminary to Swan. Trial by fire, he'd find. Highest suicide rate in the state, highest incidence of intestinal pinworms, and quite a few plain loonies. God help me, he thought, I've dealt with arson and stealing from the collection basket and pregnant twelve-year-olds. No wonder I could not face the uproar of finding that piece of paper on the ground. I did the sensible thing. I'm going to pray for them all, but I have enough on my plate.

Tony whistled as he bagged the plums. He threw in a couple of peaches for good luck and touched the blue eyeball he wore around his neck. According to his grandmother, priests sometimes cast the evil eye.

Today Father Tyson looked hot enough to pop.

Yesterday, Father Tyson had just settled Mattie Tucker in the front seat, after helping her take a vase of glads to poor Ham's grave. As he went around to his side of the car, an envelope lay at his feet. Small, dirty. In typed letters he saw the word *Catherine*. Under it, *The last day*. Around town they'd been saying Catherine Mason was buried with a letter in her hand. Here it was, blown to his feet, blown to the priest of the church to which she had belonged. Was that not auspicious, was not God sending him a message? He slipped it into his pocket and drove Mattie to her sagging house with several cats waiting on the porch. She was one of his saviors in Swan. She and four other women tended to the needs of the church as if it were their own home. Mattie, always immaculate in her brown or gray anonymous dresses, ironed the altar linen, baked cookies for the Episcopal Youth Fellowship, and sat in the third pew every time the doors of the church opened. She did not deserve for Ham to up and die like that, washing the car on a Saturday afternoon. Father Tyson did not mention to Mattie the envelope secretly shoved in his pocket.

When he got back to the church office, he took out the fragile envelope and pulled out what appeared to be a blackened-edge page ripped from a spiral notebook. In handwriting different from the envelope's he read:

Beauty is a thing beyond the grave.
That perfect bright experience
Will never fall to nothing
And time will dim the [blurred spot] sooner
Than our full consummation [blurred spot]
In this brief life will tarnish or pass away.

He held the lined page up to the light. The paper was soft, speckled with mildew. A hard shudder ran through him as he realized it had been held in the hand of a dead woman under the ground for all these years. Beneath the watery blurs he made out *moon* and *here*. He dropped the page on his desk and wiped his hands on his pant legs. *Time will dim the moon. Our full consummation here.* Could they find fingerprints on something this damaged? He thought not. Since he was a man of the cloth and had no fingerprints on file anywhere, he knew he was exempt from the law. He wrapped the letter in crumbled tissue paper he pulled out of the wastebasket. Full consummation, that sounds sexual. His mouth turned downward. I will not speculate on the meaning of this, he decided. I do not want to be involved. He put the page under his sermon notes. I do not want to know. Yes, her life was brief, but killing oneself is surely to be condemned. Shame. Her family had to walk out of Eden, covering themselves. And look what they've become. More than any visitation, he dreaded the monthly call he made on Wills Mason, who looked at him as though he were a cockroach on the wall. He had trouble enough in the present. To meddle in the past was beyond the call.

That night, reading under a circle of lamplight in the corner of the bedroom, he waited until Rosemary fell asleep, her hair wound in tight sausages secured with rubber bands, a mask of pale green cold cream on her face. He felt more serene after reading the Book of Job. Rosemary's eyes fluttered when he picked up the keys and he waited until she snorted and rolled on her side. He drove out Island 10, and on out to the Mason house, killed the lights, and stuck the letter in the mailbox.

When he coasted into his driveway, Rosemary was waiting at the back door. "Tim . . . at this time of night?" she was almost shouting. With the dim garage light shining on her green face, she looked frightening.

There was no lie to tell, nothing he could invent that she would not know was untrue by tomorrow or the next day. Any accident, death, emergency in Swan would be hers by noon. He told her the truth. "I just did not want to be pulled into their lives."

She looked at him blankly. "But you could have *offered* them . . ." The night freight rumbled by two blocks back, muffling her words. Then she said something else and went back to bed.

He thought she said *shame*.

Ginger turned the air vent toward her face as J.J. raised a cloud of dust between them and Ralph's office. She saw a lone figure in blue looking out at them from the upstairs barred window of the jail. She had an impulse to wave but did not. "If we just spring it on Daddy, maybe he will react in some revealing way."

"You think this kind of news goes straight to the reptilian brain stem?"

"It felt that way to me." Even going as far as to speculate that they might stun Wills into a reaction made her need air. Her throat felt too tight to breathe. She conjured the face of Marco, but his look, she realized, would be incredulous. Marco, she feared, could not follow this. Who could? — J.J. and I are the ones swallowed by the whale. Or do I underestimate Marco, automatically shut down? *Easiest crime in the world,* Ralph had said. "There's a rational world to live in, isn't there?" she asked, but J.J. only sighed and shook his head. I've been feeling my way toward one, she thought, and if this news is true, maybe we can reach around the past years back to the earliest world, where Daddy let me put his stethoscope to the hearts of my dolls and taught me to bandage their legs. At the very rim of her consciousness, she knew his warmth — he is running from rain, holding her, a red plaid umbrella over them, and he is laughing. Her small arm crooks around his neck and his face is next to hers. She hears and against her chest also feels his laughter. Not an ounce of her believes that her father could be a murderer. What colossal bad luck he'd had. "You look miles away, J.J., a stone on the moon, come down."

"What strikes my brain stem is all we don't know about what we know. You want to try talking to him, I'll take you." He turned in at the Gold Star Drive-In and ordered a beer brought out to the car, though it was only eleven o'clock. The Gold Star was a Mason building, but he almost never went in, just occasionally stopped to brace himself there en route to the Columns.

"Sun's not over the yardarm, J.J."

"Well, it's dark under the house."

Ginger ordered a lemonade. It was cold and sour. She thought she was getting a sore throat. She pressed the cold glass to her forehead, then emptied it on the ground.

J.J. and Ginger differed over the mental state of their father. Ginger often saw flashes of the real Wills. She saw his mind as a film exposed many times. He found fractured and layered images but couldn't put together a scene. When she probed, asking him about the cabin when he was a child, about medical school, about Big Jim and Mama Fan, at times a power came back to his face. "Your grandmother," he said, "loved the smell of a gardenia. She had a big bush of them eight feet tall."

"Where?" Ginger knew, because it still bloomed outside Lily's bedroom window, under her own.

"I don't know." But he said *grandmother*, Ginger would think; he has enough reason to know that his mother was my grandmother.

The possibility that he would come back never really left her. The chemical levels would separate or purify, leach through to the dried areas, the damaged neurons would knit again into a pattern, synapses

reconnect. She willed them to stitch together. "What in the name of God are we
supposed to do? For Christ's sake, turn up
the air." Now she sounded like J.J. If she
lived here, she'd probably become like J.J.
A Chamber of Commerce sign on the outskirts of town said in foot-high letters *If
you lived here, you'd be home now.* Wills's
two years of drinking (decline, Lily called
it) after Catherine's death Ginger and J.J.,
too, attributed to his grief, which moved
Ginger to a pity J.J. could not allow. *A pity
beyond all telling,* she'd underlined in her
copy of Yeats's poems, *is hid in the heart of
love.*

J.J. considered Wills a total goner. He
judged his father's character: weak. And
his indulgent weakness had lowered him
and Ginger to orphans. Wards of the Lily.
If you love someone, if you have a choice,
you don't let them down. Ever since they'd
been let down, down, a free-fall down, J.J.
had smoldered with a double-edged fury.
All three of them were fingered by
Catherine's death, and he could forgive
only Ginger. He was able to see her innocence but not his own and certainly not his
father's. He remembered feeling as if he
were turning into wood when Lily,
swinging into the drive at the House, sud-

denly announced, "You're home, this is home." Their own house was left closed for months before Lily decided to sell. He and Ginger would take the key off the nail on the trellis and let themselves in to find a game or a jacket. Some of their clothes still hung in the closet. Everything of Catherine's was gone. A dirt dauber built a four-chambered nest on the leg of a pair of J.J.'s jeans. No one had unplugged the refrigerator. They escaped the quiet house covered by a layer of dust and ran toward home, as they now knew it. They'd had to invent themselves after Wills flaked on them. Bird girl, J.J. thought, bird boy, mismatched socks, swingers of ropes, searchers for petroglyphs, snapping turtles, back-of-the-classroom, moon-howlers, pick a card, any card, X marks the spot. Long after they were too old, they tore through the woods yelling like Indians on the warpath in the Saturday movies. They developed with all the subtlety of kerosene-soaked rags.

At best, he attenuated his rage toward his father by seeming to humor him like a spoiled-rotten child. At worst, he went for weeks without visiting at all, then would arrive one afternoon to find Wills in a snit because he'd had to wait in his bath for help, or someone had stolen the dollar bills he kept for cigarettes. News of a car crash killing seven and a spilled glass of water received equally bland stares. J.J.'s absence troubled him not at all. J.J. would lean against the air conditioner — it diffused the smells of diapers, bandages, IV bags, pissed mattresses, fried food, and hell-bent misery absorbed in the walls of the Columns by years of dying patients — not making conversation, his lips set in a curl, sometimes wondering if he would be caught if he held a pillow over Wills's face and put him out of his misery. Whose misery? J.J.'s. His father's arrogance and imperialism he found so unbearable that in the few moments when Wills turned vulnerable, looked straight at him with the eyes of a bagged hare, or reached out a shaky hand for balance, J.J. exited as soon as possible. Driving toward the Columns, he briefly considered whether or not subconsciously he'd suspected his father. But the idea, dropped on them by Ralph, was preposterous.

There were no columns at the Columns, only squat porch posts along a low two-story building made of cinder blocks painted beige. Patients propped in rocking chairs sat silently facing the parking lot, like Easter Island carvings facing the sea. One or two fanned with cardboard Jesus fans, the rest slumped over in the trance of heat and near-death. A young man with no arms or legs was trussed into a lawn chair. "There but for the grace of God . . ." J.J. pushed Ginger's elbow forward.

"Don't," she said, "just don't."

"Let's run the gauntlet." All through high school, they dreaded the journey from car to corridor to Wills's room. All through their twenties, they'd never become inured. "Last one in is a rotten egg."

Turn left at the entrance and you faced the crazy ward; turn right and you faced the old people's area. Though he was a little bit of both now, Wills lived among the old. Most rooms were shared by two, but he had his own, with his leather reclining chair, an antique chest lined with photos, and fresh ferns Lily brought each time one curled and dried, not that he noticed. His old gabardine and linen suits hung in the closet, his *summa cum laude* medical diploma above the mirror. The institutional iron bed Lily had covered with a blue comforter. From the window he looked out onto a tennis court, absurdly constructed, with federal grants, for those who could barely stand, much less swing a racket. The net sagged and weeds sprouted through the baking clay.

Doors along the hall stood open, the occupants hoping for a passing greeting or a visit, but Ginger and J.J., familiar with the cast of characters, today looked neither right nor left. Wills kept his door closed. Ginger tapped. "Daddy, it's us." She peeped in, then opened the door wider. Wills lay on his side, his feet under the covers. His hands, pressed together as if in prayer, rested under his head. They came in quietly but he sat up.

"Who, what?" He looked wildly around the room, then recognized them. "Oh, I must have been dreaming."

"What were you dreaming?" Ginger asked.

"Dreaming of dreaming."

Ginger could be blunt, but J.J. was startled when she cut short the usual banter. "Daddy, we have learned something serious and very surprising. You know that mother was taken out of her grave? Lily told you."

He stared at her, then at J.J. "Catherine, she was a lovely woman."

"Yes, well, something even stranger has happened. The GBI examined her body and now say that she did not shoot herself."

"No? What are you talking about? J.J., speak up, what is she saying about my wife?"

"Dad, she's saying what she's saying. The police have new techniques. Mother was murdered." He said it brutally, although he was not yet sure he believed it himself.

Wills reared back as though water had been thrown in his face. He made an animal grunt, flung himself off the bed, and teetered over to the leather chair, where J.J. sat. He leaned into J.J.'s face. "Where's that rifle of mine? I know my gun went off. She went *bang.*" He held his finger to his temple.

J.J. spun toward Ginger and shouted, "She went *bang.* Did you hear that? She went bang. This is fucking unbelievable. What did we do in another life to deserve this?"

"Quit it, J.J.!" Ginger tried to lead Wills to a chair. "Daddy, listen. No, she didn't use the gun. That's the point. She did not pull the trigger." Wills sagged down, his knees flopped open. "Try to remember. Who would have shot her? Did anyone hate her?"

"I hated when she was gone." He reached over and turned on the TV. Lawrence Welk appeared and Wills smiled.

J.J. stood up and snapped off the TV. "I have to ask you this. Did you, did you kill her, kill Catherine?" He wanted to grab him by the throat, shake him until he spoke an intelligent sentence.

Wills raised his chin and looked defiant. "Don't be ridiculous."

"Who could have, goddammit, think for once. Who could have?" Wills stared at the empty screen.

"What is wrong with you? It's time for my programs."

"It's dawning on me that nothing is wrong with me or Ginger after all. What happened to her notebooks? She used to write in spiral notebooks. There were lots of them." He could see the cutout paintings and paper-covered cardboard Catherine glued on the covers, each one different.

"I don't know." Wills looked alarmed, as though something were expected but he did not know what.

"Why wouldn't you talk to Mother's friend Charlotte?" J.J. pushed on.

"I always talked to Charlotte. Charlotte. She was real nice." Wills smiled sweetly and patted Ginger on the leg. "Sugar, you're so pretty."

"Daddy, can't you come in from some-where and react to this news? Are you stunned to hear that what we always as-sumed is not true?"

"I'm tuckered out. Ring for a drink, will you, sugar? Scotch and soda. Jigger of gin."

"You can have some juice, if you want." Ginger gave up. She washed her face in Wills's bathroom. "Cold water, J.J. Splash your face and cool off. If the news reached him, I can't tell. When was the last time he helped with anything?"

"You'd have to go on one of your archae-ological expeditions to find that fact."

A tiny man on a cane opened the door. "Howdy, Doc, you want to play slapjack?" His smile exposed glistening bare gums. Ginger recognized him as Gene, the desk clerk at the Oglethorpe Hotel when she was a child. He still had cornflower-blue eyes bright with life.

"No."

"So nice to see you, Gene." Ginger quickly covered her father's rudeness. "Why don't you come in and visit? We're going to love you and leave you, Daddy. J.J. wants to go fishing and I'm going to visit with Lily." She wanted to call Marco, wake him up if necessary, just to hear the timbre of his voice, ignorant of all this chaos, still

315

thinking that they existed together just as they had three days ago.

"Hey, Dad, do you need anything? We can swing by later if you do." J.J. walked out, reaching for his keys, without waiting for an answer. Ginger kissed Wills's cheek, a gesture she had to force herself to perform. Gene took the cards out of his bathrobe pocket anyway and Wills looked interested.

"Now, Doc, when I turn up a jack, you slap it. That's all there is to it."

Ginger returned to the house with a mission, although she didn't mention it to J.J. He obviously was in his fish-out-of-water mode, almost flailing with anger and impatience. Though the drivers of cars they passed waved, he waved to no one, just slung the car around corners, then gunned it at Island 10. She felt at least twenty kinds of tiredness. At the House, she barely closed the car door before he scratched off. "Come out to the cabin later. I'll cook some birds. *Arrivederci, Roma.*" He practically fishtailed out of the driveway. Ginger was annoyed. He always did that: he went along *together,* but at a point — and she could feel that point coming — split off on his own.

One sole of the old loafers she'd found in her closet peeled back, letting dust into her shoes. She stopped in the driveway and took them off, shook out the fine silt, and walked barefoot across the grass. *JJJJJJJJJ,* the cicadas chattered in the oaks, *JJJJJJJJJJ*. Enough to drive a person mad. She flung a rock into a tree and the racket stopped, as though switched off. How can they make that much noise? What bow do they use across what strings? They started again. She would look them up in the old *Britannica* in the downstairs hall. When she travelled to the ruins on Crete, the cicadas were ten times as loud. There she'd had a memory of home, of these moss oaks vibrating in July heat, of herself in her yellow room, the noise sawing through her head as she pulled a comb through her wet hair, driving out thought, driving out everything but the grinding heat, and there on Crete she had felt simultaneously the yammering song of those cicadas in the acacias at Knossos drop back through time, a Greek chorus, a fricative beat to accompany the Minoan builders as they stacked mud bricks and swilled sour wine from amphoras cooled in underground rooms — *that,* she thought, archaeology never can uncover, that pitch and relentlessness of the cicada on summer afternoons, sounding through epochs, but memory can bring back the sweat dripping down my backbone, my young face in a foxed mirror, the eyelet dress, already limp hanging on the closet door, memory can do that when the cicada suddenly stops then starts again, that awful vibrato, memory — for as long as it lasts — then everything is archaeology, sifting layers and layers, covering the site for the winter, uncovering and starting again. Seventeen years the cicada incubates, then bursts into, not song, but raucous noise, making up for all their years underground. Mother's hideous emergence. Could I think of this in archaeological terms? What does a wrapped mummy say about those who buried her? Ancient bodies found in peat bogs say nothing good — their heads split open by an ax, so long ago that you only could ask, not why the deed, but what sort of ax? How was the stone worked? Where was it quarried? Ancillary questions.

She opened the door to the wide hall, the round table in the middle with keys, mail, and a bunch of Lily's orange nasturtiums in the blue vase with crackled glaze made by Catherine in a college pottery class. Ginger had known that vase as long as anything, as long as she'd known the splash of light at the back of the hallway way back when she played Mother, May I? with J.J. on rainy Sunday afternoons when she was very small. After the noon dinner, her mother went upstairs with Lily and

Mama Fan to look at pattern books in Lily's room. After coffee, Big Jim napped and her daddy read the paper.

In the game, you were given an instruction by the "mother": take three giant steps, or take three butterfly twirls, or take two baby steps. The goal was the French door at the end of the hall. To progress, they had to remember to ask before twirling or jumping, *Mother, may I?* Are we always going to be asking *may I, may I?* she wondered. J.J. always won because he never forgot the mythic instruction, but Ginger, anxious to perform her cartwheel, scissors step, or three somersaults, forever went back over and over to the front-door starting line.

Big Jim's clock struck one. The appalling horror of her mother being undressed, examined. Her body the subject of ghoulish jokes. The mummy at Zagreb, she remembered, that mummy wrapped in linen strips turned out to be a young girl, perhaps from Egypt, but on the linen swaddling, when they looked closely, they found faint markings that partially unlocked the Etruscan language. Her mother, unwrapped, was found innocent of the crime of self-murder. *Mother, may I,* may I take two grasshopper leaps?

★ ★ ★

Marco picked up on the first ring. "*Cara, cara,* where are you? Should I take a plane, I could come to you tomorrow. Will you tell me now what is the problem? I know you have found something serious there." Ginger told him, emphasizing that there was nothing anyone could do, she just needed to stay through the week until, she hoped, everything would be solved, her mother safe in the ground again. It was less embarrassing than she'd thought; perhaps this event finally had inured her to something as everyday as embarrassment. Maybe now she could learn to say the word *suicide* without her tongue sticking to the roof of her mouth.

"Tell me about work, tell me everything." She wanted to hear his voice, let his voice wrap around her, his voice from a place that had nothing to do with this place, a place all its own, more humane, more beautiful. Not more beautiful, she corrected herself. He had found a baby owl, still covered with down. His sisters-in-law were feeding it soup with an eye-dropper and chopping up bits of meat. The owl sat with them at dinner on the back of a chair, letting the children pet its back. The project was going well, but the heat made everyone silly. They were making up work songs with dirty words. Ginger's eyes burned and her throat went taut. She never really cried, but tears formed, spilled over. "I miss you." She tried to say it lightly but heard her voice hit a note of panic. She missed the whole world she knew because of him. "We'll talk later. More later."

In the dining room, Lily was pinning swatches of cloth to the draperies, a coral pink, a yellow cotton damask, and a hideous gold and rose stripe. "Nix that stripe, Lily. It's heavy, don't you think?" Ginger was relieved to see Lily quite put together again in a navy suit with polka-dot blouse, her glasses hanging on a beaded chain, and her hair nicely swept up in a twist. Depend on Lily to take the brunt, then roll over and move on.

"Yes, you're right. But how can I ever decide between this gorgeous pale yellow and the pure persimmon pink?" She laid larger samples on the seats of the chairs, stepping back to admire them. "Agnes would like the pink."

"Isn't this blue still fairly new?" Ginger remembered swatches from her last visit, but maybe that was in the den. Lily was always recovering, repapering, repainting, repotting. Her handbag was stuffed with color chips, bits of tile, fringe, pages torn from magazines showing bedrooms literally festooned in English chintz and foyers decorated with French bread racks and enormous turtle shells.

Let J.J. tell her. Why was she always the one? She was going to keep quiet about what Ralph had told them. She lacked the energy to handle Lily's reaction, and what if it later turned out to be false? Lily and Ginger sat down at the table, with J.J.'s empty place still set. As Tessie served chicken-fried steak and mashed potatoes, made just for Ginger, she tried to imagine Marco facing her across this table. Lily rambled on about Bonny Vinson winning a scholarship to music camp even though she faltered at high C in the high school choir, about wallpaper and the coarse tung shan material she had not chosen. Ginger was not going to bring up anything unpleasant. Enough is enough, she thought.

Lily had spent the morning at the Mill Store, which still operated, although the Mason mill was long closed. Bennie Ames had turned what had been a place to sell flawed goods and overruns into a drapery and upholstery store. She and Agnes often went together, but in times of crisis, Lily always headed there alone. Because she'd spent good childhood afternoons with Big Jim, walking behind him as he checked the women at the looms, watching the corded backs of the black men as they hoisted three-hundred-pound bales on their shoulders, and diving from the giant scale into bins of bolls, she was comforted all her life by the pure smell of flax and cotton. She liked to run fabrics through her fingers, finding the warp and weft, thinking of her mother doing the same, her closet full of flowered bolts and folded aqua linen and a dreamy green silk that Mama called "water of the Nile." Mama said, "We're fabric people, like others are Sioux people or mountain people." Her family, too, had been in the cotton business. At the Mill Store, Lily could slip closer to her parents. The shelves of watered silk and embroidered organdy, the rack of colored spools of thread, the cutting table with its precise ruler glued to the end and the *thump-thump* of the bolt unfurling across it — no trouble could accumulate there. No grotesque memory, no brutal acts, just beauty, the possibility of transforming a bed or chair, as Mama always did.

Ginger was saying something. ". . . the barn key."

"What, sugar? I'm in a heat daze today."

"I want to go look through the boxes in the barn, the boxes from our old house. You know, I never have looked at one thing from there. Not even at my character dolls or the dollhouse Daddy made for me." She stopped. She didn't mean to fall into the family habit of dissembling. "But that's not the point. What I want to see is if there are things that belonged to my mother." She wanted to search for her mother's notebooks that she'd seen mentioned in the report. She wanted to call Charlotte Crowder, who'd thrown a fit to the sheriff.

"I don't see any point in dwelling on this ghastly situation. Just let the sheriff handle it, try to enjoy your time here without riffling through old mouldy blankets and yearbooks. Let's don't be morbid." Lily held the swatches to the light. "I think I'll order the persimmon since I have yellow in my bedroom. Do you want anything else, sugar?"

"No thanks. Good choice. I like the persimmon. I'll stay until heatstroke sets in, just a few minutes."

"The key is where it has always been, hanging on the back porch. Ask Tessie. She's out there shelling butterbeans for supper."

Tessie already had gone through a colander full. "Butterbeans, Tessie, I love them."

Two of Lily's cream-colored Lincolns, a 1950 and a 1960, were still parked in the barn. In the face of her reasoning, J.J. had given up on trying to get her to sell or junk them. When asked to do so, her explanation for keeping them was simply, "Darlin', I *loved* those cars." Ginger rather liked them, too. In high school she had a few times sneaked into the '50 one with Tony Pappas to make out in the backseat.

She opened the barn's back room door, formerly a maid's room. Though it had been several years since she'd been in here — she saw boxes of wedding gifts she had not wanted — nothing had moved: Lily's headless dress mannequin, trunks with rusted locks, softened cardboard boxes, the standing wicker cornucopias Mama Fan had used for garden parties, upholstered chairs Lily rejected, a bookcase of medical journals, house magazines Lily might someday look at again, and a mildewed four-volume history of Georgia with, Ginger knew, a large photograph of Big Jim's father with bushy eyebrows, a lugubrious mustache, and fierce, staring, daring eyes that would follow you if you propped up the book.

In the first boxes she opened, she found her tin tea sets and dollhouse furniture wrapped in newspapers, a coat of J.J.'s, and Mama Fan's fine monogrammed sheets, which she decided she would take back to Italy with her. She went through old tax forms, deeds, and bank statements. Large white checks fell out with her mother's and father's handwriting. Pay to the order of Swan Water Company, seven dollars and 10/100. Under that, folded tablecloths and a jar of Bakelite and mother-of-pearl buttons. She poured them in her lap. She had loved the button jar as a child. She sifted her hand through them now as she had then. Her mother had sewn yellow curtains for Ginger's room and covered them with bright buttons. Who had packed up the house? The boxes had no order, no labels. She had brought no tape to reseal the cartons and, with her plundering, she caused more disorder. But who cared about this kitchen midden? It should all be burned. One box she opened was packed with baby clothes, her own batiste dresses, rompers with food stains on the front, bibs embroidered with bears and geese. Wrapped in a baby blanket, she found the family christening gown, with trailing skirt inserted with circles of lace. She put it with the sheets to take with her. Perhaps she would marry Marco, have a baby who would be baptized far from here. Where were her mother's things? Were her college textbooks thrown out, her letters and baby pictures, and those notebooks, so like the ones J.J. kept?

She saw a labeled box, different from the others, a red-striped box from Rich's in Atlanta. In her mother's familiar slanted handwriting, it was labeled *Maternity Clothes*. So, a box sealed prior to the packing of the house, and well sealed. In the cleaning of the house, it probably was stacked along with other packed boxes. Ginger split the crackling tape and shook out a rose velvet jumper and the satin blouse that went under it. Slacks with a stretch placket in front, a black dress with black grosgrain ribbon woven around the skirt. Beneath the clothes, she saw two sketch books and a notebook. Ginger breathed out a long sigh. It was a moment she knew. The moment the second step of the Etruscan staircase came clear under their brushes, they knew they'd found something major. Beneath the books she uncovered a reel of film and a few letters tied with ribbon. They were not addressed or stamped. In neat capitals on blue envelopes, each said *Catherine*. Clearly, she had found something Catherine had wanted to conceal long before her death. Conceal from whom?

She slid Catherine's secret things into a pillowcase and wrapped a sheet around it. Her mother, so long the arrow shot into the center of the back, now a mysterious presence completely open to revision. The remaining five boxes revealed little, although Ginger was happy to find her mother's recipe box, the red and white cookbook she remembered her mother consulting, and two church and garden club recipe collections from local women. She would lug these inside, too. Someday she would try homemade mayonnaise and icebox cookies. She imagined Marco working at the site, stripped down to his undershirt in the heat. What a miracle, a dig. That we find things still there after three *thousand* years, when even these boxes seem old. Ginger walked along the azalea border hoping for a cool current through the garden to the house. What if this were a thousand years from now and someone were searching for clues about Swan? The peculiar habits of a people who raised square white houses, procreated, and lived their short spans in the pine barrens of a place once called Georgia. The Etruscans called themselves *Rasenna*. Now they are only Etruscans, their own name almost lost. *Catherine*, the letters said. *Summer, 1943*, the notebook said. So, ready or not, I will see something of Catherine as she was to herself, she thought. She pushed her lead body through air that seemed to be turning solid. One foot, then another. She climbed the twenty-six steps to her room, turned on the fan, and closed the door.

J.J. sat under the arbor. Everything sticks to everything, he thought. His back stuck to the back of the chair. He'd ripped off his T-shirt, so sweated through that a salt rim had formed a cloud on the back. His arms felt glued to the table, his fingers tacky on the drawing pencil, and his hair lapped to the back of his neck. The Dr Pepper thermometer nailed to the house read 98 in the shade, heat close to 10 x 10. He might spontaneously combust, leave a grease spot in the dirt for Ginger to find when she came out later in the afternoon. No, no, no, no, nothing more for Ginger to find. He would always care for himself, primarily because he didn't want Ginger hurt again. He was drawing small shells he'd found in a sand-shelf outcropping by the clay road to the cabin. Bivalves that once breathed in sea-wet sand? Or just something dropped by a bird riding a long draft from the coast? He felt he had eaten heat. Since he'd eaten little of the feasts Tessie prepared for Ginger's nontriumphal return, why not eat heat? A plate of heat, a sack of heat, a glass of heat.

Last night in his room, after he'd spilled his guts to Ginger, he tried to sleep with a wet washcloth over his eyes. At four, he leapt from bed and stood under a cold shower, going back to bed wet. Lying on the damp sheet, he thought this must be what it was like to be unborn, eyes closed, heart pumping, turning in a salty undertow, awake but *not there*, twisting, jabbing against a soft wall, the sheet coiled like a rope down his stomach, between his legs, and he tried lying so still, willing sleep, but just as sleep approached, his whole body jerked and he was awake, floating in heat again.

He slapped gnats away from his eyes. The drawing was distorted. He ripped it in two, then from top to bottom. How long until Ginger arrived? He decided to go down to the bend. He had already placed himself, leaning back in the rowboat under the willow at the clear pool formed from an old half-washed-away beaver dam. Fish might be biting in that shoal. Trout. He would see clear through the water to the coarse sand and pebbled bottom.

Lily found that she couldn't lie down for a rest. The back of her head seemed to broil on the pillow. A trapped butterfly battered against the screen. None of the Masons liked air-conditioning in a house, and usually the attic fan kept them cool enough, but today the fan sucked in hot air. She wandered into the kitchen for a glass of tea. Tessie was having one, too, half dozing and looking at a magazine. "Is Ginger still out in that hot barn?"

Tessie jumped. "She's up in her room. Had a armful of stuff. Sleeping now, I imagine." Tessie gestured to a wrinkled package. "Miss Lily, this was in the mailbox this morning. I forgot about it. It sure is a poor-looking gift."

Lily unwrapped the tissue. The envelope. Speckled with age, yellowed, the envelope had found its way back into her hands.

"What is that?" Tessie looked up.

"A note. Just a note of sympathy. Thank you, Tessie."

She took a long drink of tea, then went back to her room. Inside the envelope, she found, as she knew she would, the page torn from one of Catherine's notebooks. She, not Wills, had lifted that cold hand and laid the envelope on Catherine's other hand. A gift, a good-bye, placed partly out of shame, shame Lily still felt, because the very day of the suicide, after Tessie's friends cleaned the house, when Wills was incoherent with grief, and shock and rage, crying and cursing Catherine at the same time, finally leaving the house to look for J.J., she had tried to give Ginger a sandwich but her teeth clenched and she would only lie on the bed shaking, and when she finally slept, Lily, in a rage herself — how could that bitch do this to her brother! — had gone to Catherine's sewing room. She'd filled the wastebasket with all the loose paper on the desk, pulled the half-finished skirt from the sewing machine and torn it to pieces. She ripped off the drawings tacked around the window, scooped up the row of notebooks between bookends, sketch books, the fabric-covered boxes of letters and photographs. All this she'd piled onto a blanket and dragged to the garbage beyond the garage. *Catherine had everything.* Lily had bitten her lip hard.

She had everything I wanted and she threw it away.

In her bedroom, Lily put the page under the inside flap of a book jacket. Who had left this? The insane person who dug up the grave? An unaccustomed streak of adrenaline coursed through her body. The violator of the grave was still free.

After her rampage through Catherine's private room, she'd moved to the bedroom, jerking armfuls of clothes from the closet and throwing them out the window on the garage side. Catherine was vain, no doubt about it. Lily had begun to lose a bit of her zeal by then, but still she made a pile and set everything on fire. A fitting end to the day. Still Wills did not come home. By the time the fire had cooled, she wondered if she, too, had gone crazy, like Catherine must have. She saw the edge of one notebook in the ashes and shoved it with her foot. Who cared about her egotistic ramblings, her drawings of doors? Mostly burned, the black book still smoked.

Because Ginger had kicked and lashed out with her fingernails when Lily tried to rouse her, Lily had spent the night in J.J.'s bed — not that she slept, not in that house where someone had committed a crime against nature. Early in the morning, she went out to the fire and picked up the last notebook, cooled now and wet with dew. The pile of ashes was almost all that remained of Catherine Mason, née Phillips, late of Vidalia, survived by destroyed children, destroyed husband. Ashes to ashes. Her at the morgue with a hole for a heart. Lily opened the book and read. There was some gibberish about how cashmere was made and goats and combing. She turned over pages of drawings of a chair. She recognized the chair at the cabin, a rough thing with steer-hide seat and leather thongs tying the rungs. Catherine had drawn it forty times, at least. Then she came to the page she tore out. She resisted Catherine always, but always there came a moment when Catherine won and Lily reluctantly loved her. As violently as she hated Catherine that day, she was moved by the poem, which she assumed Catherine had written, and moved more by thinking of Catherine at the cabin, out on the dock in white shorts and a halter printed with watermelons, looking at her art books, writing in her notebook, saying the poem aloud. Someone so alive — just gone. She'd dumped the charred notebook in the trash.

Ginger wouldn't go in the kitchen for orange juice. Lily had left a note for Wills saying she'd started to clean out Catherine's things.

The sooner they're gone, the better for you, she'd written. She'd packed an overnight bag, took Ginger, sullen and silent, out the front door, and drove her to the House, where they had to face Catherine's mother and several distant relatives.

Lily answered the phone in the hall. "Miss Lily, this is Ralph Hunnicutt."

"Why, yes, Sheriff." Who knows someone found the envelope? she wondered. Should I tell him about it? No.

"I just got a call from the GBI. I wanted to let you know that the tests confirmed what I told Ginger and J.J. this morning. Their mother definitely was murdered. The agent said that at this late date, of course, there's no evidence at all as to who killed her."

Lily, stunned, repeated, "Murdered." Yes, she was murdered by herself. "Do you mean *again?* She was murdered *again?*" What was he talking about?

"No, ma'am." Was he not speaking the king's English? "The first time. The death. She was murdered by someone."

Silence.

"As I explained this morning . . ." Shit,

336

they hadn't told her. "I'm sorry, Miss Lily, but J.J. and Ginger can explain everything. They must have been too upset to tell you yet. It wasn't definite," he added.

Lily held the phone without saying anything, then hung up. She went back to the kitchen. Tessie was ironing her aprons. "That was the sheriff. He said that Catherine did not kill herself, she was murdered. The GBI said so." She sat down and lighted a cigarette.

"Sweet Jesus. Is this good news or bad? I think it's good but depending on who shot her it's bad." Tessie's iron sizzled a black triangle onto the white apron. "Lord have mercy on us." Who? she thought but did not say. She carried with her the image of that kitchen she and her two friends had scrubbed down. Wiping up blood with the sponge mop, squeezing it out in the sink, the steaming-hot water swirling with blood and soap. She'd thrown out those rolled logs of Catherine's peanut butter cookies in the refrigerator, too. Who'd want to bake them with her dead? Now they were saying murder. Her friend Rosa had speculated about that while they cleaned that day, but she'd told her to hush. It couldn't be Dr. Mason, but — but who else? "What do you think, Miss Lily?"

"I think I want to tear my hair out." But instead, she put her head in her hands and cried. "A murder case. At least the suicide was . . . oh, contained. Now everyone will gossip for years." She could not bear the prospect. Wills would be drawn into this, a crime of passion? The idea of suicide flashed across Lily's mind, a handful of pills, an obliterating blast, like Catherine. But no, not now. *We all can forget her suicide as something infectious that might spread.*

"Can't J.J. hush it up?" Tessie asked. "Mr. Big Jim sure could. Mr. Big Jim, he called the shots around these parts."

"Those days are gone." Lily felt a surprising surge of hatred for Big Jim. "Where is J.J.?"

"He hightailed it to the woods, same as always."

Lily heaved herself up. Lily loved Wills. With all her strength, she said, "Tessie, please tell Ginger that I know. I'm going out to the Columns to visit my poor brother. Let me take him some of those butterbeans. He'll enjoy them so much."

It would have been nice if'n J.J. was here to drive her, Tessie thought, but she said nothing. A hundred times her husband had told her not to mind Mason business. *You don't have a dog in that fight,* he'd remind her.

Holt waited until Eleanor nodded off. They'd had a cold lunch at her house after their drive around Swan. She was settling down after her shocking experience, but the reappearance of Catherine had stirred up memories of her husband's death. She kept bringing up details of his illness until Holt Junior suggested that when something un-pleasant occurred to her, she might instead search for a moment of happiness. She'd then had a nice lunch, telling him about the drive they took up the California coast when Holt Junior was six. She'd warmed to the subject of baby seals for rather a long time. Now she was comfortable in her husband's easy chair with her feet up on the ottoman.

Holt tipped out without disturbing her and drove to his cottage opposite the high school, where he served as principal. He never tired of looking at the U-shaped rose-brick school with many small-paned windows. From the first class he took there in the ninth grade, he'd felt just right among the airy rooms and the oiled heart-pine hallways. He liked the students, the well-brought-up, sassy town girls and the earnest boys in from the surrounding farms. His teachers pleased him, too, with the exception of one drinker who sipped vile vodka and milk from a flask while trying to conjugate Latin verbs. Swan High won state one-act play competitions, debate matches, and track meets. The choir placed every year in the regionals, and he thanked Muffy Starns for holding practice three afternoons a week. The same Board of Education was voted in every three years, all friends of Holt, so the school ran with harmony. On a wall of his office hung photographs of retired teachers, including both of his parents, looking young and vibrant.

From his breakfast room window, he glanced at the school. Living so close, he kept the building under his protection. He found it a pleasure to walk across the street to work, then to go home at noon for a sandwich and a quick nap.

In truth, Catherine's reappearance had stirred memories for him, too. He had once encountered her in a situation almost as shocking for them both as Eleanor's graveside nightmare must have been. But no, he mused, I exaggerate. Nevertheless, he'd had an illusion of a successful secret life until that encounter. A moment of change arrives and you want to go behind it, make another turn, take another road, but there it is, the marker known as before and after. He replayed the small slice of time all the intervening years had not dimmed or edited, the scenes always current.

In the parking lot of Miss Bibba's Dine and Dance on the outskirts of Macon, a hundred miles from home and not a likely place for either him or Catherine to be, he'd pulled over under the billboards, the darkest edge of the lot, and slouched down. The doors of Miss Bibba's swung open and he saw a woman come out with a man about her own height, a man with medals shining on his navy pilot's uniform. As they came nearer, he recognized Catherine Mason. He caught the man's profile. Even now he would recognize that straight nose, unbridged, coming down sharply from his forehead, the sensual big lips. The way they walked in step suggested intimacy, not just a casual evening between friends. They were close, smiling, and Holt saw the man brush his lips through her hair. How curious: In memory, he saw this in black and white. Wills was off serving his air force time in North Carolina, his medical unit waiting for emergency relief orders to Europe.

Holt stretched his legs under the table. His knee sounded like a rusty zipper opening. He'd been 4F because of his football injury. He opened a beer and walked to the living room. Because he never bothered to accumulate much, his house stayed neat. Eleanor had seen to the selection of furniture and duly had things hauled away when they became too grotty.

He wished the memory ended there. They'd laughed their laugh, had their fling, that's that. He tried to conjure Catherine's face — a small dimple in the middle of her chin, pale skin, yes, she had curly hair — but he couldn't see her clearly; years had erased the whole image. He remembered better an air of, not disdain, but aloofness. J.J. must have gotten a double gene for that. She'd lived for thirteen more years, Wills building his reputation in Swan, Catherine growing all those roses. Children, trips, the whole thing — before the suicide. Who knows what goes on between people? They seemed among the blessed. But Holt always wondered if the suicide had something to do with the sharp-looking officer with the full lips. If the memory ended there, Holt thought, life would have been simpler. But the moment, instead of slipping away, exploded.

What luck. Catherine and her man were parked next to his car. As the man opened the door for her, she glanced Holt's way. At that exact moment in their fates, Lucy Waters, rushing out the side door of Bibba's, an enormous smile of anticipation lighting her face, reached Holt's car, her hand out to open the door. Catherine took in at one glance Holt's startled face. She looked at him, then at Lucy. Lucy's faltering voice quavered, "Oh, hey," over the top of the car. The navy man stepped back, quick and wary, as Catherine and Holt locked eyes. Holt saw the confusion in hers. They both were caught. Then she raised her shoulders, adjusted her coat, slid into the car, and they drove away.

As far as he knew, Catherine never told anyone that he was seeing Lucy. If she had, Holt would not be looking out at the double white door of the high school, where he loved his job as principal. Far more heinous a crime than Catherine's wartime fling, the scandal of Holt

Whitefield seen at midnight in the far corner of a parking lot beside a sleazy supper club, seen slouched in the front seat, waiting for the light-skinned eighteen-year-old, niece of Hattie, recently hired to work in the kitchen at Bibba's, to peel onions and potatoes as her mother and grandmother had done for years in Swan white folks' kitchens, that scandal would be reverberating yet in the annals of Swan. *Domino, domino.* If anyone had known, if it ever came out that he'd paid her rent on the apartment over a garage in colored town in Macon, that he drove in late, out early . . .

Often when he watched the girls' gymnastic classes, he thought of Lucy's gracile body. He could write a book, if he were so inclined, about first seeing her helping her Aunt Hattie in the kitchen when his mother was having a party. He'd come in from college. She was laughing, her head thrown back, and she stopped as he came in. How narrow she was, built thin as a pencil, with, he thought, such capable-looking hands. Of course, he noted her skin, dusky, like a pale person standing in deep shadow. In another time, he thought, she would have been a dancer. In another time, we could have walked down Corfu

344

Street together, but not in this lifetime.

Two weeks later he had seen Catherine at a wedding reception. They took cups of punch off the same serving tray and Catherine raised hers and toasted him, saying no more than what a beautiful bride Camille Stevenson was. Neither of them ever mentioned the night in Macon. We run on what's not said, he thought, at least in Swan we do. For all the talk, talk, talk we do, the crucial subjects are swallowed without a sound.

Holt had kept no pictures of Lucy. If he were run down by a watermelon truck, he didn't want his mother to find that face among his effects. Because he had crossed the color barrier, he never could separate his cultural fear and self-censorship from his feelings for Lucy. Even his memories were cauterized. For her part, she had been terrified. Finally, it was she who broke away, moved to Washington, D.C., and found a job with a political family. She never married either. If he ventured a casual "How's Lucy doing?" to Hattie, all she ever gave him was, "She's doing fine up there in the North, just fine."

Once at 3:00 a.m. he'd answered the phone to hear a heavy breather. At first he feared someone had found out about Lucy, but the voice finally said, "You should be ashamed teaching young people when you're queer as a two-dollar bill," and hung up. Let them think queer, let them think anything, but not the real truth.

The blinds were closed in Wills's room. In the dim blue TV light, he stared at the game show without looking up when Lily came in holding a covered dish. "Are you all right?" She kissed him on the forehead. He nodded but didn't look her way. She thought she'd come to comfort her brother, but, she realized, she needed comfort herself. "It's hot out there. You're lucky to be in such a cool spot." She sat down beside him and took off her shoes. The air conditioner blew directly on her legs. Together they watched. She was grateful for the idiotic buzzes and shrieks from the contestants. She could rest awhile, quiet, her hand on her brother's arm, and forget the chaos at the House. She could close her eyes and imagine that she and Wills, young again, sat in his old room listening to *The Lone Ranger* on the radio. She glanced at him. Lord, he was handsome then, best-looking boy in Georgia. Who was this old stump?

Lily drove slowly home. She thought she must have worn ruts in the road, so many times had she gone back and forth to the Columns. All of Swan languished in the afternoon heat. The gardens, lush in June, were beginning to fade, the hydrangeas visibly shriveling, the hibiscuses dropping buds before they bloomed. Tessie watered Lily's pots of trailing yellow nasturtiums twice a day, but they looked puny by three o'clock.

In backyards all over town, children ran in and out of sprinklers and pushed each other down on the wet grass. The luckier ones had talked their mothers into loading the car with friends and driving out to Lake T. For years the town pool had been closed because of segregation, and the nearest place to swim was ten miles away, where from the anchored raft, you could dive deep enough to find a layer of cold water. The mothers sat in brightly painted metal chairs under the pines, talking and dispensing change for ice cream sandwiches and Paydays.

The one-legged postmaster, Ollie Fowler, drove slowly with the window down, collecting mail dropped in the five boxes around Swan. Back at the post office he sat behind the pulled-down grates and sorted the thirty or so letters going out of town. Father Tyson, he saw, had written to the bishop again. Mildly curious, he held up the envelope to the light and made out the words *be of service*. The marble post office, closed for the afternoon, smelled of dust and brass spittoons and glue.

Eleanor, napping in her chair, woke up suddenly. Holt Junior had left. She would bake something special for him. He seemed distracted. A lemon pound cake that he loved. Later she'd drop it by his house on the way to her hair appointment with Ronnie, followed by a manicure and pedicure — she could no longer reach her toes — with his wife, Tina. She dreaded and anticipated the talk about the Masons.

Several teenagers drank milk shakes at the Sacred Pig. One was Francie Lachlan, daughter of the mayor, who had a head of blond curls the angels would envy. She was tanned after a month at Carrie's Island and wore a tight orange top which stopped above her waist, revealing just how delectable a young body could be. Her father called the boys who were always around her "flies." He had plenty to worry about — Francie was wild about Richard Rooker, who set up pins in the adjacent bowling alley. Wrong side of the tracks and full of testosterone.

Swan's tobacco warehouses rivaled the hottest places on earth. The sun bore down on the corrugated tin roofs, reflecting shimmering waves of light that could be seen from Mars. In the lighted doors at either end floated gilded particles of dust from the pungent, drying leaves stacked in long rows. For an instant you could think you were walking into a temple where gold swirled, a magic chamber where the unintelligible, musical cry of the auctioneer could herald a miracle. But a few steps inside, a biting, parched, sour stink burned your nose and cut into your lungs, the heat clamped down onto your head like a hawk onto prey. Absurdly, the auctioneers smoked. All afternoon farmers hauled in pallets for tomorrow's auction. Buyers down from North Carolina cigarette factories moved in droves across the street to Scott's store for cold drinks. Usually, they upended the first one, then drank the second one slowly. Twelve teaspoons of sugar, twenty-four. Mindy and Scott kept the coolers full and still ran out every day. They stocked plenty of ice in the freezer, though, and Mindy popped open bottles while Scott poured. Mindy liked the men. They flirted and asked her to go juking, but she knew they were all married, and just laughed. Every night she was hoping to see J.J.'s Jaguar pull up in front of her house.

The streets of Swan, once brick, but now paved over, softened, going back to their liquid petroleum origins deep in the earth's core. A small girl, running to a neighbor's house to play dolls, was half across the street before she felt the bubbling tar blistering her bare feet.

Rosemary Tyson sat at her dining room table writing, *Dear Daddy, I was thinking of you this morning, how you polished my patent-leather shoes with Vaseline before Sunday School when I was little. Remember?* When the weather turned cool, he could visit. They would take walks and come back to the kitchen and drink coffee together and eat oatmeal cookie sandwiches with sweetened cream cheese inside. If her husband had passed by, he might have noticed her lovely neck reflected in the mirror. With her hair up and her head bent over her letter, the mirror caught the creamy light falling on her. He might have leaned over to kiss that delicate curve and felt a surge of happiness from her beauty. He might have whispered, *I'm sorry.*

All down Central on the island parks, just-hatched chicks rolled in the dirt and pecked under the palm trees. Years ago a local poultry farm experimented with raising a type of Burmese chicken, an exotic rust-colored bird with fluffy legs and a blue crown. When they refused to fatten for the frying pan, they were simply released. No one foresaw how quickly they could multiply. Some people liked their plumage or presence — what town other than Swan boasted of such wildlife? Sick of chasing them from their tomato patches and flower beds, both Billie and Margaret Alice set out poisoned corn. The birds even migrated downtown, where they perched on the edge of the Oasis fountain.

The three sisters finished scrubbing down the counters. Four o'clock. Time to go home. They packed a grocery bag for supper, ham and potato salad they would enjoy with a pitcher of tea on the screened porch while they worked on crossword puzzles in the long twilight. Among the three of them, they could finish the dailies easily and even the Sunday ones in twenty minutes. By nine they'd be talking softly, listening to the crickets. They drove home, harmonizing "In the Sweet Bye and Bye." Martha pointed to high clouds blowing in from the east, possibly a squall over the Atlantic, moving in, bringing relief.

Ginger left a note for Lily propped on the dining room table. *We're reeling from the latest news from Ralph and know you are too. Sorry I didn't tell you. I think I'll spend the night at the cabin and leave you to a peaceful evening.* She hoped Lily would sit on the porch with her needlepoint, complete a few more stitches toward her lifetime project of twelve chair bottoms. Maybe she would take one of her pink pills that helped her sleep.

Ginger opened all four doors of the rented car; it would have to air out before she could touch the steering wheel. Because the House was sited on a rise, she could see across corn and cotton fields to the west. Already farmers were plowing under spent crops, sending dust into billows that faceted the beams of sunset, striating the sky lurid flamingo and purple. She took the long loop to the cabin, around Swan, passing the turnoff to the woods where Jefferson Davis finally was captured by the 1st Wisconsin and the 4th Michigan cavalries, who immortalized themselves in southern history by approaching from different directions and firing on each other. *What can you expect, damn fool Yankees?* She drove through the old-growth pines, calming herself with the scent. Will there be a third drama, one every decade or two, pulling me limb from limb, from wherever I have managed to go? she wondered. Maybe this is my path of enlightenment. Five acts with long intermissions. Just when I thought there was nothing more my parents could do to me. In the front of her mind still jangled the sound of the telephone as she sorted her boxes of stones in Monte Sant'Egidio. Ralph's call. *Squillare,* "to ring" in Italian, the shrill squeal built right into the word. Only now were the subsequent events beginning to swamp that first trauma of his gentle voice.

All afternoon at the House, she'd looked at the sketch books her mother had packed and sealed with her maternity dresses, the clothes she'd worn when pregnant with Ginger. If she lived to be a famous archaeologist, a discoverer of the Etruscans' origins or a lost city, lost continent, the *Argo,* anything, no discovery ever would mean more to her than today's. Yesterday existed, then today. Yesterday she did not know about them, and now they would be cherished. Out of long habit, she tried to attenuate her reaction. Just wait, she kept whispering. Wait for J.J. But she had sat cross-legged on her bed, turning the pages, gazing on each pencil drawing, each word in the margins, *cardinal, aquamarine, charcoal, and paint a wall with a green circle.* Her mother, she discovered, was a list maker:

Goals: research French antique roses
check into beach rental for July
Mother's recipes — Lane Cake, Wills's
    Nut Cake, Besta's Lemon Pie,
    her brown sugar muffins
call Charlotte about pastels
hedge along back?
bias tape — yellow, black

Bits of fabric were glued onto the pages beside drawings of sundresses and evening capes. She listed words she must have liked: *susurrous, prelapsarian.* Ginger had no idea what they meant, and then easier ones, *fluvial, dithyrambic.* She experienced waves of pleasure, recognizing a younger Tessie, hand on hip, drawn in colored pencils, the dining room window in their house with vines around the edges, her fa-

355

ther's profile, the House seen from a distance, several pages of roses (not so well done), her mother's friend Charlotte in some costume with a plumed hat.

Looking, she recaptured her real mother, not just the mother from her official registry of memories. The last page of the first sketch book would be her joy. In the year of Ginger's birth, Catherine had drawn a self-portrait, quite pregnant, in profile. The face, smiling — there, the tiny gap between her front teeth — is turned to the viewer, and inside the silhouette of the orange maternity dress, she sketched the coiled baby. The baby who was Ginger.

The second sketch book, she knew, would become a treasure for J.J. She would give it to him and see his face as he looked at page after page of drawings of himself from the week of his birth until his twenty-third month, when Ginger was born. J.J. in Big Jim's arms. J.J. in a basket. J.J. in a high chair with his arms over his head. J.J. on a pony. A gift, a tremendous gift of love, a bliss, not mixed with the article about Catherine in the paper, the constant blaming from Lily, the corpse, the blankness of the father, but actual pages, pristine love, drawn out of fascination with the little boy who was Catherine's firstborn child, her son. The last page had her name, Virginia Mason, lettered in red, with her birth date. Underneath, Catherine sketched J.J. holding the new baby.

Ginger had closed the book and fallen back on her pillows to sleep. A door had slammed shut downstairs, jerking her awake with the sudden feeling, on that day, of reaching for the handle of the screen door into her mother's kitchen. But it was only Tessie.

She passed the outskirts of Swan, low brick liquor stores, the drive-in theater, and the road to the mill, then hit the open road through virgin timber, wavy up ahead, with black-water swamps on either side. Beside her on the front seat were the sketch books, the film, the notebook, the packet of letters she would share with J.J. Music on the radio, sky growing more spectacular by the second, the images of the sketch books flashing in her mind, the new knowledge, scary and liberating — all enjambed, sending a rush of excitement through her body. She felt good. *Dithyrambic* was one of her mother's margin words, yes. A turkey buzzard — hideous creature — swooped down to feed on roadkill. She hit the horn and slowed, then as she sped up, she reached over to push back the sketch books on the seat.

In the moment she looked down, a pulp-wood truck passing another oncoming truck pulled out into her lane, the chrome grille magnifying, heading straight at her. She slammed on the brake and swerved off the road, held on to the steering wheel as she careened along a ditch, humped over gullies, slashed through saw palmettos, and stopped. The truck pulled over down the road, and the driver jumped out. When he saw her get out of the car, saw that she had not rolled down an embankment and broken her neck, that she had not landed in six feet of swamp water and drowned, he simply waved and jumped back in his truck. She ran to the road shouting, "Stop, wait, you son of a bitch, stop!" But he already was inching his load of pine trees back onto the road. "Bastard," she shouted. "You stupid hick idiot." He drove on, tossing out a can. "You . . . What an asshole jerk."

She again felt the truck roaring toward her. She would have been instantly dead if that logjam had jammed her. The red flag on the longest log flapped in the wind, grew smaller, disappeared. J.J. would have been summoned by the State Patrol. *I'm afraid there's been an accident.* He never would have left the woods after that. Marco, *Marco.* Lily, Tessie. Doomsday, just like the signs nailed on trees always said. Day of reckoning. God, damn, damn, damn. She stamped in the road. Wouldn't that just round it out, her own luck as bad as her mother's, her father's. The sketch books would have burned and J.J. never would have known. J.J. would have buried her and her mother at the same time. She tried to swallow her rage but turned and beat her fists on the hood. Shaking all over, she let out a scream that spiraled into the air, hanging there after she closed her mouth. Life is too accidental, I can't take it. J.J. would have been lost. One moment "Moon River" on the radio, the next oblivion. She sat down against the car and thought she'd like to strangle that idiot with a wire. Slowly, until his eyes popped. She closed her eyes. In the complete silence, she could feel her heart about to explode, hear the blood rasping in her ears. The road was empty. There was nothing to do but get back in the car.

The Pontiac wheels spun in the sandy soil but torqued and the car spurted back onto the road. As though nothing had happened.

I saved myself, Ginger thought.

J.J. had caught three trout. He was standing at the sink cleaning them when he saw Ginger round the white curve and stop. She arrived at the cabin at that late hour of the evening when the languescent river darkened to green-black satin, shimmed with gold. A faint mist rose from the water, staining the air blue under the trees.

The water looked miraculously joyous and beautiful after her scare down to the bones. Her father used to imitate Paul Robeson singing "Ol' Man River" as he put away the boat and tackle. Keeps on rolling. She stood and stared. The ebullience she felt earlier returned. Her rented stone farmhouse by the stream in Italy existed in a floating soap bubble, which might land miraculously without bursting. She imagined Marco standing behind her, her back along his body, his arms around her. What would he say?

"Hey, gal baby." J.J. was rinsing his fishy hands. His two-day beard shadowed his face. "What's all that?"

"I am bearing gifts. I am a sorceress who grants wishes. A conjure woman with voodoo to ward off gypsies, grave robbers, and family hexes. Also, I am returned from the dead. J.J., I was almost smeared into the pavement like a jackrabbit." She described what happened.

"Did you get his plate number, or the company?"

"No, I was about to ram head-on into trees. The ass looked back like a goofball and drove on. The truck was green like all the trees they're destroying."

J.J. was, after all, Big Jim's grandson. There were not that many pulpwood crews. Tomorrow J.J. would track the driver down. They were probably culling Mason land; he seemed to remember selling off rights. It would be the last time the bastard pulled a stunt like that. His boss would chew him up and spit him out. "Chivalry is dead."

"No joke. Are we having grilled trout?"

"Yes, but first we are going to swim. We're going to wash away all your fear."

"I'm fine, really. I want to tell you about what I found in the barn."

361

"A chapter for *The Secret in the Old Barn*?" He rolled a dish towel and snapped it at her.

"You write it, Mr. Faulkner. What happened to all Mother's things, do you suppose?"

"Sands of time."

After dinner, Ginger sat J.J. down on the sofa and just handed him the sketch books. She wanted him to look at them alone. "I'm going to take a bath. Then there's more I haven't looked at. Is that old movie projector still here?"

"Yeah, I can find it." He rubbed his rough face. Usually, you see your fate from behind, much later, not speeding toward you like a turpentine truck, he thought. The sketch books leaned against his chest. Volatile oil, he knew, flash point. But after what Ralph had told them, he was ready, finally, to look at the past.

Ginger came back in a pair of cotton pajamas that smelled fusty. They'd been damp and dried many times in her bottom drawer.

J.J. looked up at her. "This is amazing. I can't say how amazing. This is what *I* do." He gestured to the margin words, the drawing of three walnuts on a piece of flowered fabric. "Like mine. Mother's process — like mine, or mine so like hers. I never knew that I absorbed her daily practice by osmosis when I was nine, eleven. You think she read like I do, fell onto a book and didn't look up until the last line?" He remembered her notebooks sticking out the top of her handbag or lying on the backseat of the car. He remembered her room under the eaves of the house painted in wide blue stripes. But he must have pored over her drawings, he must have been allowed. The pages and pages of his baby face and the pregnant profile with the nascent Ginger — he could say nothing. He looked up at Ginger leaning over his shoulder. "I was one ugly white child."

"You look very jolly. I bet you were a good, good *bambino*."

In his life that stopped the day Catherine died, shunted off, and resumed on different terms later, nothing had picked him up by the back of the neck like this. "Gin, I don't think I can take in anything else for a while. Let's go out on the dock."

She put her arm around his shoulder. "Southern nights, give me a southern night anytime. Nothing like it on God's green

Ping-Pong ball. Smell the honeysuckle? Connects me directly — do not pass Go — to my first kiss out on one of these county roads with Tony Pappas in his father's fruit truck. He picked a sprig and put it behind my ear, then kissed me with his luscious Greek lips. He smelled like lemons."

"A defining moment, no doubt. He implanted you with the desire to meet foreign men."

"He was born in Swan. Daddy delivered him."

"Still." The Pappas family always would be *the Greeks* in Swan.

"J.J., do you feel that we got Mother back?"

"We did." J.J. hauled up a net. Earlier, he'd lowered a watermelon into the cool current. He split a side with his pocketknife, then pulled it open with his hands. He and Ginger only ate the heart. "Your favorite taste, after Pappas lips." He handed her a chunk. They rinsed their hands in the river, then leaned on the pilings, looking up at the Milky Way, a broad sweep of pavé diamonds.

"It looks like a sequined train on the bride of heaven's dress. If you look in the same place for eleven minutes, you'll see a falling star, guaranteed." She didn't mention Monte Sant'Egidio, where on San Lorenzo's day in August everyone came out together, walking in the hills on the night of the shooting stars, and the stars seemed intimate, maybe because they were associated with a particular saint. They're his largesse, his fireworks for his friends below. Here the barbed stars tore holes in the sky.

"If I look in the same place for twenty minutes, my neck will snap." J.J. lay back on the dock. "I come down here all the time. Just visiting with the stars, nice and immense, keeps me out of trouble. Lying here, you can unhook, drift. Let's go back."

J.J. set up the projector on the sofa table and Ginger hung a white sheet over the fireplace. The brittle film broke as soon as the reel turned. J.J. wound several turns around the reel and started again. For seconds, nothing, then trees and sky slid onto the screen. A white building they recognized as the Marshes Hotel at Carrie's Island.

"But who is that man?" Ginger wondered. Coming down the steps laughing, a man in a white suit, his face shaded by the tropical garden palms. The film cut to a fair, the World's Fair in New York, shiny exhibit booths and in the distance the New

York skyline. Then Catherine came on, the film fluttery. She wore a large straw hat which she held in a breeze. She sat on the porch railing of a yellow house, and beside her a swing moved back and forth. Someone had just risen. The camera panned to the right, a white door, then swung back, closer to Catherine. Ginger and J.J. watched her young face break into a smile. She raised her hand and waved her palm back and forth, a little wave like the queen gives when passing in a motorcade. The screen went blank, flashed a moment of a cocker spaniel with his tongue out, then the film flew off the reel.

"When we were little, I don't think I knew how pretty she was. She was just Mother." Ginger was dazzled by the smile, the *soft* look of her face.

"I knew." He rewound and played the film again. "Odd that this is one of the things she sealed in the box. I don't think it was because of the World's Fair. She must have wanted to keep the shots of the man at Carrie's Island. Or herself at that moment, wherever she was."

J.J. poured Ginger some orange juice and himself a glass of Scotch.

"They both were laughing."

The five letters, undated, were from

someone named Austin. They were a mixture of quite desperate and poetic love letters and descriptions of his travels. Apparently, he was a navy pilot who lived outside Macon. He thought of her in Philadelphia, he missed her in New York, he longed for her back at the farm, where there was a new foal he named Cathy. He wanted her the previous night on the terrace when the half moon rose and the band played "How High the Moon" and everyone was dancing. *Somewhere there's music, Cath, it's where you are.*

"What a romancer. Listen to this. *When I think of how I most want to spend my days, you are all I see. Catherine morning, Catherine noon, Catherine night.*"

"Looks like she was having an affair."

"Why do you think that? I don't see any dates. He must have been pre-Daddy."

Then Ginger opened the notebook. "Shall I read? The first sentence says, *I write in purple today, like the menus in Paris.* She never went to Paris." Ginger paged through. Quotes, doodles, drawings, and poems were interspersed with a few pages of written diary entries. She and J.J. faced each other from opposite ends of the sofa, her knees up, his feet on the coffee table, just as they'd sat for all the years they'd taken turns reading the Sunday funnies or books about the Creek Indians, *The Swiss Family Robinson*, the discovery of Troy, and *Green Mansions*.

The House has many cool big rooms. Floors smooth to the foot have been waxed and walked on and waxed until they shine like water. The screen doors bang in the afternoons when the rain gusts. When the rain starts, I jump up from my nap, from the wide bed of thick old sheets edged with crochet intricate as filigree, and run all over the house latching doors. The house is old and melancholy — smells of Big Jim's hair oil, cloves, the toast Lily burns every morning, and something dense — Florence's fruitcakes soaked in bourbon? The sofa cushions give off the heavy scent of Lily's Shalimar. I'd like to fling open all the windows and let the rain lash in. Big Jim hates staying in bed, hates being dependent on Florence, Lily, and me. He squeezes my hand and looks up mournfully from bed like a faithful bird dog locked in a pen. In his illness, he has turned sweet. I guess he was always courageous — he stared down the strikers and beat down the union. How many times have I heard that story? Visitors come and go. I spell Lily and Florence every afternoon so they can go to their bridge clubs. The baby sleeps and I write to Wills or lie down in the room where we've set up a crib. I open a drawer in this farthest bedroom and pick up an engraved yellowed card inviting me to a christening that took place sixty-four years ago. Just underneath is a photograph of that same baby, Big Jim's dead brother, Calhoun, at thirty or so, already balding and paunchy. He's long gone with the wind and rain. I can't help but balk. Feel the cutting scissors of Time, capital T.

The liquor cabinet in the sideboard has a box of nightclub swizzle sticks from the thirties. The Bartender's Guide, *published in '28, tells me how to make a Biffy, a Barking Dog, Mississippi Mule, and a Diki-Diki. But we drink only gin. I take Big Jim a big glass with lime every afternoon as the day starts to grate on his nerves, when he has nothing to do but wait for supper. Of course, he's not supposed to have alcohol after a heart attack but who can tell him anything? In the sideboard drawer, a stack of old photos. In them the now abundant garden — Florence keeps planting plumbago this year — wild with tangled vines and tumbling roses and a patch of nettles that erupt my skin — be-*

comes almost bare — orderly, clipped, planted, and edged — a background for the young wife Mary holding one, then two boys, Big Jim — James then — and Calhoun. Mary is skinnier and more serious with each child. She died young. A row of trees along the wall is now gone. Time. Mary, that whole family — dead except for Big Jim. But in the photo, Mary smiles at someone, me, she never knew. Someone who uses her hand-painted platters and monogrammed towels and recipes.

It's as if I fall through trapdoors, into old books and clippings, letters. Mary, John, and the two heirs apparent wish you a Merry Christmas before you were born. The boys, Big Jim and Calhoun, with straight arms and knee socks. A husband who likes his Yorkshire pudding and bubble-and-squeak too much. The last photos in the drawer are newer; black and white instead of brown and white with ripple-cut edges. Florence and Big Jim at Manatee Springs, pushing off in a boat. Ah, once he travelled with her! And the two of them gazing down through the water — what were they thinking? (What to think of the hulking bodies of those almost-lost manatees roaming deep-black water?) Lily and Florence in Bermuda on a pink beach, Lily in an awful woolly bathing suit. Lily in college, Wills leaning against a car, me, my arms around Florence and Big Jim. Weddings. Faces, smiling into the future, full of life, looking trustfully at the camera — and at me in the closed dining room, looking for a cocktail napkin for a sick man. Oh, here we are.

"Look, she's drawn a glass full of swizzle sticks. You got your love of writing from her, too." Ginger passed J.J. the notebook. "J.J. — we never knew anything."
"Pretty cool. I like what she wrote. It's good. Keep on."

Big Jim worsened. Wills got leave. Now Big Jim has revived. I admire him although I know he can be mean as a snake — and that he always runs around with other women. Lily thinks he will ascend into heaven to sit on the right hand of J. C. Wills could stay only four days. In uniform he seems older. The serious war in his face. When he appears in a doorway, I always feel an expansion. A light. He likes the dining room since I painted the walls bright peach. The word he used was flamingo. *Am I as real to him as a rock or wave or storm or bread?*

371

I'm going over to the House less. The baby has a rash. Lily comes for supper often but does not offer to take the baby for a walk or to stay during the day. She is lost but does not know it. She thinks the sun rises and sets for the House. I will take Baby with me to Macon.

At home again I talk to my notebook. A. L. His last gift was a pearl pendant in the shape of two crescent moons back-to-back. Baby and I go to the cabin. I love the humidity, the afternoon rain in sheets, and the passionate creeks. I run errands for Florence. We've started to call her Mama Fan for Baby. She does not like "grandmother," "grammy" — names for the old. Big Jim wants this or that. Wants to boss. I go to the office, too, and settle orders, meet payroll for him. I — or Lily — could run the mill. Florence resents him but keeps the stiff upper lip. Stiff everything. The House full of fits and starts. Many silences.

Big Jim sits on the porch in a rocker. He is allowed to walk around the yard, to the corner and back. He uses a cane. "To beat the women away," he brags. Charlotte is coming for the day. I miss her. We really talk. Chicken salad with pecans.

*Wills's letters are all about the camp —
the rumors, the wounded flown back from
abroad. Blown-off faces and legs. Our life
in Swan seems too remote to comment on.
Wills, all present tense, like all the Mason
men I've heard about. Yesterday is as over
as the Wars of the Roses. People like that
eternally renew, empty, renew. I am adored
when I am present. A dis-ease the doctor
cannot cure. Does he have pangs for us? Or
is it business at hand? I am fascinated by
this, envious, scornful. These people are too
terrible, righteous as angels. They live in a
flat world when clearly it is round and
turning.*

*The leopard has come back to my
dreams. I lie along his muscled back, my
mouth against the hot fur. He has been
running. I don't move because I'm afraid
to wake him. Who is this? I am afraid to
wake up.*

*My face in his hand felt like a cat's. I
am restless. Sometimes afraid. But of what?
Sometimes the repairman at the door is a
strangler in green. But it's only sullen
Clovis with his little sullen Sonny, sent by
Big Jim to fix the fence. I can't make them
smile and don't try. Big Jim's men worship*

or hate. The pearl crescents lie back-to-back on their bed of cotton. My favorite moon, the thinnest crescent. Wills may spot the waning gibbous from the officers' barracks tonight, lifting over the line of planes on the runway ready to go. The pearl crescents. Like two people in bed not sleeping.

Beneath love, inside sex, the climax like sheet lightning, the cry of the body flying away.

"That's steamy." Ginger looked up. "What do you make of this?"

Clovis, he thought, one of Big Jim's men who used to fix things. "Let's wait to talk. There's something she's not saying."

Like the alligators sunk up to their eyeballs, I lower myself into the cool river every afternoon. Baby likes to be dunked. He shrieks and smiles.

"Hey, you liked the river even then. Little J.J. baby, baptized by the waters. Here's a drawing of a baby foot — yours."

Leftovers, scraps, crumbs.

I won't be one of the broken. Keep right, keep the rules, don't walk on the grass, don't tread on me. If you leave the sheaf on the rib, the removed bone grows back. If the sheaf is stripped, no renewal . . . Baby crying. He's good and is beginning to want to skip his morning nap.

Took the baby to see Mother. I never knew her grandmother was named Sarah America Gray. I like each part of that name. A tiny girl named America.

If I come to you, it will only be to borrow a cup of salt.

"Am I missing something? Could you open the back door? There's not a puff of air coming in the windows. A cup of salt? This is pretty elliptical."

J.J. didn't think so. "Well, there's sadness. A cup of salt is not something you would borrow, so it's about tears. See, it's like a poem in one line. That's a big *if* she starts with." He recognized the method. A way to hide. He had many. Even if you don't think anyone will read your notebooks, you write, not what you meant, but what reminds you of what you meant.

"Not much left." Ginger flicked through

the pages. Blue, purple, black, crimson, dark green inks. She had a faint memory of reaching for small bottles on the desk and hearing *no.* As she read, she felt a spreading sorrow for her mother — obviously full of ideas and art — stuck in Swan, a war going on far away, no husband, annoying in-laws. She remembered long headache days, when her mother would not get up. Were those migraines like J.J.'s, or was she depressed? This she thought over but tactfully did not voice, since J.J., too, was, by her lights, stuck in Swan. She wondered if he saw it that way. "I always felt sorry for *us.* Mostly mad at her. Too unable to understand how that act could come out of all our lives. Now she is not a suicide; she didn't throw that blanket over our heads. Finding the sketch books, even the strange notebook — seems like this whole ordeal is a labyrinth."

"It is a labyrinth."

"You know I went to Crete last year. I was studying Knossos. The cicadas blared like maniacs and I stumbled through the ruins in hundred-degree heat. I didn't see any real labyrinth for the bull, just an added-onto, stacked, sprawled house of a thousand rooms that anyone could get lost in. Still, I love the story of Icarus flying out of there on wax wings. The moral we've been spoon-fed is 'don't fly too close to the sun,' but the real moral must be 'attach wings to your back and fly.' I like to imagine him soaring out over the island."

J.J. lifted his glass of Scotch. "Here's to Icarus, who drowned in the sea."

"Even if we don't solve every single mystery from our family, I think we have a whole history to rewrite. Mother's tragedy — ours — is shifting, turning inside out. And at least we've had all these years in the light: hers went dark so soon."

J.J. had been gripped by every word in the notebook, ever since he heard *here we are*. He felt with every word what Catherine meant. "And here's to Mother, Gin," he added in a low voice. "She was something. We don't have any idea how much silence there was between one page and the next."

"Here's the rest."

My days should be natural, like drawing a bath. Oh, to be natural. Can I be baked by the sun, moved by the wind, washed by the rain? Should I keep bees? In early morning light they are gold sparks. So

many in the catalpa — they purr.
A rose the color of a massive bruise.

Big thunder. The kind that loosens the fillings of your teeth! Tree frogs and roving clouds. Hollyhocks and Queen Anne's lace keep Baby and me company at the table. I hope my life will use all of me.

Lily green. Lampblack. Almond green. Comb of light.

Segments, particles, patches, splinters, remnants.

The gift pearls are gone. When I last opened the box, the gleam of a galaxy streaked out. Hammer this home. I am as real as bread or moss. Soon my baby will quicken. The avalanche of life force begins, sending us all forward into a new world. Wills's world. When he comes marching home. Austin's world. Blown roses. Baby's world. His toes in the river. Little X in the flux of the womb. Swimmer. Mine. The color wheel, spinning fast.

She, Allegra, Alexandra, Miss X, she, the soles of her feet smaller than grains of rice. She's in the hidden envelope at the

bottom of the drawer. Little thorn. Little al-
mond. Little finger. The briar rose.

"That means she's pregnant with me?"
"I'd say so."

It's true — I am going to have a baby.
Already it has gill slits, a primitive tiny
blob of a creature who will become
someone. How ordinary to have a baby —
to squat in the fields, drop the child, and
keep on picking. But what a miracle. I
have to think — this is my baby. I didn't
tell Mother. Will only tell myself for now.

country captain chicken
tarragon green beans
brown sugar muffins
butterscotch pie

"What an ending. I wish we had some."
Ginger closed the notebook and slid it onto
the coffee table. Neither of them spoke. A
green lizard squeezed under the window
screen and darted sideways across the fireplace stones. "Do you know it's two-thirty?"
"Austin. The big romancer. Do you
think the pearl gift was from him? I don't
remember any pearl crescents among her
jewelry."

"Must have been." J.J. wanted to read the journal to himself. As Ginger had read, he was flashing on the unsaid. The *tone* of secrecy. The past was stripping down, like those clear overlays you peel back to reveal muscle, then circulation, then bone. Was his mother pregnant by Austin?

Late, as Ginger slept, J.J. sat at the kitchen table with the notebook, the same table where years ago Catherine sat writing late at night, a cricket creeping across the floor, the kitchen quiet, the washed dishes draining by the sink. The notebook made his mother live. He was again beside her in church when her gold beads broke, rolling out of reach on the floor, the choir screeching "Jerusalem." Memory, he thought, cuts and comes again. He sees the half-moons of sweat under her arms, Ginger squirming, Dad's hands on his knees, solid as a sphinx. We all rise. Young again. The benediction. The scent of his bay lime cologne and the fetid water of the church flowers, then, soon after, we clamor for the wishbone, ask what's for dessert. Back to our coloring books, he thought, connecting the dots. The finished pictures never had resembled what was intended. He still saw the constellation of dots. He opened his own notebook. *River on Fire,* he wrote on the last blank page in the book.

★ ★ ★

Ginger, wide-eyed in the night, started going over every resemblance to her father ever mentioned. She was sure J.J. had picked up the dropped crumbs through the forest but neither of them could absorb the possibility quickly enough to talk about it. Their lifetime habits of mutual protection stalled them even now, after the knockout shocks of the week. Usually, she heard that she was the spitting image of her mother and, turning the pillow over to its cool side, she remembered, *this is my baby* in the notebook. She had her mother's rather thin lips and the same expressive shoulder gestures. But she had Wills's square fingernails and flat tight butt — surely those were identifying genes. She and J.J. called him "sackbutt," among other attempts to render him harmless. She imagined her profile in the mirror, her rear a bare curve. She ran her forefingers around her thumbnails. I'll have to look at J.J.'s nails tomorrow. Her hair, pale silky red, had come from nowhere. Big Jim, Florence, Lily with hair the color of steel wool, Catherine's parents — all dark. J.J. with hair black as a crow. There must have been an ancestor, perhaps that Sarah America Gray, with her hair.

How many more questions could arise?

Along with blunt shock ran a current of joy. She kept thinking of the word *redeem*. To redeem, meaning "to take back, to buy back." We paid. We will not, she tried to form the words, have the cicatrix *suicide* carved across our faces. We need not have practiced jungle survival for all those years, learning to make sun hats from palmetto fronds, drinking by touching our tongues to the ends of wet pine needles. Out of the staggering, stupefying horror of what happened, J.J. had found out that the deepest part of him came directly from his mother. He was, she thought, saved. Mother had managed to hand him her finest heirlooms. Was there something she handed me? Ginger, who never cried, began to cry, turning her face into the pillow. She gave in to a sense of release, complicated now, but whatever came next, her mother was freed from suicide, free to love her in the past. *My* baby. The knowledge of her mother that Ginger had as a child was true.

A few days before Catherine's death she had been sewing a circle skirt printed with sombreros. Ginger had sat cross-legged on the daybed, playing with her character dolls, probably the last day she'd ever opened the shoe box and taken out the Polish twins with their red, rickrack-trimmed skirts, their velvet ribbons, and their black aprons over their skirts. Catherine had pressed hard on the pedal and zoomed along the seams. Ginger still could feel the hard bodies of the two dolls she'd dressed, see the unnatural orangy tint of their faces and their empty eyes. Really, she'd preferred the Dutch twins.

This speck of memory — something to hold. She had been simply with her mother on a quiet afternoon at home. While she'd read the notebook aloud, she had glanced now and then at J.J., frowning slightly, looking into the fireplace or at his feet. He was so concentrated that he appeared to be in a trance.

Ginger flung back the sheet and went into the kitchen. J.J. jumped, dropped the notebook. "You remember the recipe for that grainy fudge? Want to make some?"

July 11

Mayhew, always up early, saw the article in the paper and took it into the bedroom. "Charily, Charily, wake up. This is something." She swam up from a dream of driving a race car, skirting the edge of an abyss, woke to see Mayhew leaning over her. Irrationally, she thought he looked like a boiled pig, then she focused, saw dear Mayhew, and reached for her glasses.

SPECIAL FROM *THE SWAN FLYOVER*
BY RAINEY GROVER

TWIST OF EVENTS IN
SWAN CEMETERY CASE

SWAN, GEORGIA — GBI investigator Gray Hinckle and J. E. B. Stuart County Sheriff Ralph Hunnicutt, investigating the recent exhumation of a body buried for nineteen years in Swan, Georgia, have come to the extraordinary conclusion that the original cause of death, previously presumed to be suicide, was murder. The alert officer and Swan sheriff concluded that because of the entrance angle of the bullet wound near the woman's heart, she could not have pulled the trigger of the .22-caliber automatic rifle found next to her body. Other advanced forensic techniques have supported their theory. The body is that of Catherine Phillips Mason, wife of Dr. Wills Mason, long a resident of Swan. Her disheveled body was discovered beside her grave in the family plot by her sister-in-law, Lillian Mason, and Mrs. Eleanor Whitefield, neither of whom were available for comment. Sheriff Ralph Hunnicutt says his office is pursuing all leads and he expects to capture the culprits. When asked about the unexpected turn of events, he said it is too soon to comment.

Charlotte leapt out of bed. "God Almighty, Jesus, Joseph, and Mary, this is hideous. But, Mayhew, I've waited nineteen years to read that! I *knew* Catherine would not commit suicide. Remember, I *knew*. She just would not."

"Well, it's pretty strange that someone would kill her, then years later someone *else* would dig her up. Would you say the two might be related?"

"But how, who, *who?* I never thought that anyone who knew her was involved in her death. Who knows? It's absurd. Someone broke in, broke in both times; that's the only answer."

"If it's two random crimes, I say she had shit for luck." Mayhew smoothed back her hair hard, as if he were petting a dog. "Try to keep your head screwed on." He knew she'd be spinning way out over this news.

Charlotte dialed 0. "Operator, may I have information in Swan, the number for Lillian Mason?" But what would she say to Lily after all these years? Those Masons squelched the investigation because they were ashamed. Charlotte never liked Lily, wanted, in fact, to kick her in the pants. So proprietary. So controlling. A saint, though, to raise those children.

"Well, I can give you that number, honey, but I can tell you Lily is not home 'cause I just saw her drive off from the drugstore with Eleanor Whitefield."

"Thank you, I'll try calling later." Charlotte shrieked, "Gawd that town!" If

Catherine hadn't married into that poky fiefdom. If she had chosen Austin. Charlotte pulled out the Macon phone book. Austin. Austin Larkin. His thin blue letters had arrived at the dorm daily. She could still see a stack on Catherine's dresser in their dorm room, held down with an ivory-backed mirror. Catherine lying back in bed with a textbook on her chest, kicking her legs in the air. "He says I should float down the Nile on a flower-covered barge." Catherine lined the window ledge with conch shells and amethyst geodes and ambrotypes of nineteenth-century children — all gifts he pulled from his pockets on the weekends. When she came back from that Thanksgiving wearing Wills's square emerald ring, Austin had backed down the dorm steps shaking his head. Never said a word. As far as Charlotte knew, Catherine never heard from him again, except for the event of the roses. One winter afternoon, he flew his tiny plane low over the campus, scattering roses for Catherine, thousands of roses.

Charlotte wondered if he still lived somewhere near. Despite whatever had happened in his life, he'd want to know that Catherine had not killed herself. Charlotte was sure of that. He'd been brought up forty-five minutes away, in Stonefield. She called the operator; no Larkin was listed. She would go there and try to find him. Austin, what a hunk. "Hubba hubba," Catherine used to say. Could she paint roses falling out of the sky? She had not seen them fall, only the quad after he flew over, strewn with petals, buds, full-blown blooms. To each stem was tied a thread with a small white flag attached. In black calligraphy, *CRP* was written on each. Rose — Catherine's middle name. Catherine had picked up only one. It was as if she picked up a bolt of lightning, Charlotte thought. She could see the bloodred rose against Catherine's pink angora sweater. In memory, the moments form so oddly, she thought, like a swan sculpted in ice floating in my bloodstream.

Aileen was out early. She had to drive over to Tipton to the Singer store because her last needle had snapped off. She needed more tiny pearl buttons and some ready-made tatting for edging the baby blankets of her less particular customers.

A sign on the door said *Back in fifteen minutes.* Since she didn't know when the fifteen minutes had started, she walked across the street to the Main Street Café to have coffee and wait. Someone had left the Macon paper on the table. As she slid into the booth, the story on Catherine Mason jumped off the page at her.

Not a suicide.

She read the article twice, ignoring the waitress who poured her coffee. When she tried to pick up the cup, it rattled against the saucer. She put both shaking hands on her lap and pretended to blow the hot coffee. Across the street, a woman was unlocking the Singer store. But what could now raise her from her seat and send her among the buttons and zippers?

The information in the paper, she feared, was the truth, even though she'd told herself a different version ever since Catherine Mason died. That day, when news of the death had flown through the mill village, she had been completely relieved to hear that Catherine was dead by suicide, not by murder. She'd been desperately afraid at first that Sonny had tried to rape her and then killed her. He'd often railed on about Big Jim deserving for *his* family women to get fucked, tortured. He said he'd stick knives up them and see how horny Big Jim felt then. Sonny was *always* blowing up, but Aileen was scared of him. He'd gone into details that made her fear he'd do those things to her. But Catherine's death had been simply suicide. No evidence to the contrary. No torn-up house. The sheriff knew how Catherine died, she'd thought. The sheriff could tell by how she was found, what gun was fired. They said she was holding the gun. Who knew what she was going through? Maybe her own husband screwed around. The sheriff knew those things. Sonny, she'd quickly concluded, didn't do it; he simply left, the way he said he was going to.

Aileen always felt that she walked with Sonny's shadow covering her. The preacher might explain that as her knowledge of her own sins, but Aileen never had told the preacher — or anyone, not even her sister. At work, when she'd looked at the office door, she was afraid Sonny's pointed face and fish eyes would appear in the glass. His violence would sometimes scare her during sex with Big Jim at the motel. Even when she could take her time for the luxury of a shower afterward, she feared he might burst in and rip back the curtain. Sonny could find them. Alone at home, she had dreamed over and over that he was breathing outside the door.

After Big Jim up and died, even a branch scratching against the window made Aileen gasp. Then one morning, Sonny had appeared at her door, opened the screen, and walked in. All her fears during his four-year absence suddenly took the form of his real shape. It was as if his raid on the office were continuing. She was terrified by his bushy white run-together eyebrows, the distant look in his eyes. By then Big Jim was dead a year, the wife was dead, too. But Sonny, just out of the army, had come home still ranting about revenge. He yanked her hair back and spit in her face. "You pussy bitch. You stinking whore. He's dead but he deserves to be drawn and quartered. *His* father fucked my grand-mother. Who do they think they are? You're not worth killing. But I'm going to get that family, all of them, those sorry motherfuckers. That puffed-up doctor, I'll see how he likes somebody doing his woman."

Out of fear, she lied. "It was never how you thought. Big Jim wanted me but I *didn't*. Those things you found were because he was trying to get me. You never trusted me, ever. Now he's dead. And we're divorced, for God's sake. You were dead wrong. Leave me alone. Forget it." She wanted to kick and spit at him but remained still and controlled.

Sonny sat down. To hear the name Big Jim still enraged him. He banged his fist on the kitchen table. He looked at her, wide-eyed, grinding his teeth. He slung his arm across the table, sweeping the jelly and salt and pepper onto the floor.

"Please. Go. Please leave, go. Leave those people alone — they never did anything to you. It's over, he's dead." She put her head on the table and cried.

He laughed. His eyes darted and he

blinked over and over. His top lip raised like a dog about to snarl. Suddenly he slammed out of the house "Okay. Okay. You win, you slut. I'm going out West to Arizona, and you're not ever going to see me again." He said it like a threat, emphasizing each word. He jabbed the air with his middle finger.

Aileen breathed out. To placate him, she said, "Well, I hope your life goes better now. I never meant you no harm." She rubbed her head where he'd pulled her braid. She closed the door and slid the bolt. She wished he were dead. She imagined slashing him with the turkey knife.

A month later, the night when she'd heard of Catherine Mason's suicide, she got in the car and drove forty miles to her sister's. Sometimes in the years after that, she'd imagined Catherine Mason wondering what had brought Sonny, a millworker who was sometimes sent there for repairs, to her door. Aileen imagined his attack, Catherine grabbing a gun, and Sonny turning it on her and firing, pausing only to arrange the gun in her hand while her life dripped out on the floor. But Catherine was a suicide. Sonny was long gone. Over time, her memory of Sonny receded. She began to leave her doors unlocked, like everyone else in Swan. She had not seen him since that day — nineteen years. After that long, can something still fester? Had he done this trick at the cemetery? Her mind would not stop whirling. Remembering his vacant eyes, she would not put it past him.

Aileen glanced at her face in the window's reflection. "I'm plain gaunt," she said to herself. When her face and lips had been kissed and kissed by Big Jim, she looked full and rosy in the motel mirror. Twenty years had sculpted her so that now her high cheekbones stuck out, concaving her face. Her lips looked pinched. I look like I suck lemons, she thought. Her hair remained thick and lustrous. She managed to sip the coffee, managed to light a cigarette and blow out smoke toward her own face in the glass. She looked at herself again. Her eyes looked wild. She saw a fox face, something on the edge of the woods with shining eyes — she could be Sonny's twin.

She decided she would just drive on over to her sister's in Tyler. She would have to figure out how she could go to the sheriff, Hunnicutt's grandson. She knew she should, but should, would, could, blended together in her mind. Could she think of how not to tell the whole story? She did not want her carefully hidden life to be more shamefully exposed than Catherine Mason's rotten body. And Big Jim, the bank president, mayor, owner of the mill. She would just wait and see what came to light.

Her sister, a widow now, would be glad for her company. They could make blue plum jelly, and Jeannie could help her sew. She could buy the few things she needed. If Sonny paid a visit to the mill village, there'd be no one for him to hit. Then she thought of the other Mason women — if Sonny was that crazy. But she didn't really believe he had come back after all these years. Maybe she *would* talk to someone. She liked the preacher in her sister's Primitive Baptist church. He spoke the gospel while looking at the sky, then would lower his head and bear down on the congregation with burning eyes. Aileen liked his unruly brown curls and the ropy cords in his neck. She imagined sweeping her hair over his sinless body. Last time she heard him, she'd gone to the verge of feeling saved.

I'll go, she thought. I'll get up from this booth and go. She left the newspaper on the table, Catherine Mason's photo faceup for the next reader. She walked across the street and bought the lace and pearl buttons she needed.

Ralph's phone at home and at the office would not stop ringing. With the news hitting the morning papers, reporters from all over the state and as far away as Tallahassee and Mobile kept calling for information. Gray, with backup from the GBI staff, was conducting his own investigation. He'd walked out of the Columns after interviewing Wills convinced he had nothing to do with the exhumation. "Old fart could barely brush his teeth. Now, whether he pulled the trigger years ago, we're just not going to find out unless something breaks open from an unexpected quarter," Gray said. Ralph had combed the cemetery and had found no letter. Nothing. Gray had asked him to check up on J.J. Embarrassed that he would have to phone and ask J.J. where he was last week, he stopped in Scott's store to verify their fishing trip to St. Clare's.

Scott was wiping down the sweating

sides of the ice cream freezer. He was hoping J.J. would stop in to go over some orders he wanted to make. "Yes," he told Ralph, "we chartered a boat down there, fishing for marlin." Scott gave him names and numbers, without mentioning that he'd slept on deck both nights because J.J. picked up a twenty-year-old girl named Gay Nix at the tackle shop, and they were rocking the cabin. That was nobody's bidness. A big girl, who'd brought on board a sack of fried catfish and hushpuppies from her mama's fish fry stand next to her daddy's tackle and bait place. She'd kept up a shrieking laugh, and Scott had concentrated on the slap of waves against the bow. Usually, J.J. didn't spin off like that on their trips. Had to be mighty hard up to go after that big-kneed gal. Far as he knew, she never asked them their names. J.J. kept calling her Sunshine. No need to tell the sheriff any of that.

Somebody down in St. Clare's was mounting two fish they'd caught. Scott showed Ralph the receipt. Plenty of contacts. A relief. Ralph had no reason not to believe him, but for God's sake somebody had to have dug up that body and maybe it was J.J. and this loyal buck. He didn't want to be like his grandfather, who let the Masons slide by. He had to admit, however, that no motive presented itself, aside from pure craziness. Whatever he was, J.J. was not one drop crazy.

Mindy up at the register cut her eyes at Ralph. He is cute, plenty cute, she thought. That slash of scar all down his arm is from Vietnam. Who was it said he'd been left for dead and had to walk at night through war zones to get back to his troop?

Ralph picked up a bottle of Dr Pepper and some peanuts. "Well, Miss Mindy, how's everything?" She wore a scoop-necked lavender T-shirt and he gazed down the great divide between her pushed-up breasts. She saw his look and reached to pin her hair, the gesture of raising her arms lifting her breasts. Ralph pulled on his earlobe and looked down at the change on the counter.

"I'm just fine and dandy, Ralph."

"You sure are. Hey, you want to go out to the Shack tomorrow night? They've got a band." He hadn't danced in years. This Mason mess made him want to hit balls, run, dance, fuck, drive fast. Anything to re-mind him that the world was not going crazy again. He looked into her pert face. She wouldn't have any idea about war or the horror of corpses. Ever since the war he'd been amazed by people's innocence. He looked over at the rows of dish soap and detergent to block the sudden vision of Tommy Melton crawling beside him one moment, his head blown to bits the next, blood spurting from what had been his neck, his face like a run-over cantaloupe in the mud. Mindy's old husband, Holy Roller now, with one leg two inches shorter than the other, never got drafted, like so many others — like J.J., come to think of it. Some said Mason contacts had fixed that, but Ralph didn't see how he could, with the military offices way over in Dannon.

"Let me see if my sister will keep my little girl. I think she will. You know where I live — the sea-foam-colored house in the mill village." She kept looking right into his eyes. He imagined rolling that T-shirt right off, the explosion of her flesh into his hands.

"Mindy," he said. "What's that short for?"

"Just Mindy. Mindy Marie." She would wear her low-cut white eyelet that buttoned up the front. With her Saturday paycheck, she'd buy those fuchsia sandals with wedge heels in the window of Buster's Shoes. She liked his square teeth and his golden chest hair in the V of his shirt. She hoped he didn't have furry hair on his back like her ex-husband. Who would wait around for J. J. Mason to turn up? Not her. "Mama named me after her mama, Sugar Marie, and her granny, Mindy Lou."

"That's right nice. And much better than 'Sugar Lou.' Although, come to think of it, that's a good name, too. Around eight tomorrow?"

He is damn cute, Mindy thought. Sugar Lou, who would have thought of that?

Rainey Grover pushed back her chair from her desk at *The Swan Flyover*. The famous doctor's diet promised that she wouldn't feel hungry between meals, but her stomach was roaring, as if it were trying to digest itself. After two weeks of starvation, she hadn't lost but one pound. She'd expected five by now, hoped for eight. She opened a drawer and took out a package of cheese crackers with peanut butter, 125 calories apiece. She closed her eyes and ate one of the little sandwiches slowly, throwing the rest in the wastebasket. She had forty pounds to lose. At the conservative estimate according to the diet book, she would be down to her slinky best by February. Immediately, she wished she had not eaten the poisonous-looking orange crackers spread with evil peanut butter. At lunch she would skip the allowed piece of fruit.

She'd spent the morning calling people

she met last March at the newspaper conference in Atlanta. She was bone-sure that no Mason had disrupted a grave. When, since the fabled Big Jim, had they ever shown enough energy for such an exploit? Her husband, Johnny, agreed. She wanted to be the investigative force for the case. That Lily or Wills could engineer a grave-opening was ludicrous. J.J.? But why? And besides, he was off fishing, playing the nature boy as usual, with that muscle-bound black stud who worked for him. J.J. — Swan's answer to Tarzan. Only Ginger was on the move, and she went from pillar to post, without ever settling on anything. The news that their mother didn't shoot herself must have rocked them all the way back to the cradle. When her own mother simply died of sugar diabetes, Rainey had been outraged. For years she half expected her mother to call or write.

Her colleagues scattered around Georgia were wildly curious about the case in Swan but had nothing to add, no similar activities in their towns. "Must be Martians," the editor of *The Cleveland Ledger* said. "I wish something exciting would happen here," others lamented. Rainey walked over to the long windows looking out onto the sidewalk and Main Street. Passing clouds reflected on the glass. Cliff Bryant, walking his two spaniels, Stevie and Clarkie, made her smile. His own doggish muzzle made him look as though he, too, might yap instead of speak. Agnes Burkhart, who with her cropped hair and laced, square-heeled shoes looked as though she'd been picked up by the wind from a street in old Europe and set down in Swan, came out of the drugstore with a little bag, probably medication for her sister's fits. Francie Lachlan slammed on brakes and got out of her new yellow convertible with three boys. Pied Piper of, where? Hamlin? Watch out, Francie, she thought. Rainey had been the honeypot of her day, though she'd never had the pleasure of a daddy who bribed good behavior with fancy wheels.

Such a normal day. Cusetta Fletcher, new-rich in town, swaggered into the furniture store. She waved to Bunky, her neighbor, who caught her eye as she drove by. The slow flow of cars seemed to move through a dream. Rainey loved Swan. All her life it had seemed the best place on earth to live. Even as a girl, she'd felt she never could leave. She liked working downtown with Johnny, her desk looking out at the Oasis, the noon walk over to the

Three Sisters, where she picked up most of her news. She even liked the tentacular gossip, rampant in any place where no news is no news.

She looked at her watch. Another hour until her carrot, chicken soup, and small salad. The sisters would commiserate as they plunked their coconut pies onto the sideboard. She pushed in the basketball bulge of her stomach, despising herself for fantasizing a slice of that tall, creamy pie sliding onto a plate. Now she and Johnny never made love with her on top. Too tactful to say so, he felt squished, she knew, when not many years ago, Johnny could span her waist with his fingers.

J.J. slept in, for once. It was almost nine by the time he lowered himself into the river. Four turtles, one a pretty substantial snapping turtle, sunned on a log the current had wedged against the dock. They regarded him without interest. He would let Ginger sleep as late as she could. She'd polished off the fudge at five in the morning. When she got up, they would call Charlotte Crowder in Macon. He'd already called Scott and found out that green pulpwood trucks belonged to Tall Pine Company thirty miles down the road in Flanders. That was the company to whom J.J. had sold cutting rights. He'd called Andy Foster to let him know he'd never get another tree from J. E. B. Stuart County unless they dealt with the bastard who almost ran down his sister yesterday. "Squirrelly little guy, we just hired him last week. I'll sure see about it," Andy Foster told him.

J.J. swam out to the sandbar and back, then lay flat back on the dock, his feet in the water, and looked at the sundogs and rainbows between his wet eyelashes until he fell asleep again under a clean sky.

Stonefield's one and only main drag, thought Charlotte, looked like one of those dreary WPA pictures from the Depression. Leaning, tin-roofed stores with throwback names like Bunny's Dry Goods. As opposed to wet? The wide street accommodated a sleeping hound in the middle, which the few passing cars swerved around. Now that she was here, she wasn't sure what to do. She went inside a small dime store on the corner. It smelled of stale popcorn and parakeet cages. Charlotte thought purgatory, if it existed, would be something like a dime store in a small town. Her eye was caught by the wall of embroidery threads, the skeins in figure eights silky and bright. She picked out damson, scarlet, spring green, rust. As she paid, she asked the clerk, "Do you know of a Larkin here in Stonefield?"

"I wouldn't know. I'm not from around

here. I'm from Lux." Lux was all of eight miles away.

Charlotte walked down one side of the street, crossed, and started back up the other. Three codgers sat outside the barbershop, chairs tilted back, their cheeks puffed with snuff. She glimpsed a soda fountain in the drugstore. She ordered a milk shake and the boy who made it whistled, to her joy, the Academic Festival Overture. "Do you know of any Larkins in town?" she asked.

"Yes, ma'am. Mr. Austin Larkin still owns a place off the highway out east of town, but he doesn't live here. Hasn't for a hundred years. Comes back now and then. He lives out West somewheres. Place is falling apart."

"Where's his house? Is it far? I want to leave something for him." What a lie. What could she leave, skeins of thread?

"You go out to the red light" — he pointed — "then go about a mile and you'll come to two big pines. Turn in there, and the road, nothing more than a pig track now, leads up to the house."

Charlotte found the pines, with a leaning mailbox underneath. She opened it from the car window and saw only a clutch of leaves and a thick spiderweb.

411

Branches and palmettos slashed the sides of the car. She crept forward, the car bottom scraping, and stopped under a pecan tree. Austin's house was a sprawling two-story farmhouse with wraparound porch and a round turret. Flaking white paint revealed a yellow coat underneath, probably from a happier time. Charlotte thought those who painted their houses yellow were optimists. From an open door on the right side's lower wing, a tall black woman looked out. "Hello," Charlotte called. "I'm an old friend of Austin Larkin. Is he here?" She walked up to the woman, who held strips of willow in her hand.

"Nome. He ain't here. He done been gone a long time." She gestured Charlotte in out of the heat. The table was covered with stripped willow branches. Charlotte introduced herself and the woman responded, "I'm Edwina, living here to take care of Mr. Austin's home while he be gone out West."

"You're weaving?" Charlotte looked on the benches around the table and saw a fine egg basket and several small round ones, perfect for bread — no, for her collection of old marbles. You could dip in your hand and let them run through your fingers. "How beautiful."

"Yes'm. I pass the time. It's lonesome out here. My husband's gone all day."

"I'm sorry. At least it's peaceful." Charlotte waved her hand at the window, a neglected garden with some half-dead geraniums around a birdbath, weed trees, an overgrown field swaying with grasses and black-eyed Susans. "Do you sell them?" She lifted a basket.

"Oh, no, just give them to my chirrun. They use them for this and that. Nobody would pay good money for a little ol' basket like this." She waved a taut oval basket woven from osier. "It's just a old habit I got from my granddaddy." Her long fingers looked as supple as the willow wands she wove.

"I'd like to call Mr. Larkin. We were in college at the same time, then we lost touch. Do you have his number out West?"

"Nome, I sure don't. We don't have no phone. He just turns up here now and then. I don't think he plans on coming back home to live."

"When was he here last? Did I just miss him?"

"I reckon it was last November. He came back for some bird huntin'. Would you like a glass of tea? I made some fresh this morning."

"Why, thank you." Charlotte examined the egg basket. Her church craft fair could sell these like hotcakes at Christmas. Austin or not, she'd be back to talk to Edwina later about making three dozen of these. Would she be interested? Edwina walked like a queen, stately in her big shoes. Slowly, she poured and, as though she were transporting communion wine, set down the glass in front of Charlotte. Her two bare rooms were immaculate. Through a door she saw her bed made up without a wrinkle, the white curtains (from old flour sacks?) crisp at the window. Charlotte felt a stab of admiration for her reclusive life far in the country, the practice of an art that sprang so naturally from the ground. Weaving baskets seemed a felicitous life. She imagined Edwina gathering her materials along the wet spots where willows grew. One could rest here, she thought. Her own life crowded her head — too many people, exhibits, the children, dinners, Mayhew's business, clubs, commitments. Sometimes she felt like a monkey swinging from tree to tree. And her painting squeezed in around the edges. This egg basket with its ridge up the middle to keep the eggs from knocking against each other — what a piece of necessity and beauty. If Catherine were here, she would want to stay all afternoon and learn how Edwina worked. Sometimes she thought Catherine knew everything. But how? She sprang from a tight Protestant family, just as intent on saying no as Charlotte's family had been. *The paintings, don't they tie you to them so you never want to get away?* They had looked furiously at the Matisse book, dazzled. *So divine, they rush all the way through you.* No wonder Austin had worshiped her. Or do we project on the dead a knowledge of life unchallenged by their silence? Charlotte always wondered what she would have said, what she would have been, how they would have gone forward . . . Dead, Catherine became a never-opened safe-deposit box for the imagination.

Charlotte thanked Edwina and said she must be going. She was dying to look in the windows of the main house but waved and headed for her car. Edwina again stood in the doorway. "Wait a minute." She turned back into the dark house and emerged holding the egg basket. "Take this. I'm glad you like it. Everybody's got some eggs."

As Charlotte passed the post office sign,

she had an inspiration. Austin would have left a forwarding address. Obtaining it turned out to be easy. She simply said she was an old friend, had been to his house looking for him, and now wanted to write. The postmistress looked in her pigeon-holes, took out an envelope, and copied his address. "He doesn't get any mail any-more. He's been gone too long. I think even the tax office forgot him."

"How long has he been gone?" Charlotte glanced down: 1518 Whitman St., Palo Alto, California.

"Ah, he left during the war. He warn't a plain soldier like everybody else. He flew some big planes. Then I heard he went out near San Francisco, something else to do with airplanes. So I heard. Comes back here every so often. He's still a good-looking man."

"Thank you so much." So he'd left the South long before Catherine's death. "Oh, what did he do when he lived here? I lost touch with him after college."

"I believe he used to travel in sales, equipment for cotton mills. Then all the mills went bust 'cause of the Japanese, so I guess he made other plans."

"Thanks again." Amazing what you can find out, Charlotte thought, quite pleased with her detective work. What she would do with the information she had no idea. Regardless of the span of time, she just knew that Austin should know the news about Catherine. Maybe she would call him. No, too awkward. She would write, say she remembered him well, and since they both had loved Catherine, she wanted him to know.

Seeing Edwina made Charlotte want to get back to her studio over the garage, to sit under the skylight in front of the A-shaped window looking out at expanses of trees and a big sky. She would paint not the cunning basket filled with eggs, but Edwina herself, long and big-boned, out-lined by the sun in the doorway, her eyes black as asbestos, something in her hand, something to give.

In the long summer twilights Marco walked in the fields around his archaeological site. Although the current excavation surely had more to reveal at the most conservative estimate, his guess was that the site was potentially on a vast scale. He hoped to extend funding so that he could start preliminary surveys of surrounding terrain even while his team's work continued. He wanted to begin with one group carefully walking the transects along the contours, bag whatever turned up, then pinpoint a few places for trial digs. Already Marco had picked up a few scattered sherds, probably Roman. With endless land spreading around them, it was always fascinating that the ancients built right on top of what was there before. Many local Christian churches rested on Etruscan stone foundations; below that, probably something from the earlier Umbrians. The artesian springs in this area guaranteed long habitation.

The farmer would not be pleased. A neighboring farmer last year turned up a bronze cup incised with Etruscan writing. For months he had hidden it in his hay barn but had not been able to keep quiet about it in the piazza. The police eventually made a visit and he handed it over. If Marco found funding, and the Italian ministry granted him permission, the farmer would lose his tobacco crop. Even though he would be compensated, such invasion didn't sit right with local farmers who feared for their land becoming tourist attractions.

This particular gently terraced hillside would have been appealing in any era. Wide swaths of olive trees interspersed by rangy old grapevines stepped down to flat cultivation. Marco skirted the tobacco plants, keeping to the field's edge, where the plow had left a ridge. He walked to unkink after a day at the site and to pass time until he could meet friends for dinner. Ginger had just called him at his mother's. Midday there and she was just getting up. She told him about finding the film and her mother's drawings and notebook. She and J.J. had made candy and drunk some icy vodka, then gone in the river late at night. "Don't worry, we've done it all our lives," she had said.

He missed her. During the day he was too busy, but he missed seeing her concentrating on her work, her startled look when he called to her, her hair falling around her face until she reached back, swirled it around, and pinned it up. He'd moved two interns to the area she'd been working and half hoped they would not find anything. When she returned, she would unearth a gold bee or a pot handle with datable glaze. Mostly, he found that he wanted to reach for her. Her physical absence felt solid, almost like a presence. Her life over there in the South was another world for him. The brother sounded dangerous, a man cut off like that. He unbuttoned his shirt to catch some of the breeze. That Ginger had knocked around in San Francisco, New York, had been married, all this seemed more inert as facts than the old chronology of sequential settlements on this land. He sensed her damage. He'd known her five months before she'd made love with him. Other American girls were stepping out of their clothes after coffee in a bar. Sometimes her eyes fixed somewhere beyond him — she travelled, he thought, *over there,* or she would turn silent in a group. But he felt her slowly changing, loving her work, quick to retreat but trusting him. Over time, he thought, she would simply walk away from the past, close the book on the dark story of her parents. His love would be a light to flood her bones.

"Should I go there to Georgia?" he'd asked. She insisted that she was fine. Her voice sounded remote. She would be back soon, maybe next week. The site would be closed for August, a reprieve for him to catch up on paperwork and for the team to go off on holiday. He and Ginger could go to Elba for a few days and lie in the healing sun. This made sense, but something was gnawing at him. She was the only woman he'd ever wanted to dance with in the kitchen, the pasta water coming to a boil, steaming the windows, his old albums, Johnny Mathis, Dominico Modugno, the Platters, the big crooners, a green-checked tablecloth, a bowl of sliced tomatoes, his uncle's wine in a yellow pitcher. Laughing, speculating about the dig, Ginger licking sauce on her thumb. I haven't loved her enough, he thought. What is life but this? Choices made early in a relationship determine the course. To wait for her, as she asked, is that the right choice?

When Ginger woke up, J.J. remembered to show her the bone fish spear. "I found this the day before I came home and saw Scott sitting on the dock looking hangdog, the bearer of bad tidings, which he sure as hell was." Ginger sipped the scalding-hot coffee that had sat too long while she slept an exhausted sleep. He held the tiny spear. "Isn't this something?"

Ginger jumped up. Immediately, he saw the joy in her face. "Oh, *beautiful!*" She held it in the palm of her hand. "It's so precise, so gorgeous. Where did you find it?"

"Near the dock. This is the best thing I've found since that shark's tooth on the sandbar." J.J. even showed her his drawings of the spear.

Ginger knew that since sharks regrow their teeth many times, they are the fossil most frequently found from the ancient

Eocene sea, though this far south, not many turned up. The pointed shark tooth sat on the mantel, almost as big as the palm of a hand. She picked it up, held it beside her jaw. "As old as it gets. Imagine him trolling that warm sea eons ago. Chomping on something finny. I find that incomprehensible, like black holes in space, and other galaxies."

"Incomprehensible that we can pick it up on a sandbar." Ginger is the only person who can travel with me, he thought, travel around an object, travel back and forth in time. "Gin, I think we should take a ride."

"Where? I know — to Charlotte Crowder. Let's call her."

Charlotte's neighborhood looked familiar, though they barely remembered going there. J.J. recalled a Thanksgiving, when the turkey was burned outside and raw inside. Ginger remembered the Crowder children's huge white dog.

When they got out of the car, Charlotte ran to them, hugging and exclaiming. She was breathless and immediately began telling them that her cat had been caught in a mulberry tree all morning while she'd been gone, and she came home and had to climb a ladder which slipped and sent her, one hand on the cat, sliding sideways. "I am so glad to see you. We have a lot to talk about — years to talk about." She put her hand to her throat, hoping they did not hear the catch in her voice. They had not come to see her cry. She led them into her sunroom piled with books and newspapers. The cat slept soundly on the flowered cushion of a wicker rocker. "That's Jasmine, the culprit." She brought in a tray with tea and cookies. "Ginger, when you were little, you used to drink only ice water with a spoon of cane syrup in it."

"I did? I don't remember that."

"And J.J., I still have a letter you wrote me when you were seven. You asked for two books for Christmas. You said, 'Please, may I have two this year?' I remember so many things." Again her eyes smarted as she bent over the tea glasses. Parents remember the ten thousand things a child says and does. Ginger and J.J. had no one to restore the fragments of their early days to them. "How proud your mother — and your father, I must say — would be to see you! You're both fabulously beautiful and I can still see your tiny faces — both so bright — in your faces right now. Some people lose their youngest faces . . ." She realized she was starting to chatter.

J.J. told her about seeing her name in the sheriff's report. "You were the only one who doubted the suicide. We read that you insisted that he investigate. Of course, we never knew that. What did you think at the time?"

"You *know* I never thought Wills would have done something like that in a million years, but I thought *someone* had stepped into the house, picked up the gun. Maybe a robber, a gypsy, some crazed goon or half-wit. Your mother, I knew then, never would have destroyed herself and, I imagine, a hunk of your lives."

"Understatement," J.J. said.

"Your mother, if you'd like to hear, was an extraordinary person. In all my life, I never met anyone like her. I feel I've been looking for her in my friends ever since and they all come up short."

"We would like to hear," Ginger said. "We found one of her notebooks and two sketch books yesterday and read them last night. We are just getting to know her again. It's so strange, how suicide cut her off from our memories." Ginger loved looking at Charlotte. Mother's age, this is how she would be. Welcoming us in a sunny room, telling us some anecdotes

425

about ourselves, pouring tea.

Charlotte told them about college days at GSCW, their passions for art nouveau, modern dance, clothes, and clay soul jugs. Catherine, they learned, had collected folk pottery. She told them about Catherine's toast-colored coat with a lynx collar, which made her face look wild and fresh. "Sophomore year," she told them, "Catherine was elected the Kappa Alpha Rose at Emory. She wore a sleek white evening dress and was serenaded by the entire fraternity dressed to kill in Confederate uniforms. Your daddy, a glamorous med student, was her date. She snowed him." The cat woke up and climbed onto Charlotte's lap. "Oh, and Catherine was a daddy's girl. That man doted on her, spoiled her, your grandmother thought." She wondered how she could convey what it was like to spend a simple hour in Catherine's company.

J.J. picked up the egg basket from the coffee table. He held it up for Ginger to see. "Look, this is real fine." Ginger leaned to him and together they looked intently as J.J. slowly turned the basket. Charlotte saw the look of familiar connection that passed between them. That rare, wordless bond that spoke more clearly than words. As she saw this, she felt less sad. They had lost so much of their mother, lost so much of their own childhoods. And Wills's downfall, what an H-bomb that must have been. But irrefutably Ginger and J.J. had each other. Who knows, the choice relationship of their lives. And maybe it would not have been so if their parents had been able to raise them. She wondered if they ever had realized that. Something taken, but something given.

Charlotte heard Mayhew come into the kitchen. He peered in the sunroom. "I'll be damned. I am so glad to see you children — of course you're not children." He embraced them and clapped his hands. "You're staying for dinner. I insist. I've got steaks to throw on the grill and Charlotte is a master of the baked potato." He disappeared into the pantry.

Charlotte heard herself launch into the awkward subject. "There was someone else — Austin Larkin, who went to Tech — mad for her. This may seem like a myth or a dream, but once he flew over the campus and scattered thousands of roses for Catherine. This was right after her engagement to Wills our sophomore year. I always wondered if Austin overwhelmed her, while Wills seemed more like someone to build a life around."

"Austin," Ginger faltered. "What a fabulous, fabulous gesture. I'd run away with anyone who scattered roses from an airplane for me." Marco, she thought, he's that tender, too. Ginger rubbed her lapis ring over her lips. A flash of insight hit her. Marco was *her* inheritance from her mother, maybe she now could let herself have a big love. She smiled at Charlotte.

How lovely she is, Charlotte thought. That silky hair and natural, sort of bony elegance. Ginger saw the admiration in Charlotte's eyes and felt expansive. "This Austin comes up in her notebook, which was written during the war. I wish you would read it and tell us what you think." She didn't speculate. She took the sketch books and notebook out of her bag, along with the film reel. "And this was in the box, too. Do you have a projector?"

"We do, and miles of film of the children. Let's look when it gets dark."

"We should call Lily."

"Sugar, you go up to my room and call her, and, J.J., if you would give Mayhew a hand, then I'll sit here and finish my tea and read."

From the first page of the sketch books, Charlotte was mesmerized by the prolific

428

drawings. She grasped with firsthand knowledge Catherine's hard, joyful work. By the time she started the notebook, she was so jittery she wanted to jump out of her skin from the shock of seeing her own name, reading the chronicle of that elusive time, plunging into Catherine's delicate, reserved emotional terrain, and more, imagining J.J. and Ginger discovering the notebook lying on top of all the years of silence.

Over dinner, Ginger, swamped with fatigue, leaned her elbows on the table. Mayhew's steak, doused with his own Ol' Hoss sauce, was delicious, and she didn't know how much she'd missed big baked potatoes piled with sour cream, butter, and chives. She would have to make them for Marco someday, she thought distractedly, if she ever could find sour cream in Italy. Tired, she ate slowly but with her usual relish. Charlotte seemed to forget about the plate in front of her as she described trips she and Catherine made up to Tech for dances, her plans for her garden, and the antics of her three grandchildren. Gently, she asked about Wills, not knowing whether the children had conceived of him as a possible murderer, an idea hardly to be avoided now.

J.J. said, "He's like a big, bad baby in a high chair, banging his cup. It's hard to explain. Who was he back then? What was he capable of? Maybe you'd know more than we do."

Charlotte nodded. "He never . . . He saved people. I remember many times when he got up from the table to rush out to someone passing a kidney stone or someone who'd fallen off a ladder. He ignored Big Jim's business — not many men would — in order to help people." She didn't say that in her experience she'd often found that someone's strongest characteristic has an equal and opposite component. She simply did not know how far Wills could be driven. Under the wrong circumstances, couldn't almost anyone turn murderous or cruel?

Mayhew set up the projector on the end of the table, and Charlotte pulled the draperies, closing out the night gathering on the garden. Ah, there was Austin as she remembered him, against the pink oleanders at Carrie's Island, where she and Mayhew had spent many weekends with their three children. The World's Fair footage passed, then the film abruptly shifted. When the yellow house appeared on her dining room wall, she recalled immediately the peeling paint on Austin's farmhouse. "Austin's porch," she said. Mayhew looked at her, frowning. She remembered that she had not had a chance to tell him about going to Stonefield. "I'll explain in a minute." She fell silent, they all did, when Catherine loomed on the wall, filling the space between the windows, her face incandescent in slashes of sunlight.

Charlotte brought in for dessert a plate of barely thawed lemon squares, and Mayhew put on a pot of coffee. "I went to Stonefield — only this morning, seems like a week ago." She described the house and Edwina, then her inspiration to stop at the post office. "Austin lives in California, has for umpteen years, the same town as Stanford."

"You know what they say." Mayhew pushed back his chair. "God tilted America at the Rockies and everything loose rolled west."

Ginger wondered if, twenty years from now, she would have the confidence in her instinct to pick up an action on someone's behalf the way Charlotte had this morning, when she acted on her understanding of a friend from way back in college.

J.J. was admiring Charlotte, too. No

logic, he thought. Plain blood knowledge.

Reading the notebook had confirmed everything Charlotte had not fully suspected. Catherine had met no mysterious stranger; she was seeing Austin during the war. But why? Charlotte knew she was devoted to Wills. Now this new, gaping question was opening before all their eyes. Mayhew and probably 99 percent of the people she knew would disagree, but Charlotte thought Austin as a father might be not so bad a discovery, considering the fate of Wills. If a family secret were brought into the light, which is surely a strong congenital abhorrence of all southerners, no matter how old or insignificant the secret, there might be an unexpected way forward.

Privately, in college she had longed for Austin herself, but since he already loved Catherine the possibility was totally unrealistic. She had hardly articulated her infatuation to herself. Senior year, she'd met Mayhew. They were instant friends, a friendship that strengthened on her part. On his, he'd been drawn to Charlotte with a migratory pull, the way sea turtles guide themselves back across the ocean toward their island of origin.

Charlotte opened her handbag and

found the address the postmistress had written on a forwarding slip. She handed it to J.J., insisting that they spend the night, but Ginger said they must get back to Lily. When Ginger called from upstairs earlier, Lily was having dinner with Eleanor. Then she let it slip that Tessie had spent last night at the House. Ginger and J.J., so caught up with their own emotions, hardly had considered Lily beyond her initial shock and injured hand, nor had they thought that she might be frightened to stay alone. "I feel so guilty," Ginger said as they got in the car. "She said she and Tessie sat up in their bathrobes last night watching *Wuthering Heights*. Is there something we can take her?"

"At this time of night? A fifth of Southern Comfort? Let's think about it tomorrow, Scarlett, my dear."

"J.J., the idea of Lily and Tessie drinking cocoa in the den and watching a movie. I never thought of them like that."

"Best of friends. They just don't know it."

July 12

In the night Ginger woke up. A fox barked in the distance, a high repetitive yap, answered by another fox. She lay awake, watching a cottony light begin to streak the windows. She heard J.J. moving around in his room. Vaguely, she heard something slide, then the shower running. Nothing on earth felt as comfortable as her bed in her room. The four pillows were right. She went from one to another for coolness. In the course of the night the two firm ones were flung to the floor, leaving the flat, down ones. She concentrated on Marco. If he were here, listening to the young foxes. If his leg weighed on her hips. If he woke up in the night and said *what are you dreaming now?* She fell asleep and when she woke again, full sun struck the mirror in her room and the house was quiet.

When Ginger trailed into the dining room, Lily was reading a magazine. The remains of a platter of scrambled eggs and bacon were still warm. Tessie brought in buttered toast. "Sugar, I was so worried. You two were away so long, and now J.J. has gone again."

"What? Where is he — the cabin?" Ginger reached for the jam.

Lily folded sections of the paper. "He left this note. I don't know where he is."

Top o' the morning, the note said. *I will be back in a couple of days.*

"That's it? I don't believe this."

"He probably went off fishing with Scott. You know he can only take so much."

"What about us?" Ginger kept staring at the note. Surely, surely not. She remembered that when Charlotte found Austin's address, J.J. had stuck it in his shirt pocket. She wanted to believe that J.J. had been hit too hard by the notebook and sketch books to run off downriver in his usual fashion now. But she found it difficult to believe otherwise, since he only left the county for occasional hunting and fishing forays, once with her former husband, Mitchell, to Nicaragua to hunt ducks, twice to a college friend's cabin in Colorado to hunt elk. Travel that involved only camouflage pants tucked into high boots. When she thought

438

of what *she* would have done if the notebook had raised the possibility that Austin was J.J.'s father, she knew that J.J. had gone to California. He would be almost to Atlanta by now if he left around five. He'd take the first plane smoking on the runway, fly to California, and what? As the idea began to seem feasible, Ginger was thrilled. He'd gone for her. "Lily, what if we take a little jaunt, too?"

"What a good idea. Where could we go?"

"We could go visit the Culpeppers at the island, but I'd really like to drive up to Athens and talk to Professor Schmitt about my graduate work. I need to go over all the requirements with him and see how much I have left — in case I decide to finish my degree. We can spend the night at the Inn on the Park, have a nice dinner." She wanted to make amends for deserting Lily during all the fracas. She was embarrassed to see how thrilled Lily was. "You can take your needlepoint to work on, and I want to show you Mother's sketch books that I found in the barn yesterday. It seems like a miracle." She did not mention the notebook. Lily had no need to know about Austin or any of that. For her own protection, Ginger thought. And for ours. If

Mother had a lover, we'd never hear the end of poor Wills in this lifetime or the next. Secrets are being revealed, she realized, but we keep folding others inside them. She sighed. There must be another way to live, but we don't know how.

Lily gathered her cup and plate. "Would you like more bacon, sugar?" She was thinking of the envelope someone had brought to the mailbox. Would she ever know who had found it at the cemetery? She thought it was not the criminal who had dug up the grave but someone she knew, someone who now knew something, not much, but knew that Catherine's hand had not held a confession. She did not want to discuss the contents with anyone, ever. And especially now that Catherine was no longer the weak suicide. The memory of her own act of arson burned her enough. When the graves were restored, she intended to take flowers to Catherine every week. Previously, she'd driven out to Magnolia with two vases on Saturdays, one for her mother and one for Big Jim. Nothing for Catherine, who had disgraced the Mason name. Lily had another idea, another way to make amends. She would give Holt Junior whatever money it took to send a local girl to college every year. He could name the scholarship after Catherine. But she would never tell about her burning of Catherine's private things. She did not want to hurt J.J. and Ginger with the knowledge of her crime against their mother. She could not stand it if they thought of her as someone who would do such a thing.

Rain began an hour out of town and pursued them, now sprinkling, now blinding the windshield, all the way to Athens. Ginger kept letting down the window for the black dirt scent, the waves of oak and pine spicing the steamy air, the scorched ozone smell of lightning, the dusty odor of wet fields and fertilizer. Lily looked through the sketch books without comment. Finally, Ginger asked, "What do you think? Didn't she have a gift?" Come on, Lily, she thought. Give her *something*, after all we've learned.

"Oh, I remember well. She was devoted to those books she kept." The rage that fueled the fire that burned the notebooks, obliterating Catherine from memory, had remained the strongest emotion Lily had felt in her life up until the news that her sister-in-law was not a suicide. All the years of vitriol and indignation she'd felt.

What a waste. All the poisonous remarks she'd made because she thought Catherine had destroyed her brother. "What we are capable of, we never can gauge," she said cryptically.

Ginger drove. *Capable,* she thought. What a nice, solid word. It must come from *capere.* To hold. If you're capable, you hold on to something. I want to think of myself as capable. I have to take charge. I was the screw-up who couldn't get downstairs for my wedding. The temp in San Francisco living in a studio I barely could stand up in, dating another screw-up who worked as a bicycle messenger after graduating from college. The mole in the basement apartment in New York, trudging to the insurance office like a drudge, calling in sick so many days that they fired me without paying my final check. All the bad attempts at romance and sex. See Jane run. Run, Jane, run. What floundering, what a colossal waste.

During the past two days, as their turn of fate sank in, Ginger had begun to have an inkling of herself as someone with a mother to admire. Catherine would have been like Charlotte, vital, connected, warm. She would have developed in fascinating directions. So what if she had a love

442

affair? She was passionate. Perhaps Wills had been like her husband, Mitchell, and Austin resembled Marco. Catherine had married at twenty, far too young.

Looking back a few years, Ginger could see how wrong she had been about herself at every step. When she went to college, she refused to study out of fear of failing, even though she'd scored well on the SATs and had made straight As effortlessly in high school. Going back to school after the divorce, she saw how easy the courses had been all along. Anytime she looked though photo albums, she was shocked to see that she had been thin and pretty. She often looked awkward — a hand in motion, her eyes closed, knees too close to the camera — but pretty, definitely, when she had not felt pretty. Other girls always seemed more put together, ready to take their chances with men. When Ginger heard, "You have the most beautiful eyes I've ever seen," or "You're the most interesting girl I've ever met," she assumed southern hyperbole. She'd hardly ever noticed that although she had money to buy clothes and have her hair done, she wore the same things over and over and just let her hair hang. Luck and chance, if it had been luck and chance, finally led her to that first classroom in

Athens, where Dr. Schmitt's lectures not only engaged her mind but seemed like codes for unlocking the lost secrets of the world. She loved her tiny Athens apartment with a waist-high fridge and a mattress platform on concrete blocks, a door on filing cabinets for a desk. She was in love with her textbooks and professors as she never had been in love with any man, until she went to Italy for the internship and met Marco. Propped in bed, surrounded by books, she ate saltines with mayonnaise, devouring at the same time the whole history of archaeology.

Athens, where she had lived in passive desperation with Mitchell, became a haven as soon as she was in school. She walked her landlady's dog across campus, feeling a charge from the mellow brick buildings.

As she drove into town now, she turned off on Ridge Street and pointed out to Lily the side entrance to the antebellum house where she'd lived. They had a bite in the Bide Awhile, then checked into the Inn. Dr. Schmitt agreed to meet her at his office midafternoon. Lily decided to rest while Ginger went to the university. Later she would walk to the needlepoint shop Ginger had pointed out down the street as they drove in. She'd spotted a handsome bargello pattern in the window, which would be magnificent on a wing chair.

Ginger had an hour before Dr. Schmitt would be in his office. She looped back around the university, turned down Cane Street, where she'd lived with Mitchell. Oh, glory, there he was. She stopped a hundred feet from the house and flipped down the sun visor. Mitchell was opening the door to a blue car. He looked exactly the same, except that his hair was longer and brushed back. Without a glance her way, he drove off. She exhaled, realizing that her breath had stopped while he flung his suit jacket on the backseat, closed the door, and got in the front. Ginger knew he was returning after lunch to his office downtown. Working on Saturday. How typical. At a distance, behind sunglasses and the visor, she followed him. On impulse, when he swung into his office parking lot, she followed and pulled up beside him. Still, he didn't look her way. She observed his eyes crinkle in the heat as he stepped out of the car. He reached down and pulled a weed from the sole of his shoe, his shoe polished every morning, she knew, his nails buffed, his crisp shirt unfolded from cardboard. And as he is outside, so he is inside, she knew. Clean and right. Ginger opened her door without knowing exactly why. "Mitchell, hey, Mitchell."

He looked at her blankly only for an instant, then bucked back his head in overreactive surprise. "Well, hey, Mason. Knock me over with a feather." She was the last person he expected to encounter on his way to take a Saturday deposition from a student who claimed a teacher had raped her. There Ginger was, smiling at him. Of course, he had heard from a dozen people about the exhumation and had wanted to call her and his old roommate, J.J. He had not yet summoned the courage, after not speaking to either of them in four years.

"I had to come up to see about my degree status. I decided to ride by our house. I saw you coming out."

"I've heard about your mother. My God, what in the devil do they think happened?"

"Let's get out of the sun."

Mitchell checked his watch. The deposition was scheduled in ten minutes. Let them wait. "Get in my car and I'll crank up the air. I have to go into a meeting in a minute. Maybe we could meet later?"

"Oh, I don't think so. Lily is with me." She got in the front seat. "I just wanted to say something. I'm not sure what, but something overdue. Maybe it's as simple as 'I'm sorry.' I am. I don't even know if you're married or what, or if you care to hear anything at all from me, but I've felt really terrible for you, for who I was when we were together. In hindsight — the one hundred percent clear vision of hindsight — I was a walking disaster. You didn't deserve that."

She looked to him like a child confessing a theft from her mother's handbag. "Guess what, Mason. I have figured out a lot of things over the past few years myself. I know I didn't reach out far enough for you. Sometimes I think you were unreachable, but other times I can see that you were right there, waiting for something. That something just was not me. At the time." He wondered about the circuitous journey from the news of the exhumation to this confessional in the parking lot. "Aren't you living in Italy?"

"I was. I am. But I had to come home because of all the craziness. Mitchell, you look so good. I hope everything is going well?"

"Yes, yes. I'm a partner in the firm. I have a girlfriend with a three-year-old boy. He's a pistol."

"You heard that Mother was not a suicide?"

"Yes. I can't imagine how all this must feel."

"Overall, good. For J.J., too." She told him about the sketch books and notebook, but nothing about Austin. "They probably can't find out after this long who shot her. They don't even seem able to find out who violated the grave."

He saw the other lawyer entering the office. "Speaking of violating, I've got to go inside for a bizarre case right now. Look . . ."

"This is not the last time. I'll call you next time I'm here. I'm glad we ran into each other."

"We didn't. You followed me, you crazy nut!" He kissed her on the cheek. She did not reel back. "How's your dad taking all this?" He figured Wills must be a suspect but didn't want to say so.

"He's oblivious mostly. Helpless. Still has his mean streak. He didn't always."

Mitchell remembered the chilling visits when they'd haul Wills out to the car for a Sunday ride, and he'd sit in the backseat lunging for the ashtray and burning the leather upholstery with his cigarette. Old wreck. No wonder Ginger dragged a ball and chain. J.J., too. After the divorce, Mitchell told no one, because he did not want to damage his law practice, but he'd consulted a psychiatrist in Atlanta — far enough away — for three months. He'd come to understand, looking out on Dr. Patton's walled garden with a moss-covered nymph trickling water from a basket, that because of the suicide, Ginger might not have been able to love him. She feared the surrender of a part of herself to someone. Without her knowing it, marriage reenacted a possibility of self-obliteration, her greatest fear. She would *have* to escape an intense relationship. "Witness," Dr. Patton had pointed out, "the wedding day." Sex was crucible and fire for that fear. Dr. Patton had led him by the hand from bitterness and a crushed heart, and from his jural black and white thinking, to a place where he could look at Ginger and himself and sympathize with both. He had reached around the crumbled marriage, back to the Masons as he knew them in college, when he'd gone to the cabin with J.J. and they'd swum in the river, hunted wild hogs, and played poker all night. Then J.J. asked his little sister down from college in Virginia to be his date. She wore a champagne net dress with sequins around the hem. Her hair formed a short, red-gold halo. By the end of the evening, he'd asked if he could go up to Virginia to see her. The next day he took her three of his favorite albums and walked across campus with her under the yellow sycamore trees, their feet scuffing through wet leaves.

Mitchell not only was happy to have retrieved their earlier selves, he then was able to resume his life.

His mother, however, never got beyond her fierce dislike of Ginger and berated her still whenever she was reminded of her existence. "Unnatural," she called her. "Scattered. And she cut her fingernails with clippers. I've never known a woman to cut her nails with clippers." Any little memory spurred her. "Couldn't boil water." "What a brat. She wanted to be the bride at the wedding and the corpse at the funeral at the same time." Mitchell didn't really mind the criticism. He had been hurt, and even if he'd managed forgiveness, he thought his side deserved to get in a few licks. He watched her drive away.

Ginger left Mitchell with a sense of happiness coursing through her. She'd expected never to see him again after that

January afternoon in the courthouse. He'd sat in a raincoat with his arms crossed, never looking her way.

Now she'd simply appeared, spoken, he'd kissed her, welcomed her, obviously had forgiven her, even without her apology. She'd felt like a hit-and-run driver. But clearly he was on down the road, as she was.

The thousand images of him that ran through her mind did not now have to be mentioned. She held on to one for a moment — Mitchell trying to stem the gush from a broken toilet pipe when they'd come in late and found a flood in the hall. The mighty push of the water he tried to plug with one hand, while fumbling for the shutoff valve with the other, his bright pink sweater drenched, his feet skidding, and then as he managed to turn the valve, he plopped down in a pool of water. She froze in the hall in the instant before he turned to her and laughed. She laughed, too, and could hear their laughter still.

Dr. Schmitt rose from his chair and embraced Ginger. "Ah, Pupil Number One!" He, too, had read the news. Had everyone in the state of Georgia heard? He pushed back from his desk and listened to her story.

451

"And at the end of this saga, I've decided, I *think* I've decided, that I do want to finish my Ph.D. Coming back to school was the best move I made in my very long series of false starts. And the work in Italy — I could stay there forever."

"Yes, I've heard things are going brilliantly." He hoped she bloody well had the sense to continue. He totted up her course work. They reviewed the possibilities for independent study and looked at the catalogue listings from the University of Perugia, where she could take some on-site courses and transfer the credit. "Looks like two more quarters here will do it. The rest can be done from Italy."

"Not bad. I'll be Dr. Mason! If I finish — ah, my father!" She'd never thought of taking over his title. "My father was a doctor in Swan before his stroke." Her plans were surging forward. She'd not known she could transfer units from Perugia. I'll go back to Italy for August, she calculated, then Athens for the fall. Marco can come here for a month at Christmas, then I'll stay for winter quarter. Then I'm hatched, sprung, born again, baptized in the river.

She wanted to give Dr. Schmitt something but had forgotten to buy a nice bottle

452

of wine or a bunch of flowers. She opened her handbag and felt the bottom until her fingers touched cool flint. She held out her favorite arrowhead, found when she was nine, a medium-sized ocher beauty chipped by a master. "Here's something from Swan."

Lily was waiting in the lobby with a Dubonnet. She'd met another lady in the needlepoint shop. They'd ended up having a pot of tea together. She was elated and opened her shopping bag to show Ginger the natural yarns in blue, pale orange, and caramel wool. Ginger joined her with a Dubonnet, a drink she found too sweet but she wanted to second Lily's choice. Lily looked transformed from the fright she'd been when Ginger arrived from Italy. She leaned back in the flowered armchair, relaxed. Her shoes looked rather stylish.

Lily saw her glance and laughed. "I bought shoes." She held out her feet for Ginger's approval.

"Very nice." There is something infrangible about Lily, Ginger thought. She manages to *right* herself. Maybe it's a talent to rearrange reality so that the ugly is isolated like an infection, while the good red cells move on it. She's unlike Daddy, who went belly-up. No matter what devastates us, in a few hours she has loaves of banana bread cooling on the rack. I'll invite her to Athens for a weekend. I'll insist that she come visit me in Italy.

Ginger found herself telling Lily about seeing Mitchell, which led them to a second Dubonnet and a reminiscence of the wedding. This time they could joke a little. "Tessie turned two shades darker," Lily said. Then she said, into her drink, "I've always regretted that I said you were as bad as your mother that day. You know, sugar," she added lightly, "I was a little jealous of your mother."

But Ginger was still talking about her aborted wedding. She remembered the back of Mitchell's mother as she bustled to the car. She looked as though she might burst. "Old biddy. How she brought forth someone as nice as Mitchell is a mystery."

As far as Lily knew, J.J. was rounding the bend of some river, casting a line at this moment, passing Scott a beer. Ginger wished she could call him tonight but she had no idea where he was. He *could* be on the river. Her father, on a mercy mission during the war, had once parachuted behind enemy lines into Germany. If J.J. did go to California, he was on a dangerous mission, too.

She took Lily to her favorite restaurant, the Cue-T, a barbecue shack on the edge of town. They both ordered the chipped pork doused in extra hot sauce, fried sweet potatoes, and coleslaw. Pecan pie for dessert. Ginger ate like a famine victim.

With the time difference, J.J. had lost only two hours when he landed. The sun was still high overhead, but so obscured by fog that it looked like the moon. He stepped out into what could not quite be called rain.

Cold, don't they know it's July? He studied a map at the rental car desk. Palo Alto was straight south, San Francisco straight north. In less than an hour he'd checked in at the first place he saw, a small, functional hotel in downtown Palo Alto. He looked up Whitman Street on the map and saw that it was only one street over. To unkink and decide what to do, he walked. Here the air felt balmy, the way California should. How long since he'd been in a town outside south Georgia? He'd driven up to Athens to see Ginger during her divorce. He went to the dentist in Atlanta last year to have an impacted wisdom tooth pulled, then had driven back to the cabin still numb.

He liked the streets he crossed, an old neighborhood of close-together houses with hummingbirds buzzing the fuchsias. He stopped in a place filled with the warm roasted aroma of coffee beans and sat down to have a cup. He wanted to stay there a few minutes and watch the street scene. A revival cinema that looked like a wedding cake was playing *Gone With the Wind*. If they knew the half of it, he thought. Students, professorial types, bicyclists, women in tight tops with no bras, long Indian-print skirts. The libbers, he supposed. Sexy as hell. He avoided women who were waiting to relinquish their souls to a husband. No one said hey, and hardly anyone glanced at him, though out of habit he looked at each person he passed. The custom of anonymity was new to him and he liked it. In Swan, he knew everyone and what they were thinking before they even knew it, as they did with him. He walked across the street to a stationery store and bought a new notebook and a pen. Later, he would write everything so he'd remember to tell Ginger. Maybe I should take trips to New Orleans, Richmond, Charleston, he mused. Drop in and observe and go. The places that came to mind were all southern. London, he thought. Someone had taken Indians there once and displayed them in a cage. He'd probably feel like that in a foreign country. A dancing bear. What must it have been like for Ginger, he wondered, to land in Italy and start up living a life? Start collecting the things that allow you to exist there. He imagined Ginger looking up the word *towel* in the Italian dictionary. He'd bought a notebook and pen. Sheets, frying pan, a life begins. Who are you when you know no one? Palo Alto seemed foreign enough to him. Men with shaved heads and yellow robes shaking tambourines and dancing on the corner, Indian, Chinese, Japanese restaurants, health food stores, whose vile aromas gusted out onto the sidewalk as he passed. Who was Austin Larkin here? So far from Stonefield. He doubled back to Whitman Street. 1518 would be ten blocks down. He decided to walk by Austin's house. He quickly entered a different neighborhood of Spanish-style houses mixed with a few barny Victorians and boxy houses which looked like Mondrian paintings. He walked past streets named for writers — Cowper, Melville, Byron, Hawthorne. The quaint names seemed soothing here on the last edge of the country.

At a corner house, he stopped at a row of cherry trees where jays dove for the last fruit. The perfume of star jasmine along the garden wall fused with sprawling pink trumpet vine and the raucous cries of the birds. He stood and let the sensations gather. The color of the shuttered house reminded him of the light that rocks out of a cantaloupe when you split it open. What if he lived there instead of Swan? Stepped out to clip the ferns that hung along an upstairs balcony. Far inside the house, he could see a child in the kitchen. *Their lives in a place I don't know.* Then the moment broke. He walked on. Some houses seemed to be mostly garage. This squashed together, you could hear your neighbor fart, he thought. At 1518 he stopped. A gray house, contemporary, blank across the front, with a peaked roof. 15 and 18 equals 33, his age, a calculation Ginger would make. Lemons, and what he later found out to be loquats, grew up over the windows. The two-car garage facing the street dominated the house. He stared, thinking that he had no context for this sort of house. He felt suddenly large and strange, a cardboard giant standing on the sidewalk outside the house of a man his mother had lusted for dozens of years ago. How many choices of theirs brought me here? he wondered. Austin. Someone Mother loved, though not enough to leave Dad. So is he a candidate for murder? Not likely, that many years after a short affair ended. Maybe Dad finally heard about the affair. Charlotte said Austin had moved to California during the war.

J.J. wanted a face-to-face look at Austin. He wanted a gut reaction. He wanted a no or yes to tell Ginger. That's why he was here. No time like the present, he told himself.

He stood at the front door only a moment, then lifted the knocker. Austin must be in his mid-fifties. Not the lover boy he was. J.J. braced for a puffy man with turkey-gobble neck and glasses. A young woman slipping on a shirt over her bathing suit answered the door. She was small, with dark straight hair cut in a wedge so that when she moved her head, her hair seemed to follow a second later. She buttoned one button, looking at him with raised eyebrows. He took in her thin wrists and pretty legs, her aura of self-containment. "Hi. Did you come about the pool sweep?" she asked.

"No. My name's Mason, J. J. Mason. I'd

like to speak to Austin Larkin. Is this his house?"

"Yes. Daddy's not here."

"Do you expect him soon? I should explain. I'm J. J. Mason from Swan, Georgia, not far from Stonefield, where your daddy grew up. He knew my mother in college, Catherine Mason."

"Mason," she said. "I don't remember Daddy mentioning Mason, but I do remember him mentioning Swan. Who could forget that name?"

"Well, my mother was Phillips then."

"Oh! Catherine Phillips! Oh, yes. His college love. He thought she dangled the stars from the heavens. He's talked about her."

She put out her hand. "I'm Georgia Larkin. Named for you-know-where by a loyal son of the state. Come in." Her smile went all the way back to her molars. She had perfect, movie-star teeth. Good dentist, he thought.

The front door actually opened into a courtyard. The anonymous exterior had nothing to do with the lush and blooming tropical yard with a circular pool. The U-shaped house was entirely glass on its private side. From outside, he caught a glimpse of a book-lined dining room, a bedroom with bright yellow walls. She had been lying on a mat. "It's getting late. Would you like a glass of wine?"

"Thank you, but you don't need to go to any trouble for me." She went to the kitchen and came back with a tray holding a chilled white wine, glasses, and a bunch of grapes. She'd thrown on a loose white dress down to her ankles.

"I'm afraid the grapes are hot. They sat in the backseat of my car." She poured the wine and dropped one plump grape into his glass. "Daddy won't be back until late tomorrow afternoon. Will you still be here then?"

J.J. nodded. "I have some things to do here." Just let me sit here and look at you, darlin', he thought. Georgia. Neat ankles and small feet. But her face, was she beautiful? She looked — intrinsically herself. What would she do if he reached over and touched the side of his forefinger to her thick eyelashes? So this was what they meant by California girls. She's just God damned something, he thought. "Are you an only child?" Feature by feature she didn't look anything like Ginger. But one thing about her reminded him of Ginger — how still she was.

"Yes, does it show? My mother died

when I was a senior in college. Daddy hasn't remarried but maybe he's about to. He's traveling with a woman he's been seeing for a while. She sells real estate here in Palo Alto. A grown-up, thank God. My friends' fathers are always marrying people our age."

"Well, I'm looking forward to meeting your father. Sorry about your mother. I lost mine, too." He pinched his chin. "If I could call him tomorrow . . . what would be a good time?"

"I'd say around four. What are you doing tonight? Would you like to see the sights of Palo Alto? Actually, I have to go do a little work at the store around nine but you could come if you'd like to."

"Sure. My pleasure. Where do you work?"

"I don't work there. I help sometimes. Daddy owns three bookstores in the Bay Area. Stonefield's — you recognize the name? There's an event tonight and I have to introduce the readers. Actually, right now I teach riding and train horses. I taught fourth grade for two years and I'm taking a year off to figure out what I want to do."

"May I take you to dinner first?" In all his brooding on the flight out, J.J. never

463

suspected that the trip could take such an upturn. "You're my introduction to California so I want it to make the best impression."

They met at St. Michael's Alley. He'd changed into his other white shirt and thought he might look wrong in jeans, but instead he seemed overdressed among the men in dashikis, Greek striped shirts, and T-shirts. A few men wore khaki suits and rep ties. Many women had a lot of hair and wore gauzy cotton dresses and tribal beads, though some were well dressed like the women in Swan.

Georgia was already at a table. Half turned around, she was talking to a group who had books on the table and were passing around pieces of paper. She held out her hand to him. First touch. "Hi, hi. These are all the people who're reading their work at the store tonight." She pointed. Ron, Suze, Abby, Dickie, Cady, Herbert. They waved, smiled. "This is J. J. Mason. He's out here from Swan, Georgia, down near where my dad's from."

J.J. nodded at everyone. When he sat down, he asked, "What are they, all writers?" The waiter introduced himself, to J.J.'s amusement, and took their order for wine and beef bourguignon.

"Yes, a big group of friends. There are more, you'll see. They're all older than I am. Most of them went through the writing program here or the one in the city. They're in their thirties and get together all the time to criticize each other's work and drink wine. They have a grand time."

"Any good?"

"Yes. Well, mixed. Some have published books. Herbert, I think he's the best writer in Palo Alto, never sends out anything. Kind of hangs on the edges."

"Why not? If he's that good . . ." The waiter, Kipper, brought a small loaf of warm bread and their wine.

"I don't know. Maybe he's afraid. What do you do down in Swan?"

J.J. took a sip of wine and shook his head. "Not any one thing. You could say I'm kind of a property manager. But here's to you." He raised his glass. "Thanks for coming out with me. I didn't expect to be so lucky."

"Too bad Daddy is down in L.A. What brings you out here?"

J.J. looked at her. He wasn't ready to say. But he also did not want to dissemble with her. By this point in an evening, he realized, he was used to thinking of how he could slip free. He was puzzled. Friendly as she had been, he hadn't detected a trace of flirting. She flashed the same smile on the table of writers and on the waiter and on the slice of bread she buttered and handed to him. "I love their bread. They bake every afternoon." J.J. watched her chew. Usually, he didn't like to see people eat. She was neat as a cat. Probably doted on by her daddy all her life. A little princess. And usually, he didn't go for brown eyes. He thought of Mindy, Julianne, how any little thing set him off. He felt himself veering toward his critical mode, but nothing occurred to him.

He risked one of his moves. "Your eyes — I'm trying to think what color they are. Brown, but I see flecks of gold. Like looking at the bottom of the river."

"That's so nice. My dad says they're the color of good sherry. Yours are the color of the wet agates we pick up over at Pebble Beach. They're so beautiful when they're wet but fade and powder over with salt when they dry."

"Back to your question. The answer is complicated. I've knocked on your door out of nowhere. My family has a complicated history. I thought your father might shed some light on a situation that has just come up at home." Immediately, the exhumation scene rose in his mind. He went silent.

The waiter brought their salads and ceremoniously ground pepper from on high. Georgia regarded J.J. with curiosity. She liked him. His face, chiseled, seemed tight but softened when he talked. He looked, she decided, the way marble can look, both hard and caressable. He was not saying something, and, how odd, that something had to do with her father.

J.J. poured more wine. "Let's talk about you right now. The past certainly can wait another day." In the background the writers laughed and read lines aloud. He heard several toasts. The small jammed restaurant became a swirling background for the face of Georgia, right across from him, a flush to her cheeks, her bare shoulders in shadow. I'd like to drink pure water from those delicate cups in her collarbones, he thought.

"Quick subject," she said, laughing. "I went to Stanford, moved home when Mother died. I didn't want to leave my father alone. I majored in poly sci — it was the times more than an intrinsic interest. Mostly, I majored in horses. I've always kept a horse at the Stanford Barn, ever since I was eight. I liked teaching but I'd rather be outside. I'm wild about my work at the stables, although everyone says it's a girl's passion — I shouldn't consider horses a life's occupation. But I don't want to manage one of the bookstores. I love to read but selling doesn't thrill me. So I'm searching around, I guess, but not with any urgency. I may go to vet school. I want to be sure. I'm having a good time."

He kept losing his train of thought. She roadblocked his usual habits. Because he found nothing to criticize, he turned on himself. This glimpse of another way of life, even a brief glimpse, turned the telescoping lens on his solitary existence and his own knock-headedness. I'm stalking the woods wooing perch when she's living her life three thousand miles away, he thought. If I don't get out, I'm going to turn into one of those grizzled old guys hanging around the bait shop. Not that he wanted to sit at a table and read drafts aloud while eating.

"How do you like the bourguignon? It's rich, isn't it? Tell me about you."

"I'm older than you. Jesus's age, thirty-three. They call it the age of perfection." He raised his glass in a mock toast. "I have a sister two years younger. Ginger. Let's see. I graduated, what, ten years back from Emory. I was *supposed* to study medicine like my dad but took to such useful things as literature and philosophy. Never married. Never came close." College seemed a lifetime ago. He could be describing someone else. "We've got a place out on a river, a place" — he paused — "that's special. I spend a lot of time there."

"What do you like to do?"

He started to talk about fishing and quail hunting but said, "I do some writing myself. And drawing." He motioned with his head toward the table behind her, where a fat woman with stand-up black hair stabbed the air with her fork and kept repeating, "Lousy metaphor, lousy." J.J. thought, with her heavily outlined eyes, that she looked arboreal.

Georgia had imagined him in an office going over leases, although he didn't look the part. "That's a long way from property management. Isn't that what you said you do? The South has so many great writers. Why is that?"

They talked. All through dinner, dessert, coffee. Suddenly, Georgia saw that the writers had gone. She and J.J. were going to be late, not that anyone cared. They walked the couple of blocks to Stonefield's.

In the back room, huge foam cushions were scattered around the floor. The store manager already had introduced the reading, and the hefty woman was in full swing. They sank into the cushions against the back wall. J.J., who'd never been to a reading, quickly became entranced. Georgia, who'd been taken to readings all her life, had a chance to sit back and think about J.J. She glanced at his profile, his white shirt with rolled-up sleeves, wondering what he thought of her. He had certainly looked her over. She'd never felt so exposed by a simple dinner in a restaurant. His eyes were never still. They roamed over her, hungry, though now he looked remote. Just then he threw his arm along the back of her cushion, winked at her. Winked. Did people still do that? Herbert started his reading and she tried to listen. Something about J.J. seemed from another zone entirely. Unwillingly, unwittingly, a thought kept trying to break through as she struggled to sort out her reactions to him. What she felt was not even attraction, though he was gorgeous — more that her instinct was aroused. She stared at their parallel legs, almost touching, their feet. She jerked.

He smiled at her.

She smiled back and their eyes locked. "Are you liking the reading?"

"He's good. He's got it. I think he knows it." He gave the thumbs-up gesture.

The writers were going to Abby's house to continue their argument about the use of metaphor. Ron was proclaiming it dead, Abby said he was full of shit from his year in France and metaphor was how language grew. J.J. was attracted by the heat and light of active, living writers but declined. "I'm on eastern time. It's three a.m. Thanks, though."

"In California it's always earlier and later at the same time," Herbert added.

Georgia and J.J. walked back to J.J.'s car and drove down an alley of tall palms, parking at the end. They crossed the Stanford quad, where gold tesserae in the mosaicked front of the chapel picked up the sheen of moonlight. J.J. and Georgia stood in the deserted quad. His mouth was close to her hair. He breathed in her scents. "You smell like vanilla ice cream."

"You're wild! You southern gentleman."

His eyes followed the dark rhythm of the arches enclosing the courtyard. "This seems like a place Don Quixote might ride into on his horse." They sat on the edge of a fountain. "Distinctly un-American." The impact of the California landscape, as much as he'd seen so far, hit him hard. "The hills on the way from the airport were gold. Summer in the South is green, green, a thousand shades of green. Not a criticism." The palms rattled overhead in a slight breeze. "I've been in one place so long. This is surreal."

"Someone's vision. The founders lost their son, so they built a memorial. I love it here. I love all the palms. I was born at the campus medical center, so it has to be home for me. When I go South with Dad, that lush vegetation feels exotic — vines could crawl in the window overnight. When I was little, I thought the farm was Jack and the Beanstalk land." She smiled. Their shoulders touched. "I like being here with you," she said simply. This was her navel of the world, this stone folly in a dry land. She loved it that J.J. thought of Don Quixote here. He'd touched her own sense of this place. The indistinct thought that had been swimming through her all evening turned into words. *I recognize him,* she thought. Six hours with him — preposterous. As if he heard her thought, he turned to her, inclining his head to hers.

They drove back to her car under leafy

branches arching over Hamilton, University, Whitman, the leaves already turning rusty, the white globe streetlights like a string of moons under the sycamores. They both were quiet. The empty streets seemed like streams, easily taking him toward a river. "Call me tomorrow if you'd like to see the stables. Or just come." She wrote her number on a gas receipt and jumped out. He got out on his side, starting to say something, but she waved and opened her car door in a way that did not allow him to speak.

A grand magnolia loomed over the lot where he parked. The creamy blossoms took him directly back to Big Jim's. How can they thrive in this dry air? he wondered. Betray the humid South so easily? He raised his arms and flexed. His body was carrying a tension. He wanted to lie down in his plain hotel room and go over each minute since he landed. Not a tension, he thought. The good feeling of a 110-volt current charging all the synapses. He resisted the thought that he'd like to live here, but he felt the vitality and health of the place. Ginger would like it here. Lily would find it appalling, he imagined. He looked down the street at a row of shingle cottages with lamplit, lambent windows and shadows of giant ferns. I could rent one with a squat little garden and grow two tomatoes in wine vats. I could sit outside without mosquitoes dive-bombing me. Maybe here I'd write a long, layered novel about the South. Big Jim. Top of the heap. Wills. Wonder boy, the slow explosion into bits. Hell, write it there, he thought. Dip the pen into the pools of my sweat forming on the ground. He remembered a line from one of the poets. *Change me, change me into something I am.*

July 13

Rainey left Johnny at the breakfast table reading the Sunday Atlanta paper. She did not now like to linger at the table after any meal. The last piece of toast, the three slices of ham, no. The scale showed that she'd lost another half pound, though if she drank a glass of water, the needle would flap back to its stuck position. She needed time alone to write a column she had in mind. In fact, she had the inspiration for a weekly column that would get her away from the society page entirely. What we lack, she had told Johnny, is a local perspective on the national news. She did not say *feminine* perspective because she did not want to hear him groan. If she didn't mention that, she spared them both: he would not have to take a wearisome, predictable stand, and she would not have to invent tangential reasons for what she wanted.

Increasingly, the news of women changing their lives was sifting down South as far as Swan. She, for one, welcomed every missive from marching women, women starting magazines, women taking over the helm. She thought, however, that her own voice was outside politics. She would write a purely personal weekly opinion that happened to be that of a woman.

She'd left on a fan at her desk. Her papers lifted and fell, lifted and fell — the write-up of a wedding and a recipe for sour cream muffins mixed in with her investigation of hospital conditions. Last week a cockroach was served along with the salad on a patient's dinner tray. She swung her chair around to the typewriter. What should she call the column? "Rainey at Large." No, that reminded her of her weight. She thought of a newspaper colleague in Tipton's column "Pats and Pans." Horrid. The phone rang. *"Swan Flyover,"* she answered.

"Rainey, hey, this is Angela Kinsella in Simmonsville. We met last year at the conference."

"Yes, Angela, how nice to hear your voice."

"You, too. Y'all doing okay down there? I heard about what happened in Swan, and Peter Drew over in Knightsborough told me you'd called him about it, wanting to know if anything like that had happened there."

"Yes, I did. The GBI and the sheriff here haven't found a lead." Rainey picked up her pen.

"It's nothing as bad as what happened to that lady in Swan who was dumped out in the rain and all, but I wanted to let you know that last night here in Simmonsville, somebody broke down some crosses and turned over an urn on a grave. The worst was they broke the door into one of the mausoleum-type graves — you know the kind aboveground in the shape of a cedar chest?"

"Yes, I know those. Do they know who did it?"

"No, maybe some hoodlum, some fruit-cake, or Saturday night drunk who'd read about Swan. But maybe the same person that came to Swan. This sort of thing doesn't happen every day."

"Thank you, Angela." This was small potatoes, but on the chance there might be a connection, she said, "Let me get all these details straight . . ."

Ralph had just stopped by the office after church. The bells still pealed two

479

blocks away, a joyful noise over the whole town. Father Tyson had asked the congregation to pray for Catherine Mason and for the entire community that had to experience the sorrow of such a crime in their midst. Amen, brother, Ralph had thought. He picked up Rainey's call. "Good. This is good news. It's *something* rather than nothing." He dialed Gray at home.

"Well, sounds like a fetishist on our hands. We'll look into it. Don't worry about this on Sunday; sooner or later we'll find him."

Ralph would look up *fetishist*. He thought it had to do with someone who liked feet too much. He poured coffee, forgetting it was yesterday's cold leftover. He decided to walk over to the Three Sisters. Like most of Swan, on Sunday morning, he thought nothing better on earth existed than hot doughnuts. Let the GBI track this loony tune roaming the state of Georgia.

Ralph remembered the Goat Man, who used to pass through Swan when he was a child. Maybe the grave-visitor was someone like that. The Goat Man walked alongside a wooden cart, tinkling with hanging pots and scissors. His herd of goats walked companionably along with him, each with a bell. Sometimes he stopped outside town in a field, and a few people ventured near to have their knives sharpened. Ralph went once with his grandfather, who was suspicious of the Goat Man. He could still see his bony frame, Father Time beard, and rheumy, faraway eyes. The Goat Man was clearly a character. This swine-face grave-opener was probably some oily puke holding down a job, paying taxes, passing for normal.

As Ralph crossed the street, he saw a woman waving to him. She stepped out of her car and leaned against the door. He recognized her as that woman from the mill village who sewed baby clothes. He saw her pull in her lips and cross her arms over her chest. She looked cold, which was impossible in the heat. But maybe she was sick. "Is something wrong, ma'am? Are you all right?" He recrossed the street.

"Could I talk to you? It's important. Your granddaddy helped me a couple of times. My name's Aileen Boyd."

"I'm glad to hear he was of help. Now, what can I do for you?" She was right pretty in a hardscrabble way.

"It's real private."

"Let's go to the office." He took her elbow and guided her upstairs and into the small interview room in the back. Aileen

481

sank back into the sofa cushion, resting her head, her eyes closed. "Now, what's wrong?" Ralph asked.

"Everything. It's about Catherine Mason," Aileen said. "Where do I begin? I guess with Sonny. Sonny was my husband."

Ever since Ralph read his granddaddy's report on the suicide, the doodle on the folder kept snagging in his mind. *S*, his grandfather had written, and *B* or *D*. Sonny Boyd. He'd suspected him. Bingo, bingo.

Ginger and Lily left Athens around ten, driving back to Swan through Matteson Junction, where Lily's Agnes Scott roommate came from, and where Lily once met a man at a tea dance who seemed to like her, though she never heard from him again. They looked at the street lined with old houses Sherman did not burn on his march to the sea. Then Ginger sped through the countryside snarled with kudzu to Milledgeville, where her mother and Charlotte met, where Austin scattered the roses over the campus. She kept trying to shake the dream that woke her up in the night. She had been standing on her mother's shoulders in the river, her face barely breaking the surface of the water, her breathing possible only because her submerged mother held her up. She sat up drenched, about to scream.

When they got out of the car for lunch,

the smothering humidity from yesterday's rain enveloped them. Downtown Milledgeville felt like a just-drained swamp. One minute outside town, they entered deep country again — roosters running underneath board houses perched on stones, Repent signs, telephone poles strung with gourds for birdhouses, geraniums planted in tires, wash flapping on the line, whitetail deer bounding across the road. By late afternoon they entered Swan, gleaming after another rain and bathed in blond light. As they approached the House, they saw Tessie on the porch watering the ferns and a man in the doorway. "Oh, J.J.'s back," Lily said.

Ginger squinted in the glare on the bug-glazed windshield. "That's Marco!" she shouted. "That's not J.J. — that's Marco!" She slid to a stop and leapt out.

"Oh, the Italian," Lily said aloud. "So the Italian has come to Swan." Able was I ere I saw Elba, she remembered, and Caesar crossing the Rubicon. She saw his bear hug, Ginger jumping up and down, his smile over her shoulder.

He waved to Lily as she walked up the steps. "I am made very happy," he said to her. The way he said *very* made it sound almost like *furry*. He kissed her hand like a count in an old movie.

Lily, too, felt a fine shiver of happiness. "We're so happy to have you in Swan. So you've met Tessie and CoCo?"

Palo Alto on Sunday morning reverted to the sleepy town it had always been before the invasion of hip. Bicyclists picked up the paper at Dan's, the owner of the yogurt shop turned up the jazz station and swept the sidewalk.

J.J. went back to the coffee shop he'd stopped in yesterday. He sat at a window, staring into the blank pages of the notebook he'd bought. He intended to see Austin, then catch the 9:00 p.m. flight back to Atlanta. He'd arrive at dawn, be in Swan by ten. Plenty of time to deal with the reburial.

The waitress beamed at him, definitely checking him out, as she brought his coffee and croissant. As she bent down, she smelled like fruit. He lifted his face to her entirely, smiling and looking into her eyes. Full benefit. "You're not a regular here," she said. "I'm Ariel. This is my aunt's

place. I work here to support my habits."
Crystal prisms hung from her ears. She
wore a patchwork Indian skirt and
Birkenstocks.

"What habits?"

"Oh, books and shoes. Nothing lethal.
Want anything else?"

He resisted a come-on remark. He liked
the blunt openness of California women.
"Thanks, I'm just fine." Although he
wanted to call Georgia, he held back. She
probably does not want to be awakened by
some cracker she went out of her way to
entertain, he thought. No, I know she liked
me. He was shaken by the kind of ease he
felt with her. Same comfort he felt with
Ginger without the tiger instinct for protection. Georgia seemed able to take care
of herself. Praise the Lord. He strolled
around town. In a shop window he saw
women's fall clothes. On impulse he went
in. The long green turtleneck would look
good on Ginger. The price tag stopped
him for a moment, but he bought it
anyway. He held up a pale yellow cardigan,
cashmere, and bought that for Lily. He saw
a pink terry robe and had that wrapped for
Tessie. He had suffered the agony of
buying Christmas and birthday presents
but never spontaneously had bought a gift

before. He looked at the displays, wondering what Georgia would like. He picked up a scarf, handwoven in plum and blackberry from something soft. He bought it.

Stonefield's was opening across the street. No blue laws here. At home, his books had to be ordered. He didn't mind the wait, really. When the box arrived, opening it was one of his exquisite pleasures. He left his bulky gifts at the desk and browsed, picking up more than a dozen books that appealed to him. Even the bookstore had a coffee bar. He took his stack to a table and sat with another coffee for an hour. He was happy to find the letters of Van Gogh. The powerful colors and images in his paintings talked back to J.J.'s big argument with the act of writing, which he'd tried to explain to Ginger the night she got home. Between what he wanted to write and what appeared on paper when he did, an abyss opened. Van Gogh's yellow chair, blazing out as itself, radiant with its own ability to be *chair*, did not acknowledge that gap. Maybe the letters would tell J.J. why. He leafed through, briefly wishing he were at the cabin, at his own desk, the river outside the window. He glanced up. A couple, students he guessed, kissed on the sidewalk, oblivious to passing people who smiled and stared. They were in their own floating world. He returned to Van Gogh. *Now we see the Dutch paint things just as they are, apparently without reasoning,* he read. He thought of his mother's sketch books. He glanced down the page: *we can paint an atom of the chaos, a horse, a portrait, your grandmother, apples, a landscape.* What he liked was *we can.*

He picked out a few novels for Ginger and a book on English gardens for Lily. With the gifts he'd bought, he was shocked that he'd spent almost a thousand dollars. He almost never bought anything, but when he did, he thought of Big Jim, all his wheeling, dealing, gusto, his whoring, bombasting. Thanks for the Van Gogh, Big Jim.

He asked directions to the stables and drove through the campus, past the medical center where Georgia must have first been shown to the light. Down a lane where girls in hard hats rode thoroughbreds, he came to a great red barn. He walked toward a covered ring, smelling the good scents of leather, horse manure, alfalfa, and sawdust.

He spotted Georgia up on a large gelding, bearing down on a substantial jump. She *must* have done this before, he thought, but still he frowned and held his breath as she approached, leaning stiffly forward, and the horse seemed to elongate as he left the ground and arced over the pole. "Damn," he said aloud. He was able to watch her without her knowing. She continued on course, her horse meeting each jump but not, J.J. thought, with ease. Each approach seemed tense. She saw him and trotted over.

"This is Winkie. Calm down, Wink." Her hair in back dripped with sweat under the velvet hat. In her sleeveless riding shirt buttoned up to her neck, she looked ravishing. He took in every inch of her bare arms, her tall black boots.

"That horse has some fierce eyes. He looks like he's ready to tear out of here and never stop. I knew you were beautiful, but I didn't know you were brave. I wouldn't get on him for love nor money."

"He's a dream. We bought him off the track. That's why he's antsy." *Beautiful,* he'd said. When she went South, everyone constantly told her she was beautiful.

They walked slowly along a path while she cooled down her horse. "Want to have lunch?"

"I'd like that."

"Let me brush him and take a quick

shower. I have to be back to teach the intermediate class."

She directed him to the roundup, a place near the stables. They sat at a wooden table outdoors and ordered hamburgers. Above them the craggy limbs of giant oaks squiggled against blue sky. "Do you come here every day?"

"No. I try to take my lunch. The three instructors usually eat together."

He told her about his morning. "I think I spurred the cash flow at Stonefield's today. You know there's not a bookstore within a hundred miles of Swan. And that one bookcase in the department store in Macon is going to have Charles Dickens and Kahlil Gibran."

"You're so literary. Why do you stay there?"

He felt she'd poked him with a cattle prod. "No, I'm not. I'm basically a fisherman. Do a little hunting, too. I wouldn't know what to do with myself without the river a stone's throw away."

"My dad misses the South. I left him a note saying that you are in town."

"I probably won't see you again, unless you're home then."

"My last lessons end at six today.

Sunday is actually my long day. The kids are free on the weekends."

"Call in sick. Food poisoning at the Roundup. We could drive over to the coast."

He's awfully cocky, she thought. Southern women are probably all over him. I'm not like that. If he stayed long, would I become like that? His arrogance, a quality she usually hated, didn't irritate her, because she sensed that his confidence with women was skin-deep, literally. Every time his life or his past came up he ran for cover.

They drove the long way, through the somber sequoias and hills, the road gloamy in sunlight sieved through long branches. As they turned north onto the coast road, J.J. stopped talking. The Atlantic was one thing, the Pacific another, he saw. The cupped hills, tawny as lion's fur, dipped to beaches where swags of foam scalloped the sand. Georgia pointed. "Pull in at San Gregorio. We can see seals."

They walked, hardly talking, through wild roses. In the distance J.J. saw islands, as clear cut as pieces in a jigsaw puzzle. Finally, Georgia said, "I need to get back. Cindy could only take two of my classes."

The waves breaking on rocks sent fine spray over them. He would have liked to stay all day. Walking back along the trail, Georgia was ahead of him. *I have always had the coarse lusts of a beast,* he'd read in Van Gogh's letters. No, he thought, I'd like to press my lips softly to every part of her. I'd like to lick her face. In the wind, her aqua riding jacket smelled loamy, and J.J. was sure her face like his had a rime of fine salt. He touched her elbow. "Georgia." She turned and he put his hands on her shoulders. "May I?" he asked so quietly she barely heard him. With great care, he kissed her, then gently pulled her close to him.

J.J. called the House before he checked out of the hotel. Tessie put down the phone for a good five minutes before anyone bothered to pick up. Lily, out of breath, didn't even ask where he was. "We've had a grand surprise! When we drove in from Athens, Marco was here, Ginger's beau from Italy."

"You went to Athens?"

"Yes, we had a lovely trip. Now we're making dinner. Will you be here in time?"

"In time for what?"

"The burial, J.J. At eleven tomorrow. Are you at the cabin?"

"I'll be back in the morning. I just called to tell you. Y'all all right?"

"Yes. Marco is showing Tessie how to make something out of potatoes. You drop little balls in the water, and I forgot to tell you the big news. Ralph just called. He's the nicest young man. He said he has some new information but he can't discuss it yet. He also said there was a minor grave disturbance in Simmonsville, which might be related. Ginger is so happy she's fit to be tied, but she's anxious, too, you know her. I tried calling the cabin but you weren't there. And Dr. Schmitt says Ginger can finish that Ph.D. degree pretty easily. We shall see. I'll make some biscuits. She saw Mitchell, too. We'll tell you every little thing. I always said he's as nice as they come. Not that Marco isn't. See you tomorrow."

Lily. That Lily. They only made one of her.

J.J. drove down Whitman. Four-thirty. Austin should be there. He still saw Georgia growing smaller in the rearview mirror. He had not said that she affected him with a ferocity he'd never felt. He had not said he'd call. The kiss had to say what he did not. He'd forgotten to give her the plum-colored scarf.

He wanted to face Austin and go home. He craved empty days at the cabin, where he could sort through this journey to the other side. A block away he parked by a dry creek and looked down at the pattern of the current sculpted in the sand. Georgia said that every afternoon around four, an ocean breeze came in. He lifted his head for salt wind but instead inhaled the fusty, herbal smell of eucalyptus. Dread similar to what he felt when he entered the Columns slowed him. Coming from a place where every house and street was animated by a story, he thought the neighborhood of low houses with closed facades looked barren. But Georgia had opened the door of one of those houses yesterday. Twenty-four hours ago.

Austin opened the door before J.J. knocked.

J.J. faced a man who looked younger than his years. Charlotte had said he was two years ahead of them in college, so he'd be maybe fifty-seven, fifty-eight. Under his loose silk shirt and linen pants, he was obviously fit. His combed-back silver hair accentuated his modeled face. Large lips for a white guy, was J.J.'s first thought. He took in the rigorous profile and the tan. Austin, J.J. thought, Georgia's daddy. "Mr.

Larkin." J.J. held out his hand. "I'm J. J. Mason, Catherine's son. Proverbial voice from the past. I'm sorry to interrupt when you're just home."

"No, no, I'm happy to meet you. Come in, come in. Georgia left me a note saying you'd stop by this afternoon." He had only a trace of his accent left.

"I had the pleasure of dinner with your daughter. She made me feel right at home in Palo Alto." He looked around at the living room, which he'd glimpsed through the windows yesterday. Austin gestured him to a chair. Two contemporary sofas in okra-green linen around a fireplace and bright abstract paintings. The walls were covered in pale grass cloth. So this is where Georgia lives, he thought, imagining her curled on the sofa reading by the fire, rain streaking the long glass wall.

"Can I get you a drink? Whiskey, soda, wine?"

"Thanks, Scotch, that would be great." The back wall was booklined. While Austin was in the kitchen, he looked at titles. Along the front of the shelves, rocks and gems, along with a few shells, were arranged. J.J. picked up a geode darkly sparkling with amethysts.

Austin came back holding a tray. "I'm a

rock hound. Most of my collection is at the office." He looked at the books. "I've also collected signed editions over the years. With all the authors coming through, and owning bookstores, it's been an easy collection." He took the tray to the coffee table. "What brings you to *me*, J.J.?"

"Long story. Thirty years long, or longer. But let me tell you what has happened this week. Believe me, I would not barge in like this if it were not important. I haven't left Swan in several years," he admitted. Terse and factual, he told Austin about the exhumation and the subsequent conclusion of the GBI that Catherine had not died by suicide.

Austin leaned forward, his hands in the gesture of prayer, silently parting and closing them. His eyes never left J.J.'s. "Your mother, Catherine — I met her when she was nineteen. A lovelier woman never walked. Everyone who knew her felt somehow defeated when we heard she'd killed herself. I was living out here at the time. Someone from Tech sent me the article. I couldn't take it in, but I hadn't seen her by then in several years and had no idea of the circumstances that might have provoked her."

J.J. explained that the GBI thought they

could not find the murderer by now, unless someone up and confessed. "My family is convinced it was a random crime."

"You'd have thought, if you'd known her when I did, that she'd be among the lucky ones. She went forward with a kind of simple belief that the world is a curious, wondrous place. I see the same faith in my daughter."

"This is the hardest part to say. We found some of Mother's belongings in the barn. She'd apparently sealed a box after Ginger was born. It had been stashed in the attic, otherwise it would have been thrown out with all her other things after she died. Ginger went through all the stuff that was transferred to my granddaddy's house when we moved there. She found a box of maternity clothes, a reel of film, two sketch books, and a notebook. And four or five letters from you, all undated. Mother's friend Charlotte — remember her?"

"Of course. A considerable person, too."

"We ran the film at Charlotte's house and she recognized you. Then the notebook brought up an entirely new issue, and basically I've come because of that." He told Austin about the pearl crescents, the elliptical prose, the tension, and finally his concern that Austin might be the father of

Ginger. "I'm sorry — you must feel like the Martians have landed."

"This is stupendous. All of it. Are you sure I can't get you another drink? Let's talk this through."

J.J. followed him into the kitchen. On the mantel, he saw a photo of Georgia on horseback holding up a first-place ribbon, another of a woman who looked like an older version of Georgia. "Georgia's mother?" he asked.

"Yes. She died five years ago." His eyes narrowed with hurt. "I met her on leave toward the end of the war. I was flying Wildcats in the South Pacific. Air force pilot. I didn't think I'd lose her so early. She was only fifty-two. Bone marrow disorder hit her and she was weak one month and dead the next. Let's sit outside."

Austin continued to lean forward in his chair. Behind him the aquamarine pool rippled. A white cat J.J. had not seen yesterday touched its tongue to the water, then settled at Austin's feet. "I can't explain Catherine, I know that. She was an unlikely person to have an affair — and I didn't think of it that way. I was crazy about her. The very first time I saw her, I was down from Tech for the weekend. She was acting in a Greek play. The girls all had on these toga things and were dancing. She looked like she was having fun. I know these days the idea of love at first sight is an archaic concept. But that was what happened. She had me in the palm of her hand. I was happy and miserable, miserable when she went out with other men and didn't seem to notice that I was left on the sidelines. When we were together, the main thing I remember is that we laughed at the same moments. She practically destroyed me when she got engaged to Wills."

"Charlotte told us about you scattering the roses over the campus."

"I always hoped the big romantic gestures would sway her. I was calling her even on her wedding day, begging her not to marry him. She felt terrible, she said, but said it was the right thing, she knew it." As Austin talked, more of his southern accent, neutralized by years in California, returned to his voice. "Speaking of suicide — the day after she married him, I tore off on a car trip to Carrie's Island and seriously considered ramming into the intercoastal bridge. I didn't. Gradually, I got myself together again and life moved on."

"But how . . ."

"I didn't see Catherine until about three years later. I literally ran into her at the Georgia-Alabama football game. I was on leave, recovering from an appendectomy. You were a toddler. I guess left at home. Wills was in uniform. He always looked through me as though I were made of glass. Cordial, never friendly. The next week I called Catherine. She was going to Macon and we met for lunch. After that we met several times. Everything rekindled for me. I can't say what she felt. Maybe you know from the notebook. Lonely. You know women had different lives then and your mother was meant to do something with hers. She came to the farm. Four times. I'll just say it. We slept together there. In my parents' lumpy Victorian bed. She didn't seem to feel guilty. Wills got home when he could. You mentioned the pearl crescents. They were my mother's. I gave them to Catherine the first time she came to the farm. One day she mailed them back to me. She never mentioned birth control or pregnancy. *Not to worry*, she said. Of course, I heard later that she'd had another baby."

"Ginger. My sister is thirty-one. When were you and Mother together?"

"Summer of '43. In fact, around this

501

time. First part of July. I remember being alone almost all that big July-August heat wave at the farm. I had a few weeks to recover before seeing action again."

"Ginger was born May 1, 1944."

"So" — he counted back — "highly unlikely but remotely possible." Austin lowered his face into his hands. "I only saw Catherine once after that. I had a drink with a man named Paul, who worked for your granddaddy. I briefly went back to my old job after the war. I sold spindles and did a little business with the mill. We were at the bar at the country club in Swan, and I saw Catherine alone, about to tee off. I ran out and we talked for a few minutes. Her little girl was playing. I was over her by then. This was 1950. I'd met Clare at the end of the war and was about to move permanently out here to be with her. I can't say for sure, though, if Catherine had faintly suggested it, that I wouldn't have taken her away in my car that day. She seemed the same, but I think your dad's war experience had made her more solemn."

"His war experience? He was a medic, mostly in North Carolina."

"Surely you know he was in a unit that treated the prisoners after the liberation of Dachau?"

"No." J.J. swallowed the gut-burning Scotch.

"They never told you?"

"No. A family not known for mentioning the unpleasant. I knew he once parachuted into Germany — I've always imagined him floating down."

"I'm sorry. He treated those emaciated, brutalized people for weeks. Sorry, son. A Tech friend of mine was in his unit. He's been messed up ever since."

"I'm God damned." J.J. told him about Wills's desperate drinking and the resultant stroke.

"That's a hell of a fate. He had nothing but promise before the war."

"Yeah, well. He was a good father up until. Just curious. What's your blood type?"

"A."

"That doesn't help. My dad is A, too."

"I'm ready to do whatever you think best."

"I don't know of anything to do. I'll tell Ginger there's a remote chance that you're her father. Maybe I can find out from Lily if Ginger's birth was early or late. That would seem to be definitive."

"Refill?"

"No thanks, I'm going to the airport. I

may drink a few on the flight. This Dachau news is hard to take. And they're reburying tomorrow."

"So, no one told you about Wills. That's so typical, isn't it? But those guys never liked to talk about the war, those who witnessed big-time horrors. I was in the air. Midway Island — that was bad enough."

They walked through the yard. The sun had fallen behind the lacy Chinese elms and olives. "California light," J.J. said. "It's different. The outlines of things are sharper here. I want to thank you. I apologize for all this digging in the past. Seemed important for Ginger."

"Yes. And I'm somehow unburdened to hear that Catherine did not take her own life. The other parts, I'll have to absorb. Your dad. Do they suspect him of murder?"

"I think so. Lacking anyone else. He wouldn't have, not for the world." The GBI would check on Austin if J.J. mentioned the notebook, which he would not. Austin was running bookstores, raising a family, when Catherine died. He had nothing in his eyes but honesty. J.J. could understand easily his mother's attraction to Austin. And back when they all were in college he must have been what Charlotte called him — a dreamboat. "They've got to be suspicious but the likelihood is nil."

"I'd doubt their suspicion with all my heart, son. Innocent or guilty, he's serving a life sentence, from what you've told me." J.J. felt a prick of pain. Second time Austin had said *son*. A word he hadn't heard in a long time.

"Austin, your daughter seems to me like Mother seemed to you in the Greek play. I'm hoping to see her again. Now, that's an understatement." J.J. laughed at himself.

Austin laughed, too. "Another spoke in the wheel that seems bent on turning. If Georgia has any imperfections, I don't know them. She's true blue. In my experience, you only get that kind of emotion once. Or twice if you're luckier than hell. I was one of those. Now I'm seeing someone pleasant, nice, companionable. Attractive, you know. I think I'll leave it as it is, although she's ready to move in and rearrange the furniture. I'm not sure I want to give up my privacy unless I'm convinced it's for a great piece of happiness."

"I wouldn't consider it, if that's the situation. 'Course I'm the great loner." To his surprise, Austin hugged him.

J.J. had plenty of time to get to his flight. Rush-hour traffic moved along at a clip, without tractors or yokels in pickups to slow the flow. J.J. kept right, not in his usual hurry. He'd seen Georgia on the coastal trail touch the tip of her tongue to a wave-wet shrub, something he and Ginger did. He wondered if Catherine had long ago picked it up from Austin and passed it on to them. He wondered if she'd become interested in stones through him and bequeathed that, too.

What he wanted was to turn back, drive a hundred miles an hour to that stable where he last saw Georgia sitting on the fence calling out "Post" to the girls, where sunlight, sifting through the oaks and kicked-up dust, held the covered ring in sepia light, a light from the previous century.

July 14

J.J. arrived in Swan thirty minutes before they were scheduled to meet the Ireland's hearse at Magnolia Cemetery. Ginger had told Father Tyson that there was to be no ceremony. The less focus, the better. They would witness the burial, stop to see Wills, go to the Sisters for late breakfast, then resume their lives.

With Marco here, she felt more decisive. He had made the long journey to a troubled place for her. Only for her. That he deeply cared, even she could no longer doubt. "This is a great place," he kept saying as she'd driven him around yesterday before dark. "Like a place in a dream. Everything anchored in blue air." She could tell that he liked Lily and Tessie. He'd immediately invited both of them to Italy. She and Marco had stayed up late, talking on the porch. Ginger shivered in the hot night as she told him about the day she came home from school and found her mother. She told him about Wills, his grief, stroke, and unendurable aftermath, and about her survival with J.J. "Later, we'll go out to the cabin. That's where J.J. and I could connect with a source. Here, in the House, we were at home, too, but this is always Big Jim's house. The cabin belonged to my family. We kept it as a touchstone. And will."

Motionless in the rocking chair, Marco just listened. Behind her voice, he'd never heard a night so alive. He stared into the dark yard, where for all he knew crocodiles were crawling. Now and then CoCo imitated a hammer knocking off a tailpipe or a drill gun unscrewing lug nuts. Marco had kept his hand over Ginger's on the arm of her chair and she talked and talked.

J.J. came up the porch steps with his arms full of gifts. Ginger introduced Marco quickly. "Hey, buddy, I'd have brought you one if I'd known in time that you were here. Welcome to paradise." He clapped Marco on the shoulder and nodded to Ginger, a "not bad" nod she recognized. While they opened his gifts, J.J. regarded Marco. He looks okay, he thought. Solid citizen. Of Italy, of course.

Lily and Ginger were shocked at the expensive sweaters. Tessie pressed the soft cotton robe to her face.

"Go change. We'll talk on the way. We can all go in one car." Ginger wanted to get this over with.

"Tessie, are you coming?" Lily asked.

"Nome. I done told Ginger I'm going to get dinner together."

Lily went back for her handbag.

Cass Deal had cleaned the plot, even deadheaded all the spent roses. The coffin already sat next to the hole, now neat and raked smooth. Two hours of scouring had returned Big Jim's grave to pristine white granite. Against the Mason headstone leaned a spray of red roses. Below, someone had left a vase of summer garden flowers. The four of them stood to the side while the men slowly cranked the coffin down into the ground. Could anyone ever believe the pumping red heart just stops; we go in a box and are buried, while those who love us are left to figure out how to endure this brutal subtraction from life? Ginger stooped for a handful of dirt and threw it in, then J.J. did the same.

He brushed off his hand on his trousers and said in a low voice to Ginger, "Are we the only ones to bury our mother twice, both times after fucking disasters?"

"I'd like to say something," Lily said in a quaky voice. She stepped forward, turned around, and looked at them. J.J. saw her swallow twice as she unfolded a piece of paper. Slowly she spoke.

Beauty is a thing beyond the grave.
That perfect bright experience
Will never fall to nothing
And time will dim the moon sooner
Than our full consummation here
In this brief life will tarnish or pass away.

They stood in silence. J.J. clenched his fists hard to keep tears from his eyes. "That's perfect, Lily, thank you."

Ginger put her arm around her, and she and Marco walked her back to the car. Lily started to weep a little. J.J. stood a moment, with his eyes closed and head down, wondering how Lily had happened on a poem by D. H. Lawrence. J.J. suspected there was something more behind it, something she might never tell, or something that would float to the surface in time. Odd, since Ralph had told them that their mother did not kill herself, J.J. had experienced a surge of affection for Lily, as though a stone had been shoved off a spring, allowing water to flow.

While the men shoveled dirt in a mound over the coffin, J.J. read the card on the vase of flowers. *Rest forever in peace, Eleanor Whitefield.* J.J. bent to the red roses and took off the florist's card. *With love from Austin and Georgia.* He thought of Austin flying low, the roses falling on the campus for Catherine. He pocketed the cards. So much to tell Ginger.

Ginger kept it brief in Wills's room. They did not mention Catherine or what had just happened. "Daddy, this is Marco, the man I work with in Italy."

Wills proffered his hand but didn't speak.

"I've heard about you from Ginger, and it is pleasing to me to meet you," Marco said. Lily went down the hall and brought back a Coke for Wills. Marco tried again to get a response. "Ginger tells me you are a doctor. My father is, too. He delivers all the babies in Monte Sant'Egidio."

Wills reached for the Coke, as though he were constantly deprived. Ginger told him about Marco's project, but Wills threw up both hands and said, "Okay, okay."

Abruptly, Ginger said, "We're going now, Daddy. We'll see you tomorrow." Marco extended his hand but Wills ignored him.

J.J. stayed behind. "I'll be right with you." He swung a chair around and straddled it. "Dad, listen. I want to ask you a question. Does the word *Dachau* mean anything to you?"

Wills pulled the straw from his mouth. "Dachau," he repeated. "Terrible, terrible."

"Were you there?"

Wills nodded. "Terrible."

"I heard you were there. You never told us. You were brave."

Wills wiped the sweat from his upper lip on his sleeve. "I was brave," he repeated.

After breakfast at the Sisters, Lily was exhausted. Marco said he, too, wanted to sleep because he was in confused hours. "You can't," Ginger protested. "We're all going to the cabin. And it's called jet lag."

"*Va bene, va bene.* Let me sleep on the way."

"Take me to the House. I want to go visit Eleanor." And after that, Lily thought, I want to stay in bed until dinner.

At the cabin, Marco immediately spotted the arrowhead collection around the fireplace. "Did you find all these? A natural history museum would be proud to have such a display." He admired J.J.'s new fishing spear, then turned to look at the shelves of history and anthropology books.

"We were raised in the boonies, but we did read," Ginger said. She gave Marco a tour of the rest of the cabin, then, after she took him down to the river, she let him sleep in her room. At first she lay down beside him, but she was about to fall off the narrow bed and he fell soundly asleep within seconds. She opened the window, turned the fan on him, and slipped outside, where J.J. sat at his table under the scuppernong vine, looking through a stack of new books.

"I brought you these novels. Good for the long plane trip."

"I can't get over you going shopping. I love the sweater. Sweet J.J." She kissed the top of his head. "Want a dip?"

"Sounds good. Wash away the cares of the world." As they walked down to the dock, Ginger started to sing, as she always had, *Shall we gather at the river, the beautiful, the beautiful rivvvv — eerr.* She boomed on every stress.

"Was it a week ago that I found Scott sitting here with the news that tilted our little universe? Seems like a year. What do you think Ralph has found out?"

"He was mum. He did say this news might break everything open."

"Christ, good old Sherlock. Go, Ginger."
He gave her a push and she jumped in
holding her nose.

Ginger, stretched out on a decrepit aluminum chaise, spread her hair to dry. J.J.
told her about his two days in Palo Alto.
"What if Mother had left and taken us to
California and we'd been raised there with
Austin?" Ginger wondered.
"Then Georgia would not have been
born. That would have been a fatal error."
J.J. leaned back on his elbows. He told her
everything Austin had said about the affair.
"We have to ask Lily if you arrived early or
late. It could matter, but it looks like
you're stuck with Daddyo." He tried to describe Georgia, their glass house with
lemon trees, and the big surf spuming from
the rocks when he walked the coastal trail
with her. He talked about the light at the
stable as he drove away. Finally, he told her
what Austin said about Wills. "I thought
the surprises from Austin, if there were
any, would be about Mother. Instead, I
walked out staggering over what he said
about Dad. This morning when we were at
the Columns, I asked him about it. I could
tell he remembered something horrific."
"He hardly recalls anything specific.

That must have colored every corpuscle in his body." Already she was thinking of ransacking the barn and the stuffed closet in the back room for any record of this, any old Brownie photo or letter. "So he had other sorrows. Unspeakable. I wonder if Lily knows. Probably not. Surely she would have said something, as much as she poor-Wills." She remembered her father sitting alone on the dock at night.

Ginger told J.J. about seeing Mitchell in Athens, then checking with Dr. Schmitt about finishing her degree. "I just may do it! I've gone from thinking I might to thinking how could I not? I remembered so many things about Mitchell when Lily and I were driving home, after barely thinking of him in the past couple of years. Do you know once he brought me an enormous armful of Casablanca lilies? They tinged the whole house with their white perfume. I felt so good to find out he's just fine."

They heard the screen door bang and saw Marco emerge with a large book. He waved and sat down on the porch. "Ginger, Marco seems extra-primo excellent." J.J. turned his thumbs up.

"Maybe our luck has changed. No more turning into pillars of salt. No more seasons in Hades."

"Don't think it. The gods might be huddling right now, preparing the next bolt. They're still standing, those Masons. Hey, I want to go back to California for a while," J.J. said. "I liked it there."

"Georgia on your mind? Is she pretty?"

"Flawless. Something about her."

"Marco, get down here! You've got to swim in the spring," Ginger called. "I think we might drive over to the island tomorrow so I can introduce Marco to Caroline. Want to go? Marco, come *on*. Dinner's at seven and you don't want to miss Tessie's cooking."

J.J. stood up and stretched. "No, I want some time. Take Marco. I'm going up to my room for a while. I need to write down a few notes before they evaporate."

Marco stepped warily down the path, moving through troughs of heat. Ginger had told him about rattlesnakes and water moccasins the size of her thigh. The palmettos, moss-dripping oaks, and the river looked like the Amazon jungle to him. The serene piazza in Monte Sant'Egidio flashed through his mind. He couldn't imagine that he was going to jump into that swirling green water and swim, but he did.

J.J. filled his pen with black ink. He found his new notebook in his suitcase and sat down at the window. He reached for a book from his shelves and opened it at random. His finger fell on *here where the moonflowers*. And yes, he'd seen the new curling vine of the moonflowers starting up the porch rail only today. "Marco. Polo. Marco. Polo," he heard Ginger calling. She echoed the hiding game they used to play in the river. But this time she was with a real Marco. He could see them swimming fast toward the bend, where they would get out and climb over the rise to the spring. The late sunlight flashed on their arms arrowing in and out of the water. When J.J. and Ginger were small, they used to seal notes in mayonnaise jars and fling them out as far as they could, hoping the current would sweep them to the ocean. J.J. could still feel the strain in his muscle as he tried to catapult a jar into the current. "Go," Ginger had shouted as the jar flew through the air. They stood on the dock, following each glinting glass until it bobbed under and disappeared. He thought he remembered a voice beside them, Catherine saying *What a good idea*. Someone on a beach in another country would find a jar and twist it open. *We live in Swan, Georgia. If you find this, please write to us. Love, Ginger and J. J. Mason.*

About the Author

Author of the international and *New York Times* bestsellers *Under the Tuscan Sun*, *Bella Tuscany*, and *In Tuscany*, Frances Mayes has also written five books of poetry and a reader's guide, *The Discovery of Poetry*. She edited *Best American Travel Writing*, 2002. A native of Georgia, she now lives in California and Italy with her husband, the poet Edward Mayes.

DAVID J. TEECE

Essays in Technology Management and Policy

SELECTED PAPERS OF DAVID J. TEECE

World Scientific
New Jersey • London • Singapore • Hong Kong

Published by

World Scientific Publishing Co. Pte. Ltd.

5 Toh Tuck Link, Singapore 596224

USA office: Suite 202, 1060 Main Street, River Edge, NJ 07661

UK office: 57 Shelton Street, Covent Garden, London WC2H 9HE

The author and publisher are grateful for the permission granted by the following copyright owners of the reprints found in this volume:

ABA Publishing (*Antitrust Law Journal*)
American Economic Association (*Journal of Economic Literature*)
Blackwell Publishers (*The Economic Journal*)
Elsevier Science Publishers (*Research Policy, Journal of Economic Behaviour and Organization, International Journal of Industrial Organization*)
Federal Legal Publications, Inc. (*The Antitrust Bulletin*)
Harvard Business School Publishing Corp. (*Harvard Business Review*)
Hass School of Business, University of California at Berkeley (*California Management Review*)
John Wiley and Sons (*Strategic Management Journal*)
Mohr Siebeck Verlag (*Journal of Institutional and Theoretical Economics*)
Oxford University Press (*Industrial and Corporate Change*)
Sage Publications (*The Annals of the Academy of Political and Social Science*)

ESSAYS IN TECHNOLOGY MANAGEMENT AND POLICY
Selected Papers of David Teece

ISBN 981-02-4446-0
ISBN 981-02-4447-9 (pbk)

Printed in Singapore by Multiprint Services

"Knowledge is a treasure but practice is the key to it."

Thomas Fuller

To my wife Leigh, who has graciously supported my scholarly efforts;

to my daughter Jocelyn, who fancies good prose;

and to my sons Teddy, Austin and Tennyson who care deeply about the timely commercialization of gadgets, gizmos, and electronic games.

Acknowledgements

The eleven "greats" in technology management and policy, from whom I have learned, and with whom I have enjoyed collegiality and friendship.

Kenneth Arrow	*Stanford University*
Alfred Chandler	*Harvard University*
Giovanni Dosi	*St'Anna School of Advanced Studies*
David Mowery	*University of California, Berkeley*
Richard Nelson	*Columbia University*
Nathan Rosenberg	*Stanford University*
Richard Rumelt	*University of California, Los Angeles*
Hal Varian	*University of California, Berkeley*
Oliver Williamson	*University of California, Berkeley*
Sidney Winter	*University of Pennsylvania*
and	
the late Edwin Mansfield	*University of Pennsylvania*

Contents

Introduction

It has been recognized for some time now that the key drivers of economic development and progress are well-functioning political, social and business institutions, and stable and fair governance. When the institutional fabric of society facilitates market organization and contractual stability, then investments will be made and technology will be created and/or adopted by private sector firms so that wealth generation can proceed. National States will benefit from such wealth generation.

Many of the most interesting issues in management and policy — be they firm level or at the level of the National State — involve business organization and how it impacts technology generation, development, and adoption. In this book I endeavor to pull together some of my already published articles on these topics. The treatment is necessarily selective. The focus is heavily around the implications of technological innovation for management and the organization of industry; and the implications for one element of public policy, namely competition (antitrust) policy. The latter is chosen not because it is the only or the main instrument by which public policy impacts industry, but because it is an increasingly important instrument as governments deregulate and turn to competition policy to ensure that markets function properly. Indeed, in the U.S. context at least, antitrust policy is a key component of industrial policy, such as it is.

The book is broken down into five sections, which I now outline and put into context.

Section I

In this section I deal with strategies for commercializing new technologies. Too often firms engage in inventive activities, achieve inventive success, but then fail to capture value from the innovation that they have had a hand in developing. Getting market entry strategies right makes a big difference to marketplace outcomes. When technically advanced firms bring winning technologies to market, but neglect strategic business considerations, their victories are likely to be Pyrrhic.

The main elements of business strategy analyzed in this section are intellectual property, and integration/outsourcing strategy. The latter focuses on whether to own, buy or lease the complementary assets needed to bring a product to market. The correct answer depends on many factors, but key ones identified are the intellectual property (IP) positioning of the firm and the nature of the requirements that the innovation places on complementary assets.

The key insight is that if the innovator has strong IP, or its technology/design is hard for competitors to imitate or emulate, then there is less risk that competitors will end up being the winners. Moreover, strong appropriability enables you to bargain for access to complementary assets from a privileged position, as competitors will be disadvantaged. Strong IP is one lynchpin of what I call a strong "appropriability regime." The other is the nature of knowledge itself: Is it "hard" to copy? Is it tacit or codified? Frequently the appropriability regime surrounding a new technology is weak and imitators/emulators can "swarm" around the innovator, competing away profits. Figuring out the right commercialization strategy is critical to success. In short, having the right market entry strategy is critical to success as it affects the profits that the innovator will be able to reap from new technology and new products. This section develops in some detail the decision framework that should be followed and predicts outcomes for the innovator.

Whereas in *Profiting from Technological Innovation* the focus is on the particulars of a well-articulated commercialization strategy, in *Capturing Value from Knowledge Assets* a general framework is laid out that explains why the competitive advantage of firms depends increasingly on intangible assets, of which knowledge and competences are perhaps the most critical. The fundamental idea is that open competition and market access enable firms everywhere to access markets from anywhere, making business increasingly competitive and differentiation increasingly difficult. Know-how, competence, and intellectual property are frequently the only available foundations upon which to differentiate. Hence their growing importance.

Put differently, in the global economy today more is "tradable," both domestically as well as internationally, than was the case 50 years ago. This has been fueled by vertical divestiture, which has opened up many intermediate product markets, and the removal of barriers to trade and investment. In a world where one's competitors can access most everything, it is critical to own something (hopefully a critical input) that others do not have. This is what innovators can achieve. The product of innovation is know-how and intellectual property, and in the "new" economy such intangibles are the currency that firms would hope to have.

Section II

This section contains three essays that highlight how entrepreneurial management and organizational factors affect firm level performance. In *Dynamic Capabilities and Strategic Management* a framework is developed that highlights the strategic importance associated with the skillful orchestration (by top management) of the firm's technological and business assets. Firms with excellent technological competences must not only continuously renew these competences; they must do so in a way that is sensitive to the needs of consumers as expressed in the marketplace. Questions like "what do we commercialize next" cannot be found just by looking in the research lab. One must also look at the market and match evolving market opportunities to the firm's technological and business assets.[1]

An essential role for management is to be able to adapt, integrate, and reconfigure internal and external organizational skills and resources to match the requirements of changing marketplaces. The specifics of how this gets done reside in the firm's business processes and in the vision and leadership of top management. The firm's market position and prior history are obviously limiting, but the ability of an organization to sense emerging opportunities and seize them resides in large measure with management, augmented by the business firm's organizational processes that gather up and make sense of market intelligence and technological opportunities. This type of ability is a bit like that possessed by the shrewd investor. It involves sensing the future; but whereas the investor cannot deploy, redeploy, configure, and reconfigure the firm's asset base with ease, management can. It is management's expert execution on a particular vision that is critically important to success.

Mitigating Procurement Hazards in the Context of Innovation explores contractual hazards associated with innovation. The very nature of innovation almost always leads to the innovating firm discovering that to commercialize the innovation it needs access to something — be it complementary assets or technologies — it doesn't already have. Given the fact that such assets are likely to be highly specialized, and hence the number of potential providers limited, contractual hazards can be severe, i.e. the innovator can be exposed to dependence on key

---

[1] For a short restatement of my views, see "Dynamic Capabilities," in W. Lazonick (ed.), *The International Encyclopedia of Business and Management* (Oxford: Oxford University Press, 2001.

suppliers and strategic partners. Indeed, such dependence on key suppliers, customers and distributors is frequently the hallmark of both technology-based start-up firms as well as established firms launching innovative products. One of the key points developed in this chapter is that many large firms have multiple contractual points of contact with suppliers. Such "constellations of contracts" reduce the hazards associated with dependence on any one party and enable the parties to achieve a degree of protection from recontracting hazards because there are ways to "retaliate." Should one party in one contract endeavor to rejigger terms and understandings in their favor, the firm impacted by this can retaliate in a different contractual circumstance.

In *Firm Organization, Industrial Structure, and Technological Innovation*, the linkages and relationships between market structure, internal structure and innovative performance are surveyed. The clear message is that decentralized structures with low levels of bureaucracy support innovation by enabling swift decision making. They also ensure that managerial decisions are "in synch" with the market. There is no clear advantage to scale. Whether scale and structure are a handicap or advantage depend on the situation. "Systemic" innovation is frequently facilitated in large vertically integrated organizations. "Autonomous" innovation can proceed swiftly in smaller firms because decision-making is likely to be quicker; and in today's world where venture capital financing is abundant and available globally, the "free cash flows" of the large established organization is not as critical, except perhaps for product development supported by longer-range research and development programs. Internal structure and culture (in particular, entrepreneurial culture) matter significantly. At minimum, this chapter puts in context the role of market structure as a determinant of innovation. It turns out to be relatively minor. Accordingly, market structure should not be expected to have predictable effects on innovation. Whether we are looking at a firm with or without market power, the other aspects of "structure" (especially internal structure and decision-making styles) are likely to swamp market structure as a determinant of the rate and direction of innovation.

Section III

This section explores, in some detail, markets for know-how and intellectual property. Licensing, cross licensing, or the outright sale of technology and intellectual property are of increasing significance to firms competing in the global economy. When and how to license technology and intellectual property is a subject of considerable importance.

In *When Is Virtual Virtuous?* some guidance is provided as to when firms should outsource (in the context of innovation) and when they should not. Henry Chesbrough is the co-author on this chapter. We make the point that the innovation process involves some rather severe contracting hazards that limit the efficacy of outsourcing, particularly as a way to "pace" innovation. In short, the old problem of "thin" markets gets in the way. If markets are "thin," one may not be able to procure what one wants when one wants it, and one may not be able to achieve a competitive price. Suppliers, distributors, manufacturers and the like are unlikely to anticipate the innovator needs, and may not be able to provide what is needed when it is needed. The more radical the innovation, the more likely such unavailability. This is likely to be because there has been no previous demand for the input.

Accordingly, we are skeptical of the old adage that you should outsource anything and everything. Our framework enables managers to calibrate the risk associated with outsourcing, and suggests when it can be done and when it should be avoided. Frequently, innovators will themselves need to invest in complementary technologies and assets in order to bring their products to market.

Managing Intellectual Capital: Licensing and Cross-Licensing in Semiconductors and Electronics explains the multiple motives for licensing IP — from simply achieving incremental cash flows through achieving design freedom. As technological domains develop and become established (e.g. biotech, semiconductors), newcomers must contend with the fact that others have patented much prior art. To obtain design freedom, newcomers will need to either pay cash (royalties) or offer to cross-license intellectual property with the incumbents.

Many intangibles are in fact difficult to buy and sell. *The Market for Know-how and the Efficient International Transfer of Technology* explores this. The tacit nature of knowledge is one reason transactions cannot proceed smoothly. Lack of codification confounds transfer costs and requires the transfer of people to effectuate the transfer of technology.

While recent focus has been on licensing intellectual property, which may or may not involve any transfer of technology, it must also be recognized that buying or importing know-how is one way for laggards to acquire best practice. Getting the rights to intellectual property is one thing; successfully transferring technology can be quite another. This is the subject matter of *Technology Transfer by Multinational Firms*.

Needless to say, the international transfer of technology is not a costless activity. Considerable resources must often be used to effectuate transfer. Success can sometimes be elusive. The process turns out to be easier if you have done it before for the same technology. Not surprisingly, there is a steep learning curve associated with technology transfer, particularly for process technologies. (It is best for the licensee if the licensor has transferred the technology previously.) Each startup enables the owner/licensor of the technology to better understand its own technology, and how seemingly minor variations in input quality and environmental conditions can affect yields and performance.

Section IV

This section raises important issues about competition policy in regimes of rapid technological processes. Competition policy in the United States and elsewhere has not been shaped with dynamic concerns "front-of-mind." Indeed, the fundamental lynchpin of antitrust policy — the structure, conduct and performance paradigm — has always been of questionable value in explaining firm performance. With rapid innovation, competition is enhanced, both qualitatively and quantitatively.

Some commentators maintain the view that antitrust enforcement must be more severe in the context of innovation. An alternative view advanced here is that rapid innovation in an industry will render monopoly more transient than would be the case in static environments. To be sure, collusion is still something to watch out for, and the enforcement agencies around the world clearly have an important role to play in this regard.

But in regimes of rapid technological progress, the need for government antitrust enforcement ought be lower, not higher, than in static environments, other things equal. This is because of the greater ability of competitive markets experiencing rapid innovation to quickly "heal" from the effects of monopoly, since monopoly is likely to be quickly overturned when technology is evolving rapidly. Moreover, the ability of the antitrust agencies to "surgically" intervene and make the necessary fine distinctions that need to be made is significantly impeded by the fact that the agencies do not and simply cannot readily access the information and knowledge needed to improve matters.

Section V

This section deals with certain additional elements of business organization in the context of innovation. Why do firms diversify? What efficiency gains can follow from lateral diversification?

The insight offered in *Towards an Economic Theory of the Multiproduct Firm* is that in well-managed firms seeking to build shareholder wealth, the accumulation of knowledge enables and requires firms to gradually diversify in order to fully exploit their knowledge assets. This may seem self-evident to some. Nevertheless, it is not what is commonly taught (at least in economics textbooks) if diversification is taught at all. Firms over time learn to perform certain activities. As this learning accumulates, the firm's competences expand. The relative ease with which knowledge is transferred or redeployed internally (i.e. as compared to across a market), explains why it makes sense to diversify internally or through alliances or joint ventures (rather than seeking to exploit this accumulated knowledge through technology licensing). Incentives exist to diversify because the market for know-how is rather inefficient, as discussed in section III.

It is quite hard to contract for the sale of know-how because know-how is an intangible asset with poorly defined property rights. For these and other reasons, putting know-how to better use internally is often easier than trying to sell it. *Towards an Economic Theory of the Multiproduct Firm* expands upon contractual issues to explain how resources accumulate. What emerges is a conceptualization of the corporation and "efficient" diversification that is consistent with reality[2] (the evidence suggests that sustainable diversification is related "diversification" in a technological and market sense). Knowledge and competence is viewed as being organizationally fluid (i.e. it appears generally easier to transfer competences inside the firm than across organizational boundaries). This perspective, once appreciated, helps explain why big companies continue to grow once they have exhausted standard economies of scale. It also challenges the notion that plant level economies of scale and scope explain the scope of the business enterprise. Rather, organizational competences are seen to exist not only at the plant (or office) level, but also at the corporate level.

In *Competition, Cooperation, and Innovation* I explain why the introduction of new innovative processes requires deep coordination amongst various organizational units, some inside the firm, others external to it. No firm can be an island unto itself, especially when it comes to commercializing new technology. One reason is that innovation almost always requires the utilization of assets complementary to the innovation — be it complementary technologies, manufacturing assets, or distribution platforms (see Section I above). This is particularly evident in fields like biotechnology where the new biotechnology firms have limited regulatory and market experience and can benefit from "renting the assets" of the incumbent pharmaceutical companies. In essence, the development and commercialization of new products involves considerable coordination challenges, and alliances are a

---

[2] See also Teece, Rumelt, Dosi and Winter, "Understanding Corporate Coherence: Theory and Evidence," *Journal of Economic Behavior and Organization*, 23:1 (1994).

commonly used device to achieve the required coordination when innovative firms do not possess internally all the assets needed to succeed in the marketplace. Put differently, the technical challenges involved in innovation are only a part of the game. Figuring out how to execute on the business aspects also is critically important.

In *The Dynamics of Industrial Capitalism* the relationship of innovation and "competitiveness" is surveyed through the lens of the historical analysis contained in Alfred Chandler's *Scale and Scope*. Alfred Chandler is the world's leading business historian. His view is that the firms who took leadership positions in their industries through much of the 19th and 20th centuries were not necessarily the firms that were the first to innovate. Rather, the leaders were the ones who were the first to make big financial bets on new technologies. According to Chandler, the winners have been firms with access to capital and with large free cash flows. In short, the innovators were financially strong firms with visionary management willing and able to bet big on new technology. Chandler's paradigm is supported through references to enterprise development in the United States, the United Kingdom and Japan. In each country the evolutionary path is similar, suggesting that firms shape markets just as much as markets shape firms.

Concluding Remarks

These essays will hopefully enable the reader to develop an appreciation of the business side of technological innovation. Understanding the business issues is just as important as understanding the technical issues associated with new product development. Firms prosper only when they combine technical excellence with business acumen, and can orchestrate their assets astutely. These essays will hopefully provide the reader with insights on how to do so. Readers seeking additional illumination might find my two volumes of collected papers, *Economic Performance and the Theory of the Firm*, Vol. I & *Strategy, Technology and Public Policy*, Vol. II (Edward Elgar, 1998), of some value.

I

CAPTURING VALUE
FROM
TECHNOLOGICAL INNOVATION

Profiting from Technological Innovation: Implications for Integration, Collaboration, Licensing and Public Policy

David J. Teece*

School of Business Administration, University of California, Berkeley, CA 94720, U.S.A.

This paper attempts to explain why innovating firms often fail to obtain significant economic returns from an innovation, while customers, imitators and other industry participants benefit. Business strategy — particularly as it relates to the firm's decision to integrate and collaborate — is shown to be an important factor. The paper demonstrates that when imitation is easy, markets don't work well, and the profits from innovation may accrue to the owners of certain complementary assets, rather than to the developers of the intellectual property. This speaks to the need, in certain cases, for the innovating firm to establish a prior position in these complementary assets. The paper also indicates that innovators with new products and processes which provide value to consumers may sometimes be so ill positioned in the market that they necessarily will fail. The analysis provides a theoretical foundation for the proposition that manufacturing often matters, particularly to innovating nations. Innovating firms without the requisite manufacturing

Reprinted from *Research Policy* 15 (1986), 285–305.

*I thank Raphael Amit, Harvey Brooks, Chris Chapin, Therese Flaherty, Richard Gilbert, Heather Haveman, Mel Horwitch, David Hulbert, Carl Jacobsen, Michael Porter, Gary Pisano, Richard Rumelt, Raymond Vernon and Sidney Winter for helpful discussions relating to the subject matter of this paper. Three anonymous referees also provided valuable criticisms. I gratefully acknowledge the financial support of the National Science Foundation under grant no. SRS-8410556 to the Center for Research in Management, University of California Berkeley. Earlier versions of this paper were presented at a National Academy of Engineering Symposium titled "World Technologies and National Sovereignty," February 1986, and at a conference on innovation at the University of Venice, March 1986.

and related capacities may die, even though they are the best at innovation. Implications for trade policy and domestic economic policy are examined.

1. Introduction

It is quite common for innovators — those firms which are first to commercialize a new product of process in the market — to lament the fact that competitors/ imitators have profited more from the innovation than the firm first to commercialize it! Since it is often held that being first to market is a source of strategic advantage, the clear existence and persistence of this phenomenon may appear perplexing if not troubling. The aim of this article is to explain why a fast second or even a slow third might outperform the innovator. The message is particularly pertinent to those science and engineering driven companies that harbor the mistaken illusion that developing new products which meet customer needs will ensure fabulous success. It may possibly do so for the product, but not for the innovator.

In this paper, a framework is offered which identifies the factors which determine who wins from innovation: the firm which is first to market, follower firms, or firms that have related capabilities that the innovator needs. The follower firms may or may not be imitators in the narrow sense of the term, although they sometimes are. The framework appears to have utility for explaining the share of the profits from innovation accruing to the innovator compared to its followers and suppliers (see Fig. 1), as well as for explaining a variety of interfirm activities

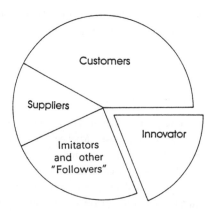

What determines the share of profits captured by the innovator?

Fig. 1. Explaining the distribution of the profits from innovation.

such as joint ventures, coproduction agreements, cross distribution arrangements, and technology licensing. Implications for strategic management, public policy, and international trade and investment are then discussed.

2. The Phenomenon

Figure 2 presents a simplified taxonomy of the possible outcomes from innovation. Quadrant 1 represents positive outcomes for the innovator. A first-to-market advantage is translated into a sustained competitive advantage which either creates a new earnings stream or enhances an existing one. Quadrant 4 and its corollary quadrant 2 are the ones which are the focus of this paper.

The EMI CAT scanner is a classic case of the phenomenon to be investigated.[1] By the early 1970s, the U.K. firm Electrical Musical Industries (EMI) Ltd. was in a variety of product lines including phonographic records, movies, and advanced electronics. EMI had developed high resolution TVs in the 1930s, pioneered airborne radar during World War II, and developed the U.K.'s first all solid-state computers in 1952.

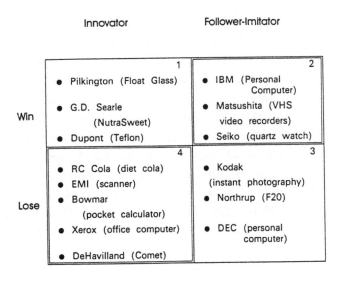

Fig. 2. Taxonomy of outcomes from the innovation process.

---

[1] The EMI story is summarized in Michael Martin, *Managing Technological Innovation and Entrepreneurship* (Reston Publishing Company, Reston, VA, 1984).

In the late 1960s Godfrey Houndsfield, an EMI senior research engineer engaged in pattern recognition research which resulted in his displaying a scan of a pig's brain. Subsequent clinical work established that computerized axial tomography (CAT) was viable for generating cross-sectional "views" of the human body, the greatest advance in radiology since the discovery of X rays in 1895.

While EMI was initially successful with its CAT scanner, within 6 years of its introduction into the U.S. in 1973 the company had lost market leadership, and by the eighth year had dropped out of the CT scanner business. Other companies successfully dominated the market, though they were late entrants, and are still profiting in the business today.

Other examples include RC Cola, a small beverage company that was the first to introduce cola in a can, and the first to introduce diet cola. Both Coca Cola and Pepsi followed almost immediately and deprived RC of any significant advantage from its innovation. Bowmar, which introduced the pocket calculator, was not able to withstand competition from Texas Instruments, Hewlett Packard and others, and went out of business. Xerox failed to succeed with its entry into the office computer business, even though Apple succeeded with the MacIntosh which contained many of Xerox's key product ideas, such as the mouse and icons. The de Havilland Comet saga has some of the same features. The Comet I jet was introduced into the commercial airline business 2 years or so before Boeing introduced the 707, but de Havilland failed to capitalize on its substantial early advantage. MITS introduced the first personal computer, the Altair, experienced a burst of sales, then slid quietly into oblivion.

If there are innovators who lose there must be followers/imitators who win. A classic example is IBM with its PC, a great success since the time it was introduced in 1981. Neither the architecture nor components embedded in the IBM PC were considered advanced when introduced; nor was the way the technology was packaged a significant departure from then-current practice. Yet the IBM PC was fabulously successful and established MS-DOS as the leading operating system for 16-bit PCs. By the end of 1984, IBM has shipped over 500,000 PCs, and many considered that it had irreversibly eclipsed Apple in the PC industry.

3. Profiting from Innovation: Basic Building Blocks

In order to develop a coherent framework within which to explain the distribution of outcomes illustrated in Fig. 2, three fundamental building blocks must first be

● Legal instruments   ● Nature of technology

    - Patents   - Product

    - Copyrights   - Process

    - Trade secrets   - Tacit

                               - Codified

Fig. 3. Appropriability regime: Key dimensions.

put in place: the appropriability regime, complementary assets, and the dominant design paradigm.

3.1. *Regime of Appropriability*

A regime of appropriability refers to the environmental factors, excluding firm and market structure, that govern an innovator's ability to capture the profits generated by an innovation. The most important dimensions of such a regime are the nature of the technology, and the efficacy of legal mechanisms of protection (Fig. 3).

It has long been known that patents do not work in practice as they do in theory. Rarely, if ever, do patents confer perfect appropriability, although they do afford considerable protection on new chemical products and rather simple mechanical inventions. Many patents can be "invented around" at modest costs. They are especially ineffective at protecting process innovations. Often patents provide little protection because the legal requirements for upholding their validity or for proving their infringement are high.

In some industries, particularly where the innovation is embedded in processes, trade secrets are a viable alternative to patents. Trade secret protection is possible, however, only if a firm can put its product before the public and still keep the underlying technology secret. Usually only chemical formulas and industrial-commercial processes (e.g. cosmetics and recipes) can be protected as trade secrets after they're "out".

The degree to which knowledge is tacit or codified also affects ease of imitation. Codified knowledge is easier to transmit and receive, and is more exposed to industrial espionage and the like. Tacit knowledge by definition is difficult to articulate, and so transfer is hard unless those who possess the know-how in question can demonstrate it to others (Teece [9]). Survey research indicates that methods of appropriability vary markedly across industries, and probably within industries as well (Levin *et al.* [5]).

The property rights environment within which a firm operates can thus be classified according to the nature of the technology and the efficacy of the legal system to assign and protect intellectual property. While a gross simplification, a dichotomy can be drawn between environments in which the appropriability regime is "tight" (technology is relatively easy to protect) and "weak" (technology is almost impossible to protect). Examples of the former include the formula for Coca Cola syrup; an example of the latter would be the Simplex algorithm in linear programming.

3.2. *The Dominant Design Paradigm*

It is commonly recognized that there are two stages in the evolutionary development of a given branch of a science: the preparadigmatic stage when there is no single generally accepted conceptual treatment of the phenomenon in a field of study, and the paradigmatic stage which begins when a body of theory appears to have passed the canons of scientific acceptability. The emergence of a dominant paradigm signals scientific maturity and the acceptance of agreed upon "standards" by which what has been referred to as "normal" scientific research can proceed. These "standards" remain in force unless or until the paradigm is overturned. Revolutionary science is what overturns normal science, as when the Copernicus's theories of astronomy overturned Ptloemy's in the seventeenth century.

Abernathy and Utterback [1] and Dosi [3] have provided a treatment of the technological evolution of an industry which appears to parallel Kuhnian notions of scientific evolution.[2] In the early stages of industry development, product designs are fluid, manufacturing processes are loosely and adaptively organized, and generalized capital is used in production. Competition amongst firms manifests itself in competition amongst designs, which are markedly different from each other. This might be called the preparadigmatic stage of an industry.

At some point in time, and after considerable trial and error in the marketplace, one design or a narrow class of designs begins to emerge as the more promising. Such a design must be able to meet a whole set of user needs in a relatively complete fashion. The Model T Ford, the IBM 360, and the Douglas DC-3 are examples of dominant designs in the automobile, computer, and aircraft industry respectively.

Once a dominant design emerges, competition shifts to price and away from design. Competitive success then shifts to a whole new set of variables. Scale and learning become much more important, and specialized capital gets deployed

---

[2] See Kuhn [4].

as incumbent's seek to lower unit costs through exploiting economies of scale and learning. Reduced uncertainty over product design provides an opportunity to amortize specialized long-lived investments.

Innovation is not necessarily halted once the dominant design emerges; as Clarke [2] points out, it can occur lower down in the design hierarchy. For instance, a "v" cylinder configuration emerged in automobile engine blocks during the 1930s with the emergence of the Ford V-8 engine. Niches were quickly found for it. Moreover, once the product of design stabilizes, there is likely to be a surge of process innovation as producers attempt to lower production costs for the new product (see Fig. 4).

The Abernathy-Utterback framework does not characterize all industries. It seems more suited to mass markets where consumer tastes are relatively homogeneous. It would appear to be less characteristic of small niche markets where the absence of scale and learning economies attaches much less of a penalty to multiple designs. In these instances, generalized equipment will be employed in production.

The existence of a dominant design watershed is of great significance to the distribution of profits between innovator and follower. The innovator may have been responsible for the fundamental scientific breakthroughs as well as the basic design of the new product. However, if imitation is relatively easy, imitators may enter the fray, modifying the product in important ways, yet relying on the fundamental designs pioneered by the innovator. When the game of musical

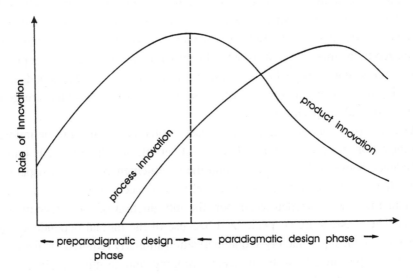

Fig. 4. Innovation over the product/industry life cycle.

chairs stops, and a dominant design emerges, the innovator might well end up positioned disadvantageously relative to a follower. Hence, when imitation is possible and occurs coupled with design modification before the emergence of a dominant design, followers have a good chance of having their modified product annointed as the industry standard, often to the great disadvantage of the innovator.

3.3. *Complementary Assets*

Let the unit of analysis be an innovation. An innovation consists of certain technical knowledge about how to do things better than the existing state of the art. Assume that the know-how in question is partly codified and partly tacit. In order for such know-how to generate profits, it must be sold or utilized in some fashion in the market.

In almost all cases, the successful commercialization of an innovation requires that the know-how in question be utilized in conjunction with other capabilities or assets. Services such as marketing, competitive manufacturing, and after-sales support are almost always needed. These services are often obtained from complementary assets which are specialized. For example, the commercialization of a new drug is likely to require the dissemination of information over a specialized information channel. In some cases, as when the innovation is systemic, the complementary assets may be other parts of a system. For instance; computer hardware typically requires specialized software, both for the operating system, as well as for applications. Even when an innovation is autonomous, as with plug compatible components, certain complementary capabilities or assets will be needed for successful commercialization. Figure 5 summarizes this schematically.

Whether the assets required for least cost production and distribution are specialized to the innovation turns out to be important in the development presented below. Accordingly, the nature of complementary assets are explained in some detail. Figure 6 differentiates between complementary assets which are generic, specialized, and cospecialized.

Generic assets are general purpose assets which do not need to be tailored to the innovation in question. Specialized assets are those where there is unilateral dependence between the innovation and the complementary asset. Cospecialized assets are those of which there is a bilateral dependence. For instance, specialized repair facilities were needed to support the introduction of the rotary engine by Mazda. These assets are cospecialized because of the mutual dependence of the innovation on the repair facility. Containerization similarly required the deployment of some cospecialized assets in ocean shipping and terminals. However, the dependence of trucking on containerized shipping was less than that of

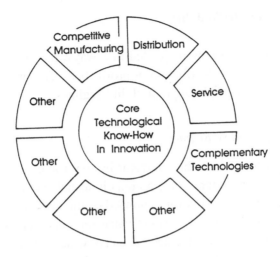

Fig. 5. Complementary assets needed to commercialize an innovation.

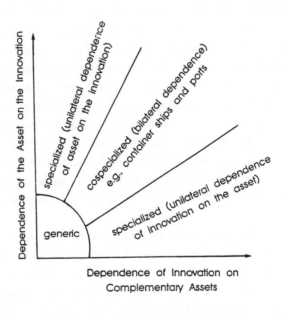

Fig. 6. Complementary assets: Generic, specialized, and cospecialized.

containerized shipping on trucking, as trucks can convert from containers to flat beds at low cost. An example of a generic asset would be the manufacturing facilities needed to make running shoes. Generalized equipment can be employed in the main, exceptions being the molds for the soles.

4. Implications for Profitability

These three concepts can now be related in a way which will shed light on the imitation process, and the distribution of profits between innovator and follower. We begin by examining tight appropriability regimes.

4.1. *Tight Appropriability Regimes*

In those few instances where the innovator has an iron clad patent or copyright protection, or where the nature of the product is such that trade secrets effectively deny imitators access to the relevant knowledge, the innovator is almost assured of translating its innovation into market value for some period of time. Even if the innovator does not possess the desirable endowment of complementary costs, iron clad protection of intellectual property will afford the innovator the time to access these assets. If these assets are generic, contractual relation may well suffice, and the innovator may simply license its technology. Specialized R&D firms are viable in such an environment. Universal Oil Products, an R&D firm developing refining processes for the petroleum industry was one such case in point. If, however, the complementary assets are specialized or cospecialized, contractual relationships are exposed to hazards, because one or both parties will have to commit capital to certain irreversible investments which will be valueless if the relationship between innovator and licensee breaks down. Accordingly, the innovator may find it prudent to expand its boundaries by integrating into specialized and cospecialized assets. Fortunately, the factors which make for difficult imitation will enable the innovator to build or acquire those complementary assets without competing with innovators for their control.

Competition from imitators is muted in this type of regime, which sometimes characterizes the petrochemical industry. In this industry, the protection offered by patents is fairly easily enforced. One factor assisting the licensee in this regard is that most petrochemical processes are designed around a specific variety of catalysts which can be kept proprietary. An agreement not to analyze the catalyst can be extracted from licensees, affording extra protection. However, even if such requirements are violated by licensees, the innovator is still well positioned, as the most important properties of a catalyst are related to its physical structure, and the process for generating this structure cannot be deduced from structural analysis alone. Every reaction technology a company acquires is thus accompanied by an ongoing dependence on the innovating company for the catalyst appropriate to the plant design. Failure to comply with various elements of the licensing contract can thus result in a cutoff in the supply of the catalyst, and possibly facility closure.

Similarly, if the innovator comes to market in the preparadigmatic phase with a sound product concept but the wrong design, a tight appropriability regime will afford the innovator the time needed to perform the trials needed to get the design right. As discussed earlier, the best initial design concepts often turn out to be hopelessly wrong, but if the innovator possesses an impenetrable thicket of patents, or has technology which is simply difficult to copy, then the market may well afford the innovator the necessary time to ascertain the right design before being eclipsed by imitators.

4.2. *Weak Appropriability Regimes*

Tight appropriability is the exception rather than the rule. Accordingly, innovators must turn to business strategy if they are to keep imitators/followers at bay. The nature of the competitive process will vary according to whether the industry is in the paradigmatic or preparadigmatic phase.

4.2.1. Preparadigmatic phase

In the preparadigmatic phase, the innovator must be careful to let the basic design "float" until sufficient evidence has accumulated that a design has been delivered which is likely to become the industry standard. In some industries there may be little opportunity for product modification. In microelectronics, for example, designs become locked in when the circuitry is chosen. Product modification is limited to "debugging" and software modification. An innovator must begin the design process anew if the product doesn't fit the market well. In some respects, however, selecting designs is dictated by the need to meet certain compatibility standards so that new hardware can interface with existing applications software. In one sense, therefore, the design issue for the micro-processor industry today is relatively straightforward: deliver greater power and speed while meeting the computer industry standards of the existing software base. However, from time to time windows of opportunity emerge for the intro-duction of entirely new families of microprocessors which will define a new industry and software standard. In these instances, basic design parameters are less well defined, and can be permitted to "float" until market acceptance is apparent.

The early history of the automobile industry exemplifies exceedingly well the importance for subsequent success of selecting the right design in the preparadigmatic stages. None of the early producers of steam cars survived the early shakeout when the closed body internal combusion engine automobile emerged as the dominant design. The steam car, nevertheless, had numerous early virtues, such as reliability, which the internal combustion engine autos could not deliver.

The British fiasco with the Comet I is also instructive. De Havilland had picked an early design with both technical and commercial flaws. By moving into production, significant irreversibilities and loss of reputation hobbled de Havilland to such a degree that it was unable to convert to the Boeing design which subsequently emerged as dominant. It wasn't even able to occupy second place, which went instead to Douglas.

As a general principle, it appears that innovators in weak appropriability regimes need to be intimately coupled to the market so that user needs can fully impact designs. When multiple parallel and sequential prototyping is feasible, it has clear advantages. Generally such an approach is simply prohibitively costly. When development costs for a large commercial aircraft exceed one billion dollars, variations on a theme are all that is possible.

Hence, the probability that an innovator — defined here as a firm that is first to commercialize a new product design concept — will enter the paradigmatic phase possessing the dominant design is problematic. The probabilities will be higher the lower the relative cost of prototyping, and the more tightly coupled the firm is to the market. The later is a function of organizational design, and can be influenced by managerial choices. The former is embedded in the technology, and cannot be influenced, except in minor ways, by managerial decisions. Hence, in industries with large developmental and prototyping costs — and hence significant irreversibilities — and where innovation of the product concept is easy, then one would expect that the probability that the innovator would emerge as the winner or amongst the winners at the end of the preparadigmatic stage is low.

4.2.2. Paradigmatic stage

In the preparadigmatic phase, complementary assets do not loom large. Rivalry is focused on trying to identify the design which will be dominant. Production volumes are low, and there is little to be gained in deploying specialized assets, as scale economies are unavailable, and price is not a principal competitive factor. However, as the leading design or designs begin to be revealed by the market, volumes increase and opportunities for economies of scale will induce firms to begin gearing up for mass production by acquiring specialized tooling and equipment, and possibly specialized distribution as well. Since these investments involve significant irreversibilities, producers are likely to proceed with caution.

Islands of specialized capital will begin to appear in an industry, which otherwise features a sea of general purpose manufacturing equipment.

However, as the terms of competition begin to change, and prices become increasingly unimportant, access to complementary assets becomes absolutely critical. Since the core technology is easy to imitate, by assumption, commercial success swings upon the terms and conditions upon which the required complementary assets can be accessed.

It is at this point that specialized and cospecialized assets become critically important. Generalized equipment and skills, almost by definition, are always available in an industry, and even if they are not, they do not involve significant irreversibilities. Accordingly, firms have easy access to this type of capital, and even if there is insufficient capacity available in the relevant assets, it can easily be put in place as it involves few risks. Specialized assets, on the other hand, involve significant irreversibilities and cannot be easily accessed by contract, as the risks are significant for the party making the dedicated investment. The firms, which control the cospecialized assets, such as distribution channels, specialized manufacturing capacity, etc. are clearly advantageously positioned relative to an innovator. Indeed, in rare instances where incumbent firms possess an airtight monopoly over specialized assets, and the innovator is in a regime of weak appropriability, all of the profits to the innovation could conceivably innure to the firms possessing the specialized assets who should be able to get the upper hand.

Even when the innovator is not confronted by situations where competitors or potential competitors control key assets, the innovator may still be disadvantaged. For instance, the technology embedded in cardiac pacemakers was easy to imitate, and so competitive outcomes quickly came to be determined by who had easiest access to the complementary assets, in this case specialized marketing. A similar situation has recently arisen in the United States with respect to personal computers. As an industry participant recently observed: "There are a huge numbers of computer manufacturers, companies that make peripherals (e.g. printers, hard disk drives, floppy disk drives), and software companies. They are all trying to get marketing distributors because they cannot afford to call on all of the U.S. companies directly. They need to go through retail distribution channels, such as Businessland, in order to reach the marketplace. The problem today, however, is that many of these companies are not able to get shelf space and thus are having a very difficult time marketing their products. The point of distribution is where the profit and the power are in the marketplace today." (Norman [8, p. 438])

5. Channel Strategy Issues

The above analysis indicates how access to complementary assets, such as manufacturing and distribution, on competitive teams is critical if the innovator is to avoid handling over the lion's share of the profits to imitators, and/or to the owners of the complementary assets that are specialized or cospecialized to the innovation. It is now necessary to delve deeper into the appropriate control structure that the innovator ideally ought to establish over these critical assets.

There are a myriad of possible channels which could be employed. At one extreme the innovator could integrate into all of the necessary complementary assets, as illustrated in Fig. 7, or just a few of them, as illustrated in Fig. 8. Complete integration (Fig. 7) is likely to be unnecessary as well as prohibitively expensive. IT is well to recognize that the variety of assets and competences which need to be accessed is likely to be quite large, even for only modestly complex technologies. To produce a personal computer, for instance, a company needs access to expertise in semiconductor technology, display technology, disk

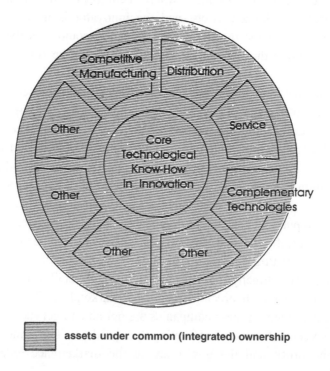

assets under common (integrated) ownership

Fig. 7. Complementary assets internalized for innovation: Hypothetical case #1 (innovator integrated into all complementary assets).

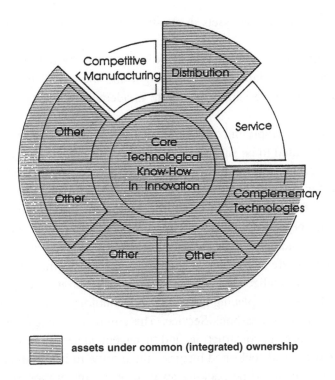

Fig. 8. Complementary assets internalized for innovation: Hypothetical case #2 (innovator subcontracts for manufacturing and service).

drive technology, networking technology, keyboard technology, and several others. No company can keep pace in all of these areas by itself.

At the other extreme, the innovator could attempt to access these assets through straightforward contractual relationships (e.g. component supply contracts, fabrication contracts, service contracts, etc.). In many instances such contracts may suffice, although it sometimes exposes the innovator to various hazards and dependencies that it may well wish to avoid. In between the fully integrand and full contractual extremes, there are a myriad of intermediate forms and channels available. An analysis of properties of the two extreme forms is presented below. A brief synopsis of mixed modes then follows.

5.1. *Contractual Modes*

The advantages of a contractual solution — whereby the innovator signs a contract, such as a license, with independent suppliers, manufacturers or distributors — are obvious. The innovator will not have to make the upfront capital expenditures needed to build or buy the assets in question. This reduces risks as well as cash requirements.

Contracting rather than integrating is likely to be the optimal strategy when the innovators appropriability regime is tight and the complementary assets are available in competitive supply (i.e. there is adequate capacity and a choice of sources).

Both conditions apply in petrochemicals for instance, so an innovator doesn't need to be integrated to be successful. Consider, first, the appropriability regime. As discussed earlier, the protection offered by patents is fairly easily enforced, particularly for process technology, in the petrochemical industry. Given the advantageous feedstock prices available in hydrocarbon rich petrochemical exporters, and the appropriability regime characteristic of this industry, there is no incentive or advantage in owning the complementary assets (production facilities) as they are not typically highly specialized to the innovation. Union Carbide appears to realize this, and has recently adjusted its strategy accordingly. Essentially, Carbide is placing its existing technology into a new subsidiary, Engineering and Hydrocarbons Service. The company is engaging in licensing and offers engineering, construction, and management services to customers who want to take their feedstocks and integrate them forward into petrochemicals. But Carbide itself appears to be backing away from an integration strategy.

Chemical and petrochemical product innovations are quite so easy to protect, which should raise new challenges to innovating firms in the developed nations as they attempt to shift out of commodity petrochemicals. There are already numerous examples of new products that made it to the marketplace, filled a customer need, but never generated competitive returns to the innovator because of imitation. For example, in the 1960s, Dow decided to start manufacturing rigid polyurethene foam. However, it was imitated very quickly by numerous small firms which had lower costs.[3] The absence of low cost manufacturing capability left Dow vulnerable.

Contractual relationships can bring added credibility to the innovator, especially if the innovator is relatively unknown when the contractual partner is established and viable. Indeed, arms-length contracting which embodies more than a simple buy-sell agreement is becoming so common, and is so multifaceted, that the term strategic partnering has been devised to describe it. Even large companies such as IBM are now engaging in it. For IBM, partnering buys access to new technologies enabling the company to "learn things we couldn't have learned

---

[3] Executive V.P. Union Carbide, Robert D. Kennedy, quoted in *Chemical Week*, November 16, 1983, p. 48.

without many years of trial and error."[4] IBM's arrangement with Microsoft to use the latter's MS-DOS operating system software on the IBM PC facilitated the timely introduction of IBM's personal computer into the market.

Smaller less integrated companies are often eager to sign on with established companies because of the name recognition and reputation spillovers. For instance Cipher Data Products, Inc. contracted with IBM to develop a low-priced version of IBM's 3480 0.5 inch streaming cartridge drive, which is likely to become the industry standard. As Cipher management points out, "one of the biggest advantages to dealing with IBM is that, once you've created a product that meets the high quality standards necessary to sell into the IBM world, you can sell into any arena."[5] Similarly, IBM's contract with Microsoft "meant instant credibility" to Microsoft (McKenna, 1985, p. 94).

It is most important to recognize, however, that strategic (contractual) partnering, which is currently very fashionable, is exposed to certain hazards, particularly for the innovator, when the innovator is trying to use contracts to access specialized capabilities. First, it may be difficult to induce suppliers to make costly irreversible commitments which depend for their success on the success of the innovation. To expect suppliers, manufacturers, and distributors to do so is to invite them to take risks along with the innovator. The problem which this poses for the innovator is similar to the problems associated with attracting venture capital. The innovator must persuade its prospective partner that the risk is a good one. The situation is one open to opportunistic abuses on both sides. The innovator has incentives to overstate the value of the innovation, while the supplier has incentives to "run with the technology" should the innovation be a success.

Instances of both parties making irreversible capital commitments nevertheless exist. Apple's Laserwriter — a high resolution laser printer which allows PC users to produce near typeset quality text and art department graphics — is a case in point. Apple persuaded Canon to participate in the development of the Laserwriter by providing subsystems from its copiers — but only after Apple contracted to pay for a certain number of copier engines and cases. In short, Apple accepted a good deal of the financial risk in order to induce Canon to assist in the development and production of the Laserwriter. The arrangement appears to have been prudent, yet there were clearly hazards for both sides. It is

---

[4] Comment attributed to Peter Olson III, IBM's director of business development, as reported in The Strategy Behind IBM's Strategic Alliances, *Electronic Business*, October 1 (1985), 126.

[5] Comment attributed to Norman Farquhar, Cipher's vice president, for strategic development, as reported in *Electronic Business*, October 1 (1985), 128.

difficult to write, execute, and enforce complex development contracts, particularly when the design of the new product is still "floating." Apple was exposed to the risk that its co-innovator Canon would fail to deliver, and Canon was exposed to the risk that the Apple design and marketing effort would not succeed. Still, Apple's alternatives may have been rather limited, inasmuch as it didn't command the requisite technology to "go it alone."

In short, the current euphoria over "strategic partnering" may be partially misplaced. The advantages are being stressed (for example, McKenna [6]) without a balanced presentation of costs and risks. Briefly, there is the risk that the partner won't perform according to the innovator's perception of what the contract requires; there is the added danger that the partner may imitate the innovator's technology and attempt to compete with the innovator. This latter possibility is particularly acute if the provider of the complementary asset is uniquely situated with respect to the complementary asset in question and has the capacity to imitate the technology, which the innovator is unable to protect. The innovator will then find that it has created a competitor who is better positioned than the innovator to take advantage of the market opportunity at hand. *Business Week* has expressed concerns along these lines in its discussion of the "Hollow Corporation."[6]

It is important to bear in mind, however, that contractual or partnering strategies in certain cases are ideal. If the innovator's technology is well protected, and if what the partner has to provide is a "generic" capacity available from many potential partners, then the innovator will be able to maintain the upper hand while avoiding the costs of duplicating downstream capacity. Even if the partner fails to perform, adequate alternatives exist (by assumption, the partners' capacities are commonly available) so the innovator's efforts to successfully commercialize its technology ought to proceed profitably.

5.2. Integration Modes

Integration, which by definition involves ownership, is distinguished from pure contractual modes in that it typically facilitates incentive alignment and control. If an innovator owns rather than rents the complementary assets needed to commercialize, then it is in a position to capture spillover benefits stemming from increased demand for the complementary assets caused by the innovation.

Indeed, an innovator might be in the position, at least before its innovation is announced, to buy up capacity in the complementary assets, possibly to its

---

[6] See *Business Week*, March 3 (1986), 57–59, *Business Week* uses the term to describe a corporation which lacks in-house manufacturing capability.

great subsequent advantage. If futures markets exist, simply taking forward positions in the complementary assets may suffice to capture much of the spillovers.

Even after the innovation is announced, the innovator might still be able to build or buy complementary capacities at competitive prices if the innovation has iron clad legal protection (i.e. if the innovation is in a tight appropriability regime). However, if the innovation is not tightly protected and once "out" is

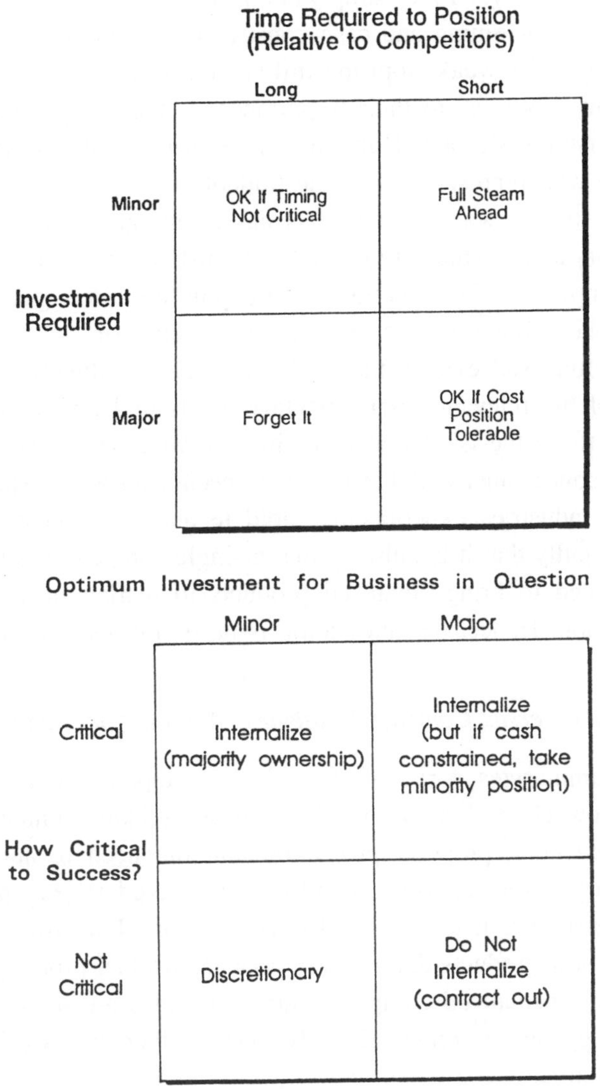

Fig. 9. Specialized complementary assets and weak appropriability: Integration calculus.

easy to imitate, then securing control of complementary capacities is likely to be the key success factor, particularly if those capacities are in fixed supply — so called "bottlenecks." Distribution and specialized manufacturing competences often become bottlenecks.

As a practical matter, however, an innovator may not have the time to acquire or build the complementary assets that ideally it would like to control. This is particularly true when imitation is easy, so that timing becomes critical. Additionally, the innovator may simply not have the financial resources to proceed. The implications of timing and cash constraints are summarized in Fig. 9.

Accordingly, in weak appropriability regimes innovators need to rank complementary assets as to their importance. If the complementary assets are critical, ownership is warranted, although if the firm is cash constrained a minority position may well represent a sensible tradeoff.

Needless to say, when imitation is easy, strategic moves to build or buy complementary assets which are specialized must occur with due reference to the moves of competitors. There is no point moving to build a specialized asset, for instance, if one's imitators can do it faster and cheaper.

It is hopefully self evident that if the innovator is already a large enterprise with many of the relevant complementary assets under its control, integration is not likely to be the issue that it might otherwise be, as the innovating firm will already control many of the relevant specialized and cospecialized assets. However, in industries experiencing rapid technological change, technologies advance so rapidly that it is unlikely that a single company has the full range of expertise needed to bring advanced products to market in a timely and cost effective fashion. Hence, the integration issue is not just a small firm issue.

5.3. *Integration versus Contract Strategies: An Analytic Summary*

Figure 10 summarizes some of the relevant considerations in the form of a decision flow chart. It indicates that a profit seeking innovator, confronted by weak intellectual property protection and the need to access specialized complementary assets and/or capabilities, is forced to expand its activities through integration if it is to prevail over imitators. Put differently, innovators who develop new products that possess poor intellectual property protection but which requires specialized complementary capacities are more likely to parlay their technology into a commercial advantage, rather than see it prevail in the hands of imitators.

Figure 10 makes it apparent that the difficult strategic decisions arise in situations where the appropriability regime is weak and where specialized assets

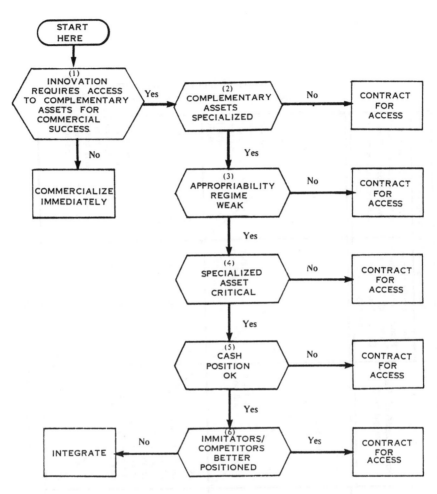

Fig. 10. Flow chart for integration versus contract decision.

are critical to profitable commercialization. These situations, which in reality are very common, require that a fine-grained competitor analysis be part of the innovator's strategic assessment of its opportunities and threats. This is carried a step further in Fig. 11, which looks only at situations where commercialization requires certain specialized capabilities. It indicates the appropriate strategies for the innovators and predicts the outcomes to be expected for the various players.

Three classes of players are of interest: innovators, imitators, and the owners of cospecialized assets (e.g. distributors). All three can potentially benefit or lose from the innovation process. The latter can potentially benefit from the additional business which the innovation may direct in the asset owners direction. Should

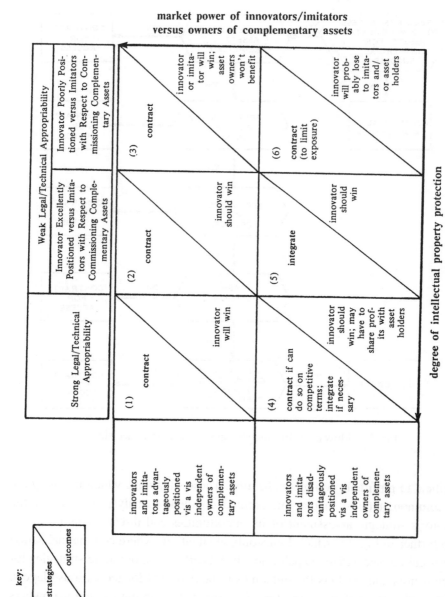

Fig. 11. Contract and integration strategies and outcomes for innovators: Specialized asset case.

the asset turn out to be a bottleneck with respect to commercializing the innovation, the owner of the bottleneck facilities is obviously in a position to extract profits from the innovator and/or imitators.

The vertical axis in Fig. 11 measures how those who possess the technology (the innovator or possibly its imitators) are positioned vis à vis those firms that possess required specialized assets. The horizontal axis measures the "tightness" of the appropriability regime, tight regimes being evidence by iron clad legal protection coupled with technology that is simply difficult to copy; weak regimes offer little in the way of legal protection and the essence of the technology, once released, is transparent to the imitator. Weak regimes are further subdivided according to how the innovator and imitators are positioned vis à vis each other. This is likely to be a function of factors such as lead time and prior positioning in the requisite complementary assets.

Figure 11 makes it apparent that even when firms pursue the optimal strategy, other industry participants may take the jackpot. This possibility is unlikely when the intellectual property in question is tightly protected. The only serious threat to the innovator is where a specialized complementary asset is completely "locked up," a possibility recognized in cell 4. This can rarely be done without the cooperation of government. But it frequently occurs, as when a foreign government closes off access to a foreign market, forcing the innovators to license to foreign firms, but with the government effectively cartelizing the potential licensees. With weak intellectual property protection, however, it is quite clear that the innovator will often loose out to imitators and/or asset holders, even when the innovator is pursuing the appropriate strategy (cell 6). Clearly, incorrect strategies can compound problems. For instance, if innovators integrate when they should contract, a heavy commitment of resources will be incurred for little if any strategic benefit, thereby exposing the innovator to even greater losses than would otherwise be the case. On the other hand, if an innovator tries to contract for the supply of a critical capability when it should build the capability itself, it may well find it has nurtured an imitator better able to serve the market than the innovator itself.

5.4. *Mixed Modes*

The real world rarely provides extreme or pure cases. Decisions to integrate or license involve tradeoffs, compromises, and mixed approaches. It is not surprising therefore that the real world is characterized by mixed modes of organization, involving judicious blends of integration and contracting. Sometimes mixed modes represent transitional phases. For instance, because of the convergence of computer and telecommunication technology, firms in each industry are discovering that they often lack the requisite technical capabilities in the other. Since the technological interdependence of the two requires collaboration amongst those who design different parts of the system, intense cross-boundary coordination and information flows are required. When separate enterprises are involved, agreement must be reached on complex protocol issues amongst parties who see their interests differently. Contractual difficulties can be anticipated since the selection of common technical protocols amongst the parties will often be followed by transaction-specific investments in hardware and software. There is little doubt that this was the motivation behind IBM's purchase of 15 percent of PBX manufacturer Rolm in 1983, a position that was expanded to 100 percent in 1984. IBM's stake in Intel, which began with a 12 percent purchase in 1982, is most probably not a transitional phase leading to 100 percent purchase, because both companies realized that the two corporate cultures are not very compatible, and IBM may not be as impressed with Intel's technology as it once was.

5.5. *The CAT Scanner, the IBM PC, and Nutra-Sweet: Insights from the Framework*

EMI's failure to reap significant returns from the CAT scanner can be explained in large measure by reference to the concepts developed above. The scanner which EMI developed was of a technical sophistication much higher than would normally be found in a hospital, requiring a high level of training, support, and servicing. EMI had none of these capabilities, could not easily contract for them, and was slow to realize their importance. It most probably could have formed a partnership with a company like Siemens to access the requisite capabilities. Its failure to do so was a strategic error compounded by the very limited intellectual property protection which the law afforded the scanner. Although subsequent court decisions have upheld some of EMI's patent claims, once the product was in the market it could be reverse engineered and its essential features copied. Two competitors, GE and Technicare, already possessed the complementary capabilities that the scanner required, and they were also technologically capable. In addition, both were experienced marketers of medical equipment, and had reputations for quality, reliability and service. GE and Technicare were thus able to commit their R&D resources to developing a competitive scanner, borrowing ideas from EMI's scanner, which they undoubtedly had access to through cooperative hospitals, and improving on it where they could while they rushed to market. GE began taking orders in 1976 and soon after made inroads on EMI. In 1977 concern for rising health care costs caused the Carter Administration to introduce "certificate of need" regulation, which required HEW's approval on expenditures on big ticket items like CAT scanners. This severely cut the size of the available market.

By 1978 EMI had lost market share leadership to Technicare, which was in turn quickly overtaken by GE. In October 1979, Godfrey Houndsfield of EMI shared the Nobel prize for invention of the CT scanner. Despite this honor, and the public recognition of its role in bringing this medical breakthrough to the world, the collapse of its scanner business forced EMI in the same year into the arms of a rescuer, Thorn Electrical Industries, Ltd. GE subsequently acquired what was EMI's scanner business from Thorn for what amounted to a pittance.[7] Though royalties continued to flow to EMI, the company had failed to capture the lion's share of the profits generated by the innovation it had pioneered and successfully commercialized.

If EMI illustrates how a company with outstanding technology and an excellent product can fail to profit from innovation while the imitators succeeded, the story of the IBM PC indicates how a new product representing a very modest technological advance can yield remarkable returns to the developer.

The IBM PC, introduced in 1981, was a success despite the fact that the architecture was ordinary and the components standard. Philip Estridge's design team in Boca Raton, Florida, decided to use existing technology to produce a solid, reliable micro rather than state of the art. With a one-year mandate to develop a PC, Estridge's team could do little else.

However, the IBM PC did use what at the time was a new 16-bit microprocessor (the Intel 8088) and a new disk operating system (DOS) adapted for IBM by Microsoft. Other than the microprocessor and the operating system, the IBM PC incorporated existing micro "standards" and used off-the-shelf parts from outside vendors. IBM did write its own BIOS (Basic Input/Output System) which is embedded in ROM, but this was a relatively straightforward programming exercise.

The key to the PC's success was not the technology. It was the set of complementary assets which IBM either had or quickly assembled around the PC. In order to expand the market for PCs, there was a clear need for an expandable, flexible microcomputer system with extensive applications software. IBM could have based its PC system on its own patented hardware and copyrighted software. Such an approach would cause complementary products to be cospecialized, forcing IBM to develop peripherals and a comprehensive library of software in a very short time. Instead, IBM adopted what might be called an

---

[7] See GE Gobbles a Rival in CT Scanners, *Business Week*, May 19 (1980), issue no. 2637.

"induced contractual" approach. By adopting an open system architecture, as Apple had done, and by making the operating system information publicly available, a spectacular output of third part software was induced. IBM estimated that by mid-1983, at least 3000 hardware and software products were available for the PC.[8] Put differently, IBM pulled together the complementary assets, particularly software, which success required, without even using contracts, let alone integration. This was despite the fact that the software developers were creating assets that were in part cospecialized with the IBM PC, at least in the first instance.

A number of special factors made this seem a reasonable risk to the software writers. A critical one was IBM's name and commitment to the project. The reputation behind the letters I.B.M. is perhaps the greatest cospecialized asset the company possesses. The name implied that the product would be marketed and serviced in the IBM tradition. It guaranteed that PC-DOS would become an industry standard, so that the software business would not be solely dependent on IBM, because emulators were sure to enter. It guaranteed access to retail distribution outlets on competitive terms. The consequences was that IBM was able to take product which represented at best a modest technological accomplishment, and turn into a fabulous commercial success. The case demonstrates the role that complementary assets play in determining outcomes.

The spectacular success and profitability of G.D. Searle's NutraSweet is an uncommon story which is also consistent with the above framework. In 1982, Searle reported combined sales of $74 million for NutraSweet and its table top version, Equal. In 1983, this surged to $336 million. In 1985, NutraSweet sales exceeded $700 million[9] and Equal had captured 50 percent of the U.S. sugar substitute market and was number one in five other countries.

NutraSweet, which is Searle's tradename for aspartame, has achieved rapid acceptance in each of its FDA approved categories because of its good taste and ability to substitute directly for sugar in many applications. However, Searle's earnings from NutraSweet and the absence of a strategic challenge can be traced in part to Searle's clever strategy.

It appears that Searle has managed to establish an exceptionally tight appropriability regime around NutraSweet — one that may well continue for some time after the patent has expired. No competitor appears to have successfully "invented around" the Searle patent and commercialized an alternative, no doubt

---

[8] F. Gens and C. Christiansen, Could 1,000,000 IBM PC Users be Wrong, *Byte*, November 1983, p. 88.

[9] See *Monsanto Annual Report*, 1985.

in part because the FDA approval process would have to begin anew for an imitator who was not violating Searle's patents. A competitor who tried to replicate the aspartame molecule with minor modification to circumvent the patent would probably be forced to replicate the hundreds of tests and experiments which proved aspartame's safety. Without patent protection, FDA approval would provide no shield against imitators coming to market with an identical chemical and who could establish to the FDA that it is the same compound that had already been approved. Without FDA approval on the other hand, the patent protection would be worthless for the product would not be sold for human consumption.

Searle has aggressively pushed to strengthen its patent protection. The company was granted U.S. patent protection in 1970. It has also obtained patent protection in Japan, Canada, Australia, U.K., France, Germany, and a number of other countries. However, most of these patents carry a 17-year life. Since the product was only approved for human consumption in 1982, the 17-year patent life was effectively reduced to five. Recognizing the obvious importance of its patent Searle pressed for and obtained special legislation in November 1984 extending the patent protection on aspartame for another 5 years. The U.K. provided a similar extension. In almost every other nation, however, 1987 will mark the expiration of the patent.

When the patent expires, however, Searle will still have several valuable assets to help keep imitators at bay. Searle has gone to great lengths to create and promulgate the use of its NutraSweet name and a distinctive "Swirl" logo on all goods licensed to use the ingredient. The company has also developed the "Equal" tradename for a table top version of the sweetener. Trademark law in the U.S. provides protection against "unfair" competition in branded products for as long as the owner of the mark continues to use it. Both the NutraSweet and Equal trademarks will become essential assets when the patents on aspartame expire. Searle may well have convinced consumers that the only real form of sweetener is NutraSweet/Equal. Consumers know most other artificial sweeteners by their generic names — saccharin and cyclamates.

Clearly, Searle is trying to build a position in complementary assets to prepare for the competition which will surely arise. Searle's joint venture with Ajinomoto ensures them access to that company's many years of experience in the production of biochemical agents. Much of this knowledge is associated with techniques for distillation and synthesis of the delicate hydrocarbon compounds that are the ingredients of NutraSweet, and is therefore more tacit than codified. Searle has begun to put these techniques to use in its own $160 million Georgia production facility. It can be expected that Searle will use trade secrets to the maximum to keep this know-how proprietary.

By the time its patent expires, Searle's extensive research into production techniques for L-phenyl-alanine, and its 8 years of experience in the Georgia plant, should give it a significant cost advantage over potential aspartame competitors. Trade secret protection, unlike patents, has no fixed lifetime and may well sustain Searle's position for years to come.

Moreover, Searle has wisely avoided renewing contracts with suppliers when they have expired.[10] Had Searle subcontracted manufacturing for NutraSweet, it would have created a manufacturer who would then be in a position to enter the aspartame market itself, or to team up with a marketer of artificial sweeteners. But keeping manufacturing inhouse, and be developing a valuable tradename, Searle has a good chance of protecting its market position from dramatic inroads once patents expire. Clearly, Searle seems to be astutely aware of the importance of maintaining a "tight appropriability regime" and using cospecialized assets strategically.

6. Implications for R&D Strategy, Industry Structure, and Trade Policy

6.1. *Allocating R&D Resources*

The analysis so far assumes that the firm has developed an innovation for which a market exists. It indicates the strategies which the firm must follow to maximize its share of industry profits relative to imitators and other competitors. There is no guarantee of success even if optimal strategies are followed.

The innovator can improve its total return to R&D, however, by adjusting its R&D investment portfolio to maximize the probability that technological discoveries will emerge that are either easy to protect with existing intellectual property law, or which require for commercialization cospecialized assets already within the firm's repertoire of capabilities. Put differently, if an innovating firm does not target its R&D resources towards new products and processes which it can commercialize advantageously relative to potential imitators and/or followers, then it is unlikely to profit from its investment in R&D. In this sense, a firm's history — and the assets it already has in place — ought to condition its R&D investment decisions. Clearly, an innovating firm with considerable assets already in place is free to strike out in new directions, so long as in doing so it is

---

[10] Purification Engineering, which had spent $5 million to build a phenylalanine production facility, was told in January 1985 that their contract would not be renewed. In May, Genex, which claimed to have invested $25 million, was given the same message, A Bad Aftertaste, *Business Week*, July 15 (1985), issue no. 2903.

cognizant of the kinds of capabilities required to successfully commercialize the innovation. It is therefore rather clear that the R&D investment decision cannot be divorced from the strategic analysis of markets and industries, and the firm's position within them.

6.2. *Small Firm versus Large Firm Comparisons*

Business commentators often remark that many small entrepreneurial firms which generate new, commercially valuable technology fail while large multinational firms, often with a less meritorious record with respect to innovation, survive and prosper. One set of reasons for this phenomenon is now clear. Large firms are more likely to possess the relevant specialized and cospecialized assets within their boundaries at the time of new product introduction. They can therefore do a better job of milking their technology, however meager, to maximum advantage. Small domestic firms are less likely to have the relevant specialized and cospecialized assets within their boundaries and so will either have to incur the expense of trying to build them, or of trying to develop coalitions with competitors/ owners of the specialized assets.

6.3. *Regimes of Appropriability and Industry Structure*

In industries where legal methods of protection are effective, or where new products are just hard to copy, the strategic necessity for innovating firms to integrate into cospecialized assets would appear to be less compelling than in industries where legal protection is weak. In cases where legal protection is weak or nonexistent, the control of cospecialized assets will be needed for long-run survival.

In this regard, it is instructive to examine the U.S. drug industry (Temin [10]). Beginning in the 1940s, the U.S. Patent Office began, for the first time, to grant patents on certain natural substances that involved difficult extraction procedures. Thus, in 1948, Merck received a patent on streptomycin, which was a natural substance. However, it was not the extraction process but the drug itself which received the patent. Hence, patents were important to the drug industry in terms of what could be patented (drugs), but they did not prevent imitation [10, p. 436]. Sometimes just changing one molecule will enable a company to come up with a different substance which does not violate the patent. Had patents been more all-inclusive — and I am not suggesting they should — licensing would have been an effective mechanism for Merck to extract profits from its innovation. As it turns out, the emergence of close substitutes, coupled with FDA regulation which had the de facto effect of reducing the elasticity of demand for drugs, placed high rewards on a product differentiation strategy. This required extensive marketing, including a sales force that could directly contact doctors, who were the purchasers of drugs through their ability to create prescriptions.[11] The result was exclusive production (i.e. the earlier industry practice of licensing was dropped) and forward integration into marketing (the relevant cospecialized asset).

Generally, if legal protection of the innovator's profits is secure, innovating firms can select their boundaries based simply on their ability to identify user needs and respond to those through research and development. The weaker the legal methods of protection, the greater the incentive to integrate into the relevant cospecialized assets. Hence, as industries in which legal protection is weak begin to mature, integration into innovation-specific cospecialized assets will occur. Often this will take the form of backward, forward and lateral integration. (Conglomerate integration is not part of this phenomenon.) For example, IBM's purchase of Rolm can be seen as a response to the impact of technological change on the identity of the cospecialized assets relevant to IBM's future growth.

6.4. *Industry Maturity, New Entry, and History*

As technologically progressive industries mature, and a greater proportion of the relevant cospecialized assets are brought in under the corporate umbrellas of incumbents, new entry becomes more difficult. Moreover, when it does occur it is more likely to involve coalition formation very early on. Incumbents will for sure own the cospecialized assets, and new entrants will find it necessary to forge links with them. Here lies the explanation for the sudden surge in "strategic partnering" now occurring internationally, and particularly in the computer and telecommunications industry. Note that it should not be interpreted in anti-competitive terms. Given existing industry structure, coalitions ought to be seen not as attempts to stifle competition, but as mechanisms for lowering entry requirements for innovators.

In industries in which technological change of a particular kind has occurred, which required deployment of specialized and/or cospecialized assets at the time,

---

[11] In the period before FDA regulation, all drugs other than narcotics were available over-the-counter. Since the end user could purchase drugs directly, sales were price sensitive. Once prescriptions were required, this price sensitivity collapsed; the doctors not only did not have to pay for the drugs, but in most cases they were unaware of the prices of the drugs they were prescribing.

a configuration of firm boundaries may well have arisen which no longer as compelling efficiencies. Considerations which once dictated integration may no longer hold, yet there may not be strong forces leading to divestiture. Hence existing firm boundaries may in some industries — especially those where the technological trajectory and attendent specialized asset requirements has changed — be rather fragile. In short, history matters in terms of understanding the structure of the modern business enterprise. Existing firm boundaries cannot always be assumed to have obvious rationales in terms of today's requirements.

6.5. *The Importance of Manufacturing to International Competitiveness*

Practically all forms of technological know-how must be embedded in goods and services to yield value to the consumer. An important policy for the innovating nation is whether the identity of the firms and nations performing this function matter.

In a world of tight appropriability and zero transactions cost — the world of neoclassical trade theory — it is a matter of indifference whether an innovating firm has an in-house manufacturing capability, domestic or foreign. It can simply engage in arms-length contracting (patent licensing, know-how licensing, co-production, etc.) for the sale of the output of the activity in which it has a comparative advantage (in this case R&D) and will maximize returns by specializing in what it does best.

However, in a regime of weak appropriability, and especially where the requisite manufacturing assets are specialized to the innovation, which is often the case, participation in manufacturing may be necessary if an innovator is to appropriate the rents from its innovation. Hence, if an innovator's manufacturing costs are higher than those of its imitators, the innovator may well end up ceding the lion's share of profits to the imitator.

In a weak appropriability regime, low cost imitator-manufacturers may end up capturing all of the profits from innovation. In a weak appropriability regime where specialized manufacturing capabilities are required to produce new products, an innovator with a manufacturing disadvantage may find that its advantage at early stage research and development will have no commercial value. This will eventually cripple the innovator, unless it is assisted by governmental processes. For example, it appears that one of the reasons why U.S. color TV manufacturers did not capture the lion's share of the profits from the innovation, for which RCA was primarily responsible, was that RCA and its American licenses were not competitive at manufacturing. In this context, concerns that the decline of manufacturing threatens the entire economy appear to be well founded.

A related implication is that as the technology gap closes, the basis of competition in an industry will shift to the cospecialized assets. This appears to be what is happening in microprocessors. Intel is no longer out ahead technologically. As Gordon Moore, CEO of Intel points out, "Take the top 10 [semiconductor] companies in the world ... and it is hard to tell at any time who is ahead of whom .... It is clear that we have to be pretty damn close to the Japanese from a manufacturing standpoint to compete."[12] It is not just that strength in one area is necessary to compensate for weakness in another. As technology becomes more public and less proprietary through easier imitation, then strength in manufacturing and other capabilities is necessary to derive advantage from whatever technological advantages an innovator may possess.

Put differently, the notion that the United States can adopt a "designer role" in international commerce, while letting independent firms in other countries such as Japan, Korea, Taiwan, or Mexico do the manufacturing, is unlikely to be viable as a long-run strategy. This is because profits will accrue primarily to the low cost manufacturers (by providing a larger sales base over which they can exploit their special skills). Where imitation is easy, and even where it is not, there are obvious problems in transacting in the market for know-how, problems which are described in more detail elsewhere [9]. In particular, there are difficulties in pricing an intangible asset whose true performance features are difficult to ascertain ex ante.

The trend in international business towards what Miles and Snow [7] call "dynamic networks" — characterized by vertical disintegration and contracting — ought thus be viewed with concern. (*Business Week*, March 3 (1986), has referred to the same phenomenon as the Hollow Corporation.) "Dynamic networks" may not so much reflect innovative organizational forms, but the disassembly of the modern corporation because of deterioration in national capacities, manufacturing in particular, which are complementary to technological innovation. Dynamic networks may therefore signal not so much the rejuvenation of American enterprise, but its piecemeal demise.

6.6. *How Trade and Investment Barriers can Impact Innovators' Profits*

In regimes of weak appropriability, governments can move to shift the distribution of the gains from innovation away from foreign innovators and towards domestic firms by denying innovators ownership of specialized assets. The foreign firm,

---

[12] Institutionalizing the Revolution, *Forbes*, June 16 (1986), p. 35.

which by assumption is an innovator, will be left with the option of selling its intangible assets in the market for know-how if both trade and investment are foreclosed by government policy. This option may appear better than the alternative (no renumeration at all from the market in question). Licensing may then appear profitable, but only because access to the complementary assets is blocked by government.

Thus when an innovating firm generating profits needs to access complementary assets abroad, host governments, by limiting access, can sometimes milk the innovators for a share of the profits, particularly that portion which originates from sales in the host country. However, the ability of host governments to do so depends importantly on the criticality of the host country's assets to the innovator. If the cost and infrastructure characteristics of the host country are such that it is the world's lowest cost manufacturing site, and if domestic industry is competitive, then by acting as a de facto monopsonist the host country government ought to be able to adjust the terms of access to the complementary assets so as to appropriate a greater share of the profits generated by the innovation.[13]

If, on the other hand, the host country offers no unique complementary assets, except access to its own market, restrictive practices by the government will only redistribute profits with respect to domestic rather than worldwide sales.

6.7. *Implications for the International Distribution of the Benefits from Innovation*

The above analysis makes transparent that innovators who do not have access to the relevant specialized and cospecialized assets may end up ceding profits to imitators and other competitors, or simply to the owners of the specialized or cospecialized assets.

Even when the specialized assets are possessed by the innovating firm, they may be located abroad. Foreign factors of production are thus likely to benefit from research and development activities occurring across borders. There is little doubt, for instance, that the inability of many American multinationals to sustain competitive manufacturing in the U.S. is resulting in declining returns to U.S. labor. Stockholders and top management probably do as well if not better when a multinational accesses cospecialized assets in

---

[13] If the host country market structure is monopolistic in the first instance, private actors might be able to achieve the same benefit. What government can do is to force collusion of domestic enterprises to their mutual benefit.

the firm's foreign subsidiaries; however, if there is unemployment in the factors of production supporting the specialized and cospecialized assets in question, then the foreign factors of production will benefit from innovation originating beyond national borders. This speaks to the importance to innovating nations of maintaining competence and competitiveness in the assets which complement technological innovation, manufacturing being a case in point. It also speaks to the importance to innovating nations of enhancing the protection afforded worldwide to intellectual property.

However, it must be recognized that there are inherent limits to the legal protection of intellectual property, and that business and national strategy are therefore likely to the critical factors in determining how the gains from innovation are shared worldwide. By making the correct strategic decision, innovating firms can move to protect the interests of stockholders; however, to ensure that domestic rather than foreign cospecialized assets capture the lion's share of the externalities spilling over to complementary assets, the supporting infrastructure for those complementary assets must not be allowed to decay. In short, if a nation has prowess at innovation, then in the absence of iron clad protection for intellectual property, it must maintain well-developed complementary assets if it is to capture the spillover benefits from innovation.

7. Conclusion

The above analysis has attempted to synthesize from recent research in industrial organization and strategic management a framework within which to analyze the distribution of the profits from innovation. The framework indicates that the boundaries of the firm are an important strategic variable for innovating firms. The ownership of complementary assets, particularly when they are specialized and/or cospecialized, help establish who wins and who loses from innovation. Imitators can often outperform innovators if they are better positioned with respect to critical complementary assets. Hence, public policy aimed at promoting innovation must focus not only on R&D, but also on complementary assets, as well as the underlying infrastructure. If government decides to stimulate innovation, it would seem important to clear away barriers which impede the development of complementary assets which tend to be specialized or cospecialized to innovation. To fail to do so will cause an unnecessary large portion of the profits from innovation to flow to imitators and other competitors. If these firms lie beyond one's national borders, there are obvious implications for the internal distribution of income.

When applied to world markets, results similar to those obtained from the "new trade theory" are suggested by the framework. In particular, tariffs and other restrictions on trade can in some cases injure innovating firms while simultaneously benefiting protected firms when they are imitators. However, the propositions suggested by the framework are particularized to appropriability regimes, suggesting that economy-wide conclusions will be illusive. The policy conclusions derivable for commodity petrochemicals, for instance, are likely to be different than those that would be arrived at for semiconductors.

The approach also suggests that the product life cycle model of international trade will play itself out very differently in different industries and markets, in part according to appropriability regimes and the nature of the assets which need to be employed to convert a technological success into a commercial one. Whatever its limitations, the approach establishes that it is not so much the structure of markets but the structure of firms, particularly the scope of their boundaries, coupled with national policies with respect to the development of complementary assets, which determines the distribution of the profits amongst innovators and imitator/followers.

References

1. W.J. Abernathy and J.M. Utterback, Patterns of Industrial Innovation, *Technology Review* 80(7) (January/July 1978), 40–47.
2. K.B. Clarke, The Interaction of Design Hierarchies and Market Concepts in Technological Evolution, *Research Policy* 14 (1985), 235–251.
3. G. Dosi, Technological Paradigms and Technological Trajectories, *Research Policy* 11 (1982), 147–162.
4. T. Kuhn, *The Structure of Scientific Revolutions*, 2nd ed. (University of Chicago Press, Chicago, 1970).
5. R. Levin, A. Klevorick, N. Nelson, and S. Winter, Survey Research on R&D Appropriability and Technological Opportunity, unpublished manuscript, Yale University, 1984.
6. R. McKenna, Market Positioning in High Technology, *California Management Review*, XXVII(3) (Spring 1985).
7. R.E. Miles and C.C. Snow, Network Organizations: New Concepts for New Forms, *California Management Review* (Spring 1986), 62–73.
8. D. A. Norman, Impact on Entrepreneurship and Innovations on the Distribution of Personal Computers, in R. Landau and N. Rosenberg (eds.), *The Positive Sum Strategy* (National Academy Press, Washington, DC, 1986).

9. D.J. Teece, The Market for Know-How and the Efficient International Transfer of Technology, *Annals of the American Academy of Political and Social Science*, November 1981.
10. P. Temin, Technology, Regulation, and Market Structure in the Modern Pharmaceutical Industry, *The Bell Journal of Economics* (Autumn 1979), 429–446.

Capturing Value from Knowledge Assets: The New Economy, Markets for Know-How, and Intangible Assets

David J. Teece

Management is always confronting new challenges. Sometimes these are simply yesterday's challenges presented anew in a slightly different context. But from time to time, new challenges emerge that have no close precedent. Managing intellectual capital in the information age is possibly one such challenge, as advanced industrial economies have entered a new epoch. Many sectors are animated by new economics, where the payoff to managing knowledge astutely has been dramatically amplified, in part because of the phenomena of increasing returns, in part because of new information technology, and in part because of the changing role of intellectual property. Moreover, the context in which knowledge assets are created and exploited is today truly global.

Knowledge and Competitive Advantage

It has long been recognized that "economic prosperity rests upon knowledge and it useful application."[1] Indeed, "the increase in the stock of useful knowledge and the extension of its application are the essence of modern economic growth."[2] Enlightened economic historians have long emphasized the role of technology and organization in economic development.

Accordingly, one must inquire about the present cacophony on knowledge management. At least two classes of explanations appear to be valid. One class is simply that policy and strategy analysts have worn intellectual blinders, so that what has been obvious to some — namely, that knowledge and its applications are at the very roots of modern economic growth and prosperity — has not been

Reprinted from *California Management Review*, 40(3) (Spring 1998), 55–79.

transparent to all. Competing theories that stressed the role of the capital stock and natural resources would appear to have received unwarranted extended play in textbooks and policy pronouncements. Meanwhile, the study of innovation and knowledge transfer has been, until quite recently, relegated to a backwater in mainstream economics as well as in the other social sciences.

However, a small cadre of dedicated economists have long emphasized the role of technological innovation, often with few accolades.[3] Now the mainstream economic theorists[4] and mainstream business have begun to recognize the importance of this literature. Moreover, the ideas have become established and disseminated to a wider audience through the efforts of insightful protagonists like Ikujiro Nonaka and Hirotaka Takeuchi.[5]

The second class of factors relates to structural changes that have occurred in the economies of advanced developed countries. These have modified the nature of what is strategic and have served to highlight the importance of knowledge and its management.

Liberalization of Markets

Since the Kennedy round of trade negotiations in the 1960s, markets for goods and services have become increasingly liberalized. Tariff and non-tariff barriers have been lowered. While the world is far from being properly characterized as having adopted free trade, significant progress has been made. Final goods, intermediate goods, and factors of production flow globally with far more freedom than in earlier times. Restrictions on knowledge transfers by both importers and exporters have also been relaxed.

Accordingly, firms cannot so rapidly earn supra-competitive returns by locating behind trade barriers. Transportation costs have also fallen, and information about market opportunities often diffuses instantaneously. Together, these developments have reduced the shelter previously afforded to privileged positions in domestic markets. Competition has been sharpened.

Expansion of What's Tradable

Markets have not only liberalized, but also have been created for many types of "intermediate" products where markets hitherto didn't exist. This has been most amplified in securities markets where swaps and swaptions, index futures, program trading, butterfly spreads, puttable bonds, eurobonds, collateralized mortgage bonds, zero-coupon bonds, portfolio insurance, and synthetic cash are now commonplace.[6] This sudden burst of financial innovation began but 20 years ago, propelled by the move to floating exchange rates and the need to protect transactions from uncertainty. It has been aided by developments in computer and information technology, which have enabled the design of new financial products and the execution of complex transactions. Also contributing has been the desire to circumvent taxation and regulation.

In addition, firms have shown greater affection for outsourcing as suppliers take advantage of the growth in the number of potential suppliers at home and abroad. In the petroleum industry, for instance, markets exist not only for many grades of crude oil and refined products, but also for a range of intermediate products (e.g., MTB) which were rarely traded, if at all, a mere decade ago. Moreover, certain forms of intellectual property are "exchanged" (cross-licensed) or sold with far greater frequency than was hitherto experienced.[7]

Whenever a market exists that is open to all qualified comers, including newcomers, then competitive advantage for firms cannot flow from participation in the market.[8] Except in rare instances where one or a few firms can "corner the market," having a market-based exchange relationship cannot yield competitive advantage because it can be so easily replicated by others, who can simply enter the same (efficient) market and secure access to the same inputs or dispose of the same outputs. In short, efficient markets are a great leveler.

Strengthening of Intellectual Property Regimes

Intellectual property is an aspect of property rights which augments the importance of know-how assets. Knowledge assets are often inherently difficult to copy; moreover, like physical assets, some knowledge assets enjoy protection against theft under the Intellectual property laws of individual nation states. In advanced nations, these laws typically embrace patents, trademarks, trade secrets, and copyright.

Intellectual property systems have been strengthened since the 1980s, both in the U.S. and abroad. Moreover, intellectual property is not just important in the new industries — such as microelectronics and biotechnology — it remains important in pharmaceuticals and chemicals and is receiving renewed interest in more mature industries such as petroleum and steel.

The growth of information technology has also amplified the importance of intellectual property and has injected intellectual property into new contexts. For example, it is not uncommon to discover the foundations of corporate success for wholesalers and retailers buried in copyrighted software and in information technology supporting order entry and logistics.

The Growing Importance of Increasing Returns

Contemporary textbook understandings of how markets operate and how firms compete has been derived from the work of economists such as Marshall and Chamberlain. These views assume diminishing returns and assign industry participants identical production functions (implying the use of identical technologies by all competitors) where marginal costs increase. Industry equilibrium with numerous participants arise because marginal-cost curves slope upwards, thereby exhausting scale advantages at the level of the firm, making room for multiple industry participants. This theory was useful for understanding 18th century English farms and 19th century Scottish factories and even some 20th century American manufacturers. However, major deficiencies in this view of the world have been apparent for some time — it is a caricature of the firm. Moreover, knowledge is certainly not shared ubiquitously and passed around at zero cost.[9]

In this century, developed economies have undergone a transformation from largely raw material processing and manufacturing activities to the processing of information and the development, application, and transfer of new knowledge. As a consequence, diminishing returns activities have been replaced by activities characterized by increasing returns. The phenomena of increasing returns is usually paramount in knowledge-based industries. With increasing returns, that which is ahead tends to stay ahead. Mechanisms of positive feed-back reinforce the winners and challenge the losers. Whatever the reason one gets ahead — acumen, chance, clever strategy — increasing returns amplify the advantage. With increasing returns, the market at least for a while tilts in favor of the provider that gets out in front. Such a firm need not be the pioneer and need not have the best product.

The increasing returns phenomena is itself driven by several factors. Consider, first, standards and network externalities. To establish networks and interoperability, compatibility standards are usually critical. If such standards are proprietary, ownership of a dominant standard can yield significant "rents." The more a protocol gains acceptance, the greater the consumer benefits (network externalities), and the better the chance the standard has of becoming dominant.

Second, consider customer lock-in. Customer learning and customer investment in high-technology products amplify switching costs. This pushes competition "forward" in the sense that providers will compete especially hard for the original sale, knowing that sales of follow-along equipment and other services will be easier. While such "lock-in" is rarely long lived, it need not be momentary.

Third, consider large up-front costs. Once a high-tech industry is established, large up-front research, development, and design engineering costs are typical. This is most amplified with software products where the first copy costs hundred of millions, and the original cost of the second copy is zero, or very nearly so.

Fourth, consider producer learning. In certain cases, producers become more efficient as experience is gained. If the underlying knowledge base is tacit, so that it resists transfer to other producers, competitors with less experience are at a comparative disadvantage. Producer learning is important where complex processors and complex assembly is involved.

The economics of increasing returns suggest different corporate strategies. In winner-take-all or winner-take-the-lion's-share contexts, there is heightened payoff associated with getting the timing right (one can be too early or too late) and with organizing sufficient resources once opportunity opens up. Very often, competition is like a high-stakes game of musical chairs. Being well positioned when standards gel is essential. The associated styles of competition are, as Brian Arthur points out, much like casino gambling.[10] Strategy involves choosing what games to play, as well as playing with skill. Multimedia, web services, voice recognition, mobile (software) agents, and electronic commerce are all technological/market plays where the rules are not set, the identity of the players poorly appreciated, and the payoffs matrix murky at best. Rewards go to those good at sensing and seizing opportunities.

Seizing opportunities frequently involves identifying and combining the relevant complementary assets needed to support the business. Superior technology alone is rarely enough upon which to build competitive advantage. The winners are the entrepreneurs with the cognitive and managerial skills to discern the shape of the play, and then act upon it. Recognizing strategic errors and adjusting accordingly is a critical part of becoming and remaining successful.

In this environment, there is little payoff to penny pinching, and high payoff to rapidly sensing and then seizing opportunities. This is what is referred to here and elsewhere[11] as dynamic capabilities. Dynamic capabilities are most likely to be resident in firms that are highly entrepreneurial, with flat hierarchies, a clear vision, high-powered incentives, and high autonomy (to ensure responsiveness). The firm must be able to effectively navigate quick turns, as Microsoft did once Gates recognized the importance of the internet. Cost minimization and static optimization provide only minor advantages. Plans are often made and junked with alacrity. Companies must constantly transform and retransform. A "mission critical" orientation is essential.

Decoupling of Information Flows from the Flow of Goods and Services

New information technology and the adoption of standards is greatly assisting connectivity. Once every person and every business is connected electronically through networks, information can flow more readily. The traditional nexus between the economics of goods and services and the economics of information can be broken, and information can be unbundled.

The traditional trade-off between reach (connectivity) and richness (customization, bandwidth) is also being transformed, or at least modified. An insurance salesman is no longer needed to sell term life policies. Sufficient information can be collected by mail or on an internet to enable customers to engage in comparative shopping, and for underwriters to do sufficient assessment of policy holders. As a result, traditional distribution channels are no longer needed for simple life or auto insurance products.

Historically, the transfer/communication of rich information has required proximity and specialized channels to customers, suppliers, and distributors. New developments are undermining traditional value chains and business models. In some cases, more "virtual" structures are viable, or shortly will be viable, especially in certain sectors like financial services. New information technology is facilitating specialization. Bargaining power will be reduced by an erosion in the ability to control information, and customer switching costs will decline, changing industry economics.

The new information technology is also dramatically assisting in the sharing of information. Learning and experience can be much more readily captured and shared. Knowledge learned in the organization can be catalogued and transferred to other applications within and across organizations and geographies. Rich exchange can take place inside the organization, obviating some of the need for formal structures.

Ramifications of New Information and Communications Technologies

Linked information and communications systems in production, distribution, logistics, accounting, marketing, and new product development have the potential to bring together previously fragmented flows of data, thereby permitting the real time monitoring of markets, products, and competitors. The requisite data can then be fed to multifunctional teams working on new product development. Networked computers using rapid communications systems thus enable major advances in corporate and intercorporate monitoring and control systems. Within organizations, computer networks can strengthen links between strategic and operations management, while also assisting linkages externally to discrete and geographically dispersed providers of complementary services.

Network computing, supported by an advanced communications infrastructure, can thus facilitate collaborative entrepreneuralism by stripping out barriers to communication. It challenges existing organization boundaries, divisions, and hierarchies and permits formal organization to be more specialized and responsive. Interorganizationally, networked organizations have blurred and shifting boundaries, and they function in conjunction with other organizations. The networked organization may be highly "virtual," integrating a temporary network of suppliers and customers that emerge around specific opportunities in fast-changing markets. Recurrent reorganization becomes the norm, not the exception.

Service firms, such as lawyers, accountants, management consultants, and information technology consultants — pose interesting issues. If knowledge and experience remain personal and are not somehow shared (either by transfer to other organization members or by being embedded in product) then the firm can at best expect to achieve constant return to scale. Larger organizations will have no advantage over boutiques and will possibly suffer bureaucratic burdens that will sap productivity.

Formalization, the sharing of personal knowledge, and the development of structural approaches as a mechanism to transfer learning throughout the firm may on the other hand sap creativity and impede learning. Ideally, one would like to develop approaches or models which have a common essential logic, but which enable customization of particular features. This is but one of the many challenges to service firms in the new economy where knowledge sharing itself can often be the basis of competitive advantage.

Product Architecture and Technology "Fusion"

With complexity becoming increasingly common, new products are rarely stand-alone items. Rather, they are components of broader systems or architectures. Innovation at the architectural level is more demanding and takes place with less frequency than at the component level, but it has greater impact.

The development of system-level integration [SLI] of ASICs — so-called systems on a chip — illustrates the point. New manufacturing processes and improved design tools have fostered SLI. Because million-gate ASICs are now possible, they can support entire systems on a single piece of silicon. If Dataquest is right, and if industry will be able to place 40 million gates on a single chip by 2000, it will be technically possible to place multiple systems on a single chip.[12]

SLI ASICs have already been designed into high-volume applications such as set-top boxes, multimedia, and wireless telephony. Dataquest estimates that SLI ASICs will pass $15 billion in revenues by the year 2000. However, what is even more significant is the ability of SLI ASICs to fuel further growth of consumer electronics through dramatic reductions in size and power usage, enhanced differentiation and functionally, quicker product development, and still lower cost. This is what the technology can deliver.

Whether the technology does in fact yield its potential depends, however, on certain organizational and managerial changes. Design reuse is of paramount importance when designing high-complexity ASICs or SLI devices. System designers must design on the block level and be able to reuse and alter intellectual property in a number of subsequent designs. As Dataquest notes, "design methodology, design reuse, and intellectual property will play vital roles in determining the winners among both suppliers and users."[13]

The organization of firms and industries and the architecture of products are interrelated. Since, the relevant intellectual property needed to effectuate SLI is almost never owned by a single firm but is widely distributed throughout the industry, new arrangements are needed to support rapid diffusion and expansion of SLI architecture. Indeed, harnessing the full potential of the technology necessarily involves cooperation amongst industry participants, many of whom might also be competitors.

A related development is the increase in convergence or integration of previously disparate technologies. One thinks not just of the convergence of computers and communications, but of mechanical industries and electronics ("mechatronics")[14] or of "robochemistry," the science of applying computerization to drug molecule research, which according to some accounts is leading to "a new age in medicine."[15] This by no means occurs automatically and requires internal structures that are flexible and permeable.

Implications

These development suggest a different dynamic to competition and competitive advantage. The expansion of markets illustrates the point. Since markets are a great leveler, competitive advantage at the level of the firm can flow only from the ownership and successful deployment of non-tradable assets. If the asset or its services are traded or tradable in a market or markets, the assets in question can be accessed by all; so the domains in which competitive advantage can be built narrows as markets expand. Not even human resources can provide the basis for competitive advantage if the skills at issue can be accessed by all in an open labor market.

One class of assets that is especially difficult, although not impossible, to trade involves knowledge assets and, more generally, competences. The market for know-how is riddled with imperfections and "unassisted markets are seriously faulted as institutional devices for facilitating trading in many levels of technological and managerial know-how."[16] Hence, the development of many types of new markets has made know-how increasingly salient as a differentiator, and therefore as a source of the competitive advantage of firms. This can be expected to remain so until know-how becomes more commodity like; and this may happen soon for some components of intellectual property.

The strengthening of intellectual property is an important counterforce to the growing ease of imitation. As the diffusion of knowledge and information accelerates, intellectual property becomes more salient. While intellectual property can be traded, and can sometimes be invented around, it can no longer be infringed with impunity and without penalty.

Increasing returns frequently sharpens the payoff to strategic behavior and amplifies the importance of timing and responsiveness. Meanwhile, the decoupling of information flows from the flow of goods and services is transforming traditional value analysis, and it is suggesting the benefits of more virtual structures and obviating some of the need for hierarchy. Simultaneously, the march of technologies such as integrated circuits is transforming the linkage between intellectual property and products. Technological innovation is requiring the unbundling of the two and the formation of more robust markets for intellectual property. It is in this new environment that a critical dimension of knowledge property. It is in this new environment that a critical dimension of knowledge management has emerged: capturing value from innovative activity.

Capturing Value from Knowledge and Competence

The proper structure, incentives, and management can help firms generate innovation and build knowledge assets. The focus here is not, however, on the creation of knowledge assets, but on their deployment and use.[17] While knowledge assets are grounded in the experience and expertise of individuals, firms provide the physical, social, and resource allocation structure so that knowledge can be shaped into competences. How these competences and knowledge assets are configured and deployed will dramatically shape competitive outcomes and the commercial success of the enterprise. Indeed, the competitive advantage of firms in today's economy stems not from market position, but from difficult to replicate knowledge assets and the manner in which they are deployed. The deployment dimension — involving as it does both entrepreneurial and strategic elements — is where dynamic capabilities are especially important.

It is always useful to distinguish between the creation of new knowledge and its commercialization. The creation of new knowledge through autonomous (specialized) innovation is a critical function. It can be the domain of the individual, or of the research laboratory, or of autonomous business units. It need not require complex organization. Indeed, one can argue that such knowledge creation is increasingly well suited to smaller organizational units.

However, the commercialization of new technology is increasingly the domain of complex organization. The new challenges require new organizational forms and the development and astute exercise of dynamic capabilities. They also require an understanding of the nature of knowledge and competence as strategic assets. The nature of knowledge and the manner in which it can or cannot be bought and sold is critical to the strategic nature of knowledge and competence.

The Nature of Knowledge

Knowledge can be thought of in many ways. In a business context, the following taxonomies are useful.

Codified/Tacit[18]

Tacit knowledge is that which is difficult to articulate in a way that is meaningful and complete. The fact that we know more than we can tell speaks to the tacit dimension. Stand-alone codified knowledge — such as blueprints, formulas, or computer code — need not convey much meaning.

There appears to be a simple but powerful relationship between codification of knowledge and the costs of its transfer. Simply stated, the more a given item of knowledge or experience has been codified, the more economically it can be transferred. This is a purely technical property that depends on the ready availability of channels of communication suitable for the transmission of well-codified information — for example, printing, radio, telegraph, and data networks. Whether information so transferred will be considered meaningful by those who receive it will depend on whether they are familiar with the code selected as well as the different contexts in which it is used.[19]

Uncodified or tacit knowledge, on the other hand, is slow and costly to transmit. Ambiguities abound and can be overcome only when communications take place in face-to-face situations. Errors of interpretation can be corrected by a prompt use of personal feedback. Consider the apprenticeship system as an example. First, a master craftsman can cope with only a limited number of pupils at a time. Second, his teaching has to be dispensed mostly through examples rather than by precept — he cannot easily put the intangible elements of his skill into words. Third, the examples he offers will be initially confusing and ambiguous for his pupils so that learning has to take place through extensive and time-consuming repetition, and mystery will occur gradually on the basis of "feel." Finally, the pupil's eventual mastery of a craft or skill will remain idiosyncratic and will never be a carbon copy of the master's. It is the scope provided for the development of a personal style that defines a craft as something that goes beyond the routine and hence programmable application of a skill.

The transmission of codified knowledge, on the other hand, does not necessarily require face-to-face contact and can often be carried out largely by impersonal means, such as when one computer "talks" to another, or when a technical manual is passed from one individual to another. Messages are better structured and less ambiguous if they can be transferred in codified form.

Observable/Non-observable in use

Much technology is (publicly) observable once sold. A new CT scanner, laser printer, or microprocessor is available for conceptual imitation and reverse engineering once it has been introduced into the market. New products are typically of this kind. Process technology, however, is often different. While in some cases the "signature" of a process may be embedded in a product and is therefore ascertainable through reverse engineering, this is generally not the case. While clues about a manufacturing process may sometimes be gleaned by closely observing the product, much about process technology can be protected if the owners of process technology are diligent in protecting their trade secrets in the factory. Thus, process technology is inherently more protectable than product technology, the patent system put to one side.

Positive/Negative knowledge

Innovation involves considerable uncertainty. Research efforts frequently go down what turns out to be a blind alley. It is well recognized that a discovery (positive knowledge) can focus research on promising areas of inquiry, thereby avoiding blind alleys. However, it is frequently forgotten that knowledge of failures ("this approach doesn't work") is also valuable as it can help steer resource allocation into more promising avenues. For this reason, firms often find it necessary to keep their failures as well as their successes secret, even holding aside issues of embarrassment.

Autonomous/Systematic knowledge

Autonomous knowledge is that which yields value without major modifications of systems in which it might embedded. Fuel injection, the self-starter, and power steering were innovations that did not require major modifications to the automobile, although the latter did enable manufactures to put more weight on the front axle and to more readily fit cars with radial tires. Systematic innovation, on the other hand, requires modification to other sub-systems. For instance, the tungsten filament light bulb would not have found such wide application without the development of a system for generating and distributing electricity.

Intellectual property regime

There are many other dimensions along which knowledge could be defined or along which innovations could be classified.[20] However, the only other key dimension to be identified here is whether or not the knowledge in question enjoys protection under the intellectual property laws.

Patents, trade secrets, trademarks provide protection for different mediums in different ways. The strongest form of intellectual property is the patent. A valid patent provides rights for exclusive use by the owner, although depending on the scope of the patent is may be possible to invent around it, albeit at some cost. Trade secrets do not provide rights of exclusion over any knowledge domain, they do protect covered secrets in perpetuity. Trade secrets can well enhance the value of a patent position. Different knowledge mediums qualify for different types of intellectual property protection. The degree that intellectual property keeps imitators at bay may depend also on other external factors, such as regulations, which may block or limit the scope for invent-around alternatives.

Replicability, Imitability, and Appropriability[21]

Replication involves transferring or redeploying competences from one concrete economic setting to another. Since productive knowledge is typically embodied, this cannot be accomplished by simply transmitting information. Only in those instances where all relevant knowledge is fully codified and understood can replication be collapsed into a simple problem of information transfer. Too often, the contextual dependence of original performance is poorly appreciated, so unless firms have replicated their systems of productive knowledge on many prior occasions, the act of replication is likely to be difficult.[22] Indeed, replication and transfer are often impossible absent the transfer of people, though this can be minimized if investments are made to convert tacit knowledge to codified knowledge. Often, however, this is simply not possible.

In short, knowledge assets are normally rather difficult to replicate. Even understanding what all the relevant routines are that support a particular competence may not be transparent. Indeed, Lippmann and Rumelt have argued that some sources of competitive advantage are so complex that the firm itself, let alone its competitors, does not understand them.[23] As Nelson and Winter[24] and Teece[25] have explained, many organizational routines are quite tacit in nature. Imitation can also be hindered by the fact that few routines are stand-alone. Imitating a part of what a competitor does may not enhance performance at all. Understanding the overall logic of organization and superior performance is often critical to successful imitation.

Some routines and competences seem to be attributable to local or regional forces that shape firm's capabilities. Porter, for example, shows that differences in local product markets, local factor markets, and institutions play an important role in shaping competitive capabilities.[26] Replication in a different geographical context may thus be rather difficult. However, differences also exist within populations of firms from the same country. Various studies of the automobile industry, for example, show that not all Japanese automobile companies are top performers in terms of quality, productivity, or product development.[27] The role of firm-specific history is a critical factor in such firm-level (as opposed to regional- or national-level) differences.[28]

At least two types of strategic value flow from replication. One is simply the ability to support geographic and product line expansion. To the extent that the capabilities in question are relevant to customer needs elsewhere, replication can confer value. Another is that the ability to replicate indicates that the firm has the foundations in place for learning and improvement. Understanding processes, both in production and in management, is the key to process improvement, so that an organization cannot improve that which it does not understand. Deep process understanding is often required to accomplish codification and replication. Indeed, if knowledge is highly tacit, it indicates that underlying structures are not well understood, which limits learning because scientific and engineering principles cannot be as systematically applied. Instead, learning is confined to proceeding through trial-and-error, and the leverage that might otherwise come from the application of modern science is denied.

Imitation is simply replication performed by a competitor. If self-replication is difficult, imitation is likely to be even harder. In competitive markets, it is the ease of imitation that determines the sustainability of competitive advantage. Easy imitation implies the rapid dissipation of rents.

Factors that make replication difficult also make imitation difficult. Thus, the more tacit the firm's productive knowledge, the harder it is to replicate by the firm itself or its competitors. When the tacit component is high, imitation may well be impossible, absent the hiring away of key individuals and the transfer of key organizational processes.

Intellectual property rights impede imitation of certain capabilities in advanced industrial countries and present a formidable imitation barrier in certain particular contexts. Several other factors, in addition to the patent system, cause there to be a difference between replication costs and imitation costs. The observability of the technology or the organization is one such important factor. As mentioned earlier, vistas into product technology can be obtained through strategies such as reverse engineering, this is not the case for process technology, as a firm need not expose its process technology to the outside in order to benefit from it. Firms with product technology, on the other hand, confront the unfortunate circumstances that they must expose what they have got in order to profit from the technology. Secrets are thus more protectable if there is no need to expose them in contexts where competitors can learn about them.

The term "appropriability regimes" describes the ease of imitation. Appropriability is a function both of the ease of replication and the efficacy of intellectual property rights as a barrier to imitation. Appropriability is strong when a technology is both inherently difficult to replicate and the intellectual property system provides legal barriers to imitation. When it is inherently easy to replicate and intellectual property protection is either unavailable or ineffectual, then appropriability is weak. Intermediate conditions also exist (see Fig. 1).

Appropriability and Markets for Know-How and Competence

Assets can be the source of competitive advantage only if they are supported by a regime of strong appropriability or are non-tradable or "sticky." As discussed

		Inherent Replicability	
		Easy	Hard
Intellectual Property Rights	Loose	Weak	Moderate
	Tight	Moderate	Strong

Fig. 1. Appropriability regimes for knowledge assets.

earlier, once an asset is readily tradable in a competitive market it can no longer be a sorce of firm-level competitive advantage. Financial assets today are of that kind.

The main classes of assets that are not tradable today are locational assets, knowledge assets, and competences.[29] Were a perfect market for know-how to someday emerge, knowledge would no longer be the source of competitive advantage. This is unlikely to happen anytime soon, but understanding the limits on the market for know-how is important to understanding how firms can capture value from knowledge assets.

Like the market for pollution right, or the market for art, buying and selling know-how and intellectual property has special challenges. These complicate exchange, and may limit in some fundamental sense the level of sophistication to which the market can ever evolve. They also explain why the market today is rather primitive.

By way of foundation, it is well recognized that markets work well when:

- there are informed buyers and sellers aware of trading opportunities,
- the objective performance properties or subjective utility of products can be readily ascertained,
- there are large numbers of buyers and sellers, and
- contracts can be written, executed, and enforced at low cost.

Thus the market for (standard) commodities like wheat, coal, stocks, bonds, and sports utility vehicles works well because these properties are largely satisfied.

However, know-how and intellectual property are "products" of an entirely different kind. These products have properties which complicate purchase and sale (see Fig. 2). These include:

- *Recognition of Trading Opportunities* — Parties typically don't know who owns what, and who might be interested in trading. This is less so for patents since they are published. But software (particularly source code) protected by copyright and trade secrets is frequently a matter of great secrecy. There are obvious reasons why even knowledge about the existence of such intellectual property is held very close. Accordingly, out of ignorance, software is often "reinvented" despite the fact that potentially advantageous trades could be consummated.
- *Disclosure of Performance Features* — Buyers must be well informed as to the availability of intellectual property but sellers may be reluctant to negotiate because their intellectual property rights are problematic. Sellers might be reluctant to negotiate because of fear that disclosure, even if pursuant to a

Characteristics	Know-How/IP	Physical Commodities
1. Recognition of trading opportunities	Inherent difficulty	Posting frequent
2. Disclosure of attributes	Relatively difficult	Relatively easy
3. Property Rights	Limited [patents, trade secrets, copyright, etc.]	Broad
4. Item of Sale	License	Measurable units
5. Variety	Heterogeneous	Homogeneous
6. Unit of consumption	Often Unclear	Weight, volume, etc.
Inherent tradeability	Low	High

Fig. 2. Inherent tradeability of different assets.

nondisclosure agreement, might inadvertently lead intellectual property rights to be jeopardized.

- *Uncertain Legal Rights* — When property rights are uncertain, and confidence in nondisclosure agreements or the law of confidences less than complete, beneficial transactions may be eschewed because of perceived risks. In addition to the disclosure issues identified above, sellers may be uncertain about factors such as the enforceability of use restrictions and sublicensing rights or simply about the ability to measure and collect royalties.

- *Item of Sale* — The "item of sale" may be know-how, or intellectual property rights, complete or partial. When intellectual property is bought and sold, what is transacted is simply a bundle of rights. While rights are frequently bought and sold [e.g., view rights, pollution rights, airspace rights, mineral rights, rights to use the electromagnetic spectrum, queuing rights], such rights are not a pure commodity. Moreover, ownership requires special policing powers for value preservation. Physical barriers to theft (e.g., locks and keys) don't suffice to protect owners; confidence in contracting and the legal system is necessary to support value.

- *Variety* — While there may be multiple transactions for a given piece of intellectual property (e.g., identical nonexclusive patent license), intellectual property is itself highly variegated. This complicates exchange by making valuation difficult and by rendering markets thin. Thin markets are likely to be less robust than thick markets. Moreover, both buyers and sellers are likely to wish to customize transactions. To the extent to which this occurs, transaction costs increase, and the difficulties of setting up an exchange increase.

- *Unit of Consumption* — Intellectual property is rarely sold lock, stock, and barrel. Hence, metering arrangements of some kind must be devised. These are by no means readily identifiable, particularly for software. Is it a component and if so, should the royalty be a function of the value of the component or the system in which it is embedded. Clearly, the value is a function of other intellectual property located alongside the intellectual property at issue. Questions of the royalty/sales base are by no means straightforward.

Some Sectoral Differences in the Market for Know-How

The inherent difficulties just identified vary according to the type of know-how/intellectual property at issue. It is instructive to compare chemicals and pharmaceuticals with electronics. Indeed, even a cursory examination would suggest that in chemicals and pharmaceuticals, the inherent difficulties associated with licensing are less than in other sectors, like electronics. Figure 3 summarizes some of these difficulties.

There are a number of reasons why the market for know-how generally works better for chemicals and pharmaceuticals. In chemicals and pharmaceuticals,

Challenge	Chemical/ Pharmaceuticals	Electronics
Recognition	Manageable	Extremely complex, often impossible
Disclosure	Handled by NDA, patents common	More difficult
Interface issues	Compatability generally not an issue	Compatability generally critical
Royalty stacking, royalty base dilemmas	Infrequent	Frequent
Value context dependent	Strongly so	Very strongly so
Patent strength	Generally high	Sometimes limited
Development cycle	Often long	Generally short
Know-How Market Works:	**Generally Well**	**Often Poorly**

Fig. 3. Some sectoral differences in the market for know-how.

patents work especially well and are ubiquitous. A survey of the efficiency of patents conducted by researchers at Yale University showed high scores for patent effectiveness in this sector.[30] Patents are in one sense the strongest form of intellectual property because they grant the ability to exclude, whereas copyright and trade secrets do not prevent firms that make independent but duplicative discoveries from practicing their inventions/innovations. Accordingly, problems of recognition and disclosure disappear when patent are at issue. Also regulation often bolsters intellectual property since "me too" misappropriators may sometimes face additional hurdles (in the U.S., FDA approval) before being able to launch a product in the market.

Compatibility/interface issues are also less severe in this sector than in some others. While technologies often must work together in chemicals and pharmaceuticals, the close coupling of the kind that characterizes electronics is usually not an absolute prerequisite. Also, the number of individual items of external intellectual property that must be brought together to design a new product is often rather limited. Indeed, the items used may all come from inside the firm, although alliances and licenses are increasingly common. Because there are less complementarities necessary to make a particular product, intellectual property is often less context dependent, and the same royalty rate is appropriate in a multitude of contexts e.g., the float glass process was licensed for the same amount (i.e., 6% of sales) to multiple jurisdictions around the world. Finally, the product life cycle is defined not in months, but often in decades. Hence, requirements for speedy execution of transactions are less severe, and the opportunity to amortize set-up costs over enormous volumes of business is often possible.

The situation in the electronics industry is different. For software, patent protection is uncommon. Hence, if purchasers receive components in source code, they can read and modify programs, thereby possibly skirting intellectual property protection. Put differently, source code can be more readily converted to new programs that don't leave fingerprints. Object code, on the other hand, must first be reverse engineered into a reasonable approximation of source code before it can be advantageously modified. Thus, disseminating software components (in source code) for external use creates misappropriation hazards. While encryption creates barriers to reverse engineering (decryption), it does not compensate for weak intellectual property. The problem of disclosure (necessary to inform buyers about what they are being offered) has clear hazards in this sector. Furthermore, interface issues are critical, as integration is paramount. Because multiple sources of intellectual property must be combined for systems on silicon, intellectual property rights must be amalgamated.[31]

The market for know-how in electronics thus creates considerable challenges and is unlikely, therefore, to be completely efficient. Accordingly, new innovations (such as system-level integration in silicon) involve new organizational challenges, orders of magnitude greater than previously encountered, and perhaps orders of magnitude greater than the technological challenges. Royalty stacking situations — where intellectual property owners fail in their pricing proposals to take into account the need for the buyer to combine other intellectual property to take into account the need for the buyer to combine other intellectual property to create value — are likely to be frequent, at least until a new business model is firmly established. Also, the tremendous premium on speed and time to market puts enormous pressure to accomplish intellectual property transactions quickly. This is impossible if intellectual property agreements are customized. However, there is at present almost no standardization in intellectual property agreements, so the market can readily become bogged down by transactional complexity.

Because of these difficulties, there is at present little if any market for software components. Estimates of the annual aggregate costs in the U.S. for "reinvention" are put at between $2 and $100 billion. These estimates, if correct, speak to the value of a properly functioning market for software intellectual property. Absent such a market, certain new product architectures (e.g., systems on Silicon) may just not happen, or may not realize but a fraction of their potential.

What was just described for know-how assets also applies to competences, which can be thought of as clusters of know-how assets. Competences include discrete business-level organizational processes fundamental to running the business (e.g., order entry, customer service, product design, quality control). But they also include generalized organizational skills such as "miniaturization," "tight tolerance engineering," and "micromotors."

Competences are tangible, and can be quite durable. They are typically supported by routines, not dependent on a single individual, and generally reside inside the business functions. Like know-how assets, they cannot be readily bought and sold, absent a transaction for the entire business.

Profiting from innovation is more readily assured when high-performance business processes and/or world-class competences support a product or process offering. This is because the asset/competences cannot be traded, and the forces of imitation are muted. Not only are such assets/competences inherently difficult to imitate because they are likely to be built on a high tacit component, but there may be opaqueness to the underlying processes and uncertainty, even within the firm, as to the organizational foundations of the competence.

Complementary Assets

The asset structure of the firm is perhaps the most relevant aspect of its positioning when the commercialization of knowledge in tangible products and processes is at issue. Such (upstream) positioning may be more important than the downstream positioning in the product markets for yesterday's product. In many cases there may be high correlation between a firm's upstream position in an asset and its downstream market position.

Complementary assets matter because knowledge assets are typically an intermediate good and need to be packaged into products or services to yield value. There are notable exceptions, of course. Software is a classic exception as it does not need to be manufactured, and with the internet, distribution becomes instantaneous and almost costless.

However, when the services of complementary assets are required, they can play an important role in the competitive advantage equation. For instance, the design for a new automobile is of little value absent access to manufacturing and distribution facilities on competitive terms.

The effort to embed knowledge in products and to bring the new product to market must confront the whole question of access to complementary assets. If already owned by the knowledge owner, there is no issue. If not, then one must build, or buy if one can. Because the market for complementary assets is itself riddled with imperfections, competitive advantage can be gained or lost on how expertly the strategy for gaining access is executed.

Circumstances of such co-specialization can benefit the asset owner, as demand for the innovation will increase demand for the co-specialized asset. If difficult to replicate or work around, the complementary asset may itself become the "choke point" in the value chain, enabling it to earn supernormal rents. Thus, ownership of difficult to replicate complementary assets can represent a second line of defense against imitators and an important source of competitive advantage.

Dynamic Capabilities

In many sectors in today's global market, competitive advantage also requires dynamic capabilities. (See Fig. 4.) This is the ability to sense and then to seize new opportunities, and to reconfigure and protect knowledge assets, competencies, and complementary assets and technologies to achieve sustainable competitive advantage.

It is relatively easy to define dynamic capabilities, quite another to explain how they are built. Part of the answer lies with the environmental and technological

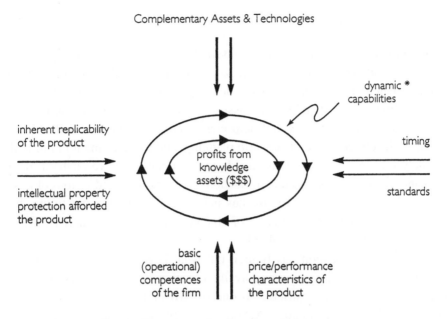

Fig. 4. Capturing value from knowledge assets.

sensing apparatus that the firm has established, and part lies with the choice of organizational form, and part lies with the ability to strategize.

External sensing

In order for an organization to exhibit dynamic capabilities, it must sense the opportunity and the need for change, properly calibrate responsive actions and investments, and move to implement a new regime with skill and efficiency. During "sensemaking," the organization receives and interprets messages about new markets, new technologies, and competitive threats. This information is necessarily evaluated in the light of the individuals' and the organization's experience and knowledge. In formulating an action plan, the organization is necessarily guided to some extent by rules and routines, which structure inquiries and responses.

Sensemaking, or interpretation, is a critical function. Well performed, it can enable the organization to connect with its environment and invest its resources wisely, thereby generating superior returns. The fundamental challenge to sensemaking is bounded rationality; one cannot learn all there is to learn about a situation or an opportunity, and action must proceed based on hunches and informed guesses about the true state of the world. In essence, business organizations and their management must interpret the world about them.

Interpretative activity is basically a form of theorizing about market and firm behavior.

Sensemaking can be assisted by sensemaking tools, like scenario planning, as well as the insights of brilliant outsiders — like a Peter Druker or Gordon Moore. Scenario planning can help managers develop mental maps of possible complex future realities. Such mental maps assist in the interpretation of new data and information from the market and help chart courses of action. Shell Oil is well known for its effective use of scenario planning, and its investment in this activity is widely recognized inside and outside the company to have enabled planners and managers to have extended conversations resulting in shared visions of possible futures. The object of the exercise has never been to predict the future, but to understand the fundamental drivers of change and to quickly chart action plans once key uncertainties are resolved.

When the organization has figured out what is going on, and calibrated the opportunity, it must choose among available action plans. These are not infinite in number, but may be restricted to one or two or maybe a handful of viable alternatives that are satisfactory. Actions are likely to be similar to those used in the past. Organizational routines — distinct ways of doing things — come into play. Actions and decision routines are part of the organization's procedural memory. Procedures and policies enable internal competition to be fair, objective, and legitimate. Organizational rationality can exist, despite individuals' bounded rationality, if rules, routines, and procedures guide individual decision making.

The openness of markets, stronger intellectual property protection, increasing returns, the unbundling of artifacts and information, and the possibilities for "integration" using new information technology are necessarily a part of the sensemaking milieu.

Information receipt and interpretation is by no means restricted in its importance to the understanding of business, market, and technological trends. There is also the need to identify relevant external technology and bring it into the firm. An organization's absorptive capacity with respect to external technology is a function of "the technical and managerial competence of the transferee."[32] Absorptive capacity is greatest when what is to be learned is related to what is already known.[33] As Mowery has explained, a firm is far better equipped to absorb the output of external R&D if one is performing some amount of R&D internally.[34] In short, internal and external R&D are complements, not substitutes.

Organizational action

Once an opportunity is sensed, it must then be seized. This is where the organization's ability to quickly contract up the requisite external resources and direct the relevant internal resources comes into play. Schumpeter referred to the importance of effectuating "new combinations." This is precisely what management must do. It increasingly involves forming alliances to access the requisite complementary technologies and complementary assets. The alliance structure is favored because markets simply don't exist for much of what must be accessed, and the alliance is a (hybrid) way to do so that shares risks and rewards but achieves a coalignment of strategy.

However, it also requires an organizational structure where decision making is immediate and action is swift. This typically implies high-powered incentives and decision making that is anything but bureaucratic. Smaller entrepreneurial companies appear to excel in many such environments, although dynamic capabilities are certainly not restricted to small companies. Larger enterprises can also deliver much of what is required if they are turned to changes in their external environments, and if they have adopted decision-making processes that both enable and require quick response.

Implications for the Theory of the Firm

The firm is a repository for knowledge — the knowledge being embedded in business routines and processes. Distinctive processes undergird firm-specific assets and competences (defined as integrated clusters of firm-specific assets). The firm's knowledge base includes its technological competences as well as its knowledge of customer needs and supplier capabilities. These competences reflect both individual skills and experiences as well as distinctive ways of doing things inside firms. To the extent that such competences are difficult to imitate and are effectively deployed and redeployed in the marketplace (reflecting dynamic capabilities), they can provide the foundations for competitive advantage.

The essence of the firm is its ability to create, transfer, assemble, integrate, and exploit knowledge assets. Knowledge assets underpin competences, and competences in turn underpin the firm's product and service offerings to the market. The firm's capacity to sense and seize opportunities, to reconfigure its knowledge assets, competencies, and complementary assets, to select appropriate organization forms, and to allocate resources astutely and price strategically all constitute its dynamic capabilities.

The knowledge perspective presented here requires us to stress the entrepreneurial rather than the administrative side of corporate governance. In high-technology industries, firms are not so much organizations designed to minimize transactions costs — although this they do — but organizational structures capable of shaping and reshaping clusters of assets in the distinct and unique combinations needed to serve ever-changing customer needs. Accordingly, boundary issues (such as vertical integration) are not determined by transactions cost considerations alone. Rather, they are strongly influenced by tacit knowledge and imitability/ replicability considerations. Even setting aside strategic and transaction cost issues, the tacit component of knowledge cannot frequently be transferred absent the transfer of personnel and organizational systems/routines. Tacit knowledge and its transfer properties help determine the boundaries of the firm and may well swamp transaction costs considerations.

Competitive advantage can be attributed not only to the ownership of knowledge assets and other assets complementary to them, but also to the ability to combine knowledge assets with other assets needed to create value. Knowing what assets to develop, and what to abandon, is a critical element in the success equation. Dynamic capabilities are critical if knowledge assets are to support sustainable competitive advantage.[35]

Thus, the competences/capabilities view of the firm sees the proper boundaries of the firm and governance structure being determined not only with reference to transactions costs, but also with reference to technological and knowledge concerns. The boundaries of the firm, and future integration and outsourcing opportunities, must clearly be made with reference to learning and knowledge issues as well as transaction cost economics.

The emphasis on the development and exploitation of knowledge assets shifts the focus of attention from cost minimization to value maximization. Governance decisions involve both questions of what assets to build inside the firm versus accessing externally, as well as how to organize internally. This perspective thus complements transaction cost economics.

Conclusion

Knowledge, competence and related intangibles have emerged as the key drivers of competitive advantage in developed nations. This is not just because of the importance of knowledge itself, but because of the rapid expansion of goods and factor markets, leaving intangible assets as the main basis of competitive differentiation in many sectors. There is implicit recognition of this with the growing emphasis being placed on the importance of intangible assets, reputation, customer loyalty, and technological know-how.

While there is some recognition of these changes, there is perhaps a failure to recognize just how deep these issues go. The value-enhancing challenges facing management are gravitating away from the administrative and towards the entrepreneurial. This is not to denigrate the importance of administration, but merely to indicate that better administration is unlikely to be where the economic "rents" (superior profits) reside. Indeed, if one looks at the sources of wealth creation today, they are markedly different from what they were barely two decades ago. The key sources of wealth creation at the dawn of the new millennium will lie with new enterprise formation; the renewal of incumbents; the exploitation of technological know-how, intellectual property, and brands; and the successful development and commercialization of new products and services.

The implications for management are clearly quite considerable. New forms of business organization — and new management styles that enable intangibles to be developed and dynamic capabilities to be practiced — are clearly critical. There is now sufficient experience with new network organizations and with alliances to sensitize management to the richness of the organizational menu that is now available. Moreover, modern information technology clearly enables a greater variety of transactional structures than was hitherto thought possible. What is apparent is the need to focus on developing a deeper understanding of imitability and replicability issues with respect to intangibles and the role of markets in undermining traditional forms of competitive advantage.

The extension of markets and growth of competition is a great benefit to the consumer and society. However, the post-war evolution of markets has powerful strategic implications for how and where firms position themselves to build competitive advantage. This does not appear to be well appreciated. It is no longer in product markets but in intangibles assets where advantage is built and defended. There is no such thing as a privileged product market position — unless it rests on some upstream intangible asset. The focus of strategy analysis must change, and is changing, as indicated by the burgeoning literature in strategic management on the resource-based theory of the firm.[36] Managers who figure this out are likely to be well positioned to build and maintain competitive advantage in the next millennium. They must recognize that in open unregulated markets, the domains in which value can be built are likely to be more and more confined. Perhaps Andy Grove is right after all when he warns that "only the paranoid survive."

Notes

1. D.J. Teece, The Market for Know-How and the Efficient International Transfer of Technology, *Annuals of the American Association of Political and Social Sciences*, November 1981, pp. 81–86.

2. S. Kuznets, *Modern Economic Growth; Rate, Structure, Spread* (Yale University Press, New Haven, CT, 1966).

3. These included the late Edwin Mansfield, Richard Nelson, Chris Freeman, Sidney Winter, Paul David, Nathan Rosenberg, Giovanni Dosi and David Mowery.

4. See P. Romer, What Determines the Rate of Growth and Technological Change, World Bank Working Papers, WPS 279, World Bank, 1989.

5. I. Nonaka and H. Takeuchi, *The Knowledge Creating Company* (Oxford University Press, New York, 1995).

6. M. Miller, *Merton Miller on Derivatives* (John Wiley & Sons, London, 1997).

7. P. Grindley and D.J. Teece, Managing Intellectual Capital: Licensing and Cross-Licensing in Semiconductors and Electronics, *California Management Review* 39/2 (Winter 1997), 8–41.

8. That's not to say that these are not opportunities to take bets against the market, but such bets represent asset plays by investors which ought not be thought of as a foundation for competitive advantage, as gains need not require involvement in operations of any kind.

9. Teece, op. cit., 1981.

10. B. Arthur, Competing Technologies: An Overview, in G. Dosi *et al.* (eds.), *Technical Change and Economic Theory* (Frances Pinter, London, 1988).

11. D.J. Teece, G. Pisano and A. Shuen, Dynamic Capabilities and Strategic Management, *Strategic Management Journal* 18/7 (1997), 509–533.

12. Following Dataquest, we define SLI as an integrated circuit that contains a compute engine, memory, and logic on a single chip and has more than 100,000 utilized gates. Two types of SLI devises can be recognized: ASICs (application-specific integrated circuits) that are sold to a single user, and ASSPs (application-specific standard product) that are sold to more than one user.

13. Dataquest, *ASIC's Worldwide*, December 18, 1995.

14. Fumito Kodama, *Analyzing Japanese High Technologies* (Pinter, London, 1991).

15. A Dynamic Mix of Chips and Biotech, *Forbes*, January 26, 1996, pp. 76–81.

16. Teece, op. cit., 1981, p. 84.

17. For analysis of the sources of innovation, see D.J. Teece, Firm Organization, Industrial Structure, and Technological Innovation, *Journal of Economic Behavior and Organization* 31 (1996), 193–224.

18. This section is based on Teece, op. cit., 1981, pp. 82–84.

19. These ideas are developed further in C.E. Shannon and W. Weaver, *The Mathematical Theory of Communication* (University of Illinois Press, Chicago, IL, 1949). I am grateful to Max Boisot for drawing them to my attention.

20. For example, we could identify innovation that were architectural or non architectural, competency enhancing or competency destroying.

21. This section is based in part on Teece, Pisano and Shuen, op cit.

22. D.J. Teece, Technology Transfer by Multinational Firms: The Resource Cost of Transferring Technological Know-How, *The Economic Journal* 87 (1977), 242–261.

23. S.A. Lippman and R.P. Rumelt, Demand Uncertainty and Investment in Industry-Specific Capital, *Industrial and Corporate Change* 1/1 (1992), 235–262.
24. R. Nelson and S. Winter, *An Evolutionary Theory of Economic Change* (Harvard University Press, Cambridge, MA, 1982).
25. D.J. Teece, Towards an Economic Theory of the Multiproduct Firm, *Journal of Economic Behavior and Organization* 3 (1982), 39–63.
26. M.E. Porter, *The Competitive Advantage of Nations* (Free Press, New York, 1990).
27. See K. Clark and T. Fujimoto, *Product Development Performance: Strategy, Organization, and Management in the World Auto Industries* (Harvard Business School Press, Cambridge, MA, 1991).
28. Nelson and Winter, op. cit.
29. Competences may in turn be embedded in other corporate assets, including assets complementary to knowledge assets.
30. S. Winter, Knowledge and Competence as Strategic Assets, in D. Teece (ed.), *The Competitive Challenge: Strategies for Industrial Innovation and Renewal* (Harper and Row, Ballinger Division, New York, 1987).
31. This isn't necessary for broad level integration of physical components, where the bundling of intellectual property in products simplifies intellectual property transactions.
32. D.J. Teece, *The Multinational Corporation and the Resource Cost of International Technology Transfer* (Ballinger, Cambridge, MA, 1976), p. 48.
33. W.M. Cohen and D.A. Levinthal, Absorption Capacity: A New Perspective on Learning and Innovation, *Administrative Sciences Quarterly* 35 (1990), 128–152.
34. D. Mowery, Firm Structure, Government Policy, and the Organization of Industrial Research, *Business History Review* 58 (1984), 504–531.
35. The astute management of the value in a firm's competence/knowledge base is a central issue in strategic management. D.J. Teece, Profiting from Technological Innovation, *Research Policy* 15/6 (1986), 285–305. The firm must therefore be understood not just in terms of its competences, but also in terms of its dynamic capabilities and the ability to orchestrate internal and external assets so as to capture value. Dynamic capabilities reflect the entrepreneurial side of management. Incentives as well as the formal and informal structure of the firm are all elements of governance affecting dynamic capabilities. These elements together help define the firm as we know it. Accordingly, competitive advantage flows from both management and structure.
36. For an excellent compendium, see Nicolai Foss (ed.), *Resources, Firms and Strategies: A Reader in the Resource-Based Perspective* (Oxford University Press, New York, 1997).

II

Sustaining Value Creation and Capture

Dynamic Capabilities and Strategic Management

David J. Teece*

*Haas School of Business, University of California,
Berkeley, California, U.S.A.*

Gary Pisano

*Graduate School of Business Administration, Harvard University,
Boston, Massachusetts, U.S.A.*

Amy Shuen

*School of Business, San Jose State University,
San Jose, California, U.S.A.*

The dynamic capabilities framework analyzes the sources and methods of wealth creation and capture by private enterprise firms operating in environments of rapid technological change. The competitive advantage of firms is seen as resting on distinctive processes (ways of coordinating and combining), shaped by the firm's (specific) asset positions (such as the firm's portfolio of difficult-to-trade knowledge assets and complementary assets), and the evolution path(s) it has adopted or inherited. The importance of path dependencies is amplified where conditions of increasing returns exist. Whether and how a firm's competitive advantage is eroded depends on the stability of market demand, and the ease of replicability (expanding internally) and imitatability (replication by competitors). If correct, the framework suggests that private wealth creation in regimes of rapid technological change depends in large measure on honing internal technological, organizational, and managerial processes inside the firm. In short, identifying new opportunities and organizing effectively and efficiently to embrace them are generally more fundamental to private wealth creation than is strategizing, if by strategizing one means engaging in business conduct

Reprinted from *Strategic Management Journal* 18(7) (1997), 509–533.

*Correspondence to: David J. Teece, Institute of Management, Innovation and Organization, Haas School of Business, University of California, Berkeley, CA 94720–1930, U.S.A.

that keeps competitors off balance, raises rival's costs, and excludes new entrants.

© 1997 by John Wiley & Sons, Ltd.

Keywords: Competences; capabilities; innovation; strategy; path dependency; knowledge assets

1. Introduction

The fundamental question in the field of strategic management is how firms achieve and sustain competitive advantage.[1] We confront this question here by developing the dynamic capabilities approach, which endeavors to analyze the sources of wealth creation and capture by firms. The development of this framework flows from a recognition by the authors that strategic theory is replete with analyses of firm-level strategies for sustaining and safeguarding extant competitive advantage, but has performed less well with respect to assisting in the understanding of how and why certain firms build competitive advantage in regimes of rapid change. Our approach is especially relevant in a Schumpeterian world of innovation-based competition, price/performance rivalry, increasing returns, and the "creative destruction" of existing competences. The approach endeavors to explain firm-level success and failure. We are interested in both building a better theory of firm performance, as well as informing managerial practice.

In order to position our analysis in a manner that displays similarities and differences with existing approaches, we begin by briefly reviewing accepted frameworks for strategic management. We endeavor to expose implicit assumptions, and identify competitive circumstances where each paradigm might display some relative advantage as both a useful descriptive and normative theory of competitive strategy. While numerous theories have been advanced over the past two decades about the sources of competitive advantage, many cluster around just a few loosely structured frameworks or paradigms. In this paper we attempt to identify three existing paradigms and describe aspects of an emerging new paradigm that we label dynamic capabilities.

The dominant paradigm in the field during the 1980s was the competitive forces approach developed by Porter (1980). This approach, rooted in the structure–conduct–performance paradigm of industrial organization (Mason, 1949; Bain,

---

[1] For a review of the fundamental questions in the field of strategy, see Rumelt, Schendel and Teece (1994).

1959), emphasizes the actions a firm can take to create defensible positions against competitive forces. A second approach, referred to as a strategic conflict approach (e.g. Shapiro, 1989), is closely related to the first in its focus on product market imperfections, entry deterrence, and strategic interaction. The strategic conflict approach uses the tools of game theory and thus implicitly views competitive outcomes as a function of the effectiveness with which firms keep their rivals off balance through strategic investments, pricing strategies, signaling, and the control of information. Both the competitive forces and the strategic conflict approaches appear to share the view that rents flow from privileged product market positions.

Another distinct class of approaches emphasizes building competitive advantage through capturing entrepreneurial rents stemming from fundamental firm-level efficiency advantages. These approaches have their roots in a much older discussion of corporate strengths and weaknesses; they have taken on new life as evidence suggests that firms build enduring advantages only through efficiency and effectiveness, and as developments in organizational economics and the study of technological and organizational change become applied to strategy questions. One strand of this literature, often referred to as the "resource-based perspective," emphasizes firm-specific capabilities and assets and the existence of isolating mechanisms as the fundamental determinants of firm performance (Penrose, 1959; Rumelt, 1984; Teece, 1984; Wernerfelt, 1984).[2] This perspective recognizes but does not attempt to explain the nature of the isolating mechanisms that enable entrepreneurial rents and competitive advantage to be sustained.

Another component of the efficiency-based approach is developed in this paper. Rudimentary efforts are made to identify the dimensions of firm-specific capabilities that can be sources of advantage, and to explain how combinations of competences and resources can be developed, deployed, and protected. We refer to this as the "dynamic capabilities" approach in order to stress exploiting existing internal and external firm-specific competences to address changing

---

[2] Of these authors, Rumelt may have been the first to self-consciously apply a resource perspective to the field of strategy. Rumelt (1984, p. 561) notes that the strategic firm "is characterized by a bundle of linked and idiosyncratic resources and resource conversion activities." Similarly, Teece (1984, p. 95) notes: "Successful firms possess one or more forms of intangible assets, such as technological or managerial know-how. Over time, these assets may expand beyond the point of profitable reinvestment in a firm's traditional market. Accordingly, the firm may consider deploying its intangible assets in different product or geographical markets, where the expected returns are higher, if efficient transfer modes exist." Wernerfelt was early to recognize that this approach was at odds with product market approaches and might constitute a distinct paradigm of strategy (1984).

environments. Elements of the approach can be found in Schumpeter (1942), Penrose (1959), Nelson and Winter (1982), Prahalad and Hamel (1990), Teece (1976, 1986a, 1986b, 1988) and in Hayes, Wheelwright, and Clark (1988). Because this approach emphasizes the development of management capabilities, and difficult-to-imitate combinations of organizational, functional and technological skills, it integrates and draws upon research in such areas as the management of R&D, product and process development, technology transfer, intellectual property, manufacturing, human resources, and organizational learning. Because these fields are often viewed as outside the traditional boundaries of strategy, much of this research has not been incorporated into existing economic approaches to strategy issues. As a result, dynamic capabilities can be seen as an emerging and potentially integrative approach to understanding the newer sources of competitive advantage.

We suggest that the dynamic capabilities approach is promising both in terms of future research potential and as an aid to management endeavoring to gain competitive advantage in increasingly demanding environments. To illustrate the essential elements of the dynamic capabilities approach, the sections that follow compare and contrast this approach to other models of strategy. Each section highlights the strategic insights provided by each approach as well as the different competitive circumstances in which it might be most appropriate. Needless to say, these approaches are in many ways complementary and a full understanding of firm-level, competitive advantage requires an appreciation of all four approaches and more.

2. Models of Strategy Emphasizing the Exploitation of Market Power

2.1. *Competitive Forces*

The dominant paradigm in strategy at least during the 1980s was the competitive forces approach. Pioneered by Porter (1980), the competitive forces approach views the essence of competitive strategy formulation as "relating a company to its environment ... [T]he key aspect of the firm's environment is the industry or industries in which it competes." Industry structure strongly influences the competitive rules of the game as well as the strategies potentially available to firms.

In the competitive forces model, five industry-level forces — entry barriers, threat of substitution, bargaining power of buyers, bargaining power of suppliers, and rivalry among industry incumbents — determine the inherent profit potential of an industry or subsegment of an industry. The approach can be used to help the firm find a position in an industry from which it can best defend itself against competitive forces or influence them in its favor (Porter, 1980, p. 4).

This "five-forces" framework provides a systematic way of thinking about how competitive forces work at the industry level and how these forces determine the profitability of different industries and industry segments. The competitive forces framework also contains a number of underlying assumptions about the sources of competition and the nature of the strategy process. To facilitate comparisons with other approaches, we highlight several distinctive characteristics of the framework.

Economic rents in the competitive forces framework are monopoly rents (Teece, 1984). Firms in an industry earn rents when they are somehow able to impede the competitive forces (in either factor markets or product markets) which tend to drive economic returns to zero. Available strategies are described in Porter (1980). Competitive strategies are often aimed at altering the firm's position in the industry vis à vis competitors and suppliers. Industry structure plays a central role in determining and limiting strategic action.

Some industries or subsectors of industries become more "attractive" because they have structural impediments to competitive forces (e.g. entry barriers) that allow firms better opportunities for creating sustainable competitive advantages. Rents are created largely at the industry or subsector level rather than at the firm level. While there is some recognition given to firm-specific assets, differences among firms relate primarily to scale. This approach to strategy reflects its incubation inside the field of industrial organization and in particular the industrial structure school of Mason and Bain[3] (Teece, 1984).

2.2. Strategic Conflict

The publication of Carl Shapiro's 1989 article, confidently titled "The Theory of Business Strategy," announced the emergence of a new approach to business strategy, if not strategic management. This approach utilizes the tools of game theory to analyze the nature of competitive interaction between rival firms. The main thrust of work in this tradition is to reveal how a firm can influence the

---

[3] In competitive environments characterized by sustainable and stable mobility and structural barriers, these forces may become the determinants of industry-level profitability. However, competitive advantage is more complex to ascertain in environments of rapid technological change where specific assets owned by heterogeneous firms can be expected to play a larger role in explaining rents.

behavior and actions of rival firms and thus the market environment.[4] Examples of such moves are investment in capacity (Dixit, 1980), R&D (Gilbert and Newberry, 1982), and advertising (Schmalensee, 1983). To be effective, these strategic moves require irreversible commitments.[5] The moves in question will have no effect if they can be costlessly undone. A key idea is that by manipulating the market environment, a firm may be able to increase it profits.

This literature, together with the contestability literature (Baumol, Panzar, and Willig, 1982), has led to a greater appreciation of the role of sunk costs, as opposed to fixed costs, in determining competitive outcomes. Strategic moves can also be designed to influence rivals' behavior through signaling. Strategic signaling has been examined in a number of contexts, including predatory pricing (Kreps and Wilson, 1982a, 1982b) and limit pricing (Milgrom and Roberts, 1982a, 1982b). More recent treatments have emphasized the role of commitment and reputation (e.g. Ghemawat, 1991) and the benefits of firms simultaneously pursuing competition and cooperation[6] (Brandenburger and Nalebuff, 1995, 1996).

In many instances, game theory formalizes long-standing intuitive arguments about various types of business behavior (e.g. predatory pricing, patent races), though in some instances it has induced a substantial change in the conventional wisdom. But by rationalizing observed behavior by reference to suitably designed games, in explaining everything these models also explain nothing, as they do not generate testable predictions (Sutton, 1992). Many specific game-theoretic models admit multiple equilibrium, and a wide range of choice exists as to the design of the appropriate game form to be used. Unfortunately, the results often depend on the precise specification chosen. The equilibrium in models of strategic behavior crucially depends on what one rival believes another rival will do in a particular situation. Thus the qualitative features of the results may depend on the way price competition is modeled (e.g. Bertrand or Cournot) or on the presence or absence of strategic asymmetries such as first-mover advantages. The analysis of strategic moves using game theory can be thought of as "dynamic" in the sense that multiperiod analyses can be pursued both intuitively and formally. However, we use the term "dynamic" in this paper in a different sense, referring to situations

---

[4] The market environment is all factors that influence market outcomes (prices, quantities, profits) including the beliefs of customers and of rivals, the number of potential technologies employed, and the costs or speed with which a rival can enter the industry.

[5] For an excellent discussion of committed competition in multiple contexts, see Ghemawat (1991).

[6] Competition and cooperation have also been analyzed outside of this tradition. See, for example, Teece (1992) and Link, Teece and Finan (1996).

where there is rapid change in technology and market forces, and "feedback" effects on firms.[7]

We have a particular view of the contexts in which the strategic conflict literature is relevant to strategic management. Firms that have a tremendous cost or other competitive advantage vis à vis their rivals ought not be transfixed by the moves and countermoves of their rivals. Their competitive fortunes will swing more on total demand conditions, not on how competitors deploy and redeploy their competitive assets. Put differently, when there are gross asymmetries in competitive advantage between firms, the results of game-theoretic analysis are likely to be obvious and uninteresting. The stronger competitor will generally advance, even if disadvantaged by certain information asymmetries. To be sure, incumbent firms can be undone by new entrants with a dramatic cost advantage, but no "gaming" will overturn the outcome. On the other hand, if firms' competitive positions are more delicately balanced, as with Coke and Pepsi, and United Airlines and American Airlines, then strategic conflict is of interest to competitive outcomes. Needless to say, there are many such circumstances, but they are rare in industries where there is rapid technological change and fast-shifting market circumstances.

In short, where competitors do not have deepseated competitive advantages, the moves and countermoves of competitors can often be usefully formulated in game-theoretic terms. However, we doubt that game theory can comprehensively illuminate how Chrysler should compete against Toyota and Honda, or how United Airlines can best respond to Southwest Airlines since Southwest's advantage is built on organizational attributes which United cannot readily replicate.[8] Indeed, the entrepreneurial side of strategy — how significant new rent streams are created and protected — is largely ignored by the game-theoretic approach.[9] Accordingly, we find that the approach, while important, is most relevant when competitors are closely matched[10] and the population of relevant

---

[7] Accordingly, both approaches are dynamic, but in very different senses.

[8] Thus even in the air transport industry game-theoretic formulations by no means capture all the relevant dimensions of competitive rivalry. United Airlines' and United Express's difficulties in competing with Southwest Airlines because of United's inability to fully replicate Southwest's operation capabilities is documented in Gittel (1995).

[9] Important exceptions can be found in Brandenburger and Nalebuff (1996) such as their emphasis on the role of complements. However, these insights do not flow uniquely from game theory and can be found in the organizational economics literature (e.g. Teece, 1986a, 1986b; de Figueiredo and Teece, 1996).

[10] When closely matched in an aggregate sense, they may nevertheless display asymmetries which game theorists can analyze.

competitors and the identity of their strategic alternatives can be readily ascertained. Nevertheless, coupled with other approaches it can sometimes yield powerful insights.

However, this research has an orientation that we are concerned about in terms of the implicit framing of strategic issues. Rents, from a game-theoretic perspective, are ultimately a result of managers' intellectual ability to "play the game." The adage of the strategist steeped in this approach is "do unto others before they do unto you." We worry that fascination with strategic moves and Machiavellian tricks will distract managers from seeking to build more enduring sources of competitive advantage. The approach unfortunately ignores competition as a process involving the development, accumulation, combination, and protection of unique skills and capabilities. Since strategic interactions are what receive focal attention, the impression one might receive from this literature is that success in the marketplace is the result of sophisticated plays and counterplays, when this is generally not the case at all.[11]

In what follows, we suggest that building a dynamic view of the business enterprise — something missing from the two approaches we have so far identified — enhances the probability of establishing an acceptable descriptive theory of strategy that can assist practitioners in the building of long-run advantage and competitive flexibility. Below, we discuss first the resource-based perspective and then an extension we call the dynamic capabilities approach.

3. Models of Strategy Emphasizing Efficiency

3.1. *Resource-Based Perspective*

The resource-based approach sees firms with superior systems and structures being profitable not because they engage in strategic investments that may deter entry and raise prices above long-run costs, but because they have markedly lower costs, or offer markedly higher quality or product performance. This approach focuses on the rents accruing to the owners of scarce firm-specific resources rather than the economic profits from product market positioning.[12]

---

[11] The strategic conflict literature also tends to focus practitioners on product market positioning rather than on developing the unique assets which make possible superior product market positions (Dierickx and Cool, 1989).

[12] In the language of economics, rents flow from unique firm-specific assets that cannot readily be replicated, rather than from tactics which deter entry and keep competitors off balance. In short, rents are Ricardian.

Competitive advantage lies "upstream" of product markets and rests on the firm's idiosyncratic and difficult-to-imitate resources.[13]

One can find the resources approach suggested by the earlier preanalytic strategy literature. A leading text of the 1960s (Learned *et al.*, 1969) noted that "the capability of an organization is its demonstrated and potential ability to accomplish against the opposition of circumstance or competition, whatever it sets out to do. Every organization has actual and potential strengths and weaknesses; it is important to try to determine what they are and to distinguish one from the other." Thus what a firm can do is not just a function of the opportunities it confronts; it also depends on what resources the organization can muster.

Learned *et al.* proposed that the real key to a company's success or even to its future development lies in its ability to find or create "a competence that is truly distinctive."[14] This literature also recognized the constraints on firm behavior and, in particular, noted that one should not assume that management "can rise to any occasion." These insights do appear to keenly anticipate the resource-based approach that has since emerged, but they did not provide a theory or systematic framework for analyzing business strategies. Indeed, Andrews (1987, p. 46) noted that "much of what is intuitive in this process is yet to be identified." Unfortunately, the academic literature on capabilities stalled for a couple of decades.

New impetus has been given to the resource-based approach by recent theoretical developments in organizational economics and in the theory of strategy, as well as by a growing body of anecdotal and empirical literature[15] that highlights the importance of firm-specific factors in explaining firm performance. Cool and Schendel (1988) have shown that there are systematic and significant performance differences among firms which belong to the same strategic group within the U.S. pharmaceutical industry. Rumelt (1991) has shown that intraindustry differences in profits are greater than interindustry differences in profits, strongly suggesting the importance of firm-specific factors and the relative unimportance

---

[13] Teece (1982, p. 46) saw the firm as having "a variety of end products which it can produce with its organizational technology."

[14] Elsewhere Andrews (1987, p. 47) defined a distinctive competence as what an organization can do particularly well.

[15] Studies of the automobile and other industries displayed differences in organization which often underlay differences amongst firms. See, for example, Womack, Jones, and Roos (1991); Hayes and Clark (1985); Barney, Spender and Reve (1994); Clark and Fujimoto (1991); Henderson and Cockburn (1994); Nelson (1991); Levinthal and Myatt (1994).

of industry effects.[16] Jacobsen (1988) and Hansen and Wernerfelt (1989) made similar findings.

A comparison of the resource-based approach and the competitive forces approach (discussed earlier in the paper) in terms of their implications for the strategy process is revealing. From the first perspective, an entry decision looks roughly as follows: (1) pick an industry (based on its "structural attractiveness"); (2) choose an entry strategy based on conjectures about competitors' rational strategies; (3) if not already possessed, acquire or otherwise obtain the requisite assets to compete in the market. From this perspective, the process of identifying and developing the requisite assets is not particularly problematic. The process involves nothing more than choosing rationally among a well-defined set of investment alternatives. If assets are not already owned, they can be bought. The resource-based perspective is strongly at odds with this conceptualization.

From the resource-based perspective, firms are heterogeneous with respect to their resources/capabilities/endowments. Further, resource endowments are "sticky": at least in the short run, firms are to some degree stuck with what they have and may have to live with what they lack.[17] This stickiness arises for three reasons. First, business development is viewed as an extremely complex process.[18] Quite simply, firms lack the organizational capacity to develop new competences quickly (Dierickx and Cool, 1989). Secondly, some assets are simply not readily tradeable, for example, tacit know-how (Teece, 1976, 1980) and reputation (Dierickx and Cool, 1989). Thus, resource endowments cannot equilibrate through factor input markets. Finally, even when an asset can be purchased, firms may stand to gain little by doing so. As Barney (1986) points out, unless a firm is lucky, possesses superior information, or both, the price it pays in a competitive factor market will fully capitalize the rents from the asset.

Given that in the resources perspective firms possess heterogeneous and sticky resource bundles, the entry decision process suggested by this approach is as follows: (1) identify your firm's unique resources; (2) decide in which markets those resources can earn the highest rents; and (3) decide whether the rents from those assets are most effectively utilized by (a) integrating into related market(s),

---

[16] Using FTC line of business data, Rumelt showed that stable industry effects account for only 8 percent of the variance in business unit returns. Furthermore, only about 40 percent of the dispersion in industry returns is due to stable industry effects.

[17] In this regard, this approach has much in common with recent work on organizational ecology (e.g. Freeman and Boeker, 1984) and also on commitment (Ghemawat, 1991, pp. 17–25).

[18] Capability development, however, is not really analyzed.

(b) selling the relevant intermediate output to related firms, or (c) selling the assets themselves to a firm in related businesses (Teece, 1980, 1982).

The resource-based perspective puts both vertical integration and diversification into a new strategic light. Both can be viewed as ways of capturing rents on scarce, firm-specific assets whose services are difficult to sell in intermediate markets (Penrose, 1959; Williamson, 1975; Teece, 1980, 1982, 1986a, 1986b; Wernerfelt, 1984). Empirical work on the relationship between performance and diversification by Wernerfelt and Montgomery (1988) provides evidence for this proposition. It is evident that the resource-based perspective focuses on strategies for exploiting existing firm-specific assets.

However, the resource-based perspective also invites consideration of managerial strategies for developing new capabilities (Wernerfelt, 1984). Indeed, if control over scarce resources is the source of economic profits, then it follows that such issues as skill acquisition, the management of knowledge and know-how (Shuen, 1994), and learning become fundamental strategic issues. It is in this second dimension, encompassing skill acquisition, learning, and accumulation of organizational and intangible or "invisible" assets (Itami and Roehl, 1987), that we believe lies the greatest potential for contributions to strategy.

3.2. *The Dynamic Capabilities Approach: Overview*

The global competitive battles in high-technology industries such as semiconductors, information services, and software have demonstrated the need for an expanded paradigm to understand how competitive advantage is achieved. Well-known companies like IBM, Texas Instruments, Philips and others appear to have followed a "resource-based strategy" of accumulating valuable technology assets, often guarded by an aggressive intellectual property stance. However, this strategy is often not enough to support a significant competitive advantage. Winners in the global marketplace have been firms that can demonstrate timely responsiveness and rapid and flexible product innovation, coupled with the management capability to effectively coordinate and redeploy internal and external competences. Not surprisingly, industry observers have remarked that companies can accumulate a large stock of valuable technology assets and still not have many useful capabilities.

We refer to this ability to achieve new forms of competitive advantage as "dynamic capabilities" to emphasize two key aspects that were not the main focus of attention in previous strategy perspectives. The term "dynamic" refers to the capacity to renew competences so as to achieve congruence with the changing business environment; certain innovative responses are required when time-to-market and timing are critical, the rate of technological change is rapid, and the nature of future competition and markets difficult to determine. The term "capabilities" emphasizes the key role of strategic management in appropriately adapting, integrating, and reconfiguring internal and external organizational skills, resources, and functional competences to match the requirements of a changing environment.

One aspect of the strategic problem facing an innovating firm in a world of Schumpeterian competition is to identify difficult-to-imitate internal and external competences most likely to support valuable products and services. Thus, as argued by Dierickx and Cool (1989), choices about how much to spend (invest) on different possible areas are central to the firm's strategy. However, choices about domains of competence are influenced by past choices. At any given point in time, firms must follow a certain trajectory or path of competence development. This path not only defines what choices are open to the firm today, but it also puts bounds around what its internal repertoire is likely to be in the future. Thus, firms, at various points in time, make long-term, quasi-irreversible commitments to certain domains of competence.[19]

The notion that competitive advantage requires both the exploitation of existing internal and external firm-specific capabilities, and developing new ones is partially developed in Penrose (1959), Teece (1982), and Wernerfelt (1984). However, only recently have researchers begun to focus on the specifics of how some organizations first develop firm-specific capabilities and how they renew competences to respond to shifts in the business environment.[20] These issues are intimately tied to the firm's business processes, market positions, and expansion paths. Several writers have recently offered insights and evidence on how firms can develop their capability to adapt and even capitalize on rapidly changing environments.[21] The dynamic capabilities approach seeks to provide a coherent framework which can both integrate existing conceptual and empirical knowledge, and facilitate prescription. In doing so, it builds upon the theoretical foundations provided by Schumpeter (1934), Penrose (1959), Williamson (1975, 1985), Barney (1986), Nelson and Winter (1982), Teece (1988), and Teece et al. (1994).

---

[19] Deciding, under significant uncertainty about future states of the world, which long-term paths to commit to and when to change paths is the central strategic problem confronting the firm. In this regard, the work of Ghemawat (1991) is highly germane to the dynamic capabilities approach to strategy.

[20] See, for example, Iansiti and Clark (1994) and Henderson (1994).

[21] See Hayes et al. (1988), Prahalad and Hamel (1990), Dierickx and Cool (1989), Chandler (1990), and Teece (1993).

4. Toward a Dynamic Capabilities Framework

4.1. *Terminology*

In order to facilitate theory development and intellectual dialogue, some acceptable definitions are desirable. We propose the following.

4.1.1. Factors of production

These are "undifferentiated" inputs available in disaggregate form in factor markets. By undifferentiated we mean that they lack a firm-specific component. Land, unskilled labor, and capital are typical examples. Some factors may be available for the taking, such as public knowledge. In the language of Arrow, such resources must be "non-fugitive."[22] Property rights are usually well defined for factors of production.

4.1.2. Resources[23]

Resources are firm-specific assets that are difficult if not impossible to imitate. Trade secrets and certain specialized production facilities and engineering experience are examples. Such assets are difficult to transfer among firms because of transactions costs and transfer costs, and because the assets may contain tacit knowledge.

4.1.3. Organizational routines/competences

When firm-specific assets are assembled in integrated clusters spanning individuals and groups so that they enable distinctive activities to be performed, these activities constitute organizational routines and processes. Examples include quality, miniaturization, and systems integration. Such competences are typically viable across multiple product lines, and may extend outside the firm to embrace alliance partners.

4.1.4. Core competences

We define those competences that define a firm's fundamental business as core. Core competences must accordingly be derived by looking across the range of a

---

[22] Arrow (1996) defines fugitive resources as ones that can move cheaply amongst individuals and firms.

[23] We do not like the term "resource" and believe it is misleading. We prefer to use the term firm-specific asset. We use it here to try and maintain links to the literature on the resource-based approach which we believe is important.

firm's (and its competitors) products and services.[24] The value of core competences can be enhanced by combination with the appropriate complementary assets. The degree to which a core competence is distinctive depends on how well endowed the firm is relative to its competitors, and on how difficult it is for competitors to replicate its competences.

4.1.5. Dynamic capabilities

We define dynamic capabilities as the firm's ability to integrate, build, and reconfigure internal and external competences to address rapidly changing environments. Dynamic capabilities thus reflect an organization's ability to achieve new and innovative forms of competitive advantage given path dependencies and market positions (Leonard-Barton, 1992).

4.1.6. Products

End products are the final goods and services produced by the firm based on utilizing the competences that it possesses. The performance (price, quality, etc.) of a firm's products relative to its competitors at any point in time will depend upon its competences (which over time depend on its capabilities).

4.2. *Markets and Strategic Capabilities*

Different approaches to strategy view sources of wealth creation and the essence of the strategic problem faced by firms differently. The competitive forces framework sees the strategic problem in terms of industry structure, entry deterrence, and positioning; game-theoretic models view the strategic problem as one of interaction between rivals with certain expectations about how each other will behave;[25] resource-based perspectives have focused on the exploitation of firm-specific assets. Each approach asks different, often complementary questions. A key step in building a conceptual framework related to dynamic capabilities is to identify the foundations upon which distinctive and difficult-to-replicate advantages can be built, maintained, and enhanced.

A useful way to vector in on the strategic elements of the business enterprise is first to identify what is not strategic. To be strategic, a capability must be honed

---

[24] Thus Eastman Kodak's core competence might be considered imaging, IBM's might be considered integrated data processing and service, and Motorola's untethered communications.

[25] In sequential move games, each player looks ahead and anticipates his rival's future responses in order to reason back and decide action, i.e. look forward, reason backward.

to a user need[26] (so there is a source of revenues), unique (so that the products/ services produced can be priced without too much regard to competition) and difficult to replicate (so profits will not be competed away). Accordingly, any assets or entity which are homogeneous and can be bought and sold at an established price cannot be all that strategic (Barney, 1986). What is it, then, about firms which undergirds competitive advantage?

To answer this, one must first make some fundamental distinctions between markets and internal organization (firms). The essence of the firm, as Coase (1937) pointed out, is that it displaces market organization. It does so in the main because inside the firms one can organize certain types of economic activity in ways one cannot using markets. This is not only because of transaction costs, as Williamson (1975, 1985) emphasized, but also because there are many types of arrangements where injecting high-powered (market like) incentives might well be quite destructive of cooperative activity and learning.[27] Inside an organization, exchange cannot take place in the same manner that it can outside an organization, not just because it might be destructive to provide high-powered individual incentives, but because it is difficult if not impossible to tightly calibrate individual contribution to a joint effort. Hence, contrary to Arrow's (1969) view of firms as quasi markets, and the task of management to inject markets into firms, we recognize the inherent limits and possible counter-productive results of attempting to fashion firms into simply clusters of internal markets. In particular, learning and internal technology transfer may well be jeopardized.

Indeed, what is distinctive about firms is that they are domains for organizing activity in a nonmarket-like fashion. Accordingly, as we discuss what is distinctive about firms, we stress competences/capabilities which are ways of organizing and getting things done which cannot be accomplished merely by using the price system to coordinate activity.[28] The very essence of most capabilities/competences is that they cannot be readily assembled through markets (Teece, 1982, 1986a; Zander and Kogut, 1995). If the ability to assemble competences using markets is what is meant by the firm as a nexus of contracts (Fama, 1980), then we

---

[26] Needless to say, users need not be the current customers of the enterprise. Thus a capability can be the basis for diversification into new product markets.

[27] Indeed, the essence of internal organization is that it is a domain of unleveraged or low-powered incentives. By unleveraged we mean that rewards are determined at the group or organization level, not primarily at the individual level, in an effort to encourage team behavior, not individual behavior.

[28] We see the problem of market contracting as a matter of coordination as much as we see it a problem of opportunism in the fact of contractual hazards. In this sense, we are consonant with both Richardson (1960) and Williamson (1975, 1985).

unequivocally state that the firm about which we theorize cannot be usefully modeled as a nexus of contracts. By "contract" we are referring to a transaction undergirded by a legal agreement, or some other arrangement which clearly spells out rights, rewards, and responsibilities. Moreover, the firm as a nexus of contracts suggests a series of bilateral contracts orchestrated by a coordinator. Our view of the firm is that the organization takes place in a more multilateral fashion, with patterns of behavior and learning being orchestrated in a much more decentralized fashion, but with a viable head-quarters operation.

The key point, however, is that the properties of internal organization cannot be replicated by a portfolio of business units amalgamated just through formal contracts as many distinctive elements of internal organization simply cannot be replicated in the market.[29] That is, entrepreneurial activity cannot lead to the immediate replication of unique organizational skills through simply entering a market and piecing the parts together overnights. Replication takes time, and the replication of best practice may be illusive. Indeed, firm capabilities need to be understood not in terms of balance sheet items, but mainly in terms of the organizational structures and managerial processes which support productive activity. By construction, the firm's balance sheet contains items that can be valued, at least at original market prices (cost). It is necessarily the case, therefore, that the balance sheet is a poor shadow of a firm's distinctive competences.[30] That which is distinctive cannot be bought and sold short of buying the firm itself, or one or more of its subunits.

There are many dimensions of the business firm that must be understood if one is to grasp firm-level distinctive competences/capabilities. In this paper we merely identify several classes of factors that will help determine a firm's distinctive competence and dynamic capabilities. We organize these in three categories: processes, positions, and paths. The essence of competences and capabilities is embedded in organizational processes of one kind or another. But the content of these processes and the opportunities they afford for developing competitive advantage at any point in time are shaped significantly by the assets the firm possesses (internal and market) and by the evolutionary path it has adopted/inherited. Hence organizational processes, shaped by the firm's asset

---

[29] As we note in Teece *et al.* (1994), the conglomerate offers few if any efficiencies because there is little provided by the conglomerate form that shareholders cannot obtain for themselves simply by holding a diversified portfolio of stocks.

[30] Owners' equity may reflect, in part, certain historic capabilities. Recently, some scholars have begun to attempt to measure organizational capability using financial statement data. See Baldwin and Clark (1991) and Lev and Sougiannis (1992).

positions and molded by its evolutionary and co-evolutionary paths, explain the essence of the firm's dynamic capabilities and its competitive advantage.

4.3. *Processes, Positions, and Paths*

We thus advance the argument that the competitive advantage of firms lies with its managerial and organizational processes, shaped by its (specific) asset position, and the paths available to it.[31] By managerial and organizational processes, we refer to the way things are done in the firm, or what might be referred to as its routines, or patterns of current practice and learning. By position we refer to its current specific endowments of technology, intellectual property, complementary assets, customer base, and its external relations with suppliers and complementors. By paths we refer to the strategic alternatives available to the firm, and the presence or absence of increasing returns and attendant path dependencies.

Our focus throughout is on asset structures for which no ready market exists, as these are the only assets of strategic interest. A final section focuses on replication and imitation, as it is these phenomena which determine how readily a competence or capability can be cloned by competitors, and therefore distinctiveness of its competences and the durability of its advantage.

The firm's processes and positions collectively encompass its competences and capabilities. A hierarchy of competences/capabilities ought to be recognized, as some competences may be on the factory floor, some in the R&D labs, some in the executive suites, and some in the way everything is integrated. A difficult-to-replicate or difficult-to-imitate competence was defined earlier as a distinctive competence. As indicated, the key feature of distinctive competence is that there is not a market for it, except possibly through the market for business units. Hence competences and capabilities are intriguing assets as they typically must be built because they cannot be bought.

4.3.1. Organizational and managerial processes

Organizational processes have three roles: coordination/integration (a static concept); learning (a dynamic concept); and reconfiguration (a transformational concept). We discuss each in turn.

---

[31] We are implicitly saying that fixed assets, like plant and equipment which can be purchased off-the-shelf by all industry participants, cannot be the source of a firm's competitive advantage. In asmuch as financial balance sheets typically reflect such assets, we point out that the assets that matter for competitive advantage are rarely reflected in the balance sheet, while those that do not are.

Coordination/integration. While the price system supposedly coordinates the economy,[32] managers coordinate or integrate activity inside the firm. How efficiently and effectively internal coordination or integration is achieved is very important (Aoki, 1990).[33] Likewise for external coordination.[34] Increasingly, strategic advantage requires the integration of external activities and technologies. The growing literature on strategic alliances, the virtual corporation, and buyer–supplier relations and technology collaboration evidences the importance of external integration and sourcing.

There is some field-based empirical research that provides support for the notion that the way production is organized by management inside the firm is the source of differences in firms' competence in various domains. For example, Garvin's (1988) study of 18 room air-conditioning plants reveals that quality performance was not related to either capital investment or the degree of automation of the facilities. Instead, quality performance was driven by special organizational routines. These included routines for gathering and processing information, for linking customer experiences with engineering design choices, and for coordinating factories and component suppliers.[35] The work of Clark and Fujimoto (1991) on project development in the automobile industry also illustrates the role played by coordinative routines. Their study reveals a significant degree of variation in how different firms coordinate the various activities required to bring a new model from concept to market. These differences in coordinative routines and capabilities seem to have a significant impact on such performance variables as development cost, development lead times, and quality. Furthermore, Clark and Fujimoto tended to find significant firm-level differences in coordination routines and these differences seemed to have persisted for a long time. This suggests that routines related to coordination are firm-specific in nature.

---

[32] The coordinative properties of markets depend on prices being "sufficient" upon which to base resource allocation decisions.

[33] Indeed, Ronald Coase, author of the pathbreaking 1937 article "The nature of the firm," which focused on the costs of organizational coordination inside the firm as compared to across the market, half a century later has identified as critical the understanding of "why the costs of organizing particular activities differs among firms" (Coase, 1988, p. 47). We argue that a firm's distinctive ability needs to be understood as a reflection of distinctive organizational or coordinative capabilities. This form of integration (i.e. inside business units) is different from the integration between business units; they could be viable on a stand-alone basis (external integration). For a useful taxonomy, see Iansiti and Clark (1994).

[34] Shuen (1994) examines the gains and hazards of the technology make-versus-buy decision and supplier codevelopment.

[35] Garvin (1994) provides a typology of organizational processes.

Also, the notion that competence/capability is embedded in distinct ways of coordinating and combining helps to explain how and why seemingly minor technological changes can have devastating impacts on incumbent firms' abilities to compete in a market. Henderson and Clark (1990), for example, have shown that incumbments in the photolithographic equipment industry were sequentially devasted by seemingly minor innovations that, nevertheless, had major impacts on how systems had to be configured. They attribute these difficulties to the fact that systems-level or "architectural" innovations often require new routines to integrate and coordinate engineering tasks. These findings and others suggest that productive systems display high interdependency, and that it may not be possible to change one level without changing others. This appears to be true with respect to the "lean production" model (Womack *et al.*, 1991) which has now transformed the Taylor or Ford model of manufacturing organization in the automobile industry.[36] Lean production requires distinctive shop floor practices and processes as well as distinctive higher-order managerial processes. Put differently, organizational processes often display high levels of coherence, and

---

[36] Fujimoto (1994, pp. 18–20) describes key elements as they existed in the Japanese auto industry as follows: "The typical volume production system of effective Japanese makers of the 1980s (e.g. Toyota) consists of various intertwined elements that might lead to competitive advantages. Just-in-Time (JIT), Jidoka (automatic defect detection and machine stop), Total Quality Control (TQC), and continuous improvement (Kaizen) are often pointed out as its core subsystems. The elements of such a system include inventory reduction mechanisms by Kanban system; levelization of production volume and product mix (heijunka); reduction of "muda" (non-value adding activities), "mura" (uneven pace of production) and "muri" (excessive workload); production plans based on dealers' order volume (genyo seisan); reduction of die set-up time and lot size in stamping operation; mixed model assembly; piece-by-piece transfer of parts between machines (ikko-nagashi); flexible task assignment for volume changes and productivity improvement (shojinka); multi-task job assignment along the process flow (takotei-mochi); U-shape machine layout that facilitates flexible and multiple task assignment, on-the-spot inspection by direct workers (tsukurikomi); fool-proof prevention of defects (poka-yoke); real-time feedback of production troubles (andon); assembly line stop cord; emphasis on cleanliness, order and discipline on the shop floor (5-S); frequent revision of standard operating procedures by supervisors; quality control circles; standardized tools for quality improvement (e.g. 7 tools for QC, QC story); worker involvement in preventive maintenance (Total Productive Maintenance); low cost automation or semi-automation with just-enough functions); reduction of process steps for saving of tools and dies, and so on. The human-resource management factors that back up the above elements include stable employment of core workers (with temporary workers in the periphery); long-term training of multi-skilled (multi-task) workers; wage system based in part on skill accumulation; internal promotion to shop floor supervisors; cooperative relationships with labor union; inclusion of production supervisors in union members; generally egalitarian policies for corporate welfare, communication and worker motivation. Parts procurement policies are also pointed out often as a source of the competitive advantage.

when they do, replication may be difficult because it requires systemic changes throughout the organization and also among interorganizational linkages, which might be very hard to effectuate. Put differently, partial imitation or replication of a successful model may yield zero benefits.[37]

The notion that there is a certain rationality or coherence to processes and systems is not quite the same concept as corporate culture, as we understand the latter. Corporate culture refers to the values and beliefs that employees hold; culture can be a de facto governance system as it mediates the behavior of individuals and economizes on more formal administrative methods. Rationality or coherence notions are more akin to the Nelson and Winter (1982) notion of organizational routines. However, the routines concept is a little too amorphous to properly capture the congruence amongst processes and between processes and incentives that we have in mind. Consider a professional service organization like an accounting firm. If it is to have relatively high-powered incentives that reward individual performance, then it must build organizational processes that channel individual behavior; if it has weak or low-powered incentives, it must find symbolic ways to recognize the high performers, and it must use alternative methods to build effort and enthusiasm. What one may think of as styles of organization in fact contain necessary, not discretionary elements to achieve performance.

Recognizing the congruences and complementarities among processes, and between processes and incentives, is critical to the understanding of organizational capabilities. In particular, they can help us explain why architectural and radical innovations are so often introduced into an industry by new entrants. The incumbents develop distinctive organizational processes that cannot support the new technology, despite certain overt similarities between the old and the new. The frequent failure of incumbents to introduce new technologies can thus be seen as a consequence of the mismatch that so often exists between the set of organizational processes needed to support the conventional product/service and the requirements of the new. Radical organizational reengineering will usually be required to support the new product, which may well do better embedded in a separate subsidiary where a new set of coherent organizational processes can be fashioned.[38]

Learning. Perhaps even more important than integration is learning. Learning is a process by which repetition and experimentation enable tasks to be performed

---

[37] For a theoretical argument along these lines, see Milgrom and Roberts (1990).

[38] See Abernathy and Clark (1985).

better and quicker. It also enables new production opportunities to be identified.[39] In the context of the firm, if not more generally, learning has several key characteristics. First, learning involves organizational as well as individual skills.[40] While individual skills are of relevance, their value depends upon their employment, in particular organizational settings. Learning processes are intrinsically social and collective and occur not only through the imitation and emulation of individuals, as with teacher – student or master – apprentice, but also because of joint contributions to the understanding of complex problems.[41] Learning requires common codes of communication and coordinated search procedures. Second, the organizational knowledge generated by such activity resides in new patterns of activity, in "routines," or a new logic of organization. As indicated earlier, routines are patterns of interactions that represent successful solutions to particular problems. These patterns of interaction are resident in group behavior, though certain subroutines may be resident in individual behavior. The concept of dynamic capabilities as a coordinative management process opens the door to the potential for interorganizational learning. Researchers (Doz and Shuen, 1990; Mody, 1993) have pointed out that collaborations and partnerships can be a vehicle for new organizational learning, helping firms to recognize dysfunctional routines, and preventing strategic blindspots.

Reconfiguration and transformation. In rapidly changing environments, there is obviously value in the ability to sense the need to reconfigure the firm's asset structure, and to accomplish the necessary internal and external transformation (Amit and Schoemaker, 1993; Langlois, 1994). This requires constant surveillance of markets and technologies and the willingness to adopt best practice. In this regard, benchmarking is of considerable value as an organized process for accomplishing such ends (Camp, 1989). In dynamic environments, narcissistic organizations are likely to be impaired. The capacity to reconfigure and transform is itself a learned organizational skill. The more frequently practiced, the easier accomplished.

Change is costly and so firms must develop processes to minimize low pay-off change. The ability to calibrate the requirements for change and to effectuate

---

[39] For a useful review and contribution, see Levitt and March (1988).

[40] Levinthal and March (1993), Mahoney (1992) and Mahoney and Pandian (1995) suggest that both resources and mental models are intertwined in firm-level learning.

[41] There is a large literature on learning, although only a small fraction of it deals with organizational learning. Relevant contributors include levitt and March (1988), Argyris and Schon (1978), Levinthal and March (1981), Nelson and Winter (1982), and Leonard-Barton (1995).

the necessary adjustments would appear to depend on the ability to scan the environment, to evaluate markets and competitors, and to quickly accomplish reconfiguration and transformation ahead of competition. Decentralization and local autonomy assist these processes. Firms that have honed these capabilities are sometimes referred to as "high-flex".

4.3.2. Positions

The strategic posture of a firm is determined not only by its learning processes and by the coherence of its internal and external processes and incentives, but also by its specific assets. By specific assets we mean for example its specialized plant and equipment. These include its difficult-to-trade knowledge assets and assets complementary to them, as well as its reputational and relational assets. Such assets determine its competitive advantage at any point in time. We identify several illustrative classes.

Technological assets. While there is an emerging market for know-how (Teece, 1981), much technology does not enter it. This is either because the firm is unwilling to sell it[42] or because of difficulties in transacting in the market for know-how (Teece, 1980). A firm's technological assets may or may not be protected by the standard instruments of intellectual property law. Either way, the ownership protection and utilization of technological assets are clearly key differentiators among firms. Likewise for complementary assets.

Complementary assets. Technological innovation require the use of certain related assets to produce and deliver new products and services. Prior commercialization activities require and enable firms to build such complementarities (Teece, 1986b). Such capabilities and assets, while necessary for the firm's established activities, may have other uses as well. These assets typically lie downstream. New products and processes either can enhance or destroy the value of such assets (Tushman, Newman, and Romanelli, 1986). Thus the development of computers enhanced the value of IBM's direct sales force in office products, while disk brakes rendered useless much of the auto industry's investment in drum brakes.

Financial assets. In the short run, a firm's cash position and degree of leverage may have strategic implications. While there is nothing more fungible than cash, it cannot always be raised from external markets without the dissemination of considerable information to potential investors. Accordingly, what a firm can do

---

[42] Managers often evoke the "crown jewels" metaphor. That is, if the technology is released, the kingdom will be lost.

in short order is often a function of its balance sheet. In the longer run, that ought not be so, as cash flow ought be more determinative.

Reputational assets. Firms, like individuals, have reputations. Reputations often summarize a good deal of information about firms and shape the responses of customers, suppliers, and competitors. It is sometimes difficult to disentangle reputation from the firm's current asset and market position. However, in our view, reputational assets are best viewed as an intangible asset that enables firms to achieve various goals in the market. Its main value is external, since what is critical about reputation is that it is a kind of summary statistic about the firm's current assets and position, and its likely future behavior. Because there is generally a strong asymmetry between what is known inside the firm and what is known externally, reputations may sometimes be more salient than the true state of affairs, in the sense that external actors must respond to what they know rather than what is knowable.

Structural assets. The formal and informal structure of organizations and their external linkages have an important bearing on the rate and direction of innovation, and how competences and capabilities co-evolve (Argyres, 1995; Teece, 1996). The degree of hierarchy and the level of vertical and lateral integration are elements of firm-specific structure. Distinctive governance modes can be recognized (e.g. multiproduct, integrated firms; high "flex" firms; virtual corporations; conglomerates), and these modes support different types of innovation to a greater or lesser degree. For instance, virtual structures work well when innovation is autonomous; integrated structures work better for systemic innovations.

Institutional assets. Environments cannot be defined in terms of markets alone. While public policies are usually recognized as important in constraining what firms can do, there is a tendency, particularly by economists, to see these as acting through markets or through incentives. However, institutions themselves are a critical element of the business environment. Regulatory systems, as well as intellectual property regimes, tort laws, and antitrust laws, are also part of the environment. So is the system of higher education and national culture. There are significant national differences here, which is just one of the reasons geographic location matters (Nelson, 1994). Such assets may not be entirely firm specific; firms of different national and regional origin may have quite different institutional assets to call upon because their institutional/policy settings are so different.

Market (structure) assets. Product market position matters, but it is often not at all determinative of the fundamental position of the enterprise in its external environment. Part of the problem lies in defining the market in which a firm competes in a way that gives economic meaning. More importantly, market position in regimes of rapid technological change is often extremely fragile. This is in part because time moves on a different clock in such environments.[43] Moreover, the link between market share and innovation has long been broken, if it ever existed (Teece, 1996). All of this is to suggest that product market position, while important, is too often overplayed. Strategy should be formulated with regard to the more fundamental aspects of firm performance, which we believe are rooted in competences and capabilities and shaped by positions and paths.

Organizational boundaries. An important dimension of "position" is the location of a firm's boundaries. Put differently, the degree of integration (vertical, lateral, and horizontal) is of quite some significance. Boundaries are not only significant with respect to the technological and complementary assets contained within, but also with respect to the nature of the coordination that can be achieved internally as compared to through markets. When specific assets or poorly protected intellectual capital are at issue, pure market arrangements expose the parties to recontracting hazards or appropriability hazards. In such circumstances, hierarchical control structures may work better than pure arms-length contracts.[44]

4.3.3. Paths

Path dependencies. Where a firm can go is a function of its current position and the paths ahead. Its current position is often shaped by the path it has traveled. In standard economics textbooks, firms have an infinite range of technologies from which they can choose and markets they can occupy.

---

[43] For instance, an Internet year might well be thought of as equivalent to 10 years on many industry clocks, because as much change occurs in the Internet business in a year that occurs in say the auto industry in a decade.

[44] Williamson (1996, pp. 102–103) has observed, failures of coordination may arise because "parties that bear a long term bilateral dependency relationship to one another must recognize that incomplete contracts require gap filling and sometimes get out of alignment. Although it is always in the collective interest of autonomous parties to fill gaps, correct errors, and affect efficient realignments, it is also the case that the distribution of the resulting gains is indeterminate. Self-interested bargaining predictably obtains. Such bargaining is itself costly. The main costs, however, are that transactions are maladapted to the environment during the bargaining interval. Also, the prospect of ex post bargaining invites ex ante prepositioning of an inefficient kind."

Changes in product or factor prices will be responded to instantaneously, with technologies moving in and out according to value maximization criteria. Only in the short run are irreversibilities recognized. Fixed costs — such as equipment and overheads — cause firms to price below fully amortized costs but never constrain future investment choices. "Bygones are bygones." Path dependencies are simply not recognized. This is a major limitation of micro-economic theory.

The notion of path dependencies recognizes that "history matters." Bygones are rarely bygones, despite the predictions of rational actor theory. Thus a firm's previous investments and its repertoire of routines (its "history") constrain its future behavior.[45] This follows because learning tends to be local. That is, opportunities for learning will be "close in" to previous activities and thus will be transaction and production specific (Teece, 1988). This is because learning is often a process of trial, feedback, and evaluation. If too many parameters are changed simultaneously, the ability of firms to conduct meaningful natural quasi experiments is attenuated. If many aspects of a firm's learning environment change simultaneously, the ability to ascertain cause — effect relationships is confounded because cognitive structures will not be formed and rates of learning diminish as a result. One implication is that many investments are much longer term than is commonly thought.

The importance of path dependencies is amplified where conditions of increasing returns to adoption exist. This is a demand-side phenomenon, and it tends to make technologies and products embodying those technologies more attractive the more they are adopted. Attractiveness flows from the greater adoption of the product amongst users, which in turn enables them to become more developed and hence more useful. Increasing returns to adoption has many sources including network externalities (Katz and Shapiro, 1985), the presence of complementary assets (Teece, 1986b) and supporting infrastructure (Nelson, 1996), learning by using (Rosenberg, 1982), and scale economies in production and distribution. Competition between and amongst technologies is shaped by increasing returns. Early leads won by good luck or special circumstances (Arthur, 1983) can become amplified by increasing returns. This is not to suggest that first movers necessarily win. Because increasing returns have multiple sources, the prior positioning of firms can affect their capacity to exploit increasing returns. Thus, in Mitchell's (1989) study of medical diagnostic imaging, firms already controlling the relevant complementary assets could in theory start last and finish first.

---

[45] For further development, see Bercovitz, de Figueiredo and Teece (1996).

In the presence of increasing returns, firms can compete passively, or they may compete strategically through technology-sponsoring activities.[46] The first type of competition is not unlike biological competition amongst species, although it can be sharpened by managerial activities that enhance the performance of products and processes. The reality is that companies with the best products will not always win, as chance events may cause "lock-in" on inferior technologies (Arthur, 1983) and may even in special cases generate switching costs for consumers. However, while switching costs may favor the incumbent, in regimes of rapid technological change switching costs can become quickly swamped by switching benefits. Put differently, new products employing different standards often appear with alacrity in market environments experiencing rapid technological change, and incumbents can be readily challenged by superior products and services that yield switching benefits. Thus the degree to which switching costs cause "lock-in" is a function of factors such as user learning, rapidity of technological change, and the amount of ferment in the competitive environment.

Technological opportunities. The concept of path dependencies is given forward meaning through the consideration of an industry's technological opportunities. It is well recognized that how far and how fast a particular area of industrial activity can proceed is in part due to the technological opportunities that lie before it. Such opportunities are usually a lagged function of foment and diversity in basic science, and the rapidity with which new scientific breakthroughs are being made.

However, technological opportunities may not be completely exogenous to industry, not only because some firms have the capacity to engage in or at least support basic research, but also because technological opportunities are often fed by innovative activity itself. Moreover, the recognition of such opportunities is affected by the organizational structures that link the institutions engaging in basic research (primarily the university) to the business enterprise. Hence, the existence of technological opportunities can be quite firm specific.

Important for our purposes is the rate and direction in which relevant scientific frontiers are being rolled back. Firms engaging in R&D may find the path dead

---

[46] Because of huge uncertainties, it may be extremely difficult to determine viable strategies early on. Since the rules of the game and the identity of the players will be revealed only after the market has begun to evolve, the pay-off is likely to lie with building and maintaining organizational capabilities that support flexibility. For example, Microsoft's recent about-face and vigorous pursuit of Internet business once the Net-Scape phenomenon became apparent is impressive, not so much because it perceived the need to change strategy, but because of its organizational capacity to effectuate a strategic shift.

ahead closed off, though break-throughs in related areas may be sufficiently close to be attractive. Likewise, if the path dead ahead is extremely attractive, there may be no incentive for firms to shift the allocation of resources away from traditional pursuits. The depth and width of technological opportunities in the neighborhood of a firm's prior research activities thus are likely to impact a firm's options with respect to both the amount and level of R&D activity that it can justify. In addition, a firm's past experience conditions the alternatives management is able to perceive. Thus, not only do firms in the same industry face "menus" with different costs associated with particular technological choices, they also are looking at menus containing different choices.[47]

4.3.4. Assessment

The essence of a firm's competence and dynamic capabilities is presented here as being resident in the firm's organizational processes, that are in turn shaped by the firm's assets (positions) and its evolutionary path. Its evolutionary path, despite managerial hubris that might suggest otherwise, is often rather narrow.[48] What the firm can do and where it can go are thus rather constrained by its positions and paths. Its competitors are likewise constrained. Rents (profits) thus tend to flow not just from the asset structure of the firm and, as we shall see, the degree of its imitability, but also by the firm's ability to reconfigure and transform.

The parameters we have identified for determining performance are quiet different from those in the standard textbook theory of the firm, and in the competitive forces and strategic conflict approaches to the firm and to strategy.[49] Moreover, the agency theoretic view of the firm as a nexus of contracts would put no weight on processes, positions, and paths. While agency approaches to the firm may recognize that opportunism and shirking may limit what a firm can do, they do not recognize the opportunities and constraints imposed by processes, positions, and paths.

Moreover, the firm in our conceptualization is much more than the sum of its parts — or a team tied together by contracts.[50] Indeed, to some extent individuals can be moved in and out of organizations and, so long as the internal processes and structures remain in place, performance will not necessarily be impaired. A shift in the environment is a far more serious threat to the firm than is the loss

---

[47] This is a critical element in Nelson and Winter's (1982) view of firms and technical change.

[48] We also recognize that the processes, positions, and paths of customers also matter. See our discussion above on increasing returns, including customer learning and network externalities.

[49] In both the firm is still largely a black box. Certainly, little or no attention is given to processes, positions, and paths.

[50] See Alchian and Demsetz (1972).

of key individuals, as individuals can be replaced more readily than organizations can be transformed. Furthermore, the dynamic capabilities view of the firm would suggest that the behavior and performance of particular firms may be quite hard to replicate, even if its coherence and rationality are observable. This matter and related issues involving replication and imitation are taken up in the section follows.

4.4. *Replicability and Imitatability of Organizational Processes and Positions*

Thus far, we have argued that the competences and capabilities (and hence competitive advantage) of a firm rest fundamentally on processes, shaped by positions and paths. However, competences can provide competitive advantage and generate rents only if they are based on a collection of routines, skills, and complementary assets that are difficult to imitate.[51] A particular set of routines can lose their value if they support a competence which no longer matters in the marketplace, or if they can be readily replicated or emulated by competitors. Imitation occurs when firms discover and simply copy a firm's organizational routines and procedures. Emulation occurs when firms discover alternative ways of achieving the same functionality.[52]

4.4.1. Replication

To understand imitation, one must first understand replication. Replication involves transferring or redeploying competences from one concrete economic setting to another. Since productive knowledge is embodied, this cannot be accomplished by simply transmitting information. Only in those instances where all relevant knowledge if fully codified and understood can replication be collapsed into a simple problem of information transfer. Too often, the contextual dependence of original performance is poorly appreciated, so unless firms have replicated their systems of productive knowledge on many prior occasions, the act of replication is likely to be difficult (Teece, 1976). Indeed, replication and transfer are often impossible absent the transfer of people, though this can be minimized if investments are made to convert tacit knowledge to codified knowledge. Often, however, this is simply not possible.

---

[51] We call such competences distinctive. See also Dierickx and Cool (1989) for a discussion of the characteristics of assets which make them a source of rents.

[52] There is ample evidence that a given type of competence (e.g. quality) can be supported by different routines and combinations of skills. For example, the Garvin (1988) and Clark and Fujimoto (1991) studies both indicate that there was no one "formula" for achieving either high quality or high product development performance.

In short, competences and capabilities, and the routines upon which they rest, are normally rather difficult to replicate.[53] Even understanding what all the relevant routines are that support a particular competence may not be transparent. Indeed, Lippman and Rumelt (1992) have argued that some sources of competitive advantage are so complex that the firm itself, let alone its competitors, does not understand them.[54] As Nelson and Winter (1982) and Teece (1982) have explained, many organizational routines are quite tacit in nature. Imitation can also be hindered by the fact few routines are "stand-alone"; coherence may require that a change in one set of routines in one part of the firm (e.g. production) requires changes in some other part (e.g. R&D).

Some routines and competences seem to be attributable to local or regional forces that shape firms' capabilities at early stages in their lives. Porter (1990), for example, shows that differences in local product markets, local factor markets, and institutions play an important role in shaping competitive capabilities. Differences also exist within populations of firms from the same country. Various studies of the automobile industry, for example, show that not all Japanese automobile companies are top performers in terms of quality, productivity, or product development (see, for example, Clark and Fujimoto, 1991). The role of firm-specific history has been high-lighted as a critical factor explaining such firm-level (as opposed to regional or national-level) differences (Nelson and Winter, 1982). Replication in a different context may thus be rather difficult.

At least two types of strategic value flow from replication. One is the ability to support geographic and product line expansion. To the extent that the capabilities in question are relevant to customer needs elsewhere, replication can confer value.[55] Another is that the ability to replicate also indicates that the firm has the foundations in place for learning and improvement. Considerable empirical evidence supports the notion that the understanding of processes, both in production and in management, is the key to process improvement. In short, an organization cannot improve that which it does not understand. Deep process understanding is often required to accomplish codification. Indeed, if knowledge

---

[53] See Szulanski's (1995) discussion of the intrafirm transfer of best practice. He quotes a senior vice president of Xerox as saying "you can see a high performance factory or office, but it just doesn't spread. I don't know why." Szulanski also discusses the role of benchmarking in facilitating the transfer of best practice.

[54] If so, it is our belief that the firm's advantage is likely to fade, as luck does run out.

[55] Needless to say, there are many examples of firms replicating their capabilities inappropriately by applying extant routines to circumstances where they may not be applicable, e.g. Nestle's transfer of developed-country marketing methods for infant formula to the Third World (Hartley, 1989). A key strategic need is for firms to screen capabilities for their applicability to new environments.

is highly tacit, it indicates that underlying structures are not well understood, which limits learning because scientific and engineering principles cannot be as systematically applied.[56] Instead, learning is confined to proceeding through trial and error, and the leverage that might otherwise come from the application of scientific theory is denied.

4.4.2. Imitation

Imitation is simply replication performed by a competitor. If self-replication is difficult, imitation is likely to be harder. In competitive markets, it is the ease of imitation that determines the sustainability of competitive advantage. Easy imitation implies the rapid dissipation of rents.

Factors that make replication difficult also make imitation difficult. Thus, the more tacit the firm's productive knowledge, the harder it is to replicate by the firm itself or its competitors. When the tacit component is high, imitation may well be impossible, absent the hiring away of key individuals and the transfers of key organization processes.

However, another set of barriers impedes imitation of certain capabilities in advanced industrial countries. This is the system of intellectual property rights, such as patents, trade secrets, and trademarks, and even trade dress.[57] Intellectual property protection is of increasing importance in the United States, as since 1982 the legal system has adopted a more pro-patent posture. Similar trends are evident outside the United States. Besides the patent system, several other factors cause there to be a difference between replication costs and imitation costs. The observability of the technology or the organization is one such important factor. Whereas vistas into product technology can be obtained through strategies such as reverse engineering, this is not the case for process technology, as a firm need not expose its process technology to the outside in order to benefit from it.[58]

---

[56] Different approaches to learning are required depending on the depth of knowledge. Where knowledge is less articulated and structured, trial and error and learning-by-doing are necessary, whereas in mature environments where the underlying engineering science is better understood, organizations can undertake more deductive approaches or what Pisano (1994) refers to as "learning-before-doing."

[57] Trade dress refers to the "look and feel" of a retail establishment, e.g. the distinctive marketing and presentation style of The Nature Company.

[58] An interesting but important exception to this can be found in second sourcing. In the microprocessor business, until the introduction of the 386 chip, Intel and most other merchant semi producers were encouraged by large customers like IBM to provide second sources, i.e. to license and share their proprietary process technology with competitors like AMD and NEC. The microprocessor developers did so to assure customers that they had sufficient manufacturing capability to meet demand at all times.

Firms with product technology, on the other hand, confront the unfortunate circumstances that they must expose what they have got in order to profit from the technology. Secrets are thus more protectable if there is no need to expose them in contexts where competitors can learn about them.

One should not, however, overestimate the overall importance of intellectual property protection; yet it presents a formidable imitation barrier in certain particular contexts. Intellectual property protection is not uniform across products, processes, and technologies, and is best thought of as islands in a sea of open competition. If one is not able to place the fruits of one's investment, ingenuity, or creativity on one or more of the islands, then one indeed is at sea.

We use the term appropriability regimes to describe the ease of imitation. Appropriability is a function both of the ease of replication and the efficacy of intellectual property rights as a barrier to imitation. Appropriability is strong when a technology is both inherently difficult to replicate and the intellectual property system provides legal barriers to imitation. When it is inherently easy to replicate and intellectual property protection is either unavailable or ineffectual, then appropriability is weak. Intermediate conditions also exist.

Conclusion

The four paradigms discussed above are quite different, though the first two have much in common with each other (strategizing) as do the last two (economizing). But are these paradigms complementary or competitive? According to some authors, "the resource perspective complements the industry analysis framework" (Amit and Schoemaker, 1993, p. 35). While this is undoubtedly true, we think that in several important respects the perspectives are also competitive. While this should be recognized, it is not to suggest that there is only one framework that has value. Indeed, complex problems are likely to benefit from insights obtained from all of the paradigms we have identified plus more. The trick is to work out which frameworks are appropriate for the problem at hand. Slavish adherence to one class to the neglect of all others is likely to generate strategic blindspots. The tools themselves then generate strategic vulnerability. We now explore these issues further. Table 1 summarizes some similarities and differences.

4.5. *Efficiency versus Market Power*

The competitive forces and strategic conflict approaches generally see profits as stemming from strategizing — that is, from limitations on competition which

Essays in Technology Management and Policy

Table 1. Paradigms of Strategy: Salient Characteristics

Paradigm	Intellectual Roots	Representative Authors Addressing Strategic Management Questions	Nature of Rents	Rationality Assumptions of Managers	Fundamental Units of Analysis	Short-Run Capacity for Strategic Reorientation	Role of Industrial Structure	Focal Concern
(1) Attenuating competitive forces	Mason, Bain	Porter (1980)	Chamberlinean	Rational	Industries, firms, products	High	Exogenous	Structural conditions and competitor positioning
(2) Strategic conflict	Machiavelli, Schelling, Cournot, Nash, Harsanyi, Shapiro	Ghemawat (1986) Shapiro (1989) Brandenburger and Nalebuff (1995)	Chamberlinean	Hyper-rational	Firms, products	Often infinite	Endogenous	Strategic interactions
(3) Resource-based perspectives	Penrose, Selznick, Christensen, Andrews	Rumelt (1984) Chandler (1966) Wernerfeld (1984) Teece (1980, 1982)	Ricardian	Rational	Resources	Low	Endogenous	Asset fungibility
(4) Dynamic capabilities perspective	Schumpeter, Nelson, Winter, Teece	Dosi, Teece and Winter (1989) Prahalad and Hamel (1990) Hayes and Wheelwright (1984) Dierickx and Cool (1989) Porter (1990)	Schumpeterian	Rational	Processes, positions, paths	Low	Endogenous	Asset accumulation, replicability and inimitability

firms achieve through raising rivals' costs and exclusionary behavior (Teece, 1984). The competitive forces approach in particular leads one to see concentrated industries as being attractive — market positions can be shielded behind entry barriers, and rivals costs can be raised. It also suggests that the sources of competitive advantage lie at the level of the industry, or possibly groups within an industry. In text book presentations, there is almost no attention at all devoted to discovering, creating, and commercializing new sources of value.

The dynamic capabilities and resources approaches clearly have a different orientation. They see competitive advantage stemming from high-performance routines operating "inside the firm," shaped by processes and positions. Path dependencies (including increasing returns) and technological opportunities mark the road ahead. Because of imperfect factor markets, or more precisely the nontradability of "soft" assets like values, culture, and organizational experience, distinctive competences and capabilities generally cannot be acquired; they must be built. This sometimes takes years — possibly decades. In some cases, as when the competence is protected by patents, replication by a competitor is ineffectual as a means to access the technology. The capabilities approach accordingly sees definite limits on strategic options, at least in the short run. Competitive success occurs in part because of policies pursued and experience and efficiency obtained in earlier periods.

Competitive success can undoubtedly flow from both strategizing and economizing,[59] but along with Williamson (1991) we believe that "economizing is more fundamental than strategizing ... or put differently, that economy is the best strategy."[60] Indeed, we suggest that, except in special circumstances, too much "strategizing" can lead firms to underinvest in core competences and neglect dynamic capabilities, and thus harm long-term competitiveness.

4.6. *Normative Implications*

The field of strategic management is avowedly normative. It seeks to guide those aspects of general management that have material effects on the survival and

---

[59] Phillips (1971) and Demsetz (1974) also made the case that market concentration resulted from the competitive success of more efficient firms, and not from entry barriers and restrictive practices.

[60] We concur with Williamson that economizing and strategizing are not mutually exclusive. Strategic ploys can be used to disguise inefficiencies and to promote economizing outcomes, as with pricing with reference to learning curve costs. Our view of economizing is perhaps more expansive than Williamson's as it embraces more than efficient contract design and the minimization of transactions costs. We also address production and organizational economies, and the distinctive ways that things are accomplished inside the business enterprise.

success of the business enterprise. Unless these various approaches differ in terms of the framework and heuristics they offer management, then the discourse we have gone through is of limited immediate value. In this paper, we have already alluded to the fact that the capabilities approach tends to steer managers toward creating distinctive and difficult-to-imitate advantages and avoiding games with customers and competitors. We now survey possible differences, recognizing that the paradigms are still in their infancy and cannot confidently support strong normative conclusions.

4.6.1. Unit of analysis and analytic focus

Because in the capabilities and the resources framework business opportunities flow from a firm's unique processes, strategy analysis must be situational.[61] This is also true with the strategic conflict approach. There is no algorithm for creating wealth for the entire industry. Prescriptions they apply to industries or groups of firms at best suggest overall direction, and may indicate errors to be avoided. In contrast, the competitive forces approach is not particularly firm specific; it is industry and group specific.

4.6.2. Strategic change

The competitive forces and the strategic conflict approach, since they pay little attention to skills, know-how, and path dependency, tend to see strategic choice occurring with relative facility. The capabilities approach sees values augmenting strategic change as being difficult and costly. Moreover, it can generally only occur incrementally. Capabilities cannot easily be bought; they must be built. From the capabilities perspective, strategy involves choosing among and committing to long-term paths or trajectories of competence development.

In this regard, we speculate that the dominance of competitive forces and the strategic conflict approaches in the United States may have something to do with observed differences in strategic approaches adopted by some U.S. and some foreign firms. Hayes (1985) has noted that American companies tend to favor "strategic leaps" while, in contrast, Japanese and German companies tend to favor incremental, but rapid, improvement.

4.6.3. Entry strategies

Here the resources and the capabilities approaches suggest that entry decisions must be made with reference to the competences and capabilities which new

---

[61] On this point, the strategic conflict and the resources and capabilities are congruent. However, the aspects of "situation" that matter are dramatically different, as described earlier in this paper.

entrants have, relative to the competition. Whereas the other approaches tell you little about where to look to find likely entrants, the capabilities approach identifies likely entrants. Relatedly, whereas the entry deterrence approach suggests an unconstrained search for new business opportunities, the capabilities approach suggests that such opportunities lie close in to one's existing business. As Richard Rumelt has explained it in conversation, "the capabilities approach suggests that if a firm looks inside itself, and at its market environment, sooner or later it will find a business opportunity."

4.6.4. Entry timing

Whereas the strategic conflict approach tells little about where to look to find likely entrants, the resources and the capabilities approach identifies likely entrants and their timing of entry. Brittain and Freeman (1980) using population ecology methodologies argued that an organization is quick to expand when there is a significant overlap between its core capabilities and those needed to survive in a new market. Recent research (Mitchell, 1989) showed that the more industry-specialized assets or capabilities a firm possesses, the more likely it is to enter an emerging technical subfield in its industry, following a technological discontinuity. Additionally, the interaction between specialized assets such as firm-specific capabilities and rivalry had the greatest influence on entry timing.

4.6.5. Diversification

Related diversification — that is, diversification that builds upon or extends existing capabilities — is about the only form of diversification that a resources/ capabilities framework is likely to view as meritorious (Rumelt, 1974; Teece, 1980, 1982; Teece *et al.*, 1994). Such diversification will be justifiable when the firms' traditional markets decline.[62] The strategic conflict approach is likely to be a little more permissive; acquisitions that raise rivals' costs or enable firms to effectuate exclusive arrangements are likely to be seen as efficacious in certain circumstances.

4.6.6. Focus and specialization

Focus needs to be defined in terms of distinctive competences or capability, not products. Products are the manifestation of competences, as competences

---

[62] Cantwell shows that the technological competence of firms persists over time, gradually evolving through firm-specific learning. He shows that technological diversification has been greater for chemicals and pharmaceuticals than for electrical and electronic-related fields, and he offers as an explanation the greater straight-ahead opportunities in electrical and electronic fields than in chemicals and pharmaceuticals. See Cantwell (1993).

can be molded into a variety of products. Product market specialization and decentralization configured around product markets may cause firms to neglect the development of core competences and dynamic capabilities, to the extent to which competences require accessing assets across divisions.

The capabilities approach places emphasis on the internal processes that a firm utilizes, as well as how they are deployed and how they will evolve. The approach has the benefit of indicating that competitive advantage is not just a function of how one plays the game; it is also a function of the "assets" one has to play with, and how these assets can be deployed and redeployed in a changing market.

4.7. *Future Directions*

We have merely sketched an outline for a dynamic capabilities approach. Further theoretical work is needed to tighten the framework, and empirical research is critical to helping us understand how firms get to be good, how they sometimes stay that way, why and how they improve, and why they sometimes decline.[63] Researchers in the field of strategy need to join forces with researchers in the fields of innovation, manufacturing, and organizational behavior and business history if they are to unlock the riddles that lie behind corporate as well as national competitive advantage. There could hardly be a more ambitious research agenda in the social sciences today.

Acknowledgements

Research for this paper was aided by support from the Alfred P. Sloan Foundation through the Consortium on Competitiveness and Cooperation at the University of California, Berkeley. The authors are grateful for helpful comments from two anonymous referees, as well as from Raffi Amit, Jay Barney, Joseph Bower, Henry Chesbrough, Giovanni Dosi, Sumantra Goshal, Pankaj Ghemawat, Connie Helfat, Rebecca Henderson, Dan Levinthal, Richard Nelson, Margie Peteraf, Richard Rosenbloom, Richard Rumelt, Carl Shapiro, Oliver Williamson, and Sidney Winter. Useful feedback was obtained from workshops at the Haas

---

[63] For a gallant start, see Miyazaki (1995) and McGrath *et al.* (1996). Chandler's (1990) work on scale and scope, summarized in Teece (1993), provides some historical support for the capabilities approach. Other relevant studies can be found in a special issue of *Industrial and Corporate Change* 3(3) (1994), that was devoted to dynamic capabilities.

School of Business, the Wharton School, the Kellogg School (Northwestern), the Harvard Business School, and the International Institute of Applied Systems Analysis (IIASA) in Vienna, the London School of Economics, and the London Business School.

References

W.J. Abernathy and K. Clark, Innovation: Mapping the Winds of Creative Destruction, *Research Policy* 14 (1985), 3–22.

A.A. Alchian and H. Demsetz, Production, Information Costs, and Economic Organization, *American Economic Review* 62 (1972), 777–795.

R. Amit and P. Schoemaker, Strategic Assets and Organizational Rent, *Strategic Management Journal* 14(1) (1993), 33–46.

K. Andrews, *The Concept of Corporate Strategy*, 3rd ed. (Dow Jones-Irwin, Homewood, IL, 1987).

M. Aoki, The Participatory Generation of Information Rents and the Theory of the Firm, in M. Aoki, B. Gustafsson and O.E. Williamson (eds.), *The Firm as a Nexus of Treaties* (Sage, London, 1990), pp. 26–52.

N. Argyres, Technology Strategy, Governance Structure and Interdivisional Coordination, *Journal of Economic Behavior and Organization* 28 (1995), 337–358.

C. Argyris and D. Schon, *Organizational Learning* (Addison-Wesley, Reading, MA, 1978).

K. Arrow, The Organization of Economic Activity: Issues Pertinent to the Choice of Market versus Nonmarket Allocation, in *The Analysis and Evaluation of Public Expenditures: The PPB System*, 1. U.S. Joint Economic Committee, 91st Session, U.S. Government Printing Office, Washington, DC, 1969, pp. 59–73.

K. Arrow, Technical Information and Industrial Structure, *Industrial and Corporate Change* 5(2) (1996), 645–652.

W.B. Arthur, Competing Technologies and Lock-in by Historical Events: The Dynamics of Allocation Under Increasing Returns, working paper WP-83-90, International Institute for Applied Systems Analysis, Laxenburg, Austria, 1983.

J.S. Bain, *Industrial Orgainzation* (Wiley, New York, 1959).

C. Baldwin and K. Clark, Capabilities and Capital Investment: New Perspectives on Capital Budgeting, Harvard Business School working paper #92-004, 1991.

J.B. Barney, Strategic Factor Markets: Expectations, Luck, and Business Strategy, *Management Science* 32(10) (1986), 1231–1241.

J.B. Barney, J.-C. Spender and T. Reve, *Crafoord Lectures*, Vol. 6 (Chartwell-Bratt, Bromley, U.K. and Lund University Press, Lund, Sweden, 1994).

W. Baumol, J. Panzar and R. Willig, *Contestable Markets and the Theory of Industry Structure* (Harcourt Brace Jovanovich, New York, 1982).

J.E.L. Bercovitz, J. M. de Figueiredo and D.J. Teece, Firm Capabilities and Managerial Decision-Making: A Theory of Innovation Biases, in R. Garud, P. Nayyar and Z. Shapira (eds.), *Innovation: Oversights and Foresights* (Cambridge University Press, Cambridge, U.K., 1996), pp. 233–259.

A.M. Brandenburger and B.J. Nalebuff, *Coopetition* (Doubleday, New York, 1996).

A.M. Brandenburger and B.J. Nalebuff, The Right Game: Use Game Theory to Shape Strategy, *Harvard Business Review* 73(4) (1995), 57–71.

J. Brittain and J. Freeman, Organizational Proliferation and Density-Dependent Delection, in J.R. Kimberly and R. Miles (eds.), *The Organizational Life Cycle* (Jossey-Bass, San Francisco, CA, 1980), pp. 291–338.

R. Camp, *Benchmarking: The Search for Industry Best Practices that Lead to Superior Performance* (Quality Press, Milwaukee, WI, 1989).

J. Cantwell, Corporate Technological Specialization in International Industries, in M. Casson and J. Creedy (eds.), *Industrial Concentration and Economic Inequality* (Edward Elgar, Aldershot, 1993), pp. 216–232.

A.D. Chandler, Jr., *Strategy and Structure* (Doubleday, Anchor Books Edition, New York, 1966).

A.D. Chandler, Jr., *Scale and Scope: The Dynamics of Industrial Competition* (Harvard University Press, Cambridge, MA, 1990).

K. Clark and T. Fujimoto, *Product Development Performance: Strategy, Organization and Management in the World Auto Industries* (Harvard Business School Press, Cambridge, MA, 1991).

R. Coase, The Nature of the Firm, *Economica* 4 (1937), 386–405.

R. Coase, Lecture on the Nature of the Firm, III, *Journal of Law, Economics and Organization* 4 (1988), 33–47.

K. Cool and D. Schendel, Performance Differences Among Strategic Group Members, *Strategic Management Journal* 9(3) (1988), 207–223.

J.M. de Figueiredo and D.J. Teece, Mitigating Procurement Hazards in the Context of Innovation, *Industrial and Corporate Change* 5(2) (1996), 537–559.

H. Demsetz, Two Systems of Belief About Monopoly, in H. Goldschmid, M. Mann and J.F. Weston (eds.), *Industrial Concentration: The New Learning* (Little, Brown, Boston, MA, 1974), pp. 161–184.

I. Dierickx and K. Cool, Asset Stock Accumulation and Sustainability of Competitive Advantage, *Management Science* 35(12) (1989), 1504–1511.

A. Dixit, The Role of Investment in Entry Deterrence, *Economic Journal* 90 (1980), 95–106.

G. Dosi, D.J. Teece and S. Winter, Toward a Theory of Corporate Coherence: Preliminary Remarks, unpublished paper, Center for Research in Management, University of California at Berkeley, 1989.

Y. Doz and A. Shuen, From Intent to Outcome: A Process Framework for Partnerships, INSEAD working paper, 1990.

E. F. Fama, Agency Problems and the Theory of the Firm, *Journal of Political Economy* 88 (1980), 288–307.

J. Freeman and W. Boeker, The Ecological Analysis of Business Strategy, in G. Carroll and D. Vogel (eds.), *Strategy and Organization* (Pitman, Boston, MA, 1984), pp. 64–77.

T. Fujimoto, Reinterpreting the Resource-Capability View of the Firm: A Case of the Development-Production Systems of the Japanese Automakers, draft working paper, Faculty of Economics, University of Tokyo, 1994.

D. Garvin, *Managing Quality* (Free Press, New York, 1988).

D. Garvin, The Processes of Organization and Management, Harvard Business School working paper #94-084, 1994.

P. Ghemawat, Sustainable Advantage, *Harvard Business Review* 64(5) (1986), 53–58.

P. Ghemawat, *Commitment: The Dynamics of Strategy* (Free Press, New York, 1991).

R.J. Gilbert and D.M.G. Newberry, Preemptive Patenting and the Persistence of Monopoly, *American Economic Review* 72 (1982), 514–526.

J.H. Gittell, Cross Functional Coordination, Control and Human Resource Systems: Evidence from the Airline Industry, unpublished Ph.D. Thesis, Massachusetts Institute of Technology, 1995.

G.S. Hansen and B. Wernerfelt, Determinants of Firm Performance: The Relative Importance of Economic and Organizational Factors, *Strategic Management Journal* 10(5) (1989), 399–411.

R.F. Hartley, *Marketing Mistakes* (Wiley, New York, 1989).

R. Hayes, Strategic Planning: Forward in Reverse, *Harvard Business Review* 63(6) (1985), 111–119.

R. Hayes and K. Clark, Exploring the Sources of Productivity Differences at the Factory Level, in K. Clark, R.H. Hayes and C. Lorenz (eds.), *The Uneasy Alliance: Managing the Productivity — Technology Dilemma* (Harvard Business School Press, Boston, MA, 1985), pp. 151–188.

R. Hayes and S. Wheelwright, *Restoring Our Competitive Edge: Competing Through Manufacturing* (Wiley, New York, 1984).

R.S. Hayes, S. Wheelwright and K. Clark, *Dynamic Manufacturing: Creating the Learning Organization* (Free Press, New York, 1988).

R.M. Henderson, The Evolution of Integrative Capability: Innovation in Cardiovascular Drug Discovery, *Industrial and Corporate Change* 3(3) (1994), 607–630.

R.M. Henderson and K.B. Clark, Architectural Innovation: The Reconfiguration of Existing Product Technologies and the Failure of Established Firms, *Administrative Science Quarterly* 35 (1990), 9–30.

R.M. Henderson and I. Cockburn, Measuring Competence? Exploring Firm Effects in Pharmaceutical Research, *Strategic Management Journal,* Summer Special Issue, 15 (1994), 63–84.

M. Iansiti and K.B. Clark, Integration and Dynamic Capability: Evidence from Product Development in Automobiles and Mainframe Computers, *Industrial and Corporate Change* 3(3) (1994), 557–605.

H. Itami and T.W. Roehl, *Mobilizing Invisible Assets* (Harvard University Press, Cambridge, MA, 1987).

R. Jacobsen, The Persistence of Abnormal Returns, *Strategic Management Journal* 9(5) (1988), 415–430.

M. Katz and C. Shapiro, Network Externalities, Competition and Compatibility, *American Economic Review* 75 (1985), 424–440.

D.M. Kreps and R. Wilson, Sequential Equilibria, *Econometrica* 50 (1982a) 863–894.

D.M. Kreps and R. Wilson, Reputation and Imperfect Information, *Journal of Economic Theory* 27 (1982b), 253–279.

R. Langlois, Cognition and Capabilities: Opportunities Seized and Missed in the History of the Computer Industry, working paper, University of Connecticut. Presented at the conference on Technological Oversights and Foresights, Stern School of Business, New York University, March 11–12, 1994.

E.C. Learned, C. Christensen, K. Andrews and W. Guth, *Business Policy: Text and Cases* (Irwin, Homewood, IL, 1969).

D. Leonard-Barton, Core Capabilities and Core Rigidities: A Paradox in Managing New Product Development, *Strategic Management Journal,* Summer Special Issue, 13 (1992), 111–125.

D. Leonard-Barton, *Wellsprings of Knowledge* (Harvard Business School Press, Boston, MA, 1995).

B. Lev and T. Sougiannis, The Capitalization, Amortization and Value-Relevance of R&D, unpublished manuscript, University of California, Berkeley, and University of Illinois, Urbana–Champaign, 1992.

D. Levinthal and J. March, A Model of Adaptive Organizational Search, *Journal of Economic Behavior and Organization* 2 (1981), 307–333.

D.A. Levinthal and J.G. March, The Myopia of Learning, *Strategic Management Journal,* Winter Special Issue, 14 (1993), 95–112.

D. Levinthal and J. Myatt, Co-Evolution of Capabilities and Industry: The Evolution of Mutual Fund Processing, *Strategic Management Journal,* Winter Special Issue, 15 (1994), 45–62.

B. Levitt and J. March, Organizational Learning, *Annual Review of Sociology* 14 (1988), 319–340.

A.N. Link, D.J. Teece and W.F. Finan, Estimating the Benefits from Collaboration: The Case of SEMATECH, *Review of Industrial Organization* 11 (October 1996), 737–751.

S.A. Lippman and R.P. Rumelt, Demand Uncertainty and Investment in Industry-Specific Capital, *Industrial and Corporate Change* 1(1) (1992), 235–262.

J. Mahoney, The Management of Resources and the Resources of Management, *Journal of Business Research* 33(2) (1995), 91–101.

J.T. Mahoney and J.R. Pandian, The Resource-Based View Within the Conversation of Strategic Management, *Strategic Management Journal* 13(5) (1992), 363–380.

E. Mason, The Current State of the Monopoly Problem in the U.S., *Harvard Law Review* 62 (1949), 1265–1285.

R.G. McGrath, M.-H. Tsai, S. Venkataraman and I.C. MacMillan, Innovation, Competitive Advantage and Rent: A Model and Test, *Management Science* 42(3) (1996), 389–403.

P. Milgrom and J. Roberts, Limits Pricing and Entry Under Incomplete Information: An Equilibrium Analysis, *Econometrica* 50 (1982a), 443–459.

P. Milgrom and J. Roberts, Predation, Reputation and Entry Deterrence, *Journal of Economic Theory* 27 (1982a), 280–312.

P. Milgrom and J. Roberts, The Economics of Modern Manufacturing: Technology, Strategy, and Organization, *American Economic Review* 80(3) (1990), 511–528.

W. Mitchell, Whether and When? Probability and Timing of Incumbents' Entry into Emerging Industrial Subfields, *Administrative Science Quarterly* 34 (1989), 208–230.

K. Miyazaki, *Building Competences in the Firm: Lessons from Japanese and European Optoelectronics* (St. Martins Press, New York, 1995).

A. Mody, Learning Through Alliances, *Journal of Economic Behavior and Organization* 20(2) (1993), 151–170.

R.R. Nelson, Why do Firms Differ, and How does it Matter? *Strategic Management Journal*, Winter Special Issue, 12 (1991), 61–74.

R.R. Nelson, The Co-Evolution of Technology, Industrial Structure, and Supporting Institutions, *Industrial and Corporate Change* 3(1) (1994), 47–63.

R. Nelson, The Evolution of Competitive or Comparative Advantage: A Preliminary Report on a Study, WP-96-21, International Institute for Applied Systems Analysis, Luxemburg, Austria, 1996.

R. Nelson and S. Winter, *An Evolutionary Theory of Economic Change* (Harvard University Press, Cambridge, MA, 1982).

E. Penrose, *The Theory of the Growth of the Firm* (Basil Blackwell, London, 1959).

A.C. Phillips, *Technology and Market Structure* (Lexington Books, Toronto, 1971).

G. Pisano, Knowledge Integration and the Locus of Learning: An Empirical Analysis of Process Development, *Strategic Management Journal*, Winter Special Issue, 15 (1994), 85–100.

M.E. Porter, *Competitive Strategy* (Free Press, New York, 1980).

M.E. Porter, *The Competitive Advantage of Nations* (Free Press, New York, 1990).

C.K. Prahalad and G. Hamel, The Core Competence of the Corporation, *Harvard Business Review* 68(3) (1990), 79–91.

G.B.H. Richardson, *Information and Investment* (Oxford University Press, New York, 1960, 1990).

N. Rosenberg, *Inside the Black Box: Technology and Economics* (Cambridge University Press, Cambridge, MA, 1982).

R.P. Rumelt, *Strategy, Structure, and Economic Performance* (Harvard University Press, Cambridge, MA, 1974).

R.P. Rumelt, Towards a Strategic Theory of the Firm, in R.B. Lamb (ed.), *Competitive Strategic Management* (Prentice-Hall, Englewood Cliffs, NJ, 1984), pp. 556–570.

R.P. Rumelt, How Much Does Industry Matter? *Strategic Management Journal* 12(3) (1991), 167–185.

R.P. Rumelt, D. Schendel and D. Teece, *Fundamental Issues in Strategy* (Harvard Business School Press, Cambridge, MA, 1994).

R. Schmalensee, Advertising and Entry Deterrence: An Exploratory Model, *Journal of Political Economy* 91(4) (1983), 636–653.

J.A. Schumpeter, *Theory of Economic Development* (Harvard University Press, Cambridge, MA, 1934).

J.A. Schumpeter, *Capitalism, Socialism, and Democracy* (Harper, New York, 1942).

C. Shapiro, The Theory of Business Strategy, *RAND Journal of Economics* 20(1) (1989), 125–137.

A. Shuen, Technology Sourcing and Learning Strategies in the Semiconductor Industry, unpublished Ph.D. Dissertation, University of California, Berkeley, 1994.

J. Sutton, Implementing Game Theoretical Models in Industrial Economies, in A. D. Monte (ed.), *Recent Developments in the Theory of Industrial Organization* (University of Michigan Press, Ann Arbor, MI, 1992), pp. 19–33.

G. Szulanski, Unpacking Stickiness: An Empirical Investigation of the Barriers to Transfer Best Practice Inside the Firm, *Academy of Management Journal*, Best Papers Proceedings, 1995, pp. 437–441.

D.J. Teece, *The Multinational Corporation and the Resource Cost of International Technology Transfer* (Ballinger, Cambridge, MA, 1976).

D.J. Teece, Economics of Scope and the Scope of the Enterprise, *Journal of Economic Behavior and Organization* 1 (1980), 223–247.

D.J. Teece, The Market for Know-How and the Efficient International Transfer of Technology, *Annals of the Academy of Political and Social Science* 458 (1981), 81–96.

D.J. Teece, Towards an Economic Theory of the Multiproduct Firm, *Journal of Economic Behavior and Organization* 3 (1982), 39–63.

D.J. Teece, Economic Analysis and Strategic Management, *California Management Review* 26(3) (1984), 87–110.

D.J. Teece, Transactions Cost Economics and the Multinational Enterprise, *Journal of Economic Behavior and Organization* 7 (1986a), 21–45.

D.J. Teece, Profiting from Technological Innovation, *Research Policy* 15(6) (1986b), 285–305.

D.J. Teece, Technological Change and the Nature of the Firm, in G. Dosi, C. Freeman, R. Nelson, G. Silverberg and L. Soete (eds.), *Technical Change and Economic Theory* (Pinter Publishers, New York, 1988), pp. 256–281.

D.J. Teece, Competition, Cooperation, and Innovation: Organizational Arrangements for Regimes of Rapid Technological Progress, *Journal of Economic Behavior and Organization* 18(1) (1992), 1–25.

D.J. Teece, The Dynamics of Industrial Capitalism: Perspectives on Alfred Chandler's Scale and Scope (1990), *Journal of Economic Literature* 31(1) (1993), 199–225.

D.J. Teece, Firm Organization, Industrial Structure, and Technological Innovation, *Journal of Economic Behavior and Organization* 31 (1996), 193–224.

D.J. Teece. and G. Pisano, The Dynamic Capabilities of Firms: An Introduction, *Industrial and Corporate Change* 3(3) (1994), 537–556.

D.J. Teece, R. Rumelt, G. Dosi and S. Winter, Understanding Corporate Coherence: Theory and Evidence, *Journal of Economic Behavior and Organization* 23 (1994), 1–30.

M.L. Tushman, W.H. Newman and E. Romanelli, Convergence and Upheaval: Managing the Unsteady Pace of Organizational Evolution, *California Management Review* 29(1) (1986), 29–44.

B. Wernerfelt, A Resource-Based View of the Firm, *Strategic Management Journal* 5(2) (1984), 171–180.

B. Wernerfelt and C. Montgomery, Tobin's Q and the Importance of Focus in Firm Performance, *American Economic Review* 78(1) (1988), 246–250.

O.E. Williamson, *Markets and Hierarchies* (Free Press, New York, 1975).

O.E. Williamson, *The Economic Institutions of Capitalism* (Free Press, New York, 1985).

O.E. Williamson, Strategizing, Economizing, and Economic Organization, *Strategic Management Journal*, Winter Special Issue, 12 (1991), 75–94.

O.E. Williamson, *The Mechanisms of Governance* (Oxford University Press, New York, 1996).

J. Womack, D. Jones and D. Roos, *The Machine that Changed the World* (Harper-Perennial, New York, 1991).

U. Zander and B. Kogut, Knowledge and the Speed of the Transfer and Imitation of Organizational Capabilities: An Empirical Test, *Organization Science* 6(1) (1995), 76–92.

Mitigating Procurement Hazards in the Context of Innovation

John M. de Figueiredo and David J. Teece

Haas School of Business, University of California, Berkeley, CA 94720-1930, U.S.A.

This paper extends the transaction cost economics framework to examine the contractual hazards that arise in the course of technological innovation. We identify three main strategic hazards related to future technological opportunities that may develop in business transactions: loss of technological pacing possibilities on the technological frontier, loss of technological control at or behind the frontier, and design omissions. In examining these hazards we focus on the increasingly common phenomenon of vertically integrated firms supplying downstream competitors. We then analyze how constellations of safeguards, particularly relational safeguards, can augment transaction-specific safeguards in many instances to ensure high-powered incentives are maintained. We also consider under what conditions downstream divestiture is a desirable economizing option. Supportive illustrations are drawn from the desktop laser printer and telecommunications industries.

> *I have spoken to many audiences about the benefits of AT&T being a vertically integrated business that had both services and equipment. ... There have been many advantages to our current structure. But the dramatic changes in our markets driven by our customers, new technologies like wireless, and public policy decisions, have opened up so many new opportunities that we need to simplify and more sharply focus our businesses to respond swiftly and effectively to those opportunities. It is not a secret that our Network Systems business has been affected by the conflicts that out Communication Services Group has been having with the RBOCs both in the public policy arena and increasingly in the marketplace as we entered the intra-LATA market. These conflicts foreshadow similar issues with some PTTs around the world. In recent months, it has become clear*

Reprinted from *Industrial and Corporate Change* 5(2) (1996), 537–559.

*that the advantage of our size ... is starting to be offset by the
amount of time, energy, and expense it takes to manage conflicting
business strategies ... So, in this spirit, we prepare to launch three
strong businesses... .*

(Bob Allen, Chairman, AT&T,
Message to Employees on the Restructuring of AT&T,
20 September 1995).

1. Introduction

Mitigating contractual hazards is one of the core functions of the business enterprise (Williamson, 1975, 1985, 1996a; Teece, 1980a, 1986). Vertical integration and other complex organizational arrangements often arise to safeguard transactions against the hazards of *ex post* opportunism. Nevertheless, hazards that arise in the course of business vary in gravity and magnitude. These can be severe when technological innovation is involved. Yet there have been few attempts to elucidate and enumerate innovation-driven hazards in a systematic way.

In this paper, we focus on the contractual hazards and organizational mechanisms that arise in the context of pacing, controlling and directing, current and future technological development and the products that emanate from innovation. We discuss three specific hazards that may occur in high technology transactions: poor sequencing (pacing) of developments in complementary technologies, loss of control over knowledge and intellectual property, and technological "foreclosure".

We limit our analysis to a class of cooperative and competitive transactions that have been largely neglected in the strategic management literature to date — vertically integrated firms supplying their downstream, non-integrated competitors. Antitrust analysis has often been suspicious of such types of transactions, viewing them as mechanisms to effectuate predatory acts, such as vertical price squeezes, by the integrated firm. However, if the integrated supplier achieves upstream efficiencies through some economies of scale or core capabilities that are difficult for independent suppliers to replicate, then it may be efficient and desirable for a non-integrated downstream competitor to source from such vertically integrated competitors. The problem that arises for the buyer is that there may be incentives for the integrated supplier, if it is dominant upstream, to disadvantage the buyer at contract renegotiation or to otherwise handicap the buyer. In many cases, the incentives of the integrated firm to act strategically may be higher than those of independent suppliers. Even if the supplier does not behave strategically, buyers may be concerned that the supplier might do so at some future date and act accordingly.

Assessing the magnitude of technological hazards for the buyer requires examination of two factors: first, whether the upstream firm possesses market power and/or the ability to appropriate quasi-rents, and second, whether there is complexity and unobservability in the transaction, in that the performance dimensions of the intermediate good being supplied is only over time revealed, thus creating monitoring problems for the customer. If these two conditions hold in a transaction involving leading edge technology, then technological hazards suggest particular organizational arrangements which provide strong safeguards.

In some contexts, transaction-particular safeguards may not suffice. Rather, individual, transaction-specific safeguards need to be augmented by a constellation of safeguards developed within the context of a broader business relationship that spans numerous transactions. Malfeasance in one transaction may then have repercussions on other transactions in the current relationship, or severe reputation effects with other exchange partners. Thus, in a number of circumstances, relational safeguards that span multiple transactions may be employed to protect against technological hazards, thereby facilitating exchange. However, if complexity, uncertainty and unobservability are sufficiently high, situations may arise when even a constellation of safeguards will not be adequate protection against contracting hazards. In these situations, vertical integration — with the associated possible loss of upstream economies — is sometimes necessary to protect against the hazards of incomplete contracting and the problematic incentives which are sometimes occasioned when a downstream firm sources from a competitor. Alternatively, integrated firms can take the "ultimate" form of credible commitment not to behave strategically in the downstream market. The upstream integrated firm may decide to simply divest (or not integrate downstream) in order to signal that it will not behave strategically.

It should be noted at the outset that this paper does not address public policy responses. Rather, it examines how managerial solutions accomplished through contractual safeguards and organizational design can act to protect transactions against technological hazards that may arise. Its purpose is to elucidate the hazards that ensue in the context of an integrated firm supplying a non-integrated, downstream competitor, and to examine safeguards which are employed to support contractual relationships in such circumstances. The next section reviews the phenomenon of cross-competitive supply and examines the development and shortcomings of the current literature. Section 3 unravels some of the types of technological hazards that occur in the context of high technology transactions.

Section 4 reviews the safeguards that firms employ to protect against these hazards in cross-competitive supply relationships. Section 5 closes with some concluding remarks.

2. Background

The Phenomenon: Buying from Integrated Competitors

Buying from one's competitor is not uncommon, and may be increasing in frequency. In this paper, we examine sourcing by non-integrated firms from integrated competitors in high technology markets. Figure 1 illustrates this relationship. While Firms 1 and 2 both compete in the downstream market, only Firm 1 is vertically integrated into the upstream component market. However, Firm 2 sources components, sometimes exclusively, from Firm 1. Often there may be independent component suppliers who provide feasible alternative sources of the component at the outset, yet are not awarded the supply contract by firm 2.

There are a number of reasons a firm would want to source from a competitor. The most advanced or most reliable technology may be possessed by the competitor. The cheapest component may be provided by a competitor. Mere

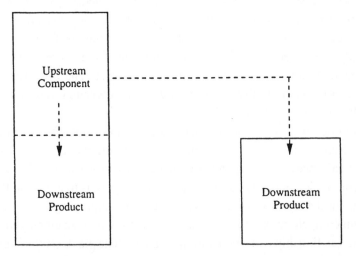

Fig. 1. Supply.

transportation cost considerations may call for competitor supply. These and other reasons often make competitor supply a sensible strategy, provided contractual safeguards can be erected.

Examples of this abound. Consider the laser printer industry. The engines of laser printers determine, among other things, print speed and print quality;

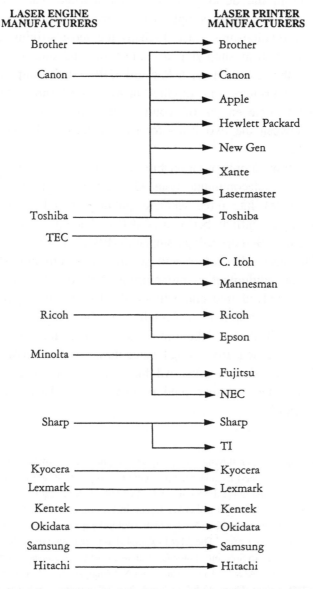

Fig. 2. Supply chain in the desktop laser printer industry, circa 1990.

the laser printer industry contains many firms that make engines, some firms which are present only downstream, some firms which are present only upstream. It is common to see vertically integrated firms supplying engines on a contractual basis to non-integrated companies against whom they compete. Figure 2, illustrates this point. The left-hand column identifies some of the engine manufacturers. The right-hand column identifies some of the firms that are present in the desktop laser printer market. The arrows indicate which engine manufacturers supply which printer manufacturers. Clearly, several types of relationships exist. Perhaps the most striking example of a vertically integrated firm supplying a competitor (and one to which we will return later), is the Canon-Hewlett-Packard (HP) relationship. Canon makes both engines and printers and supplies nearly all of (non-integrated) HP's very significant volume engine of requirements. This contractual relationship has persisted between the two firms for over a decade, despite the apparent strategic hazards.

Cross-competitor supply relationships can also been seen in electronics, semiconductors, and telecommunications. One of the reasons enumerated for the recent split of AT&T into three separate, publicly traded companies was the problem of strategic conflicts between AT&T Technologies (the manufacturing arm) and the regional Bell operating companies (RBOCs), who were its traditional customers. The recent divestiture will separate the communications systems (AT&T) from the equipment manufacturing (Network Systems). As AT&T and the RBOCs evolved into competitors, the RBOCs were reluctant to buy telecommunications equipment, especially switches, from AT&T. Overseas, companies such as Deutsch Telekom in Germany and France Telecom were also wary of buying equipment from AT&T since they expected AT&T to emerge as a competitor in their national market. All this meant that competitors were passing their equipment dollars to other vendors, even when AT&T equipment might have been superior.[1]

---

[1] "There's always tension when buying a majority of equipment from somebody who is also your biggest competitor", said Robert Barada, vice-president for corporate strategy and development, for Pacific Telesis Group. Spinning off the equipment arm "will alleviate that [problem] in a big way". Moreover, Brian Adamik, an analyst at Yankee Group in Boston, commented, "After the break-up, Network Systems could now even sell to MCI, which wouldn't buy equipment from AT&T in the past because of the its long-distance arm." The AT&T example has been drawn from: John Keller, Defying Merger Trend, AT&T Plans to Split into Three Companies, *Wall Street Journal*, September 21, 1995, pp. A1, A16; Leslie Cauley, AT&T's Rivals Shrug, but Not Analysts, *Wall Street Journal*, September 21, 1995, p. A6; Jeff Pelline, Giant AT&T to Break into 3 Companies, *San Francisco Chronicle*, September 21, 1995, pp. A1, A15.

These examples, and those that follow, serve to elucidate a common phenomenon that has been little studied — vertically integrated firms supplying competitors in the downstream market in high technology industries. We examine the conditions under which this is a stable outcome and inquire as to when contractual safeguards will be inadequate to sustain this type of relationship. Although both parties may face contractual hazards, our focus is on understanding the strategic hazards that the non-integrated firm faces.

Theoretical Antecedents

Chicago School analysts conducted the first systematic theoretical investigation into cross-competitive supply (for example, Posner, 1976, pp. 196–207; Bork, 1978; Posner and Easterbrook, 1981).[2] They pointed out that because monopoly rents could only be taken once in the supply chain, a firm with monopoly (or market) power had two options to retain monopoly rents. First, it could vertically integrate and charge monopoly prices in the downstream market. Equivalently, it could set the price for the intermediate good at the monopoly level and extract all the rents without forward integration. Thus, a vertically integrated firm with upstream monopoly power has little incentive to exclude downstream rivals, since forward integration is not necessary to extract upstream rents. Accordingly, vertical mergers pose no problems. If upstream Firm A and downstream Firm B merge, the merger ought not change concentration or prices. Thus monopoly power will not and cannot be extended. Vertical leveraging is simply impossible.

This view of cross-competitor supply, as it relates to business strategy, has been extended on two fronts. First, game theorists have argued that this Chicago School analysis is not a subgame perfect equilibrium (Hart and Tirole, 1990; Ordover *et al.*, 1990). Other firms in the industry may respond to a competitor's integration decision with integration and price strategies of their own. Under a

---

[2] This phenomenon is quite different from the voluminous writing on strategic alliances (for example, Parkhe 1993; Contractor and Lorange 1988; Gulati 1995). With strategic alliances, partners typically have expertise in different functional or technological areas, and the strategic alliance facilitates teaming to create new products. The success of the alliance hinges on strategic alignment and the ability of the two firms to combine their resources and capabilities to build a single product. If either firms fails, both firms lose. Our analysis differs from the strategic alliance literature in that we are primarily concerned with those transactions where the firms are competitors in the downstream market and only one firm possesses the upstream facilities which it supplies to the downstream competitor. One firm, in our analysis, possesses the resources to build and possibly to market the product before the two firms come together.

variety of strategies, the subgame perfect equilibrium can result in inefficiency and a refusal to deal (Hart and Tirole, 1990, p. 212). One insight that is gleaned from this literature is that vertically disintegrated structures or parallel vertical integration may be equilibrium outcomes.

A second extension was the development of transaction cost economic analysis (Williamson, 1971, 1975, 1983, 1985). In *Markets and Hierarchies* (1975), Williamson introduced the notion of contractual hazards and contractual safeguards, primarily flowing from the possibility of *ex post* opportunism in an incomplete contracting regime. His analysis revised and enriched the Chicago approach, and added an efficiency dimension. Williamson (1975) and later Klein *et al*. (1979), showed how asset specificity could cause contractual hazards. Common ownership of such assets could ease those hazards and facilitate efficient investment. Williamson (1983) subsequently highlighted the importance of reciprocity and "exchange of hostages" as ways to attenuate hazards which might otherwise destroy the basis for exchange. The transaction cost economics framework, because of its focus on hazards and safeguards, is a useful point of departure for our analysis. We show that transaction cost economics can in turn be extended to embrace organizational questions when changing technology is at issue.

In much of the work of transaction cost economics, hazards are developed in a rather particular manner, often illustrated by price renegotiation, and quality degradation. These usually augment costs. We seek to expand the framework by examining contracting hazards related to the (usually partial) denial by one party of future technological and associated market opportunities.

Transaction cost economics posits that firms can protect against hazards through contractual safeguards such as penalty for premature termination, dispute resolution mechanisms, and bilateral exchange of hostages (Williamson, 1985, pp. 33–34, 1996b). While these types of safeguard do assist transactions, we go beyond the analysis of strictly discrete transactional safeguards that frequently preoccupies transaction cost economics. In cases when vertical integration is costly, a constellation of safeguards transcending the traditional, discrete transaction safeguards may be effective.[3] This constellation may include transaction specific safeguards in the traditional transaction cost sense, but also may encompass broader relational and multi-transactional structures that safeguard groups of transactions. It is the relational safeguards that may insure adequate protection of transactions, and void the need for vertical integration.

---

[3] Nickerson (1996) explores how hazards are interrelated in the trucking industry.

Relevance for Strategic Management

One conceptual argument we put forward is that transaction cost economics can be usefully informed by expanding the notion of hazards and safeguards. Specifically, we view contractual relationships as generating bundles of hazards, and governance structures as providing bundles of safeguards. The task of management is to identify the hazards that are attendant to a business relationship and then to create and insure that the economizing bundle of safeguards necessary for effective execution of transactions and exploitation of opportunities are in place.

We examine the contractual hazards that arise when developing and commercializing new technology, and show that discrete transactional safeguards may be usefully supplemented by multi-transactional relational safeguards. This is especially so when non-integrated firms buy from integrated competitors. Though many of our concepts are applicable to a variety of transactional arrangements, we limit our analysis to cross-competitor supply.

3. Technological Hazards in Competitor Supply

Several well recognized contractual hazards occur in supply situations. First, when a downstream firm must make some specific investment in order to support efficient production, it exposes its non-redeployable assets to *ex post* recontracting hazards (Williamson, 1985). If investment in specific assets is not required for efficient production, then the non-integrated downstream firm can costlessly switch suppliers and avoid all hazards. If the buyer must invest in non-redeployable assets, it could avoid the hazards associated with *ex post* recontracting through vertical integration.

Second, the characteristics of the intermediate component that is being delivered to the downstream firm might not be readily observable. This may occur because of the extreme complexity of the product or may be due to other non-observable characteristics. In short, there may be an acute monitoring problem for the downstream firm that only resolves itself over the long-run. While these two classes of problems are important, we focus instead on circumstances where new technology is at stake.

In business transactions when new technology is at stake, a less understood set of hazards may arise. This class of contracting hazards stems not so much from the extraction of quasi-rents, but from the guarding of future strategic opportunities. Integrated suppliers can, for example, exclude firms from immediate access to new knowledge, and future possibilities for technological progress.

These types of situations may arise when an integrated firm has the ability to use its upstream technological prowess to exclude a downstream rival from a transaction that will open up future technological and commercial opportunities.[4] The seller's ability to pace, direct, control, and guard the development of new products and technologies are all hazards to the buyer that arise in this context. It is these technological hazards that we examine in more depth.

Out-Sourcing and Competitive Advantage: Key Components and Pacing Technology at the Frontier[5]

Technological hazards exist if a downstream firm has failed to accumulate the capabilities needed to make critical components, or has opted, for other (normally sound) business reasons, such as scale, cost, or risk, to forego production of these components. The firm may then have no choice but to purchase critical components from its competitors. Some components, whether commodity or customized to the producer's own downstream requirements, are simply not all that important to competitive advantage. The only strategic advantage to the integrated supplier-competitor flowing from opportunistic behavior with respect to these components is the one time benefit associated with capturing quasi-rents associated with irreversible investments already made. Loss of quasi-rents associated with employing idiosyncratic physical assets may have considerable short-run implications, but if the firm's balance sheet is strong, it need not impair long-run competitive advantage.

Contrast this to new components based on leading edge technology that convey strategic advantage. If firms wish to pace or direct the evolution of new products, then these types of components should, *ceteris paribus*, be developed internally. If such products are outsourced, the supplier gets to pace and direct the development of the technology. Transactions cost and recontracting hazards are not the core considerations; rather, it is the failure to accumulate critical competences important to the firm's overall new product development strategy which matters.

Consider Motorola as it attempts to develop battery technology for their mobile communications products.[6] Motorola can obtain nickel-cadmium (Ni-Cd)

---

[4] This notion can also be viewed as a dynamic extension of the raising rival's cost literature (Salop and Scheffman, 1983).

[5] When we speak about the frontier, we refer to a component or service being procured which enlists technology that is not ubiquitously employed in the industry. Frontier technologies are those leading edge innovations being incorporated into subsystems and components.

[6] See Chesbrough and Teece (1996) for a more detailed description of Motorola case.

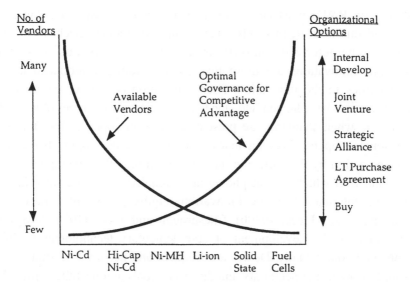

Fig. 3. Available sources and organizational options for Motorola in battery cell technology.

batteries from a host of suppliers. However, because the bottleneck technology for Motorola is the battery, there is benefit to accelerating/controlling the development of more long-lasting and lighter weight batteries (e.g. fuel cells). Motorola can safely source standard Ni-Cad batteries externally, but more advanced batteries may need to be developed and sourced internally (see Fig. 3). The reasons do not flow from exposure to recontracting hazards as such. Rather, control of the development process is critical to coordinate and accomplish the roll-out of new products.

Microsoft provides another illustration of how an integrated firm can pace technological development downstream. Microsoft not only retains control over the operating system (Windows) for the majority of personal computers, but also commercializes some key applications downstream. Other independent application designers rely on Windows for their applications to run. Thus, Windows acts as a constraint on some of the technological features of the downstream applications (e.g. speed and protocol of data exchange). Microsoft's ability to pace the upstream technology and its ability to exploit its operating system technology in its applications software, has helped it to become one of the dominant players in applications.

A second source of competitive advantage related to technological pacing (that may require integration) is the difficulty of accomplishing what Richardson (1960) and Williamson (1975) have called 'convergence of expectations'.

Investment (in R&D) must be coordinated between upstream and downstream entities, and this is difficult to effectuate using contractual mechanisms. Teece (1988) has characterized innovations as either autonomous or systemic. Autonomous innovations are those that do not require coordinated activities between parties to the innovation. Each innovation can occur within its own walls and can then be "plugged into" the bigger project. These types of innovations are pervasive when standards are present, such as the open architecture of the IBM personal computer. Systemic innovations are those developments that require coordinated action by the parties to the innovation (e.g. the development of new cameras and film which instant photography required). In order to achieve the coordinated outcomes systemic innovation requires, it is often necessary to vertically integrate (Teece, 1980b). Chesbrough and Teece (1996) have argued that coordinating the development of complementary technologies is difficult when pursued contractually. Delays are frequent and need not be strategic; they may simply flow from uncertainty and divergent goals amongst the parties. MIPS encountered this with their failed attempted to promote their Advanced Computing Environment (ACE) to compete with Sun's Scalable Processor Architecture (SPARC). MIPS set up alliances with Compaq, DEC, Silicon Graphics and other firms to pursue a RISC-based computing standard. However, as DEC and Compaq announced that they were going to reduce their commitment to ACE, the alliance soon fell apart because MIPS could not pick up the slack in some of the upstream activities. It failed to understand and develop competencies in key aspects of the technology, and was not able to create a common expectation for the alliance (Gomes-Casseres, 1994).

Technological Control at or Behind the Frontier

A second hazard that arises where new technology (at or even behind the frontier) is utilized, is the leakage of technology to competitors. Arrow (1962) first brought to light the disclosure problem in the market for know-how, and others have since elaborated on this and related technology transfer problems (Goldberg, 1977; Teece, 1981, 1985, 1986). Appropriability hazards are of concern when property rights are difficult to establish and enforce and when the knowledge is not retained entirely at the organizational level (Oxley, 1995). The leakage we have in mind can occur vertically (upstream and downstream) as well as horizontally (Silverman, 1996).

Proprietary knowledge that leaks from buyer (supplier) to supplier (buyer) in the course of fulfilling a purchase contract is especially problematic when the supplier (buyer) is integrated downstream (upstream). The argument is of course symmetric. Although an independent supplier who obtains knowledge from the buyer may choose to integrate into the downstream product, the likelihood that this will occur is small. However, a firm which is already vertically integrated downstream and supplies a downstream competitor may be able to take the know-how that has leaked to its upstream division and incorporate it into the downstream products and processes relatively quickly.[7] Downstream investments in manufacturing have already been made and small modifications may be all that is necessary to enhance competitiveness in the downstream operations. Staff engineers who understand the downstream process and product can take the know-how and improve upon the current product or process.

In the digital switching business, AT&T has had difficulty selling switches to some of the RBOCs because of fear that it will misuse commercial secrets it learns from the RBOCs. This happens because many switches are configured to the needs of each customer. In order to customize the switch, the RBOC must reveal its telephone traffic patterns, capacity utilization, infrastructure layout, and other extremely sensitive information to the switch supplier. While contractual mechanisms can be designed to protect this information, information flows through informal channels and internal movement of personnel, combined with the cost and difficulty of enforcement of such contractual clauses, create hazards for the buyer.[8] The ability of a competitor to use and improve upon know-how which has been inadvertently leaked may be higher for integrated suppliers that for non-integrated suppliers.

Guarding Technological Capabilities

Another disadvantage buyers may experience when market power exists upstream and intellectual property regimes are strong (Teece, 1986), is that the integrated supplier may be in a position to guard its know-how advantage and if it chooses, simply refuse to sell to its competitors. The integrated firm may have incentives to exclude its rivals from its most advanced components if this will hinder the ability of the downstream rival to participate in related or future business. By protecting its competitive advantage in this way, the integrated firm can advance its competitive position downstream. Thus, integrated suppliers may have a higher incentive to withhold (or degrade) supply than would independent

---

[7] When we use the term leakage, we do not mean to imply that intellectual property rights have necessarily been violated. We have in mind the quite legal imitation and emulation that takes place in the normal course of business.

[8] We thank James Dalton of Bell South for making this point.

firms.[9] The downstream division of the integrated firm may be able to advance its position in related and emerging markets if the upstream division does not assist downstream competitors.

For example, in digital telecommunications equipment supply, the switches hold the key to competitive advantage for many future service innovations (such as value-added network services). The purchase of switches and other equipment from AT&T has the potential for creating many hazards for the RBOCs, who may be foreclosed from the opportunity to participate in the future technological innovations if their switch supplier chooses not to add features that would enhance the RBOC's ability to compete against AT&T in telecommunication service markets. The incentives of an integrated AT&T, if it has some market power in switch manufacturing, may be to act in a manner that might disadvantage the RBOCs in domains where they currently compete or are likely in the future to compete with AT&T. The problem evaporates, however, if there are abundant actual or potential competitive supply alternatives. Vertical integration into manufacturing is just one among many possible solutions.

4. Safeguarding Against Technological Hazards

The need to safeguard incomplete contracts against *ex post* opportunistic behavior is not a new or novel concept. The need to monitor effort under technological non-separability (Alchian and Demsetz, 1972), assert control when property rights are not well-defined (Coase, 1960; Demsetz, 1967), and protect streams of quasi-rents in a competitive contracting process (Klein *et al.*, 1978) has long been recognized. Most of these analyses, however, have been concerned with vertical integration as a way to safeguard specific investments. Indeed, the paradigmatic safeguard, and the one which has received the majority of attention in the literature, is vertical integration (Williamson, 1975).

Although vertical integration is normally an effective safeguard, it is not always desirable. When poorly implemented, vertical integration can be fraught with low-powered incentives and bureaucratic costs which will impair performance

---

[9] We stress features rather than an entire product. If an independent supplier could monopolize the downstream market, then it might integrate downstream or it might charge a price for the intermediate good so that it obtains a monopoly rent. This result is less likely if only certain features of the product are not available, as in the digital switching example. For an example of this at the national level, see General Accounting Office, International Trade: US Business Access to Certain State-of-the-Art Technology, *GAO Report* (GAO/NSIAD-91-278), September 1991, p. 33.

and make it unattractive (Williamson, 1975, 1985, 1991; Teece, 1976, 1996). A superior alternative in many instances is to rely on contracts and develop a constellation of safeguards, enveloping many aspects of the firm's business with such protections, so that a contractual exchange that might otherwise be considered risky, can flourish.

Constellations of Safeguards

In the original concept of hostages as safeguards (Williamson, 1983), each firm places a hostage that has an *ex ante* (screening) or *ex post* (bonding) effect to support exchange. The parties' incentive to perform when bonds are held is high because exit would entail forfeiture of the hostage.[10] Thus hostages can, in many circumstances, be more cost effective than integration in supporting exchange.

However, incomplete contracting and bounded rationality make hostage exchange difficult in many circumstances where there is uncertainty as to outcomes, such as with innovation. The amount of the bond to be placed in custody is difficult to determine *ex ante* because unforeseen contingencies may render the hostage inefficiently large or, of more concern, too low in value. This is especially likely to be a problem when technological innovation and new product development is involved. In these circumstances, firms may exit the transaction — appropriating the technology, and leaving the insufficient hostage on the table for the other party. Alternatively, the hostage may itself become the subject of the oppotunistic bargaining as the ante is renegotiated.[11] While hostages may support market transactions, they do so over a limited range of situations, or in conjunction with other safeguards.

Our interest in this paper is in demonstrating the efficacy of constellations of safeguards in cross-competitive supply situations, including ones where technological hazards exist. Although contracts give guidance as to how transactions

---

[10] Williamson (1983, p. 527) has noted: "… a king who is known to cherish two daughters equally [one beautiful and one ugly] and is asked, for screening purposes, to post a hostage is better advised to offer the ugly one".

[11] Sequential hostages often face the same problem. Some type of contractual and hybrid relationships require a number of hand-offs of a project between parties in order to achieve the goal. Both firms are better off if the project goal is reached, but incentives may exist to expropriate the other partner at each stage of development. Although the hostage is the project itself, interim knowledge gained may prove to be more valuable than the successful completion of the project. Moreover, in the last stage of the project, the last firm has the incentive to expropriate the partner because the game has come to an end. The game then unravels under most conditions.

can proceed, constellations of arrangements can create a larger context in which contracts can operate. In this sense, multilateral and multi-transactional relationships are akin to relational contracts (Macneil, 1978) where contracts occur against the background of the relationship, where changes to a contract are adopted 'only in the overall context of the whole relation' (p. 890) and where often 'preservation of the relation' (p. 895) is the concern.

The Canon-HP relationship, with special reference to the laser printer industry, is illustrative. As mentioned earlier, Canon, a vertically integrated firm that makes both laser engines and laser printers, supplies all of HP's engine requirements. At first glance, it would seem there would be many contractual hazards facing HP. However, the Canon-HP transaction is embedded in a larger relationship that displays a constellation of safeguards.

Relational safeguards. The Canon-HP relationship began long before the advent of the desktop laser engine.[12] Throughout much of the 1970s and early 1980s, Canon not only supplied laser engines for HP's midrange laser printer systems, but also engaged in some joint development with HP of floor-model printer technology. The move from midrange to desktop laser printers was only one of many steps in the printer market that the two firms took together. This historical relationship provides important context. Canon and HP had (and still have) a web of ties in numerous transactions and technologies that serve as the basis for exchange. We understand that these discrete transactions are linked through a position created in each firm referred to as the "relationship manager".[13] Although this manager does not have formal authority to compel divisions to cooperate, this person does have tremendous informal authority, reports to a division head, and has responsibility for the smooth running of the broader strategic relationship. Moreover, as overseer of the strategic relationship between the two firms, this manager also becomes a mediator should disputes develop. Through this central mechanism, transactions are 'bundled' together, albeit imperfectly, for what is a relational governance scheme. Opportunistic behavior and conflict in one transaction may change how the other contracting party views the potential for opportunism in other transactions. Bundling transactions therefore raises the cost of cheating. There is the threat that there will be loss of the entire relationship if there is substantial malfeasance in the specific transaction. Usually, loss of the entire relationship is more costly than the gains from expropriation available from a single transaction. As firms enter

---

[12] See Mowery and Beckman (1995) for a more detailed discussion of HP's strategy.

[13] We thank Lee Rhodes of Hewlett-Packard for bringing this to our attention.

into larger types of relationships that involve multiple transactions, the individual transaction becomes subsumed in a web of current and future transactions. Indeed, Williamson has noted, "... interdependencies among series of related contracts may be missed or undervalued as a consequence [of examining each trading nexus separately.] Greater attention to the multi-lateral ramifications of contract is sometimes needed" (1985, p. 393).

Transaction-specific safeguards. In addition to these relational safeguards, HP possesses some discrete transactional safeguards that support exchange. One flows from the fact that HP purchases annually hundreds of millions of dollars in printer engines from Canon, representing nearly 50% of Canon's engine output. Hence, it is highly unlikely that Canon would act opportunistically with HP in laser engine supply because of the volume of business that HP represents. While this capacity is not technically transaction-specific, there is little doubt that at least some assets that support it would be stranded if HP suddenly stopped buying engines from Canon. Thus, if the non-integrated buyer represents a significant portion of the purchases of the integrated supplier, and there does not exist excess demand in the market, then it is unlikely that the supplier will opt to engage in expropriation at contract renegotiation.[14]

A second transaction-specific safeguard that protects HP from opportunism is the reputation effects that Canon would suffer if it acted opportunistically to expropriate HP or provide HP with a consistently sub-standard product. If HP effectively publicized and detailed malfeasance by Canon in laser engines, Canon might lose a large portion of its remaining customers. At best, remaining customers might update their probabilities of opportunistic behavior (Crocker and Reynolds, 1993) in their own transactions with Canon. Given the short lifetime of a laser printer model (1–3 years), product model turnover acts to favor printer manufacturers. The printer manufacturer is therefore only committed to the current laser engine for the current printer (though there is the need for some continuity between models). If malfeasance occurs, the downstream buyer can obtain a new supplier for its subsequent models. The result in the extreme case, then, is that Canon could lose its entire customer base in 2–3 years. This is extreme, but illustrates how short product turns (with reasonable discount rates) enhance the need for suppliers to maintain a good reputation. Williamson discusses reputation effects and argues, "Suffice it to observe here that reputation effect are no

---

[14] Williamson (1985, p. 93) addresses this in the context of "dedicated assets" which he defines as a "discrete investment in generalized (as contrasted with special purpose) production capacity that would not be made but for the prospect of selling a significant amount of product to a specific customer".

contracting panacea" (1985, pp. 395–396). Indeed, we argue that reputation acts in concert with other safeguards to ensure exchange.

Mixed-mode safeguards. HP's proprietary control of most aspects of its ink-jet technology provides HP's laser printer division with considerable protection against possible opportunism from Canon. The possibility that an altogether different technology can be developed, at reasonable cost, which effectively substitutes for the technology of the transaction will serve to keep the contract sustainable. Most core capabilities for the rapid roll-out of the alternative technology must exist within the boundaries of the non-integrated firm if this is to be a credible threat. The degree of protection such a safeguard provides is directly related to the degree and cost of substituting the alternative technology. The ink-jet technology that HP has developed was not created as an intentional safeguard to laser technology, but rather as an alternative technology with an independent marketing strategy. However, ink-jet technology has evolved. If Canon were to refuse to supply engines or to escalate prices, HP might credibly shift its focus from laser jet technology to the improvement of the current ink-jet technology. No doubt, HP would prefer to stay with laser printers. However, it might be able to push ink-jet technology so as to seriously challenge the laser technology. Ink-jet printers already cannibalize laser printers on the lower end of the market. The impetus given to ink-jet technology could have a substantial detrimental effect on the laser printer market and specifically on Canon, the largest supplier of laser engines in the world.

Canon has many customers for its laser engines, yet HP has (asymmetrically) exposed itself to contractual hazards with Canon if HP is looked at in isolation. However, by employing constellations of relational, transaction-specific, and mixed-mode safeguards, HP appears to have protected itself against possible opportunism by Canon and, market exchange continues between the two firms. Thus, a more global view of safeguards appears to be warranted.

Vertical Integration, Divestiture and Credible Commitments

Maintenance of high powered incentives and avoidance of bureaucratic costs are benefits retained if safeguards short of vertical integration will suffice (as described above). However, sometimes contractual and relational safeguards do not suffice. In such instances, both integration (by the purchaser) and divestiture (by the seller) serve to correct some of the hazards we have identified. They are not perfect alternatives, but they do paradoxically provide some degree of remedy to the (strategic) hazards we have identified. We consider circumstances where vertical integration may be the better solution.

Controlling the rate and direction of innovation. Where there is a need to be on the frontier of the technological possibility curve, technological pacing becomes most important. The firm that chooses (for whatever reasons) to eschew vertical integration, yet endeavors to direct the rate and direction of development using contracts, may find it difficult. As noted earlier, reliance on one's competitor for supply is problematic because of the misaligned incentives of the integrated firm. In some cases, even independent supply could be problematic. In these instances, vertical integration (internal development) may be the best way to confidently pace interrelated technological developments. This is particularly true when solutions inside an existing technological paradigm (Dosi, 1982) will suffice. This is because investment in R&D will yield a degree of predictability as to outcomes. When this is not the case (i.e. required solutions require radical advances unlikely within the paradigm), vertical integration (internal development) may be ineffective.[15]

To illustrate this point, we accumulated data on a sample of PC compatible, desktop laser printers introduced in 1992 and 1993.[16] Two characteristics often cited as determinants of the proximity of a laser printer to the technological frontier are print speed, measured by pages per minute (PPM), and print resolution, measured by the number of dots per inch (DPI) it prints. High performance is associated with greater speed and greater dot density. Figure 4, places all of these printers on a scatter plot graph. Each point is assigned an ▲, ❑ or ○, which designates who makes the engine for the printer: the same firm that makes the printer (▲ = hierarchy), an independent upstream supplier that does not make printers (❑ = independent), or a vertically integrated competitor that makes engines and printers (○ = competitor). On the outer technological frontier of desktop laser printers (represented by the AB curve), there is a high proportion of firms vertically integrated into engine and printer production.[17] This suggests that technological pacing (as well as technological control) may

---

[15] For a related discussion of competency-enhancing and competency-destroying innovation in centralized versus decentralized firms, see Bercovitz *et al.*, 1996.

[16] This data set is being compiled from trade magazines such as *PC World* and *PC Magazine*.

[17] The 14 printers on the frontier represent the integration strategies of eight firms. We drew the frontiers by analyzing each printer by its list price and features. We then derived the technological frontiers by constructing a curve for each segment that approximated the leading edge technology available at each price.

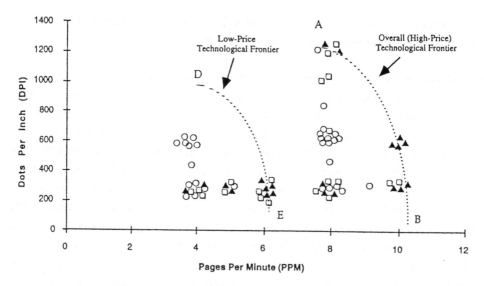

Fig. 4. Desktop laser engine-laser printer transaction: governance decisions, 1992–1993.

play a role in this industry. The second largest number of printers on the frontier source engines from independent suppliers. Only one of the 14 "frontier" printers has an engine manufactured by a competitor. This is consistent with our analysis that competitor relationships are fraught with hazards that independent supply, and certainly integrated supply, avoid.

It is also interesting to note that there is a second group of firms near 6 PPM which share the same governance characteristics as the outside frontier firms. This seems to occur because the desktop laser market has split into two segments — a high end, full feature, high-priced segment; and a low end, low feature, low-priced segment.[18] In the low-price segment, firms seem to be trying to create a printer that is technologically advanced with as many features as possible, but constrained by an upper limit on list price of approximately $2,000. Hierarchical firms (and independent suppliers) show up en masse on this frontier of the low end printers (represented by the secondary "frontier" CD), followed by a high

---

[18] Beginning in 1990, the desktop laser printer market began to diverge into two segments. Preliminary analysis of the data indicates that the lower-priced printers have fewer features, less processing paper, and, in some cases, longer duty cycles.

preponderance of competitor supply. Thus, on both frontiers, firms that seem to be pacing the development of the technologies tend to be vertically integrated in the first instance, and tend not to source engines from a competitor. We must stress, however, that while suggestive, these results are highly preliminary. The data set is not complete, and controls for other independent variables have not been included.

Sustaining technological capabilities. Maintaining technological control, even when behind the technology frontier, sometimes requires vertical integration. The two key components that technologically differentiate products in the laser printer market are the engine and the controller card. From 1984 to 1988, HP outsourced the controller cards for its laser printers to Canon. Although HP designed these cards, Canon actually manufactured the cards on its own board line in Japan. However, in 1988, HP chose to integrate this activity into their printer division in Boise. Two concerns seem to have led to this decision. First, HP felt integration would allow them to respond to changes in technological and market conditions in a real-time manner.[19] Second, we understand that HP feared that if the controller cards and engines for its laser printers were both sourced from Canon, it might lose its technology to Canon and, in effect, create a formidable competitor. The need to retain control over its own technology and ensure sustained access to key components seem to be key motivating factors in the change of HP strategy. Moreover was also the time when DRAM chips were in short supply. This may also have had an influence on HP's decision to internalize controller card production.

Design omissions. Finally, vertical integration may be desired to guard against strategic product design manipulation. It is not surprising that in the digital telecommunications switching equipment industry with continued deregulation bringing AT&T and the RBOCs into competition, that non-integrated suppliers have emerged (e.g. DSC and Motorola). It is also not surprising to see RBOCs abandon traditional purchase relations with AT&T in favor of purchases from Northern Telecom, Ericsson, NEC, and others for whom there is no strategic conflict downstream. Indeed, with the impending entry of the inter-exchange carriers into the local exchange, and the local exchange companies into the inter-exchange business, AT&T may have the incentive to guard its technology jealously, if by doing so it can delay the RBOCs offering new services which

---

[19] Hewlett Packard Begins Making Component of Top-Selling Laserjet Printer, *Business Wire*, December 7, 1988.

would require the use of AT&T product technology. Whether meritorious or not, concerns along these lines cost AT&T significant equipment sales, and appears to be a major factor behind its tripartite divestiture.

5. Conclusion

Thinking of contracts and governance structures as generating hazards and providing safeguards enriches our understanding of the theory of the firm. In this paper, we argued that identifying technological considerations that arise in the context of innovation gives a different perspective on the organizational problems. We have discussed a variety of safeguards. Although these may be transaction specific, many times relational or mixed-mode safeguards will be employed that span transactions and serve as a cost-effective mechanism of governance. When the parties are linked by a broad constellations of contracts, vertical integration can be avoided and high-powered incentives retained. There will be times, however, when even a rich constellation of safeguards will be insufficient. In these circumstances, we can expect to see both parallel vertical integration, or in the alternative, divestiture.

Our focus on the future opportunities and appropriability considerations that arise in technology transactions suggests a need to move to a more dynamic and evolutionary approach to organizations. Indeed, changes in governance structures over time may reflect not only the shifts in traditional economic incentives to integrate, but also exposure to strategic hazards and the need to accumulate capabilities necessary for current and future competitive advantage. An industry's structure could change over time as knowledge accumulation and diffusion change the hazards associated with sourcing from a competitor. Thus, vertical structures may be reshaped as these conflicting forces wax and wane.

Acknowledgements

We wish to acknowledge helpful comments and assistance of Sara Beckman, Janet Bercovitz, Glenn Carroll, David Mowery, Jackson Nickerson and Oliver Williamson. A much earlier draft of this paper was presented at the "Firms, Markets and Organizations" Conference held at Berkeley, 6–8 October 1995. We also wish to thank the Sloan Foundation and the Ameritech Foundation for their generous financial support.

References

A.A. Alchian and H. Demsetz, Production Costs, Information Costs, and Economic Organization, *American Economic Review* 62 (1972), 777–795.

K.J. Arrow, Economic Welfare and the Allocation of Resources of Invention, in National Bureau of Economic Research (ed.), *The Rate and Direction of Inventive Activity: Economic and Social Factors* (Princeton University Press, Princeton, NJ, 1962), pp. 609–625.

J.E.L. Bercovitz, J.M. de Figueiredo and D.J. Teece, Firm Capabilities and Managerial Decision-Making: A Theory of Innovation Biases, in R. Garud, P. Nayaar and Z. Shapira (eds.), *Technological Learning, Foresights, and Oversights* (Cambridge University Press, New York, 1996), forthcoming.

R.H. Bork, *The Antitrust Paradox* (Basic Books, New York, 1978).

H.W. Chesbrough and D.J. Teece, When is Virtual Virtuous: Organizing for Innovation, *Harvard Business Review* 74 (1996), 65–73.

R.H. Coase, The Problem of Social Cost, *Journal of Law and Economics* 3 (1960), 1–44.

F.J. Contractor and P. Lorange (eds.), *Cooperative Strategies in International Business* (Lexington Books, Lexington, MA, 1988).

K.J. Crocker and K.J. Reynolds, The Efficiency of Incomplete Contracts: An Empirical Analysis of Air Force Engine Procurement, *Rand Journal of Economics* 24 (1993), 253–264.

H. Demsetz, Toward a Theory of Property Rights, *American Economic Review* 57 (1967), 347–359.

G. Dosi, Technological Paradigms and Technological Trajectories, *Research Policy* 11 (1982), 147–162.

V. Goldberg, Competitive Bidding and the Production of Precontract Information, *Bell Journal of Economics* 8 (1977), 250–261.

B. Gomes-Casseres, Group Versus Group: How Alliance Networks Compete, *Harvard Business Review*, July 1994, pp. 62–74.

R. Gulati, Does Familiarity Breed Trust — The Implications of Repeated Ties for Contractual Choice in Alliances, *Academy of Management Journal* 38 (1995), 85–112.

O. Hart and J. Tirole, Vertical Integration and Market Foreclosure, *Brookings Papers: Microeconomics*, 1990, pp. 205–276.

B. Klein, R.A. Crawford and A.A. Alchian, Vertical Integration, Appropriable Rents, and the Competitive Contracting Process, *Journal of Law and Economics* 21 (October 1978), 297–326.

I.R. Macneil, Contracts: Adjustments of Long-Term Economic Relations Under Classical, Neoclassical, and Relational Contract Law, *Northwestern University Law Review* 72 (1978), 854–906.

D.C. Mowery and S.L. Beckman, Corporate Change and Competitiveness: The Hewlett-Packard Company, CCC Working Paper No. 95-13, University of California, Berkeley, 1995.

J. Nickerson, Strategy and Structure: The Role of Transactional Interdependencies on Organizational Form, Ph.D. dissertation, University of California, Berkeley, 1996.

J.A. Ordover, G. Saloner and S. Salop, Equilibrium Vertical Foreclosure, *American Economic Review* 80 (1990), 127-142.

J.E. Oxley, International Hybrids: A Transaction Cost Treatment and Empirical Study, Ph.D. dissertation, University of California, Berkeley, 1995.

A. Parkhe, Strategic Alliance Structuring — A Game Theoretic and Transaction Cost Examination of Interfirm Cooperation, *Academy of Management Journal* 36 (August 1993), 794-829.

R.A. Posner, *Antitrust Law* (University of Chicago Press, Chicago, IL, 1976).

R.A. Posner and F.H. Easterbrook, *Antitrust: Cases, Economic Notes, and Other Materials*, 2nd edn (West Publishing, St. Paul, 1981)

G.B.H. Richardson, *Information and Investment* (Oxford University Press, Oxford, 1990).

S. Salop and D. Scheffman, *Raising Rival's Costs*, *American Economic Review* 73 (May 1983), 267-271.

B.S. Silverman, Technical Assets and the Logic of Corporate Diversification, Ph.D. Dissertation, University of California, Berkeley, 1996.

D.J. Teece, *Vertical Integration and Divestiture in the U.S. Oil Industry* (The Stanford University Institute for Energy Studies, Stanford, CA, 1976).

D.J. Teece, Economies of Scope and the Scope of the Enterprise, *Journal of Economic Behavior and Organization* 1 (September 1980a), 223-245.

D.J. Teece, Vertical Integration and Procurement, unpublished Working Paper, University of California, Berkeley, 1980b.

D.J. Teece, The Market for Know-How and the Efficient Transfer of Technology, *The Annals of the Academy of Political and Social Science* (1981), 81-96.

D.J. Teece, Multinational Enterprise, Internal Governance and Industrial Organization, *American Economic Review* 75 (1985), 233-238.

D.J. Teece, Profiting from Technological Innovation: Implications for Integration, Collaboration, Licensing, and Public Policy, *Research Policy* 15 (1986), 285-305.

D.J. Teece, Technological Change and the Nature of the Firm, in G. Dosi (ed.), *Technical Change and Economic Theory* (Pinter Publishers, London, 1988), pp. 256-281.

D.J. Teece, Firm Organization, Industrial Structure, and Technological Innovation, *Journal of Economics, Behavior, and Organization* (1996), forthcoming.

O.E. Williamson, The Vertical Integration of Production: Market Failure Considerations, *American Economic Review* 61 (May 1971), 112-123.

O.E. Williamson, *Markets and Hierarchies: Analysis and Antitrust Implications* (The Free Press, New York, 1975).

O.E. Williamson, Credible Commitments: Using Hostages to Support Exchange, *American Economic Review* 73 (September 1983), 519–540.

O.E. Williamson, *The Economic Institutions of Capitalism* (The Free Press, New York, 1985).

O.E. Williamson, Comparative Economic Organization: The Analysis of Discrete Structural Alternatives, *Administrative Science Quarterly* 36 (1991), 269–296.

O.E. Williamson, *The Mechanisms of Governance* (Oxford University Press, New York, 1996a).

O.E. Williamson, Revisiting Legal Realism: The Law, Economics and Organization Perspective, *Industrial and Corporate Change* 5 (1996b), 383–420.

Firm Organization, Industrial Structure, and Technological Innovation[1]

David J. Teece

Mitsubishi Bank Professor, Walter A. Haas School of Business, University of California, Berkeley, CA 94720-1930, U.S.A.

Received 29 July 1994

The formal and informal structures of firms and their external linkages have an important bearing on the rate and direction of innovation. This paper explores the properties of different types of firms with respect to the generation of new technology. Various archetypes are recognized and an effort is made to match organization structure to the type of innovation. The framework is relevant to technology and competition policy as it broadens the framework economists use to identify environments that assist innovation.

Keywords: Organizational structure; Innovation; Market structure-innovation relationships; Proprietary technology; Vertical Integration; Flexible hierarchy.

1. Introduction

It is increasingly recognized that the dynamism of a competitive private enterprise system flows from the development and application of new technology and the adoption of new organizational forms. As a result, attention is being focused on trying to develop a better understanding of the institutional environment in which these activities take place. In market economies, the business firm is clearly the

Reprinted from *Journal of Economic Behavior and Organization* 31 (1996), 193–224.

[1] I am grateful for helpful comments and conversations with Glenn Carroll, Hank Chesbrough, Niel Kay, Ralph Landau, Richard Nelson, Nathan Rosenberg, Oliver Williamson, and two anonymous referees.

leading player in the development and commercialization of new products and processes.[2] However, much of the literature in economics proceeds as if the identity of the firm in which innovation is taking place is of little moment. Moreover, the links between firm structure and strategy and the innovation process are poorly understood.[3]

In this paper, it is suggested that the formal and informal structures of the firm, as well as the network of external linkages that they possess, has an important bearing on the strength as well as the kind of innovative activity conducted by private enterprise economies.[4] Frameworks are presented to indicate how firm structure and the nature of innovation are linked. The approach adopted eschews optimality and embraces comparative analysis, in the spirit of Williamson[5] (1975, 1985), whereby alternatives are compared to each other rather than to hypothetical ideals. The institutional context is also considered. In particular, the role of capital markets is at least addressed, and the legal infrastructure is not assumed away completely. Indeed, various aspects of the legal system, and in particular intellectual property law, are explicitly considered.

The general approach adopted involves (1) identifying the fundamental characteristics of technological development, (2) determining the factors that affect innovation at the level of the firm, (3) identifying distinctive archetypes or governance modes for firms, and (4) choosing from available alternatives the organizational forms better suited to deal with various types of innovation. It is hoped that analyzing innovation in this manner will help broaden the agenda for industrial organization economists and organization theorists as they begin to grapple with understanding one of the most distinctive features of modern capitalism.

---

[2] In fact, there are governments, universities, and also professional societies in the system, and certain activities that firms cannot be expected to do on their own because the returns are so low, are picked up by other institutions, or receive public monies, or both.

[3] For a review, see Dosi *et al.* (1988).

[4] The following statement by Little (1985, p. 14) is representative of accepted views: "Our work among innovative companies indicates that the management decision on how to organize for innovation is critical."

[5] The approach rejects assumptions of temporal equilibrium. The framework does not assume that the selection process immediately weeds out all organizations that do not match the business environment at a particular point in time. While the organizational system is seen as gravitating toward an end point or equilibrium, it takes so long to reach it that the environment is likely to change again in the interim, leading to a state of perpetual disequilibrium.

2. Fundamental Characteristics of Technological Development

It is impossible to identify the organizational requirements of the innovation process without first specifying underlying properties of technological innovation. Fortunately, there appears to be on emerging consensus among scholars who study the innovation process with respect to the stylized facts. In the main, these appear to characterize innovation independently of the organizational context in which it takes place.

2.1. *Uncertainty*

Innovation is a quest into the unknown. It involves searching and the probing and reprobing of technological as well as market opportunities. With hindsight, much effort is spent traveling down blind alleys. Serendipity and luck play an important role. There are various types of uncertainty. Tjalling Koopmans (1957) has made a useful distinction between primary and secondary uncertainty. Both are critical in the context of innovation. Secondary uncertainty arises "from lack of communication, that is, from one decision-maker having no way of finding out the concurrent decisions and plans made by others." Primary uncertainty arises from "random acts of nature and unpredictable changes in concurrent preferences" (1957, pp. 162, 163). Williamson recognizes a third kind of uncertainty, which he calls behavioral uncertainty, which is attributable to opportunism. Such uncertainty can lead to ex post surprises.[6] It is important to note that secondary uncertainty can be affected by changing the boundaries of the organization. As Richardson (1990) and Williamson (1975) have explained, vertical integration can facilitate the coordination of complementary investments through the sharing of investment plans. Secondary uncertainty is thus a function of organizational form.

2.2. *Path Dependency*

Technology often evolves in certain path dependent ways, contoured and channeled by what might be thought of as technological paradigms (Dosi, 1982, 1982). A

---

[6] Uncertainty also makes information a valuable commodity. Information about which outcomes will occur, or are more likely to occur, will obviously have great value. Information, of course, itself has very special characteristics. It is not only an indivisible commodity, in which case the classic problems of allocation in the presence of indivisibilities will be present, but it is also highly tacit, as discussed below. Often it cannot be readily articulated and codified in language. Combined with the absence of legal protection, these features make it difficult to trade.

technological paradigm is a pattern of solutions to selected technical problems which derives from certain engineering relationships. A paradigm identifies the problems that have to be solved and the way to inquire about them; within a paradigm, research efforts become channeled along certain trajectories.[7] Relatedly, new product and process developments for a particular organization are likely to lie in the technological neighborhood of previous successes.

2.3. *Cumulative Nature*

Technology development, particularly inside a particular paradigm, proceeds cumulatively along the path defined by the paradigm. The fact that technological progress builds on what went before, and that much of it is tacit and proprietary, means that it usually has significant organization-specific dimensions. Moreover, an organization's technical capabilities are likely to be "close in" to previous technological accomplishments.[8]

2.4. *Irreversibilities*

Technological progress exhibits strong irreversibilities. This follows not just because innovation typically requires specialized investments, but because the evolution of technologies along certain trajectories eliminates the possibility of competition from older technologies, even if relative prices change significantly. Thus mechanical calculators are unlikely to ever replace electronic ones, even if the relative prices of silicon and steel were to switch by a factor of 1000[9] in favor of steel.

---

[7] Examples of technological paradigms include the internal combustion engine, biotechnology, and tungsten filament lighting. Technological discontinuities occur when new paradigms emerge. Thus new technologies are more threatening to existing skills and capabilities if they embody a new paradigms emerge. Thus new technologies are more threatening to existing skills and capabilities if they embody a new paradigm. The emergence of microelectronics, which carried with it a new paradigm, was far more threatening to the skills of incumbents than the emergence of the facsimile, which fused the technology of the telephone and the copier.

[8] Specific technological skills in one field (e.g. pharmaceuticals) may be applicable in closely-related fields (e.g. pesticides) but they are unlikely to be of use in distant fields (e.g. aircraft). See Teece (1988), Teece *et al.* (1994).

[9] If sailing ships ever replace propeller-driven ships, it will be with such a different sailing technology as to be almost unrecognizable from nineteenth century counterparts. And if the prop-fan recaptures markets from the fan-jet, it will also be with a markedly different prop and engine.

2.5. *Technological Interrelatedness*

Innovation is characterized by technological interrelatedness between various subsystems. Linkages to other technologies, to complementary assets, and to users must be maintained if innovation is to be successful. If recognizable organizational subunits such as R&D, manufacturing, and marketing exist, they must be in close and continuous communication and engage in mutual adaptation if innovation in commercially relevant products and processes is to have a chance of succeeding. Moreover, successful commercial innovation usually requires quick decision making and close coupling and coordination among research, development, manufacturing, sales and service. Put differently, organizational capacities must exist to enable these activities to be closely coordinated, and to occur with dispatch.

2.6. *Tacitness*

The knowledge developed by organizations is often highly tacit. That is, it is difficult if not impossible to articulate and codify (Polanyi, 1962, Winter, 1987). A corollary is that technology transfer is often difficult without the transfer of key individuals. This simultaneously explains why imitation is often costly, and why the diffusion of new technology often depends on the mobility of engineers and scientists (Teece, 1977, Nelson and Winter, 1977). Relatedly, an organization's technology ought not to be thought of as residing in some hypothetical book of blueprints, or with some hypothetical chief engineer, but in an organization's system and habits of coordinating and managing tasks. These systems and habits have been referred to as organizational routines (Nelson and Winter, 1982). It is the performance of these routines that is at the essence of an organization's technological capacity.

2.7. *Inappropriability*

Under many legal systems, the ownership rights associated with technical know-how are often ambiguous, do not always permit rewards that match contribution,[10] vary in the degree of exclusion they permit (often according to the innate patentability or copyrightability of the object or subject matter) and

---

[10] For instance, it is possible to receive a patent which is arguably too narrow or too broad in relation to the patent holder's contribution to economic welfare. Moreover, in many cases legal protection for technical contributions may simply not be available, or if available may be difficult to enforce.

are temporary. Or as Arrow (1996) put it, technical information is a "fugitive resource, with limited property rights." Accordingly, investment in innovative activity may not necessarily yield property which can be reserved for the exclusive use of the innovator. But the activity may nevertheless still be valuable enough to attract some investment, depending in part on other institutional arrangement to be examined later. The degree to which new products and processes are protectable under intellectual property law will henceforth be referred to as the intellectual property regime. For expositional simplicity, regimes will be classified as strong if patents and copyrights are effective, and weak otherwise. Clearly, the industrial world does not readily bifurcate, and there exists a continuum of appropriability regimes, as data assembled by Levin *et al.* (1987) make apparent.

The market for know-how is further confounded because in order to provide full information to the buyer, the seller of know-how may have to disclose the object of the exchange, but in so doing the basis for the exchange evaporates, or at least erodes, as the potential buyer might now have in its possession that which he was seeking to acquire. Hence, transactions in the market for know-how must proceed under conditions of ignorance. Accordingly, at least until reputations become established, exchange is likely to be exposed to hazards. Optimal resource allocation is unlikely to result.

3. Organizational and Market Determinants of the Rate and Direction of Innovation

While our understanding of innovation has been enriched in recent years, the basic framework employed in policy debates about innovation, technology policy, and competition policy are often remarkably naive and highly incomplete. Even elementary considerations such as those identified in Sec. 2 are frequently neglected. In economics, for instance, it is not uncommon to find debate about innovation policy collapsing to a rather outmoded discussion of the relative virtues of competition and monopoly, as if they were the key determinants of innovation. Clearly there is much more at work. In this section, various classes of variables — some economic, some organizational — are identified that impact the rate and direction of innovation. Subsequent sections will identify distinct types of organizations based on various organizational attributes. A final section will then endeavor to match these organizations to different types and levels of innovation.

3.1. *Monopoly Power*

One reason why our understanding of innovation has not proceeded faster in the last half century is that many researchers, particularly industrial organization economists, have overly focused on just one variable: the degree of market power that a firm or firms may have. The evidence is unequivocal that competition and rivalry are important for innovation; but few believe that the world of perfect competition in which firms compete in highly fragmented markets using identical nonproprietary technologies is an organizational arrangement that any advanced economy would aspire to achieve. Nevertheless, many policy debates proceed on the assumption that fragmented markets assist innovation.[11]

Schumpeter was among the first to declare that perfect competition was incompatible with innovation. He noted, "The introduction of new methods of production and new commodities is hardly conceivable with perfect — and perfectly prompt — competition from the start. And this means that the bulk of what we call economic progress is incompatible with it."[12] However, the Schumpeterian notion that small entrepreneurial firms lack financial resources seems archaic, at least in countries with a vigorous venture capital market. In any case, the Schumpeterian debate seems a little beside the point, as there is an enormous number of variables that can potentially intervene between the generation of monopolistic rents and the allocation of resources to the development of new products and processes. Consider, first, single product firms. The notion that innovation requires the cash flow generated by the exercise of monopoly power assumes both that (1) capital markets are inefficient, and (2) that monopolistic levels of internal cash flows are adequate to fund the requisite R&D programs. If capital markets are operating according to what Fama (1970) has called *strong form efficiency*, then cash flow is unimportant because firms with high yield projects will be able to signal their profit opportunities to the capital market and the requisite financing will come forth on competitive terms. Thus if there is strong form efficiency and zero transaction costs (its corollary), cash will get matched to projects whether or not the cash is internally generated.

In fact, the world is not properly characterized by zero transaction costs, but that does not mean that the availability of internal cash flows from monopoly (as compared to competitive) product market positions is what makes the difference

---

[11] Clearly rivalry and competition are important to innovation, but belief in the virtues of perfectly competitive systems is lore, reflecting casual empiricism and prejudice and not careful theorizing and empirical study. The same is true for monopoly.

[12] Schumpeter (1934, p. 105).

between being able to fund a project and not being able to fund it. Significant innovative efforts involve expenditures in a particular year which may be many times the available cash flows. So the availability of marginally higher cash flows occasioned by monopoly power are unlikely to grossly change the financial picture, except in unusual circumstances.

Furthermore, even in the absence of adequate internal cash flow, firms need not go to the capital market to find the requisite financing. The "Schumpeterian" view of the innovation processes appears to be one that involves full integration, from research, development, manufacturing and marketing. But the financial requirements associated with developing and commercializing new products and processes can be accomplished with a myriad organizational arrangements including research joint ventures, co-production, and co-marketing arrangement. With such arrangements, there is the possibility that the capital requirements associated with a new project could be drastically reduced for the innovator. Economies of scale and scope can often be captured through interfirm arrangements. In some instances they cannot.[13]

The link between market power and innovation in specific markets is further undone if the multidivisional multiproduct firm is admitted into the scene.[14] The basic function and purpose of the multiproduct structure is to allocate cash generated everywhere to high-yield purposes anywhere. If a multidivisional multiproduct firm does operate this way, and there is plenty of evidence to suggest that they can and do, then the link between market power in a particular market and the funding of innovation in that market is undone. In a multiproduct firm selling products in markets A through Z, the cash generated by virtue of power in market A can indeed fund innovation relevant to market A, but it can equally well fund innovative activity in market Z. The capital market inside the multiproduct firm thus unlocks the relationship between market structure and innovation proposed by Schumpeter.

When firms do go into the capital market they generally have multiple sources of funding available. Generically, these can be split into debt and equity. The various types of debt and equity can on the one hand be thought of as financial instruments or, as Williamson suggests, as different "governance structures" (Williamson, 1988, 1996). Williamson explains that the decision by firms to use debt or equity to support individual investment projects is likely to be linked to the redeployability of the underlying investment. Since new product development

---

[13] For a managerially oriented analysis of the limits of outsourcing in the context of innovation, see Chesbrough and Teece (1996).

[14] See Kay *et al.* (1990), undated working paper.

programs commonly involve investment in assets that are substantially irreversible (like R&D) and/or non-redeployable (like specialized equipment), debt is only of limited value in financing innovation, unless a firm has collateral and is under-leveraged to begin with. Accordingly, the fund sources generally available to support new product development are internal cash flow and new equity. In instances when a firm does not already have substantial cash flows, then equity is the major source of new funds. The role of equity is made distinct if it is considered in the context of "start-up" firms which do not already have free cash flows. Investors have obvious problems in evaluating the prospects for new products and processes, and the best investees have problems, though less serious, in identifying the best investors.[15]

Now consider internally generated cash flow. Even in the United States where there is a vibrant venture capital market, internal "free" cash flow is the major source of private financing for innovation. A firm's cash flow is not just a function of price-cost margins in the product markets (sometimes suggested as a proxy for monopoly power) but its existing asset structures and the need for new investment in existing businesses. A business can clearly be a "cash cow" even if it is earning only competitive returns. This would be true if the firm was gradually divesting itself, or simply harvesting its position in a particular market. Internally generated cash can be readily allocated by management and is not typically constrained by covenants.

Over the last half decade, a controversial body of literature has emerged which, in essence, argues that free cash flows must be distributed to shareholders, rather than being invested internally in discretionary projects, if firms are to operate efficiently (Jensen, 1989). The basic idea is that the discipline of debt is needed to cause capital to be channeled to high-yield uses in the economy, as well as in the firm. There are severe problems with this thesis, not least of which

---

[15] The investors' problems are rather obvious. The investor has the difficult challenge of calibrating investment prospects in an environment where there is usually high market uncertainty, high technical uncertainty, and bountiful opportunism and optimism. Several kinds of opportunism are possible. One is simply that the technology can be misrepresented. This tendency, however, can be checked if the investor hires technical consultants to validate the entrepreneurs' claims. Another is that the tenacity and veracity of the entrepreneur are difficult to calibrate, with consequences much more unfortunate for the investor than for the entrepreneur. Ascertaining whether the entrepreneurs' optimism is honest yet misplaced is perhaps even more difficult. There is "much evidence that in the context of planning and action most people are prone to extreme optimism in their forecasts of outcomes, and often fail to appreciate the chances of an unfavorable outcome" (Kahneman and Lovalla, 1995, p. 2). Decision makers often take risks because they deny their existence or underestimate their extent (March and Shapira, 1987).

is that debt holders are loss averse and not at all business-opportunity driven. While it may indeed be the case that free cash flows do sometimes get misallocated by managers, to delimit them in the manner proposed by advocates of the free cash flow hypothesis is to force the firm into equity markets to finance innovation. For reasons explained earlier, this is not always desirable because the new issues markets, both public and private, have disabilities with respect to recognizing and funding new opportunities.

To summarize, innovation clearly requires access to capital. The necessary capital can come from cash flows or from equity. At least with respect to early stage activity, debt financing is unlikely to be viable, unless the firm has other assets to pledge. However, certain downstream investments needed to commercialize innovation can be debt financed if they are redeployable. Alternatively, alliances can be entered which reduce the need for new investment in complementary assets. The point, however, is that there are many factors besides firm size, and the presence or absence of market power, that affect an innovator's capacity to access capital.[16]

3.2. *Hierarchy*

Hierarchy arose to help in the administration of military, religious, and governmental activities.[17] While hierarchies are old, deep hierarchies are relatively new. Anthropologists point out that most tribes, clans and agricultural enterprises have rather flat hierarchies. The Roman Catholic Church, for instance, has only four levels. Centralizing and decentralizing are not genuine alternatives for organization; the key issue is to decide the mix. Hierarchies can accomplish complex organizational tasks, but they are often associated with organizational properties inimical to innovation, such as slow (bureaucratic) decision making and weak incentives.

3.2.1. Bureaucratic decision making

Decision making processes in hierarchical organizations almost always involve bureaucratic features. In particular, a formal expenditure process involving

---

[16] For an expanded discussion, see Day *et al.* (1993), part I.

[17] Hierarchical subdivision is not a characteristic that is peculiar to human organization. It is common to virtually all complex systems of which we have knowledge (Simon, 1973, p. 202). The advantages of hierarchy are well understood. In particular, among systems of a given size and complexity, hierarchical systems require much less information transmission among their parts than do other types of systems.

submissions and approvals is characteristic. Decision making is likely to have a committee structure, with top management requiring reports and written justifications for significant decisions. Moreover, approvals may need to be sought from outside the organizational unit in which the expenditure is to take place. While this may ensure a matching up of expenditures to opportunities across a wider range of economic activity, it unquestionably slows decision making and tends to reinforce the status quo.

The latter characteristic follows from committee decision making structures, which almost always tend toward balancing and compromise. But innovation is often ill served by such structures, as the new and the radical will almost always appear threatening to some constituents. Put differently, representative structures, bureaucratic or political, often tend to endorse the status quo. Strong leaders can often overcome such tendencies, but such leaders are not always present and their capacities are often thwarted by the organization.[18]

One consequence is what Williamson (1975) has referred to as a "program persistence bias," and its corollary the "anti-innovation bias." Program persistence refers to the funding of programs beyond what can be sustained on merits, and follows from the presence or influence of program advocates in the resource allocation process. This proclivity almost automatically has the countervailing effect of reducing funds available to new programs, which are unlikely to be well represented in the decision making process. As Anthony Downs points out, "the increasing size of the bureau leads to a gradual ossification of operations — since each proposed action must receive multiple approvals, the probability of its being rejected is quite high — its cumbersome machinery cannot produce results fast enough, and its anti-novelty bias may block the necessary innovation" (p. 160)

The sharpening of global competition, and diversification (organizationally and geographically) in the sources of new knowledge compels firms to make decisions faster, and to reduce time to market in order to capture value from technological innovation. It seems clear that to accomplish such responsiveness, organizations need new structures and different decision-making protocols to

---

[18] Crozier (1964, p. 225) puts it this way: "People on top theoretically have a great deal of power and often much more power than they would have in other, more authoritarian societies. But these powers are not very useful, since people on top can act only in an impersonal way and can in no way interfere with the subordinate strata. They cannot, therefore, provide real leadership on a daily basis. If they want to introduce change, they must go through the long and difficult ordeal of a crisis. Thus, although they are all-powerful because they at the apex of the whole centralized system, they are made so weak by the pattern of resistance of the different isolated strata that they can use their power only in truly exceptional circumstances."

facilitate entrepreneurial and innovative behavior. Burgelman (1984) identifies a menu of such arrangements which include: special business units, new ventures department, new venture divisions, and independent business units. Clearly, all of these designs imply smaller, flatter and more specialized structures within which to conduct activities where speed and responsiveness are critical. In the limit, the spinoff or spinout of a new division signifies that the enterprise's (or at least the individuals associated with it) chances of success are greater outside rather than inside an established hierarchy. In addition to the creation of semi-autonomous units, firms can attempt to "delayer" by stripping out layers of middle management. But flattening organization need not fundamentally redefine the relationships between people and functions in the organizations. Functions may still work sequentially, with decisions being made from fragmented perspectives.

In essence, the organizational challenge appears to be that activities are not as decomposable as they used to be, and that cross-functional interaction must take place concurrently, rather than sequentially, if firms are to cut time-to-market for new products and processes. Cross-functional and cross-departmental networks must be strengthened without causing information overload. Computer networks can assist cross-functional interaction by project teams, concurrent engineering teams, network teams, task forces and the like. If such activity becomes completely unstructured, it augments rather than displaces bureaucracy. Instead of random ad hoc approaches, what is needed are well-defined cross-functional teams, which can be redefined as needed. With organizational subunits cross-linked in this way, authority occurs as much from knowledge as position in the organizational hierarchy. The challenge is to develop a culture which supports the establishment of cross-functional teams which draw on the requisite knowledge, wherever it may be located.

3.2.2. Low-powered incentives

As they grow, organizations often become characterized by what Williamson (1985, p. 153) calls "low powered incentives." Low-powered incentives can be defined as those where the co-variance of employee compensation with business unit performance is low. One reason is that compensation structures inside large organizations need to be sensitive to relative as well as absolute levels of compensation. If the compensation structure itself has value through the relativities it establishes, then the enterprise will be reluctant to disturb the structure to support innovation. Another reason is that stock options cannot be granted to reflect divisional performance since it is generally the case that the division's shares are nontradeable in public markets. The absence of a public equity market for subunit shares thus deprives the firm of the opportunity to provide an objective capital market-based augmentation to compensation.[19] If the employee is rewarded instead through stock in the total enterprise, the impact of divisional, departmental, and individual performance is likely to be severely diluted.[20]

3.2.3. Principal-agent distortions

Business firms of great size are rarely owner managed. Inasmuch as managers (agents) trade-off enterprise performance for their own welfare, innovation is likely to be impaired. This is because the interests of managers are sometimes at odds with what innovation requires, because the tenure of top management is usually much shorter than the gestation period for major innovations. Moreover, principals must invest in costly information collection and monitoring activities in order to check up on the performance of agents. These costs can be considerable. Moreover, principals may insist on certain expenditure controls which themselves slow decision making and thwart innovation.

3.2.4. Myopia

Organizations can become closed to changes in the market and business environment and to new sources of technology. Individuals in organizations, including chief executive officers, can fall into the trap of adopting a citadel mentality. The availability of free cash flows can help sustain that mentality and behavior for considerable periods of time. Closed systems may be able to hone existing routines, but they will lose the capacity to engage in new routines. Organizations can become closed through administrative arrangements (as when the firm's boundaries are delimited by its organization chart), through legalistic (rather than relational) contracting with suppliers and customers, and through social and cultural norms which stress the importance of inside rather than outside considerations.

3.3. *Scope*

The scope of product market activities may impact the innovative performance of firms in at least three ways. One has just been discussed in the context of finance: the multidivisional multiproduct firm is in a position to re-allocate cash from businesses that have positive cash flow to new businesses with negative cash flow. A second hypothesis, put forward at various times by Joseph Schumpeter,

---

[19] Surrogate valuation indexes can sometimes be created based on the use of "yardstick" companies, but they typically do not convey liquidity.

[20] For further discussion on measurement problems, see Holmstrom (1993, pp. 144–146).

Richard Nelson and others, is that the product market portfolios of multiproduct firms will increase the payoff to uncertain R&D by increasing the probability that new products and processes resulting from corporate R&D can be commercialized inside the firm. Neither of these will be the main focus here.

Instead, it is suggested that multiproduct firms can more readily develop and commercialize "fusion" technologies which involve the melding of technological capacities relevant to disparate lines of business. This fusion — as with mechanics and electronics (what Kodama, 1986 calls "mechatronics") — by no means occurs automatically, and requires internal structures which are flexible and permeable.[21] Indeed, there appears to be less diversity in firms' products than in their technologies (Pavitt *et al.* 1989). Nevertheless, the multiproduct firm does afford opportunities for economies of scope based on transferring technologies across product lines and melding them to create new products (Teece, 1980, 1982). Despite the path dependent-nature of technological change, the diversity of application areas for a given technology are often quite large, and it is often feasible and sometimes efficient to apply the firm's capabilities to different market opportunities.

Suppose application areas outside of the core business do in fact open up. The question arises as to whether potential scope economies deriving from the application of proprietary know-how in new markets add more to the innovating firm's value if they are served through licensing and related contractual arrangements to unaffiliated firms who then serve the new product markets in question, or by direct investment, either de novo or by merger/acquisition. This is an important question, the answer to which ought to help shape a positive theory of the scope of the firm's activities.

Whether the firm integrates or not is likely to depend critically on four sets of factors: (1) whether the technology can be transferred to an unaffiliated entity at higher or lower cost than it can be transferred to an affiliated entity; (2) the degree of intellectual property protection afforded to the technology in question by the relevant statutes and laws; (3) whether a contract can be crafted which will regulate the sale of technology with greater or less efficiency and effectiveness or whether department-to-department or division-to-division sales can be regulated by internal administrative procedures; and (4) whether the set of complementary competences possessed by the potential licensee can be assessed by the licensor at a cost lower than alternatives. If they are lower, the available returns from the market will be higher, and the opportunity for a satisfactory royalty or profit-sharing arrangement accordingly greater.

---

[21] This is discussed in Sec. 4.3.

These matters are explored in more detail elsewhere (Teece, 1980, 1984, 1986, Chesbrough and Teece, 1996). Suffice to say that contractual mechanisms are often less satisfactory than the alternative. Proprietary considerations are more often than not assisted by integration, and technology transfer is difficult both to unaffiliated and affiliated partners, with the consequence that integration (or multiproduct diversification) is the more attractive alternative, except where incumbents are already competitively established in downstream activities, and are in a position to render de novo entry by the technology-based firms unattractive because of the excess capacity it would generate. Hence, multiproduct firms can be expected to appear as efficient responses to contractual, proprietary and technology transfer problems in an important set of circumstances. Mixed modes, such as joint ventures and complex forms of profit-sharing collaboration, will also be common according to how the set of transactions in question stacks up against the criteria identified above.

3.4. *Vertical Integration*

The characteristics of technological development identified earlier also have important implications for the vertical structure of the firm, and vice versa. Economic historians have long suggested that there may be links between vertical structures and the rate and direction of innovation. For instance, Frankel (1955) has argued that the slow rate of diffusion of innovations in the British textile and iron and steel industries around the turn of the century was due to the absence of vertically integrated firms. Kindleberger (1964) has gone so far as to suggest that the reason why West Germany and Japan have overtaken Britain may be due to "the organization of [British] industry into separate firms dealing with each other at arm's length." This "may have impeded technological change because of the possibility that part of the benefits of that change would have been external to the separate firms" (pp. 146, 147). Kindleberger also studied the reasons for the failure of the British railroads to abandon the 10-ton coal wagon in favor of the more efficient 20-ton wagon, and concludes (1964) that the reason for the slow rate of diffusion was institutional and not technical. In short, it stemmed from the absence of vertical integration.[22] General Motors' early dominance in

---

[22] Technical aspects of interrelatedness do not seem to have held up the movement to more efficient size, either through making such a change uneconomic because of the enormity of the investment required or by adding amounts too great for any one firm to borrow. The sums involved were not large, and railway finance was rarely a limiting factor in the period up to 1914. Private ownership of the coal cars by the collieries, on the other hand, posed a type of interrelatedness that was institutional rather than technical.

the diesel electric locomotive industry has also been attributed to the fact that it was integrated into electrical supply while its competitors were not (Marx, 1976). A systematic exploration of the relationship between technological innovation and enterprise boundaries is needed.

For present purposes, it is useful to distinguish between two types of innovation: autonomous (or "stand-alone") and systemic. An autonomous innovation is one which can be introduced without modifying other components or items of equipment. The component or device in that sense "stands alone." A systemic innovation, on the other hand, requires significant readjustment to other parts of the system. The major distinction relates to the amount of design coordination which development and commercialization are likely to require. An example of a systemic innovation would be electronic funds transfer, instant photography (it required redesign of the camera and the film), front-wheel drive, and the jet airliner (it required new stress-resistant airframes).

With systemic innovation, internal organization (integration) can often assist the workings of the market. Integration facilitates systemic innovations by facilitating information flows, and the coordination of investments plans. It also removes institutional barriers to innovation where the innovation in question requires allocating costs and benefits, or placing specialized investments into several parts of an industry.

Comprehensive evidence with respect to these propositions has yet to be assembled. Vignettes can be found in Chesbrough and Teece (1996). The only statistical test performed to date relates to the petroleum industry (Armour and Teece, 1978). These findings indicated that firm and R&D expenditures for basic and applied research in the U.S. petroleum industry between 195–1975, were statistically related to the level of vertical integration which the enterprise possessed.[23]

3.5. *Organizational Culture and Values*

Market power is an element of industrial structure; scale, scope, integration and hierarchy can be thought of as elements of the formal structure of an organization. Of equal if not greater importance is the informal structure of an organization.

---

[23] Despite the fact that the ultimate objective of R&D programs is to produce innovations, not simply to dissipate resources on R&D activities, expenditure data can be viewed as a useful proxy for innovative performance in that they reveal the intensity of innovative activity. Furthermore, if the discount rate facing non-integrated firms is similar to that facing integrated firms and if similar risk preferences exist across the management of these firms, the higher productivity per dollar of research expenditure posited in vertically integrated firms implies that, ceteris paribus, such firms will devote more resources to R&D.

Organizational culture is the essence of an organization's informal structure. It is "the pattern of beliefs and expectations shared by the organization's members. These beliefs and expectations produce norms that powerfully shape the behavior of individuals and groups" (Schwartz and Davis, 1981, p. 33).

Organizational culture can be thought of as the "central norms that may characterize an organization" (O'Reilly, 1989, p. 305). A strong culture is a system of informal rules that spells out how people are to behave most of the time. By knowing what is expected of them, employees will waste little time deciding how to act in a given situation (Deal and Kennedy, 1982). There need not be consensus within an organization with respect to these beliefs, as the guiding beliefs or vision held by top management and by individuals lower down in the organization may not congruent. It is the latter, however, which define an organization's culture (O'Reilly, 1989, p. 305).

There seems to be an emerging consensus (Deal and Kennedy, 1982, Peters and Waterman, 1982, O'Reilly, 1989) that the following set of norms assists the development and commercialization of new products and processes. With respect to development, these include: the autonomy to try and fail; the right of employees to challenge the status quo; open communication to customers, to external sources of technology, and within the firm itself. With respect to commercialization or implementation, teamwork, flexibility, trust and hard work are considered to be critically important. The right culture is not just an important asset to assist in technological development; it may be a requirement.

With a few notable exceptions (North, 1990), economists have given almost no attention, and little sympathy, to the topic of organizational culture.[24] Occasionally, economists may speak to the importance of trust and consciousness. Thus Arrow (1974, p. 28) notes that "social demands may be expressed through formal rules and authorities, or they may be expressed through internalized demands of conscience. Looked at collectively, these demands may be compromises which are needed to increase the efficacy of all."[25] If Arrow is right in his claim that

---

[24] North's discussion (chapter 5) is almost exclusively limited to societal culture rather than organizational culture. He does however note that informal constraints flowing from the broader societal culture are pervasive. Veblen (1972, p. 174) notes that "at least since mankind reached the human plane, the economic unit has been not a solitary hunter, but a community of some kind."

[25] Moreover, there is a tendency to squeeze such concepts into "externalities," where it is not clear they belong. Thus Arrow (1974, p. 23) notes that: "Trust and similar values, loyalty or truth-telling, are examples of what the economist would call 'externalities'. They are good, they are commodities; they have real, practical economic value; they increase the efficiency of the system, enable you to produce more goods or more whatever values you hold in high esteem. But they are not commodities for which trade on the open market is technically possible or even meaningful."

values can increase efficiency, it is unfortunate that the topic has been left to organizational sociologists and psychologists, and that economic science ignores what appears to be an important set of variables in the understanding of organizational performance.

One way for economists to begin grappling with organizational culture is to see it as control on the cheap; reduction in shirking is just one element.[26] If individuals can be motivated and directed without pecuniary incentives and (and disincentives) and the exercise of authority, tremendous resource savings can ensue, and innovation processes can avoid the burdens of bureaucracy. Conversely, if a firm's culture and strategy do not align, it is likely to be unable to implement its strategy, especially strategies which involve innovation. For instance, a declaration by top management of a firm that the firm is now going to be more open to external sources of technological ideas will not ensure that the strategy will be successful if there is a well entrenched "not invented here" culture inside the organization. The failure to develop new norms supportive of a particular strategy "means that changes will persist only where they are closely monitored and directly rewarded" (O'Reilly, 1989, p. 310).

3.6. *External Linkages*

Economists, as well as many organization theorists, have traditionally thought of firms as islands of hierarchical control embedded in a market structure and interacting with each other through the price mechanism. Indeed. Coase (1937) has referred to firms as "islands of conscious power." Coase's metaphor needs to be transformed from islands to archipelagos to capture important elements of business organization. This is because firms commonly need to form strategic alliances, vertically (both upstream and downstream), laterally, and sometimes horizontally in order to develop and commercialize new technologies.[27] Compared to arm's-length market contracts, such arrangements have more structure, involve constant interaction among the parts, more open information channels, greater trust, rely on voice rather than exit, and put less emphasis on price. Compared to hierarchies, such alliances or networks among firms call for negotiation rather

---

[26] Alchien and Demsetz (1972).

[27] Imai (1988, p. 2) notes that "corporate networks in a broad sense are the vital economic institution which has led the Japanese economic development. The long history of cooperation between firms may be a crucial factor to explain the special adaptability of the Japanese economy." Imai uses the term, as it is used in this paper, to indicate interfirm relationships in general, including zaibatsu and business groups.

than authority and put great emphasis on boundary-spanning roles. Although firms connected through alliances have a high degree of autonomy, the relationship may well be anchored by a minority equity position. These arrangements can be used to provide some of the benefits of integration while avoiding some of the costs. This undoubtedly helps explain the proliferation of alliances in recent decades.

The variety of such arrangements to link organizations is almost unlimited, and the resultant forms quite diverse. A constellation of lincensing, manufacturing and marketing agreements will typically characterize many interorganizational arrangements. R&D joint ventures, manufacturing joint ventures, co-marketing arrangements and consortia are just a few of the resultant forms. Some of these arrangements constitute extremely complex open systems, and some may be unstable. The managerial functions in these interorganizational networks are quite different from the authority relationship which commonly exists in hierarchies. Managers have to perform boundary-spanning roles, and learn to manage in circumstances that involve mutual dependency.

3.7. *Assessment*

The above discussion of the variables which impact firm-level innovation suggests that economic and organizational research needs a richer framework if the innovation process is to be better understood. Economic research needs to pay greater attention to organizational structure, both formal and informal, and organizational research needs to understand the importance of market structure, internal structure, and the business environment. Figure 1 is a diagrammatic presentation of the various classes of variables that have been identified, as well as considerations deemed to be important but assumed away in this analysis. For instance, the firm's human resources/capital and the mechanism by which firms attract, train, and hold first-rate people has not been deeply analyzed. Nor has the role of government in the support of the scientific and technological infrastructure been analyzed. Another major omission has been the strategy by which firms identify what projects to engage and what assets to build or buy in order to commercialize technology.

In Secs. 4 and 5 consideration is given to identifying particular organizational forms that have distinct implications for certain types of innovation. The treatment is illustrative and not comprehensive. It suggests that there are a variety of organizational modes that can support innovation, but that there are important differences amongst organizations in the types of innovation they can support.

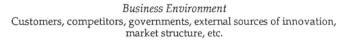

Business Environment
Customers, competitors, governments, external sources of innovation, market structure, etc.

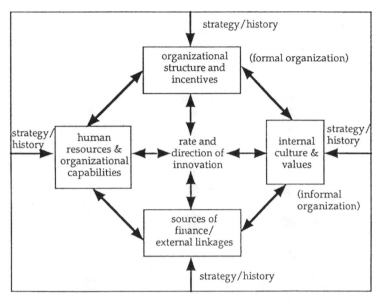

Fig. 1. A determinants of the rate and direction of firm level innovation.

4. Distinctive Governance Modes (Archetypes)

In the previous section, various organizational characteristics were identified. Distinctive governance modes arise when these characteristics are represented to greater or lesser degrees. The specification of the governance mode requires attention to at least four classes of variables: firm boundaries, internal formal structure, internal informal structure, and external linkages. What immediately becomes clear is that for purposes of considering the innovative potential of various organizational forms, one can no longer simply specify the type by reference to one or two aspects of structure. For example, it is no longer meaningful to discuss the innovative potential of conglomerates, vertically integrated firms, etc. without specifying much more. Rather than specify all possible permutations and combinations of these variables in this paper, the focus will be on the following archetypes: (1) stolid, multiproduct, integrated hierarchies; (2) high flex "Silicon Valley"-type firms; (3) hollow corporations of various types; and (4) conglomerates of various types. There will also be a brief discussion of the individual inventor (not really an organizational form).

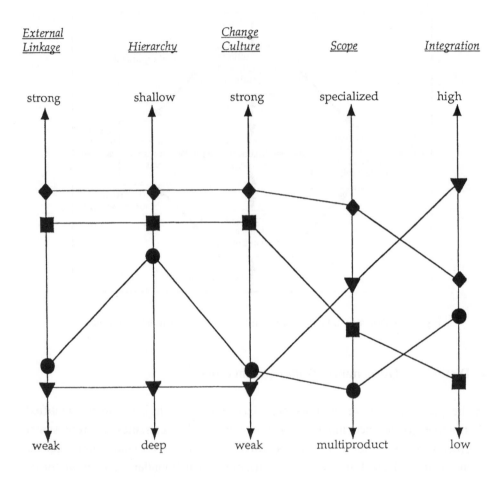

Fig. 2. Identifying archetypical firms by scope, structure, and integration.

Figure 2 graphs these structures on ordinal scales measuring various structure variables plus scope and external linkages.

4.1. *The Individual Inventor and the Stand-Alone Laboratory*

Many still cling to the notion that the individual inventor, standing outside of an organization, is responsible for the lion's share of innovation in today's economy. This myth springs in part from the first industrial revolution when invention was the province of the individual or pairs. But since the last quarter of the 19th century and the emergence of R&D labs, and more recently venture capital, innovation has become more the domain of organizations, not individuals.[28]

The problems that the inventor-entrepreneurs have in extracting value from new technology are considerable. However, when an inventor (or an enterprise) can rely on the instruments of intellectual property protection to protect invention from imitation, theory suggests that the inventor can appropriate a substantial fraction of the invention's market value. When property rights are weak (the normal case), the inventors' ability to capture value are dramatically circumscribed (Teece, 1986). In the case where the individual inventor has a patent but little else, then the patent holder's options include: (i) licensing the technology to incumbent firms who already have the necessary complementary assets in place; (ii) using the patent as collateral to raise debt funds to help develop an organization to exploit the technology; (iii) exchanging the patent for equity in a start-up, equity-funded firm; (iv) exchanging the patent for equity in an established firm.

None of these options avoid the problem of valuing the patent and the concomitant leakage problems which this process exposes. Valuation is likely to require disclosure and the triggering of what Arrow (1971, p. 152) has referred to as the *fundamental paradox* of information: Its value for the purchaser is not known until one has the information, but then one has in effect acquired it without cost. While this problem is somewhat softened when there is good patent protection, most non-industrial providers of funds are going to need technical experts to evaluate the technology, in which case the risk of leakage remains. A wealthy inventor can of course overcome some of these problems by signaling value to financiers and joint venture partners through providing collateral, performance guarantees, or by co-investing.

---

[28] That is not to say that individual inventors are not sometimes very important and very successful. My argument is that when they are successful commercially, it is generally in an organizational setting.

If imitation is easy, the problem are more difficult. In those instances the granting of low royalty, non-exclusive output-based licenses (i.e. royalties rather than up-front fees) are likely to yield higher rents to the inventor. In this way, the inventor does not provide much incentive for firms to invent around (in the case of a weak patent) or otherwise invest resources in imitation; these costs can be extracted in part by the licensor.

Even when the valuation problem is overcome the parties must meet another challenge — transferring the technology to the buyers. As discussed earlier, the tacit nature of knowledge (which helps make imitation difficult) also makes transfer difficult (Teece, 1980, 1982). Hence the circumstances where imitation is difficult are also the circumstances where transfer is often difficult. The only clear circumstance where the inventor can succeed alone is when (1) the technology is well protected by intellectual property law, (2) the technology can be transferred from the inventor to an organization, and (3) the inventor already has great wealth. The circumstances where these factors occur together is likely to be relatively rare.

The stand-alone research laboratory faces many of the same challenges as the individual inventor. The main difference is that the laboratory can bring multiple organizational skills to bear on the R&D process, and the probabilities of fusing multiple technologies is likely to be enhanced from the bringing together of multiple research disciplines. Moreover, if scale economies exist in R&D, the laboratory is better able to capture these than the individual. But the framework would suggest that stand-alone laboratories cannot be viable, unless they happen to work in areas where strong intellectual property protection is assured.[29]

4.2. Multiproduct, Integrated, Hierarchical Firms

It is not uncommon to find such enterprises on the industrial scene. N.V. Phillips and General Motors in the 1980s were good examples. Hierarchical is meant to signal the presence of bureaucratic decisions, and absence of a powerful change culture and high-powered incentives. Such enterprises are also likely to be internally focused. As a consequence, external changes in the market as well as in the science and technology establishment are unlikely to get recognized in a timely fashion. Decision making is slow and ponderous.

---

[29] Even setting aside protection issues, stand-alone R&D laboratories have problems in developing information channels to their sponsors to understand their sponsors' needs, and in transferring technology back to the sponsor if in fact useful technology is developed. Moreover, because of leakage problems, competitors are likely to be reluctant to use a common R&D laboratory.

However, if such organizations are able to achieve what Downs (1967, p. 160) calls "breakout" — where a new organization, possibly a new venture division, is set up for a special task — it may be able to overcome the anti-innovation bias, at least temporarily. Burgelman (1984) has argued that "autonomous strategic behavior" can take place inside large firms, if management sets up the appropriate internal structures. The range of enabling structures is quite large and includes venture teams' "skunk-works," new venture divisions and the like. The suitability of these various structures depends on a variety of technological, market and organizational factors which will not be explored here.

Nevertheless, integrated firms overcome some basic problems associated with relying on an economy of Lilliputian firms. Integrated firms can readily support systemic innovation as discussed earlier. They can also adapt to uncertainty (Williamson, 1975) in a sequential fashion as events unfold. (Managerial hierarchies are often better at adjudicating disputes inside the firm than courts are at adjudicating disputes between and among firms.) Large multiproduct, multidivisional integrated firms can take on large projects and can help set standards important to the continued evolution of a technology. In the early years of the PC industry, IBM drove floppy-disk drive capacity. The 5.25 in. floppy diskettes initially held 180 KB each when IBM introduced its PC in 1981. By 1983, capacity had doubled to 360 KB, and a year later had increased to 1.44 MB. But they stayed stuck at 1.44 MB for over a decade. The explanation does not lie in inherent limits to the technology, but in IBM's declining ability to coordinate choices of follow-along standards. A new standard requires PC manufacturers to agree to accommodate it in their machines, that diskette manufacturers tool up for it, and that software publishers agree to supply programs in the new format. IBM's leadership is no longer sufficient to convert the industry over.[30]

There are also appropriability benefits. If it is a process technology which is at issue, the vertically integrated firm is capable of using the technology in-house and taking profits not by selling the technology directly, but by selling products that embody or use the process. Thus inasmuch as this type of firm does not have to utilize the market for know-how to capture value from the technology, the appropriability problem is softened. Inasmuch as contracting is internal, specialized assets are protected and recontracting hazards are attenuated. The technology transfer process is likely to be internal, so the tacitness problem is eased considerably, as the redeployment of personnel internally raises far fewer default issues than does external redeployment.

---

[30] I wish to thank Henry Chesbrough for helping develop the facts on this point.

Such firms are likely to need alliance structures in order to tap into external sources of new knowledge. If large integrated firms are able to successfully team up with other firms[31] that have the entrepreneurial structures in place to promote creativity, then such firms are likely to be able to access a pipeline of new product and process concepts. The benefits here are a corollary to the benefits associated with strategic alliances.[32] However, the absence of a change culture and an outward orientation mean that such relationships may not be sought.

4.3. *High Flex "Silicon Valley"-Type Firms*

The distinguishing features of such firms are that they will possess a change culture upon which there is great consensus.[33] They will have shallow hierarchies and significant local autonomy. Such firms will resist the hierarchical accouterments of seniority and rank found in Category 2 above, and they will resist functional specialization which restricts the flow of ideas and destroys the sense of commonality of purpose. Examples of firms that started this way and still reflect much of this style are Intel, Hewlett Packard, Sun Microsystems, Motorola, Raychem, Genentech, and 3M.

Decision making in these firms is usually simple and informal. Communication and coordination among functions is relatively quick and open. Early on in their development, one or two key individuals, typically the founders, make the key decisions. In the early stages, these firms, however, typically do not have a steady stream of internally generated cash with which to fund new opportunities. Hence, connections to the venture capital community or to other firms with cash available are important. These firms are likely to be highly innovative. But they are also likely to be cash-constrained. Those that are not, are likely to do very well.

---

[31] Such as the one described in VI.3.

[32] It is important to recognize, based on historical experience in the United States in the period up to 1980, that the acquisition of a multiproduct, integrated, hierarchical company by high-flex "Silicon Valley"-type company is often extremely difficult to achieve without destroying the creative and entrepreneurial capacity of the small companies. This is because the organizational controls of the large organization tend to destroy the innovative capacities of small firms, as discussed earlier.

[33] Indicative of this spirit is a statement by Andy Grove, CEO of Intel, "You need to try to do the impossible, to anticipate the unexpected. And when the unexpected happens, you should double your efforts to make order from the disorder it creates in your life. The motto I am advocating is, Let chaos reign, then rein in chaos. Does that mean that you shouldn't plan? Not at all. You need to plan the way a fire department plans. It cannot anticipate fires, so it has to shape a flexible organization that is capable of responding to unpredictable events."

The highly specialized nature of such firms and the absence of good intellectual property protection create strategic risks. The ability to capture the rents from innovation is by no means assured. But if such firms are able to develop and manage their external relationships without losing their distinct culture and responsive structures, then many of the problems stemming from uncertainty,[34] indivisibilities,[35] inappropriability,[36] asset specificity,[37] and tacitness[38] can be overcome, while organizational failure issues are held at a distance because much is outsourced and alliances are used frequently. By providing considerable autonomy and strong incentives, this organizational form is likely to be able to support many different types of innovation.

4.4. *Virtual Corporations*

The term virtual corporation has been used in business parlence in the 1980s and 1990s to refer to business enterprises that subcontract anything and everything.

---

[34] Primary uncertainty can never be reduced, but organizations can adapt to it. Secondary uncertainty, due to ignorance of complementary investment plans, can obviously be much reduced through bilateral agreements which involve mutual commitments and the maintenance of reciprocity through the exchange of hostages (Williamson, 1985).

[35] It is perhaps in the realm of indivisibilities that bilateral exchange comes closest to the perfect solution of a market failure problem. As discussed elsewhere (Teece, 1980, 1982), interfirm agreements are a relatively straightforward way to access complementary assets, particularly if they are already in place, are in excess capacity, and do not involve a high degree of asset specificity. Even when asset specificity is involved, the incentives for opportunistic recontracting can be attenuated by reputation effects, repeat contracting, or exchange of hostages.

[36] Inasmuch as firms can use bilateral contracts to access existing industry capacities so that new capacity does not have to be put in place de novo, product commercialization time can be reduced and lead time lengthened. Thus a major strategic advantage, lead time, can often be enhanced through the use of bilateral contracts. While the innovator may have to share part of the rent stream with the provider of complementary assets, investment risk for the innovator is typically reduced and imitators can be outpaced.

[37] Bilateral contracts enable specialized assets to be protected. While the degree of protection may not be as great as is provided under vertical integration, it is likely to be significantly higher than under unilateral contracts. A "hostage," or its economic equivalent, including specific investments which are mutually dependent, can be used to help support exchange. Thus if a manufacturer installs dedicated equipment to serve the developer, and the developer makes specialized investments which dovetail with the manufacturer, both can be assured that transactions will have a better chance of continuing in the face of adversity or superior opportunities.

[38] Tacitness is less a problem if a bilateral relationship exists, particularly if it is supported by equity. If repeated transactions are contemplated, spillovers and costs associated with seconding technical staff are less severe as adjustments can be made in subsequent transactions, as long as spillovers and costs are perceived similarly by both parties.

A key question is whether the innovative capacities of such companies are impaired by the absence of in-house manufacturing and other capabilities. Virtual corporations are of course smaller than they might otherwise be (by virtue of the absence of vertical integration) and thus generally have shallow hierarchies. They might well have innovative cultures and external linkages to competent manufacturers.

Defined this way, virtuals have the capacity to be very creative and to excel at early stage innovation activities. If they do indeed establish a strong alliance with a competent manufacturer, they may also have the capacity to be first to market, despite the absence of the requisite internal capabilities.

The hazards associated with virtual structures are not unlike the hazards facing the individual inventor. The problem is that unless the firm is operating in a regime of tight appropriability, the innovator may not be able to capture value from the innovation, and the manufacturer, by integrating into research and distribution, is likely to become the firm's competitor (Teece, 1986). Accordingly, the virtual corporation is not seen to be a viable long-run organizational form, except in limited circumstances.

The RCA color television experience demonstrates the downside of the *virtual* approach to innovation.[39] When RCA developed the color television, it made no attempt to keep the innovation to itself.[40] Rather, it licensed its color TV technology aggressively, and outsourced the manufacturing of key components of the television itself. It utilized a network of retailers to market the sets. Its licensees, however (particularly the Japanese licensees), made major investments in the integration of the television components, and then integrated forward and made the entire television set. In the 1970s, RCA had to abandon the manufacturing and development of color television sets, leaving the Japanese as world leaders in consumer electronics.

The RCA experience is not an anomaly. There are real risks in contracting everything out to the market and functioning as the hub or nexus of contracts. Research and development markets, in particular, are fraught with contractual hazards that undercut the ability of firms to coordinate arms-length purchases of R&D through markets (Teece, 1988). Consider the problem of using fixed price contracts to develop new products and processes. With fixed price contracts, one hazard is the inability to adequately specify in advance the desired output of the contract. Another hazard is that, if the R&D supplier shares too much

---

[39] See Yamamura and Vendenberg (1986). I am not suggesting that RCA was or is a virtual organization; but merely that at various times it has embraced key elements of the virtual approach to innovation.

[40] Peters (1990), for example, advises firms to License your most advanced technology as well as Subcontract anything and everything.

knowledge ex ante, the buying firm can appropriate the knowledge without any payment. A third concern is the specific nature of most R&D activity. The R&D supplier and buyer confront hold-up hazards from each other, and there are strong lock-in effects once a relationship is begun. These hazards are softened with cost-plus contracts, but these contracts create other problems. The supplying R&D firm has no incentive to control costs, which creates the possibility of a blank check agreement for the buyer.

For these reasons, R&D is usually linked with manufacturing inside the firm.[41] For a similar set of reasons, the marketing function is also joined with these two functions. The desired output of an R&D process depends critically on the perceived user requirements for the product. This is highly impacted information, which cannot be contracted for in advance. And usually there is iteration between the emerging design and user reactions to the design, requiring an ongoing flow of information between the marketing and R&D functions. As a result, firms find it necessary to combine these complementary functions, not through the high-powered incentives of the market, but through the low-powered incentives of the firm.

Another dimension of this is that while markets are very efficient at coordinating adjustments where the technological coordination is low in terms of the interdependence of one technology on another, as the technologies become more interdependent, the hazards of coordinating through the market rise quickly. Internal organization often incurs greater costs than markets when technological interdependence is low. While coordination costs do rise as interdependence grows, those costs rise much more slowly than the market's costs. Accordingly, as interdependence rises, more integrated structures displace virtuals. Clearly, virtual is not always virtuous (Chesbrough and Teece, 1996).

4.5. *Conglomerates*

In the framework developed here, the conglomerate is not an especially distinctive organizational form. It is likely to be decentralized, and this favors the innovation process. It can also use the internal capital market to fund the development of new technologies. However, the importance of this is likely to be reduced the more (i) access to capital, including venture capital, is available for new stand-alone businesses, and (ii) headquarters management acts much like external

---

[41] Mowery (1982) also finds that the contract research laboratories in the first half of the 20th century confined their work to simple testing and materials analysis, while internal R&D laboratories conducted the more sophisticated and firm-specific research.

capital market agents. Accordingly, on grounds of access to capital and diversity of activities, one would not expect the conglomerate to look too different from a portfolio of stand-alone firms with respect to its innovative capacity.[42]

However, there are two ways in which one might expect the conglomerate to underperform a portfolio of stand-alone firms with respect to innovation. One is that it is difficult for conglomerates to develop distinctive company-wide corporate cultures. Accordingly, it may be quite difficult to build a strong internal change culture at the corporate level. Certainly, as compared to a stand-alone firm, getting across to employees the notion that the unit must ultimately "stand on its own bottom" will be quite a challenge. As a consequence free riding may well be accentuated. Likewise, the design of high-powered incentives for top management and employees will be hindered by the absence of an equity instrument geared to divisional performance. In short, the conglomerate does not appear to offer distinctive advantages in environments characterized by rapid technological change.

4.6. *Alliance Enterprise*

We define an alliance enterprise as a *virtual corporation* that has developed strong commitments to other enterprises, usually through equity-based links to affiliated enterprises lying upstream, downstream, horizontal, and lateral from its core business. Such structures include consortia (e.g. Airbus, Sematech) as well as semipermanent teaming arrangements that transcend particular projects. Many new biotech firms in the United States are heavily alliance-dependent to fund their R&D move drugs to the market.

The viability and desirability of alliances and other external linkage arrangements depend, not just on the efficacy of this form of contract, but also on the resources/capabilities which can be accessed in this fashion. Alliances were essential in the 1980s and 1990s to the pharmaceutical industry as a mechanism to tap into the drug development capabilities of new biotech firms. Since the biotechnology revolution has occurred outside the organizational gambit of the

---

[42] There has been very little discussion of the relationship between the conglomerate and technological innovation. The arguments advanced by Williamson (1975) that conglomerate firms possess miniature capital markets would suggest that the conglomerate is an ideal form for identifying new investment opportunities, including process and product innovations, and funding them until they become cash-flow positive. In the absence of market-for-venture capital, this argument would seem to imply that the conglomerate form ought to be associated with a stream of new product and process launches. The best evidence (Kline, 1995) indicates that relative to appropriately defined yardsticks, conglomerates did not underinvest in R&D, and indeed before 1970 they may well have overinvested.

established pharmaceutical industry, alliances have been embued with virtues they might not otherwise possess. Put differently, the value of a contract can easily be confused with what it enables one to access. The comparative institutional approach used here imputes to the alliance only that which it can uniquely access as compared to other arrangements.

5. Matching Innovation and Organizational Archetypes[43]

The diversity of organizational forms observed is semipermanent and not a transitional feature of modern industrial economies. The diversity of observed forms in and of itself suggests that different organizational arrangements are suited to different types of competitive environments and differing types of innovation.

One cannot possibly expect to be comprehensive in developing a taxonomy of innovations and organizational archetypes. However, illustrations are developed below which involve matching organizational form to the locus of existing capabilities, and to the type of innovation (autonomous or systemic).

As the interdependence between technologies increases, pure market forms are less effective at achieving the requisite coordination. The more systemic the innovation, the greater the interdependence. Exposure to recontracting hazards is likely to be frequent.

The discussion in Sec. 4.4 noted the distinction between autonomous and systemic innovation. Autonomous innovations (Teece, 1984) create improved products and processes that fit comfortably into existing systems. These innovations not only fit well within current industry standards, but they reinforce those standards. An example would be the introduction of a faster microprocessor using the same architecture, such as the Intel 80×86/Pentium family. Systemic innovations, however, change technological requirements and offer new opportunities so that the resulting configuration of both the innovation and its related technologies (which comprise a system of technology) are different; for example, audio CD plays require the abandonment of vinyl records and the manufacture of CD discs. Innovations of this type require that the design of the subsystems be coordinated in order for the gains from the innovation to be realized. Since these innovations span current technology boundaries, a complex coordination problem arises.

The other key dimension in organization form is the extent to which the capabilities needed to exploit the innovation exist within the firm already, and if

---

[43] This section draws in part on Chesbrough and Teece (1996).

autonomous   systemic

	autonomous	systemic
Capabilities Exist Inhouse	**S**	**M**
Capabilities Exist Outside	**V**	**A**
Capabilities Must be Created	**A,S**	**S**

Key:

S= Silicon Valley type

M= Multiproduct integrated

A= Alliances (virtual with equity)

V= Virtual (outsource everything & anything)

Fig. 3. A proposed matrix of innovation, capabilities and preferred organization forms.

not, whether those capabilities are available outside the firm. It has been argued elsewhere (Teece *et al.* 1994) that the firm is best regarded as a bundle of distinctive capabilities that enables it to perform functions more efficiently than its historical competitors. The presence or absence of critical complementary assets affects the prospects for appropriating the gains from innovation when the appropriability regime is not tight (Teece, 1986). These two dimensions motivate the simple framework presented in Fig. 3.

5.1. *Autonomous Innovation*

Alliances and virtual structures will work well when the technology can be sourced externally, and the high-flex Silicon Valley-type will work well if it must be developed internally. When the technology can be sourced externally, the required coordination takes place with known technologies, so that no special hazards in contracting arise and adjustments to related technologies to realize the benefits of innovation are minimal. Indeed, when firms use bureaucratic centralized structures inappropriately to manage autonomous innovations, small firms and more decentralized large firms are likely to outperform them.

As noted, there are important nuances with respect to the particulars of how to organize for autonomous innovation. (1) The first circumstance is when the technology exploits capabilities already present within the firm. In these circumstances, internal development by high-flex Silicon Valley-type firms will work well. (An example here would be the introduction of a faster microprocessor using the same architecture, such as the Intel 80 × 86/Pentium family.) (2) The second is when innovation remains autonomous, but exploitation requires the firm to access capabilities outside its boundaries. Innovating firms must craft relational structures such as alliances to obtain access, thereby sharing the gains from innovation. Such firms must also overcome hold-up problems between the innovator and the owner of relevant outside capabilities. This is where virtual structures are often virtuous. Sun Microsystems pursued this strategy quite successfully with its SPARC microprocessor architecture. Sun defined the basic architecture, and then licensed out the design to other firms. This strategy induced enough entry by SPARC licensees to develop a standard, and attracted outside software developers to support the architecture. Sun later split its organization so that its hardware was separated from its software and its microprocessor design.[44]

(3) A third circumstance is when innovation remains autonomous, but requires new capabilities to be created to exploit its potential. Virtual structures are not quite enough. Consider biotechnology. New products can continue to pass through the same regulatory procedures and sell to physicians through the same marketing and distribution channels as yesterday's ethical drugs. But the underlying technology draws from a different science base. Here, internal development or alliances with equity are required to manage contractual problems between the young biotechnology companies developing new products and the older pharmaceutical companies seeking to add new products to their lineup. These additional structures provide a credible ex ante basis for dividing the gains from innovation between the two types of firms.[45]

---

[44] Note that Sun's strategy of defining a standard microprocessor architecture, and then licensing it, created a well-defined technical interface and resulted in transforming what would have been a systemic innovation to an autonomous innovation. Sun's approach facilitated decentralized innovation around its standard. The downside to this approach was experienced by IBM in the PC market.

[45] Pisano (1988) detailed the practice of using joint equity agreements to facilitate these relations in the biotechnology industry.

5.2. *Systemic Innovations*

By their nature, systemic innovations require coordinated adjustment throughout the system to realize the gains from innovation. The potential from systemic innovations cannot be fully realized until adjustments are made throughout the system. Unaffiliated enterprises with weak internal integration will not suffice. The problem is that tight coordination is needed. Without the close integration of personnel, necessary coordination may be forsaken. Property rights issues may also arise if multiple enterprises are involved. Information sharing can be reduced or biased, as each seeks to get the most at the expense of the other. The party that commits first can be held-up by the other parties, while the party that waits until the others have committed themselves can extract more rents from the other partners. Even if such opportunism is contained, the rate of advance of complementary technologies may not be properly matched, so that product release dates slip and co-investment schedules of the parties are mismatched.

Lockheed's failure in the wide-bodied civilian airliner market can be attributed in part to the debacle it had with Rolls Royce. Rolls Royce committed to develop the RB-211 engine to power the L-1011, but technical problems that took time to be revealed to Lockheed caused major delays in commercialization, and took both Lockheed and Rolls Royce into bankruptcy. Similarly, GM's success with the diesel electric locomotive, and the failure of the GE/Alco co-development efforts can properly be tied to the inability of GE and Alcoa to properly coordinate and integrate their development efforts (Marx, 1976).

What is needed to successfully develop and commercialize systemic innovations are institutions with low-powered incentives, where information can be freely shared without worry of expropriation, where entities can commit themselves and not be exploited by that commitment, and where disputes can be monitored and resolved in a timely way. This is precisely what multi-product integrated firms achieve.

While systemic innovation favors integrated structures from a coordination perspective, it may nevertheless be the case that the relevant technological capabilities are resident in unaffiliated enterprises.[46] Alliances are then the best arrangement. Virtuals and even small Silicon Valley-type firms will not survive. NeXT and MIPS, for example, were dependent of the autonomous decisions of other firms in order to be able to realize the benefit of their technology. When these other firms delayed their supporting investments, each company was forced to narrow

---

[46] For a discussion of capabilities, see Teece and Pisano (1994), Teece *et al.* (1997).

its focus and retrench.[47] This is where larger firms may have an advantage, by being able to secure minority investment positions in smaller firms with necessary capabilities, or by using their scale to create sufficient momentum so that complementary innovations are developed.[48] Japanese *keiretsu* commonly leverage strong relationships to access needed capabilities outside the firm, and they fit this model. For example, Toyota's successful introduction of the *kanban* production system (a truly systemic innovation) required tremendous coordination with its network of suppliers. Since Toyota was much larger than its suppliers, and because until recently it was the largest customer of virtually all of its suppliers, it had sufficient leverage to compel its suppliers to make radical changes to their business practices without exposing itself to hold-up.[49]

Another circumstance considered is where the systemic innovation requires entirely new capabilities in order for the innovation's potential to be realized. This is precisely the situation Chandler (1990) describes in *Scale and Scope* for the leading industries of the late 19th and early 20th centuries. The leading industries of that era — chemicals, steel, and railroads — were all transformed by systemic innovation (Teece, 1993). The winners were the companies that made major investments to shape the markets, and simply did not rely upon them. Today one sees leading companies like Intel and Microsoft making extensive investments to enhance their current capabilities and spur the creation of new ones.[50] Network arrangements among unaffiliated enterprises are exactly the wrong

---

[47] NeXT has completely withdrawn from the hardware side of its workstation business, focusing entirely on its NeXTStep operating system. MIPS was acquired by Silicon Graphics, and is no longer a significant player as a workstation microprocessor architecture developer.

[48] The contrast between MIPS and DEC's Alpha chip is one example. By committing to supply Alpha on its own workstations, DEC is gathering greater commitment from third-party developers than did MIPS. Apple and IBM's PowerPC chip are garnering even more support, as Apple and IBM together claim to have shipped over one million systems with the PowerPC chip. Scale and integration are the key differences here.

[49] According to Gerlach (1992), Japanese manufacturers also place managers on the boards of its supplier firms and usually share their main bank with them. This allows a manufacturer such as Toyota to wield control over the supplier's strategic decisions and control the supplier's access to capital without requiring Toyota to have complete ownership of its suppliers. It is this which creates functional control. These structures provide a blend of market incentives (high-powered incentives, external measures of prices, profits and value added) with internal coordination capability.

[50] Intel, for example, has just committed itself to building the largest fab in the world in New Mexico to improve its manufacturing prowess. Microsoft is competing in virtually every segment of the PC software business with internally-developed products, rather than licensing or buying outside products. It recently announced plans to spend over $900 million in its current fiscal year, a 50% increase over last year's spending (San Francisco Chronicle, September 10, 1994, p. D2).

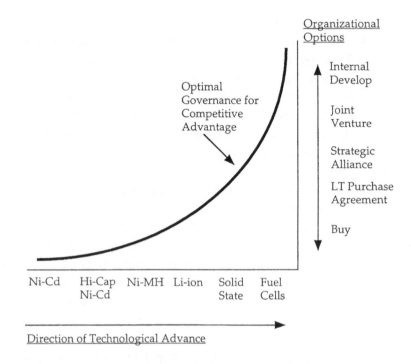

Fig. 4. Available technologies and organizational options for Motorola in battery cell technology.

organizational strategy when firms are trying to commercialize and appropriate the gains of systemic innovation. An excellent illustration of this is an example often held to support the benefits of decentralization — the IBM PC. While the PC's early years highlighted the benefits of the *virtual* approach, the passage of more time has revealed the downside of that approach. This example is examined elsewhere (Chesbrough and Teece, 1996).

The process of matching organizational form to underlying technological and market conditions is of course a dynamic one. This aspect is somewhat expressed in Fig. 4. An illustration of some of the dynamics is provided by Motorola which continues to innovate in hand-held communication devices, including cellular phones. Future improvements on cellphone designs, and in particular, weight reduction and extended operation, requires lighter and more long-lived batteries. Motorola is in a position to advance these technologies through its own internal R&D programs, which have historically been very productive. As the older more established battery technologies like Nickel Cadmium have been widely diffused, Motorola can reasonably rely on outsourcing from numerous existing suppliers to access its requirements in the Ni–Cd domain. However, solid state and fuel cells are still in their infancy as technologies to support personal communication devices. Moreover, Motorola is as well placed as others to advance the development of such technologies. With reliance on unaffiliated parties leading to obvious contractual hazards (Teece, 1988), internal development, or at the minimum joint venture development, is suggested for such technologies. In Fig. 4, this suggests that desirable governance arrangements will migrate toward *internal development* as the technology becomes more *state-of-the-art* and the population of outsider vendors diminishes.[51] It is likely to do so one confronts more advanced technological options.

6. Conclusions

If this analysis is correct, it has rather strong implications for theory building, for management, and for public policy. With respect to theory building, it suggests the inadequacy of standard economic approaches that have market structure as the key if not the only determinant of the rate and direction of innovation. Clearly, such approaches are poor guides to policy. At the minimum, firm boundaries (the level of integration), the structure of financial markets, and formal and informal organizational structure must be recognized as major determinants. This paper indicates that firm organization (not just product market structure) is an important determinant of innovation, a point made by Williamson (1975) that has largely gone unheeded by industrial organization economists.

The framework developed here is designed to shift the market structure — innovation debate in industrial organization beyond the domain where Schumpeter (1942), Galbraith (1952), Mansfield (1968), Scherer (1980) and others have put it, and into a new domain where internal structure, interfirm agreements, and capital market structures attain new significance. This also has obvious policy significance. The opening up of financial markets and the emergence of a vibrant venture capital industry have "provided new forms of finance for innovative activity again on a scale never seen before, effectively reducing barriers to innovative, competitive entry, across the industrialized world" (Rybczynski, 1993). Put differently, product market structure is not the main and possibly not the key factor in determining the rate and direction of innovation.

The framework also has strong implications for business history. It suggests the possible viability of new hybrid organizational arrangement — such as complex

---

[51] LT purchase agreement in Fig. 4 is an abbreviation for long-term agreement.

forms of interfirm agreements linking firms with complementary capabilities and capacities — over both the integrated alternatives and the small firm alternatives. These organizational forms may well represent a new and dramatic organizational innovation in business history. Firms are continuing to learn how and when to use them, and scholars are trying to understand them. In retrospect, the emergence and growth of these new forms, dating from about 1970, may turn out to be as significant an organizational innovation as the moving assembly line and the multidivisional firm.

References

A. Alchien and H. Demsetz, Production, Information Cost, and Economic Organizations, *American Economic Review* 62 (1972), 777–795.

H. Armour and D.J. Teece, Organizational Structure and Economic Performance: A Test of the Multidivisional Hypothesis, *The Bell Journal of Economics* 9(2) (1978), 106–122.

K.J. Arrow, *Essays in the Theory of Risk-Bearing* (North-Holland, Amsterdam, New York, 1971).

K.J. Arrow, *The Limits of Organization* (Norton, New York, 1974).

K.J. Arrow, Technical Information and Industrial Structure, *Industrial and Corporate Change* 5(2) (1996).

R.A. Burgelman, Designs for Corporate Entrepreneurship, *California Management Review* 26(3) (Spring 1984), 154–166.

H.W. Chesbrough and D.J. Teece, When is Virtual Virtuous: Organizing for Innovation, *Harvard Business Review*, January–February 1996.

R. Coase, Nature of Firm, *Economica* 4, pp. 386–405.

M. Crozier, *The Bureaucratic Phenomenon* (University of Chicago Press, Chicago, 1964).

R.H. Day, G. Eliasson and C. Wihlborg (eds.), *The Markets for Innovation, Ownership and Control* (North-Holland, Amsterdam, New York, 1993).

T.E. Deal and A. Kennedy, *Corporate Culture* (Addison-Wesley, Reading, MA, 1982).

G. Dosi, Technological Paradigms and Technological Trajectories, *Research Policy*, 1982a.

G. Dosi, Technological Paradigms and Technological Trajectories: A Suggested Interpretation of the Determinants and Directions of Technical Change, *Research Policy* 11(3) (June 1982b), 147–162.

G. Dosi, C. Freeman, R. Nelson, G. Silverberg and L. Soete, *Technical Change and Economic Theory* (Pinter, London, 1988).

A. Downs, *Inside Bureaucracy* (Little Brown, Boston, 1967).

E. Fama, Efficient Capital Markets: A Review of Theory and Empirical Work, *American Economic Review* 60 (1970), 163–174.

M. Frankel, Obsolence and Technological Change in a Maturing Economy, *American Economic Review*, 1955.

J.K. Galbraith, *American Capitalism* (Houghton-Mifflin, Boston, 1952).

M.L. Gerlach, *Alliance Capitalism: The Social Organization of Japanese Business* (University of California Press, Berkeley, 1992).

B. Holmström, Agency Costs and Innovation, in R.H. Day *et al.*, *The Markets for Innovation, Ownership and Control* (North-Holland, Amsterdam, New York, 1993).

Imai, Japan's Corporate Networks, unpublished working paper (Hitotsubashi University, Tokyo, 1988).

C. Jensen, Eclipse of the Public Corporation, *Harvard Business Review* 67(5) (September–October 1989), 61–74.

D. Kahneman and D. Lovallo, Timid Decisions and Bold Forecasts: A Cognitive Perspective on Risk Taking, in R. Rumelt, D. Schendel and D. Teece (eds.), *Fundamental Issues in Strategy* (Harvard Business School Press, Boston, MA, 1990).

N. Kay, Industrial Structure, Rivalry, and Innovation: Theory and Evidence, undated working paper, Department of Economics (Herriot-Watt University, Edinburgh, Scotland).

C.P. Kindleberger, *Economic Growth in France and Britain, 1851–1950* (Harvard University Press, Cambridge, MA, 1964).

P. Kline, Conglomerate Organizations and Economic Performance: Evidence from the 1960s, unpublished doctoral dissertation (University of California, Berkeley, 1995).

F. Kodama, Japanese Innovation in Mechatronics Technology, *Science and Public Policy* 13(1) (1986), 44–52.

T.C. Koopmans, *Three Essays in the State of Economic Science* (McGraw-Hill, New York, 1957).

R. Levin, A. Klevorick, R. Nelson and S. Winter, Appropriating the Returns from Industrial R&D, Brookings Papers on Economic Activity, 1987.

A.D. Little, *Management Perspectives on Innovation* (Harvard University Press, Cambridge, MA, 1985).

E. Mansfield, *The Economics of Technical Change* (Norton, New York, 1968).

J. March and Z. Shapira, Managerial Perspectives on Risk and Risk Taking, *Management Science* 33(11) (1987), 1404–1418.

T. Marx, Vertical Integration in the Diesel-Electric Locomotive Building Industry: A Study in Market Failures, *Nebraska Journal of Economics and Business* 15(4) (Autumn 1976), 37–51.

D. Mowery, The Relationship between Contractual and Intrafirm Forms of Industrial Research in American Manufacturing, 1900–1940, *Exploration in Economic History* (October 1982), 351–374.

R.R. Nelson and S.G. Winter, In Search of a Useful Theory of Innovations, *Research Policy* 6(1) (1977), 36–76.

R.R. Nelson and S.G. Winter, *An Evolutionary Theory of Economic Change* (Harvard University Press, Cambridge, MA, 1982).

D. North, *Institutions, Institutional Change, and Economic Performance* (Cambridge University Press, Cambridge, 1990).

C.A. O'Reilly, Corporate Culture Considerations Based on an Empirical Study of High Growth Firms in Silicon Valley, *Economia Aziendale*, Vol. III, 3 (1989).

K. Pavitt, M. Robson and J. Townsend, Accumulation, Diversification and Organisation of Technological Activities in U.K. Companies, 1945–1983, in M. Dodgson (ed.), *Technology Strategy and the Firm* (Longman, London, 1989).

T. Peters, Get Innovative or Get Dead, *California Management Review* (Fall 1990), 9–21.

T. Peters and R. Waterman, In Search of Excellence, 1982.

G.P. Pisano, Innovation through Markets, Hierarchies, and Joint Ventures: Technology Strategy and Collaborative Arrangements in the Biotechnology Industry, unpublished Ph.D. dissertation, Haas School of Business (University of California, Berkeley, 1988).

M. Polanyi, *Personal Knowledge: Toward a Post Critical Philosophy* (Harper and Row, New York, 1962).

G.B. Richardson, *Information and Investment* (Oxford University Press, Oxford, 1990).

T. Rybczynski, Innovative Activity and Venture Financing: Access to Markets and Opportunities in Japan, the U.S. and Europe, in Day *et al.*, *The Market for Innovation, Ownership and Control* (North-Holland, Amsterdam, New York, 1993).

F.M. Scherer, *Industrial Market Structure and Economic Performance*, 2nd edn. (Rand McNally, Chicago, 1980).

J.A. Schumpeter, *The Theory of Economic Development* (Harvard University Press, Cambridge, MA, 1934).

J.A. Schumpeter, *Capitalism, Socialism and Democracy* (McGraw-Hill, New York, 1942).

H. Schwartz and S. Davis, Matching Corporate Culture and Business Strategy, *Organizational Dynamics* (1981), 30–48.

H. Simon, Decision Making and Organizational Design, in D.S. Pugh (ed.), *Organizational Theory* (Penguin, London, 1973).

D.J. Teece, Technology Transfer by Multinational Firms: The Resource Cost of Transferring Technological Know-How, *Economic Journal* 87(346) (June 1977), 242–261.

D.J. Teece, Economics of Scope and the Scope of the Enterprise, *Journal of Economic Behavior and Organization* 1(3) (1980), 223–247.

D.J. Teece, Toward an Economic Theory of the Multiproduct Firms, *Journal of Economic Behavior and Organization* 3(1) (1982), 39–63.

D.J. Teece, Economic Analysis and Strategic Management, *California Management Review* 26(3) (Spring 1984), 87–110.

D.J. Teece, Profiting from Technological Innovation, *Research Policy* 15(6) (1986), 285–306.

D.J. Teece, The Nature of the Firm and Technological Change, in G. Dosi *et al.* (eds.), *Technical Change and Economic Theory* (Pinter, London, 1988).

D.J. Teece, The Dynamics of Industrial Capitalism: Perspectives on Alfred Chandler's Scale and Scope, *Journal of Economic Literature* 31 (March 1993).

D.J. Teece and G. Pisano, The Dynamic Capabilities of Firms: An Introduction, *Industrial and Corporate Change* 3(3) (1994).

D.J. Teece, G. Pisano and A. Shuen, Dynamic Capabilities and Strategic Management, *Strategic Management Journal* (1997), forthcoming.

D.J. Teece, R. Rumelt, G. Dosi and S. Winter, Understanding Corporate Coherence: Theory and Evidence, *Journal of Economic Behavior and Organization* 23 (1994), 1–30.

T. Veblen, Professor Clark's Economics, in E.K. Hunt and J. Schwartz, *A Critique of Economic Theory*, 1972.

O.E. Williamson, *Markets and Hierarchies* (Free Press, New York, 1975).

O.E. Williamson, *The Economic Institutions of Capitalism* (Free Press, New York, 1985).

O.E. Williamson, Corporate Finance and Corporate Governance, *Journal of Finance* 43 (July 1988), 567–591.

O.E. Williamson, *The Mechanisms of Governance* (Oxford University Press, New York, 1996).

S.G. Winter, Knowledge and Competence as Strategic Assets, in D. Teece (ed.), *The Competitive Challenge: Strategies for Industrial Innovation and Renewal* (Ballinger, Cambridge, MA, 1987).

K. Yamamura and J. Vandenberg, Japan's Rapid Growth Policy on Trial: The Television Case, in G. Saxonhouse and K. Yamamura (eds.), *Law and Trade Issues of the Japanese Economy: American and Japanese Perspectives* (University of Washington Press, Seattle, WA, 1986).

III

LICENSING, TECHNOLOGY TRANSFER, AND THE MARKET FOR KNOW-HOW

When is Virtual Virtuous?

Organizing for Innovation

Henry W. Chesbrough* and David J. Teece

1. Introduction

Champions of virtual corporations are urging managers to subcontract anything and everything. All over the world, companies are jumping on the bandwagon, decentralizing, downsizing, and forging alliances to pursue innovation. Why is the idea of the virtual organization so tantalizing? Because we have come to believe that bureaucracy is bad and flexibility is good. And so it follows that a company that invests in as little as possible will be more responsive to a changing marketplace and more likely to attain global competitive advantage.

There is no question that many large and cumbersome organizations have been outperformed by smaller "networked" competitors. Consider the eclipse of IBM in PCs and of DEC in workstations by Packard Bell and Sun Microsystems. But while there are many successful virtual companies, there are even more failures that don't make the headlines. After many years of studying the relationship between organization and innovation, we believe that the virtues of being virtual

Reprinted from *Harvard Business Review*, January–February 1996, pp. 65–73.

*Henry W. Chesbrough, a former computer industry executive, is a faculty member at the Harvard Business School. David J. Teece is the Mitsubishi Bank Professor and director of the Institute of Management, Innovation and Organization at the Haas School of Business.

have been oversold. The new conventional wisdom ignores the distinctive role that large integrated companies can play in the innovation process. Those rushing to form alliances instead of nurturing and guarding their own capabilities may be risking their future.

What's Special about Virtual?

What gives the virtual company its advantage? In essence, incentives and responsiveness. Virtual companies coordinate much of their business through the marketplace, where free agents come together to buy and sell one another's goods and services; thus virtual companies can harness the power of market forces to develop, manufacture, market, distribute, and support their offerings in ways that fully integrated companies can't duplicate. As William Joy, vice president of research and development at Sun Microsystems, puts it, "Not all the smart people [in the workstation industry] work for Sun." Because an outside developer of workstation software can obtain greater rewards by selling software to Sun customers than by developing the same software as a Sun employee, he or she will move faster, work harder, and take more risks. Using high-powered, market-based incentives such as stock options and attractive bonuses, a virtual company can quickly access the technical resources it needs, if those resources are available. In situations where technology is changing rapidly, large companies that attempt to do everything inside will flounder when competing against small companies with highly trained and motivated employees.

But the incentives that make a virtual company powerful also leave it vulnerable. As incentives become greater and risk taking increases, coordination among parties through the marketplace becomes more and more difficult, precisely because so much personal reward is at stake. Each party to joint development activity necessarily acts in its own self-interest. Over time, innovation can generate unforeseen surprises that work to the advantage of some parties and to the disadvantage of others. The result: Once-friendly partners may be unwilling or unable to align strategically, and coordinated development activity falters. In contrast, integrated, centralized companies do not generally reward people for taking risks, but they do have established processes for settling conflicts and coordinating all the activities necessary for innovation.

This trade-off between incentives and control lies at the heart of the decision that managers must make about how to organize for innovation. (See the graph "Finding the Right Degree of Centralization.") If virtual organizations and integrated companies are at opposite ends of the spectrum, alliances occupy a

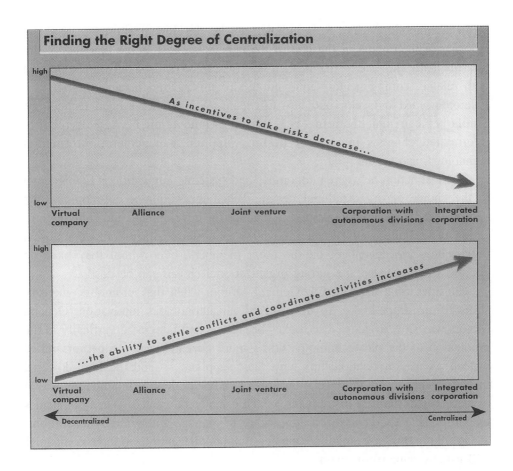

kind of organizational middle ground. An alliance can achieve some of the coordination of an integrated company, but, like players in a virtual network, the members of an alliance will be driven to enhance their own positions, and over time their interests may diverge. The challenge for managers is to choose the organizational form that best matches the type of innovation they are pursuing.

Types of Innovation

When should companies organize for innovation by using decentralized (or virtual) approaches, and when should they rely on internal organization? The answer depends on the innovation in question.

Some innovations are *autonomous* — that is, they can be pursued independently from other innovations. A new turbocharger to increase horsepower in an automobile engine, for example, can be developed without a complete redesign of the engine or the rest of the car. In contrast, some innovations are fundamentally *systemic* — that is, their benefits can be realized only in conjunction with related, complementary innovations. To profit from instant photography, Polaroid needed to develop both new film technology and new camera technology. Similarly, lean manufacturing is a systemic innovation because it requires interrelated changes in product design, supplier management, information technology, and so on.

The distinction between autonomous and systemic innovation is fundamental to the choice of organizational design. When innovation is autonomous, the decentralized virtual organization can manage the development and commercialization tasks quite well. When innovation is systemic, members of a virtual organization are dependent on the other members, over whom they have no control. In either case, the wrong organizational choice can be costly.

Consider what happened to General Motors when the automobile industry shifted from drum brakes to disc brakes, an autonomous innovation. General Motors was slow to adopt disc brakes because it had integrated vertically in the production of the old technology. GM's more decentralized competitors relied instead on market relationships with their suppliers — and the high-powered incentives inherent in those relationships. As a result, they were able to beat GM to market with the new disc brakes, which car buyers wanted. When companies inappropriately use centralized approaches to manage autonomous innovations, as GM did in this case, small companies and more decentralized large companies will usually outperform them.

To understand why the two types of innovation call for different organizational strategies, consider the information flow essential to innovation. Information about new products and technologies often develops over time as managers absorb new research findings, the results of early product experiments, and initial customer feedback. To commercialize an innovation profitably, a tremendous amount of knowledge from industry players, from customers, and sometimes from scientists must be gathered and understood. This task is easier if the information is codified.

Codified information — for example, specifications that are captured in industry standards and design rules — can often be transferred almost as effectively from one company to another as it can within a single company. Because such information is easily duplicated, it has little natural protection. Sometimes bits and pieces can be protected by intellectual property rights, but those pieces, especially trade secrets and patents, are small islands in a broad ocean of knowledge.

Other information does not travel as easily between companies. Tacit knowledge is knowledge that is implicitly grasped or used but has not been fully articulated, such as the know-how of a master craftsman or the ingrained perspectives of a specific company or work unit. Because such knowledge is deeply embedded in individuals or companies, it tends to diffuse slowly and only with effort and the transfer of people. Established companies can protect the tacit knowledge they hold, sharing only codified information. They can be quite strategic about what they disclose and when they disclose it.

The information needed to integrate an autonomous innovation with existing technologies is usually well understood and may even be codified in industry standards. Systemic innovations, on the other hand, pose a unique set of management challenges regarding information exchange. By their very nature, systemic innovations require information sharing and coordinated adjustment *throughout an entire product system*. Here is where a market-based, virtual approach to innovation poses serious strategic hazards. Unaffiliated companies linked through arm's-length contracts often cannot achieve sufficient coordination. Each company wants the other to do more, while each is also looking for ways to realize the most gain from the innovation. Information sharing can be reduced or biased, as each seeks to get the most at the other's expense. In most cases, the open exchange of information that fuels systemic innovation will be easier and safer within a company than across company boundaries. The inevitable conflicts and choices that arise as a systemic innovation develops can best be resolved by an integrated company's internal management processes.

The Case of Industry Standards

Coordinating a systemic innovation is particularly difficult when industry standards do not exist and must be pioneered. In such instances, virtual organizations are likely to run into strategic problems. Consider how technical standards emerge. Market participants weigh many competing technologies and eventually rally around one of them. There are winners and losers among the contestants, and potential losers can try to undermine the front-runner or to fragment the standard by promoting a rival. Until a clear winner emerges, customers may choose to sit on the sidelines rather than risk making the wrong choice.

By virtue of its size and scope, an integrated company may be able to advance a new standard simply by choosing to adopt a particular technology. If a large company commits itself to one of a host of competing technologies, consumers as well as companies promoting rival technologies will probably be persuaded to follow suit. Virtual companies, however, which may be struggling to resolve conflicts within their networks, won't be able to break a deadlock in a complicated standards battle. Players in a network won't be able to coordinate themselves to act like a large company.

Once a new standard has been established, virtual organizations can manage further innovation quite well. But when an industry begins to advance technology to a new level, the cycle can begin anew. Again, technically feasible choices present new strategic trade-offs. Suppliers, competitors, and customers may fail to agree on a common path. Unless a big player emerges to break the logjam among rival technologies, the existing standard will prevail long past its usefulness.

Today computer floppy disks are frozen in an old standard because no single company has been able to establish a new one. IBM pioneered the 3.5-inch hard-case diskette in 1987 when it introduced its new line of PS/2 personal computers. Within two years, the memory capacity of 3.5-inch diskettes doubled from 720 kilobytes to 1.44 megabytes, where it has remained ever since.

Why? The technical capability to expand diskette capacity is available, but no company has the reputation and strength to set a new standard. Through the 1980s, IBM was large enough to coordinate standards among the key participants in the industry: personal computer manufacturers, diskette makers, and software publishers. If IBM told the industry it would use a particular capacity on its next generation of machines, others did the same. But in the 1990s, IBM's leadership of the PC market came to an end, perhaps permanently. Today IBM is not strong enough to move the industry by itself, and it won't move ahead of the other industry players and risk being stranded if they don't follow.

A simple rule of thumb applies: When innovation depends on a series of interdependent innovations — that is, when innovation is systemic – independent companies will not usually be able to coordinate themselves to knit those innovations together. Scale, integration, and market leadership may be required to establish and then to advance standards in an industry.

The IBM PC: Virtual Successor or Failure?

IBM's development of the personal computer is a fascinating example of both the advantages and disadvantages of using virtual approaches to pursue innovation. When IBM launched its first PC in 1981, the company elected to outsource all the major components from the marketplace. By tapping the capabilities of other companies, IBM was able to get its first product to market in only 15 months.

The microprocessor (the 8088) was purchased from Intel, and the operating system (which became PC-DOS) was licensed from a then fledgling software company, Microsoft. In effect, the IBM PC had an "open" architecture: It was based on standards and components that were widely available. The high-powered incentives of the marketplace could coordinate the roles of component manufacturers and software vendors. IBM successfully promoted its open architecture to hundreds of third-party developers of software applications and hardware accessory products, knowing that those products would add to the appeal of the PC.

IBM also relied on the market to distribute the product. Although IBM launched its own IBM Product Centers as retail storefronts and had its own direct sales force for large corporate customers, the majority of the company's systems were distributed through independent retailers, initially Computer-Land and Sears. Eventually, there were more than 2000 retail outlets.

By using outside parties for hardware, software, and distribution, IBM greatly reduced its investment in bringing the PC to market. More important, those relationships allowed IBM to launch an attack against Apple, which had pioneered the market and was growing quickly. The IBM PC was an early success, and it spawned what became the dominant architecture of the entire microcomputer industry. By 1984, three years after the introduction of the PC, IBM replaced Apple as the number one supplier of microcomputers, with 26% of the PC business. By 1985, IBM's share had grown to 41%. Many observers attributed the PC's success to IBM's creative use of outside relationships. More than a few business analysts hailed the IBM PC development as a model for doing business in the future.

Indeed, IBM's approach in its PC business is exactly the kind of decentralized strategy that commentators are urging large, slow-moving companies to adopt. The early years of the IBM PC show many of the benefits of using markets and outside companies to coordinate innovation: fast development of technology and tremendous technological improvements from a wide variety of sources.

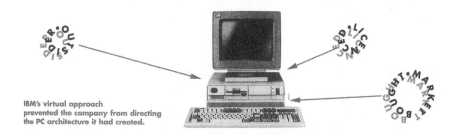

IBM's virtual approach prevented the company from directing the PC architecture it had created.

With the passage of time, though, the downside of IBM's decentralized approach has become apparent. IBM failed to anticipate that its virtual and open approach would prevent the company from directing the PC architecture it had created. The open architecture and the autonomy of its vendors invited design mutinies and the entry of IBM-compatible PC manufacturers. At first, competitors struggled to achieve compatibility with IBM's architecture, but after several years compatibility was widespread in the industry. And once that happened, manufacturers could purchase the same CPU from Intel and the same operating system from Microsoft, run the same application software (from Lotus, Microsoft, WordPerfect, and others), and sell through the same distribution channels (such as ComputerLand, BusinessLand, and MicroAge). IBM had little left on which to establish a competitive advantage.

To maintain technological leadership, IBM decided to advance the PC architecture. To do that, IBM needed to coordinate the many interrelated pieces of the architecture — a systemic technology coordination task. However, the third-party hardware and software suppliers that had helped establish the original architecture did not follow IBM's lead. When IBM introduced its OS/2 operating system, the company could not stop Microsoft from introducing Windows, an application that works with the old DOS operating system, thereby greatly reducing the advantages of switching of OS/2. And third-party hardware and software companies made investments that extended the usefulness of the original PC architecture. Similarly, Intel helped Compaq steal a march on IBM in 1986, when Compaq introduced the first PC based on Intel's 80386 microprocessor, an enhancement over the earlier generations of microprocessors used in IBM and compatible machines. Even though IBM owned 12% of Intel at the time, it couldn't prevent Intel from working with Compaq to beat IBM to market. This was the beginning of the end of IBM's ability to direct the evolution of PC architecture.

By the third quarter of 1995, IBM's share of the PC market had fallen to just 7.3%, trailing Compaq's 10.5% share. Today its PC business is rumored to be modestly profitable at best. Most of the profits from the PC architecture have migrated upstream to the supplier of the microprocessor (Intel) and the operating system (Microsoft), and to outside makers of application software. The combined market value of those suppliers and third parties today greatly exceeds IBM's.

IBM's experience in the PC market illustrates the strategic importance of organization in the pursuit of innovation. Virtual approaches encounter serious problems when companies seek to exploit systemic innovation. Key development activities that depend on one another must be conducted in-house to capture the rewards from long-term R&D investments. Without directed coordination, the necessary complementary innovations required to leverage a new technology may not be forthcoming.

The Virtuous Virtuals

How have the most successful virtual companies accomplished the difficult task of coordination? The virtual companies that have demonstrated staying power are all at the center of a network that they use to leverage their own capabilities. Few virtual companies that have survived and prospered have outsourced everything. Rather, the virtuous virtuals have carefully nurtured and guarded the internal capabilities that provide the essential underpinnings of competitive advantage. And they invest considerable resources to maintain and extend their core competencies internally. Indeed, without these companies' unique competencies and capabilities, their strategic position in the network would be short-lived.

Consider the well-known battle between MIPS Technologies and Sun Microsystems for control of workstation processors. (See Benjamin Gomes–Casseres, "Group Versus Group: How Alliance Networks Compete," HBR July–August 1994.) MIPS was trying to promote its Advanced Computing Environment (ACE) against Sun's Scalable Processor Architecture (SPARC). Sun had strong internal capabilities, whereas MIPS tried to compete as a more virtual player, leveraging off of the competencies of partners such as Compaq, DEC, and Silicon Graphics. MIPS had a good technical design, but that was literally all it had, and this hollowness left the company at the mercy of its partners. As soon as DEC and Compaq reduced their commitment to the ACE initiative, the network fell apart and pulled MIPS down with it. The very reliance of virtual companies on partners, suppliers, and other outside companies exposes them to strategic hazards. Put another way, there are plenty of small, dynamic companies that have not been able to outperform larger competitors. In particular, a hollow company like MIPS is ill equipped to coordinate a network of companies. Although Sun also worked with alliance partners, it had strong internal capabilities in systems design, manufacturing, marketing, sales, service, and support. As a result, Sun can direct and advance the SPARC architecture, a dominant technology in the industry.

Many companies with superior capabilities have prospered as the dominant player in a network. Japanese keiretsu are structured that way. Consider Toyota, whose successful introduction of the lean production system — a truly systemic innovation — required tremendous coordination with its network of suppliers. Because Toyota was much larger than its suppliers, and because, until recently, it was the largest customer of virtually all of them, it could compel those suppliers to make radical changes in their business practices. In a more egalitarian network, suppliers can demand a large share of the economic benefits of innovations, using what economists call hold-up strategies. Strong central players like Toyota are rarely vulnerable to such tactics and are thus in a better position to drive and coordinate systemic innovation.

The most successful virtual companies sit at the center of networks that are far from egalitarian. Nike may rely on Asian partners for manufacturing, but its capabilities in design and marketing allow it to call all the shots. In the computer industry, Intel has effective control of the 80X86 microprocessor standard, Microsoft dominates PC operating systems, and Sun is driving the SPARC architecture. Those companies control and coordinate the advance of technologies in their areas, and in this regard they function more like integrated companies than like market-based virtuals.

Choosing the Right Organizational Design

Today few companies can afford to develop internally all the technologies that might provide an advantage in the future. In every company we studied, we found a mix of approaches: Some technologies were "purchased" from other companies; others were acquired through licenses, partnerships, and alliances; and still other critical technologies were developed internally. Getting the right balance is crucial, as IBM's disastrous experience in PCs illustrates. But what constitutes the right balance?

Consider how a successful innovator such as Motorola evaluates the trade-offs. Motorola, a leader in wireless communications technology, has declared its long-term goal to be the delivery of "untethered communication" — namely, communication anytime, anywhere, without the need for wires, power cords, or other constraints. In order to achieve that goal, Motorola must make important decisions about where and how to advance the required technologies. Those decisions turn on a handful of questions: Is the technology systemic or likely to become systemic in the future? What capabilities exist in-house and in the current supplier base? When will needed technologies become available?

For Motorola, battery technology is critical because it determines the functionality that can be built into a handheld communications device and the length of time that the device can be used before recharging. Batteries have been a pacing technology in this area for many years.

As Motorola scans the horizon for improved battery technology, it encounters a familiar trade-off between the degree of technological advancement and the number of reliable volume suppliers. Conventional battery technologies such as nickel cadmium (Ni-Cd) have become commodities, and there are many suppliers. But few if any suppliers can offer the more advanced technologies Motorola needs. And the most exotic technologies, such as fuel cells and solid-state energy sources, are not yet commercially viable from any supplier. How should Motorola organize to obtain each of the technologies it might need? Under what circumstances should the company buy the technology from a supplier and when should it form alliances or joint ventures? When should Motorola commit to internal development of the technology? (See the matrix "Matching Organization to Innovation.")

For Ni-Cd technology, the clear choice for Motorola is to buy the technology, or to use the market to coordinate access to this technology, because Motorola can rely on competition among many qualified suppliers to deliver what it wants, when needed, for a competitive price. Motorola faces a more complex decision for fuel cells and solid-state battery technologies should Motorola wait until those technologies are more widely available, or should the company opt for a joint venture or internal development?

Before deciding to wait for cutting-edge battery technologies to be developed, Motorola must consider three issues. One is that Motorola could lose the ability to influence the direction of the technology; the early commercial forms may be designed for applications that do not benefit Motorola, such as electric automobiles. The second problem is that Motorola might lose the ability to pace the technology, to bring it to market at a competitively desirable time. The third issue is that if such technologies are — or become — systemic and Motorola

Nike relies on Asian partners for manufacturing, but its design and marketing capabilities allow it to call all the shots.

Ameritech's Strategy for Emerging Technologies

Ameritech, a Regional Bell Operating Company with wire and fiber assets in the Midwest, has the potential to be a major player in the development of on-demand video and interactive information services for home use. In emerging technologies such as multimedia, no one has all the information to determine what capabilities a company must develop internally or access through the market. The only certainty is that the promise of this market will depend on the co-development of many technologies, including data formats, throughput rates, wiring topologies, billing systems, and user interfaces.

Because the eventual configuration of the multimedia industry is unknown (and arguably unknowable ex ante), organizations such as Ameritech must become insiders to the discussions among a range of potential industry players. In emerging markets that are dependent on evolving technologies, considerable information sharing among a wide variety of companies will ultimately result in a road map for the industry. Virtual organizations can serve as catalysts to the development of industry directions and standards in ways that fully integrated organizations cannot.

Consider the role of alliances in Ameritech's multimedia strategy. By allying its own capabilities with those of companies with relevant and complementary skills, Ameritech can participate directly in defining and developing an architecture that will ultimately manage the emerging technologies. One such alliance is with Random House, a leading print publisher of books and magazines, with properties such as the *New Yorker*, Condé nast, Fodor's, and Arthur Frommer Travel Guides. Random House is capable of supplying significant "content" over Ameritech's wires into the home.

This alliance allows both companies to begin to explore the business and technical requirements of providing content into the home.

Ameritech and Random House have formed a joint venture to acquire a start-up virtual company called Worldview Systems, which publishes an electronic monthly current-events database of travel information about more than 170 destinations around the world. While Worldview Systems' products are now sold primarily through travel agents and an 800 telephone number, Ameritech and Random House believe that this type of product may turn out to be ideal for delivery to the home. As Thomas Touton, Ameritech Development's vice president for venture capital notes, such exploratory investments "require support from senior management willing to move fast in investing but be paitent in waiting for returns, and an investment focus that is strongly synergistic with the company's operations."

When and if the promise of the multimedia market becomes real, Ameritech will doubtless be competing against other powerful players. But Ameritech may already have an inside track in the race to deliver information and video on demand into the home. Through alliances such as the one with Random House and exploratory investments in virtual companies such as Worldview Systems, Ameritech has been able to share information and know-how with other potential industry participants and become an insider with the potential to influence the direction of this nascent industry. Until a technological direction becomes clear, companies must invest in capabilities and become active participants in the information dissemination process. Virtual organizations can be an extremely valuable tool at this early stage of market evolution.

has no control over them, the company may not be able to advance related technologies and design features to achieve its goal of untethered communication.

Those issues suggest that Motorola cannot simply wait for the technologies to be provided by the market. Rather, Motorola needs to build strong ties to suppliers with the best capabilities, thus increasing its ability to direct the path of future systemic innovation. Where Motorola itself has strong capabilities, the company should pursue the technologies on its own.

To retain its leadership over the long term, Motorola must continue to develop the critical parts of its value chain internally and acquire less critical technologies from the market or from alliances. Although networks with their high-powered incentives may be effective over the short term for an unchanging technology, they will not adapt well over the long term as technology develops and companies must depend on certain internal capabilities to keep up. The popularity of networked companies and decentralization arises, in part, from observations over a time horizon that is far too short. Remember the enthusiasm that greeted IBM's early success in PCs.

Scale and Scope

Business history presents us with a lesson of striking relevance to the organizational decisions managers face today. In the classic *Scale and Scope*, Alfred Chandler details how the modern corporation evolved in the United States, Germany, and Great Britain at the end of the nineteenth century. Managers who invested the capital to build large-scale enterprises blazed the trail for the leading industries of the second industrial revolution. Markets in railroads, steel, chemicals, and petroleum were developed and shaped by major companies, not the other way around. The most successful of those companies were the first in their industries to make the massive investments in manufacturing, management, and distribution that were needed to realize the gains from innovation.

Companies that failed to make such coordinated, internal commitments during this period were soon thrust aside. The experience of British companies provides a cautionary tale for the champions of the virtual company. Many enjoyed early technological leads in their industries, but the reluctance of those family-run companies to relinquish control to outside investors prevented them from investing to build the capabilities they needed to commercialize their technologies. When German or U.S. competitors made the requisite investments, British companies lost their leadership position. In chemicals, for example, the British lead in the 1870s was completely lost by 1890. History even provided British chemical

Matching Organization to Innovation

The capabilities you need...

Type of Innovation

Autonomous — Systemic

	Autonomous	Systemic
...exist outside	go virtual	ally with caution
...must be created	ally or bring in-house	bring in-house

companies with a second chance when Germany's defeat in World War I temporarily cost German chemical manufacturers their plants and distribution networks. But by 1930, German chemical companies regained the lead because the British again failed to invest adequately. The lesson is that companies that develop their own capabilities can outperform those that rely too heavily on coordination through markets and alliances to build their businesses.

The leading industries of the late nineteenth and early twentieth centuries — chemicals, steel, and railroads — all experienced rapid systemic innovation. The winners were the companies that made major internal investments to shape the markets, rather than those that relied on others to lead the way. While business conditions have certainly changed, many of the principles that worked a century ago still pertain.

Today leading companies like Intel and Microsoft make extensive investments to enhance their current capabilities and spur the creation of new ones. Because so many important innovations are systemic, decentralization without strategic leverage and coordination is exactly the wrong organizational strategy. In most cases, only a large company will have the scale and scope to coordinate complementary innovations. For both the chemicals industry 100 years ago and the microcomputer industry today, long-term success requires considerable and sustained internal investment within a company. The lessons of the second industrial revolution apply to the third: Adept, well-managed companies that commit the right internal resources to innovation will shape the markets and build the new industries of the twenty-first century.

Managing Intellectual Capital: Licensing and Cross-Licensing in Semiconductors and Electronics

Peter C. Grindley and David J. Teece

One of the most significant emerging business developments in the last decade has been the proactive management of intellectual capital by innovating firms. While firms have for decades actively managed their physical and financial assets, until quite recently intellectual property (IP) management was a backwater. Top management paid little attention and legal counsel did not participate in major managerial decisions. This is changing. High-technology firms now often have "IP" managers as well as "IT" managers.[1] In some firms considerations of intellectual capital management have expanded from the mere licensing of residual technology to become a central element in technology strategy. This development is spurred by the increasing protection afforded IP worldwide and by the greater importance of technological know-how to competitive advantage. These developments herald a new era for management.

Patents and trade secrets have become a key element of competition in high-technology industries. In electronics and semiconductors, firms continually make large investments in R&D in their attempts to stay at the frontier and to utilize technological developments external to the firm. Fierce competition has put a premium on innovation and on defending IP from unlicensed imitators. As IP owners have taken a more active stance regarding their patent portfolios, industry participants increasingly find it necessary to engage in licensing and cross-licensing.[2] Moreover, and relatedly, royalty rates have risen. The effect has been positive for firms with strong portfolios, who are now able to capture considerable, benefit from their patent estates. Firms that are high net users of others' patents have a choice. They must increasingly pay royalties, or they must develop their own portfolios so as to bring something to the table in cross-licensing negotiations.

Reprinted from *California Management Review* 39(2) (Winter 1997), 1–34.

The new environment affords new challenges. If a firm is to compete with advanced products and processes, it is likely to utilize not only its own technology, but also the patents of others. In many advanced products, the range of technology is too great for a single firm to develop its entire needs internally. In cumulative technology fields such as electronics and semiconductors, one innovation builds on another. There are inevitably overlapping developments and mutually blocking patents. It is likely that firms will need to cross-license patents from others to ensure that they have freedom to manufacture without infringement. Thus in many industries today, firms can generate value from their innovation not only by embedding it in new products and processes, but also through engaging in licensing and cross-licensing.

In electronics and semiconductors, cross-licensing is generally more complex than the exchange of individual patent rights. The size of the patent portfolios of some firms is often too great for it be feasible to identify individual infringements. Companies may own thousands of patents, used in literally tens of thousands of products, and may add hundreds more each year. With this degree of overlap of technology; companies protect themselves against mutual infringement by cross-licensing portfolios of all current and future patents in a field-of-use, without making specific reference to individual patents. It is simply too cumbersome and costly to license only the specific patents you need for specific products. The portfolio approach reduces transactions costs and allows licensees freedom to design and manufacture without infringement.[3]

An important dimension of field-of-use cross-licensing is the calculation of balancing royalty payments, according to the relative value of the patent portfolios of each party. This calculation is made prospectively, based on a sample of each firm's leading patents. Weight is given to the quality and market coverage of the patents. Desirable portfolios have excellent patents covering technology widely used in the industry. A quality portfolio is a powerful lever in negotiating access to required technology and may lead to significant royalty earnings or, at a minimum, to reduced payments to others. Obviously, a firm which is a large net user of other firms' patents, without contributing comparable IP in exchange, is likely to have to pay significant royalties.

Many managers now understand the use of licensing and cross-licensing as part of business strategy as well as the importance of a valuable patent portfolio. The key to successful cross-licensing is a portfolio of quality patents that covers large areas of the partner's product markets. Significantly, for the balancing process, the firm should not necessarily emulate the portfolio of its cross-licensing partner. Rather it should concentrate R&D in those areas in which it does best and has the most comparative advantage to develop patents that its partners need. This will give maximum leverage in negotiating access and balancing royalties. This might be in product design, software, or manufacturing processes, wherever the firm's R&D is most effective and its IP most widely used. In this sense, cross-licensing has a double positive effect on innovation. It allows firms greater means of earning a return on innovation (to help fund further R&D), while allowing firms to concentrate their innovation and patenting activities according to their comparative advantage. In this way, firms can develop complementary rather than duplicative technology, thereby benefiting the public interest.

The unprecedented rates of technological development in the electronics industries have been made possible by a combination of the ability to capture value from innovation and the freedom to design and manufacture. Cross-licensing has been crucial. A key lesson for managers is to be aware of the value of developing a strong, high-quality IP portfolio and the effect this can have on licensing and cross-licensing strategies. This protects the firm's innovations and may significantly reduce royalty payments and fund further R&D.

The Licensing Legacy

Background — The Formation of RCA

Cross-licensing is not a new phenomenon in electronics; it goes back almost to the beginning of the industry. Cross-licensing is typical of industries involved in "cumulative systems technologies," where one innovation builds on another and products may draw on several related technologies. Multiple firms develop patented innovations in the same technological fields, and the "state of the art" of the technology tends to be covered by a large number of different patents held by different firms. Because of the potential for mutually blocking patents, firms typically cross-license all patents in a field-of-use to ensure adequate access to technology. The strongest examples of cumulative systems technologies are in electronics, including computers and semiconductors, where extensive cross-licensing ensures "design freedom" or "freedom-to-manufacture."[4] Note that this is a different situation than in some other industries not characterized by cumulative systems technologies, such as chemicals and pharmaceuticals, where cross-licensing, or, rather, reciprocal licensing, is typically aimed at exchanging technology rather than avoiding patent interference.[5]

An important instance of field-of-use cross-licensing is the development of radio in the first quarter of this century.[6] It epitomizes the complexities surrounding intellectual property arrangements that may be encountered with cumulative systems technologies. Also, many of the cross-licensing ideas used later by the electronics industry were pioneered during the early days of radio.

The commercialization of radio required a number of basic inventions. The scientific basis for wireless was developed by university scientists such as Maxwell, Hertz, and Lodge in the 19th century. Their discoveries were first applied to practical communication with the development of wireless telegraphy by Marconi in Britain in 1896. The first speech transmissions were made in the U.S. by Fessenden in 1900, using a high-frequency alternator. Further basic innovations were made over the next two decades.[7]

Many of these inventions were initially developed by individuals working independently of each other. Indeed, many carry the name of the inventor, such as the Poulsen arc, the Fleming valve, and the de Forest triode.[8] As the potential for radio became apparent, and the need for large-scale R&D and investment grew, large corporations entered the field. The pace of development accelerated and the number of patents multiplied. The companies involved included Marconi, General Electronic (GE), Westinghouse, AT&T, Telefunken, and others. In addition to their considerable R&D effort, these corporations also acquired key patents where appropriate.[9] There was considerable competition, and with research teams in different companies working in parallel, patent interferences were common.[10] By 1918, it was apparent that several technologies were needed to manufacture radio systems, and each of these technologies itself involved multiple patents from different firms. In the words of Armstrong, one of the pioneers of radio, "It was absolutely impossible to manufacture any kind of workable apparatus without using practically all of the inventions which were then known."[11]

The result was deadlock. A number of firms had important patent positions and could block each other's access to key components. They refused to cross-license each other. It was a "Mexican standoff," with each firm holding up the development of the industry.[12] The situation arose in large part as a result of the way radio had developed. Key patent portfolios had been developed by different individuals and corporations, who were often adamant about refusing to cross-license competitors. Also, in a new industry in which large scale interference was a novel problem, there was no well developed means of coordinating cross-licensing agreements between these groups.

The situation was resolved in the U.S. only when, under prompting by the U.S. Navy, the various pioneers formed the Radio Corporation of America (RCA) in 1919.[13] This broke a key source of the deadlock. RCA acquired the U.S. rights to the Marconi patents, and cross-licensed the U.S. rights for other major patent portfolios.[14] The major U.S. patent holders became shareholders in RCA. In this way, RCA acquired the U.S. rights to all the constituent radio patents under one roof — amounting to over 2000 patents.[15] It established RCA as the technical leader in radio, but also enabled the other cross-licensees to continue their own development of the technology for use in other fields or as suppliers to RCA. The RCA cross-licenses to continue their own development of the technology for use in other fields or as suppliers to RCA. The RCA cross-licensing agreements became a model for the future.[16]

The case shows that because of the reluctance of the parties to cross-license, technological progress and the further commercialization of radio was halted. In this case, the debacle was resolved only by the formation of RCA, a rather radical organizational solution. However, it became clear from the experience that the same ends — namely design freedom — may be achieved more simply, without such fundamental reorganization, by cross-licensing alone. This helped set the stage for further development of cross-licensing in electronics.

AT&T's Cross-Licensing Practices

The need to achieve design freedom was soon experienced in other fields of electronics and resulted in patent cross-licensing agreements. One of the most influential firms in shaping the industry practices was AT&T, whose licensing and cross-licensing policy, especially from the 1940s until its breakup in 1984, has been crucial to the development of similar practices in U.S. electronics and semiconductor industries.

Over its long history, AT&T's licensing policy has had three phases, reflecting changes in its overall business strategy. First, from AT&T's establishment in 1885 until its first antitrust-related commitment in 1913, it used its IP rights in a forthright fashion to establish itself in the service market.[17] In the second phase, from 1914 until 1984, AT&T became a regulated monopoly. Its policy (as a matter of law under the 1956 antitrust consent decree) was to openly license its IP to everyone for minimal fees. Reasons of technology access similar to those in radio led to patent cross-license agreements between the major producers of telephone equipment, starting in the 1920s. This developed into a more widespread policy. It was during this period that the transistor was invented at Bell Labs. This and other breakthroughs laid the foundation for the semiconductor industry and shaped the development of the telecommunications, computer, and electronics industries. In the current phase, dating from divestiture in 1984, AT&T is no longer bound by the consent decree, and its IP licensing can be aligned with its proprietary needs.[18]

The 1956 antitrust consent decree required AT&T to openly license all patents controlled by the Bell System to any applicant at "reasonable royalties," provided that the licensee also grant licenses at reasonable royalties in return. AT&T was also required to provide technical information with the licenses on payment of reasonable fees; licenses had the right to sublicense the technology to their associates.[19] The impact of AT&T's liberal licensing on the industry was considerable, especially when considered in parallel with that at IBM.[20]

To a large extent, the licensing terms in AT&T's 1956 decree simply codified what was already AT&T policy. As an enterprise under rate-of-return regulation, it had little reason to maximize royalty income from its IP. Instead, it used its technology and IP to promote new services and reduce costs. It procured a tremendous amount of equipment and materials on the open market and apparently figured that its service customers would be better off if its technologies were widely diffused amongst its actual and potential suppliers, as this would lower prices and increase the performance of procured components.[21] It was the first company we are aware of to have "design freedom" as a core component of its patent strategy. It did not see licensing income as a source of funds for R&D, as Bell Labs research was largely funded by the "license contract fee," assessed on the annual revenues of the Bell operating companies. This very stable source of research funding supported a constant stream of basic innovations.[22] Using its own portfolio as leverage, AT&T was able to obtain the (reciprocal) rights it needed to continue to innovate, unimpeded by the IP of others. It successfully accomplished this limited objective.

An interesting aspect of AT&T's IP strategy was that technologies (though not R&D programs) were often selected for patent protection based on their potential interest to other firms generating technology of interest to AT&T. Since the legal requirement for open licensing specifically did not extinguish all of AT&T's intellectual property rights, the company was able to gain access to the external technology that it needed, while contributing enormously to innovation in telecommunications, computers, and electronics worldwide.[23]

The terms of AT&T's licenses set a pattern that is still commonplace in the electronics industries. The "capture model" was defined in the consent decree.[24] Under this arrangement, the licensee is granted the right to use existing patents and any obtained for inventions made during a fixed capture period of no more than five years, followed by a survivorship period until the expiration of these patents and with subsequent agreement renewals. The open licensing regimes this led to were persistent, since with the long survivorship period on many of the basic patents, there was limited scope to introduce more stringent conditions for new patents.

AT&T's licensing policy had the effect of making its tremendously large IP portfolio available to the industry worldwide for next to nothing. This portfolio included fundamental patents such as the transistor, basic semiconductor technology, and the laser, and included many other basic patents in telecommunications, computing, optoelectronics, and superconductivity. Shaped under antitrust policy reflecting the needs and beliefs of an era in which U.S. firms did not have to worry much about foreign competition, such a liberal policy appears quite anachronistic today. However, there is no doubt that it provided a tremendous contribution to world welfare. It remains as one of the most unheralded contributions to economic development — possibly far exceeding the Marshall Plan in terms of the wealth generation capability it established abroad and in the United States.

The traditional cross-licensing policy of AT&T was greatly extended following the invention of the transistor. Widespread "field-of-use" licenses in the semiconductor industry is a legacy, as the industry was founded on the basic semiconductor technology developed by AT&T. In the early days of semiconductor technology, AT&T controlled most of the key patents in the field. It soon realized that, given the importance of semiconductor technology, other electronics companies were developing their own technologies and could eventually invent around the AT&T patents. Cross-licensing ensured that AT&T would have reciprocal access to this technology and be able to develop its own technology without risking patent interference.[25]

AT&T's liberal licensing allowed the semiconductor industry to grow rapidly, and members of the industry did not care much about individual patents. The culture of the industry still reflects this, with a tradition of spin-outs and new ventures, open communications and frequent job changes.[26] The continued speed of technological use are reasons why there is still a need for the transactional simplicity associated with "lump-sum" or bundled licensing.[27] With individual product life cycles short compared with the long patent lives, any new innovation is likely to infringe several existing patents. Licensing thus typically involves clusters of patents.

Not surprisingly, AT&T now uses its IP more strategically. No longer bound by the consent decree, and with R&D funding no longer guaranteed by the telephone subscribers, its IP policy is necessarily linked more closely to individual business opportunities. This is especially true of trade secret licensing, which is often a key component of international joint ventures, involving omnibus IP agreements combining patents, trademarks, and know-how.

Cross-Licensing in the Computer Industry — IBM

A second major influence on licensing practice across the electronics industry has been IBM. It has long been heavily involved in licensing and cross-licensing its technology, both as a means of accessing external technology and to earn revenues. In many ways, it has been in a similar position to AT&T in that it has been a wellspring of new technology but was also subject to a consent decree in 1956 that had certain compulsory licensing terms. Under the IBM consent decree, IBM was required to grant non-exclusive, non-transferable, world-wide licenses for any or all of its patents at reasonable royalties (royalty free for existing tabulating card/machinery patents) to any applicant — provided the applicant also offered to cross-license its patents to IBM on similar terms. The provision covered all existing patents at the time of the decree (i.e., as of 1956) plus any that were filed during the next five years. The rights lasted for the full term of the patents.[28]

IBM's cross-licensing activity continues today. IBM states that it is "exploiting our technology in the industry through agreements with companies like Hitachi, Toshiba, Canon, and Cyrix." Patent and technology licensing agreements earned $640 million in cash for IBM in 1994.[29] IBM is one of the world's leading innovators, with more U.S. patents granted in each of the three years from 1993 to 1995 than any other company (see Table 1).

Table 1. Top Ten U.S. Patent Recipients (1990–1995)

Company	U.S. Patents Received					
	1990	1991	1992	1993	1994	1995
IBM	608	684	851	1088	1305	1383
Canon	868	831	1115	1039	1100	1088
Motorola	396	614	662	731	839	1012
NEC	448	441	462	602	901	1005
Mitsubishi	862	964	977	944	998	971
Toshiba	891	1031	1036	1064	985	970
Hitachi	902	962	973	949	1002	909
Matsushita	351	467	616	722	782	852
Eastman Kodak	720	863	778	1008	890	772
General Electric	785	818	943	942	973	757

Source: IFI/Plenum Data Corp., USPTO

The central importance IBM attaches to its patent portfolio in providing an arsenal of patents for use in cross-licensing and negotiating access to outside technology has been borne out in public statements by the company.[30] For IBM, the main object of its licensing policy has been "design freedom," to ensure "the right to manufacture and market products." To be able to manufacture products, IBM needs rights to technology owned by others:

> Market driven quality demands that we shorten our cycle times. This means we have to speed up the process of innovation. And that means there is less time to invent everything we need. We can't do everything ourselves. IBM needs to have access to the inventions of others.[31]

It acquires these rights "primarily by trading access to its own patents, a process called 'cross-licensing'."[32] IBM has often had the reputation of being a "fast follower" in some areas of technology, and it has used the power of its patent portfolio to negotiate the access needed. The company notes that:

> You get value from patents in two ways: through fees, and through licensing negotiations that give IBM access to other patents. Access is far more valuable to IBM than the fees it receives from its 9000 active [U.S.] patents. There is no direct calculation of this value, but it is many times larger than the fee income, perhaps an order of magnitude larger.[33]

The effect of the consent decree for IBM, as for AT&T, was in large part to formalize policies that were already partly in effect. While IBM already used cross-licensing for design freedom where appropriate, the consent decree expanded the scope and in a sense prodded IBM into treating licensing and cross-licensing as a central aspect of its business.

Impact of Consent Decrees on Industry Development

The combined cross-licensing of basic technology by the technologically leading firms — AT&T, IBM, and others — had a profound influence on the development of the post-war electronics industry. The effect of the 1956 AT&T and IBM consent decrees was to make a huge range of basic semiconductor and telecommunications technology widely available for next to nothing to domestic and foreign firms. Even so, for AT&T and its existing cross-licensing partners, the AT&T 1956 consent decree merely formalized what was already established corporate policy.

This was exchanged for rights to related technology where this was available; otherwise it was offered at low royalty payments. The availability of the basic technology formed the basis for the rapid growth of the semiconductor industry. Given the common technological base, firms relied on the rapid development and introduction of new products to succeed.

Yet the very prevalence of AT&T, IBM, and others in licensing at low royalties also created a mind set in the industry that became accustomed to artificially low royalties. This contributed to some initial agitation, if not outrage, in some quarters when in the 1980s some intellectual property owners such as Texas Instruments began to seek market returns on their IP.[34]

Licensing Practice at a Semiconductor Company — Texas Instruments[35]

Licensing Objectives

In the semiconductor industry, IP licensing is an integral and essential element of competition, and a corollary of innovation. As noted above, the industry was launched with the invention of the transistor by Bell Laboratories in 1947. First commercial transistor production took place in 1952. By 1995, worldwide sales of the industry were over $150 billion. Like other parts of the electronics industry, the semiconductor industry is characterized by wide use of cross-licensing. The main purpose of cross-licensing is to ensure "freedom-to-operate" or "design freedom" in an industry where there are likely to be large numbers of overlapping patents. Given rapid technological development and many industry participants, the probability is high that any new product or process will overlap technology developed by other firms pursuing parallel paths. Also, the technology often overlaps that developed in related industries, such as computers and telecommunications.

The licensing procedures and royalty rate determination process at Texas Instruments (TI) illustrates the ways in which cross-licensing agreements are used in practice. TI has two main licensing objectives. The first and primary objective is to ensure freedom to operate in broad areas of technology supporting given product markets, without running the risk of patent infringement litigation by other firms with similar technology. Agreements cover groups of patents within designated "fields-of-use," including existing and new patents developed within the fixed term of the agreement. The second objective is to obtain value from the firm's IP, in the form of its patent portfolio, by generating royalty income. The purpose and result of royalty payments received under cross-licensing

Table 2. U.S. Patents Granted in Semiconductor Devices and Manufacture (1969–1994)

Company*	Patents Granted (1969–1994)	Patents Granted (1994)
IBM	3435	220
Toshiba	2492	245
Texas Instruments	2366	231
AT&T	2342	110
Hitachi	2218	170
Motorola	1882	210
Mitsubishi	1691	275
RCA	1601	0
Siemens	1518	46
U.S. Philips	1482	61
General Electric	1446	48
NEC	1360	261
Fujitsu	1335	125

*Companies with over 1000 semiconductor patents granted (1969–1994).
Source: USPTO, 1995

agreements is "competitive re-balancing," which equalizes the net cost and profit advantage for imitators who otherwise might free-ride on technology TI developed.

Buying "freedom-to-operate" is vital in the semiconductor industry, with its rapid innovation, short product life cycles, and ubiquity of patents. In a typical technological field, there may be as many as a half dozen other firms with patents that an innovator could potentially infringe while implementing its independent research strategy. In semiconductor devices and manufacture, there are huge numbers of patents to consider, with many more generated each year, as seen in Table 2. Bear in mind that a particular product can utilize technology from several other technology fields, such as computers, software, materials, communications, and general systems, each with large patent establishments.

At the start of an R&D program, possible infringements cannot be easily predicted, as firms are quite ignorant of the R&D and product development plans of competitors. Yet a firm investing in R&D and product development needs to be confident that patents developed through independent R&D efforts by others will not hinder commercialization of its technology. Consider that a water production facility now costs $1 billion.[36] The facility may have a five-year life or longer, and it is not known in advance what products will be developed for manufacture during that time. R&D is similarly becoming more expensive. Companies need to be able to develop new products to fill the wafer fabrication facilities without being concerned that startup may be blocked by patents owned by competitors and other companies inside and outside the industry.

One approach for a developer to deal with the IP rights of others would be simply to identify all infringements as they arise, and negotiate separate licenses for each. However, the transactions costs of such an approach would be inordinate.[37] Moreover, it would expose the potential licensee to large risks.

A typical cross-license includes all patents that licensees may own in a given field-of-use, giving each firm the freedom to infringe the other's existing and future patents for a given period, typically five years. Such licenses are typically non-exclusive and rarely include any trade-secret or know-how transfer or sublicensing rights.[38]

In a cross-license, technology is not usually transferred, as the parties each are capable of using the technology in question without assistance. Firms will usually gain access to the relevant technology either by developing it themselves, or by other means such as reverse engineering, hiring consultants, other technical agreements, or technical publications.[39] In either case, the cross-license primarily confers the right to use the patented technology without being sued for infringement. This avoids monitoring costs and adjusts royalty payments to reflect overall contributions to the stock of IP currently in use.[40]

In the semiconductor industry, licensing agreements sometimes go further, and may include transfer of trade secrets and know-how. However, trade secret licenses are quite different, typically involve technology transfer, and often accompany a joint venture or strategic alliance. Technology transfer involves significant costs and managerial effort, and often "creates competitors', as it frequently transfers to the licensee important technological capabilities otherwise inaccessible.[41]

Types of Cross-Licenses

There are two main models for cross-licensing agreements in the semiconductor industry: "capture" and "fixed period." In the "capture" model the licensee has rights to use, in a given field-of-use, all patents within a technological field which exist or are applied for during the license period, usually five years, and, importantly, retains "survivorship" rights to use the patents until they expire, up to 20 years later. The agreement does not generally list individual patents, but some patents of particular strategic importance to the licensor may be excluded. In the "fixed period" model the licensee has similar rights to use patents existing or applied for during the license period, but with no survivorship rights once the license period has expired. This requires full renegotiation of the cross-license for succeeding periods.

TI has been a leader in the use of fixed period licensing, which is becoming more widely used. The capture model became widespread through the industry following its use by AT&T and IBM. It gives broad rights to patents for a long period. The fixed period model allows more flexible commercialization of patent portfolios, since licensing terms can be periodically adjusted to account for changes in competitive conditions and the value of the technology. This increases strategic flexibility and allows the parties more freedom to negotiate royalty terms so that they more closely mirror the value of the patents. It is a logical evolution of licensing practices reflecting the difficulties and changes in the market for know-how.

"Proud List" Royalty Valuation Process

Balancing payments are negotiated as part of the agreement, to account for the relative value of the IP contributed by two firms. Each firm's contribution is evaluated by estimating the value of a firm's patent portfolio to its licensing partner, with the net royalty payment to the one with the greater contribution. Where both firms contribute similar portfolio values, the net payment will be small or zero. Where one firm has developed little technology and the other a great deal, the payments may be significant. Occasionally, cross-licenses are royalty-free because contributions are either very close or difficult to assess. However, even in royalty-free agreements it should not be assumed that a detailed patent balancing process has not taken place. Also, the cross-license may be included as part of a larger joint venture.

Royalty balancing is performed according to a "proud list" procedure. In this procedure, each firm identifies a sample list of its most valuable patents and this is used as a representative proxy group for estimating the value of the entire portfolio. There is a great deal of preparation before the negotiations. Having identified a potential cross-licensing candidate, TI first performs extensive reverse engineering of the other's products to assess the extent of any infringement — called "reading" the patents on the infringer's products — and identifies product market sizes involved. This may take a year of effort.[42] As part of this effort, it generates the proud list of about 50 of its major patents which it believes are being infringed, and which apply over a large product base of the other firm. The other firm also prepares a proud list of its own strongest patents.

In the negotiations, each of the sample patents is evaluated by both sides according to its quality and coverage. Quality measures include: the legal validity and enforceability of the patent; the technological significance of this feature to the product compared with other (non-infringing) ways of achieving the same end; and the similarity between the infringing features and the patent. These determine quality weighting factors for each patent so that a legally strong patent, which is hard to invent-around and is close to the infringing feature, has a high relative weight. The coverage is the size of the infringer's product market using the patent. Each patent is assigned a nominal royalty rate, which is then multiplied by its quality weighting factor and the annual sales of the affected product base to arrive at a dollar amount. Certain patents of particular strategic significance to the technology are assigned a flat rate as a group and do not go through the weighting process.

The dollar amounts are summed for all the listed patents and expressed as a royalty rate percentage of the licensee's total sales. Typically, the values of each side's estimated royalty payments are netted out to give a single royalty rate paid by the firm with the less valuable portfolio.[43] This royalty rate applies to the licensee's sales for the term of the license. When the license expires the same procedure will be used to reevaluate the relative portfolio values for the next five years.[44]

Strategic Considerations

TI's procedures provide a formal mechanism for determining royalty rates based on best estimates of the economic and technological contribution of the patent portfolios of the two firms. These procedures have been applied to a wide variety of relative IP contributions, both where these are roughly in balance and where not. Even so, there are often other considerations to include in final negotiations of a licensing agreement. Much depends on the individual needs of the parties, their negotiating strength, and the broader strategic considerations of each firm. Individual rates and the overall rates also tend to recognize overall competitive effects of the royalty payments, as well as "what the market will bear."[45]

There is obviously an upper limit on royalties, since royalties that are too high will cripple the competitive capacities of the licensee, causing royalty payments to decline. If a potential problem in this respect exists, it is usually not with an individual agreement, which is likely to be set at reasonable royalty rates. Rather, problems may arise when a licensee is subject to claims from several licensors and the cumulative royalty payments become onerous. This can create serious problems in negotiating agreements with would-be licensees. There does not seem to be an easy solution to this problem, given that agreements are negotiated individually.[46]

Royalty rates may also be affected by longer-term strategic considerations. For one thing, both parties are likely to need to renew the agreement in future, and an aggressive royalty rate now may make negotiations more difficult later, when the balance of IP may have shifted in a different direction. The firms may have, or expect to have, overlapping interests in other market areas, which will also condition negotiations. Licenses often may also be part of a cooperative venture of some kind. Patents can often be traded for know-how, or used as an entry ticket to a joint development arrangement. For example, rather than seek royalties, TI has had technology development agreements with Hitachi. It also has several manufacturing joint ventures around the world.

Strategic considerations may also affect the usual licensing process where the technology is intended to become part of an industry standard. Industry standards bodies sometimes require that patent holders agree to license their patents with low or zero royalty fees, often on a non-discriminatory basis: Similarly, when trying to establish a de facto market standard, a firm may charge low royalty rates.[47] The aim is to ensure the wide adoption of the technology as an industry-wide standard. Value from the technology may then be earned through product sales in an expanded market. The "reasonable rate" royalty involved is likely to be low, though need not be zero.[48]

Impact of TI's Licensing Strategy

TI has led industry moves to take a more active stance on licensing and cross-licensing. The impact of its licensing strategy on its capability to compete and innovate is of particular interest. TI instituted its current licensing strategy in 1985. Cumulative royalty earnings of over $1.8 billion had been achieved during the period from 1986 to 1993. Among other effects, this enabled TI to maintain a high level of R&D spending during 1989-91, when the semiconductor market was in a downturn, as shown in Fig. 1. However, moving to a more active licensing strategy and the aggressive assertion of its IP rights was a major step for the company — and the industry — and involved considerable risk.[49] TI's strategy was enhanced by the stronger U.S. treatment of IP after 1982.

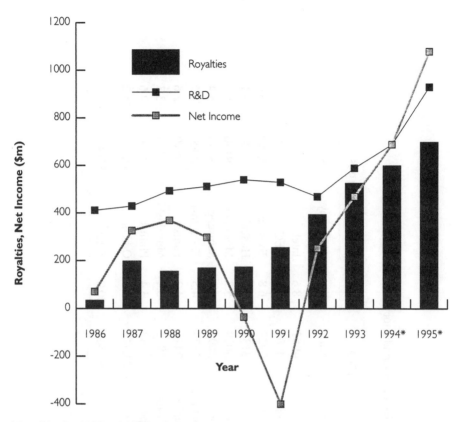

*Royalties for 1994 and 1995 estimated.
Source: Annual Reports

Fig. 1. Texas instruments: Royalty earnings, net income and R&D.

TI's IP portfolio has been valuable in negotiating R&D cooperation. For example, TI has had a series of ventures with Hitachi for the joint technological development of DRAM memory chips. TI's ability to supply technology, supported by its IP rights, was a crucial component in making these agreements.[50] TI's changed IP strategy has allowed it to implement new product market strategies to expand its manufacturing capacity by means of joint ventures, based partly on the negotiating value of its IP portfolio, and expanding its development of high value added components. It has been a partner in a number of international manufacturing joint ventures to set up production facilities for memory chip production.[51] TI and Hitachi also entered a joint venture in 1996 to manufacture DRAMs in Texas.

Table 3. Top 10 Merchant Semiconductor Firms: 1980–1995

	1980			1990			1995		
	Company	$m	%	Company	$m	%	Company	$m	%
1.	Texas Inst.	1580	12.2	NEC	4952	8.6	Intel	13,830	8.9
2.	Motorola	1110	8.5	Toshiba	4905	8.5	NEC	11,360	7.3
3.	Philips	935	7.2	Hitachi	3927	6.8	Toshiba	10,190	6.6
4.	NEC	787	6.1	Intel	3135	5.5	Hitachi	9420	6.1
5.	National	747	5.7	Fujitsu	3019	5.3	Motorola	9170	5.9
6.	Toshiba	629	4.8	Motorola	3692	6.4	Samsung	8340	5.4
7.	Hitachi	622	4.8	Texas Inst.	2574	4.5	Texas Inst.	8000	5.2
8.	Intel	575	4.4	Mitsubishi	2476	4.3	Fujitsu	5510	3.6
9.	Fairchild	566	4.4	Matsushita	1945	3.4	Mitsubishi	5150	3.3
10.	Siemens	413	3.2	Philips	1932	3.4	Philips	4040	2.6
	Others	5036	38.7	Others	24,943	43.4	Others	69,990	45.2
	Total	13,000	100.0	Total	57,500	100.0	Total	155,000	100.0

Source: Dataquest

These changes have had a major impact on TI's performance, helping the company to grow and to increase its world market share since the mid 1980s. This helped reverse a relative decline in its position beginning in the mid-1970s due to inroads made in world markets by foreign producers, as seen in Table 3.

IP Management and Cross-Licensing in an Electronics Company — Hewlett-Packard[52]

Innovation Strategy

Many aspects of licensing elsewhere in electronics are similar to those described for semiconductors. The electronics industry shares many of the basic features of the semiconductor industry: rapid technological innovation, short product life cycles, and significant patenting. The computer, telecommunications, electronics, and semiconductor industries also use many of the same technologies and have been influenced by the practices of AT&T and other major corporations. Field-of-use cross-licensing is used widely.

However, a difference between many electronics firms outside of semiconductors is the breadth of technologies that are practiced. In addition to semiconductor technology, product development may involve integrating many aspects of computing, telecommunications, software, systems design, mechanical engineering, ergonomics and so forth. There are also likely to be complex manufacturing and marketing requirements. Thus, IP strategies in such firms are likely to involve broader considerations.

Hewlett-Packard (HP) produces many different types of products, from laser printers and computers to hand-held calculators and electronic instruments. HP is currently organized into Computer Products, Systems, Measurement Systems, and Test and Measurement organizations.

To maintain its high rate of innovation, a high priority for HP in its IP strategy is maintaining "design freedom." It has two principal objectives: ensuring that its own technology is not blocked by competitor's patents; and ensuring that it has access to outside technology. HP's products include complex systems that typically involve several different technologies, some of which may be developed by other firms and other industries. HP alone cannot develop the complete range of technologies used in its products. To obtain access to needed technologies, Hewlett-Packard needs patents to trade in cross-licensing agreements. The company has a huge portfolio of patents and know-how in leading-edge technologies, developed as part of its extensive R&D programs. This IP portfolio is the basis for protecting HP's own products; it is also invaluable as leverage to ensure access to outside technology.

Licensing Objectives

One type of HP cross-licensing takes place as "program licensing," which is aimed at acquiring access to specific technologies. The company identifies firms with technologies of interest. There may be several different technologies at a given firm so the strategic overlaps must be considered in assessing each licensing opportunity.

HP's licensing activities are not focused primarily on cash income. With a wide range of products, the company's interests in one area are likely to overlap with those in other areas. It may encounter licensing partners in several different markets in a variety of circumstances — a competitor in one field may be a supplier or customer in another. HP does not want negotiations in one product group to interfere with those in another. This leads to a long-term bias towards meaningful cross-licensing agreements and a soft approach to royalties. HP recognizes that it is likely to deal with the same partners repeatedly and therefore normally does not require high royalty rates that could be used as a precedent against it in the future.

There are some exceptions in that some strategic patents are only licensed at high royalty rates, or more likely are not licensed at all. In products where HP has a strong leadership position (e.g. printers), it is unlikely to license out its core IP rights. HP's IP policy in this area is aimed, as it must be, at the aggressive protection of a key source of competitive advantage. The company would normally consider licensing such IP rights only as part of a specific strategic alliance and would normally exclude such technology from cross-licensing agreements.

The form of the cross-license agreements is quite standard, with a limited capture period, usually with survivorship rights. The objective is to estimate the relative value of the infringements that are likely to take place over a five-year period. Other inputs to the licensing decision include the expected R&D spending in the field by each firm, the number of patents held by each party in the particular field, and determination of the value to the infringer of a limited number of pertinent patents. Each side to the agreement may select a limited number of patents which it has determined are being infringed by the other party's products. This may be as few as six to twelve patents each. The imputed royalty fee for these patents over the next five years becomes one of the inputs to the negotiation. In general, this balancing process is not unlike that which exists in the semiconductor industry.

Royalties are often paid as a lump sum. Agreements almost never include sublicensing rights, since the company could lose control of its own technology if sublicensing were permitted. Exclusive licensing is also rare, partly because of potential antitrust concerns, but also because the historical practice of non-exclusive cross-licensing leaves fewer innovations that could be treated as exclusive.

Even after a patent cross-license agreement is concluded, HP policy is not to over-use the technology of the other party to the agreement. This is again related to a long-term view of licensing. The agreement will probably need to be renewed in the future and the more of the other party's technology HP uses, the greater the leverage the other party would have the next time around. Also, patents are lagging indicators of research, so that to be at the forefront of technology each party will need to have developed its own application of the technology well before the patents are issued. One purpose of the agreement is to be able to use the technology in the development of new products without worrying about "accidental infringement."

Licensing is only secondarily seen as a source of royalty earnings. Royalty earnings are significant but not material, given the overall size of HP's operations. However, there are some cases where licensing for revenue is pursued. One is where the company has world-class technology and is approached by others seeking a license. If the technology is not of strategic importance to HP, the company may license it out for profit. Another is the "rifle short" license, where a single patent may be licensed, if it has specific value to a licensee. Licensing terms in either case are usually very simple, amounting to an agreement to allow use of the innovation for a royalty payment or lump sum without being subject to an infringement claim.

IP Management

Given the importance of IP to Hewlett-Packard, a formal IP strategy has been developed for managing its large and diverse IP portfolio. Since products combine many technologies, IP may need to be even more closely integrated with business strategy than at a single product corporation. HP has a series of procedures for identifying technological areas to stress for patent protection and for making individual decisions about the best method of protecting innovations. Obtaining and maintaining patent protection is costly, and hence only selected innovations are patented. This process starts with "templates" to guide what IP should be protected. The templates are updated each year to protect technologies that will be strategically important to the company in the future. These templates are developed by a process that rates and prioritizes products and technologies and reviews patent needs throughout the world. This does not go as far as targeting R&D programs at innovations that will be useful in negotiating cross-licenses; rather it aims to make maximum use of innovations by creating patent portfolios that will be strategically valuable. This supports rather than directs corporate strategy.

The IP protection decision process for individual innovations is shown in Fig. 2. When a product or process innovation is developed, a determination is made whether to patent it, to keep it as a trade secret, or, if it not believed worthwhile to patent, to publish it. The inputs to this decision take place in an internal committee process, with inputs from engineering management and the legal (IP) department. Innovations that are likely to be of strategic value are either patented immediately or, if they are not yet completed or proven, are reviewed again at a later time. If the innovation is valuable but its use by an imitator would be undetectable (such as for some process innovations), then the innovation may be kept as a trade secret. Marginal ideas are published immediately to preempt patenting by a competitor who might later block their use by HP. "Vanity publishers" for publicly disclosing the results of research exist for this purpose.[53]

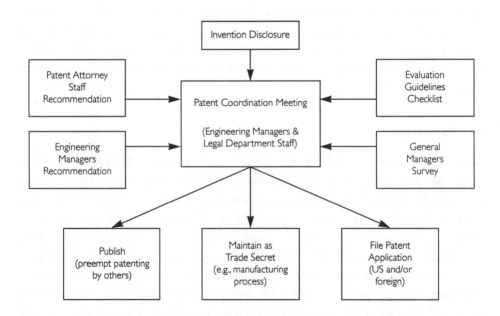

Fig. 2. Intellectual property and patenting decision process at HP.

Managing Intellectual Capital in the Electronics Industry

Contrasting IP Management Objectives

The case studies indicate several similarities in the way firms in the electronics industry use licensing and cross-licensing to ensure design freedom as well as some level of licensing earnings. They also illustrate how differences in management objectives are reflected in cross-licensing strategies.

RCA represents a rather complex organizational response to the problem of design freedom, in which a single company acquired exclusive cross-licensed rights to all the patents needed for radio manufacture. It then licensed out these rights to other manufacturers. Partly as a result, RCA was able to dominate the radio market for many years.

AT&T, as a regulated monopoly before 1984, was primarily interested in the dissemination of technology to as many producers as possible, to develop technologies that would be useful in its telecommunications services — as purchased components or in its own systems development. It was barred from competing in product markets, so it cross-licensed on liberal terms with the aim of stimulating development and obtaining access to new technology.

A primary concern of IBM in cross-licensing has been design freedom. As one of the world's leading innovators it has been very active in using its IP for competitive advantage, both in products and to obtain the widest possible access to other technology. IBM's interests have spanned a wide range of computer related markets and it has needed broad access to many different technologies. It also obtains significant income from its licenses.

TI's interests have generally been more specific to the semiconductor industry, although it also has interests in other areas of electronics. Its concerns have been to obtain freedom-to-operate given the dense patent concentration in semi-conductors, and to obtain cash from cross-licensing its IP, to help fund R&D and to equalize any advantage it would otherwise be allowing competitors using its IP.

Finally, HP is in a somewhat similar position to IBM in having a broad range of interests in different markets and being especially interested in design freedom for products spanning many technologies. HP's breadth of interests — in which a competitor in one field may be a customer, supplier, or venture partner in another — moderates its approach to seeking high royalties. IP is central to its business, needed to support its rapid product innovation and to trade for technology access. It has well developed procedures for developing and protecting IP across its diverse fields.

Changing IP Modes in the Semiconductor Industry

The strengthening of IP rights and increased licensing and cross-licensing have extended the ability of the innovator to earn a reward from R&D. In addition to providing better IP protection for new products, there are greater opportunities for earning value via access to technology, joint ventures, technology exchanges, and R&D collaboration. Royalty earnings have become more significant. Much of this is a recent development and there are many questions as to how much strategic emphasis firms should place on licensing and cross-licensing compared with manufacturing, and on the importance of licensing revenue earning compared with freedom-to-operate.

It may help put these questions in context by reviewing the changing modes of competition in semiconductors, where firms have gradually needed to place increased stress on innovation, IP protection, and licensing and cross-licensing as a basis for product competition. There have been major changes in the way firms have obtained value from innovation as the industry has developed. The weak IP regime in effect during the first two or three decades of the industry was not a barrier to R&D and investment, and the liberal licensing practices used by AT&T and others accelerated the initial diffusion of the technology. This nurtured the early growth of a new industry. However, firms could not operate successfully in today's technological and competitive environment with the strategies and policies in place in the 1950s and 1960s. Competition to stay at the forefront of innovation is sharper and R&D and investment take place on a much bigger scale. AT&T no longer has a franchise monopoly, the market power of other industry participants is at best a phantom, and the industry is global.

Initial growth phase

From 1950 until the late 1970s, semiconductor and electronics firms used technology to open up new markets. Semiconductor technology was new and developing rapidly, and was too big and too important to be developed and commercialized adequately within one organization. There were benefits from having multiple sources of innovation. This was epitomized by AT&T's policy. As a major consumer of semiconductors, it wished to spread the use of the technology as widely as possible. Elements of this reasoning applied to other firms, who benefited from the rapid expansion of technology and markets. And, given the weak protection of IP afforded by the courts at this time, patents were not seen as a major factor in building competitive advantage.[54]

At that time, firms relied primarily on time-to-market advantages to keep ahead. The basic semiconductor patents were already widely licensed, so any individual patent had limited power.[55] Product life cycles were short and often firms would simply not bother to patent inventions, believing that there was no point in patenting products and processes that would soon be obsolete. The fragmented structure of the new "merchant" semiconductor industry (which had grown up around spin-offs from Bell Labs and others), the rapidity of innovation, and the high level of competition reflected the fact that not much attention was paid to protecting IP.[56] The predominant strategy for capturing value from technology involved "riding the experience curve" — reducing prices rapidly as unit costs fell with the hope of earning enough to fund the next round of development.[57]

Second sourcing, licensed or not, was often required by many of the large customers to ensure continuous and competitive supplies. There was significant cross-licensing (often associated with second sourcing), but it rarely involved significant royalty payments.[58]

Customers like the Department of Defense (DOD) had sufficient clout to force small suppliers like Intel to second source. During this period, licenses were mainly used to get some residual value from an innovation when it could not be recovered via the product market because of investment restrictions or trade restrictions. An example is the difficulty U.S. firms had selling products in Japan. Faced with effective trade protection, most U.S. firms' only recourse was to license technology to Japanese firms.[59]

At this time, TI was one of the first firms to make strategic use of its IP. It established a production plant in Japan in 1968, one of the very few foreign firms to do so. It achieved these rights from MITI by using the power of its patent portfolio.[60] This heralded a new role for IP in global commerce and firm competitiveness.

Increased global competition

The competitive environment began to change during the 1970s. The complexity of the technology and the scale of investment in R&D and capacity were rising, increasing the business risk of each new development. Moreover, as requirements for specialized investment increased, the business risk associated with a patent holder's ability to obtain an injunction (in the case of inadvertent or intentional infringement) increased.

Managers were at first distracted by the increasing size of the total market when new mass markets opened up in the 1970s for consumer electronics (including calculators, watches, and later personal computers) and computer memories. By the early 1980s, new competitors from Japan (and later Korea) had entered the world markets and were challenging the U.S. firms, using technology largely developed in the United States. Changes were most dramatic in the manufacture of "commodity" DRAM memory chips, in which U.S. manufacturer's share of the world market fell from 75% in 1980 to 17% in 1986, while over the same period Japanese memory share rose from 25% to 79%.[61] U.S. firms could no longer rely on success in the product market alone to obtain returns from innovation.

The new entrants to the industry depended on access to existing technology and often sought to cross-license it. Yet nominal or royalty-fee cross-licenses, which had been common in the industry prior to the 1980s, came to be seen as unfair when the entrants from outside the industry offered to pay the nominal cross-license fees, but with no balancing portfolios of patents to offer. Royalty fees also reflect payment for access to technology accumulated in prior years, often at great expense. TI and others realized that more detailed evaluation of relative contributions to cross-licenses were required.

Innovation leadership

The situation today is that, with numerous qualified competitors, competitive advantage requires more emphasis on strong IP rights. Stronger IP protection calls for dual strategies for capturing value from technology — the simultaneous use of product manufacturing using the IP in question together with IP licensing. Market developments have put more emphasis on chip design, developed close to the customer, and on being able to protect this and leading-edge process technology from imitation by fully able competitors. The increase in cooperative R&D and manufacturing joint ventures, often underpinned by IP rights, represent a market response to increased costs and the risks of development.

A regime shift occurred when many of the once small semiconductor firms such as Intel could no longer be forced into second sourcing their products. The demise of contractually required second sourcing suddenly made the value of IP more significant. The successful blunting of buyer's demand for second sourcing made IP more important — so much so that many companies, such as Intel, now have designated IP managers.

Many in the semiconductor industry have been opposed to stronger assertion of IP rights, having grown accustomed to a relatively open exchange of ideas and personnel. Not surprisingly, advocates of this view include start-ups, who claim that if they pay the full price of technology, it would limit their ability to compete. This may be true, but it is also trite. We observe that supporters of open ideas often become more protective once they have invested heavily in R&D. Most significantly, there has been a change in the global competitive reality. What may have been a useful model in the early days of the industry (in which it may be argued that all firms in a local market benefit from mutual exchange of ideas), becomes a different equation when firms are global.[62]

Lessons for Innovation Management

To an extent, management today has little choice but to adopt a more active IP and licensing stance. IP rights have been strengthened and, not surprisingly, firms have become more strategic about commercializing IP. Cross-licensing enables firms to protect their IP while at the same time obtaining freedom to manufacture. The new IP and licensing circumstances have increased incentives to build IP portfolios and to innovate. In these new circumstances, there are some key lessons for innovation management.

Using IP to support core business

Despite, or because of, the growing importance of licensing and cross-licensing, IP strategy should still be designed primarily to support technological developments and strategies surrounding the firm's core business. The global marketplace still rewards firms primarily for developing and commercializing products and processes as such, not for developing IP. Accordingly, few firms target technologies primarily for their value in earning royalties or for trading IP rights in future cross-licensing agreements.

Furthermore, for long-term success, firms typically need to be closely involved with the markets in which they operate and to develop core capabilities (in manufacture and design) closely linked to the products and processes. Maintaining a stream of valuable innovations requires extensive, up-to-date information about market demand and technological possibilities, especially in industries where technology is changing rapidly. Although this depends on the nature of the product, it usually also calls for close functional links between design, production, and marketing. These needs are typically best served by active participation in the product market.[63]

The alternative — becoming a pure "licensing company" not directly involved in the product market and increasingly remote from the manufacture and design of the product itself — can be a risky strategy. Such a strategy, on its own, not only risks the erosion of the dynamic capabilities of the firm to continue innovating, it also is likely to be less financially rewarding than developing and commercializing products.[64]

Importance of developing a valuable patent portfolio

Developing a valuable patent portfolio is an increasingly important part of strategy. In the electronics industry, patents are valuable because they provide protection from imitation for new proprietary products and services; they provide bargaining chips in negotiating access to other firms' technology (to avoid patent blocking and ensure freedom-to-operate); and patents may be an additional source of earnings or of reduced royalty fees the firm might otherwise have to pay.

The value of a portfolio is greatest when it has a high-quality patents that cover significant product markets. These patents affect each of the reasons for holding a portfolio, but are seen most directly in the effect on cross-licensing. Patents have greatest cross-licensing value when they give the firm maximum leverage to obtain a favorable cross-license. This means that the patents should be legally and technically strong and should cover key aspects of the licensee's product base.

Concentrate R&D where the firm is strongest

In developing its patent portfolio, the firm can concentrate its R&D in those areas where it has the greatest competitive advantage in developing valuable innovations, provided these are also areas needed by other firms. It need not focus on those technological areas where its cross-licensee is strongest in an attempt to duplicate or avoid the licensee's patents — a hopeless task with complex cumulative technology, such as electronics, where infringement is almost inevitable.[65] This might be in the same fields that it wishes to cross-license from its partners, or it might be in a more specialized area. For cross-licensing with a multidivisional corporation with interests in several markets, it might be in a different business area or field-of-use than the one from which it wishes to access technology. As argued above, a firm is most likely to create valuable IP where it is actively involved in the market, i.e., its core business. Provided this is also a commercially important field to cross-licensing partners, the firm can concentrate on developing and protecting IP in this field, rather than seeking another.

Licensing and cross-licensing enable firms to capture value from technology so long as they contribute to the common pool of industry knowledge. Innovators who are contributors have every incentive to avoid duplicative R&D investments, since a contribution to an industry's useful stock of proprietary knowledge is recognized no matter what the precise domain of applicability. Firms are advised to focus on innovating where they can best make a contribution to the development of quality patents they and other firms are likely to need. Cross-licensing thus enables firms to play to their technological strengths.

Although the number of patents a firm holds is important, of even greater importance is their quality. A single key patent is often worth more than a portfolio of questionable ones when it comes to assessing the ability of a patent owner to stop an infringer. The most effective way to acquire a portfolio of valuable patents is likely to be through in-house R&D. Occasionally, firms can purchase a portfolio of patents with which to establish cross-licensing relationships; but quality patents often are not available in this fashion.

In summary, the reality of the global marketplace today indicates that firms should proactively develop IP portfolios with an eye towards value in the market for know-how. A corollary is that to create a valuable patent portfolio for cross-licensing, it matters little where R&D is aimed, so long as it creates quality patents in a field that one's competitors need to license.

Policy Issues

Intellectual property is more critical than ever to competitive advantage and, as a result, is being given increasing attention by strategists and policy makers. IP protection has been strengthened and firms are more actively defending and exploiting their IP. Coincident with the increased importance of patents is the increased importance of licensing and cross-licensing. Cross-licensing has become a significant dimension of competition. Absent the ability to offer an equivalent IP portfolio, licensees must incur considerable costs. This in and of itself is a spur to innovation.

Cross-licensing outcomes do not, however, tilt towards the large firm at the expense of the small. Rather, they favor firms with significant IP regardless of size. In a particular market niche where patents from two firms overlap, a small firm may have as many patents as a large firm, and as much bargaining power as the large firm. It may have sufficient IP leverage to block a larger competitor by pursuing a claim in court (or credibly threatening to do so). Indeed, in the evaluation process, a small innovator with a strong patent may be the net gainer, if the patent applies to a high-volume product of a large corporation.[66] Some competitors may possess "equal patents but unequal products." Nor need the licensing process disadvantage a new entrant firm. If a new entrant has significant relevant technology, it can in principle be a beneficiary of the cross-licensing regime.

Those investing in R&D need to ensure that they earn an adequate return, and royalties from licensing are an increasingly significant part. A company that develops technology will be at a competitive disadvantage in the market if its competitors are free to use its technology without incurring any expenses. Licensing fees on patented technology help ensure that the innovator earns an adequate return, which helps support future R&D. Cross-licensing helps balance the costs for developers and imitators. Thus, products manufactured by imitators who have not performed R&D do not have a competitive advantage merely by virtue of engaging in "copycat" imitation. If both parties to a licensing agreement have contributed similarly to a product field-of-use — in terms of the number, quality, product base coverage, and commercial significance of the patents included in the agreement — then the net royalty payments will be small, or possibly zero. In short, royalty payments help level the playing field, thereby ensuring competition on the merits.

The result is that IP now often has great value, both as a lever to obtain design freedom and as a vehicle to assist innovators in capturing value from innovation. This is of considerable consequence to firms without much IP — they must expect to pay — and also for firms with significant IP portfolios. IP and other knowledge assets are the core assets of many high-technology companies.

However, and perhaps because IP rights have become more valuable, infringers do not always step forward and offer to pay royalties. Accordingly, patent owners must often be proactive in obtaining royalty payments. Litigation or the threat of it may sometimes be necessary to enforce one's rights. Unfortunately, at least in the U.S., litigation is often slow and costly, and antitrust and patent misuse defenses are often raised, sometimes frivolously. The archaic state of the law on patent misuse may further handicap the chances of efficient and socially desirable outcomes.[67] Moreover, antitrust attorneys are often ready to argue that a package license is a tying arrangement with anticompetitive effects, and/or that cross-licensing is a front for collusion. However, the truth of the matter is that such arguments are out of step with the new competitive order.

Such arrangements are pro-innovation and pro-competitive. There would appear to be a significant knowledge gap in some circles with respect to the nature, purposes, and effects of cross-licensing. For instance, the field-of-use cross-licensing of patents in widespread use today is quite different from the traditional practice of licensing and cross-licensing involving individual patents. In the electronics industries, it is simply too cumbersome and transactionally costly to license specific patents for specific products, and so licensing commonly proceeds on a portfolio basis. Yet patent misuse and patent antitrust arguments often assume a world where infringement is easy to detect and costless to enforce. This is rarely the case in the electronics industry today.

At the most elementary level, licensing and cross-licensing involve merely the sale or exchange of property rights. Indeed, it often involves precisely that and no more. However, such arrangements ensure that firms have freedom-to-operate in developing and using innovations, without risking infringement claims from holders of patents in the same field of technology. In industries experiencing rapid technological innovation, patents, even when developed independently, will inevitably overlap technological domains worked by other firms. Cross-licensing agreements provide firms active in R&D with protection against inadvertent infringement and the rights to use the licensee's patents. Cross-licensing arrangements provide a mechanism for recognizing contributions through the establishment of balancing royalty payments. Royalty flows thus recognize the relative contributions to the product technology of the parties, thereby providing a mechanism for net takers to compensate net contributors. The arrangements thereby provide some limited protection against "free riders" who wish to use an industry's stock of proprietary knowledge without contributing. Balancing royalty payments are part of most cross-licenses, even when the main purpose is freedom-to-operate. "Pure" royalty free cross-licenses are rare for some companies and nowadays tend only to apply where the patent portfolios of both firms are large and the overall technological balance is both hard to assess and roughly equal.

Conclusion

Licensing is no longer a marginal activity in semiconductors and electronics. Whereas the management of patents and other forms of IP have always been of great importance in some industries like chemicals and pharmaceuticals, the ascendancy of IP in electronics is relatively recent. This is not just because the industry is new, but because regulatory and judicial distortions which impaired the value of IP have now been substantially rectified. The U.S. Department of Justice (DOJ) and the Courts forced AT&T, and to a lesser extent IBM, to license their technologies way below market value.[68] Not surprisingly, the electronics industry worldwide grew up with a distorted view of the value of intellectual property. This was reinforced by second sourcing requirements imposed by the DOD and other large buyers of integrated circuits that could, and did, insist on licensing for second sourcing purposes at low or zero royalties. Moreover, AT&T itself, being a significant purchaser of telecommunications and electronic equipment, and with protected service markets, had private incentives to diffuse technology rather than use it to build competitive advantage.

This confluence of very special factors has ended. The AT&T consent decree is gone, and AT&T must now be far more proprietary with its technology. The

IBM patent provisions ended in 1961. Intel, TI, and other integrated circuit producers are no longer forced to second source. Moreover, the courts are more inclined to enforce IP rights than ever before. In these respects, hopefully the DOJ/FTC 1995 Antitrust Guidelines for the Licensing of IP, which include statements regarding the potential efficiency benefits of licensing and cross-licensing, are an important step in the right direction and reflect more modern thinking about IP.[69] However, these guidelines are non-binding in litigation, though one would of course hope that the courts would take them into account.

The old regime — whereby the antitrust authorities pressed major IP owners to give up whatever rights they held, where the courts were reluctant to enforce IP rights and were eager to see IP as a barrier to competition rather than as an instrument of it — has faded away. Meanwhile, the ability of the buyers of electronic componentry to bargain for and achieve second source arrangements (which indirectly lowered the value of IP by causing owners to create their own competition) has declined. As a result of these developments, a new order has emerged in which IP rights are valuable. Firms must either invest in R&D and develop patentable technology, or pay to license the patent portfolios of others. The free ride appears to be coming to an end, and IP management is now critical to the success of new entrants and incumbents alike.

Notes

1. By "IT," we refer of course to information technology.
2. In cross-licensing, two or more firms license their IP to each other.
3. Cross-licensing is not the same as a patent pool, in which member firms contribute patents to a common pool and each member accesses them on the same conditions. In cross-licensing, firms agree one-on-one to license their IP to each other and retain control over their proprietary technology, which is used for competitive advantage via product manufacturing and further licensing.
4. Other examples of "cumulative systems" include aircraft and automobiles. In aircraft, problems of blocking patents, stemming from different approaches by pioneers such as the Wright Brothers and Curtiss, were only resolved during World War II when automatic cross-licensing was introduced. In automobiles, the Association of Licensed Automobile Manufacturers (although formed to exploit the Selden patent) developed means for automatic cross-licensing of patents early this century. In both cases, the lack of cross-licensing probably held up industry development. R. Merges and R. Nelson, On the Complex Economics of Patent Scope, *Columbia Law Review* 90 (1990), 839–916.

5. In chemicals and pharmaceuticals, although patenting is extensive, individual technology development paths are less likely to overlap, and cross-licensing may be used to ensure broad product lines. For licensing strategy in the chemicals industry, see P. Grindley and J. Nickerson, Licensing and Business Strategy in the Chemicals Industry, in R. Parr and P. Sullivan (eds.), *Technology Licensing Strategies* (Wiley, New York, 1996), pp. 97–120.

6. The early history of radio is described in: G. Archer, *History of Radio to 1926* (American Historical Society, New York, 1938); W. Maclaurin, *Invention and Innovation in the Radio Industry* (Macmillan, New York, 1949); J. Jewkes, D. Sawers and R. Stillerman, *The Sources of Innovation* (Norton, New York, 1969), pp. 286–288; G. Douglas, *The Early Days of Radio Broadcasting* (McFarland, Jefferson, NC, 1987); Merges and Nelson, op. cit., pp. 891–896.

7. These included the high-frequency alternator, high-frequency transmission arc, magnetic amplifier, selective tuning, crystal detector, heterodyne signal detection, diode valve, triode valve, high vacuum tube, and directional aerials.

8. Not all early inventors were independent. Alexanderson — who improved the Fessenden alternator, invented a magnetic amplifier, electronic amplifier, and multiple tuned antenna, and co-invented the "Alexanderson-Beverage static eliminator" — was a General Electric employee.

9. AT&T acquired the de Forest triode and feedback patents in 1913–1914 for $90,000, and his remaining feedback patents in 1917 for $250,000; Westinghouse cross-licensed the Fessenden heterodyne interests in 1920, and acquired the Armstrong super heterodyne patents in 1920 for $335,000. Archer, op. cit., p. 135; Maclaurin, op cit., p. 106.

10. The fact that GE and AT&T alone were each devoting major research attention to the vacuum tube led to no less than twenty important patent interferences in this area. Maclaurin, op. cit., p. 97.

11. Federal Trade Commission, *The Radio Industry* (FTC, Washington DC, 1923); Maclaurin, op. cit., p. 99.

12. To cite one important example, Marconi and de Forest both had critical valve patents. Marconi's diode patent was held to dominate de Forest's triode patent. Both technologies were vital to radio, yet the interests refused to cross-license. [Archer, op. cit., pp. 113–114; Douglas, op. cit., p. 12.] The application of the triode (audion) to feedback amplification was also the subject of a long-running patent priority dispute between de Forest and Armstrong (finally resolved in de Forest's favor by the Supreme Court in 1934). Its use in transmission oscillation was the subject of four-way patent interference between Langmuir, Meissner, Armstrong, and de Forest. [Maclaurin, op. cit., p. 77.] These problems held up the use of the triode — a crucial component of signal transmission, detection, and amplification, which has been called "the heart and soul of radio" [Douglas, op. cit., p. 8], and "so outstanding in its consequences it almost ranks with the greatest inventions of all time" [Nobel Prize physicist Rabi, quoted in Maclaurin, op. cit., p. 70].

13. A main concern of the U.S. Navy was that international wireless communications were dominated by the British firm Marconi, and the patent impasse helped perpetuate this. It favored the establishment of an "All American" company in international communications. RCA was formed by GE in 1919, and simultaneously acquired the American Marconi Corp. Major shareholders included GE, AT&T (1920) and Westinghouse (1921). Archer, op. cit., pp. 176–189; Maclaurin, op. cit., p. 105.

14. As part of its role in the formation of RCA, the U.S. Navy also initiated cross-licensing to resolve the patent situation in radio manufacture. It wished to have clear rights to use the radio equipment it purchased, without risking litigation due to the complex patent ownership — noting in 1919 that "there was not a single company among those making radio sets for the Navy which possessed basic patents sufficient to enable them to supply, without infringement, ... a complete transmitter or receiver." A formal letter suggesting "some agreement between the several holders of permanent patents whereby the market can be freely supplied with [vacuum] tubes," sent from the Navy to GE and AT&T in January 1920, may be seen as an initiating point for cross-licensing in the industry. Archer, op. cit., pp. 180–186; Maclaurin, op. cit., pp. 99–110.

15. RCA concluded cross-license agreements with firms including GE, Westinghouse, AT&T, United Fruit Company, Wireless Specialty Apparatus Company, Marconi (Britain), CCTF (France), and Telefunken (Germany). Archer, op. cit., p. 195; Maclaurin, op. cit., p. 107.

16. A distinction was that the RCA cross-licenses typically granted (reciprocal) exclusive rights to use the patents in given territories or markets, compared with the non-exclusive cross-licenses that became the norm later. The cross-license with GE (and later Westinghouse) included provisions for the supply of components to RCA. The RCA cross-licenses were for very long terms — many for 25 years, from 1919 to 1945. They covered current and future patents. Other radio manufacturers took licenses with RCA, starting in the late 1920s. Some of RCA's cross-licensing policies were later questioned on antitrust grounds, and modified following a consent decree in 1932. Archer, op. cit., pp. 381–387; Maclaurin, op. cit., pp. 107–109, 132–152.

17. Historical perspective on competition in the telecommunications industry is given in: M. Irwin, The Telephone Industry, in W. Adams (ed.), *The Structure of American Industry*, 5th ed. (Macmillan, New York, 1977), pp. 312–333; G. Brock, *The Telecommunications Industry: The Dynamics of Market Structure* (Harvard University Press, Cambridge, MA, 1981); Office of Technology Assessment, *Information Technology Research and Development: Critical Trends and Issues* (Pergamon Press, New York, 1985); R. Noll and B. Owen, The Anticompetitive Uses of Regulation: United States v. AT&T, in J. Kwoka and L. White (eds.), *The Antitrust Revolution* (Macmillan, New York, 1989); G. Rosston and D. Teece, Competition and "Local" Communications: Innovation, Entry, and Integration, *Industrial and Corporate Change* 4/4 (1995).

18. OTA, op. cit.; M. Noll, Bell System R&D Activities: The Impact of Divestiture, *Telecommunications Policy* 11 (1987), 161–178; R. Harris, Divestiture and Regulatory Policies, *Telecommunications Policy* 14 (1990), 105–124.

19. The two substantive provisions of the 1956 consent decree were that (a) it confined AT&T to providing regulated telecommunications services, and its manufacturing subsidiary Western Electric to making equipment for those services (effectively prohibiting it from selling semiconductors in the commercial market), and (b) all patents controlled by the Bell System should be licensed to others on request. Licenses for the 8600 patents included in existing cross-licensing agreements were royalty free to new applicants, and licenses to all other existing or future patents were to be issued at a non-discriminatory "reasonable royalty" (determined by the court if necessary). AT&T was also to provide technical information along with the patent licenses for reasonable fees. Licenses were unrestricted, other than being non-transferable. [*U.S.A. v. Western Electric Co. Inc. and AT&T*, Civil Action, 17–49, Final Judgement, January 24, 1956; Brock, op. cit., pp. 166, 191–194; R. Levin, The Semiconductor Industry, in R. Nelson (ed.), *Government and Technical Progress* (Pergamon, New York, 1982), pp. 9–101.] In fact, AT&T went beyond the Consent Decree in its efforts to diffuse transistor technology, including symposia and direct efforts to spread know-how. [Levin, op. cit., pp. 76–77.]

20. See section later in this article on "Lessons for Innovation Management."

21. "We realized that if [the transistor] was as big as we thought, we couldn't keep it to ourselves and we couldn't make all the technical contributions. It was to our interest to spread it around." AT&T executive, quoted in Levin, op. cit., p. 77, after J. Tilton, *International Diffusion of Technology: The Case of Semiconductors* (The Brookings Institution, Washington, DC, 1971).

22. By 1983, Bell Labs had received 20,000 patents. This may be compared to about 10,000 currently at IBM and 6000 at Texas Instruments.

23. W. Kefauver, Intellectual Property Rights and Competitive Strategy: An International Telecommunications Firm, in M. Wallerstein, M.E. Mogee and R. Schoen (eds.), *Global Dimensions of Intellectual Property Rights in Science and Technology* (National Academy Press, Washington, DC, 1993), pp. 236–240.

24. For the capture model, see section below on "Policy Issues." The survivorship period could be as much as 17 years from the grant date (possibly several years after filing), under U.S. patent rules prior to 1995, or 20 years from the filing date, after 1995.

25. In the U.S., during 1953–1968, 5128 semiconductor patents were awarded. Bell Laboratories was granted 16% of these; the next five firms were RCA, General Electric, Westinghouse, IBM, and Texas Instruments. Tilton, op. cit.

26. E. von Hippel, Cooperation Between Rivals: Informal Know-How Trading, *Research policy* 16 (1987), 416–424; A. Saxenian, Regional Networks and the Resurgence of Silicon Valley, *California Management Review* 33/1 (Fall 1990), 89–112.

27. There are also transactions costs reasons for using bundled licensing, as noted previously.

28. If the parties could not agree on a reasonable royalty rate, the court could impose one. Patent rights could be very long lived, since, at that time, patent life was 17 years from the grant date, which might be some years after the filing date. The patent licensing provisions ended in 1961. The decree also included other provisions related to the sale of IBM products and services. U.S.A. v. International Business Machines Corporation, CCH 1956 Trade Cases para. 68, 245, SDNY 1956.

29. This increased from $345 million in 1993 [IBM Annual Report, 1994]. IBM initiated a more active approach to licensing in 1988, when it increased the royalty rates sought on its patents from 1% of sales revenue on products using IBM patents to a range of 1% to 5%. Computerworld, April 11, 1988, p. 105.

30. R. Smith, Management of a Corporate Intellectual Property Law Department, *AIPLA Bulletin* (April/June 1989), pp. 817–823; C. Boyer, The Power of the Patent Portfolio, *Think* 5 (1990), 10–11.

31. Gary Markovits, IBM patent process manager, in Boyer, op. cit., p. 10.

32. Jim McGrody, IBM VP and director of research, in Boyer, op. cit.

33. Roger Smith, IBM assistant general counsel, in Boyer, op. cit. In all, IBM has about 11,000 active inventions, with about 35,000 active patents around the world. Smith, op. cit.

34. Many firms in the U.S. semiconductor industry were reported to be "dismayed" and "outraged" over the higher royalties and more active IP strategies of TI and others. [S. Weber, The Chip Industry is Up in Arms Over TI's Pursuit of Intellectual Property Rights at the ITC, *Electronics*, February 1991, p. 51.] For example, T.J. Rodgers, CEO of Cypress Semiconductor described the practice of increased litigation over patent rights as a "venture capital investment." [*Upside*, December 1990.] Others have questioned whether the strengthening of patent rights might be hindering innovation, by enabling IP holders to demand "crippling royalties from young companies." Several small Silicon Valley semiconductor firms, including Cypress Semiconductor, LSI Logic, and VLSI Technology, formed a consortium to defend themselves against patent suits. [B. Glass, Patently Unfair: The System Created to Protect the Individual Inventor May be Hindering Innovation, *InfoWorld*, October 29, 1990, p. 56.] Although some Japanese manufacturers reportedly described royalty demands as "possibly exorbitant," the Japanese response has generally been to increase their own patenting effort. [*Computergram*, September 14, 1990; Weber, op. cit.] Similar objections to increased patent strength and licensing activity have also been evident in resistance to the growing use of patents for computer software, which it has been claimed may restrict innovation by small enterprises. [B. Kahin, The Software Patent Crisis, *Technology Review*, April 1990, pp. 53–58.] However, here too, many software firms who at first resisted the trend have now accepted the need to build their own patent portfolios. [M. Walsh, Bowing to Reality, Software Maker Begins Building a Patent Portfolio, *The Recorder*, August 17, 1995, p. 1.]

35. This section is based in part on discussions with Texas Instruments executives. However, the views expressed here are those of the authors and should not be seen as necessarily reflecting those of Texas Instruments.

36. The costs of manufacturing facilities have risen dramatically. A new wafer fabrication plant cost $10–20 million in 1975 (4-kilobit DRAM), $300–400 million in 1990 (16-megabit DRAM) and over $1 billion in 1991 (256-megabit DRAM). SEMATECH, *Annual Report*, 1991; Foreign Alliances Which Make Sense, *Electronic Business*, September 3, 1990, p. 68.

37. Without field-of-use cross-licenses, a typical semiconductor firm might need to reverse engineer an average of two or three competitors' products a day, as each is introduced over the course of a five-year license, to ascertain whether these are infringing its patents. It must do the same for its own products. This would be prohibitively expensive. Tracking sales by each of hundreds of affected products, on a patent by patent basis, to ascertain royalties, would be virtually impossible.

38. In some cases, where there are only a few very specific overlaps between two firms' technology needs, firms may choose to license single patents. Although an option, it is rarely convenient compared with field-of-use cross-licensing when there are substantial technology overlaps.

39. R. Levin, A. Klevorick, R. Nelson and S. Winter, Appropriating the Returns to Industrial R&D, *Brookings Papers on Economic Activity* 3 (1987), 783–820. Of course, even reading the patent is a helpful guide to someone knowledgeable in the field.

40. The most powerful threat to enforce a patent is an injunction to close down the infringer's production line. This could be ruinous for a manufacturing corporation, especially in fast developing markets such as electronics and semiconductors. The threat of damages may also be important, but as these are often based on projected royalties (and hence may be little worse than freely negotiated licensing terms) they are less potent, unless multiplied by the court.

41. For the economics of technology transfer see D. Teece, The Market for Know-How and the Efficient International Transfer of Technology, *Annals of the American Academy of Political and Social Science* 458 (1981), 81–96.

42. Reverse engineering a semiconductor product is not a simple matter, involving as it does decapping and microscopic examination at the submicron level. Although the process is by now largely automated, it can take 400–500 man-hours per device.

43. For cross-licenses with firms outside the semiconductor industry, such as the personal computer industry, the process used is simpler. In this case, there may be few patents to balance against the proffered patents. Licensing follows precedents long established in the computer industry, primarily under the leadership of IBM, as the holder of many of the patents used in the industry. The negotiations are similar, but the weighting process is not involved. Royalty rates are influenced by industry norms.

44. In some cases licensees may only wish to license a few selected patents, rather than all patents in a field-of-use. For this reason licenses are generally also offered for

individual or specific patents, as well as for all patents in a given field. However, there are significant transactions savings to both sides from a field-of-use license, and the cost per patent is likely to be higher when only a few patents are licensed.

45. For general considerations affecting royalty rates, see M. Lee, Determining Reasonable Royalty, *Les Nouvelles* 27 (1992), 124–128; R. Parr, *Intellectual Property Infringement Damages: A Litigation Support Handbook* (Wiley, New York, 1993).

46. To an extent this may be a transactional problem. As licensing becomes more widespread, individual licenses are more likely to be negotiated in the knowledge that other licenses, potential or actual, must be taken into account.

47. For strategies to establish standards see R. Hartman and D. Teece, Product Emulation Strategies in the Presence of Reputation Effects and Network Externalities, *Economics of Innovation and New Technology* 1 (1990), 157–182; L. Gabel, *Competitive Strategies and Product Standards* (McGraw-Hill, London, 1991); P. Grindley, *Standards, Strategy, and Policy: Cases and Stories* (Oxford University Press, Oxford, 1995).

48. However liberal the licensing terms, the patent holder should not inadvertently assign away IP rights beyond those specifically needed to operate the standard, and may need to condition rights over its IP to uses related to the standard. The innovator might otherwise be deterred from participating in standards setting. There is a balance to be drawn between committing to an open standard and limiting that commitment to what is needed for the standard and to keep access open in future.

49. Risks include the likelihood that the validity of the patents would be challenged in court, that firms — and nations — would retaliate, and that the corporate image with customers would suffer. Patent assertion against customers and partners is an especially sensitive area.

50. R&D agreements with Hitachi have ranged from a 4-megabit DRAM know-how exchange in 1988 to a 256-megabit DRAM co-development agreement in 1994. According to Yasutsugu Takeda of Hitachi, "You can't create [a successful cooperative venture] just because you sign up a lot of companies that are barely committed and don't have anything to bring." The Hitachi-TI collaboration on 256-megabit memory chips has been successful because it is a "meeting of equals" [*Business Week*, June 27, 1994, p. 79]. Complementary capabilities are generally considered important factors in selecting international collaborative venture partners. D. Mowery, "International Collaborative Ventures and the Commercialization of New Technologies," in N. Rosenberg, R. Landau and D. Mowery, *Technology and the Wealth of Nations* (Stanford University Press, Stanford, CA, 1992), pp. 345–380.

51. TI entered joint ventures during 1989–1990 to build manufacturing plants with total investments over $1 billion: with the Italian government; Acer (Taiwan); Kobe Steel (Japan); and the Singapore government, HP, and Canon (Singapore).

52. This section is based in part on discussions with Hewlett-Packard executives. However, the views expressed here are those of the authors, and should not be seen as necessarily reflecting those of Hewlett-Packard.

53. Examples include *Research Disclosure* and other publications. Such journals charge fees to authors, yet often have large circulations for reference libraries and research laboratories.
54. Surveys of executives in a range of industries taken in the early 1980s typically rated methods such as lead time and superior sales and service effort as the most effective means of protecting innovations, rather than patent protection, which was considered relatively ineffective. Levin *et al.*, op. cit.
55. The original transistor process patents were held by AT&T, so that all transistor manufacturers needed to cross-license their own patents at least with AT&T. Similarly, the key patents for the integrated circuit (IC) technology were held by two firms, TI and Fairchild, ensuring that these too were widely licensed. With the critical patents widely available, the cumulative nature of innovation guaranteed broad cross-licensing. Levin, op. cit., pp. 79–82.
56. The first commercial producers of transistors in the 1950s, using AT&T licenses, included Shockley Labs, Fairchild, Motorola and TI. These gave rise to a wave of spin-off companies in the 1960s, such as National Semiconductor, Intel, AMD, Signetics and AMI, which in turn gave rise to subsequent waves of new companies, such as, Cypress Semiconductor, Cyrix, LSI Logic, Chips and Technologies, Brooktree Semiconductor, and others.
57. At TI this approach was formalized in the Objectives, Strategies, and Tactics (OST) product development management process, including "design to cost" methods formalizing experience curve pricing procedures. *Business Week*, September 18, 1978; B. Uttal, TI Regroups, *Fortune*, August 9, 1982, p. 40; M. Martin, *Managing Technological Innovation and Entrepreneurship* (Reston, Reston, VA, 1984); R. Burgelman and M. Maidique, *Strategic Management of Technology and Innovation* (Irwin, Homewood, IL, 1988).
58. Tilton, op. cit.; M. Borrus, J. Millstein and J. Zysman, *International Competition in Advanced Industrial Sectors: Trade and Development in the Semiconductor Industry* (U.S. Department of Commerce, Washington, DC, 1982).
59. Borrus *et al.*, op. cit.
60. The same is broadly true of IBM's entry into Japan.
61. Dataquest figures, quoted in United Nations Organization (UNO), *The Competitive Status of the U.S. Electronics Sector* (United Nations Organization, New York, 1990). For comments on the U.S. recovery since the late 1980s, see W. Spencer and P. Grindley, SEMATECH After Five Years: High-Technology Consortia and U.S. Competitiveness, *California Management Review* 35/4 (Summer 1993), 9–32; P. Grindley, D. Mowery and B. Silverman, SEMATECH and Collaborative Research: Lessons in the Design of High-Technology Consortia, *Journal of Policy Analysis and Management* 13 (1994), 723–758.
62. For contrasting views on the responses of Silicon Valley to international competition, see R. Florida and M. Kenney, Why Silicon Valley and Route 128 Can't Save Us, *California Management Review* 33/1 (Fall 1990), 66–88; Saxenian, op. cit.

63. Hazards for innovation when a firm is remote from business transactions, and hence from the technological frontier, are outlined in J. de Figueiredo and D. Teece, Strategic Hazards and Safeguards in Competitor Supply, *Industrial and Corporate Change*, Vol. 5.2 (1996). The similar vulnerability of the "virtual corporation," which contracts out development and manufacturing, is discussed in H. Chesbrough and D. Teece, When Is Virtual Virtuous: Organizing for Innovation, *Harvard Business Review*, January/February 1996, pp. 65–73.

64. For the nature of dynamic capabilities of firms and their relationship to innovation, see D. Teece and G. Pisano, The Dynamic Capabilities of Firms: An Introduction, *Industrial and Corporate Change* Vol. 3.3 (1994), 537–556; D. Teece, G. Pisano and A. Shuen, Dynamic Capabilities and Strategic Management, *Strategic Management Journal* (forthcoming in 1997). For the role of complementary assets in commercializing innovation, see D. Teece, Profiting from Technological Innovation, *Research Policy* 15 (1986), 285–305.

65. Indeed, in some cases the firm might conceivably do better if it has strengths in an area where the licensee is relatively weak, since it will have greatest difficulty avoiding their patents in those areas, whereas where it is strongest it may have more ability to invent around the patents.

66. An example is Brooktree Corporation, a small semiconductor design company in San Diego, which concluded a favorable cross-licensing agreement with TI in 1993.

67. See E. Sherry and D. Teece, The Patent Misuse Doctrine: An Economic Reassessment, in *Antitrust Fundamentals*, ABA Section of Antitrust Law, Chicago (forthcoming).

68. IP rights to the transistor were given away to U.S. and foreign firms for very small amounts. Levin, op. cit.

69. DOJ/FTC, *Antitrust Guidelines for the Licensing of IP*, April 6, 1995 (U.S. Department of Justice and the Federal Trade Commission, Washington, DC, 1995).

The Market for Know-How and the Efficient International Transfer of Technology

David J. Teece*

This article explores the nature of international technology transfer and the operation of the market for know-how. It begins by examining the relationship between codification and transfer costs and then analyzes various imperfections in the market for know-how. The special properties of know-how are shown to confound various aspects of the exchange process when arms-length contracting is involved. The internalization of the exchange process within multinational firms serves to bypass many of these difficulties, and explains why the multinational firm is of such importance. Several forms of regulation of technology imports and exports are examined. It is discovered that the process is insufficiently well understood to permit the design of effective regulation that, moreover, appears unlikely to eliminate inefficiency. An efficiency focus is maintained throughout since I feel no qualification on pontificate on complex and confused distributional issues.

1. Introduction

ECONOMIC prosperity rests upon knowledge and its useful application. International, interregional, and interpersonal differences in levels of living can

Reprinted from *AAPSS* 458 (November 1981), 81–96.

*David J. Teece is associate professor of business economics at the Graduate School of Business, Stanford University. He has a bachelor's and master's degree from the University of Canterbury, Christchurch, New Zealand, and a doctorate in economics from the University of Pennsylvania, which he received in 1975. Professor Teece specializes in the fields of industrial organization and the economics of technological change, and has published numerous scholarly articles and monographs on the multinational firm, the organization of the petroleum industry, the behavior of the Organization of Petroleum Exporting Countries (OPEC), and the relationship between the internal organization and performance of large enterprises.

Note: The financial support of the National Science Foundation is gratefully acknowledged, together with the valuable comments from Max Boisot, Almarin Phillips and Oliver Williamson.

be explained, at least in part, by differences in the production techniques employed. Throughout history, advances in knowledge have not been uniformly distributed across nations and peoples, but have been concentrated in particular nations at particular times. According to Kuznets, (... the increase in the stock of useful knowledge and the extension of its application are of the essence of modern economic growth ... . No matter where these technological and social innovations emerge ... the economic growth of any given nation depends on their adoption. In that sense, whatever the national affiliation of resources used, any single nation's economic growth has its base somewhere outside its boundaries — with the single exception of the pioneering nations.[1])

The rate at which technology is diffused worldwide depends heavily on the resource costs of transfer — both transmittal and absorption costs — and on the magnitude of the economic rents obtained by the seller. The resource costs of transfer depend on the characteristics of the transmitter, the receiver, the technology being transferred, and the institutional mode chosen for transfer.[2] These are matters explored in the following section.

The rents obtained are a function of the working of the market for know-how, a matter explored in a subsequent section. The last two sections explore regulatory issues with respect to this market from the perspective first of less-developed country (LDC) importers and from the perspective of the United States as a net exporter of know-how. What emerges is an understanding of the technology transfer process, the role of the multinationals, and the difficulties and occasional contradictions associated with regulation. In no sense can the market for know-how and the transfer process be said to operate in an ideal fashion. However, internalization of the process appears to offer considerable efficiencies, and "codes of conduct" are likely to confound the very objectives of importers, while export controls can be expected to yield only limited benefits, and then only under special conditions.

Codification and Transfer Costs

The fact that different individuals, organizations, or nations possess different types of knowledge and experience creates opportunities for communication and

---

[1] S. Kuznets, *Modern Economic Growth: Rate, Structure, Spread* (Yale University Press, New Haven, 1966).

[2] The concept and measurement of the resource cost of transfer can be found in David Teece, *The Multinational Corporation and the Resource Cost of International Technology Transfer* (Ballinger, Cambridge, 1976), and in "Technology Transfer by Multinational Firms: The Resource Cost of International Technology Transfer," *Economic Journal*, June 1977.

mutually profitable transfer. Yet, paradoxically, such transfer as does take place among individuals and organizations, can only do so on the basis of similarities in the knowledge and experience each possess. A shared context appears necessary for the formulation of meaningful messages. Transmittal and receiving costs are lower the greater the similarities in the experience of the transmitting unit and the receiving unit; for the greater these similarities, the easier it is to transfer technology in codified form, such as blueprints, formulas, or computer languages.

Furthermore, there appears to be a simple but powerful relationship between codification[3] of knowledge and the costs of its transfer. Simply stated, the more a given item of knowledge or experience has been codified, the more economically it can be transferred. This is a purely technical property that depends on the ready availability of channels of communication suitable for the transmission of well-codified information — for example, printing, radio, telegraph, and data networks. Whether information so transferred will be considered meaningful by those who receive it will depend on whether they are familiar with the code selected as well as the different contexts in which it is used.[4]

Uncodified or tacit knowledge, on the other hand, is slow and costly to transmit. Ambiguities abound and can be overcome only when communications take place in face-to-face situations. Errors of interpretation can be corrected by a prompt use of personal feedback. Consider the apprenticeship system as an example. First, a master craftsman can cope with only a limited number of pupils at a time; second, his teaching has to be dispensed mostly through examples rather than by precept — he cannot easily put the intangible elements of his skill into words; third, the examples he offers will be initially confusing and ambiguous for his pupils so that learning has to take place through extensive and time-consuming repetition, and mastery will occur gradually on the basis of "feel"; finally, the pupil's eventual mastery of a craft or skill will remain idiosyncratic

---

[3] Codification — the transformation of experience and information into symbolic form — is an exercise in abstraction that often economizes on bounded rationality. Instead of having to respond to a hopelessly extensive and varied range of phenomena, the mind can respond instead to a much more restricted set of information. At least two obstacles stand in the way of effective codification. First, abstracting from experience can be accomplished in an almost infinite number of ways. Ask a group of painters to depict a given object and each will select different facets or features for emphasis. Furthermore, the choice of what to codify and how to codify it is often personal. Second, to structure and codify experience one way can make it difficult, subsequently, to do so in an alternative way. The conceptual channels through which experience is made to flow appear to run deep and resist rerouting.

[4] These ideas are developed further in C. E. Shannon and W. Weaver, *The Mathematical Theory of Communication* (University of Illinois Press, Chicago, 1949). I am grateful to Max Boisot for drawing them to my attention.

and will never be a carbon copy of his master's. It is the scope provided for the development of a personal style that defines a craft as something that goes beyond the routine and hence programmable application of a skill.

The transmission of codified knowledge, on the other hand, does not necessarily require face-to-face contact and can often be carried out largely by impersonal means, such as when one computer "talks" to another, or when a technical manual is passed from one individual to another. Messages are better structured and less ambiguous if they can be transferred in codified form. Take for example Paul Samuelson's introductory textbook for students of economics. Year after year, thousands of students all over the globe are introduced to Samuelson's economic thinking without being introduced to Samuelson himself. The knowledge acquired will be elementary and standardized, and idiosyncratic approach at this level being considered by many as a symptom of error rather than of style. Moreover the student can pick up the sage's book or put it down according to caprice; he can scan it, refer to it, reflect upon it, or forget it. This freedom to allocate one's attention or not to the message source is much more restricted where learning requires interpersonal contact.

With respect to the international transfer of technology, the costs of transfer are very much a function of the degree to which know-how can be codified and understood in that form by the recipient. Typically, only the broad outline of technical knowledge can be codified by non-personal means of intellectual communication or communication by teaching outside the production process itself. Accordingly, the transfer of technology generally requires the transfer of skilled personnel, even when the cultural and infrastructural differences are not great. History has illustrated this time and time again. For instance, the transfer of technological skills between the United States and Britain at the end of the nineteenth century was dependent upon the transfer of skilled personnel. One also observes that the diffusion of crafts from one country to another depends on the migration of groups of craftsmen, such as when the Huguenots were driven from France by the repeal of the Edict of Nantes under Louis XIV.

The costs of transfer so far examined are simply the resource costs of transfer — the costs of the labor and capital that must be employed to effect transfer. An empirical investigation of these issues based upon a sample of 26 international transfers indicated that the resource cost of international transfer is nontrivial.[5] Transfer costs ranged from 2.25 percent to 59 percent of total project costs with a mean of 19.16 percent. They declined with each subsequent application

---

[5] See David Teece, Technology Transfer by Multinational Firms: The Resource Cost of International Technology Transfer, *Economic Journal*, June 1977.

of the technology and were typically lower the greater the amount of related manufacturing experience possessed by the transferee. Experience with transfer and experience with the technology appear to be key considerations with respect to the ease with which technology can be transferred abroad. In order to understand these costs, as well as other aspects of the transfer process, it will be necessary to examine the market for know-how. In so doing, the focus is on private transactions between firms of different national origins.

Characteristics of the Market for Know-How

The differential distribution of know-how and expertise among the world's enterprises means that mutually advantageous opportunities for the trading of know-how commonly exist. However, these opportunities will be realized only if the institutional framework exists to provide the appropriate linkage mechanisms and governance structures to identify trading opportunities and to surround and protect the associated know-how transfers. Unfortunately, unassisted markets are seriously faulted as institutional devices for facilitating trading in many kinds of technological and managerial know-how.

The imperfections in the market for know-how for the most part can be traced to the nature of the commodity in question. Know-how has some of the characteristics of a public good, since it can often be used in another enterprise without its value being substantially impaired. Furthermore the marginal cost of employing know-how abroad is likely to be much less than its average cost of production and transfer. Accordingly the international transfer of proprietary know-how is likely to be profitable if organizational modes can be discovered to conduct and protect the transfer at low cost.

An examination of the properties of markets for know-how readily leads to the identification of several transactional difficulties. These difficulties can be summarized in terms of recognition, disclosure, and team organization. Consider a team that has accumulated know-how that can potentially find application in foreign markets. If there are firms abroad that can apply this know-how with profit, then according to traditional microeconomic theory, trading will ensue until the gains from trade are exhausted. Or, as Calabresi has put it, "if one assumes rationality, no transactions costs, and no legal impediments to bargaining, all misallocations of resources would be fully cured in the market by bargains."[6]

---

[6] G. Calabresi, Transactions Costs, Resource Allocation, and Liability Rules: A Comment, *Journal of Law and Economics*, April 1968.

However, one generally cannot expect this happy result in the market for proprietary know-how. Not only are there high costs associated with obtaining the requisite information, but there are also organizational and strategic impediments associated with using the market to effect transfer.

Consider the information requirements associated with using markets. In order to carry out a market transaction, it is necessary to discover potential trading partners and acceptable terms of trade. It is also necessary to conduct negotiations leading up to the bargain, to draw up the contract, to undertake the inspection needed to make sure that the terms of the contract are being observed, and so on. As Kirzner has explained, (for an exchange transaction to be completed it is not sufficient merely that the conditions for exchange which prospectively will be mutually beneficial be present; it is necessary also that each participant be aware of his opportunity to gain through the exchange. ... It is usually assumed ... that where such scope is present, exchange will in fact occur. ... In fact, of course, exchange may fail to occur because knowledge is imperfect, in spite of the presence of the conditions for mutually profitable exchange.[7])

The transactional difficulties identified by Kirzner are especially compelling when the commodity in question is proprietary information. One reason is that protecting the ownership of technological know-how often requires the suppression of information on exchange possibilities. By its very nature, industrial R&D requires that the activities and outcomes of the R&D establishment be disguised or concealed.

Even where the possessor of the technology recognizes the opportunity and has the capability to absorb know-how, markets may break down. This is because of the problems of disclosing value to buyers in a way that is convincing and that does not destroy the basis for exchange. Due to informational asymmetries, the less informed party must be wary of opportunistic representations by the seller. Moreover, if there is sufficient disclosure to assure the buyer that the information possesses great value, the "fundamental paradox" of information arises: "its value for the purchases is not known until he has the information, but then he has in effect acquired it without cost."[8]

Appropriability issues emerge not only at the negotiating state but also at all subsequent stages of the transfer. Indeed, as discussed elsewhere in this issue, Magee has built a theory of multinational enterprise around the issue of appropriability, hypothesizing that multinational corporations are specialists in

---

[7] I. Kirzner, *Competition and Entrepreneurship* (University of Chicago Press, Chicago, 1962), p. 215.

[8] K.J. Arrow, *Essays in the Theory of Risk Bearing* (Chicago University Press, Chicago, 1971).

the production of information that is less efficient to transmit through markets than within firms.[9]

However, the transactional difficulties in the market for know-how that provide an incentive for firms to internalize technology transfer go beyond issues of recognition and appropriability. Thus suppose that recognition is no problem, that buyers concede value and are prepared to pay for information in the seller's possession, and that enforceable use restrictions soften subsequent appropriability problems. Even if these assumptions are satisfied, there is still the problem of actually transferring the technology.

In some cases the transfer of a formula or a chemical compound, the blueprints for a special device, or a special mathematical algorithm may be all that is needed to effect the transfer. However, more is frequently needed. As mentioned earlier, know-how cannot always be codified, since it often has an important tacit dimension. Individuals may know more than they are able to articulate.[10] When knowledge has a high tacit component, it is extremely difficult to transfer without intimate personal contact, demonstration, and involvement. Indeed, in the absence of intimate human contact, technology transfer is sometimes impossible. In a slightly different context Polanyi has observed, "It is pathetic to watch the endless efforts — equipped with microscopy and chemistry, with mathematics and electronics — to reproduce a single violin of the kind the half literate Stradivarius turned out as a matter of routine more than 200 years ago."[11]

In short, the transfer of knowledge may be impossible in the absence of the transfer of people. Furthermore, it will often not suffice just to transfer individuals. While a single individual may sometimes hold the key to much organizational knowledge, team support is often needed, since the organization's total capabilities must be brought to bear upon the transfer problem. In some instances the transfer can be effected through a one-time contract providing for a consulting team to assist in the startup. Such contracts may be highly incomplete and may give rise to dissatisfaction during execution. This dissatisfaction may be an unavoidable — which is to say, an irremediable — result. Plainly, foreign investment would be a costly response to the need for a one-time international exchange. In the absence of a superior organizational alternative, one-time, incomplete contracting for a consulting team is likely to prevail.

---

[9] See Stephen Magee, Information and Multinational Corporation: An Appropriability Theory of Direct Foreign Investment, in Jagdish Bhagwati (ed.), *The New International Economic Order* (MIT Press, Cambridge, MA, 1977), p. 318.

[10] See Michael Polanyi, *Personal Knowledge: Towards a Post Critical Philosophy* (University of Chicago Press, Chicago, 1958).

[11] Polanyi.

Reliance on repeated contracting is less clearly warranted, however, where a succession of transfers is contemplated, or when two-way communication is needed to promote the recognition and disclosure of opportunities for information transfer as well as the actual transfer itself. In these circumstances a more cooperative arrangement for joining the parties would enjoy a greater comparative institutional advantage. Specifically, intrafirm transfer to a foreign subsidiary, which avoids the need for repeated negotiations and attenuates the hazards of opportunism, has advantages over autonomous trading. Better disclosure, easier agreement, better governance, and more effective team organization and reconfiguration all result. Here lies the incentive for internalizing technology transfer within the multinational firm.

The preceding discussion has emphasized that an important attribute of the multinational firm is that it is an organizational mode capable of internally transferring know-how among its various business units in a relatively efficient and effective fashion. Given the opportunities that apparently exist for international trade in know-how, and given the transactional difficulties associated with relying on markets, one should expect to find multinational enterprises (MNEs) frequently selecting internal channels for technology transfer. However, when problems of recognition, disclosure, and team transfer are not severe, one should expect that market processes will be utilized, in which case the licensing of know-how among nonaffiliated enterprises will be observed.

Recognition, disclosure, and team transfer problems will be modest, it would seem, when the following exist: (1) the know-how at issue is not recent in origin so that knowledge of its existence has diffused widely; (2) the know-how at issue has been commercialized several times so that its important parameters and performance in different situations are well understood, thereby reducing the need for start-up assistance; and (3) the receiving enterprise had a high level of technological sophistication. Some evidence supportive of these propositions has recently been presented. Mansfield, employing a sample of 23 multinationals, discovered that foreign subsidiaries were the principal channel of transfer during the first five years after commercialization.[12] For the second five-year period after commercialization, licensing turned out to be more important. Larger firms also tended to rely more on internal transfer than did smaller firms, although this

---

[12] See Edwin Mansfield, "Statement to the Senate Commerce Committee Concerning International Technology Transfer and Overseas Research and Development," Hearings before the Subcommittee on International Finance of the Committee on Banking, Housing, and Urban Affairs of the Committee on Commerce, Science, and Transportation, United States Senate, Ninety-fifth Congress, Second Session, Part 7: Oversight on U.S. High Technology Exports (Government Printing Office, Washington, DC, May 1978).

might not reflect relative efficiency considerations but rather the sunk costs larger firms have already made in foreign subsidiaries.

One implication for a potential technology purchaser is that it will have to look among the smaller firms in the industry, and at firms in different industries, to find willing technology suppliers. This does not result in an easy search process. It is made more difficult by the fact that few firms actively market their know-how. Thus the apparent size and nature of the market is likely to be a function of the search costs buyers are willing to incur.

Another implication is that because the marginal cost of successive applications of a technology is less than the average cost of production and transfer, and because know-how is often unique — implying that trading relations are characterized by small numbers — there is often a high degree of indeterminacy with respect to price. Killing's field research confirmed that "neither buyer nor seller of technology seems to have a clear idea of the value of the commodity in which they are trading," fueling speculation that "royalty rates may simply be a function of negotiating skills of the parties involved."[13] This is because the market for know-how commonly displays aspects of bilateral monopoly, at least at the level of the individual transaction. So in many important cases there is likely to be a wide range of indeterminacy.

The existence of elements of bilateral monopoly has led some countries to advocate regulation of the market for know-how. Indeed, some Third World countries, as well as the antitrust authorities in some developed countries, have already imposed various regulatory regimes.

By 1974, over 20 countries had enacted specific legislation to control and direct foreign capital and technology. Their actions and regulations focused on lowering the royalties paid for foreign technology, forcing local participation in management and ownership, and in increasing the government capability to screen and direct foreign activities — the major focus of the governments was initially to limit the kind of restrictive clauses allowed in contracts for technology transfer with foreign firms.[14]

Governmental and intergovernmental intervention in the market for know-how appears to be growing in significance. In the following sections, several dimensions of this phenomenon are explored in more detail.

---

[13] Peter Killing, Technology Acquisition: License Agreement or Joint Venture, *Columbia Journal of World Business* (Fall 1980).

[14] See Harvey Wallender, Developing Country Orientations Towards Foreign Technology in the Eighties: Implications for New Negotiation Approaches, *Columbia Journal of World Business* (summer 1980), 21–22.

Codes of Conduct and the Regulation of Technology Imports

Since the United Nations Conference on Trade and Development (UNCTAD) IV decided to set up an intergovernmental group of experts to prepare a draft of an international code of conduct on the transfer of technology, discussion has intensified on matters associated with the transfer and development of technology, particularly on topics of concern of developing countries.[15] A number of draft codes have emerged in which representatives from less-developed countries have argued that technology is part of the universal heritage of mankind and that all countries have right of access to technology in order to improve the standards of living of their peoples. Such contentions obviously involve fundamental challenges to the world's industrial property system. They also fail to recognize the constitutional restraints in countries such as the United States that prevent the government from confiscating private property.

The stated objective of the UNCTAD code is "to encourage the transfer of technology transactions, particularly those involving developing countries, under conditions where bargaining positions of the parties to the transaction are balanced in such a way so to avoid abuses of a stronger position and thereby to achieve mutually satisfactory agreement." One of the principal mechanisms by which this is to be achieved is through the elimination of "restrictive business practices."[16] A long litany of these is typically advanced, including tying or packaging, use restrictions, exclusive dealing, and territorial restrictions. An examination of recent legislation on the transfer of technology, particularly in Latin America and Yugoslavia, shows that many of these ideas have been uncritically accepted into national law.[17]

It is not possible to attempt a comprehensive review of restrictive business practices in this article. However, I submit that insufficient analysis has been

---

[15] The movement toward an international code on the transfer of technology is but a reflection of larger, exceedingly complex political problems that have been engendered by an international society undergoing profound changes. Demands for a new international economic order, international regulation of transnational enterprises, and the like form the backdrop of UNCTAD's activities in the technology transfer area. These broader demands raise the possibility that the work now being carried on by UNCTAD in moving toward a code of conduct for the transfer of technology will be subsumed by the development of a more comprehensive code of conduct for transnational enterprises by the U.N. Commission on Transnational Corporations.

[16] See UNCTAD, "Draft International Code of Conduct on the Transfer of Technology," TD/CODE/TOT/20.

[17] See UNCTAD, "Selected Legislation, Policies and Practices on the Transfer of Technology," TD/B/C.6/48.

given to the efficiency-enhancing attributes of many practices surrounding the generation and transfer of technology. Many restrictive clauses in licensing and know-how agreements are designed to protect the transaction and the underlying know-how; in their absence less technology might be transferred, to the mutual detriment of all, or technology might be transferred less efficiently. In the space that follows, two "restrictive business practices" — use restrictions and tying — are analyzed in order to illustrate that "restrictive business practices" can be in fact procompetitive and may serve to promote economic efficiency.

Use Restrictions

The interesting question associated with use restrictions is whether they are anticompetitive, designed merely to extract monopoly rents, or whether they are efficiency instruments, the removal of which might leave both parties worse off. Since know-how is the principal resource upon which the value of many private enterprise firms is based, firms facing market competition are not going to sell it carte blanche to a firm that might use it to compete with their own products, for to do so would reduce the value of the firm. Thus reasonable limitations on use are commonly necessary to provide adequate incentives for transfers to occur and for those transfers to operate efficiently. This is especially true when the transferor and the transferee are competitors or potential competitors.

When know-how is transferred by a market transaction (contract) the buyer does not acquire the asset to the exclusion of use by the seller in the same sense as occurs when a physical item is bought and sold. The seller of know-how retains the knowledge even after it has been transferred to a buyer. Furthermore, technology is constantly evolving. Indeed, static technology is generally obsolete technology. Accordingly, a buyer of intangible know-how typically needs ongoing, future cooperation from the seller to obtain the full benefit of the know-how purchased, since all of the learning and experience of the developer of the know-how cannot be captured in the codified descriptions, drawings, and data that are amenable to physical transfer.

Limitations on the use of technological know-how are often needed to provide adequate incentives for the buyer and the seller to effect a continuous transfer of the knowledge in question. If the seller is limited in his use of the know-how, the buyer can rely more confidently on the seller's full disclosure and cooperation in the buyer's use of the know-how. Where the seller contemplates some use of the know-how himself, limitations on the buyer's use of the know-how in competition with the seller are necessary to provide the seller with the incentive to transfer this know-how and to share fully in his mental perceptions, understandings, working experience, and expertise.

A partial analogue to these principles is when business enterprises are sold. These transactions have traditionally included ancillary limitations on the economic activities of the seller after the business is sold. Such limitations bring about economically efficient transfers of ongoing businesses by ensuring that the buyer acquires exclusively the enterprise — or part of the enterprise — he is contracting to purchase, including its intangible goodwill. Similarly, in the sale of a business the seller is often retained as a consultant for the purpose of ensuring that the intangible knowledge that comes from the seller's experiences is conducting the business is fully transferred in the transaction. Without contractual or other limitations on the seller's use of the assets being transferred, and without the seller's continued cooperation, a buyer would not pay the full economic value of those assets. As a result, the efficient transfer of the assets would be inhibited.

Use limitations are particularly beneficial when two or more uses exist for the products that can be derived from know-how and when some of the uses are for some reason foreclosed to the developer of the know-how. In this instance, transfer of the know-how to a buyer having access to one or more of these otherwise foreclosed uses may be beneficial to both parties, since economies of scope will be generated. The seller of the know-how requires adequate incentives to transfer his knowledge, however. The seller will not transfer the know-how to a buyer for the otherwise foreclosed uses if, in doing so, he is likely to lose more in the uses that are available to him with no transfer than he gains through the expanded uses made possible by transfers. The availability of limitations on the buyer's use of the know-how provides possible means to prevent such losses.

Use limitations are also beneficial in providing incentives for the contracting parties to share complementary know-how in order to reach a new market that neither acting independently could efficiently serve. If each of the parties has one or more of the technology elements critical for a particular new use, if neither of the parties has all of the critical technology elements for that use, and if through sharing of the complementary technologies for the new use one or both of the parties could enter markets that neither party could serve without sharing, then use limitations are necessary to effect the bilateral technology transfers. Without use limitations, one or both of the parties may lack the incentive to share, since the losses that might occur in an existing market through sharing could exceed the gains derived from reaching the new market.

Tying and Packaging

In a tying arrangement, the seller requires the buyer to purchase a second product as a condition of sale of the first, such as when a petrochemical firm licenses its process technology to another firm on the condition that it purchase certain inputs on a continuous basis, or when an automobile company agrees to build a facility abroad so long as it is able to select equipment and designs for the whole facility and not just for part of it.

In the context of the international transfer of technology, there are often very genuine managerial and technical reasons for tying the sale of products. For instance, coordinated design and construction might allow important systems engineering functions to be carried out more efficiently. Furthermore, processing facilities may require raw materials and components that meet certain narrow technological standards, and tying may be necessary to ensure that the requisite amount of quality control is exercised. These problems are likely to be especially severe when the technological distance between the transferor and transferee is great.

It is only under rather special circumstances that tying will enable a monopolist to expand the amount of monopoly profit that would be obtained in the absence of tying. One such circumstance is if tying can be used as a method of price discrimination.

Accordingly, blanket prohibitions against tying and packaging are likely to be costly to the country imposing the prohibitions. Technology suppliers may have good reasons for wanting to supply know-how and other products and services in a package. Certainly some striking examples exist of problems that have arisen when adequate packaging and systems design have not been performed. Consider the Soviet Union's experience in constructing and starting up its Kama River truck plant, as related by Lee Iacocca, then with Ford Motor Company:

Well, one example of acquiring technology in its unbundled state is the Kama River truck plant in Russia. After first attempting to get a foreign company to build the plant (we were approached but decided against it) the Russians decided to do it themselves and to parcel out contracts to foreign firms for various parts of the project. That was in 1971. As of December 1976, the project was almost two years behind schedule. By year's end, only about 5000 trucks were expected to roll off the line, instead of the 150,000 vehicles and 100,000 diesel engines and transmissions originally scheduled for annual production. According to published reports, only four of nine projected furnaces in the iron foundry were operating and those only at half capacity. What's more, 35 percent of the castings were being rejected as unserviceable. There were bottlenecks on the assembly line, and because the components and designs were bought from different suppliers all over the world, replacement parts were not interchangeable.

Now compare that with Ford's recent investment in Spain. It took us just three years to the day to build a complex that includes an assembly plant, a stamping and body plant and an engine plant on a manufacturing site 2½ miles long and half a mile wide, with 55 acres under roof. The first Fiesta, our new minicar, was driven off the assembly line last August, well ahead of schedule. To get from farmland to an annual capacity of 250,000 cars and 400,000 engines in three years, we drew on the experience of our personnel and our technological resources from all over the world — experience and resources that couldn't be bought and that we probably wouldn't even know how to sell.[18]

Regulation of Technology Exports

Pressures for restricting trade in technological know-how have also come from technology exporters. The reasons advanced for controls are almost the complete opposite of those advanced by the LDCs. In the United States concern is often expressed in industry and government that the United States is either selling its technology for far less than its economic value, or allowing it to be stolen through industrial espionage, principally to other developed countries, or simply transferring it abroad too soon. According to J. Fred Bucy, the president of Texas Instruments:

Today our toughest competition is coming from foreign companies whose ability to compete with us rests in part on their acquisitions of U.S. technology. … The time has come to stop selling our latest technologies, which are the most valuable things we've got.[19]

Labor groups in the United States go further and argue that not only is the know-how underpriced, but that one consequence of the export of technology is the export of jobs.[20] According to one labor leader:

---

[18] See Lee Iacocca, Multinational Investment and Global Purpose, speech delivered before the Swiss-American Chamber of Commerce, Zurich, June 17, 1977. Reprinted in *Vital Speeches*, September 15, 1977.

[19] See, Those Worrisome Technology Exports, *Fortune*, May 22, 1978, p. 106.

[20] An example commonly cited is that of Piper aircraft. Until a few ears ago, Brazil was the leading purchaser of light aircraft manufactured in the United States. However, the Brazilian government levied prohibitive taxes on the import of American-produced light aircraft and it invited an American manufacturer, Piper, to bring in U.S. technology and produce with Brazilian workers. As a result, hundreds of U.S. citizens who were directly employed in light aircraft production became unemployed, some permanently. Now Brazil is selling light aircraft to other Latin American countries and is also planning to export planes to the United States in competition with American producers.

I recognize that technology will flow across national lines no matter what we do. But certainly we do not have to cut our own throats with aid, trade, tax and tariff policies that actively encourage and promote the export of American jobs and technology, without regard for the impact on either those who give or those who receive.[21]

Before proceeding further, it will be helpful to outline the available evidence with respect to these considerations. Unfortunately, only very sketchy data are available. Conclusive evidence on the net impacts of foreign investment and technology transfer on U.S. jobs and welfare does not exist. The available evidence suggests that the impact is likely to vary from one instance to another. Baranson has presented case studies that suggest that U.S.-based firms, driven by competitive necessity, are transferring their newest technology abroad more frequently than in the past.[22] To investigate this issue further, Mansfield and Romeo obtained information concerning the age of the technology transferred abroad in a sample of 65 transfers taken from 31 U.S.-based multinationals.[23] As shown in Table 1, they found that the mean age of the technologies transferred to overseas subsidiaries in developed countries was about 6 years, which was significantly less than the mean age of technologies transferred to overseas subsidiaries in developing countries — about 10 years. Table 1 also suggests that the mean age of the technologies transferred through licenses, joint ventures, and

Table 1. Mean and Standard Deviation of Number of Years between Technology's Transfer Overseas and its Initial Introduction in the United States, for 65 Technologies

Channel of Technology Transfer	Mean (Years)	Standards Deviation (Years)	Number of Cases
Overseas subsidiary in developed country	5.8	5.5	27
Overseas subsidiary in developing country	9.8	8.4	12
Licensing or joint venture	13.1	13.4	26

Source: Edwin Mansfield and Anthony Romeo, "Technology Transfer to Overseas Subsidiaries by U.S.-Based Firms," Research Paper, University of Pennsylvania, 1979.

---

[21] William Winpisinger, The Case Against Exporting U.S. Technology, *Research Management*, March 1978, p. 21.

[22] Jack Baranson, Technology Exports Can Hurt, *Foreign Policy* 25 (Winter 1976–1977).

[23] See Edwin Mansfield and Anthony Romeo, "Technology Transfer to Overseas Subsidiaries by U.S.-Based Firms," Research Paper, University of Pennsylvania, 1979.

channels other than subsidiaries is commonly higher than the mean age of the technologies transferred to subsidiaries, indicating that firms tend to transfer their newest technology overseas through wholly owned subsidiaries rather than via licenses or joint venture, but the latter channels become more important as the technology becomes older.

Another concern of countries that generate new technology is that the transfer of technology to overseas subsidiaries will hasten the time when foreign producers have access to this technology. Some evidence has recently become available on the speed with which technology "leaks out" and the extent to which international transfer actually hastens its "leaking out." The evidence, which is based on a sample of 26 technologies transferred abroad, indicated that the mean lag between the transfer and the time when foreign firms had access to the technology was about four years.[24] In over half the cases, the technology transfer was estimated to have had no effect at all on how quickly foreign competitors had access to the technology. On the other hand, in about one-fourth of the cases, it was estimated to have hastened their access to the technology by at least three years.

Technology transfer hastened the spread of process technologies to a greater degree than it did the spread of product technologies. According to the study, the most frequent channel by which the technology "leaked out" was reverse engineering.[25] That is, foreign competitors took apart and analyzed the new or modified product to gain insights into the relevant technology. Clearly, this evidence gives only a very sketchy impression of the level and nature of the returns from international technology transfer, and the role that technology exports are having on the U.S. competition position. However, there is little evidence that the technological lead of the United States in various industries is about to disappear as a result of the technology transfer activities of American firms. Indeed, there is some evidence, admittedly of a conjectural nature, that the

---

[24] *Ibid.*

[25] Reverse engineering is very common in the semiconductor industry, it involves stripping down a competitor's chip to recreate an outright copy, to figure out how a chip works in order to design a functionally equivalent emulator chip, or merely to determine whether a new chip contains any new ideas that might be adaptable to other products. Creating a copy is surprisingly simple: the necessary tools include a microscope, acid to etch away the circuits layer by layer, and a camera to record the successive steps; $50,000 of equipment will suffice. Reverse engineering enables a rival to obtain the same advantages as could be obtained by pirating the masks — the negatives that are used to lay down the circuit elements on silicon wafers — used in manufacturing the product. Intel Corporation of California has accused the Soviet Union of copying one of its 4K memory chips and Japan's Toshiba Corporation of making a "dead ringer" of another. See *Business Week*, April 21 1980, p. 182.

international transfer of technology stimulated R&D activities by multinational firms.[26]

From a public policy perspective the interesting question is whether the United States could increase its economic welfare through restrictions on technology exports. It is a well-known theorem of international trade that if a country has monopoly (monopsony) power in world markets, then imposing a tax (tariff) on exports (imports) will serve to improve welfare in the absence of retaliation. This, of course, assumes that such a policy can be effectively administered.

The economic intuition behind this theorem is fairly apparent. By transferring technology abroad, American firms increase the likelihood of foreign competition in the future. While firms face incentives to consider this when setting prices at which technology is transferred, each firm will evaluate the future effects on themselves, not on the rest of the economy. The company that exports the technology is not usually the one that loses out. It receives payment of some kind. The victim is likely to be another American company, one that prior to the technology transfer enjoyed a competitive advantage over the foreign company. Fujitsu, for example, has used the technology it got from Amdahl to compete with IBM. Therefore, in strictly nationalist terms, private firms will have a tendency to set the price of technology too low and to transfer too much technology abroad. Where several U.S. firms have similar technology that does not exist abroad, their competition will tend to lower the price of technology transfers. The United States could prevent this by reducing competition and by establishing monopoly prices through control of such transfers. For instance, an export tax would serve to restrict exports, thereby driving up the price and enabling the United States economy to capture monopoly rents from the export of know-how. A similar result could be obtained by enabling domestic industry to cartelize foreign markets.[27]

There is, in fact, a long history of government attempts to limit the export of technology and trade secrets. A prime example is England during the Industrial Revolution. There are serious disadvantages in limiting technology transfers, however. One problem is that while levels of restriction that are optimal on nationalist grounds can be determined in theoretical models, there is little reason to be confident that government policies will approach such optima in practice.

---

[26] See Edwin Mansfield, Anthony Romeo and Samuel Wagner, Foreign Trade and U.S. Research and Development, *Review of Economics and Statistics*, 1979.

[27] One difference is that with a cartel as compared with a tax, the industry would capture a larger portion of the economic rents, as there would be no revenues accruing to the government.

Domestic firms seem able to circumvent restrictions on the export of know-how,[28] while foreign firms can engage in "reverse engineering of products and designs" to circumvent many controls.

An alternative approach to technology controls might involve placing more emphasis on technical data and critical manufacturing equipment and less on commodities.[29] However, it is enormously difficult to control the export of technical data, since it can move in many informal ways that are often difficult to detect.[30] Clearly the transfer of highly visible turnkey plants is more readily controlled than are surreptitious, casual conversations. Furthermore, the effectiveness of controls depends on the degree of monopoly power possessed by the United States. In most instances where controls are applicable, the United States does not have a clear superiority vis-a-vis other Western countries. The effectiveness of controls therefore depends upon cooperation with other suppliers and potential suppliers.[31]

Conclusion

In the foregoing discussion, the arms-length market for know-how has been shown to be exposed to a number of hazards and inefficiencies, many of which can be overcome by internalizing the process within the multinational firm. Despite the shortcomings identified, it was not apparent that regulation by either technology importers or exporters could substantially improve the efficiency with which this market operates; indeed, for the instances examined it appeared that the impairment of efficiency through regulation was the more likely outcome. Yet the strongest

---

[28] In 1980, allegations of export control violations in the United States numbered 350, up from 200 in 1979. *Business Week*, April 27, 1981, p. 131.

[29] On the other hand, some authorities suggest that Soviet spies might do better acquiring consumer products in large department stores. Buying consumer and industrial products such as toys, appliances, and industrial tools in many cases may be more useful than technical data because of the delays in Defense Department procurement of new chips and the rapidity with which new chips become incorporated into consumer products.

[30] According to one source, the KGB has 30 agents in California's Silicon Valley, plus others in Phoenix and Dallas, charged with obtaining data on microeconomics technology. *Business Week*, April 27, 1980, p. 128.

[31] The Coordinating Committee on Export Controls (COCOM), an organization consisting of all NATO members plus Iceland and Japan, is the forum usually chosen to attempt the necessary coordination. However, the members have no legal obligation to participate in COCOM or to abide by its recommendations.

argument against controls on the transfer of technology is the same as the argument for liberal trade policies in general. Many kinds of economic restrictions can be used to bring gains to some at the expense of others. But almost everyone is likely to end up worse off if they all succeed. This holds just as true for nations within the world economy as for individuals and groups within a national economy. The basic case for liberal policies is not that they always maximize short-run gains, but that they serve enlightened and longer-run interests in avoiding a world riddled with restrictions.

Technology Transfer by Multinational Firms: The Resource Cost of Transferring Technological Know-How*

David J. Teece

1. Introduction

The essence of modern economic growth is the increase in the stock of useful knowledge and the extension of its application. Since the origins of technical and social innovations have never been confined to the borders of any one nation, the economic growth of all countries depends to some degree on the successful application of a transnational stock of knowledge (Kuznets, 1966). In other words, the economic growth of every nation is inextricably linked to the successful international transfer of technology. Nevertheless, economists have been remarkably slow in addressing themselves to the economics of international technology transfer. The result is that "at both the analytic and factual level very little is known about the international transfer of knowhow" (Reynolds, 1966).

This paper addresses itself to this need. The starting-point is Arrow's suggestion that the cost of communication, or information transfer, is a fundamental factor influencing the world-wide diffusion of technology (Arrow, 1969).[1] The purpose

Reprinted from *The Economic Journal* 87 (June 1977), 242–261.

*The findings described in this paper resulted from research undertaken for my Ph.D. dissertation, "The Multinational Corporation and the Resource Cost of International Technology Transfer" (Ballinger, Cambridge, Mass., 1976). The trenchant comments of Professor Edwin Mansfield were much appreciated during all phases of the study. My particular gratitude goes to the participating firms, without whose co-operation this paper would not have been possible. I should also like to acknowledge the financial support provided for this study by the National Science Foundation, under a grant to Professor Edwin Mansfield of the University of Pennsylvania.

[1] Arrow asks: "If one nation or class has the knowledge which enables it to achieve high productivity, why is not the other acquiring that information? ... The problem turns on the differential between costs of communication within and between classes" (or nations), p. 33.

of the paper is to examine the level and determinants of the costs involved in transferring technology. The value of the resources which have to be utilised to accomplish the successful transfer of a given manufacturing technology is used as a measure of the cost of transfer. The resource cost concept is therefore designed to reflect the ease or difficulty of transferring technological know-how from manufacturing plants in one country to manufacturing plants in another.

2. Technology Transfer and the Production of Knowledge

The literature on technological change recognises that it takes substantial resources to make a new process or product feasible (Mansfield, 1968). However, it is common to assume that the cost of transferring the innovation to other firms is very much less, so that the marginal costs of successive application is trivial compared to the average cost of research, development, and application. This paradigm is sometimes extended to international as well as domestic technology transfer (Rodriguez, 1975).[2] Buttressing this view is a common belief that technology is nothing but a set of blueprints that is usable at nominal cost to all. Nevertheless, it has been pointed out that generally "only the broad outlines of technical knowledge are codified by non-personal means of intellectual communication, or communication by teaching outside the production process itself" (Berrill, 1964). The cost of transfer, which can be defined to include both transmission and absorption costs, may therefore be considerable when the technology is complex and the recipient firm does not have the capabilities to absorb the technology. The available evidence is unfortunately very sketchy. From the case studies of Mueller and Peck, Arrow inferred that transfer costs must be high (Arrow, 1962). From the Hall and Johnson study of the transfer of aerospace technology from the United States to Japan, it is not clear that this is true (Hall and Johnson, 1970). Robinson believes that economists' views on transfer costs are exaggerated (Robinson, 1973) while Mansfield and Freeman take the opposite view (Freeman, 1965; Mansfield, 1973). The lack of compelling evidence is apparent, and the appeals for further research (Mansfield, 1974; UNCTAD, 1970) seem to be well founded.

---

[2] Transmission of technology between countries is assumed costless. Thus, it is possible for the country which owns the technology to operate a plant in a foreign country without any transfer of factors, p. 122.

Table 1. Twenty-Six Technology Transfer Projects: 3 Digit ISIC Category and Transferee Location

Location	Chemicals and Petroleum Refining			381: Fabricated Metal Products Machinery and Equipment	Machinery		Total
	351: Industrial Chemicals	353: Petroleum Refineries	356: Plastic Products		382: Machinery Except Electrical	383: Electrical Machinery, Appliances, and Supplies	
Canada	1	1	0	1	0	0	3
Northern and Western Europe	3	1	0	0	4	1	9
Australia	0	0	1	0	0	0	1
Japan	3	0	0	0	1	0	4
Eastern Europe	2	0	0	0	0	0	2
Latin America	3	0	0	0	0	1	4
Asia (excluding Japan)	0	1	0	0	0	1	2
Africa	1	0	0	0	0	0	1
Total	13	3	1	1	5	3	26

3. The Sample

The domain of this study is the transfer of the capability to manufacture a product or process from firms in one country to firms in another. Consequently the transfers can be considered as horizontal,[3] and in the design phase.[4] Data on 26 fairly recent international technology transfer projects were obtained. The proprietary nature of much of the data meant that sampling costs were high, which in turn severely limited the size of the sample that could be collected. All 26 transfers were conducted by firms which were multinational in the scope of their manufacturing activity, although they varied considerably in sales value (10–20 billion U.S. dollars) and R&D expenditures (1.2–12.5% of sales value). All had headquarters in the United States. The transferees were on the average much smaller and less research-intensive. In 12 instances they were wholly owned subsidiaries of the transferor, in 8 instances the transferor and transferee were joint ventures partners, in 4 instances transfers were to wholly independent private enterprises, and the remaining 3 were to government enterprises. Table 1 shows that 17 of the projects fall into a broad category which will be labelled "chemicals and petroleum refining." The remaining 9 projects fall into a category which will be labelled "machinery".[5] Table 1 also indicates the wide geographical dispersion of the transferees.

4. Definition of Technology Transfer Costs

An economic definition of transfer cost is developed below. The emphasis is on the resources which must be utilised to transfer technological know-how. Of course royalty costs or rents must be incurred merely to secure access to the technology, but these costs are not the focus of attention of this paper.[6]

---

[3] Horizontal transfer refers to the transfer of technical information from one project to another. It can be distinguished from vertical transfer, which refers to the transfer of technical information within the various stages of a particular innovation process, e.g. from the basic research stage to the applied research stage.

[4] For the distinctions between materials transfer, design transfer, and capacity transfer, see Hayami and Ruttan (1971).

[5] Chemicals and petroleum refining thus embrace ISIC categories (United Nations, 1968), 351, 353, and 356, while "machinery" embraces categories 381, 382, and 383.

[6] Many observers equate the cost of technology with royalty fees (Mason, 1973; Gillette, 1973). Royalty costs are considered in the dissertation from which this paper was taken.

In order to appreciate the importance of the definition that will be presented, a distinction must first be made between two basic forms in which technology can be transferred. The first form embraces physical items such as tooling, equipment, and blue prints. Technology can be embodied in these objects. The second form of technology is the information that must be acquired if the physical equipment or "hardware" is to be utilised effectively. This information relates to methods of organisation and operation, quality control, and various other manufacturing procedures. The effective conveyance of such "peripheral" support constitutes the crux of the process of technology transfer, and it typically generates the associated information flows. It is towards discovery of the cost of transfer of this "unembodied"[7] knowledge that the attention is directed.

Technology transfer costs are therefore defined as the costs of transmitting and absorbing all of the relevant unembodied knowledge. The costs of performing the various activities which have to be conducted to ensure the transfer of the necessary technological know-how will represent the cost of technology transfer.[8] Clearly, a great many skills from other industries (e.g. design engineering) will be needed for plant design, plant construction, and equipment installation. However, not all of these skills will have to be transferred to ensure the success of the project. As defined, the costs of transfer clearly do not include all of the costs of establishing a plant abroad and bringing it on stream.

The definition of transfer costs presented at the conceptual level can be translated into operational measures by considering the nature of a given project activity. At the operational level the subset of project costs identified as transfer costs fall into four groups. The first group is the cost of pre-engineering technological exchanges. During these exchanges the basic characteristics of the technology are revealed to the transferee, and the necessary theoretical insights are conveyed. The second group of costs included are the engineering costs associated with transferring the process design and the associated process engineering[9] in the case of process innovations, or the product design and

---

[7] Unembodied knowledge is the term used here to denote knowledge not embodied in capital goods, blueprints, and technical specifications, etc.

[8] All of the relevant costs are included, irrespective of which entity initially or eventually incurs them.

[9] Process engineering for continuous flow technology involves the compilation of flow diagrams, heat balances, control instrumentation, etc. It can be distinguished from detailed engineering which involves the translation and elaboration of the process engineering into a manufacturing facility.

production engineering[10] in the case of product innovations. If the technology has already been commercialised,[11] transmission may simply involve transferring existing drawings and specifications with the minimum of modification. However, the process of absorption may be more difficult, requiring the utilisation of considerable consulting or advisory resources. "Engineering" costs not falling into the specified categories[12] are excluded from transfer costs. The excluded engineering costs are essentially the plant or detailed engineering costs, net of advisory or consulting costs. This residual is assumed to correspond with routine drafting costs. Routine drafting is generally performed by technicians under the supervision of engineers. Drafting skills do not have to be transferred for the viability of the project to be assured. Accordingly, drafting is not considered to represent a transfer activity.[13]

The third group of costs are those of R&D personnel (salaries and expenses) during all phases of the transfer project. These are not the R&D costs associated with developing the underlying process or product innovations. Rather, they are

---

[10] Production engineering for a specified item can be divided into two phases: production design and process planning. Production design is the modification of the functional design in order to reduce manufacturing costs. (Functional product design is the design of a product to fulfil certain specifications and requirements.) Given the design, process planning for manufacture must be carried out to specify, in careful detail, the processes required and their sequence. The production design first sets the minimum possible costs that can be achieved through the specification of materials, tolerances, basic configurations, methods of joining parts, etc. Process planning then attempts to achieve that minimum through the specification of processes and their sequence to meet the exacting requirements of the design specifications. The accepted end-point for production design is manifested by the drawing release. Process planning takes over from this point and develops the broad plan of manufacture of the part or product. A distinction can also be drawn between process planning and the layout of the physical facilities. Some process planning will take place during the layout phases of the design of a production system, Process plans can be regarded as inputs to the development of a layout. (*McGraw-Hill Encyclopedia*. 1960.)

[11] An innovation is said to have been commercialised if it has already been applied in a facility of economic size which is essentially non-experimental in nature. Thus pilot plant or prototype application is not considered to represent commercialisation.

[12] These categories are (a) process or design engineering costs and related consultation for process innovations or (b) production engineering expenses for product innovations; and (c) costs of engineering supervision and consultation (salaries plus travel and living) for the plant engineering.

[13] Drafting costs can be considered an implementation cost rather than a transfer cost, the implication being that if the host country does not have these skills, the viability and cost of the project is unlikely to be affected. The advisory and consulting costs, on the other hand, represent transfer costs since these activities are necessary if the technology is to be adjusted to the local circumstance and requirements. Clearly, if an existing plant was to be duplicated in its own environment, consulting costs could be expected to go to zero, whereas routine drafting would still have to be performed.

the R&D costs associated with solving unexpected problems and adapting or modifying the technology. For instance, research scientists may be utilised during the transfer if new and unusual technical problems are encountered[14] with the production inputs. These R&D costs are generally small or non-existent for international transfers falling into the "design transfer" category.

The fourth group of costs are the pre-start-up training costs and the "excess manufacturing costs". The latter represent the learning and debugging costs incurred during the start-up phase, and before the plant achieves the design performance specifications. It is quite possible that no marketable output will be produced during the initial phases of the start-up. Nevertheless, normal labour, materials, utilities, and depreciation costs will be incurred, together with the costs of the extra supervisory personnel that will inevitably be required to assist in the start-up. The operating losses incurred during initial production are very often a close approximation to excess manufacturing costs.[15]

5. Transfer Costs: Data and Hypotheses

5.1. *The Level of Transfer Costs*

The above definition was used to calculate the transfer costs for 26 projects. The results are presented in Table 2. The costs are given in absolute dollars,

---

[14] Referring to process technologies, it is possible that differences in feedstocks amongst various locations may create problems that only research scientists can effectively handle. Similarly, changes in atmospheric conditions or water supply could have unexpected consequences for some highly complex processes.

[15] An important consideration is the extent to which excess manufacturing costs correctly reflect technology transfer costs rather than the costs of discovering and overcoming the idiosyncrasies of a new plant. One way to confront this issue is to consider the level of excess manufacturing costs when an absolutely identical plant is constructed in a location adjacent to an existing plant. Further, assume the second plant embodies the same technology as the first plant, and the labour force from the first is transferred to the second for the purpose of performing the manufacturing start-up. The assumption is that under these circumstances excess manufacturing costs in the second plant will be zero, or very nearly so. The correctness of this assumption was corroborated by a subsample of project managers subsequently questioned about this matter. The postulated circumstance would be identical to shutting down the first plant and then starting it up again. Some excess manufacturing costs might be incurred during the initial hours of operation if the plant embodies flow process technology. (For the projects in the sample the average duration of the manufacturing start-up was 8.2 months.) However, these costs are unlikely to be of sufficient magnitude to challenge the validity of classifying excess manufacturing costs as a component of technology transfer costs.

Table 2. Sample Data on the Resource Costs of Technology Transfer: 26 International Projects

Chemicals and Petroleum Refining		Machinery	
Transfer Costs: Dollar Amount (Thousands)	Transfer Costs: Dollar Amount / Total Project Cost	Transfer Costs: Dollar Amount (Thousands)	Transfer Costs: Dollar Amount / Total Project Cost
49	18	198	26
185	8	360	32
683	11	1,006	38
137	17	5,850	45
449	8	555	10
362	7	1,530	42
643	6	33	59
75	10	968	24
780	13	270	45
2,142	6		
161	2		
586	7		
877	7		
66	4		
2,850	19		
7,425	22		
3,341	4		

and then normalised by total project costs.[16] For the sample as a whole, transfer costs average 19% of total project costs. Clearly, the data do not support the notion that technology is a stock of blueprints usable at nominal cost to all. Nevertheless, there is considerable variation in the sample data, with transfer costs ranging from 2% to 59% of total project costs. The number of factors influencing transfer costs is undoubtedly very great,[17] but some

---

[16] Total project costs are measured according to the inside boundary limits definition commonly employed by project accountants. Installations outside the plant perimeter are thereby excluded.

[17] For a broader view of the spectrum of hypotheses, see the author's Ph.D. dissertation.

factors are likely to have a more pervasive influence than others. The discussion to follow is restricted to hypotheses for which statistical testing is feasible, given the available data. Two groupings of testable hypotheses can be identified: characteristics of the technology/transferor, and characteristics of the transferee/ host country.

5.2. Technology/Transferor Characteristics

A critical factor in the transfer of technology is the extent to which the technology is completely understood by the transferor. The number of manufacturing start-ups[18] or applications which the transferor has already conducted with a specific technology can be used as an index of this knowledge.[19] An increase in the number of applications is likely to lower transfer costs since with each start-up additional knowledge about the technology is acquired. Since no two manufacturing start-ups are identical, each start-up provides the firm with the opportunity to observe the effects of different operating parameters and differences in equipment design. Each application can be regarded as a new experiment which yields new information and new experience.[20] Transfer will be facilitated the more fully the technology is understood. Besides these engineering economies, additional applications provide expanded opportunities for the pre-start-up training of the labour force. Clearly, if identical or similar plants exist elsewhere, then experienced operators from these plants can be used to assist the start-up in the new plant. In addition, untrained operators can be brought into existing plants for pre-start-up training.

The second variable to be considered is the age of the technology. The age of the technology is defined as the number of years since the beginning of the first commercial application of the technology[21] anywhere in the world, and

---

[18] Manufacturing start-ups are synonymous with the number of applications of the technology. If a new plant is built for each application, it would also by synonymous with the number of plants that are built which utilise the technology.

[19] Corporations engaged in technology transfer ventures not grounded on their own technology are known to have encountered massive transfer problems and costs.

[20] The first application represents first commercialisation of the technology. This will result in the creation of a set of basic engineering drawings and specifications. Duplication and alteration of these for a subsequent start-ups will involve a modest cost compared to the initial cost of constructing them.

[21] If there is more than one key innovation embodied in the technology, then the date of commercial application of the most recent key innovation is the reference date.

the end[22] of the technology transfer programme. The age of an innovation will determine the stability of the engineering designs and the transferor's knowledge of the manufacturing procedures. The older the technology, *ceteris paribus*, then the greater have been the opportunities for interaction between the development groups and the manufacturing and operating groups within the firm. Problems stand a better chance of already being ironed out, and the drawings are likely to be more secure. Further, since technology is not embodied in drawings alone, there is a great deal of uncodified information — the relevant "art". This kind of knowledge is carried by the supervisors, engineers, and operators. As the age of the technology increases, more individuals in the firm have the opportunity to acquire this non-codified information, and hence are potentially available to assist in the transfer. There will, however, be some point after which greater age will begin to increase the cost of transfer. When the length of stay of corporate personnel begins to be outstripped by the age of technology, then the non-codified dimensions of design knowledge may be lost to the firm.[23]

It is necessary to distinguish the cost reductions resulting from additional start-ups from the cost reductions resulting from greater age of the technology. For continuous flow technologies, additional applications of an innovation in entirely new plants will allow experimentation with scale and with the basic parameters of the design. This will generate a greater understanding of the technology. On the other hand, greater age, given the number of applications or start-ups, generally permits experimentation only with operating parameters, the design of the plant remaining fixed throughout.

The third technology variable to be considered is the number of firms utilising the technology, or one that is "similar and competitive". This is taken to represent the degree to which the innovation and the associated manufacturing technology is already diffused throughout the industry. The greater the number of firms with the same or similar and competitive technology, then the greater the

---

[22] Age is defined up to the end of the transfer programme since any knowledge about the technology acquired up to this point is potentially useful for the transfer. For the very first start-up, age will be the length of the transfer minus the development overlap.

[23] In the limit, the firm could terminate its utilisation of a particular technology, and the non-codified information associated with it could be gradually lost for ever as the technology becomes historic. Further, the drawings associated with technology that is very old may suffer from so many small alterations that the very essence of even the codified technology may suffer from so many small alterations that the very essence of even the codified technology may become quite obscure. Since none of the technology transfer projects in the sample were historic in the above sense, the relevant range of the hypothesised age-transfer cost function involves an inverse relationship between the age of the technology and the cost of transfer.

likelihood that technology is more generally available, and can therefore be acquired at lower cost.[24]

These technology variables and the attendant hypotheses begin to take on some extra significance when viewed together. Taken singly they define the technology to only a limited degree. Together, they hypothesise, *ceteris paribus*, that the most difficult and hence costly technology to transfer is characterised by very few previous applications, a short elapsed time since development, and limited diffusion. Technology displaying such characteristics can be termed "leading-edge" technology. "Leading-edge" technology is likely to be in a state of flux; the engineering drawings will be constantly altering, thus frustrating the transfer. In comparison, state-of-the-art technology is hypothesised, *ceteris paribus*, to involve lower transfer costs since the engineering drawings are more likely to be finalised and the fundamentals of the technology stand a better chance of being more fully understood.

5.3. Transferee and Host Country Characteristics

The technical and managerial competence of the transferee will be presented as an important determinant of the ease with which technology can be absorbed. The years of manufacturing experience of the transferee in a given 4-digit ISIC industry (United Nations, 1968) is used as an index of the extent to which managers, engineers, and operators have command over the general manufacturing skills of an industry. A firm skilled in the manufacture of a group of products is likely to have less difficulty absorbing a new innovation in that industry group than is the firm which has had no previous experience manufacturing products in a particular industry group (Rawski, 1975). Older enterprises, with their skilled manufacturing personnel, seem more likely to be able to understand and apply codified knowledge to the manufacture of a new product, or the utilisation of a new process.[25]

---

[24] An identification problem may exist here because more firms may have applied the technology because the transfer cost is low.

[25] According to Rawski, recent experience of the People's Republic of China shows that during at least some phases of industrialisation, production experience may be a key determinant of the level and fungibility of industrial skills. Rawski notes that "with their skilled veteran workers and experienced technical persons, old industrial bases and old enterprises find it easier to tackle complicated technical problems than new enterprises and new industrial bases. With these advantages, it is the established centers which are best able to copy foreign equipment samples, to extract useful information from foreign technological publications, and to apply it to current domestic problem areas." (Rawski (1975), p. 386.)

Another variable to be considered is the size of the transferee. Although less compelling, the reasoning behind the hypothesis that transfer costs decline with firm size is that larger firms generally have a wider spectrum of technical and managerial talent which can be called on for assistance during the transfer. A small firm may be technically and managerially quite competent yet unable to absorb new technology easily because of the extra demands placed on its scare managerial and technical manpower. Consultants may have to be engaged by the smaller firms to perform tasks that are typically handled internally in larger firms.

A third variable considered is the R&D activity of the transferee. When unusual technical problems are unexpectedly encountered, an in-house R&D capability is likely to be of value. Oshima has argued that the R&D capability of Japanese firms facilitated the low-cost importation of foreign technology by Japanese firms (Oshima, 1973). The R&D to sales ratio of the transferee is taken as an index of its R&D capability, and an inverse relationship between this and transfer cost is postulated.

The final variable considered is designed to reflect the level of development of the host country infrastructure, which is hypothesised to be a determinant of the cost of transfer. For example, the level of skill formation in the host country will influence the amount and type of training that the labour force will require. Similarly, if the new venture is to acquire its inputs domestically, the quality of the inputs available will undoubtedly influence the level of start-up costs. There are many other considerations of similar kind which could be discussed. However, the high degree of cross-sectional collinearity between indices of development (Kuznets, 1966) makes the identification of separate effects statistically difficult. However, GNP *per capita*, a measure of productive capacity, can be expected to capture some of the above considerations, and it will be used in this study as an index of economic development. A negative relationship between transfer cost and GNP/*per capita* is postulated.[26]

6. Determinants of the Cost of International Technology Transfer: Tests and Results

6.1. *The Model*

The basic model to be tested is

$$C_i = f(U_i, G_i, E_i, R_i, S_i, N_i, P_i, Z_i), \tag{1}$$

---

[26] The sample did not include countries where high GNP statistics were grossly dependent on oil revenues.

where C_i is the transfer cost divided by the total project cost for the ith transfer; U_i is the number of previous applications or start-ups that the technology of the ith transfer has undergone by the transferor;[27] G_i is the age of the technology in years; E_i is the number of years of manufacturing experience that the recipient of the ith transfer has accumulated; R_i is the ratio of research and development to sales for the recipient of the ith transfer, calculated for the year the transfer commenced; S_i is the volume of sales, measured in millions of dollars, of the recipient of the ith transfer; N_i is the number of firms identified by the transferer as having a technology that is identical or "technically similar and economically competitive" to the technology underlying the ith transfer; P_i is the level of GNP per capita of the host country (International Bank, 1973); Z_i is the random error term for the ith transfer. The expected derivatives are:

$$\frac{\partial C_i}{\partial U_i} < 0, \quad \frac{\partial C_i}{\partial G_i} < 0, \quad \frac{\partial C_i}{\partial E_i} < 0, \quad \frac{\partial C_i}{\partial R_i} < 0, \quad \frac{\partial C_i}{\partial S_i} < 0, \quad \frac{\partial C_i}{\partial N_i} < 0, \quad \frac{\partial C_i}{\partial P_i} < 0.$$

Since one of the best tests of any hypothesis is to look for the convergence of independent lines of evidence, the testing of this model will proceed in two phases. First, cross-section data on 26 completed projects is utilised in a linear version of the model estimated by ordinary least-squares procedures. Secondly, cost estimates provided by project managers for comparable projects are pooled to test a more specific non-linear version of the model.

6.2. Statistical Tests: Phase I

The model to be tested is

$$C_i = \alpha_0 + \alpha_1 \bar{U}_i + \alpha_2 G_i + \alpha_3 E_i + \alpha_4 R_i + \alpha_5 S_i + \alpha_6 N_i + \alpha_7 P_i + Z_i, \qquad (2)$$

where $\bar{U}_i$ is a dummy variable taking the value 1 if the transfer represents the first manufacturing start-up, and zero otherwise. $\bar{U}_i$ is used rather than U_i for empirical reasons, since the first start-up is often of critical importance. The sample was dichotomised because of the large differences between continuous flow process technology, and product technology. One category includes chemicals and petroleum refining and the other includes machinery (see Table 1).

---

[27] The number of previous manufacturing start-ups was significant in Phase 1 only when it was included as a dummy variable taking the value 1 if there had been no previous manufacturing start-ups of this technology by the transferring firm, and zero otherwise.

Table 3. Regression of Coefficients and t Statistics in Regression Equations to Explain C (The Cost of Transfer)

Independent Variable	Chemicals and Petroleum Refining		Machinery	
	Equation (1)*	Equation (2)*	Equation (1)*	Equation (2)*
Constant	12.79	13.42	16.67	65.98
	(6.82)	(6.98)	(8.27)	(6.60)
Novelty dummy variable $\bar{U}^{\dagger}$	6.73	6.11	—	1.62
	(1.92)	(1.75)		(0.15)
Number of firms variable	−0.37	−0.39	−1.29	−1.26
	(−2.06)	(−2.22)	(−2.28)	(−1.95)
Age of technology variable (years)	—	—	−2.43	−2.35
			(−3.53)	(−2.51)
Experience of transference variable (years in 4-digit ISIC)	−0.09	−0.08	−0.84	−0.85
	(−1.66)	(−1.42)	(−3.37)	(−2.95)
Size of transferee variable (thousands of dollars of sales)	—	−0.0009	—	—
		(−1.18)		
Number of observations	17	17	9	9
R^2	0.56	0.61	0.78	0.78
F	5.66	4.73	6.00	3.22
Significance level of F	0.01	0.02	0.04	0.12

*Omitted coefficient indicates variable dropped from the regression equation.
†Note 2, p. 251.

The results in Table 3 indicate that in chemicals and petroleum refining $\bar{U}_i$, N_i, and E_i are significant at the 0.05 level and carry the expected signs. In the machinery category the variables N_i, G_i, and E_i all carry the expected signs and are significant at the 0.05 level. N_i and E_i are thus significant in both industry groupings, strongly supporting the hypothesis that transfer costs decline as the number of firms with identical or "similar and competitive" technology increases, and as the experience of the transferee increases. However, R_i and P_i were not significant in any of the equations, and although S_i carries the expected sign and approaches significance in one of the regressions it is not possible to be more than 85% sure that the sign is correct or that the coefficient is different from zero.[28]

The results therefore generally support the hypotheses advanced earlier, but there are differences in the size of coefficients as well as in the specification of the equations between the industry groups. In particular, the novelty variable $\bar{U}_i$ is significant in chemicals and petroleum refining, but insignificant in machinery. The converse is true for the age variable G_i. The reason may be that there exists relatively less latitude for production experimentation with continuous flow process technology than with product technology. Once the plant is constructed, the extent to which the design parameters can be changed is rather minimal because of the degree of interdependence in the production system. In comparison, many product technologies allow greater design flexibility. Innumerable small changes to the technology are very often possible without massive reconstruction of the plant. It is also of interest that the coefficient of the experience variable E_i is considerably larger in machinery than in chemicals and petroleum refining. This is consistent with other findings that reveal important learning economies in fabrication and assembling (Tilton, 1971).

6.3. Statistical Tests: Phase II

The above analysis is handicapped by the small sample size and the very high costs of adding additional observations. Limited variation in exogenous variables coupled with the problem of omitted variables can imply difficulties with bias and identification. For the projects in the sample, a procedure was therefore devised to hold the missing variables constant while generating large variation in the exogenous variables. The respondent firms were asked to estimate how the

---

[28] Multicollinearity does not appear to be a serious problem in any of the equations. Correlations amongst pairs of the independent variables were never significant at the 0.05 level. The stability of the regression coefficients further suggests that multicollinearity is not a serious problem. Dummy variables were introduced to test for the effects of the organisational relationship between transferor and transferee (affiliate/non affiliate, public enterprise/private enterprise), but they were not found to be statistically significant determinant of transfer costs. Application of a forward step by step procedure did not reveal a preferred subset of variables. However, it is possible that the correct model is the simultaneous equation model $C_i = f(N_i,...)$, $N_i = f(C_i,...)$. To eliminate simultaneous equation bias it would be desirable to use a two-stage procedure. A predictor of N could first be obtained by regressing N_i on arguments other than C_i. This could then be used as an argument in the transfer cost regression. It was not possible to obtain a good predictor of N using the available cross-section data, so this procedure was not employed. Consistency was sacrificed for efficiency. It is therefore possible that simultaneous equation bias remains in the model. Therefore, the estimates of the parameters may not be consistent.

total transfer costs would vary for each project if one particular exogenous variable happened to take a different value, assuming all other variables remain constant. The responses were taken into account only if the exercise generated circumstances within the bounds of an executive's experience. Given these limitations, the change specified was quite large in order to provide a robust sample. Generally the actual value of a selected variable was hypothesised first to halve and then to double. The estimated impact on transfer costs was noted. The exercise was performed for the following independent variables; the number of applications or start-ups that the technology has undergone; the age of the technology; the number of years of previous manufacturing experience possessed by the transferee in a given four-digit industry; the research and development expenditures to sales ratio for the transferee; the size (measured by sales value) of the transferee. For each variable this exercise generated at most three observations (including the actual) or transfer costs for each project. Pooling across projects produces enough observations for ordinary least-squares regression analysis.

The estimation procedure is commenced by assuming that the shape of the cost function can be represented by the following relatively simple but quite specific equation

$$C_j = V e^{\phi/X_j}. \tag{3}$$

C is the estimated transfer cost as a percentage of total project cost, X represents the value of various independent variables, j refers to the jth observation.

With this specification, the transfer cost for a project asymptotically approaches a minimum non-zero value as the value of each X increases. That is, as X goes to infinity, C goes to V. Therefore V is the minimum transfer cost with respect to the X variable. However, there is no maximum cost asymptote for the range of the data. The expression for the elasticity of transfer cost with respect to X is given by

$$\frac{-X}{C}\frac{dC}{dX} = \frac{\phi}{X}. \tag{4}$$

Thus for a specified value of X, the elasticity of transfer cost with respect to X is determined by ϕ Hence the elasticity depends only on ϕ and X. In order to estimate the function, the log of the arguments in (3) are taken:

$$\log C_j = \log V + \frac{\phi}{X_j}. \tag{5}$$

Dummy variables are used to pool the observations across projects. Inclusion of dummy variables allows the minimum cost asymptote to vary from project to project. It is assumed that ϕ is constant across projects. These assumptions provide a pooled sample with intercepts which vary across projects.

Ordinary least-squares regressions of log C_j on the dummy variables and I/X_j then proceeded for five different X variables, and for five data sets. These were: total transfers; transfers within the chemical and petroleum refining category; transfers in the machinery category; transfers of chemicals and petroleum refining technology to developed countries; and transfers of chemical and petroleum refining technology to less developed countries.[29] The Chow test (Chow, 1960) of equality between sets of coefficients in two linear regressions revealed that the separation of the sample along industry lines was valid, except for the research and development variable. However, there was no statistically valid reason for disaggregating the chemical and petroleum refining subsample according to differences in GNP *per capita* in the host countries.

Table 4. Estimated Values of ϕ (Obtained from Regressing Log C_j on log $V + \phi/X_j$) Together with Corresponding *t*-Statistics, Sample Size, Degress of Freedom, and Coefficient of Determination R^2

Variable	ϕ	*t*-Statistic	Sample Size	Degrees of Freedom	R^2
Start-ups					
Chemicals and petroleum refining	0.46	4.23	45	25	0.92
Machinery	0.19	1.76	20	10	0.91
Age					
Chemicals and petroleum refining	0.04	1.29	47	30	0.89
Machinery	0.41	2.19	21	13	0.94
Experience					
Chemicals and petroleum refining	0.007	0.85	52	33	0.78
Machinery	0.57	6.08	23	14	0.91
Size					
Chemicals and petroleum refining	0.008	1.17	54	35	0.88
Machinery	0.081	5.18	17	10	0.99
R&D sales					
Total sample	0.06	1.58	59	30	0.90

---

[29] A purely arbitary classification was used where less developed countries were defined as those with GNP/*per capita* less than $1000.

Table 5. Arc or Point Elasticity of Transfer Costs with Respect to Number of Start-Ups, Age of Technology, Experience, Size and R&D/Sales of Transferee

Independent Variable	Chemicals and Petroleum Refining	Machinery
	Arc elasticity	
Number of start-ups		
1–2	0.34	0.14
2–3	0.19	0.08
3–4	0.13	0.05
9–10	0.05	0.02
14–15	0.03	0.01
Age of technology	Point elasticity	
(years)		
1	0.04	0.41
2	0.02	0.20
3	0.01	0.14
10	0.00	0.04
20	0.00	0.02
Experience of transferee	Point elasticity	
(years)		
1	0.007	0.57
2	0.003	0.28
3	0.002	0.19
10	0.001	0.06
20	0.000	0.03
Size of transferee	Point elasticity	
(millions of sales dollars)		
1.0	0.008	0.081
10	0.001	0.008
20	0.000	0.004
100	0.000	0.001
1000	0.000	0.000
R&D/Sales of transferee	Total sample	
(%)	point elasticity	
1	0.06	
2	0.03	
3	0.02	
4	0.01	
5	0.01	
6	0.01	

The results of the estimation are contained in Table 4. The high R^2 values are partly because the large across-project variation in costs is being captured by the project dummies. The intercept term was always highly significant and the coefficients are significantly different from each other. All of the coefficients are significantly greater than zero at the 0.20 level and the age of the technology, the number of manufacturing start-ups, transferee size and experience achieve at least the 0.05 significance level in one or other of the subsamples. In several cases the coefficients are highly significant, providing strong statistical support for the hypotheses that have been advanced. The number of previous applications once again has a sizeable impact. Diffusion and manufacturing experience are particularly important in the machinery category.

The calculation of elasticities allows interpretation and comparisons of estimated effects. Average or point elasticities for some typical sample values of X are presented in Table 5. These estimates suggest that in the chemicals and petroleum-refining category, the second start-up could lower transfer costs by 34% over the first start-up, other variables held constant. The corresponding change for conducting a third start-up is 19%. The other elasticities can be interpreted similarly.

7. Defferences between International and Domestic Technology Transfer

Although this is primarily a study of international technology transfer, it is apparent that many of the characteristics of international technology transfer are also characteristic of the technology transfer that occurs within national borders, but there are differences. For instance, distance and communication costs very often differentiate international from domestic transfers. Although the communications revolution of the twentieth century has enormously reduced the barriers imposed by distance,[30] the costs of international communciation are often significant.[31] Language differences can also add to communication costs, especially if the translation of engineering drawings is required. The experience of Polyspinners Ltd at Mogilev in the Soviet Union (Jones, 1973) is ample testimony to the extra costs that can be encountered.[32] International differences in units of measurements

---

[30] Facsimile equipment exists which can be used to transmit messages and drawings across the Atlantic instantaneously.

[31] One of the participating companies indicated that travel, telegraph, freight, and insurance added about 10% to the total cost of a project established in New Zealand.

[32] The project manager estimated that documentation alone cost £500,000, and the translation a similar amount.

and engineering standards can compound the problems encountered (Meursinge, 1971). Additional sources of difficulty are rooted in the cultural and attitudinal differences between nations, as well as differences in the level of economic development and the attendant socioeconomic structure.

It is of interest to know the magnitude and determinants of the "international component" of the transfer cost. Unfortunately, foreign and domestic transfers are rarely identical in scope or in timing, and so it is not possible to gather comparative data on implemented projects at home and abroad. It was therefore

Table 6. International Component* of Transfer Cost

Chemicals and Petroleum Refining		Machinery	
Dollar Amount (Thousands)	As % of Actual Transfer Cost	Dollar Amount (Thousands)	As % of Actual Transfer Cost
3.03	6.07	35.55	17.88
0.00	0.00	−399.37	−110.93
−12.81	−1.87	−50.06	4.93
43.90	31.00	830.70	14.20
0.00	0.00	−4.59	−0.02
5.17	1.42	226.80	14.82
132.75	20.63	0.67	1.99
0.00	0.00	−134.40	13.87
342.00	43.84	34.98	12.95
0.00	—		
0.00	—		
0.00	0.00		
−10.77	−6.66		
−50.16	−8.52		
0.00	—		
637.32	72.60		
−1.33	−1.99		
1723.81	60.48		
1370.25	18.45		
15.69			

*Amount of actual transfer costs attributable to the fact that transfer was international rather than domestic. (Accordingly negative values indicate that firms estimated that transfer costs would be higher had the transfer been domestic.) In general, these numbers were derived from taking the weighted average of estimated changes in the various identifiable components of transfer costs.

found necessary to rely on estimates provided by the firms involved in international transfers. For the projects in the sample, project managers were asked to estimate the dollar amount by which transfer costs would be different if the international transfers in the sample had occurred domestically, holding firm and technology characteristics constant. The procedure was designed to highlight the effects of country characteristics such as differences in language, differences in engineering and measurement standards, differences in economic infrastructure and business environment, and geographical distance from the transferor. The international component of the transfer cost for the projects in the sample could be obtained by subtracting the estimated transfer cost from the actual transfer cost. The data, contained in Table 6, reveal that the difference in cost is not always positive. This indicates that in at least some of the cases, the international transfer of an innovation was estimated to cost less than a comparable domestic transfer. This may seem paradoxical at first, given that international technology transfer generally augments the transfer activities that have to be performed.[33] An analysis of the determinants of the international component of transfer costs may yield an explanation.

Several hypotheses are presented and tested. The first is that the difference is large and positive when the technology has not been previously commercialised. National boundaries are often surrogates for cultural and language barriers, differences in methods and standards of measurement, and distance from the home country. During first commercialisation of a product or process, there are generally enormous information flows across the development-manufacturing interface. The hypothesis is that placing a national boundary at this interface can complicate matters considerably, and escalate the costs enormously. The second hypothesis is that transfers to government enterprises in centrally planned economies will involve higher transfer costs. Transferors can expect numerous delays and large documentation requirements (Jones, 1973). The third hypothesis is that the less the diffusion of the technology, measured as before by the number of firms utilising the innovation, the greater the positive differential associated with international technology transfer. The fourth hypothesis is that whereas, in general, low levels of economic development are likely to add to transfer costs because of inadequacies in the economic infrastructure, this may be more than offset, in some circumstances, by low labour costs. Labour costs can have a substantial impact on excess manufacturing costs, especially in relatively labour intensive industries. Since machinery manufacture is relatively labour intensive,

---

[33] The source of the apparent paradox may be differences in labour costs. Nevertheless, the identification of the transfer for which international transfer costs less than domestic transfer is an issue of importance.

the hypothesis is that the GNP per capita in the host country is positively related to the transfer cost differential in this classification, but is negatively associated with the differential in the chemicals and petroleum refining category.

To test these hypotheses it is assumed that

$$D_i = \alpha_0 + \alpha_1 d_i + \alpha_2 \bar{U}_i + \alpha_3 N_i + \alpha_4 P_i + Z_i,$$

where D_i is the "international component" as a percentage of actual transfer cost for the ith transfer. d_i is a dummy variable which takes the value 1 if the recipient of the ith transfer is a government enterprise in a centrally planned economy, and zero otherwise. The other variables carry the same definitions as previously. The expected derivations are:

$$\frac{\partial D_i}{\partial d_i} > 0, \quad \frac{\partial D_i}{\partial U_i} > 0, \quad \frac{\partial D_i}{\partial N_i} < 0;$$

$\partial D_i / \partial P_i \gtrless 0$ according to the industry category (the partial is postulated positive for the machinery category, and negative otherwise). Least-squares estimates of the α's were obtained, the results being:

Chemicals and petroleum:

$$D_i = 0.285 + 3.84 d_i + 4.46 \bar{U}_i \quad (n = 17, \ r^2 = 0.71).$$
$$\quad\;\; (0.91) \quad\; (5.01) \quad\;\; (4.89)$$

Machinery:[34]

$$D_i = -8.59 - 1.39 N_i + 0.005 P_i \quad (n = 9, \ r^2 = 0.94).$$
$$\quad (-1.96) \; (-5.98) \quad\;\; (3.90)$$

The hypotheses are to some extent borne out by the data, but the small sample size must counsel caution in the interpretation of these results.[35] In chemicals and petroleum, the results indicate that transfers to government

---

[34] O_i was omitted from the machinery regression since none of the actual transfers in this category were to government enterprises in centrally planned economies.

[35] If the second observation on D_i in the machinery category is excluded, and the regression results recomputed, the estimates of the coefficients exhibit considerable instability and the "goodness of fit" deteriorates. The estimated equation is

$$D_i = -4.96 - 0.66 N_i + 0.003 P_i \quad (n = 8, \ r^2 = 0.45).$$
$$\quad\;\; (1.14) \quad (2.40) \quad\;\; (1.94)$$

These estimates are nevertheless significant at the 0.05 level for a one-tail test.

enterprises, and transfers before first commercialisation, involve substantial extra costs. Furthermore, both N_i and P_i are significant in the machinery category, despite the small number of observations, yet they are insignificant in chemicals and petroleum refining, where there are more than twice as many degrees of freedom. Apparently, the level of host country development and the degree of diffusion of an innovation have no bearing on the international-domestic transfer cost differential in the chemicals and petroleum grouping. This calls for an explanation. The diffusion variable N_i is taken to indicate the degree to which the requisite skills are generally available. The statistical results suggest that the relevant skills for highly capital intensive industries, such as chemicals and petroleum refining, are more easily transferred internationally than are the requisite skills in the machinery category.[36] Furthermore, P_i was not significant in chemicals and petroleum refining, suggesting that costs of transfer are independent of the level of economic development in this category. This is consistent with speculation that international transfer is no more difficult than domestic transfer when the underlying technology is highly capital intensive. The perceived reluctance of multinational firms to adapt technology to suit the capital-labour endowments of less developed countries could well be rooted in the desire to avoid escalating transfer costs to unacceptable levels.

8. Conclusion

The resources required to transfer technology internationally are considerable. Accordingly, it is quite inappropriate to regard existing technology as something that can be made available to all at zero social cost. Furthermore, transfer costs vary considerably, especially according to the number of previous applications of the innovation, and how well the innovation is understood by the parties involved. It is equally inappropriate, therefore, to make sweeping generalisations about the process of technology transfer and the costs involved. For instance, technology transfer in chemicals and petroleum refining displayed relatively low transfer costs, presumably because it is possible to embody sophisticated process technology in capital equipment, which in turn facilitates the transfer process.

The analysis of the determinants of technology transfer costs provided some interesting findings with development implications. The success of the more

---

[36] This is consonant with the views expressed by several project managers in the chemical industry. It was asserted that technology could be transferred with equal facility to almost anywhere in the world, including less developed countries, assuming host government interference is held constant.

experienced enterprises, indicated by lower transfer costs, points towards economic models which emphasis the accumulation of skills, rather than fixed assets or capital, in facilitating the technology transfer process. This seems consonant with the findings of several economic historians (Rosenberg, 1970; Rawski, 1975).

The results also provide some managerial implications for the multinational firm. Consider the costs associated with separating production from development (Arditti, 1968). The results indicate that the international transfer of technology is most likely to be viable when production runs are long enough to allow second sourcing. The especially high cost of transfer before first application favours the development location, at least for production of initial units. However, transfer costs will be lowered once the first production run has been commenced, and international transfer then becomes more likely, a finding consistent with the product cycle model (Vernon, 1966). However, inter-industry differences are important, and the costs involved in separating first production from development did not prove to be an insurmountable transfer barrier for an important subset of the sample projects.

A second implication is that since transfer costs decline with each application of a given innovation, technology transfer is a decreasing cost activity. This can be advanced as an explanation for the specialisation often exhibited by engineering firms in the design and installation of particular turnkey plants,[37] a characteristic particularly noteworthy of the petrochemical industry.

A third set of managerial implications relate to the criteria which might be used for the selection of a joint venture or licensing partner to utilise the innovating firm's technology abroad. While the manufacturing experience, size, and R&D to sales ratio of the transferee were identified as statistically significant determinants of transfer costs for the sample, there was also evidence to suggest that, *ceteris paribus*, any firm moderately matured in these dimensions is a good candidate to absorb the technology at the minimum possible transfer cost. It is not clear, therefore, that super gaint firms have any advantage in this respect over moderately sized firms. Nor it is clear that highly research intensive firms have more than a slight cost advantage in absorbing technology over firms with a minimal commitment to research and development activity. However, manufacturing experience is important, especially for transferring machinery technology. In addition, there is evidence that transfers to governments in centrally planned economies involve substantial extra costs, perhaps because of high documentation requirements, or differences in language and managerial procedures.

---

[37] Turnkey plants generally embody state-of-the-art technology.

Technology transfer by multinational firms is clearly a complex matter. Collection and analysis of proprietary data has provided some helpful insights. Few issues have been settled although many have been raised. Further analytic research and more extensive data collection is required if our understanding of international technology transfer is to be improved.

D.J. Teece
Stanford University, California
Date of receipt of final typescript: November 1976

References

K. Arrow, Classificatory Notes on the Production and Transmission of Technological Knowledge, *American Economic Review; Papers and Proceedings* 52 (May 1969), 29–35.

_____, Comment in Universities-National Bureau Committee for Economic Research, *The Rate and Direction of Inventive Activity* (Princeton University Press, Princeton, 1962).

F. Arditti, On the Separation of Production from the Developer, *Journal of Business* 41 (July 1968), 317–28.

J. Baranson, Manufacturing Problems in India: The Cummings Diesel Experience (Syracuse University Press, Syracuse, New York, 1967).

K. Berrill (ed.), *Economic Development with Special Reference to East Asia* (St. Martins Press, New York, 1964).

G.C. Chow, Tests of Equality between Sets of Coefficients in Two Linear Regressions, *Econometrica* 28 (July 1960), 591–605.

C. Freeman, Research and Development in Electronic Capital Goods, *National Institute Economic Review* 34(34) (November 1965), 1–70.

R. Gillette, Latin America: Is Imported Technology Too Expensive? *Science* 191 (6 July 1973), 4–44.

G.R. Hall and R.E. Johnson, Transfers of United States Aerospace Technology to Japan, in R. Vernon (ed.), *The Technology Factor in International Trade* (National Bureau of Economic Research, New York, 1970).

Y. Hayami and V. Ruttan, *Agricultural Development and International Perspective* (Johns Hopkins, Baltimore, 1971).

International Bank for Reconstruction and Development, *World Bank Atlas* (I.B.R.D, Washington, DC, 1973).

D. Jones, The 'Extra Costs' in Europe's Biggest Synthetic Fiber Complex at Mogilev, U.S.S.R., *Worldwide Projects and Installations* 7 (May/June 1973), 30–35.

S. Kuznets, *Modern Economic Growth: Rate, Structure, Spread* (Yale University Press, New Haven, 1966).

E. Mansfield, Technology and Technical Change, in J. Dunning (ed.), *Economic Analysis and the Multinational Enterprise* (Allen and Unwin, London, 1974).

_____, *The Economics of Technological Change* (Norton, New York, 1968).

_____, Discussion of the Paper by Professor Griliches, in B.R.Williams (ed.), *Science and Technology in Economic Growth* (John Wiley, New York, 1973).

E. Mansfield, J. Rapoport, J. Schnee, S. Wagner and M. Hamburger, *Research and Innovation in the Modern Corporation* (W.W. Norton, New York, 1971).

R. Hal Mason, The Multinational Firm and the Cost of Technology to Developing Countries, *California Management Review* 15 (Summer 1973), 5–13.

J. Meursinge, Practical Experience in the Transfer of Technology, *Technology and Culture* 12 (July 1971), 469–470.

McGraw-Hill Encyclopedia of Science and Technology, Vols. 4, 10, pp. 639–644 (McGraw-Hill, New York, 1960).

K. Oshima, Research and Development and Economic Growth in Japan, in B.R. Williams (ed.), *Science and Technology in Economic Growth* (John Wiley, New York, 1973).

T. Rawski, Problems of Technology and Absorption in Chinese Industry, *American Economic Review* 65 (May 1975), 363–388.

L. Reynolds, Discussion, *American Economic Review* 56 (May 1966), 112–114.

E.A.G. Robinson, Discussion of the Paper by Professor Hsia, in B.R.Williams (ed.), *Science and Technology in Economic Growth* (John Wiley, New York, 1973).

C.A. Rodriguez, Trade in Technical Knowledge and the National Advantage, *Journal of Political Economy* 93 (February 1975), 121–135.

N. Rosenberg, Economic Development and the Transfer of Technology: Some Historical Perspectives, *Technology and Culture* 11 (October 1970), 550–575.

D. Teece, *The Multinational Corporation and the Resource Cost of International Technology Transfer* (Ballinger, Cambridge, 1976).

_____, Time–Cost Tradeoffs: Elasticity Estimates and Determinants for International Technology Transfer Projects, *Management Science* 23 (April 1977).

J. Tilton, *International Diffusion of Technology: The Case of Semiconductors* (Brookings Institution, Washington, DC, 1971).

United Nations, *International Standard Industrial Classification of all Economic Activities.* United Nations Statistical Papers, Series M., Number 4 (United Nations, New York, 1968).

UNCTAD, The Transfer of Technology, *Journal of World Trade Law* 4 (September/ October 1970), 692–718.

R. Vernon, International Investment and International Trade in the Product Cycle, *Quarterly Journal of Economics* 80 (May 1966), 190–207.

IV

TECHNOLOGICAL CHANGE AND COMPETITION POLICY

Antitrust Policy and Innovation: Taking Account of Performance Competition and Competitor Cooperation*

Thomas M. Jorde

School of Law, University of California at Berkeley,
Berkeley, CA 94720-2499, U.S.A.

David J. Teece

Hass School of Business, University of California at Berkeley,
Berkeley, CA 94720, U.S.A.

1. Overview

The beginning of a new decade is a good time for stock taking — to reflect upon past accomplishments and to survey challenges. In the field of antitrust, 1990 has special significance because this year marks the centennial of the Sherman Act. Our own reflections on antitrust policy, particularly as practiced in the United States, cause us to express certain concerns about the relevance of today's antitrust policy for the future and for the global economic environment. Though we certainly do not advocate its abolition, we suggest that antitrust may be anachronistic in certain contexts, and indeed, may actually inhibit effective competition.

Antitrust law has undergone significant changes since the passage of the Sherman Act in 1890. But the U.S. and world economies have undergone even

Reprinted from *Journal of Institutional and Theoretical Economics* (JITE) 18(7) (1991), 118–144.

*This paper is based in part on Jorde and Teece [1989a], [1990a], [1990b] and Teece [1986]. We are extremely grateful for financial support from the Alfred P. Sloan Foundation, the Smith-Richardson Foundation, The Pew Foundation, and the Sasakawa Peace Foundation. Bill Baxter, Oliver Williamson, and Dick Nelson made helpful comments on earlier drafts and oral presentation. We implicate none of the above in our conclusions.

greater changes. We do not intent in this paper to recount the major developments in antitrust over the past century. Nor do we intend to survey comprehensively the many changes that have occurred in our economic system and in the global economy. Rather, we will describe in general terms ways in which antitrust law and policy can be "out of touch" with other important goals. In particular, we suggest that if society wishes to promote competition, the best way to do so is to promote innovation. That in turn may require dismantling portions of our antitrust laws. To be sure, other policies affecting innovation are also important, such as savings rates, investment in education and technological skills, and appropriate financial and tax incentives. Our focus, however, is upon antitrust and its impact on innovation and competitiveness.

In our view, antitrust is being rendered increasingly superfluous by dispersion in the sources of innovation and the associated growth in international competition. So long as U.S. markets remain open to global competition, antitrust may soon become an expensive ornament that more often than not gets in the way of competition, though it need not in an ideal world with an efficient system of adjudication and enforcement. The basis of our argument is that technological innovation drives competition, that the sources of innovation are remarkably diverse, and the antitrust laws which we have inherited are informed by static theories of market performance and therefore are as likely to throttle innovation as to stimulate it. In short, we believe (1) that stimulating rivalry ought to be an important policy goal, (2) that the form of competition the antitrust laws should embrace is Schumpeterian dynamic competition, (3) that current antitrust is not designed to achieve this, (4) that the best guarantor of dynamic competition is a system that is open to international trade and has policies which facilitate innovation, and (5) that internal organization and intercorporate links, and not government intervention, is important for successful innovation and commercialization. Accordingly, we are uncomfortable with an approach to antitrust which measures market power from a static perspective and is inhospitable to a great deal of cooperative behavior among competitors. If economic welfare is the goal of antitrust, then the promotion of innovation may henceforth need to take precedence over standard antitrust concerns. At minimum, we offer certain modest changes in the antitrust laws which would alter the way that market power is measured and cooperation among competitors assessed, when credible claims of innovation and its commercialization are present.

The organization of this paper is as follows. In the next section we discuss the nature of competition and its importance to a properly functioning market economy. We distinguish between two types of competition. The first we call "price competition." This kind of competition occurs among firms in mature industries and stems from differences in scale economies and the like. The second kind of competition we simply label "performance competition." This competition originates from innovations which fuel the introduction of new products, or old products at drastically lower prices. Performance competition stimulates rivalry and promotes economic welfare far more effectively than does price competition. Yet it is not what U.S. antitrust laws seem to emphasize. We discuss the implications of this for market definition and market power analysis in Sec. 3, and for the antitrust treatment of agreements among competitors in Sec. 4. Our conclusion in Sec. 5 discusses the benefits we believe would flow from an antitrust jurisprudence that was more Shumpeterian.

2. The Nature and Importance of Competition and the Goals of Antitrust

Americans have a long-standing and well-founded belief in competition. This tradition is rooted in part in political beliefs. Competitive systems that are open to newcomers provide important checks and balances on monopoly power; monopoly power sometimes impairs resource allocations and is often seen as being correlated with political influence. Promoting competition can thus be seen as a corollary of democracy. Indeed, it was concern about the political power of the trusts that helped motivate the passage of the Sherman Act in the first place.

But while political concerns helped motivate passage of the Sherman Act, the economics profession has, particularly in the post-war period, spilled a great deal of economic content into the various antitrust vessels which Congress created. Antitrust law and policy have generally benefitted. The economic theory that has been supplied falls into two broad classes: neoclassical (text-book) microeconomics, and to a much more limited but growing extent, transaction cost economics. Neoclassical microeconomics is a very powerful lens for analyzing the behavior of certain types of markets. It is particularly useful for explaining commodity-type markets characterized either by perfect competition or pure monopoly. Textbook microeconomic analysis often rests on the following assumptions: (1) markets are characterized by perfect information; (2) economic agents are hyper-rational; (3) markets are always in equilibrium; and (4) technology is uniformly available to all firms (and therefore costlessly transferrable among them).

This results in a view of competition that is highly stylized: firms compete primarily by offering lower prices; competition is characterized by the zero profit condition; adjustments from equilibrium occur instantaneously; new entry is always good; technology is uniformly available to all firms; communication among competitors is probably for the purpose and will have the effect of cartelizing. Unfortunately, this view of economics, which informs antitrust analysis today, overlooks important aspects of the competitive process, and distorts others. Indeed, as Schumpeter suggested half a century ago, the kind of competition that really matters if enhancing economic welfare is the goal of antitrust. Rather, it is dynamic competition that really counts.[1]

Dynamic competition is the competition that comes from the new product or the new process. There are at least two types of innovative regimes which stimulate rivalry. First, there is incremental innovation. In this type of innovative system new products are introduced in rapid succession, each one such an improvement on the prior product that the new drives out the old. In regimes characterized by incremental innovation, the population of firms in an industry is likely to be relatively stable. However, established firms will fall into relative decline if they do not keep up with changing technology. Good examples of industrial regimes characterized by incremental innovation today are the aircraft, chemical, and VCR industries.

The other regime is one where radical innovation is predominant. Few industries are characterized by this for long periods of time. However, when the transistor arrived it clearly did more to invigorate competition and provide economic benefits than did any level of rivalrous behavior among the manufacturers of vacuum tubes. Likewise, the invention of the video disc and compact disc engendered competition into the recording business of a kind that firms competing with the standard vinyl records could not supply. And the arrival of the steamship sharpened competition on ocean freight in ways that intense competition among sail ships could never engender.

Recognizing these forms of dynamic competition would not cause any tension with existing antitrust laws if the world of competition envisaged in the textbook was the ideal structure from which innovation and its successful commercialization would emerge. However, there is no evidence that the world of perfect competition to which antitrust doctrine often aspires is in fact ideal for promoting innovation. The weight of the evidence appears to suggest that the structure of markets — whether competitive or monopolized — is relatively unimportant in impacting innovation.[2] The evidence does suggest that current monopoly is usually transitory and is rarely a barrier; most truly radical innovations emerge from outside an established industry, and access to the infrastructure provided by incumbent firms is rarely critical for ultimate success. Incremental innovation is not much impacted by market structure either.

---

[1] See Joseph Schumpeter [1942].

[2] See Baldwin and Scott [1987], and Teece [1990].

What, then, does innovation require? The evidence is sketchy. However, we can identify several classes of factors that are important: availability of a labor force with the requisite technical skills; economic structures which permit considerable autonomy and entrepreneurship; economic systems which permit and encourage a variety of approaches to technological and market opportunities; access to "venture" capital, either from a firm's existing cash flow or from an external venture capital community; good connections between the scientific community, especially the universities, and the technological community, and between users and developers of technology; strong protection of intellectual property; the availability of strategies and structures to enable innovating firms to capture a return from their investment; in fragmented industries, the ability to quickly build or access cospecialized assets inside or outside the industry.

Few of these considerations are impacted positively by antitrust policy. However, we contend that antitrust negatively affects the ability of innovating firms to cooperate in the development and commercialization of innovation, or engage in business strategies or interfirm agreements to keep "me too"-type imitators at bay.[3] In our view, dynamic, not static, competition is what the antitrust laws should be seeking to promote if enhancing economic welfare over time is the goal. We believe that the implicit acceptance of current antitrust law, and infatuation with the inherently short run model of perfect competition, may be counterproductive long run. There is no good theoretical reason nor any evidence to support the contention that present antitrust policy advances dynamic competition and economic growth. In Secs. 3 and 4, we explore areas in which we believe antitrust is likely to stand in the way.

We take it as axiomatic that innovation and its rapid and profitable commercialization is the key factor driving productivity improvement in the economy.[4] Accordingly, the focus of antitrust on consumer welfare is possibly misplaced. Consumer welfare is enhanced long term only if productivity increases; and that requires technological innovation. Hence, an economic welfare calculus which includes future benefits, appropriately discounted of course, requires the promotion of innovation. Modern efforts to promote consumer welfare as the goal of antitrust fall wide of the mark whenever the focus is on present consumer welfare.[5a] This is unfortunately exactly what the standard static analysis accomplishes. Accordingly, if consumer welfare is to be the goal of

---

[3] See generally, Jorde and Teece [1989a] for a detailed assessment of antitrust law and enforcement.

[4] For a brief review of this literature, see Jorde and Teece [1989].

[5a] Bork [1978] has been a strong advocate of the consumer welfare approach.

antitrust, it needs to be couched in a forward-looking, innovation-centered context.[5b] Otherwise, antitrust policy may unwittingly diminish a nation's economic welfare.

Alternatively, one might consider the abandonment of a consumer welfare orientation, and the substitution of innovation and its rapid diffusion as the goal of antitrust policy. At minimum, we would propose that when the promotion of static consumer welfare and innovation are in conflict, the courts and administrative agencies should favor innovation. Adopting dynamic competition and innovation as the goal of antitrust would, in our view, serve consumer welfare over time more assuredly than would the current focus on short-run consumer welfare. We will return to this topic in our discussion of industrial policy in Sec. 5. We next turn to two areas of antitrust law that are insufficiently sensitive to dynamic competition and its benefits: market power assessment and competitor agreements.

3. Innovation and Market Power Assessment[6]

There is no area where antitrust policy so clearly displays its focus on static competition than in the treatment of market definition. Market definition is the key pillar to antitrust theory and enforcement policy. In the absence of market power, practically every form of business behavior, other than price fixing and its economic equivalents, is legal. Once market power is proven, business practices will be closely scrutinized to determine whether they are reasonable.

Standard approaches to competition can assign market power incorrectly to an innovating firm. Even though the market power associated with innovation is often quite transitory, standard entry barrier analysis — with its one to two year fuse for entry[7] — will often not undo a finding of market dominance and associated market power for an innovator. Accordingly, innovators may need to constrain severely their business conduct in order to avoid violating the antitrust laws or the threat of private treble damage actions. Ironically, in today's global economy, with low or nonexistent tariffs, one of the few ways to build market share in the United States is through innovative success.

[5b] Interestingly, in the economic analysis of international trade policy, both producer and consumer welfare are advanced, along with tariff revenues, as legitimate components of domestic economic welfare.

[6] This section is based on Jorde and Teece [1988] and Hartman, Teece, Mitchell and Jorde [1990].

[7] See *U.S. Department of Justice Merger Guidelines*, June 14, p. 1984.

With a Schumpeterian concept of competition in mind, one finds the current methodology for defining product markets troublesome. This is because, in the Schumpeterian conception of things, market power can be ephemeral in industries characterized by rapid technological change. Schumpeterian competition is not readily incorporated into the standard analytical frameworks used to define relevant antitrust markets.

For example, consider how the U.S. Department of Justice (DOJ) approaches market definition.[8] As explained in the *Merger Guidelines* [1984], the DOJ will include in the product market a group of products such that "a hypothetical firm that was the only present and future seller of these products ('the monopolist') could profitably impose a small but significant and nontransitory increase in price — generally five percent lasting one year." Our focus here is not so much on the 5 percent threshold, but on the fact that the implicit assumption adopted is that products in a market are homogeneous and competitors compete on price. Such is often not the case. As a result, application of the 5 percent test in an industry where competition is Schumpeterian rather than neoclassical is likely to create a downward bias in the definition of the size of the relevant product market, and a corresponding upward bias in the assessment of market power.

Consider the minicomputer industry. In the minicomputer industry, a variety of systems compete on price and performance while exhibiting price differences of several 100 percent.[9] Too literal an application of the DOJ's 5 percent test would suggest that each manufacturer is in a different market, because otherwise product substitution would occur which would stimulate pressures for price equalization.

Such an interpretation, however, would ignore the realities of competition in the computer industry. A variety of systems with quite different price-performance attributes successfully occupy the same market at a given point in time. As new systems are introduced and the prices of existing systems change, it takes some time for resulting price-performance implications to be digested and understood by the market. One reason is simply that it takes time for users to experience and test the products. Moreover, to the extent that the product is durable and a replacement for existing equipment, purchase decisions are complicated by the need to retire existing equipment. In addition, new computer systems usually require new supporting systems to be developed and acquired, so that even computer systems that are consensually superior on price and performance

---

[8] While frequently criticized, this approach is widely accepted by scholars and the courts. For a critique, see Harris and Jorde [1983].

[9] See Hartman and Teece [1990].

dimensions will take time to diffuse and be adapted. In such situations, 5 percent or even 25 percent price increases may be met with no substitution until the performance of the products can be assessed and existing equipment can be economically replaced. Even a 25 percent price increase may seem insignificant if accompanied by a performance enhancement. In such circumstances, where competition is performance based, the DOJ's 5%-one-year rule is not likely to identify markets that are in any way meaningful.[10] We outline our approach to this problem, which is more fully developed in Hartman, Teece, Mitchell and Jorde [1990].

When competition proceeds primarily on the basis of features and performance, the pertinent question to ask is whether a change in the performance attributes of one commodity would induce substitution to or from another. If the answer is affirmative, then the differentiated products, even if based on alternative technologies, should be included in the relevant product market. Furthermore, when assessing such performance-induced substitutability, a one-year or two-year period is simply too short, because enhancement of performance attributes involves a longer time to accomplish than price changes. While it is difficult to state precisely (and generally) what the length of time should be, it is clear that the time frame should be determined by technological concerns. As a result, it may be necessary to apply different time frames to different products/technologies.

When assessing performance-based competition among existing producers, the product changes to be included as a metric should involve re-engineering of existing products using technologies currently known to existing competitors. Product changes which depend on anticipated technologies, that are not currently commercial, should be excluded. Thus if firm A, by modifying its product X using its existing proprietary product and process technology and public knowledge, could draw sales away from product Y of firm B, such that B would need to improve its products to avoid losing market share to A, then X and Y are in the same relevant market. If such changes are likely to occur yet would take longer than one year, the one-year rule should be modified.

When assessing potential competition and entry barriers, the two-year-5% rule must also be modified to include variations in performance attributes in

---

[10] In Sec. 3.411, the *U.S. Department of Justice Merger Guidelines* state that with heterogeneous products "the problems facing a cartel become more complex. Instead of a single price, it may be necessary to establish and enforce a complex schedule of prices corresponding to gradations in actual or perceived quality attributes among competing products. ... Product variation is arguably relevant in all cases, but *practical considerations dictate a more limited use of the factor.*" As a rule of thumb, if the product is completely homogeneous (very heterogeneous), "the Department of Justice is more (less) likely to challenge the merger."

existing and new technologies. In high-technology innovative industries, it is this competition that is often most threatening, often the most important from a welfare standpoint,[11] takes the longest time to play out, and is the most difficult to fully anticipate. A more realistic time frame must be determined over which the new products/technologies may be allowed to enter. The precise length of time allowed for the entry of potential competitors must also reflect technological realities. Hence, it too may vary by product and technology.

The need to assess performance competition argues for the use of "hedonic methods." A growing hedonic literature has addressed the importance of product attributes in economic behavior. This literature has been both theoretical and empirical. It has focused upon product demand and production cost. The demand literature has addressed the importance of product attributes in determining prices[12] and market share.[13] The cost literature demonstrates and measures the impact of product attributes on production costs.[14]

Thus assume that several firms offer various products with different attributes. Assume that one producer improves the performance of a certain attribute, holding price and other attributes constant. If the demand of a similar product decreases, there exists a performance cross-elasticity between the two products. If this cross elasticity is high enough, the products are in the same market. However, if the producer were to improve the performance of a certain attribute, but simultaneously raises the product's price such that no substitution occurs, this does not necessarily mean that the products are in different markets.

This framework allows one to analyze and quantify both price and performance (attribute) competition. Using it, one can retain the 5 percent price rule while extending the DOJ approach to incorporate performance competition. Using

---

[11] As noted earlier, Schumpeter [1942] stressed that potential competition from new products and processes is the most powerful form of competition, stating "in capitalist reality, as distinguished from its textbook picture, it is not that kind [price] of competition that counts but the competition that comes from the new commodity, the new technology, the new source of supply ... This kind of competition is as much more effective than the other as bombardment is in comparison with forcing a door, and so much more important that it becomes a matter of comparative indifference whether competition in the ordinary sense functions more or less promptly."

[12] See Brown and Mendelsohn [1984]; Brown and Rosen [1982]; Epple [1987]; Hartman [1987]; Hartman and Doane [1987]; Hartman and Teece [1990]; Ohta and Griliches [1976]; and Rosen [1974].

[13] See Atkinson and Halvorsen [1984]; Hartman [1982]; Hausman [1979]; and Mannering and Winston [1984].

[14] See Epple [1987]; Friedlaender *et al.* [1983]; Fuss [1984]; Fuss and Waverman [1981]; and Spady and Friedlaender [1978].

it, one can retain the 5 percent price rule while extending the DOJ approach to incorporate performance competition. For example, the analogous to the 5 percent price rule, one could assess the effects of percentage changes in performance. However, such an extension is far from straightforward. One needs to carefully specify rules of thumb regarding the threshold size of performance competition and the time period over which such competition is allowed to unfold.

In general, performance changes are more difficult to quantify than price changes because performance is multi-dimensional. As a result, quantification requires measuring both the change in an individual attribute and the relative importance of that attribute. Unlike price changes which involve altering the value of a common base unit (dollars), performance changes often involve changing the units by which performance is measured. Nonetheless, rough quantification is possible, based on the pooled judgements of competent observers, particularly product users.

In terms of threshold effects, we tentatively suggest introducing a 25 percent rule for a change in any key performance attribute. This threshold implies the following. Assume that an existing manufacturer lowers the quality of a key performance attribute of an existing product up to 25 percent, *ceteris paribus*. If no substitution to other products does occur, then those other products share the market with the original product. Conversely, assume that a new product is introduced that is identical to an existing product in all ways except that it offers up to a 25 percent improvement in a key performance attribute. If there is no substitution to the new product, then the products represent distinct markets. If there is substitution from the existing product to the new product, then the two products share the same antitrust market.

The criterion of 25 percent performance improvement for a single key performance attribute is conservative. Not only is a 25 percent improvement small compared to those that commonly occur in industries experiencing rapid technological change, but a 25 percent improvement in a single attribute is likely to imply an overall performance improvement of considerably less than 25 percent. This performance threshold must furthermore be judged in terms of feasibility. While it is always possible to raise prices, it is not always possible to increase performance. This problem is most severe in the case of quantum changes, such as the introduction of a special application for a device. Following introduction, however, most product changes take place along a relatively continuous trajectory of technological improvement. Many product users are familiar with the key development programs of their suppliers and are able to assess the likelihood that a particular product change will emerge in the near future.

An effective measurement procedure, therefore, would be to rely on the informed judgements of users of existing products. This procedure would involve identifying market experts, asking them to list key performance attributes. The sample of product users could be supplemented by a corresponding sample of commercial participants, although care would be required to avoid introducing competitive bias into the judgements.[15] A sample of such participants could be asked whether a 25 percent change in the performance of any one attribute would lead to product substitution.

In addition to threshold rules regarding performance changes, market definition requires an identification of a time frame for the competitive product changes — that is, the definition of the "near future." We argued above that the DOJ one-year and two-year rules are too short for almost any case of serious technical advance. Indeed, because there is significant variation among products, no single number will be appropriate for all cases. Nonetheless, we suggest that a four-year period be established as a default time frame, with the option of adjusting the period if strong evidence suggests that would be appropriate in an individual case. Like the DOJ's one-year rule, or the patent law's 17-year grant, a fixed four-year rule will not be optimal in all cases. It could provide too broad a market definition in some cases and too narrow a definition for others; however, its unambiguous nature has the advantage of being easily understood and not requiring negotiation or litigation to determine an appropriate frame.

Finally, one needs to address the question of the appropriate HHI thresholds. The Merger Guidelines selects critical HHIs at 1000 and 1800. It is difficult to hypothesize and propose alternative HHIs for technologically dynamic markets. However, the inclusion of performance competition and the extension of the time frame of competitive response may mean that it is not necessary to change these critical HHIs. Furthermore, we believe that with technologically dynamic markets, the dynamics of market structure in the past should provide some guidance to assessing market definition and predicting likely changes in market concentration. Key factors are the change in concentration and the trend in the number of competitors.

Failure to recognize that competition is often on the basis of performance attributes and not price will lead courts and the Department of Justice to

---

[15] If an employee of a competitor of a firm for which market power was being determined were included in the sample, for instance, that person would have incentives to overestimate the difficulty of performance improvement. The need to inform these economic decisions with technological reality would argue for a closer working relationship between the Antitrust Division of the Justice Department and the National Science Foundation and/or the Office of Technology Assessment.

underestimate the breadth of product markets in industries characterized by rapid technological change. This process, in turn, will lead courts and the DOJ to exaggerate antitrust dangers.[16]

4. Innovation and Cooperative Agreements among Competitors

A second area in which traditional antitrust analysis may impede innovation is in the analysis of cooperative agreements among competitors. The problem arises because of a naïve view of innovation, embedded in current antitrust economics and jurisprudence, that fails to recognize that innovating firms may need to cooperate to promote innovation. We next briefly explain two different models of the innovation process and explore implications for antitrust policy.

4.1. The (Traditional) Serial Model

Traditional descriptions of the innovation process commonly break it down into a number of stages which proceed sequentially. This view is reflected in theoretical treatments of R&D in industrial organization. According to this view the innovation process proceeds in a linear and predictable fashion from research to development, design, production, and then finally to marketing, sales, and service.[17] In simple models, there is not even any feedback or overlap between and among stages.

The serial model of innovation is an analytic convenience which no longer adequately characterizes the innovation process, except in special circumstances, such as in some scale-intensive industries. The initial development of nylon at Dupont perhaps fits this model. The Manhattan project during World War II is also illustrative. The serial model does not address the many small but cumulatively important incremental innovations that are at the heart of technological change in many industries, especially well-established industries like semiconductors, computers, and automobiles.

The serial model has enabled economists to model innovation as a vertical process. Inasmuch as antitrust policy toward vertical restraints is very permissive, many economists and legal scholars do not understand how U.S. antitrust laws could stand in the way of the various kinds of standard and non-standard contracting often needed to support the commercialization of innovation. But matters are not so simple.

---

[16] One example was the Justice Department's challenge to the sale of EMI's U.S. operations to General Electric.

[17] See Grossman and Shapiro [1986].

4.2. The Simultaneous Model

The simultaneous model of innovation recognizes the existence of tight linkages and feedback mechanisms which must operate quickly and efficiently, including links between firms, within firms, and sometimes between firms and other organizations like universities. From this perspective, innovation does not necessarily begin with research; nor is the process serial. But it does require rapid feedback, mid-course corrections to designs, and redesign.[18] This conceptualization recognizes aspects of the serial model — such as the flow of activity, in certain cases through design to development, production and marketing — but also recognizes the constant feedback between and among activities, and the involvement of a wide variety of economic actors and organizations that need not have a simple upstream-downstream relationship to each other.[19] It suggests that R&D personnel must be closely connected to manufacturing and marketing personnel and to external sources of supply of new components and complementary technologies, so that supplier, manufacturer and customer reactions can be fed back into the design process rapidly. In this way new technology, whether internal or external, becomes embedded into designs which meet customer needs quickly and efficiently.

The simultaneous model visualizes innovation as an incremental and cumulative activity that involves building on what went before, whether it is inside the organization or outside the organization, and whether the knowledge is proprietary or in the public domain. The simultaneous model also stresses the importance of the speed of the design cycle, and flexibility. IBM followed this model in developing its first PC, employing alliances with Microsoft and others to launch a successful personal computer system. Sun Microsystems and NeXT Computer launched themselves in this way and have remained in this mode for subsequent new product development. Microprocessor development at Intel often follows this logic too.

When innovation has this character, the company which is quickest in product design and development will appear to be the pioneer, even if its own contribution to science and technology is minimal, because it can be first

---

[18] This process has also been termed "cyclic." See Gomory [1987].

[19] Moreover, the linkage from science to innovation is not solely or even preponderantly at the beginning of typical innovations, but rather extends all through the process. "Science can be visualized as lying alongside development processes, to be used when needed." (Kline and Rosenberg [1986]) Design is often at the center of the innovation process. Research is often spawned by the problems associated with trying to get the design right. Indeed, important technological breakthroughs can often proceed even when the underlying science is not understood.

to "design in" science and technology already in the public domain. Both small and large organizations operate by this model, reaching out upstream and downstream, horizontally and laterally to develop and assemble leading edge systems.

In short, much innovation today is likely to require lateral and horizontal linkages as well as vertical ones. As we discuss below, and particularly for small firms, innovation may require accessing complementary assets which lie outside the organization. If innovating firms do not have the necessary capabilities in-house, they will need to engage in various forms of restrictive contracts with providers of inputs and complementary assets. The possibility that antitrust laws could be invoked, particularly by excluded competitors, thus arises. Lying ready to snare these firms are plaintiffs' attorneys appealing to cartel and "raising rivals' costs" theories. With the required forms of contracting necessarily complex, and an understanding of the requirements of the innovation process largely absent from antitrust doctrine, the possibility of judicial error is significant. Paradoxically, it is not the giant integrated enterprise which is most exposed to these risks. Most at risk are mid-sized enterprises that have developed and commercialized important innovation, because such firms are likely to have market power (under orthodox definitions) and have the need to engage in complex forms of interfirm cooperation.

4.3. *Organizational Requirements of Innovation*

Whether innovation is serial or simultaneous, it requires the coordination of various activities. The serial model suggests a rather simple organizational problem; the simultaneous model a more complex one, often employing various forms of non-standard contracting. To the extent that economists employ just the serial model, they greatly oversimplify the organizational challenges which innovation provides and underestimate potential antitrust problems. Also, they probably exaggerate the importance of research and downplay the importance of other factors. Except in special cases, a firm's R&D capability is for naught if it cannot organize the rest of the innovation process efficiently and effectively, particularly if that innovation is taking place in an already-established industry.

For innovations to be commercialized, the economic system must somehow assemble all the relevant complementary assets and create a dynamically-efficient interactive system of learning and information exchange. The necessary complementary assets can conceivably be assembled by administrative processes, or by market processes, as when the innovator simply licenses the technology to firms that already own the relevant assets, or are willing to create them. These organizational choices have received scant attention in the context of innovation. Indeed, the serial model relies on an implicit belief that arms-length contracts between unaffiliated firms in the vertical chain from research to customer will suffice to commercialize technology. In particular, there has been little consideration of how complex contractual arrangements among firms can assist commercialization — that is, translating R&D capability into profitable new products and processes. The one partial exception is a tiny literature on joint R&D activity;[20] but this literature addresses the organization of R&D and not the organization of innovation.

If innovation takes place in a regime of tight appropriability — that is, if the technological leader can secure legal protection (as when it obtains an ironclad patent[21]) — and if technology can be transferred at zero cost as is commonly assumed in theoretical models, the organizational challenge that it created by innovation is relatively simple. In these instances, the market for intellectual property is likely to support transactions enabling the developer of the technology simply to sell its intellectual property for cash, or at least license it to downstream firms who can then engage in whatever value-added activities are necessary to extract value from the technology. With a well-functioning market for know-how, markets can provide the structure for the requisite organization to be accomplished.

But in reality, the market for know-how is riddled with imperfections.[22] Simple unilateral contracts — where technology is sold for cash — are unlikely to be efficient.[23] Complex bilateral and multilateral contracts, internal organization or various hybrid structures are often required to shore up obvious market failures.[24]

4.4. *Governance Alternatives for Innovation*

The previous section has argued that innovation often requires firms to entrepreneur complex contracts and relationships with other firms in order to bring technology to the market, and to hold "me too" imitators at bay. This section considers in more detail the range of organizational alternatives available to the innovator to generate, coordinate and control such complementary assets.

---

[20] See Frossman and Shapiro [1986] and Ordover and Willig [1985].

[21] See Teece [1986].

[22] See Arrow [1962].

[23] See Teece [1980], [1982].

[24] See Williamson [1985] and Teece [1986].

4.4.1. The price mechanism

Consider first the price mechanism. Theoretical treatments generally assume that the requisite coordination and control can be achieved by the invisible hand. Efficient levels of investment in complementary assets are brought forward at the right time and place by price signals. Entrepreneurship is automatic and costless. This is the view implicit in textbook presentations; in turn, the textbook view often influences U.S. antitrust law.

However, many scholars have been rather critical of what Tjalling Koopmans calls the "overextended belief" of many economists regarding the efficiency of competitive markets as a means of allocating resources in a world characterized by ubiquitous uncertainty. Market failures are likely to arise because of the ignorance which firms have with respect to their competitors' future actions, preferences, and states of technological information.[25] In reality, there is no special means to ensure that investment programs are made known to all concerned at the time of their inception. This uncertainty is especially high for the development and commmercialization of new technology. Accordingly, innovating firms need to achieve greater coordination than the price system alone appears to be able to effectuate.

4.4.2. Internal organization

A second mechanism for effectuating coordination is the administrative processes within the firm. A company's internal organization can serve to shore up some market imperfections and provide some of the necessary coordination. As Alfred Chandler [1977] has explained, the modern multidivisional business enterprise "took over from the market the coordination and integration of the flow of goods and services from the production of raw materials through the several processes of production to the sale to the ultimate consumer ... administrative coordination replaced market coordination in an increasingly large portion of the economy." Oliver Williamson [1985] has developed a framework, both elegant and powerful, to explain the relative efficiencies of markets and administrative processes. One property of large integrated structures is that they have the potential to become excessively hierarchical and less responsive to market needs.[26] Accordingly, at least for some aspects of innovative activity, smaller organization are often superior. Unfortunately, as we discuss below, antitrust law appears to favor merger over interfirm agreements

---

[25] See Koopmans [1957, part II].

[26] See Teece [1989].

and thus burdens innovation by attaching disincentives to otherwise appropriate organizational forms.

4.4.3. Strategic alliances

Lying in between pure market and full administrative solutions are many intermediate and hybrid possibilities, including interfirm agreements. Interfirm agreements can be classified as unilateral (where A sells X to B) or bilateral (whereby A agrees to buy Y from B as a condition for making the sale of X, and both parties understand that the transaction will be continued only if reciprocity is observed). Such arrangements can also be multilateral if they involve more than two parties.

An especially interesting interfirm agreement is the strategic alliance, which can be defined as a bilateral or multilateral relationship characterized by the commitment of two or more partner firms to a common goal. A strategic alliance might include (1) technology swaps, (2) joint R&D or co-development, and/or (3) the sharing of complementary assets, such as where one party does manufacturing and the other distribution for a co-developed product. Of course, if the common goals were simply price-fixing or market-sharing, then such an agreement would constitute a cartel, especially if the agreement included substantially all members of an industry.

By definition, a strategic alliance can never have one side receiving cash alone; it is not a unilateral exchange transaction. Nor do strategic alliances include mergers, because alliances by definition cannot involve acquisition of another firm's assets or controlling interest in another firm's stock. Alliances need not involve equity swaps or equity investments, though they often do. Strategic alliances without equity typically consist of contracts between or among partner firms that are nonaffiliated. Equity alliances can take many forms, including minority equity holdings, consortia, and joint ventures. Such interfirm agreements are usually temporary, and are assembled and disassembled as circumstances warrant. Typically, only a limited range of the firm's activities are enveloped in such agreements, and many competitors are excluded.

Strategic alliances, including consortia and joint ventures, are often as effective and efficient way to organize for innovation, particularly when an industry is fragmented. Whereas full-blown national planning entails the abolition of the market as an organizing mechanism, and large hierarchies are exposed to bureaucratic limits, interfirm cooperation preserves market selection and responsiveness. In a sense, interfirm cooperation is the pure private enterprise solution. The case for planning and industrial policy recedes if a degree of operational and strategic coordination can be attained through private agreements. The benefits associated with less hierarchical structures can be obtained without incurring the disadvantages of insufficient scale and scope.

4.5. Antitrust Treatment of Agreements Among Competitors[27]

Current U.S. antitrust law needlessly inhibits agreements among competition designed to develop and commercialize new technology. The problem is that the legal standards for interfirm agreements are ambiguous. While it is generally true that "rule of reason" analysis — rather than per se rules — will be applied to contractual arrangements designed to advance innovation, the elements of rule of reason analysis are muddled. In addition, although current law, as a practical matter, recognizes a "safe harbor" for mergers between firms that will have less than 20 percent market share, it does not recognize a similar safe harbor for horizontal contractual arrangements among firms.

The Clayton Act also permits private parties to sue for treble damages for alleged antitrust injuries, and allows state attorney generals to recover treble damages on behalf of persons residing in the state. Successful plaintiffs can also recover attorneys' fees. These remedies are available only in the United States. They provide a powerful incentive for plaintiffs to litigate, and given the current state of the law, a powerful disincentive for businesses to form cooperative innovation arrangements and strategic alliances. While it is difficult to measure the missed opportunities for cooperative innovation caused by the threat of treble damage litigation, we believe it is substantial. Moreover, it works to the particular detriment of small and medium-sized innovative firms in industries where the innovative process is simultaneous.

Congress has recognized that these provisions may inhibit technological innovation, and the National Cooperative Research Act (NCRA) of 1984 took two significant steps to remove legal disincentives to cooperative research. First, the NCRA provides that "joint research and development ventures" must not be held illegal per se, and that such ventures instead should be "judged on the basis of [their] reasonableness, taking into account all relevant factors affecting competition, including, but not limited to, effects on competition in properly defined, relevant research and development markets." Second, the NCRA establishes a registration procedure for joint research and development ventures, limiting antitrust recoveries against registered ventures to single damages, interest, and costs, including attorneys' fees. Thus, Congress eliminated the threat of treble damages for litigation

---

[27] See generally, Jorde and Teece [1989a] for a detailed assessment of antitrust law and enforcement.

challenging cooperative R&D arrangements, provided that the parties to the arrangement first register their venture. But R&D is only a small piece of the innovation puzzle.

In our view, the NCRA is not sufficiently permissive. The substantive protection provided by the NCRA — guaranteed rule of reason treatment and reduction of damages — extend only to research, and downstream commercial activity "reasonably required" for research and narrowly confined to marketing intellectual property developed through a joint R&D program. Treatment of other agreements designed to facilitate innovation is thus left uncertain, to be determined only by interpretation of the "reasonably required" standard. The NCRA unwisely precludes joint manufacturing and production of innovative products and processes, which is often necessary to provide the cooperating ventures with significant feedback information to aid in further innovation and product development, and to make the joint activity profitable. The NCRA implicitly accepts the serial and not the simultaneous model of innovation.

In addition, the NCRA gives little guidance concerning the substantive content of its rule of reason approach. While the Act did require that markets be defined in the context of research and not the products that might result from it, the NCRA fails to specify factors to be considered within rule of reason analysis. It simply requires consideration of "all relevant factors affecting competition," paying no special attention to the special characteristics of the innovation process in a quickly changing industry.

Finally, while the NCRA's elimination of treble damages for registered ventures is an important step forward, cooperating firms are still not protected from antitrust litigation. Even after the NCRA, antitrust laws still permit private plaintiffs to engage in treble damage litigation against cooperative arrangements facilitating commercialization. Moreover, single damages are still available even against those registered under NCRA. The cost of defending antitrust suits is not materially reduced by the exceedingly narrow circumstances in which the Act permits an award of attorneys' fees to prevailing defendants. The threat of litigation, with attendant managerial distraction, can be extremely damaging to the competitive performance of a fast-paced industry.

Businesses seem to have recognized the limited nature of the steps taken by the NCRA. Not surprisingly, only 111 separate cooperative ventures registered under the NCRA between 1984 and June 1988. Our review of these filings indicates that they are very modest endeavors that are aimed at solving industry problems and are not of great competitive moment. We believe that if an approval procedure existed under which procompetitive arrangements could obtain exemptions from further antitrust exposure to private damage actions, then many more competitively beneficial ventures would utilize the NCRA.

In contrast to this picture of U.S. antitrust law, the antitrust and business environments in Japan and Europe are more hospitable to strategic alliances and cooperative arrangements for innovation. The basic Japanese attitude is that joint R&D activities are procompetitive and thus should not be touched by the Antimonopoly Act. Significantly, the literal Japanese translation of "R&D" — *kenkyu kaihatsu* — implicitly includes commercialization; there is no semantic distinction between the concepts of R&D and commercialization.

In Japan, the Fair Trade Commission is responsible for executing and enforcing the Antimonopoly Act of 1947, which (like the Sherman Act) broadly prohibits unreasonable restraints of trade. While there is no specific legislative exemption for joint innovation arrangements under the Act, Japan's FTC has been able to exempt cooperative innovation efforts from the scope of the law by virtue of its power as the primary enforcer of the Act.[28] FTC policy also states that if anticompetitive effects are alleged, the procompetitiveness benefits of innovation must be balanced, too. Balancing will take place not only within a particular market but also across markets,[29] because "there is a possibility of the emergence of competition at the intersection of industrial sectors as a result of joint R&D between firms in different sectors."

In considering anticompetitive effects of cooperative innovation arrangements, Japan's FTC analyzes market shares and market structure. The FTC specifically recognizes the needs of innovators and articulates procompetitive justifications that include: (1) the difficulty of single-firm innovation; (2) the faster innovation created by cooperation and specialization between joint participants; (3) the pursuit of innovation in new fields by utilizing shared technology and know-how; and (4) enhancement of the technological level of each participant through the interchange of technology.

---

[28] The basic administrative policy outlining the standards by which such joint innovation efforts are to be scrutinized is contained in a Report of Japan's Fair Trade Commission [1984, 37–39]. The Report states that the evaluation of the anticompetitive effect of joint R&D at the product market stage will depend significantly "on the competition and market shares among the participants and the market structure of the industry to which the participants belong ... In cases where the market shares of the participants are small ... the effects will be small." Although "small" is not defined in the Report, Japan's Merger Guidelines state that the FTC is not likely to closely examine cases in which the combined market share of the merging parties is less than 25 percent. See Iyori and Yesugi [1983, 86–88]. Our discussions with MITI and FTC officials confirm that the horizontal merger safe harbors would be equally applicable to cooperative contractual arrangements.

[29] *Fair Trade Commission* (Japan) [1984].

When MITI seeks to promote cooperative R&D activities (for example, as authorized by the Act for Facilitation of Research in Key Technology, or the Research Association for Mining and Manufacturing Technology Act), the FTC is consulted in advance. Once the activities are cleared by the FTC, it is extraordinarily unlikely that the FTC would pursue antitrust remedies at a future time. Significantly, treble damages are not available to private parties seeking to enforce Japanese antitrust laws, and private suits for single damages are very rare and usually unsuccessful. Thus, Japanese firms cooperating on innovation and commercialization of innovation have little to fear from Japanese antitrust laws.

Under this type of antitrust environment, it is not surprising that there is frequent collaboration for innovation. Although regular statistics are not kept in Japan, because there is no reporting requirement for collaborative research and commercialization activities, a Fair Trade Commission report issued in 1984 contains statistics suggestive of the quantity and variety of joint innovation activities in Japan. The survey results indicate that joint R&D projects among corporations in the same industrial sector, which might be classified as horizontal collaboration, represent 19.1 percent of total projects.[30] The antitrust environment shaping cooperation in the European Community is also markedly different from the United States. In 1968, the European Commission issued a "Notice of Cooperation between Enterprises" which indicates that horizontal collaboration for purposes of R&D is normally outside the scope of antitrust concerns as defined in Articles 85 and 86 of the EEC Treaty. The Commission has consistently taken a favorable position on R&D agreements unless the large entities involved imply serious anticompetitive consequences.

In 1984, the European Commission adopted Regulation No. 418/85 (hereafter Reg. 418) expanding the favorable antitrust treatment of R&D. For firms whose total market share does not exceed 20 percent, it provides blanket exceptions for horizontal R&D arrangements, including commercialization — which the Commission views as "the natural consequence of joint R&D" — up to the point

---

[30] Questionnaires were sent to 484 manufacturing corporations in the fields of electronics, tele-communications, automobiles, chemicals, ceramics, steel and nonferrous metals, whose stocks were listed in Tokyo and Osaka Stock Exchanges. Data was provided by 242 corporations, representing 1.9 percent of the total manufacturing industry that engage in R&D activities in terms of the number of corporations and 16.7 percent in terms of sales. As to the nature of the joint R&D projects, 54.3 percent of the total cases were developmental research. Basic and applied research were 13.6 and 32.1 percent respectively. In the case of large corporations with capital of more than 10 billion yen, the total basic and application research amounted to 52.1 percent.

of distribution and sales.[31] In addition, the Commission is authorized to grant exemptions for cooperative efforts that do not fall within the automatic safe harbor.

4.6. *Proposed Modifications to U.S. Antitrust Law Affecting Cooperative Agreements Among Competitors*

To insure that antitrust law is responsive to the needs of innovating firms and does not inhibit U.S. firms' from competing effectively in global markets experiencing rapid technological change, we believe the following changes are in order:

First, as discussed in Sec. 3, market definition should be tailored to the context of innovation and should focus primarily on the market for know-how. Specific product markets become relevant only when commercialization is included within the scope of the cooperative agreement.

Second, the rule of reason should be clarified to take specific account of the appropriability regime, the pace of technological change, the diversity of sources of new technology, the need to access complementary assets and technologies, and the need to have cheek-by-jowl cooperation to manage the innovation process simultaneously rather than serially.

Third, a safe harbor defined according to market power should be expressly adopted that would shield from antitrust liability interfirm agreements among competitors that involve less than 20 to 25 percent of the relevant market.

Fourth, antitrust law should not bias the selection of interfirm organizational forms; at a minimum, integration by contract or alliance should be treated no less favorably than full mergers.[32]

---

[31] Regulation No. 418/85 of 19 December 1984 on the application of Art. 85(3) of the Treaty to categories of research and development agreement, *O. J. Eur. Comm.* (No. L 53) 5 [1985], entered into force March 1, 1985, and applicable until December 31, 1997. The statutory framework of Reg. 418 is complex. It applies to three categories of agreements involving R&D: (1) joint research and development of products of processes and joint exploitation of the results of the R&D; (2) joint exploitation of the results of R&D product or processes pursuant to a prior agreement between the same parties; and (3) joint research and development of products without joint exploitation should the agreement fall within the purview of Art. 85(1). Under Reg. 418, joint exploitation is interpreted to mean joint manufacturing and licensing to third parties. Joint distribution and sales, however, are not covered and require individual exemptions pursuant to Art. 85(3).

[32] At present, the *U.S. Department of Justice Merger Guidelines* provide a degree of certainty for cooperation achieved by merger, which is absent for cooperation achieved contractually.

Fifth, the NCRA should be amended to include joint production and commercialization efforts to exploit innovation.

Sixth, an administrative procedure should be created, involving both the Justice and Commerce Departments, to allow evaluation and possible certification of cooperative arrangements among firms with market shares higher than 20 to 25 percent, when dynamic efficiency gains are likely and rivalry robust.

Seventh, private antitrust suits challenging cooperative innovation arrangements should be limited to equitable relief, and attorneys' fees should be awarded to the prevailing party.

The first four of these proposals could be accomplished by courts interpreting the rule of reason and the National Cooperative Research Act. We hope courts will not hesitate to employ the tools of evolutionary, common law interpretation and development to achieve these changes. However, to achieve the complete package of substantive and procedural changes most quickly, and thus assure certainty and predictability, legislation is the best overall solution. At a U.C. Berkeley Conference on "Antitrust, Innovation and Competitiveness" in October 1988, we distributed a draft of legislation that combined a "registration" and "certification" approach for cooperative commercialization ventures. Shortly thereafter, Congressman Edwards (H.R. 1025) and Congressman Fish (H.R. 2264) advanced a "registration" approach to cooperative commercialization efforts and Congressman Boucher and Campbell (H.R. 1024) proposed a "certification" approach. After three hearings on these bills, Chairman Jack Brooks of the House Judiciary Committee introduced and the Judiciary Committee passed the National Cooperative Production Amendments of 1990 (H.R. 4611). H.R. 4611 would amend the National Cooperative Research Act to extend its registration approach to joint production ventures.[33] At the same time, Attorney General Richard Thornburgh and Commerce Secretary Robert Mosbacher announced the Bush Administration's support of a registration approach for production joint ventures.[34]

---

[33] Professor Jorde testified on July 26, 1989, in favor of both a registration and certification approach. See Jorde and Teece [1989c]. Legislation advancing a registration approach for production joint ventures has also been introduced in the Senate by Senators Patrick Leahy (D-VT) and Strom Thurmond (R-SC) (S. 1006). Three aspects of H.R. 4611 bear noting. First, relevant market definition under rule of reason analysis would specifically consider the worldwide capacity of suppliers. Second, foreign participation in a production joint venture would be limited to 30 percent of the voting securities or equity interests, and all production facilities would have to be located in the United States or its territories. Third, apparently production joint ventures would not be limited to efforts designed to commercialize joint R&D, nor need they be related to innovation.

[34] See *Department of Justice* release, May 10, 1990, p. 701.

5. Conclusion

The case for changes in the way antitrust law analyzes and assesses market power and agreements among competitors rests on three fundamental pillars. The first is that the innovation process is terribly important to economic growth and development, because it yields social returns in excess of private returns, and because innovation is a powerful spur to competition. Hence, if antitrust policy is going to err, it ought to do so by being on the facilitating rather than on the inhibiting side of innovation. This principle is well-understood in Europe and Japan. Second, economic theory tells us that if certain organizational arrangements are exposed to governmentally-imposed costs while others are not, firms will substitute away from the burdened forms (in this context, interfirm agreements) and in favor of the unburdened forms (in this context, hierarchy), even when the former are potentially economically superior. According to Aoki,[35] the slowdown in total factor productivity in the United States can be attributed in large part to a mismatch between organizational form and the requirements of new technology; in particular, he is concerned that hierarchical solutions are overused, at least in the United States. We are concerned that present law does not give full recognition to the interorganizational requirements of the innovation process; failure to do so is damaging when innovation must proceed according to the simultaneous model. Third, cartelization of industries experiencing rapid technological change, and which are open to international trade and investment, is very difficult. So long as these industries remain open and innovative, antitrust policy should err on the side of permitting rather than restricting interfirm contracts.

There are several classes of circumstances where beneficial cooperation will eventually expand if antitrust laws are revised along the lines we propose. The response may not be immediate, particularly with respect to consortia, because the experience base in U.S. industry in this area is thin, because of our antitrust history, and because U.S. firms, at least in the post-war period, have been large relative to their foreign competitors. Accordingly, the need to cooperate has not been as powerful in the past as it is now. However, once organizational learning accumulates, we expect consortia to begin to flourish even in the absence of government funding. We also expect the reinforcement of bilateral alliances already common in U.S. industry. We briefly discuss the kinds of activities that might take place.

---

[35] See Aoki [1989].

(1) *Cooperative Manufacturing and Commercialization*. There are a number of circumstances where cooperative activity beyond early stage activity is beneficial to innovating firms. As discussed, sometimes this is true because of scale, risk, and appropriability considerations. Sometimes it is true because prohibition of cooperative commercialization imposes a significant technology transfer problem, for instance from the research joint venture (if there is one) back to the funding companies. In most cases firms will not wish to cooperate all the way from research through to commercialization. But in some instances they will, or they will wish to cooperate simply on a downstream production venture. When cartelization of the industry is not a threat, we see no reasons for antitrust restraints. The now defunct U.S. Memories, Inc. consortium wanted to invest $500 million to $1 billion to develop and manufacture for its members and for the market advanced dynamic random access memories (DRAMs). With fabrication facilities costing hundreds of millions, acting alone is beyond the financial resources of many companies in this industry who might otherwise wish to have some control over their DRAM supply. This proposed consortium had to contend with a number of difficulties including threats of third party litigation.[36] While antitrust was probably not the main reason for the failure of this enterprise, the antitrust environment did nothing to help. A certification procedure would have provided important certainty to this venture, and others like it. A registration procedure would provide less certainty, but still would be a significant advance over current antitrust law.

Similarly, in the area of superconductors, it is likely that the real challenges will come not in developing superconductors, but in their commercialization. Applying superconductors in systems like railroads, computers, and electricity distribution will require great amounts of time, resources, and capital — probably greater than any single business can muster internally. Accordingly, a public policy stance that treats only early stage activity as potentially requiring cooperation is misguided and will thwart both early and later stage activities. Most firms will not have much incentive to engage in early stage, joint development if later stage, stand-alone commercialization appears too expensive to accomplish profitably.

(2) *Cooperative Innovation Designed to Achieve Catch-up*. Cooperative activities in Japan and Europe have frequently been motivated by a desire to catch-up with the world's technological frontier, which in the postwar years was usually the technology of U.S. firms. However, U.S. firms are increasingly slipping behind the frontier. For instance, U.S. firms are now behind in areas like ceramics

---

[36] See Jorde and Teece [1989b].

and robotics, and in products like VCRs, facsimiles, and HDTV. Just as foreign firms have found cooperative ventures useful for catch-up in the past, U.S. firms could utilize cooperation for this purpose. For example, U.S.-based firms, acting together and with foreign firms, may still have a slender chance of competing in the market for high definition televisions (HDTV) and related products expected to evolve in the 1990s. In the absence of cooperative interfirm agreements, we doubt that development of HDTV systems is possible in the United States. If America's potential "re-entrants" to the consumer electronics business combine to attempt re-entry, they cannot be sure of avoiding serious antitrust problems involving treble damages, particularly if they are successful.

At minimum, the legislative changes proposed would facilitate unfettered information exchange and strategic coordination with respect to re-entry strategies. If such efforts facilitated profitable re-entry into high technology businesses when re-entering would otherwise not occur, or would occur in a more limited and unprofitable way, we do not see why antitrust concerns ought to interfere.

(3) *Cooperation in Response to Foreign Industrial and Technology Policy.* In high technology industries, both European and East Asian nations have active industrial and technology policies that significantly impact market outcomes, both in their own countries and abroad. Airbus is a case in point. The dominant U.S. attitude is one of laissez-faire, and many economists are of the view that the United States send a letter of thanks to foreign governments who subsidize exports to the United States. Such a view is insensitive to the dynamics of technological change, to the importance of cumulative learning, and to re-entry costs.

Some U.S. policy makers, however, favor retaliation against foreign countries which have active industrial policies. We support a modification of U.S. antitrust laws which in some circumstances would permit a competitive response by U.S. industry acting collectively. The proposals we advance to encourage greater cooperation among U.S. firms do not require government expenditures nor do they involve the government "picking winners." But they would soften the tensions emerging in the United States between technology, antitrust and trade policies.

U.S. antitrust policy, like so much of our economic policy, has been preoccupied with static rather than intertemporal concerns. Despite important recent developments, it is informed by naïve theories of the innovation process, and in particular is insensitive to the organizational needs of innovation. U.S. antitrust scholars still harbor suspicion of cooperative agreements among competitors, and do not appreciate the benefits. This suspicion helps fuel uncertainty about how the courts would view interfirm arrangements to promote technological progress and competition.

The model policy changes we advance are certainly no panacea for the severe problems U.S. high-technology industry is currently experiencing. But in bringing our policy closer to Europe and Japan in the way we propose, we will at least purge dogma that no longer deserves a place in our industrial policy. In time, reduced antitrust exposure will help clear the way for beneficial cooperation, thereby reducing incentives for mergers and acquisitions.

The 1990 centennial of the Sherman Act provides a good occasion to begin to set things right. The economics profession, which in the past has had a significant impact on the law of vertical restraints, can provide the intellectual leadership necessary to propel adjustments in the manner in which market power and horizontal agreements are assessed, thereby helping to align U.S. policies with the technological and competitive realities of today's global economy.

But scholarship should not rest once such modest goals are accomplished. Antitrust policy, like much of our economic policy, needs more serious overhaul. We challenge scholars and ourselves to tease out more fully the implications of Schumpeterian competition for antitrust policy.

Summary

Technological innovation drives the competitive process. It yields new products and processes, and sharpens the performance attributes of existing products and processes. Yet economic analysis, infatuated with price competition, too often ignores the role of innovation in the competitive process. The static bias is manifested in antitrust policy, at least in the United States. Accordingly, markets may be defined too narrowly in high technology industries, because price competition is the only form of competition that is recognized. Moreover, antitrust law is hostile to cooperation of effectuate innovation, unless it is strictly vertical, because of the spectre of cartels. This paper suggests how in context of innovation market definition techniques need to be modified to avoid error, and how the law affecting cooperation among competitors needs to be adjusted to ensure that antitrust policy assists rather than impedes competition.

Zusammenfassung

Technologische Innovation ist der wesentliche Motor des Wettbewerbsprozesses. Durch Innovation entstehen neue Produkte und Verfahren und die Qualität existierender Produkte und Verfahren wird erhöht. Dennoch hat sich die ökonomische Analyse überwiegend mit Preiswettbewerb beschäftigt und dabei die Rolle von Innovationen im Wettbewerbsprozeß häufig ignoriert. Die einseitig statische Sichtweise hat sich zumindest in der Wettbewerbspolitik der Vereinigten Staaten niedergeschlagen. Im Bereich der Hochtechnologie können Märkte zu eng definiert sein, wenn Preiswettbewerb die einzige Wettbewerbsform ist, der Beachtung geschenkt wird. Darüber hinaus steht die Wettbewerbsgesetz-gebung wegen des Schreckgespenstes der Kartellbildung eine Kooperation zur Durchführung von Innovationen zumindest dann ablehnend gegenüber, wenn sie nicht rein vertikaler Natur ist. In diesem Beitrag wird ein Vorschlag unterbreitet, wie bei Berücksichtingung des Innovationsaspektes bestehende Praktiken der Marktdefinition modifiziert werden müssen, um Fehler zu vermeiden. Ferner wird aufgezeigt, wie Gesetze, die Kooperation unter Wettbewerbern betreffen, zu verändern sind, damit die Wettbewerbspolitik den Wettbewerb fördert und nicht behindert.

References

M. Aoki, Global Competition, Firm Organization, and Total Factor Productivity: A Comparative Micro Perspective, Paper presented at the International Seminar on Science, Technology, and Economic Growth, OECD, Paris (June 1989).

K.J. Arrow, Economic Welfare and the Allocation of Resources for Invention, in National Bureau of Economic Research, *The Rate and Direction of Inventive Activity* (Princeton University Press, Princeton, 1962), pp. 609–625.

S.E. Atkinson and R. Halvorsen, A New Hedonic Technique for Estimating Attribute Demand: An Application to the Demand for Automobile Fuel Efficiency, *Review of Economics and Statistics* 66(3) (1984), 417–426.

W. Baldwin and J.T. Scott, *Market Structure and Technological Change* (Harwood Publishers, Chur, Switzerland, 1987).

R. Bork, *The Antitrust Paradox: A Policy at War with Itself* (Basic Books, New York, 1978).

G. Jr. Brown and R. Mendelsohn, The Hedonic Travel Cost Method, *Review of Economics and Statistics* 66(3) (1984), 427–433.

J.N. Brown and H.S. Rosen, On the Estimation of Structural Hedonic Price Models, *Econometrica* 50(3) (1982), 765–768.

A.D. Jr. Chandler, *The Visible Hand: The Managerial Revolution in American Business* (Harvard University Press, Cambridge, 1977).

D. Epple, Hedonic Prices and Implicit Markets: Estimating Demand and Supply Functions for Differentiated Products, *Journal of Political Economy* 95(1) (1987), 59–80.

Fair Trade Commission (Japan) [1984], *Research and Development Activities in Private Enterprises and Problems They Pose in the Competition Policy (Minkan kigyo ni okeru kenkyu kaihatsu katsudo na jttai to kyoso seidaku jo no kaidai).*

A.F. Friedlaender, C. Winston and K. Wand, Costs, Technology and Productivity on the U.S. Automobile Industry, *Bell Journal of Economics* 14(1) (1983), 1–20.

M.A. Fuss, Cost Allocation: How Can the Costs of Postal Services be Determined?, in Roger Sherman (ed.), *Perspectives on Postal Service Issues* (American Enterprises Institute, Washington, DC, 1984), pp. 30–52.

_____, and L. Waverman, Regulation and the Multiproduct Firm: The Case of Telecommunications in Canada, in G. Fromme (ed.), *Studies in Public Utility Regulation* (MIT Press, Cambridge, MA, 1981).

R. Gomory, Dominant Science Does Not Mean Dominant Product, *Research and Development* 29(11) (1987), 72–74.

G.M. Grossman and C. Shapiro, Research Joint Ventures: An Antitrust Analysis, *Journal of Law and Economics* 2(2) (1986), 315–337.

G. Harris and T.J. Jorde, Market Definition in the Merger Guidelines: Implications for Antitrust Enforcement, *California Law Review* 71(2) (1983), 464–496.

R.S. Hartman, A Note on the Use of Aggregate Data in Individuals Choice Models: Discrete Consumer Choice Among Alternative Fuels for Residential Appliances, *Journal of Econometrics* 18(3) (1982), 313–336.

_____, Product Quality and Market Efficiency: The Effect of Product Recalls on Resale Prices and Firm Valuation, *Review of Economics and Statistics* 39(2) (1987), 367–371.

_____ and J. Doane, The Use of Hedonic Analysis for Certification and Damage Calculations in Class Action Complaints, *The Journal of Law, Economics and Organization* 32(2) (1987), 351–372.

_____ and D.J. Teece, Product Emulation Strategies in the Presence of Reputation Effects and Network Externalities: Some Evidence from the Minicomputer Industry, *Economics of Innovation and New Technology* 1 (1990), 157–182.

_____ and _____, W. Mitchell and T. Jorde, Product Market Definition in the Context of Innovation, unpublished working paper, September 1990.

A. Hausman, Individual Discount Rates and the Purchase and Utilization of Energy-Using Durables, *Bell Journal of Economics* 10(1) (1979), 33–54.

H. Iyori and A. Yesugi, *The Antimonopoly Laws of Japan*, 1983.

T.M. Jorde and D.J. Teece, Product Market Definition in the Context of Innovation, Working Paper No. BPP-29, Center for Research in Management, University of California at Berkeley, February 1988.

_____ and _____, Innovation, Cooperation, and Antitrust, *High Technology Law Review* 4(1) (1989a), 1–113.

_____ and _____, To Keep U.S. in the Chips, Modify the Antitrust Laws, *Los Angeles Times*, July 24, 1989b.

_____ and _____, Legislative Proposals to Modify the U.S. Antitrust Laws to Facilitate Cooperative Arrangements to Commercialize Innovation, in Hearings Before the Subcommittee on Economics and Commercial Law, Committee on the Judiciary, U.S. House of Representatives, July 26, 1989c.

T.M. Jorde and D.J. Teece, Innovation and Cooperation: Implications for Competition and Antitrust, *Journal of Economic Perspectives* 4(3) (1990a), 75–96.

_____ and _____, Innovation, Dynamic Competition, and Antitrust Policy, *Regulation* 13(3) (1990b), 35–44.

S.J. Kline and N. Rosenberg, An Overview of Innovation, in N. Rosenberg and R. Landau (ed.), *The Positive Sum Strategy* (National Academy Press, Washington, DC, 1986), pp. 275–305.

T. Koopmans, *Three Essays on the State of Economic Science*, part II (McGraw Hill, New York, 1957).

F. Mannering and C. Winston, Consumer Demand for Automobile Safety, *American Economic Review* 74(2) (1984), 316–318.

M. Ohta and Z. Griliches, Automobile Prices Revisited: Extensions of the Hedonic Hypothesis, in Nester E. Terleckyi (ed.), *Household Production and Consumption* (National Bureau of Economic Research Conference on Research in Income and Wealth, Studies in Income and Wealth, Washington, DC, 1976), pp. 325–390.

J. Ordover and R. Willig, Antitrust for High Technology Industries: Assessing Research Joint Ventures and Mergers, *Journal of Law and Economics* 28 (1985), 311–333.

J.A. Schumpeter, *Capitalism, Socialism and Democracy* (Harper and Row, New York, 1942).

R.H. Spady and A.F. Friedlaender, Hedonic Cost Functions for the Regulated Trucking Industry, *Bell Journal of Economics* 9(1) (1978), 159–179.

D.J. Teece, Economies of Scope and the Scope of the Enterprise, *Journal of Economic Behavior and Organization* 1(3) (1980), 223–247.

_____, Towards an Economic Theory of the Muliproduct Firm, *Journal of Economic Behavior and Organization* 3 (1982), 39–63.

_____, Profiting from Technological Innovation, *Research Policy* 15(6) (1986), 285–305.

_____, Innovation and the Organization of Industry, CCC Working Paper No. 90-6, Center of Research in Management, University of California at Berkeley, 1990.

_____, Competition, Cooperation, and Innovation: Organizational Arrangements for Regimes of Rapid Technological Progress, *Journal of Economic Behavior and Organization*, forthcoming.

U.S. Department of Justice, Antitrust Division, *U.S. Department of Justice Merger Guidelines*, June 14, 1984.

O.E. Williamson, *The Economic Institutions of Capitalism: Firms, Markets, Relational Contracting* (Free Press, New York, 1985).

Information Sharing, Innovation, and Antitrust

David J. Teece*

1. Introduction

Antitrust analysis of vertical and horizontal agreements has evolved considerably in recent years. In the horizontal restraints area, this evolution is reflected in the Supreme Court's move away from the automatic application of the per se rule and toward a greater willingness to consider the context in which conduct occurs, employing rule of reason analysis to assess the reasonableness of behavior.[1] Both the Federal Trade Commission and the Department of Justice have developed tests that reflect in one way or another the evolution of the Supreme Court's analysis.[2] The passing of the traditional per se rule against horizontal restraints is widely recognized by economists as a desirable development.[3]

However, the implementation of rule of reason analysis requires that cooperative activity among firms be understood in a more fundamental way than is currently the case.[4] Of course there is nothing redeeming about some types of

Reprinted from *Antitrust Law Journal* 62(2) (Winter 1994), 465–481.

*Mitsubishi Bank Professor, Haas School of Business, University of California at Berkeley. The author thanks James Clifton, Ronald Davis, Thomas Jorde, and Robert Lande for helpful comments.

[1] See, e.g., Northwest Wholesale Stationers, Inc. v. Pacific Stationery & Printing Co., U.S. 472 (1985), 284, 294; NCAA v. Board of Regents, U.S. 468 (1984), 85, 103–104; Jefferson Parish Hospital Dist. No. 2 v. Hyde, U.S. 466 (1984), 2.

[2] For an excellent survey, see Joseph H. Winterscheid and James E. Thompson, Developments in the Rule of Reason Analysis of Horizontal Restraints: The FTC, DOJ and Supreme Court Approaches, in Eleanor M. Fox and James T. Halverson (eds.), *Collaborations among Competitiors — Antitrust Policy and Economics*, 1992.

[3] See, e.g., Richard Schmalansee, Agreements Between Competitors, in Thomas M. Jorde and David J. Teece (eds.), *Antitrust, Innovation & Competitiveness* 98 (1992).

[4] According to one economist, the acquisition and dissemination of information among competitors imposes "ticklish problems" for antitrust analysis. See Douglas F. Greer, *Industrial Organization and Public Policy*, 1980.

horizontal activity, such as price-fixing restraints, no matter how they are disguised, and it is not the purpose of this article to attempt to justify them. Price fixing and output prorationing agreements ought to be and are illegal. Rather, this article will focus on certain forms of cooperation that relate to innovation and have received scant treatment in the literature. Such practices may superficially appear to restrict competition, when in a more fundamental way they in fact enhance it.

The context in which I have particular interest in examining cooperation and, in particular, information collection, dissemination, and exchange among "competitors"[5] is that of dynamic environments where markets are experiencing rapid change, often induced by technological innovation. This article presents examples of certain types of beneficial information exchange that have received limited review in the antitrust literature. Needless to say, that which promotes innovation also promotes competition, as innovation remains the primary driver of competition and economic welfare in all advanced economies.[6] Also analyzed are certain circumstances in which cooperation and information exchange among U.S.-based competitors at home may help strengthen their competitive posture vis à vis foreign firms at home and abroad.[7]

Certain kinds of efficient collaboration, if recognized and disseminated to the public, make antitrust exemptions unneeded. As Anne Bingaman, Assistant Attorney General for Antitrust, recently stated:

> I am not aware of any situation where existing law is not sufficiently flexible to allow desirable economic cooperation. To be sure, I have heard the argument that even if the antitrust laws are flexible, efficient collaboration nevertheless is deterred by legal uncertainty or un-warranted fear of antitrust liability or litigation. To the extent that is true, the preferable approach is to provide the public with accurate information rather than to create antitrust exemptions.[8]

---

[5] I define competitors as firms operating in the same relevant market. However, not all exchanges among competitors are strictly horizontal, as when a firm's downstream unit cooperates with an upstream unit of another firm in the same market. Thus while much of what is said about information exchange in this article may involve vertical flows, the flows may nevertheless involve competitors.

[6] See Thomas M. Jorde and David J. Teece, Innovation, Cooperation, and Antitrust, in *Antitrust, Innovation & Competitiveness* 47, *supra* note 3.

[7] Eleanor Fox is of the view that "if, by its nature, the restraint goes to the process of rivalry, it requires weighty justification." Eleanor Fox, Competitors Collaboration: A Methodology for Analysis, in *Collaborations Among Competitiors — Antitrust Policy and Economics* 829, *supra* note 2.

[8] See Anne K. Bingaman, Assistant Attorney General, Antitrust Division, Remarks to the Antitrust Section of the American Bar Association Annual Meeting, New York, August 10, 1993.

2. Prices as "Sufficient" Statistics[9]

The reason why cooperation and information exchange are regarded suspiciously in many commercial contexts seems to have its origins in two suppositions, one correct and one false. The first is the obvious one that cartel activity requires coordinated activity and the sharing of information to construct, monitor, and police agreements. Needless to say, information exchange for such purposes is anticompetitive and ought to be condemned. The second supposition commonly accepted is that information exchange among competitors is not necessary to achieve efficient outcomes; after all, prices are "sufficient" statistics and are all that firms need to know to make good decisions. If firms know market prices and adjust their output accordingly, the market will ensure that resources will be allocated efficiently. Cooperation is not needed. This proposition is false, or at best a gross caricature of economic organization, particularly in the context of innovation.

To understand why economists often have intellectual blinders when it comes to recognizing the affirmative characteristics of information transfer and exchange, one must appreciate the limitations of the economic theory of market adjustment that is still accepted wisdom in many elementary textbooks. In elementary treatments of market processes, knowledge of market prices is considered necessary but also sufficient for the efficient operation of markets, but if the "invisible" hand is going to properly guide resource allocation, then economic agents must know not only today's supply and demand but supply and demand for all future periods. That is because efficiency requires that the future as well as the present be taken into account in resource allocation decisions. In reality, competitors need a good deal of knowledge about each other's prices and plans and intentions for the economic system to be efficient.[10] Judge Richard Posner notes:

> [T]he producer's need to have information about his competitors ... including the prices they charge, their output, the quality and reliability of their services, their investment plans, their costs ... is not obviously less important from the standpoint of efficiency than the consumer's interest in knowing what the market has to offer.[11]

---

[9] For a more complete development, see David J. Teece, Competition, Cooperation, and Innovation: Organizational Arrangements for Regimes of Rapid Technological Progress, *Journal of Economic Behavior Organization* 18 (1992), 1.

[10] See G.B. Richardson, *Information and Investment*, 2d ed. (1990).

[11] Richard A. Posner, Information and Antitrust: Reflections on the *Gypsum* and *Engineers* Decisions, *Geo. L. J.* 67 (1979), 1187, 1194.

In short, producers must be well informed about competitor's prices and plans if resources are to be allocated efficiently. Ignorance is rarely a virtue. This is not to deny that prices summarize a remarkable amount of information. They signal changes in demand and supply in ways that enable consumers and producers to respond independently and quickly. Prices unquestionably work extremely well as signals of resource scarcity, at least compared to the clumsy apparatus of central planning.[12] However, while prices are useful summary statistics, and facilitate high levels of decentralization, the price system alone is not sufficient to guide efficient resource allocation in real world economies. One obvious reason is the absence of a complete set of markets (and hence a complete set of prices), future and current, for many commodities, particularly contingent commodities.[13] There are many reasons for the failure of the theoretically desirable contingent markets and their associated prices to exist. They include complexity (there are just too many relevant contingencies) and asymmetric information (which leads to moral hazard problems).[14] It follows that the information channels that supplement prices are important. As Nobel Laureate Kenneth Arrow notes:

> The possibility of using the price system to allocate uncertainty, to insure against risks, is limited by the structure of the information channels in existence. Put the other way, the value of nonmarket decision-making, the desirability of creating organizations of a scope more limited than the markets as a whole, is partially determined by the characteristics of the network of information flows.[15]

Put differently, there is an incentive for firms to engage in information collection and dissemination activities if by so doing superior information about relevant economic fundamentals can be generated.

The requirements of producers and consumers for information beyond that contained in available prices, always considerable, depend significantly on the

---

[12] F.A. Hayek, The Use of Knowledge in Society, *American Economic Review* 35 (1945), 519.

[13] An example of a contingent commodity would be a sightseeing helicopter flight with the fare refundable if visibility turns out to be poor.

[14] Moral hazard problems occur when economic agents refuse to self-reveal relevant aspects of their motivation and personal attributes.

[15] See Kenneth J. Arrow, *The Limits of Organization* (1974), 37. Note that Arrow uses the term "organization" very broadly to include formal organizations (firms, labor unions, universities) and informal organizations (ethical codes, etc.). *Id.* at 33.

rapidity of change that the economy is experiencing and the importance of the decisions that are being made. With an extremely stable industry (with, let us say, zero demand growth and no innovation) and for industries which do not need much specific investment, the informational requirements — and therefore the need for information collection — will be less severe than for an industry experiencing turbulence and requiring specialized, risky investments. Once gathered, information will not decline in its value over time if the industry is static. Accordingly, the need for information transfer is limited. On the other hand, uncertainty and the turbulence it creates simultaneously increases the value of timely information while increasing the cost of information collection.

There is no arena in which uncertainty is higher and the need to gather information greater than in the development and commercialization of new technology. Adam Smith's warning — "[p]eople of the same trade sledom meet together, even for merriment and diversion, but the conversation ends in a conspiracy against the public, or in some contrivance to raise prices"[16] — is a bit anachronistic in such contexts. Moreover, the oft-quoted statement fails to recognize that in global industries experiencing rapid change, the difficulty of assembling all the relevant parties to effectuate an international conspiracy is an almost insurmountable challenge absent governmental assistance.

3. Information Exchange and Systems of Innovation

3.1. *National Systems of Innovation*

One's appreciation for the need for information networks that go beyond observing prices is deepened if one recognizes the importance of innovation to competition and economic development, and if one also recognizes that innovation is often associated with multifaceted networks in which information exchange is frequent. Even the casual observer of global enterprise will notice that innovating firms are not distributed uniformly across nation states. The firms and industrial sectors introducing successful innovation and profiting from them are located in a small number of countries (United States, Britain, Germany, France, and Japan). Each innovating country has some sectors of greater competitive advantage, e.g., software, semiconductors, and biotechnology in the United States; machine tools and chemicals in Germany; automobiles and photographic equipment in

---

[16] Adam Smith, *The Wealth of Nations*, Edwin Cannan (ed.), 1976, p. 144.

Japan. Moreover, the configuration of successful innovators in the world economic system tends to show a considerable stability.

Put differently, there is a strikingly localized and asymmetric distribution of innovative performance in the world economic system. This specificity cannot be explained by factor endowments (land, labor, and capital) but arises from specific institutional configurations, the character of the knowledge that the institution possesses, and by the patterns of interaction and information sharing among firms and supporting institutions. It is the collective and interactive aspects of organizations (including firms) that causes them to be effective innovators. Firms and other institutions contributing to the generation of innovations in particular countries do not act independently but are linked into networks of various kinds; firms and their supporting institutions constitute a system that might be called a National System of Innovation.[17] French writers have advanced an industry-level analogue called "filieres."[18]

The implication is that interactions among firms and institutions are important to the innovation process and that these interactions are much easier within a short geographical distance, and especially within the same social and cultural context. Information sharing lies at the very foundation of these systems (networks). Consider Silicon Valley where, one observer notes, "information-exchange is a dominant, distinguishing characteristic."[19] Information exchange and cooperative relationships of various kinds lie at the heart of this tremendously innovative assemblage of physical and human assets. Needless to say, rapid advances in communications and transportation technologies are undermining some of the geographical basis of national and regional systems. The institutional and cultural aspects of systems of innovation, however, are likely to remain even as geographical boundaries become permeable.

The concept of national (and regional) systems implies differential barriers to the flow of information between systems as compared to across systems. The information flows in question may be of many kinds: knowledge about customer needs, knowledge about new components and other technological opportunities, and knowledge about market developments, including the actions of competitors. The information flows supporting systems of innovation are

---

[17] Richard R. Nelson and Nathan Rosenberg, Technical Innovation and National Systems, in Richard R. Nelson (ed.), *National Innovation Systems: A comparative Analysis* (1993), 4–5.

[18] G. Dosi *et al.*, *The Economics of Technical Change and Internation Trade* (1990). Silicon Valley might well contain one or more filieres.

[19] Everett M. Rogers and Judith K. Larsen, *Silicon Valley Fever: Growth of High-Technology Culture*, 1984, p. 80.

by no means unilateral and are not always vertical. In Silicon Valley, for instance, Rogers and Larsen note that "[i]nformation must be given in order for it to be obtained. The nature of the technical information-exchange process in the micro-electronics industry demands a high degree of reciprocity among the participants."[20] Such information exchange is often mutually beneficial (perhaps more beneficial than unilateral transfers) as it supports incremental improvement with technological developments in one firm building on those of competitors reciprocally, with a general and rapid advance in technological capability resulting.

None of this is to say that anticompetitive purposes cannot be served by the exchange of information, particularly if the information is on prices and output. Rather, the purpose here is to indicate that information sharing is essential to economic organization, and that the frequency with which transfer will be required and the complexity of information exchanged are likely to increase with the rate and complexity of technological innovation. Accordingly, unless one is simply looking at the naked exchange of information on prices and output, information sharing should be viewed neutrally, if not favorably: it lies at the heart of highly dynamic and competitive economic systems.

3.2. *Industrial Clusters*

The role of cooperation and information sharing among industrial and technical communities has recently been highlighted by research on global competitiveness, including the influential work of Michael Porter in *The Competitive Advantage of Nations*.[21] "Industry clusters" are central to Porter's analysis. These are "industries related by links of various kinds,"[22] both vertical and horizontal, connecting users and suppliers, and enterprises that have common customers, employ related technologies, and use the same channels of communication. In Porter's framework, "groups of domestic rivals" are integral to the operation of industry clusters.

---

[20] *Id.* at 81.

[21] Michael Porter seems reluctant to draw this conclusion from his work, stressing instead the need for domestic rivalry rather than cooperation. Michael E. Porter, *The Competitive Advantage of Nations* (1990), 143–144. However, in my view, the only legitimate interpretation of his anecdotes is that competition and cooperation are both important for competitive advantage. I share this view with William Lazonick whose writings on this point are compelling and are summarized here. See William Lazonick, Industry Clusters Versus Global Webs: Organizational Capabilities in the American Economy, *Industrial and Corporate Change* 2(1) (1993), 1–10.

[22] Porter, *supra* note 21, at 131.

Cooperation, not competition, is implied by the interchange that needs to take place within industry clusters to build national advantage. According to Porter "[m]echanisms that facilitate interchange within clusters are conditions that help information to flow more easily, or which unblock information as well as facilitate coordination by creating trust and mitigating perceived differences in economic interest between vertically and horizontally linked firms."[23] Porter goes on to list a number of "facilitators of information flow" in which he includes: "[p]ersonal relationships due to schooling, military service"; "[t]ies through the scientific community or professional associations"; "[c]ommunity ties due to geographic proximity"; "[t]rade associations encompassing clusters"; and "[n]orms of behavior such as belief in community and long-term relationships."[24] He also lists a number of "sources of goal congruence or compatibility within clusters" that include family ties, common ownership, interlocking directors, and national patriotism, and that facilitate information exchange.[25] Porter states, "Mechanisms that facilitate interchange within clusters are generally strongest in Japan, Sweden, and Italy, and are generally weakest in the United Kingdom and the United States ... ."[26]

In the United States, the best-functioning clusters appear to be in health care and computing, sectors that contain some of America's premier global competitors. "Here," Porter observes, "scientific ties often overcome the natural reticence of American managers toward interchange."[27] Porter argues, and I agree, that such cooperation should not go so far as to blunt competition in any particular industry within the cluster. Rather, cooperation and competition must coexist. In Porter's words, when "the exchange and flow of information about the needs, techniques and technology among buyer, suppliers and related industries ... occurs *at the same time that active rivalry is maintained in each separate industry*, the conditions for competitive advantage are most fertile."[28]

Porter provides an instructive example of how cooperation among domestic competitors centered around the town of Sassuolo has contributed to the global competitive advantage attained by the Italian ceramic tile industry over the past four decades. Indeed, as Lazonick[29] points out, Porter's analysis of "Sassuolo

---

[23] *Id.* at 152–153.

[24] *Id.* at 153.

[25] *Id.*

[26] *Id.* at 154.

[27] *Id.*

[28] *Id.* at 152.

[29] Lazonick, *supra* note 21, at 6–7.

Rivalry" reveals the importance of intra-industry cooperation to the industry's ability to develop and utilize productive resources.

> Competition among Italian tile producers was intensely personal. All of the producers were located close together ....
>
> Assopiastrelle, the ceramic tile industry association, with membership concentrated in the Sassuolo area, gradually began offering services of common interest including bulk purchasing, foreign market research, and consulting on fiscal and legal matters. The association also took the lead in government and union relations. The growing Italian tile cluster stimulated wider mechanisms for factor creation.[30]

Given this dynamic interaction of organization and technology, the rapid interfirm diffusion of product and process innovations that Porter identifies in Sassuolo are attributable to the existence of cohesive industrial and technological communities, rooted in cooperation. Indeed, Porter's analysis as well as research by others suggest that cooperation, not competition, is the root cause of Sassuolo success.[31] For example, Brusco likewise reports that "in the [Sassuolo] ceramic tile industry, the machines which move the tiles uninterruptedly along the glazing lines, or which detect breakages through the use of sonic waves, were not the product of formal research, but were rather developed through the collaboration of the tile firms with a number of small engineering firms."[32]

The role of cooperation is again highlighted when Porter summarizes the Italian ceramic tile case: "Foreign firms must compete not with a single firm, or even a group of firms, but with an entire subculture. The organic nature of this system is the hardest to duplicate and therefore the most sustainable advantage of Sassuolo firms."[33]

The ceramic tile case study is recounted here not to argue that domestic rivalry was absent, or that it did not create pressures on individual enterprises to respond to the innovations of their competitors. Rather, it is that rivalry in and of itself cannot explain the ability of an enterprise to respond innovatively to competitive challenges. Thus Porter's own case studies suggest that the basic problem many industries face in the United States is not insufficient rivalry but insufficient cooperation and information sharing.

---

[30] *Id.* (quoting Porter, *supra* note 21, at 216).

[31] Michael H. Best, *The New Competition: Institutions of Industrial Restructuring*, 1990.

[32] Sebastiano Brusco, The Emilian Model: Productive Decentralization and Social Integration, *Cambridge Journal of Economic* 6 (1982), 167, 179.

[33] Porter, *supra* note 21, at 225.

4. Some Additional Circumstances in which Information Sharing Can Support Innovation and/or Competition

4.1. *Establishing Dominant Standards through Information Sharing and Coordination*[34]

Compatibility standards are essential if products and their complements are to be used in a system. Computers need software, compact disc players need compact discs, televisions need programs, and bolts need nuts. Compatibility standards define the format for the interface between the core and complementary goods, so that, for example, compact disc players from any manufacturer may use compact discs from any music company.

The advantage of a standard is that the greater the installed base of the core product, the more complementary goods are likely to be produced by independent vendors, in turn increasing demand for the core good. In the compact disc example, the more households that have disc players, the more titles record companies are likely to publish on compact disc. The same mechanism applies when the complement is a service, such as a maintenance network for aircraft, or when the complement is other users of the same product, as with a telephone network.

Standards apply not only to many products that use digital electronics but also to such mundane articles as ski bindings, flashlight batteries, bank cards, stapling guns, and petroleum products, and more generally to knowledge of how to use a product, such as prescribing a pharmaceutical or operating a computer. In each case the demand for the core product increases the larger the base of products using the same standard. The standard increases the total market for the product because it enables network externalities to be enjoyed.[35] Although the standard may only define the interface between core and complementary goods, this has a deep influence on the internal design of products so that common standards may require that compatible products employ similar technology.

The dynamics of a new standard are that once the installed base achieves critical mass, both core and complement producers join the bandwagon, often

---

[34] The discussion of standards here is largely confined to compatibility standards. For an excellent survey, see Shane Greenstein, Invisible Hands Versus Invisible Advisors: Coordination Mechansim in Economic Networks (Department of Economics, University of Illinois, Champaign-Urbana, Working Paper No. 93-0111, 1993). This section draws heavily on Greenstein. See also Peter Grindley, *Standards, Business Strategy and Policy: A Casebook* (1992), for some useful case studies.

[35] Peter Grindley, Managing Technology: Organizing for Competitive Advantage, in P. Swann (ed.), *New Technologies and the Firm*, 1993.

driving the rapid adoption of a new design, as happened recently with compact discs displacing the old vinyl records. The result is that a successful standard will usually dominate the whole market, leaving few if any niches for nonstandard products. An open standard, which is licensed cheaply to other manufacturers, is more likely to dominate the market than a protected standard, where the owner of the design must provide more of both core and complementary goods itself or sponsor others to do so.

To establish common standards, meetings and exchanges of technical information are often necessary.[36] Such meetings can cause antitrust suspicion. However, so long as prices are not the subject of discussion, and so long as an agreement on standards does not disguise coordinated effots to reduce output, there is little that should warrant antitrust concern.[37] The advantages to society associated with the widespread adoption of common standards can be very large, as network externalities are often considerable. It is, therefore, critical that antitrust law and litigation do not stand in the way of such activities.

Trade associations, consortia, and professional societies often sponsor standards. Consortia also often have the capacity to stimulate nonaffiliated firms to produce complementary components, as the consortia's existence and mandate can help ensure that the standards' integrity will be met. Sometimes downstream (upstream) groups can help sponsor standards for suppliers (distributors). For instance, trade associations from the grocery business helped encourage manufacturers to support bar coding their packaging.[38] Consortia may also help overcome regional separations, as was necessary, for instance, to establish national automatic teller networks.[39]

Professional organizations have had a long history assisting in the formation and adoption of standards. The International Telegraph and Telephone Consultative Committee (CCITT), Institute of Electrical and Electronic Engineers (IEEE), American Society for Testing and Materials (ASTM), American National Standards Institute (ANSI), and other groups have had especially visible involvement in the

---

[36] Standards can be set by noncooperative means as well, by a dominant firm, or from a battle for a standard in an oligopoly.

[37] It is usually very difficult to mask a cartel with a standard-setting ruse. Cartels require the involvement of senior management and require agreement on variables not normally part of the standard-setting activity.

[38] S.A. Keen, Adoption and Interfirm Diffusion of Innovation (Department of Economics, Stanford University Working Paper, 1988).

[39] Stephen C. Salop, Deregulating Self-Regulated ATM Networks, *Economic, Innovation and New Technology* 1 (1990), 85.

development of techical standards.[40] These associations serve as forums for standards, development, and dissemination of information about standards.[41] Sometimes such groups merely ratify standards determined by market processes. Usually they are more active, often even anticipating technical change in network industries and helping to guide design.[42]

One feature of these organizations is that many are voluntary.[43] Therefore, designers of new products must have some incentive for embedding a technical standard in their products since use is optional. Knowledge that the standard will become dominant is often sufficient motivation. Though most firms belong to the relevant associations and societies, their desire to participate in the development of standards can vary for a variety of technical and strategic reasons. This can lead to "free riding" on the involvement of others in the standard-setting function. It can sometimes also lead to the opposite.

Voluntary standards organizations play many useful roles in solving network coordination problems, especially those related to lack of communication. They can serve as a forum for providers or for users to educate each other about the nature of the problems to be solved.[44] They may also serve as a forum to discuss

---

[40] Walter V. Cropper, The Voluntary Development of Consensus Standards in ASTM, ASTM *Standardization News* 8 (1980), 14; D. Hemenway, *Industrywide Voluntary Product Standards,* 1975; C.F. Cargill, *Information Technology Standardization: Theory, Process, and Organizations,* 1983; M.B. Spring, Information Technology Standards, in M. Williams (ed.), *Annual Review of Information Science & Technology,* 1991, p. 26.

[41] M.B.H. Weiss and Marvin A. Sirbu, Technological Choice in Voluntary Standards Setting Committees: An Empirical Analysis, *Economic, Innovation & New Technology* 1 (1990), 111.

[42] I.H. Witten, Welcome to the Standard Jungle: An in Depth Look at the Confusing World of Computer Connections, *Byte* 8 (1983), 146–178; C.F. Cargill, *supra* note 40; P.A. David and S. Greenstein, Compatibility Standards and Information Technology — Business Strategy, Market Development and Public Policies: A Synopsis of Panelists' Statements and the Discussion at the CEPR Compatibility Standards Workshop (Stanford University Center for Economic Policy Research Publication No. 159, 1989); Stanley M. Besen, The European Telecommunications Standards Institute: A Preliminary Analysis, *Telecommunications Policy* 14 (1990), 521; *OECD Committee for Information, Computers and Communication Policy, Information Technology Standards: The Economic Dimension,* 1991, p. 9.

[43] The major exception in the United States is when standards written by voluntary standards groups are required by law or administrative fiat, as with building codes. Ernest S. Rosenberg, Standards and Industry Self-Regulation, *California Management Review* 19 (1976), 79. When governments get involved, it is often for the purpose of writing or choosing a standard directly. On occasion government bodies will also rely on those standards determined by an industry umbrella group.

[44] Marvin A. Sibru and K. Hughes, Standardization of Local Area Networks (unpublished manuscript, Department of Engineering and Public Policy, Carnegie Mellon University, 1986).

and plan the development of a system of compatible components.[45] They may also serve to document and disseminate agreements about technical specifications of standards.[46] Standards developed by such groups can serve as a focal point for designers who must choose among many technical solutions when embedding a standard in a component design. Such groups are most likely to succeed when market participants desire interoperability, need to establish a mechanism for communication, and lack an alternative means to develop or choose one of many technical alternatives.[47]

However, when technology is changing rapidly, standard-setting activities may get bypassed because cooperative efforts may simply be too slow.[48] When events become too technically complex and fluid, a focal point is easily lost. This problem is already arising in telecommunications as private networks proliferate. Reaching agreement on an Integrated Services Digital Network (ISDN), for instance, is complicated if once ISDN standards are written, the nature of technology has changed so that the standard is no longer ideal from a technical standpoint. Standards do not serve as a guide to component designers if the standards organization is overwhelmed by technical changes and must frequently amend its standards.

In sum, voluntary standard setting can improve outcomes for participants and society, particularly when markets are fragmented. Standard setting organizations are one more avenue through which a system may develop. They are an important forum in which competitors may communicate. Since the societal benefits associated with capturing the network externalities made possible by common standards are considerable, antitrust analysts must be especially careful not to construe beneficial information sharing as collusion, which warrants legal interference.

4.2. Benchmarking[49]

Another reason firms competing with each other may seek linkages and communication is to capture the stimulative benefits of benchmarking. Benchmarking

---

[45] Weiss and Sirbu, *supra* note 41.

[46] Marvin A. Sirbu and Laurence E. Zwimpfer, Standards Setting for Computer Communication: The Case of X.25, *IEEE Communications* 23 (1985), 35.

[47] Stanley M. Besen and Leland L. Johnson, *Compatibility Standards, Competition, and Innovation in the Broadcasting Industry*, 1986.

[48] W. Lehr, *ISDN*: An Economist's Primer for a New Telecommunications Technology (unpublished manuscript, 1989).

[49] This section is based in part on Thomas M. Jorde and David J. Teece, Rule of Reason Analysis of Horizontal Arrangements: Agreements Designed to Advance Innovation and Commercialize Technology, *Antitrust L. J.* 61 (1993), 579.

is the process by which firms discover the degree to which they are not world-class in their various functional activities and institute programs to emulate best practices. Typically, benchmarking involves collecting information from excellent companies inside as well as outside the industry, either directly or through third parties.

While some aspects of benchmarking are little more than competitive intelligence gathering, what makes benchmarking distinctive is the focus on sharing information. As Robert Camp, an early champion of benchmarking, points out, "We're beginning to recognize that sharing benchmarking data benefits everyone," and "getting companies to share information readily is a significant directional change in the corporate culture of this country."[50] It involves a recognition that cooperation in the sharing of information and experiences, even with one's competitors, is generally a stimulus to improvement.

Benchmarking, by bringing in external information to the firm, has a salutary effect in galvanizing companies to compete once they recognize how far behind they are and what they can do to improve. Benchmarking at the pace and scale now ongoing in the United States is a relatively new phenomenon. To some, benchmarking activities may appear contrary to sound antitrust policy because they often involve information sharing with competitors.[51] However, there is no evidence to support the notion, common in antitrust thinking, that ignorance of one's competitors' costs and/or internal quality programs is procompetitive. To the contrary, knowledge that one's competitors are ahead can be and has been a tremendous stimulus to action.[52] Moreover, knowledge of how competitors achieved success can help guide a company committed to renovating its structures and systems, lowering costs, and achieving maximum efficiency.

By sharing benchmarking information with one or a small number of competitors, a firm might better position itself against other competitors. Sharing information of one's own successes may lead to the receipt of information from other firms concerning their successes. Overall, the exchanging firms are likely

---

[50] See Robert C. Camp, *Benchmarking: The Search for Industry Best Practices that Lead to Superior Performance*, 1989, p. 3.

[51] Practitioners have recognized the potential for antitrust problems. As one practical guide notes, "Some types of data sharing (e.g., with out-of-industry companies) are clearly legal. Other types of data sharing go on all the time, with some corporations considering them proper and legal, and other corporations thinking overwise. Your own company rules and advice of your corporate attorney should be your guideline." Kaiser Associates, Inc., *Beating the Competition: A Practical Guide to Benchmarking*, 1988, p. 41.

[52] These types of behavioral considerations, while obvious to most, are not part of the apparatus of neoclassical price theory. Accordingly, they tend to be unnecessarily denigrated.

to be better off. Firms that are better at benchmarking will display superior financial performance.

As the number and market shares of the firms in an industry exchanging information increase, antitrust concerns may arise that will require careful assessment and balancing. Rule of reason analysis is the appropriate vehicle. Yet, in almost all circumstances there will be no anticompetitive harm. Indeed, were agencies and third parties to litigate over information exchange in bona fide benchmarking programs, it would have its own long run anticompetitive effects, throttling down one of the major forces of organizational renewal currently at work in America.

4.3. Information Exchanges on "Common Values"

There are often benefits when firms exchange or otherwise share information on "common values." Common values are industry or market aggregates. In the petroleum industry, an example would be industry (national or international) oil and gas reserves; in the hotel industry, it might be upcoming conferences and conventions in a particular city; in the auto industry, it might be changes in demand or in external technological developments; in the semiconductor industry, it might be the identity of future technologies and the limits of the present. Sharing such information improves forecasts of future supply and demand, and enables operations and investments to be scheduled more confidently and efficiently.

This phenomenon can be explained statistically. Suppose a firm has the task of estimating some parameter of great importance, such as future demand, the weather, or possibly even the price of a key input. The statistic of interest is quite uncertain. Each firm in the industry has some separate foundation for estimating its value. By sharing such imperfect knowledge, firms in an industry are likely to increase the accuracy of their judgments because their modal observations are likely to be better predictors than any one firm's observation. With better estimates of uncertain common values, operations and investments can be scheduled more confidently and efficiently, thereby lowering long-term costs. Basically, cost savings are generated because overinvestment and underinvestment are minimized, and operations are better tuned to supply and demand than might otherwise be the case.

Information sharing of this kind may tend to homogenize beliefs about key industry parameters. One consequence is that the quality of investment decisions is improved. Another may well be the reduction of price dispersion in an industry because firms will tend to make pricing errors less often. The level of prices is also likely to be reduced in the long term because of the efficiency consequences noted above, which competition will force to be passed on to consumers. These types of information exchanges do not constitute price-fixing agreements, and the benefits obtained by the firm in question do not come at the expense of the consumer. Similar observations regarding the effects of information exchange on prices have been advanced by Judge Richard Posner, who notes that the purpose of legitimate exchange of information is to narrow the dispersion of prices — that is, to eliminate, as far as possible, those prices in the tails of the price distribution that reflect the ignorance of buyers or sellers concerning the conditions of supply and demand. There is no reason to expect the price level — the average price in the market — to change.[53]

4.4. *Industry Visions*

Ministry of International Trade and Industry (MITI) vision statements, an attempt by industry and government to identify emerging industries, are a recognized component of Japanese industrial policy. In the U.S. semiconductor industry, vision statements have now become a reality, along with plans for their implementation. A new form of industrial policy initiated not by government but by the private sector has thus now arrived in the United States. Its creation and implementation requires considerable information exchange.

The need for an industry vision in the U.S. semiconductor industry can be understood in terms of the common values discussion above; but it goes one step further. It takes into account Japanese competition and how to respond to it collectively. Cooperation is sought not only between industry, government, and academia but implicitly within industry as well, albeit for "precompetitive" activities where the definition of precompetitive is stretched to embrace certain basic manufacturing processes.

Currently, the U.S. semiconductor industry could claim to be the first U.S. electronics industry to have recaptured leadership from the Japanese in the postwar period. Cooperation within the industry and between the industry and government, including the use of an industrial consortium, Semiconductor Manufacturing Technology Consortium (SEMATECH), appears to deserve some part of the credit. In 1993, the industry, through the Semiconductor Industry Association, published a fifteen-year "shared vision" for technological development, which was advanced as a "technological roadmap." Following the roadmap would require

---

[53] Posner, *supra* note 11, at 1197.

"a new infrastructure" to a new period of cooperation. This cooperation requires a common vision that spans the entire semiconductor industry (including its suppliers and customers) and extends as well to academia, government, and electronics users. The pervasive importance of semiconductor-based electronics, coupled with the high cost, complexity, and sophistication of integrated circuit technology of the late 1990s, compel the creation of this new shared vision. Success requires expanded teamwork and cooperation throughout the private and public domestic semiconductor infrastructure.

The essence of a common vision is strategic coordination, or at least strategic alignment. As Gordon Moore, Chairman of Intel, puts it, "We must create a common national plan from these separate approaches so that the industry is all singing from the same sheet of music."[54] He might also have added that effective coordination of government policy and private strategies is also critical. To my knowledge, the semiconductor industry's roadmaps, which include technological characteristics and cost targets, are the first time in recent history that a U.S. industry has engaged in a process to identify common objectives and has sought to align public and private investment behind it.

Old school antitrust analysts might view such activities inhospitably. Yet, such behavior should not be objectionable under current conditions. The most important reason that such activities should be supported is the existence of significant foreign competition, particularly from Japan. The existence of multiple centers of competition in an industry clearly softens any concerns that cooperation of this kind is the harbinger of cartelization. Antitrust theory and jurisprudence must accommodate rather than resist the new reality.

5. Conclusion

Concerted action among otherwise independent actors — contracts, combinations, and conspiracies — is judged sternly under Sec. 1 of the Sherman Act. Though the per se rule of horizontal restraints is almost dead, and rule of reason reigns, there are few guidelines with respect to what are legitimate rule of reason defenses and what are not. This vacuum exists because economic theory provides too few hints as to the efficiency properties (or lack thereof) of various forms of cooperation. The reason is that in economic theory the price system performs miracles. Extraordinary coordinating functions are imputed that it generally cannot

---

[54] Jack Robinson, Moore: Unity Tech Strategy, *Electronic News*, July 27, 1992, at 1, 23.

attain, at least in the context of innovation, without being augmented by networks, information flows, and associated cooperation. Hence, economic arguments based on neoclassical theory often come up short in explaining the rationale for various forms of cooperation that either are or ought to be ubiquitous. Industrial clusters, benchmarking, and the formation of technology visions are striking examples of phenomena that seem quite anomalous if the only lens through which one is looking is neoclassical price theory.

If, however, one looks to organizational economics and puts innovation and change center stage, it can be seen that many forms of industrial cooperation and information sharing — just a few of which have been examined here — are very understandable and, in fact, desirable. One should not assume that one is looking at the innards of a cartel just because some economists with a limited understanding of business institutions and the role of cooperation may be stumped in explicating the rationale for complex organizational arrangements and forms of business behavior.

The Meaning of Monopoly: Antitrust Analysis in High-Technology Industries

David J. Teece* and Mary Coleman[†]

1. Introduction

The centennial of the Sherman Act passed with considerable commentary coupled with self-congratulation by antitrust lawyers and economists. However, not everyone expressed comfort that the analytic approaches of mainstream competition policy were really up to the task of properly understanding and analyzing competition and monopoly in high-technology industries. Jorde and Teece predicted that "antitrust policy in the 1990's — will be shaped more by concerns about innovation and competitiveness than in any other period in recent history"[1] and worried aloud that "the analytic lenses still commonly employed today in antitrust analysis were more suitable in a world where competition was less global, where innovation was less of a multinational phenomenon, and where time to market was less critical."[2] Recommended was a retooling of the analytics to recognize the new competitive landscape, because of the high risk of policy error associated with an antitrust regime that proceeds with a "highly stylized, static, and inaccurate view of the nature of competition."[3]

Reprinted from *The Antitrust Bulletin* (Fall–Winter 1998), 801–857.

*Director, Institute of Management, Innovation and Organization, University of California at Berkeley, and Chairman of LECG, Inc.
[†]Senior Managing Economist, LECG, Inc.
Authors' note: The authors wish to thank participants in the interdisciplinary studies workshop at U.C. Berkeley for helpful comments. Special thanks to Richard Gilbert, Douglas Kidder, Henry Kahwaty, James Langenfeld, Jeff Machler, Jackson Nickerson, James Ratliff, Carl Shapiro, Pablo Spiller and Oliver Williamson.

[1] Thomas M. Jorde and David J. Teece, *Antitrust, Innovation, and Competitiveness*, 1992, p. 234.
[2] *Id.* at 233.
[3] *Id.*

But the call for increased scholarship[4] has been largely unanswered, and the antitrust agencies appear to be moving forward in uncharted territory assisted only by a meager amount of scholarly research on innovation and competition.[5] Other than recent work on increasing returns and network externalities, antitrust economics and jurisprudence displays at best limited recognition of the nature of competition in high-technology industries, how high-technology industries evolve, the nature and sources of economic rents, and the implications for public policy.

This is not to suggest that this article will come up with all the answers, although we will present some new conceptual approaches and analytical methods that we believe are helpful. Rather, we flag large zones of ignorance. Our focus will be primarily on monopoly and monopolization issues. While our framework is relevant to the analysis of mergers and acquisitions, we do not explicitly consider policy toward mergers and acquisitions in this article.[6]

Based on our assessment of the state of the art in antitrust economics, we respectfully suggest that the lawyers and economists in both the private and public sectors recognize the severe limitations of existing analytical tools. Unless they do so, we are extremely concerned that the antitrust agencies in particular will end up taking actions that could harm competition in the computer software industry as well as in other high-technology industries. The opportunities for the agencies to harm competition are far greater than their opportunities to improve competition in sectors where there is rapid innovation,[7] given the poor

---

[4] *Id.* at 234.

[5] In this regard we note that some economists believe that work on network effects yields sufficient guidance for enforcement policy, at least with respect to sofware. See Michael Katz and Carl Shapiro, Antitrust in Software Markets (unpublished Working Paper, Department of Economics, UC Berkeley, March 17, 1998) state the following: "we disagree with those who say that antitrust enforcers lack the economic tools to understand software markets" (p. 1). Despite important work by Katz, Shapiro and others, the amount of serious scholarly inquiry on software markets is very limited.

[6] For a recent assessment of the antitrust treatment of mergers and acquisitions in the software industry, see *id.*

[7] This is the message we tried to convey a decade ago in Jorde and Teece, *supra* note 1. We warned that competitive regimes propelled by innovation would outclass other regimes in the benefits they could bring to the consumer, and that the agencies and the courts should be very cautious about intervening. To our dismay, the agency viewpoint, at least as expressed publicly by former Assistant Attorney General Anne Bingaman on several occasions, is that the importance of innovation requires additional vigilance and intervention on the part of the agencies. Such hubris displays a lack of appreciation for the complexity of the issues, and optimism — completely unsupported by the historical record — with respect to what regulators can accomplish with respect to improving outcomes in regimes of rapid technological change. The historical record, not just in antitrust but in other regulatory contexts, indicates that regulatory processes are fundamentally limited in the context of innovation because of complexity and regulatory lags.

(though nevertheless improved) state of society's understanding of the economics of innovation.

2. Characteristics of Industries Experiencing Rapid Technological Change

2.1. *The Episodic Nature of Competitive Disruption*

2.1.1. The phenomena

Competition in high-technology industries is fierce, frequently characterized by incremental innovation, punctuated by major paradigm shifts. These shifts frequently cause incumbents' positions to be completely overturned. Andy Grove, CEO of Intel, has referred to these as major inflexion points. Their frequency means that business risk is high. As James Utterback has observed,[8] competition is not unlike the game of Chutes and Ladders. A player may arrive at the bottom of a ladder, and then rapidly ascend to a higher level and obtain higher stakes. The converse is also true, and bad luck and special circumstance can cause one to suddenly fall. In high-technology industries, a firm not fully alert to changing circumstances can find itself in this predicament.

Sensing and then seizing the opportunities and threats afforded by these major shifts is critical to a firm's survival and subsequent prosperity. Such action requires that the firm possess considerable entrepreneurial capacity in its top management. Established firms often find it difficult to change their trajectory, as they are apt to approach discontinuities and conflicting corporate interests with compromises. "Bridging a technological discontinuity by having one foot in the past and the other in the future may be a viable solution in the short run, but the potential success of hybrid strategies is diluted from the outset compared to rivals with a single focus."[9]

The opening up of a new technological regime — what Utterback calls a "technolgical ensemble" — affords opportunities for new entrants. Success for the incumbent is difficult, but not impossible. It requires that the incumbent be able to monitor and respond to new customer demands and technological opportunities, forming new alliances and relationships as appropriate. Elsewhere we refer to this as the firm's dynamic capabilities; such capabilities are critical to success in rapidly changing high-technology contexts.[10]

---

[8] James Utterback, *Mastering the Dynamics of Innovation*, 1996.

[9] *Id.* at 191.

[10] Gary Pisano, Amy Shuen and David J. Teece, Dynamic Capabilities and Strategic Management, *Stragetic Management Journal* 18 (1997), 509.

However, even if a firm is entrepreneurial, change can be either competency-enhancing (the new regime increases the demand for the competence, or competence-destroying (the new regime diminishes the demand for the competence). Dynamic capabilities thus will not necessarily suffice to help a firm transition from the old to the new. But they can certainly help. Incumbents have to be willing and able to abandon the old and embrace the new. It's frequently a property of organization that constituents inside the firm protect the old far too long, thereby compromising their commitment to the new. Only the best managed firms make these transitions with alacrity; the frequent failure of incumbents thus opens up considerable opportunities to newcomers. Sometimes the inability of firms in an industry to bridge a discontinuity is extreme. When Henderson and Clark studied the semiconductor photolithographic alignment equipment industry over five product generations, they found that no firm that led in one generation of product figured prominently in the next.[11] The reasons were as much organizational as technological, as innovation tends to destroy the usefulness of the information processing procedures inside the firm. Examples of discontinuities identified by Utterback (not all of them high tech) are presented in Table 1. In Utterback's empirical work, in only one-fourth of the cases studied (forty-six in total) did existing competitors either introduce

Table 1. Product and Process Discontinuities in Four Industries

Industry	Discontinuities
Typewriters	Manual to electric; to dedicated word processors; to personal computers
Lighting	Oil lamps to gas; to incandescent lamps; to fluorescent lamps
Plate glassmaking	Crown glass to cast glass through many changes in process architecture; to float process glass
Ice and refrigeration	Harvested natural ice to mechanically made ice; to refrigeration; to asceptic packaging
Imaging	Daguerreotype to tintype; to wet plate photography to dry plate; to roll film; to electronic imaging; to digital electronic imaging

Source: James Utterback, *Mastering the Dynamics of Innovation*, 1996, at 201

---

[11] Rebecca M. Henderson and Kim B. Clark, Architectural Innovation: The Reconfiguration of Existing Product Technologies and the Failure of Established Firms, *Administrative Science Quarterly* 35 (1990), 9.

Table 2. Technological Discontinuities in Electronic Computing

Time Frame	1960s	1970s	1980s	1990s
Computing paradigm	Mainframe	Minicomputer	Personal computing	Enterprise network
Computer platform	Mainframe	Minicomputer	Personal computer/workstation	Mainframe, minicomputer PC/workstation, LANs
Technology advance	Batch processing	Interactive processing	Desktop processing	Desktop access to all computer resources on the network
Computing environment	Single vendor	Single vendor	Single vendor	Multiple vendors
Application source	In-house and third party*	In-house and third party*	Shrink-wrapped	In-house and third party*
Primary applications	Enterprise	Enterprise	Personal productivity	Enterprise and information, E-commerce
Computer buyers	Corporate MIS	Corporate MIS	Departments/end users	Corporate MIS and departments/end users
New distribution channel	Direct sales	OEMs/VARs	Retail	Systems integrators, internets and intranets

*Third Party = Independent software vendor or system integrator.

Source: Robertson, Stephens and Company, Enterprise Software Applications in the '90'S (June 2, 1992).

radical innovation or were able to initiate them quickly and survive as major players in the market.

Discontinuities are relatively frequent in the computer industry. Indeed, as Table 2 indicates, major paradigm shifts have occurred in each of the last four decades. The paradigms are more disruptive the more they require organizational linkages (internally and externally) to be reconfigured. In computing, for instance, each new computing paradigm had introduced a significant new distribution channel.[12]

We do not mean to imply that each paradigm is hermetically sealed from the other. Indeed, there may be underlying trends that accompany the transition from one paradigm to another. For instance, computers, originally designed for number crunching and applied to "computing" tasks for nearly 50 years, are being increasingly used for communicating.[13] Moreover, the Internet is transforming computing because it is, but design, a force of decentralization. As Bill Joy, a legendary computer technologist and cofounder of Sun pointed out, "the Internet defies being controlled by any one entity, it doesn't discriminate. There are no wrong types of computers or software for the Net, as long as they follow some very basic communications rules."[14]

With the paradigm shifts, there are significant risks, not only for incumbents who don't recognize the significance of the shift, but also to newcomers that may have a good technological foundation in the new paradigm, but lack the relevant complementary assets needed to compete. Commenting on recent paradigm shifts in computing, one analyst wrote:

> We expect to see the same type of carnage on the current software industry "playing field" as we did over the past few years among companies who woke up too late (or not at all) to the realities of the shift from legacy systems to enterprise network computing. We also believe this shift will have an even greater impact on existing software vendors than did the shift to enterprise network computing from legacy systems.... getting there this time is only part of the

---

[12] With the advent of global network computing, the industry is finding that the network itself can be a distribution channel — both the Internet and corporate intranets. Electronic distribution is a new channel that is having a major impact on the software industry because there are zero barriers to firms using this as a means of distribution. Moreover, distribution costs are low, suggesting that access to distribution is unlikely to impair entry.

[13] The harbinger of this metamorphosis was the prescient statement by Sun's Scott McNealy in the mid 80s that, "the network is the computer."

[14] Bill Joy, quoted in *Fortune*, December 11, 1995, at ____.

challenge — global network computing entails both new business models for software pricing and new distribution.[15]

A paradigm shift of this nature devalues the assets of incumbents, particularly distribution assets, triggering new competition. The race will be won by the intelligent and the swift.

2.1.2. Implication for antitrust

The paradigmatic nature of industrial and technological evolution, with waves of creative destruction occurring episodically, suggests an antitrust enforcement regime that is not hair trigger in its operation. While each wave of creative destruction is by no means predictable as to timing and strength, antitrust authorities need to be cognizant of the self-corrective nature of dominance engendered by regime shifts. This is true even when there are significant network externalities and installed base effects. Except for the intelligent and the swift, market dominance is likely to be transitory, as regime shifts dramatically lower entry costs. When incumbents survive such shifts, it's usually a good indicator of their competitive fettle.

The utter destruction that can be wrought by firms embracing the new paradigm means that competition in high-technology industries is often orders of magnitude stronger than in mature industries, and the risk associated with operating in high-technology environments is correspondingly high.[16] Accordingly, one should expect to see far higher margins in high-technology businesses to compensate for this risk and the up-front investment in R&D.[17]

Moreover, antitrust intervention is likely to be rendered both unnecessary and undesirable, except in the most unusual of circumstances. One reason is that paradigm shifts periodically enable new entrants to upset the existing order — something rather rare in mature industries. A second reason is that efforts to hobble the winner in one round of innovations will be seen as diminishing the returns available from competing in such high-risk environments, thereby diverting resources to other sectors of the economy displaying less risk and affording less innovation. A third reason is that even highly expert antitrust agencies are unlikely to understand industry dynamics very well at all.

---

[15] Robertson, Stephens and Company, Enterprise Software Applications in the 90's (June 2, 1992), at 7.

[16] Competition from firms outside the established paradigm also probably needs to be weighted more heavily than competition from firms operating within a paradigm, particularly if firms operating "outside the paradigm" have products whose price/performance attributes are superior to the incumbent's.

[17] An additional factor supporting high margins is the shorter life-time-before-obsolescence during which the initial R&D investment must be recovered.

There are also significant implications with respect to the feasibility and the profitability of anticompetitive conduct. It is not unusual for economists, particularly those with well-honed theoretical capabilities, to posit complex predation stategies for which financial viability requires recoupment in some future period. These strategies, often Byzantine in their complexity, require a high degree of predictability with respect to the future structure of the industry to make them profitable in an expectational sense. The greater the likelihood of a paradigm shift, the less the expected profitability of predatory strategies relying on recoupment in a future period. While this need not establish the impossibility of predation and other forms of anticompetitive behavior, in many instances it will suggest that other factors will be better candidates to explain the conduct at hand. Furthermore, litigation lags are likely to be long compared to the speed at which competitive forces reshape the industry, possibly rendering antitrust action at best superfluous, and at worst damaging to competition.

2.2. *Increasing Returns and Network Externalities*

2.2.1. The phenomenon of increasing returns

Contemporary textbook understandings of how markets operate and how firms compete has been derived from the work of economists such as Chamberlain, Mason, and Bain. These frameworks frequently assume diminishing returns, and assign industry participants identical production functions (implying the use of identical technologies by all competitors) where marginal costs increase. Industry equilibrium with numerous participants arise because marginal costs curves slope upward, thereby exhausting scale advantages at the level of the firm, and making room for multiple industry participants. This theory was useful for understanding 18th-century English farms and 19th-century Scottish factories, and even some 20th-century American manufacturers. However, major deficiencies in this view of the world have been apparent for some time — it is a caricature of the firm. Moreover, knowledge is certainly not shared ubiquitously and transferred at zero cost.[18]

---

[18] See David J. Teece, Technology Transfer by Multinational Firms: The Resource Cost of Transferring Technological Know-How, *Economic Journal* 87 (1977), 242; also reprinted in Edward Mansfield and Elizabeth Mansfield (eds.), *The Economics of Technical Change*, 1993; also reprinted in Mark Casson (ed.), *Multinational Corporations, the International Library of Critical Writings in Economics*, 1990, p. 1, at 185–204. See also David J. Teece, The Market for Know-How and the Efficient International Transfer of Technology, *Annals of the Academy of Political and Social Science* 458 (1981), 81.

In this century, developed economies have undergone a transformation from largely raw material processing and manufacturing activities to the processing of information and the development, application, and transfer of new knowledge. As a consequence, diminishing return activities have become increasingly replaced by activities characterized by increasing returns. The phenomena of increasing returns is usually paramount in knowledge-based industries. With increasing returns, that which is ahead tends to stay ahead, until interception by a major paradigm shift. Mechanisms of positive feedback reinforce the winners and challenge the losers. Whatever the reason one gets ahead — acumen, chance, clever strategy — increasing returns amplifies the advantage. With increasing returns, the market at least for a while tilts in favor of the provider that gets out in front. Such a firm need not be the pioneering one, and need not have the best product.

The economics of increasing returns suggest different corporate strategies. In winner-take-all or winner-take-the-lion's-share contexts, there is heightened payoff associated with getting the timing right (one can be too early or too late), and organizing sufficient resources once opportunity opens up. Very often, competition is like a high stakes game of musical chairs. Being well positioned when standards gel is essential. The associated styles of competition are, as Brian Arthur[19] points out, more like casino gambling. Strategy involves choosing what games to play, as well as playing with skill. Multimedia, Web services, voice recognition, mobile (software) agents, electronic commerce are all technological/market plays where the rules are not set, the identity of the players poorly appreciated, and the payoffs' matrix murky at best. Rewards go to those good at sensing and seizing opportunities.

Seizing opportunities frequently involves identifying and combining the relevant complementary assets needed to support the business. Superior technology alone is rarely enough upon which to build competitive advantage. The winners are the entrepreneurs with the cognitive and managerial skills to discern the shape of the play, and act upon it. Recognizing strategic errors and adjusting accordingly is a critical part of becoming and remaining successful.

In this environment, there is little payoff to penny pinching, and high payoff to rapidly sensing and then seizing opportunities. This is what we refer to here and elsewhere[20] as dynamic capabilities. Dynamic capabilities are most likely to be resident in firms that are highly entrepreneurial, with flat hierarchies, a clear

---

[19] Brian Arthur, Competing Technologies: An Overview, in G. Dosi *et al.*, *Technical Change and Economic Theory*, 1988.

[20] Pisano, Shuen and Teece, *supra* note 10.

vision, high-powered incentives, and high autonomy (to insure responsiveness). The firm must be able to effectively navigate quick turns, as Microsoft did once Gates recognized the importance of the Internet. Cost minimization and static optimization provide only minor advantages. Plans must be made and junked with alacrity. Companies must constantly transform and retransform. A "mission critical" orientation is essential.

2.2.2. Implications for antitrust

If one believes in the inexorable march of increasing returns, one would predict monopoly as the eventual industry structure.[21] However, if monopolization is inevitable, then the main basis for criticizing an outcome is that the market anointed the wrong monopolist. Accordingly, even total faith in increasing returns as a governing economic principle does not necessarily lead to any clear path of antitrust intervention. It is only if one could in an ex ante sense pick the "good" potential monopolists from the "bad" ones that antitrust intervention would appear to have obvious benefit. But there is no analytical apparatus to guide the government in anointing the more benign.

There are other factors that soften the concern anyway. First, even if increasing returns do lead to the elimination of competitors who use a particular supply technology, it need not establish a monopoly if there are competing products available from suppliers who use alternative technologies. Even if the competing technologies themselves display increasing returns, the outcome is duopoly or oligopoly, not monopoly.

Furthermore, as discussed earlier, technological paradigms are eventually overturned. In some cases, it may be relevant to ask whether an incumbent's actions are designed to delay or prevent a paradigm shift that would be competency destroying. In our view, such conduct is unlikely to be effective and could not prevent a paradigm shift that offers significant improvement. The vacuum tube manufacturers could not have stemmed the tide of the transistor, no matter how hard they might have tried. In software, access to complementary assets and an installed base could not block the newcomer if the newcomer has a truly revolutionary product. Intermediate cases are of course more difficult. In general, however, efforts by incumbent firms to block rather than embrace the new paradigm are extremely risky, as failure results in annihilation because it is likely to prevent incumbents from transitioning from the old to the new. Technological change

---

[21] When there are large up-front costs, entry may be difficult because new entrants must consider postequilibrium entry and because the development costs are typically sunk and this adds to the entry risk.

external to the industry or business at hand can thus more often than not undo dominance should it arise. Accordingly, any dominance is likely to be temporary — certainly more so than in a less technologically dynamic context. The arrival of a new technological ensemble epoch/paradigm is of course unpredictable; but we do note that in the computer industry, new competing paradigms seem to have emerged each decade, certainly faster than the legal system can typically identify, analyze, and then litigate major antitrust issues.

Finally, if there are increasing returns because of large up-front development costs for new "add on" features, it may well be efficient to provide these to all customers, because the marginal cost of doing so will be low. This means that the "tying" and "bundling" of certain features is likely to be highly efficient, thereby upsetting specialist suppliers of such items.

2.3. Network Effects

2.3.1. The phenomenon

Another characteristic often found in conjunction with increasing returns, but analytically distinct from it, is network effects.[22] Increasing returns is a production-side characteristic describing the increase in output as all inputs are scaled up. Network effects are a demand-side phenomenon associated with value to the customer. Network effects result in markets where customer's valuation of a particular product is enhanced when it is employed in a system. For instance, the value of a telephone network to an individual user increases with the number of other individuals who are connected to that network. Similarly, the value of a computer platform may increase with the number of users because users share files and different files may not be compatible with different platforms. Again, with more users on a given platform, any individual user is more likely to be able to share files with another user. Network effects lead to positive feedback. The more users on a system, the more valuable it is. Network effects are a form of demand-side economies of scope. With feedback, the strong get stronger and the weak weaker.

Network effects can also be indirect. Users frequently invest in complementary goods. Given economies of scale in the manufacture of complementary goods, the more users of a given platform, the more complementary goods that will likely be supplied to that platform. This will lower the cost or increase the value of the platform.

---

[22] See Michael Katz and Carl Shapiro, Network Externalities, Competition, and Compatibility, *American Economic Review* 75 (1985), 424.

Network effects can thus lead the market to select one platform (or standard) because the benefits of having one platform are greater than the costs from less diversity in platform offerings. A major emphasis of the literature regarding network effects has been whether markets will choose the right platform (or standard) and whether new "improved" platforms will be able to supplant the existing platform.

2.3.2. Implications for antitrust

When network effects are strong, they constitute an important dimension of industry structure, or at least the structure, of demand. The degree of compatibility and the strength of network effects shapes the nature of competition, industry evolution, and paths of innovation. In the presence of strong network effects, there are good theoretical reasons to believe that "optimal" platforms and "optimal" transitioning may not be achieved by the market (although it is not clear what can be done to change this result).

It is not at all obvious that antitrust intervention can improve matters. This is because antitrust policy cannot realistically aspire to produce "optimal" outcomes, where "optimality" is measured against some theoretically defined efficiency or consumer welfare criteria. Rather, antitrust can only aspire toward helping guarantee outcomes from a competitive process, even if the outcome is not the theoretically most appealing.[23] The presence of network effects may result in the incumbent firm being favored by new customers. It could eventually become dominant through positive feedback. This could last for several generations of products, although it is unlikely to survive a major paradigm shift unless the gap between the "good enough" and the "best" is quite small.

There are several reasons why the incumbent's dominance might persist. For new customers, the incumbent supplier's existing platform may provide a better price/performance ratio even if the "platform" is inferior or higher cost because the complementary products are more numerous or lower cost. For upgrades to existing users, the incumbent supplier might have an advantage (apart from switching costs) if it is easier for producers of complementary products to upgrade existing products to the incumbent supplier's new platform (rather than an alternative new platform) or if vendors believed more users would upgrade to the incumbent supplier because of switching costs. This would make the vendors more likely to invest in the existing platform or offer lower priced products.

---

[23] We are not sanguine that antitrust policy can assist transitions in any meaningful way. The stronger the network externalities, the less impact antitrust action is likely to have. Antitrust action is simply not capable of "fine-tuning" industry outcomes in the face of strong network effects.

These advantages, however, simply reflect the characteristics of the market and the fact that the incumbent supplier succeeded at winning in the previous round of competition for platforms. The fact that an incumbent supplier wins the next generation even with a somewhat inferior product is not necessarily an anticompetitive outcome. Denying network externalities to produce a fragmented market is certainly no solution.

Moreover, the advantage conferred by network effects is not absolute. New platforms can and do supplant existing platforms even when network effects seem significant. If another platform is truly better and the only concern is lack of complementary goods, there is a gain from everyone switching. The platform owner can subsidize complementary goods manufacturers. A few suppliers of complementary goods are likely to see the market potential if the platform is truly superior.

2.4. *Decoupling of Information Flows from the Flow of Goods and Services*

2.4.1. The phenomena

New information technology and the adoption of standards is greatly assisting connectivity. Once every person and every business is connected electronically through networks, information can flow more readily. Historically, the transfer/ communication of rich information has required geographic proximity, and specialized channels to customers, suppliers, and distributors.

New developments are undermining traditional value chains and business models. In some cases, more "virtual" structures are viable, or shortly will be viable, especially in certain sectors like financial services. New information technology is facilitating specialization. Bargaining power is being reduced by an erosion in the ability to control information. Search costs and switching costs are also declining, changing industry economics. Quick and low cost access to new mass markets are now often possible.

The concomitant expansion of markets for intermediate products (and associated vertical disintegration) is lowering entry costs into many businesses. The rapid growth of virtual corporations (which perform integration roles using markets rather than administrative process inside corporations) reflects the growth in the number of intermediate product markets for all kinds of components and inputs.

The new information technology is also dramatically assisting in the sharing of information. Learning and experience can be much more readily captured and shared. Knowledge learned in the organization can be catalogued and transferred to other applications within and across organizations and geographies. Rich exchange can take place inside the organization, obviating some of the need for formal structures.

2.4.2. Implications for antitrust

The decoupling of the flow of information from the flow of goods and the expansion and liberalization of markets is sharpening competition, and lowering search costs and switching costs. New entrants benefit. The premium on quick response time is increasing, favoring smaller business units. Trends such as this are sharpening competition almost everywhere. While in and of itself this does not imply that antitrust agencies can be less vigilant, the phenomenon is easing the burden on antitrust policy, as competitive response time is being shortened.

3. Scarcity Rents, Schumpeterian Rents, and Monopoly Rents

3.1. *General*

There has long been a recognition in economics that high profits may not reflect market power. There are not only serious measurement problems associated with using accounting profits, but as Demsetz[24] and Peltzman[25] pointed out decades ago, superior profitability may reflect superior efficiency.

However, it is of some interest to break the sources of rents down more finely. In the context of innovation, Ricardian (scarcity) rents reflect difficult to expand competences; Schumpeterian (entrepreneurial) rents occur because imitation does not occur instantaneously, even though imitators might well "swarm" around the innovators' key technologies and products. Both are benign sources of rent from an antitrust perspective; from a public policy perspective they are beneficial as they encourage investment in valuable knowledge assets and in innovation.

We believe these distinctions are quite fundamental; yet to our knowledge there is no literature in antitrust economics that recognizes them. This is because of the static nature of mainstream antitrust analysis, and its gross neglect of

---

[24] Harold Demsetz, Industry Structure, Market Rivalry, and Public Policy, *Law and Economic* 16 (1973), 1.

[25] Sam Peltzman, The Gains and Losses from Industrial Concentration, *Law and Eonomic* 20 (1977), 229.

innovation. The distinctions we draw do exist in the economics literature, and they are of quite some importance in the field of strategic management.[26] The welfare implications of each are markedly different, as we will discuss.

3.2. *Ricardian (Scarcity) Rents*

In many contexts where knowledge and other specialized assets underpin a firm's competitive advantage, additional inputs cannot simply be purchased on the market to expand output. Hence, at least in the short run, a firm's output is limited by the available stocks of the scarce inputs. Over time, however, the firm can typically augment its stocks of scarce inputs. However, such replication typically involves the use of the firm's existing stock of idiosyncratic resources, because productive knowledge is not fully codified and labor inputs available on the market do not have the requisite firm-specific skills. This can be a major restraint on the firm's growth.

If the firm in question owns 100% of the world's supply of the unique input (e.g., a unique engineering skill) and if the input is necessary to produce the output, the firm could be a (transitory) "monopolist" in the output market until it is able to expand the availability of such skills. It could fully utilize the constrained input, and yet still end up with price in the final product market being above cost. While the firm might be thought of as a monopolist, its profits are scarcity rents properly attributed to the scarce input. The firm has no incentive to restrict output; but output is nevertheless below the "competitive" level — a hypothetical condition in which more of the scarce input were available. However, if the scarce input (here on engineering competence) were somehow to be broken up and distributed amongst a group of competitors, the price in the final product market would not decrease, and might well increase.[27] In this case, the scarcity rent is simply the normal return to the scarce asset, and there is no efficiency loss to monopoly. Moreover, it is of course the existence of scarcity rents that engenders expansion of output through replication of the underlying skills.

It is somewhat puzzling that the impact of Ricardian rents has not been analyzed in the antitrust literature. Perhaps the answer lies with the fact that, historically at least, economists have associated Ricardian rents with scarce natural resources, like land or iron ore. Scarcity rents then tend to flow upstream to the

---

[26] See, for example, Pisano, Shuen and Teece, *supra* note 10.

[27] This is because valuable routines could be broken, and knowledge could be "lost." See Richard Nelson and Sidney winter, *An Evolutionary Theory of Economic Change* (1982) for a discussion of routines.

owners of the scarce inputs. Profits to downstream firms then get competed away. However, when the scarce input is knowledge — embedded in a team or in a small group — rents do not get bid away to the owners of the scarce inputs, for several rather subtle reasons. One is that the market for know-how/knowledge is rather imperfect,[28] so all the rents need not accrue to the owners of the scarce inputs, simply because the market is imperfect. Secondly, the productivity of knowledge assets may depend in part on the presence of certain cospecialized assets, the services of which must be employed for the knowledge assets in question to have value. This can prevent all of the rents from accruing to the scarce inputs themselves.[29]

To summarize, an innovating firm seeking to operate on a larger scale, but temporarily constrained by its stock of idiosyncratic resources, may be highly profitable, but this in no way implies that it is exercising socially undesirable restraint over its output. It is likely that the innovator is simply collecting sufficient Ricardian rents to cover its initial investment and offer encouragement to other innovators and entrepreneurs.

3.3. *Schumpeterian (Entrepreneurial) Rents*

Other situations may generate supranormal returns that are also not properly thought of as monopoly rents. A firm may develop product and process innovations and/or unique business routines (knowledge assets), but these eventually are imitated by competitors. However, there may be a period of temporary excess returns enjoyed by the developer/owner of the knowledge assets in question. These returns are once again not monopoly rents, but Schumpeterian rents. "Low investment and slow imitation spell greater financial success for the innovator."[30] In the absence of imitation, or the absence of the fear of imitation, the innovating firm has significant control over the scale at which the innovation is implemented in the long run.

---

[28] See David J. Teece, The Market for Know-How and the Efficient International Transfer of Technology, *Annals* 458 (1981), 81 and David J. Teece, Capturing Value from Knowledge Assets: The New Economy, Markets for Know-How, and Intangible Assets, *California Management Review* 40 (1998), 8.

[29] See David J. Teece, Profiting from Technological Innovation: Implications for Integration, Collaboration, Licensing and Public Policy, *Research Policy* 15 (1986), 6.

[30] Sidney Winter, Four R's of Profitability: Rents, Resources, Routines, and Replication in Cynthia Montgomery (ed.), *Resources-Based and Evolutionary Theories of the Firm: Towards a Synthesis*, 1995, pp. 147–177.

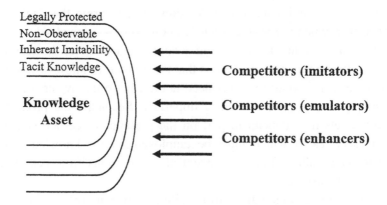

Fig. 1. Defenses against appropriation by competitors.

There are a number of factors that prevent competitors from appropriating the rents from innovation instantaneously (see Fig. 1). An obvious one is that much of the knowledge at issue may be highly tacit, rendering the product/process difficult to imitate. Secondly, the knowledge at issue may not be observable in use, and so reverse engineering is not feasible as an imitation pathway. Furthermore, the process/product in question may enjoy a certain amount of intellectual property protection, rendering imitation more costly, and possibly impossible (in the case of a broad-scope patent), at least for a period of time.

Nevertheless, barriers to imitation such as these are almost always temporary, and afford the owner of knowledge assets a certain period of time within which to earn supernormal profits. However, these profits are the return to innovation (more specifically, they are a return too difficult to imitate knowledge assets) and are generally necessary to induce investment in the creation of such knowledge assets. Such rents are accordingly necessary and desirable, and should not be the target of antitrust action.

3.4. *Monopoly (Porterian[31]) Rents*

The type of rent that ought to be the target of antitrust concern stems from the naked exercise of market power by a firm (or firms). These circumstances might

---

[31] Michael E. Porter has developed a theory of strategy around conduct designed to impair competition. As Porter notes "public policy makers could use their knowledge of the sources of entry barriers to lower them, whereas business strategists could use theirs to raise barriers." Michael Porter, The Contributions of Industrial Organization to Strategic Management, *Academy of Management Review* 6 (1981), 612.

arise because of exclusionary conduct lacking efficiency justifications, from predatory conduct, or from governmentally conferred privileges (e.g., licenses).

In the context of innovation, anticompetitive conduct is extremely chancy as an efficacious strategy. This is because the payoff from such conduct is likely to be minuscule in the total scheme of things, because of the power of new technology to shape competitive outcomes. New technology can change the price/performance profile of a product by several orders of magnitude, whereas anticompetitive conduct is likely to have at most a minor impact on the total scheme of things. History shows that commercially relevant and value-enhancing technologies triumph, even in the face of considerable adversity.

4. The Hallmarks of Monopoly Power in High Technology

4.1. *Introduction*

The competitive landscape is so different in high-technology industries that the traditional hallmarks of monopoly (reduction in output or increases in prices) are rarely seen. This is either because (1) monopoly power is so difficult to acquire in high-technology industries or (2) the traditional hallmarks of monopoly are no longer operational because the benchmarks (the competitive levels of price and output) are unobservable and very difficult to estimate, raising anew the question of how to identify monopoly, and how to measure market power. This is obviously one of the most basic questions in antitrust; but our answers to it leave much to be desired in the context of high-technology industries.

Irving Fisher defined monopoly as an "absence of competition."[32] Subsequent treatments have done little to improve the definitions. Consider modern textbooks. Pindyck and Rubinfeld define it as follows: "a monopoly is a market that has only one seller ... ."[33] "Firms may be able to affect price and may find it profitable to charge a price higher than marginal costs."[34] Carlton and Perloff point out that a "monopolist recognizes that the quantity it sells is affected by the price it sets."[35] The emphasis should of course be on whether the monopolist can profitably raise price.

Economists must admit that their criteria for defining monopoly are far from perfect. The issue is further complicated because lawyers and the laity all think

---

[32] Irving Fisher, *Elementary Principles of Economics*, 1923.

[33] Robert Pindyck and Daniel Rubinfeld, *Microeconomics*, 2d ed., 1992, p. 327.

[34] *Id.* at 328.

[35] Dennis Carlton and Jeffrey Perloff, *Modern Industrial Organization*, 1990, p. 97.

they know the meaning of monopoly. The difficulty is amplified because economists often use words that are in everyday use for which the everyday meaning is quite different from the technical definition. Even some economists have erred in labeling as a monopoly a situation where a firm controlled 100% of its own output![36]

In the context of innovation, the task is especially complicated. Competition is a dynamic process and takes place over time, often following the punctuated processes described earlier. The commercialization of innovation will at first generate high profits, which may be either of the Ricardian or the Schumpeterian kind described above. The presence of such profits will (in the case of Ricardian rents) cause the innovator to endeavor to expand output, or (in the case of Schumpeterian rents) lure imitators into the business. This will cause the price to come down, or the performance to improve, since the imitator/emulator will need to provide something to lure customers away from the innovator to the imitator. The innovator must respond by lowering price or improving performance to hold onto its customers.

What is clear is that profits are necessary to grease the competitive process. It is the quest for profits that encourages innovation in the first place; it is the quest for profits by imitators that spurs competition. And if the innovator responds to the imitator with lower prices it need not be predation but merely the process of competition at work.

In the high-technology context, a monopolist cannot therefore be identified by traditional (textbook) marginal cost pricing tests, such as the Lerner index. Perhaps a more meaningful approach to monopoly pricing is to ask whether consumers are paying a price higher than is needed to draw forth the products and services they desire over time. The price cannot therefore be analyzed statically; it must be viewed dynamically, and across products. If, for instance, prices are not high enough to cover R&D costs for both the successful and the unsuccessful products, innovation will wither.

What then is monopoly in such an environment? It is not a situation of high market share; nor is it a situation where profits are high, or where prices are above marginal cost. Rather, a monopolist would be a firm shielded from entry, i.e., insulated from competition from other innovators and imitators. The monopolist could stay ahead without innovating or lowering prices. The crucial difference between monopoly and competition is that with competition market

---

[36] An economist at the University of Washington once claimed, in the context of litigation, that Chevron had a monopoly in the sale of Chevron gasoline.

forces compel improvement in the product offerings available to the customer. With monopoly, there is no such compulsion from the marketplace.

4.2. Market Power

Since a pure monopoly circumstance (100% of an economically relevant market) is rare in the absence of governmental control, as a practical matter antitrust economists tend to analyze monopoly in terms of market power. If a firm has high market power, it faces minimal compulsion from the marketplace.

The courts have defined monopoly as the "ability to price without regard to competition" or "the power to set prices and exclude competitors." Properly understood, these are good definitions, and from an operational prospective, perhaps better than what is contained in many economics textbooks.

In order to measure market power, the field of antitrust had developed a methodology (which the Superior Court endorses) whereby one must first define a relevant antitrust market, and then assess competition within it. In a fundamental sense, this is not required of course. One could in principle figure out whether a firm has the ability to act in an unconstrained way without defining a market. However, we agree that market definition, done correctly, is a useful aid to analysis. One must place in the relevant market those products and services, and their providers, whose presence and actions serve to check the behavior of the tentatively identified monopolist.

4.3. Market Definition

4.3.1. General

The primary question in defining a relevant market remains whether there are constraints on the tentatively designated monopolist. One must always be careful to insure that the market definition exercise does not obscure the fundamental question of constraints on power. The principal constraints can be of two types: (1) those relating to demand and (2) those relating to supply. The concepts of demand and supply substitutability are useful in assessing whether there are constraints in a tentatively identified monopolist. So are some related concepts.

But the analysis of supply and demand substitution possibilities and opportunities is quite complicated in regimes of rapid technological change. Simply analyzing the market from a static perspective will almost always lead to the identification of markets that are too narrow. Because market power is often quite transitory, standard entry barrier analysis — with its 1-to-2-year fuse for entry — will often find that an innovator has power over price when its position is in fact extremely fragile. Further, much of the data on which courts and antitrust regulators rely are necessarily backward-looking,[37] meaning that firms at the end of an innovation-based period of dominance are actually more likely to be the subject of antitrust scrutiny than be in a position to exercise market power.[38] The evidence presented earlier suggests that not all firms in existing product markets are well-positioned to compete in next-generation product markets. If a firm is unable to keep up with a shift in the technological basis of the market, whether because of path dependencies or problems in replicating technical success, market analysis should dramatically discount that firm's participation in the market in evaluating market power. Unfortunately, for the most part courts are content to use past success as a proxy for future viability.[39] In many cases, doing so will overstate (understate) the competitive forces at work in a market.

These problems with the assessment of power in a dynamic market are compounded by difficulties in even defining what the relevant market is in high-technology industries. The rather monolithic approach that the FTC and Antitrust Division's 1992 Horizontal Merger Guidelines take to market definition and the assessment of market power risks defining high-technology markets too narrowly, especially if applied too mechanically. As explained in the Merger Guidelines, the agencies will include in the product market a group of products such that a hypothetical firm that was the only present and future seller of these products ("monopolist") could profitably impose a "small but significant and nontransitory increase in price" (SSNIP) — generally five percent lasting 1 year.[40] The implicit assumption adopted by the Guidelines is that products in a market are homogeneous

---

[37] The fundamental test for market definition is the reasonable interchangeability of goods — the substitutability of good x for good y in response to a change in the price of good y. See United States v. E.I. duPont de Nemours & Co., U.S. 351 (1956), 377, 380, 395–400. This cross elasticity of demand is most commonly tested by looking at the historical evidence — what has happened to sales of good x in the past when the price of good y went up.

[38] For a discussion of this problem in the context of the markets for Internet software, see Mark A. Lemley, Antitrust and the Internet Standardization Problem, *Conn. L. Rev.* — (1996), 28.

[39] See United States v. General Dynamics Corp., U.S. 45 (1974), pp. 486, 501 ("In most situations, of course, the unstated assumption is that a company that has maintained a certain share of a market in the recent past will be in a position to do so in the immediate future"). On occasion, courts will take into account factors suggesting that a current market participant is unlikely to be an effective future competitor. For example, in *General Dynamics*, the Court allowed a merger that significantly concentrated the coal industry in Illinois, because the purchased firm was running out of coal reserves and so would not be an effective competitor for future long-term coal supply contracts. *Id.* at 503–504.

[40] 1992 Horizontal Merger Guidelines, Issued by the U.S. Department of Justice and the Federal Trade Commission, April 2, 1992, at Sec. 1.11.

and competitors compete on price. Application of the SSNIP test in an industry where competition is performance-based (almost always true when product innovation is present) rather than purely price-related is likely to create a downward bias in the definition of the size of the relevant product market, and a corresponding upward bias in the assessment of market power. This can be illustrated by looking at a couple of businesses where competition is performance-based. (See Appendix A.) However, deficiencies in the standard approach can possibly be remedied with a multi-attribute SSNIPP. (See Appendix B.)

4.3.2. A note on switching costs

Whether using a SSNIP or a SSNIPP test (Appendix B), demand-side substitution is of some importance to market definition. In the context of high-technology industries, where technical compatibility and/or interoperability issues are of importance, the issue of switching costs frequently come to the fore.

In many high-technology industries, customers purchase systems of components including a platform and complementary products. The platform is only valuable (or is more valuable) if the customer acquires or creates complementary goods, services and know-how. For instance, consumers who purchase a computer (with a particular operating system) also acquire applications, and create files and knowledge of how to use that system. Other examples include CD players and CDs, VCRs and videotapes.

Suppliers of new platforms (or new versions of the platform), be they existing or new suppliers, will sell to two groups of potential customers. The first group includes new users who do not have existing systems and thus face no switching costs. The second group of customers includes users with existing systems who are seeking to replace the platform component of their existing system because technology in the platform has changed or the product has worn out. A potential consideration for customers when upgrading is whether their existing investments in complementary goods, services and know-how will be usable with the new platform or will they need to make an investment in the new complementary products in addition to the platform. If new investments in complementary goods must be made, the new base product will have to provide enough improvements over the existing platform, given the cost of the new system, to justify those investments. Thus, to attract this user group, suppliers of new platforms must not only provide improvements over existing products but also assess how switching costs might affect the purchase decision. Platform suppliers might be able to impact the level of switching costs through the manner in which they develop their product or through the development of complementary products that ease migration.

The importance of switching costs to the upgrade decision (1) increases as the existing investment in complementary goods increases; (2) decreases the more likely the customer will purchase new complementary goods; (3) decreases the more complementary goods that can be used with the new platform; and (4) decreases the greater the difference in functionality between new platforms and the existing platform. Whether the incumbent platform supplier has an advantage over other suppliers for next-generation products depends on whether the existing supplier can produce more easily a next-generation product with lower switching costs than could other suppliers. If so, the incumbent could make fewer improvements than other suppliers (or charge higher prices) and still retain customers. In essence, the firm can earn a rent equal to its advantage in switching costs. The size of this rent is constrained by the size of switching costs and the extent to which other suppliers can provide products that ease the transition of complementary goods to the new platforms; or such an increase in performance to justify investment in new complementary goods.

Consider the example of CD players. When CD players were introduced, consumers had large inventories of records and records could not be made to work on a CD player. To have a CD player be useful, therefore, consumers had to purchase a whole new inventory of CDs to replace their existing record collections. However, CD sound quality relative to records was so superior and the price for such systems dropped so rapidly that consumers switched en masse to CDs within a few years.

Similarly, many businesses have switched from proprietary closed systems to open systems running UNIX or other software to run their business applications software. The open systems were generally not directly compatible with the proprietary system. However, open-system vendors frequently provide migration tools to help port the existing files and applications to the new system, and customers were willing to purchase new applications that took advantage of the advanced features of the new system. In some cases, suppliers switched vendors; in others, customers decided to migrate to new systems from their existing vendors.

Again, it must be emphasized that the source of this advantage, to the extent it exists, is not due to anticompetitive actions taken by the existing supplier.[41] Rather this advantage is due to the nature of the products sold. The fact that new suppliers with "better" products do not supplant existing suppliers is not necessarily inefficient. Consumers will make decisions about whether to upgrade to new platforms based on the cost and advantages of switching to the new platform. A new platform should not succeed unless its advantages are greater than the full

---

[41] Unless the methods used by the supplier to win its existing customers were anticompetitive.

costs associated with switching to that platform.[42] Thus, it is important to emphasize that it is not necessarily reflective of anticompetitive actions if new "better" technologies do not succeed — rather it can be that the advantages of these technologies do not justify the investments in new complementary goods that allow transition of existing investments to the new platforms.

In dynamic industries, an incumbent supplier cannot rest on its laurels and expect to be able to retain its customers. To sell new products it must upgrade its products, or risk losing new and existing customers to other suppliers who offer better products. In addition, the supplier must take into account that the level of switching costs is not a given. Rivals can invest in means to reduce switching costs and thus reduce the incumbent supplier's advantage. In fact if the rival has developed a truly superior technology it has the incentive to do so.

The existing supplier may in fact be at a disadvantage for new-generation technology if switching costs are an issue. Implementing new technologies may cause incompatibilities for its existing customers but supporting multiple platforms may be costly. The existing supplier may not wish to "strand" its existing customer base and thus might be at a disadvantage in seeking to implement new technologies. All of these factors indicate that in a dynamic industry, switching costs may provide an advantage, but this advantage is likely to be limited particularly as regards the potential for significant "leaps" in technology.

The extent of lock-in also relates to the pace of technological change. The more rapid the pace of change, the more quickly customers are likely to switch to new base and complementary products to take advantage of new advanced features. While compatibility of existing files may still be important, the need to purchase new applications or other complementary goods may be less important since the customer would probably upgrade those in any event. Thus, the more rapid the rate of change, the lower the switching costs, and the broader the market.

4.4. *A Note on Barriers to Entry*

Entry analysis plays a major role in market definition and the assessment of market power. In terms of the apparatus of antitrust analysis, this occurs either through the identification of competitors already in the market, or whether such firms could enter the market in a timely fashion to discipline the exercise of

---

[42] Not all customers are likely to face the same switching costs or have the same valuation of the improvements in the new platforms versus the old platforms. Thus the new platform may be able to attract some but not all customers.

market power by an incumbent. Where rents are monopoly rents, or where entry is difficult, and there are not already many existing competitors in the market, monopoly power can survive. The correct analysis of entry (and expansion of firms already in the market) is thus important to the assessment of market power.

Any factor that stands in the way of an entrant is not a barrier to entry, but could simply be a cost of entry. An entry barrier exists only when entry would be socially beneficial but is somehow blocked. Unnecessarily high profits result, and society (and not just new entrants) would be better off if they were competed away.

The innovation context is most important. After a superior product has been invented, society might be better off in the short run if imitators could produce it right away. Just because they cannot does not imply the existence of economically meaningful barriers to entry. The profits earned are likely to be Schumpeterian profits, and reflect a return to investment in R&D, and to creative activity and risk taking.

4.5. *Market Share*

4.5.1. General

After a market has been defined, and the competitors in a market have been identified, the next step in traditional antitrust analysis is the computation of share. Plaintiffs in antitrust cases wish to make them high, defendants tend to point out that they are low. If a market is defined narrowly, it is more likely that shares will be high, and vice versa if the market is defined broadly.

However, the meaning of market share is a function of how one has defined the market. Define it too narrowly or too broadly, and a high share doesn't carry much information. Not everything that is in the market need be weighed equally in terms of constraining the power of the dominant firm; not all that is excluded is irrelevant for explaining the constraints on the dominant firm.

Market share is not the end of the story, particularly in high-technology industries. Many economists, drawing on their understanding of static contexts, tend to believe that a small share shows the absence of market power while a larger share indicates its presence. This is frequently not the case where there is rapid innovation. (Our presumption here is that markets have been defined correctly.)

The more fundamental question is what happens to the firm's business when (if) monopoly profits are sought. This is traditionally analyzed through entry barriers, if not already analyzed in the market definition exercise when looking at the supply-side response. Absent entry barriers, even a high level of concentration does not convey market power. This is commonly recognized in antitrust analysis. Thus a firm with a large market share in a relevant market may simply be efficient or innovative. It could be sustaining its position through lower prices and/or superior products. One should not for a moment necessarily infer market power from such a large share.

To determine whether one is looking at a firm exercising antitrust market power (a monopolist) one has to go deeper and analyze the nature of rents. Are they Ricardian (scarcity rents), Schumpeterian (entrepreneurial rents), as defined earlier, and as elaborated in more detail below. Our position is of course akin to the legal question as to whether the monopoly is acquired and maintained by superior skill, foresight, and efficiency. If it is, the antitrust law recognizes it as a legal monopoly; we would prefer to say that a large share and associated high profits are not a monopoly if the source of the rents are Ricardian or Schumpeterian. It is only a monopoly if it earns monopoly rents. Put differently, in our view a true monopolist is a firm that is earning monopoly rents and not Ricardian or Schumpeterian rents. Ricardian and Schumpeterian rents may be considerable, but they tend to be transitory unless renewed by continuous innovation.

4.5.2. Industrial dynamics and concentration levels

When an industry is in ferment, a proper definition of the market must include a variety of competing technologies, and concentration will then generally be quite low. But suppose the antitrust analyst is quite wooden and stubbornly adheres to a static framework, refusing to recognize the (Schumpeterian) gales of creative destruction blowing in an industry. Then one must surely be flexible with respect to the concentration levels that indicated market power.

For merger analysis, the Justice Department has traditionally used Herfindahl-Hirschman thresholds (HHIs).[43] The Merger Guidelines select critical HHIs at 1000 and 1800.[44] But consider a snapshot of two markets with the same HHI: one in ferment because the regime is characterized by rich opportunity and weak

---

[43] The HHI is measured by taking the sum of the squares of the market share of all market participants, expressed as percentages. Thus, an industry with two firms, each of which has 50% of the market, has an HHI of $50^2 + 50^2 = 5000$. HHIs range from numbers approaching 0 (in perfectly competitive markets) to a theoretical maximum of 10,000 (monopoly).

[44] These numbers are thresholds — the Department is unlikely to challenge a merger if the postmerger HHI is below 1000, and is likely to challenge a merger if the postmerger HHI is above 1800 and the change in HHI is greater than 50. HHIs between 1000 and 1800 occupy a middle range in which the discretion of the Department is considerable. However, it is rare for the agencies to challenge a merger where the HHIs are below 2200–2500.

appropriability, and where the incumbents lack complementary assets; the other stable because the technology is mature, appropriability is strong, and the incumbent owns the complementary assets. Clearly, competition circumstances in these two markets are quite different, even though the level of concentration is the same. In short, market concentration thresholds that are insensitive to industrial dynamics are likely to be somewhat misleading.[45] When the technological regime is in ferment, market power, even if it exists momentarily, is likely to be transient because of changes in enabling technologies and in demand conditions.

Consider as an example the diagnostic imaging industry. Teece *et al.* documented that with the possible exception of nuclear imaging, all modalities displayed rapid reductions in HHIs over time.[46] In the case of CT scanners, concentration fell from 10,000 to 2200 within 5 years. Magnetic resonance fell from 10,000 to 2489 in 5 years. Each had fallen below 1800 within a decade.[47] An antitrust analyst endeavoring to understand competitive conditions would surely be misled by a snapshot taken early in the history of this industry. Moreover, if all identified modalities are put into the same market for purposes of market definition, the HHI is in the 928–1637 range for the period 1961–1987.[48] This vividly demonstrates the importance of static versus dynamic analysis in making a market power determination.

A second example shows that dynamic analysis in antitrust can work both ways. In the telecommunications industry, alternative technologies have historically been separated by regulatory barriers, and often given exclusive franchises within a particular territory. Cable television, local telephony, long-distance telephony, satellite communications, and broadcast were all distinct regulatory categories. That began to change in the middle of this decade as technical and regulatory barriers separating the different technologies dissolved. A market power analysis of the telecommunications industry conducted in 1992 that did not anticipate these changes would have been seriously in error. The opening of telecommunications markets to competition should result in a broader market, one in which any one firm cannot maintain significant power for long. At the same time, the broadening of this market means that antitrust regulators

---

[45] The same problem exists to an even greater degree with court decisions whose measurements of market share have tended to use four-firm concentration ratios (sum of the percentage share of the four largest firms in the market), a measure that is even less sensitive to industry conditions than the HHI.

[46] David J. Teece, Raymond Hartman and Will Mitchell, Assessing Market Power in Regimes of Rapid Technological Change, *Industrial and Corporate Change* 2 (1993), 317.

[47] *Id.* at 347.

[48] *Id.*

should rightly be concerned about mergers that would have raised no antitrust issues in 1992 if the market were viewed in static terms. If a franchised cable company buys the dominant local telephone company in its geographic region, for example, the potential for competition between the technologies may be reduced in that region.[49] A static market analysis might improperly discount such potential competition and treat the merger as a conglomerate.[50] Here, the problem with the HHI is that it assumes a proper (static) market definition is already in place. It is next to impossible to measure the postmerger HHIs of two companies who are not yet in the same market. Of course, the fact the HHIs do not tell the whole story does not mean that they should be discarded entirely. But it does suggest that their use should be tempered by the economic learning discussed in this article.

5. Implications for Conduct Analysis

5.1. *General*

Anticompetitive conduct must differ from action that would be expected under competition; it is conduct that makes no sense without the monopoly profits that can be made after competition is eliminated or reduced. In the U.S., courts have been reluctant, and wisely so, to impose the penalties of Sec. 2 of the Sherman Act on firms that have gained substantial market power without having engaged in conduct that otherwise violates the antitrust laws. The law does not penalize firms that have succeeded because of superior "skill, foresight, and industry." To find a violation of Sec. 2, courts faced with a defendant possessing monopoly power must find that the defendant engaged in troublesome "anticompetitive" or "exclusionary" conduct.

---

[49] See Laura Land Sigal, Challenging the Telco-Cable Cross-Ownership Ban: First Amendment and Antitrust Implications for the Interactive Information Superhighway, *Fordham Urb. L.J.* 22 (1994), 207; Darin Donovan, Competition for All, Security for None: Antitrust and Market Definition Problems of Future Telecommunications Industries (unpublished manuscript 1994).

[50] See John M. Stevens, Antitrust Law and Open Access to the NREN, *Vill. L. Rev.* 38 (1993), 571. Cf. Bruce A. Olcott, Will They Take Away My Video-Phone if I Get Lousy Ratings?: A Proposal for a "Video Common Carrier" Statute in Post-Merger Telecommunications, *Colum. L. Rev.* 84 (1994), 1558 (suggesting that mergers between different media were critical to effective competition, and therefore that media should be integrated and regulated as a whole). Subsequent events have effectively disproven the need for (and desirability of) mergers between companies in different media.

Our earlier analysis showed that in the context of innovation, market power need not be monopoly power in the economic sense. This is not going further than the Supreme Court has so far gone. What the Court has found to be blameless we would not call monopoly. Conduct that is objectionable is thus reduced to circumstances where true monopoly power exists (as evidenced by monopoly rents rather than Ricardian or Schumpeterian rents) and the monopolist is using "bad acts" to limit the expansion of competitors.

From an economic perspective, conduct must satisfy at least three criteria to be anticompetitive:[51]

1. The conduct must not be a sort that society seeks to encourage, today, such as nonpredatory price reductions. Absent this criterion the antitrust laws could be used to discourage socially beneficial conduct.
2. The conduct must be socially inefficient, in the sense that it tends to inhibit industry innovation or otherwise create distortions inconsistent with (long-run) consumer welfare.
3. The conduct must be substantially related to the maintenance or acquisition of monopoly power, and ought to be a substantial cause of the monopoly power under scrutiny. It is not enough that the conduct exploit market power derived from other sources. The reason for this is administrative. In the absence of such a criterion, any action by the firm with substantial market power could be challenged.

The first criterion is obvious if competition is to be encouraged. The second criterion is necessary since in the context of innovation, it is not uncommon that conduct of an incumbent (especially an incumbent innovator) will tend to impair the progress of competitors (but not necessarily of competition). Given the difficulties associated with applying traditional antitrust lenses, we think it is increasingly important to break through to fundamentals and ask what is the impact on economic efficiency over time. This will assist one in arriving at more confident and more accurate answers than one would obtain from asking questions such as Does the practice increase price of reduce output? The third criterion is likewise obvious in that if the conduct is ineffectual, it is irrelevant. Failure to pass this third criterion ought to be dispositive. (This

---

[51] We purposefully avoid the "less restrictive means" criterion sometimes advanced in antitrust analysis. This is because there is almost always a less restrictive contractual mechanism for achieving any economic outcome; the creative mind can always find an arrangement that is less restrictive; but if it is less efficient or effective from an economic perspective, then it is less desirable. Note also that while our framework endeavors to be general, our focus here is on high-technology industries.

criterion is not unlike Professor Areeda's definition of exclusionary conduct, which he defined as conduct "other than competition on the merits ... that reasonably [appears] capable of making a significant contribution to creating or maintaining monopoly power."[52]) Conduct is neither anticompetitive nor exclusionary if it fails these criteria.

5.2. *The Importance of Innovation*

In the context of high-technology industries, the second criterion is almost equivalent to determining whether the conduct reduces innovation in the industry. This is because it is innovation that will most assuredly undo an incumbent monopolist's position, and it is innovation that is fundamental to the generation of benefits to the consumer, and to the economy more generally. It promotes both competition and economic welfare. Conduct that does not in the aggregate affect innovation negatively does not assist the fundamental ability of the firm to charge monopoly prices. Consequently, if conduct is to be subjected to antitrust scrutiny on the ground that it contributed to market power, then the critical inquiry is whether it impedes aggregate innovation in the industry.

The difficulties of implementing this test need not in most instances lessen its utility. Many practices can be shown by theoretical analysis alone to have no negative effect on industry innovation. In any case, it is always better to answer the right questions relatively well then to answer the wrong questions precisely correctly.

The focus on impacts on industry innovation as the linchpin of conduct analysis is perhaps novel, but it is not without foundation. As we argued strongly in earlier work,[53] innovation is the most powerful force animating competition. Throttle innovation, and one throttles the most fundamental factor driving competition and insuring superior products and competitive prices for the consumer.

Our focus and our benchmark is industry innovation, by which we mean the sum of the incumbents and new entrant innovation. Conduct need not be anticompetitive, for instance, if it limits the freedom of clones, if the clones would have the effect of reducing industry innovation.

---

[52] Philip Areeda and Donald F. Turner, *Antitrust Law* ¶ 626c (1978). See also Philip Areeda and Herbert Hovenkamp, *Antitrust Law* ¶ 651c (1996).

[53] See Thomas Jorde and David J. Teece, Antitrust Policy and Innovation: Taking Account of Performance Competition and Competitor Cooperation, *Journal of Institutional and Theoretical Economic* 147 (1991), 118.

5.3. *Predatory Pricing*

It should be noted that pricing that excludes competitors is not necessarily anticompetitive, and may in fact be procompetitive. Monopoly power is the power to keep prices artificially high, earn monopoly (as compared to Ricardian and Schumpeterian) profits, and still exclude competitors. Firms that are more efficient than their rivals always have the power to exclude competitors by setting prices low. Indeed, that is what competition is supposed to achieve.

In many high-technology contexts, prices are set low for a variety of reasons, most of which reflect competition at work. For instance, innovators may set the price of hardware low to encourage the sale of software, or vice versa. Many would agree that if a price is set so that anticipated revenue is above avoidable cost, the price in question is certainly not predatory. A firm pricing below avoidable cost might be incurring losses that it could have avoided, unless it is developing a new market or promoting a new product.

Consider innovation more generally. When the innovator has a first-mover advantage, the innovator may well price high at first ("cream skimming"), but drop prices when the "me too's" arrive and undercut the innovator's price. The innovator must respond, or possibly face a disastrous loss of market share. The innovator must lower prices precisely because it does not have market power. If the innovator's costs are lower than the imitators', the imitators may not be able to make a profit in this particular line of business.

To condemn such behavior as anticompetitive is to condemn the very process of Schumpeterian competition. To use antitrust to protect such competitors is to confound the protection of competitors with the protection of competition. Fully efficient firms will not be deterred because they will still be able to compete if prices are still above the incumbent's avoided costs. Certainly innovation isn't harmed if inefficient imitators are kept out by prices too low for them to survive.

5.4. *Tying and Bundling*

Tying occurs when the sale of one product (the tying product) is conditioned on the sale of another (the tied product). Examples include the sale of replacement parts by the manufacturer on the condition that the buyer also purchases repair service. Bundling occurs when the price of two or more products are sold together as a package is less than the sum of their individual prices.

Welfare-enhancing motivations for tying and bundling (such as economies of scope, protection of reputation, and risk sharing) have been well developed in the literature.[54] Efficiencies of various kinds are often paramount. Some relate to performance and quality. In circumstances where the various items are used in a system, separate supply may confound the determination of systems failure. Whenever complex systems are involved — be it in telecommunications, computers, or aircraft engines — the consumer/user may be hard pressed to uncover the reasons for system failure, and the reputation of the vendor of quality parts suffers, along with the reputation of the vendor of the part or subsystem that caused the system to fail. Tying thus benefits qualified firms, and will be objected to by vendors with less salutary reputations. Tying can thus be, and frequently is, the handmaiden of economic efficiency.[55]

Bundling is likewise frequently beneficial. It results in lower prices to consumers. In the high-technology context it may also enable experience to be obtained in the use of certain goods that might not otherwise sell on a stand-alone basis. Once experience is obtained, the product in question might be viable on a stand-alone basis.

Moreover, economic analysis has shown that the standard leveraging arguments — that tying is used to lever monopoly in one market into a second — fail as a matter of logic, at least in most cases. If monopoly power exists in one market, it can generally be extracted there. While theoretical possibilities suggesting otherwise can be constructed, the assumptions required are rarely met in real-world circumstances.

5.5. *Integration of Function*

In the context of high-technology industries, various plaintiffs have from time to time insisted that it is anticompetitive for an alleged monopolist to meld into a single product two or more products that were previously offered separately, or could have been offered separately. The argument is commonly made that design integration of this kind restricts entry or growth by the specialized suppliers of one or both of the separate products. It is indeed common in the computer and the software industry for new products to combine functionality, which may well have been provided by separate vendors or by separate products offered by the vendor in the past.

---

[54] See Michael Whinston, Tying, Foreclosure, and Exclusion, *American Economic Review* 80 (1990), p. 837 and William Baxter and Daniel Kessler, Toward a Consistent Theory of the Welfare Analysis of Agreements, *Stan. L. Rev.* 47 (1995), 615.

[55] Tying can also assist in the diffusion of new technology in circumstances where consumers are not quite sure of the value of a new product. See John Lunn, Tie-in Sales and the Diffusion of New Technology, *Journal of Institutional and Theoretical Economic* 146 (1990), 249.

Such integration of function implies no threat to an incumbent's rivals unless consumers prefer products integrated in this fashion (rather than being forced to integrate the products themselves). If consumers prefer buying separate products, and integrating them themselves, then the innovator who joins the functionality in just one product will fail to gain sales. So to insist that it is anticompetitive to give consumers what they want is to once again fall into the trap of using antitrust to protect competitors rather than competition and consumers.

Determining the legitimacy of design choices by innovative firms requires more than just economic analysis. It requires an evaluation of technical choices and consumer preferences. Such data, even if available to antitrust enforcement agencies, cannot typically be adequately processed and understood by them. Accordingly, enforcement agencies are likely to make serious errors if they endeavor to second-guess design decisions of innovators in regimes of rapid technological change and/or product redefinition.

5.6. *"Vaporware" and the Premature Announcement of New Products*

In industries like autos, computer hardware, and computer software, vendors announce new products expected to be available in the future. It is sometimes alleged that firms engage in this practice to discourage customers from switching to their competitors during the period before the new product becomes available.

It is clear, however, that consumer choice is assisted by timely information about future product availability. Such information enables consumers to plan their product acquisitions. We cannot see how this practice could have any anticompetitive effect. There are two obvious circumstances to evaluate: First, the announcement turns out to be accurate. Clearly, if the issue is simply that a vendor signals early on its future product releases, and does in fact release products consistent with its announcements, there cannot possibly be any antitrust or consumer protection issues. Consumer welfare is unambiguously enhanced. Second, the announcement turns out to be inaccurate or misleading. These cases are a little more complex. Both competitors, customers, and the vendor could be injured by such mistakes. The injury does not, however, enhance market power if consumers are well informed and rational. This is because consumers and the market-place will quickly calibrate the announcement/forecasting errors of the vendor, and discount its announcements accordingly. This is not unlike how investors discount a company's (and its analyst's) earnings forecasts on Wall Street. A firm that misses the analyst's forecasts, even occasionally, will have its market value discounted in short order. Customers in product markets act in much the same way.

6. Luck, Incentives, and Ignorance

With increasing returns and network effects, some antitrust analysts may be led to the view that the leading firm in an industry, while performing in a fully credible though possibly unexceptional (technological) manner, has been thrust ahead of its competitors merely by chance events. Market outcomes achieved by luck need not be easily undone for some period, although our discussion of paradigms earlier suggested that in high-technology industries (e.g., computer and computer software) good luck would carry one for only a short period. Indeed, the more recent literature on first movers suggests that first-mover advantages aren't durable.[56] Competences built-up need not be easily transferred, however. So once obtained, dominance, if underpinned by specialized competences, can sometimes be maintained — but usually only until the next paradigm shift.

There are two classes of reasons why absent unambiguous anticompetitive conduct by a firm with market power, the antitrust agencies shouldn't intervene. One is that the antitrust action might produce severe disincentive affects throughout the entire economy. The possibility of success through superior skill, foresight, and acumen, or just dumb luck, induces entry, investment, and unparalleled even maniacal effort. To penalize success with poorly reasoned antitrust intervention is dangerous. Oliver Williamson[57] reminds us of Robin Marris'[58] comments almost three decades ago:

> ... trust busting effectively contradicts the most fundamental principle of capitalism. Whatever may be said of the liberty of the individual, capitalism insists on the liberty of the organization. That liberty includes the right to grow, and the system rewards, with growth, the fruits of both good luck and good guidance. I cannot conceive how any political or other mechanism can sustain that principle if it is

---

[56] Marvin Lieberman and David Montgomery, First-Mover Advantages, *Strategic Management Journal* 9 (1988), 41; and David J. Teece, Profiting from Technological Innovation: Implications for Integration, Collaboration, Licensing and Public Policy, *Research Policy* 15 (1986), 285.

[57] Oliver Williamson, *Market and Hierarchies: Analysis and Antitrust Implications*, 1975, p. 219.

[58] Robin Marris, Is the Corporate Economy a Corporate State?, *American Economic Review* 62 (1972), 103, 113.

modified to read "You shall continue to be rewarded for success, but for successive success you shall be punished."

In high-technology contexts, we do not need to suggest that one should reward the tortoise for the foibles of the hare, for the selection environments in high-technology industries simply do not allow tortoises to survive. Contemporary high-technology industries attract and utilize the best, the brightest, and the fleet footed, and display a genre of competition completely unparalleled in the history of capitalism.

In any case, as indicated earlier, the risk of error associated with the agencies and the courts endeavoring to intervene in high-technology contexts is high. As Judge Easterbrook has aptly stated:

> if any economic institution survives long enough to be studied by scholars and stamped out by law, it probably should be left alone, and if an economic institution ought to be stamped out, it is apt to vanish by the time the enforcers get there.[59]

Moreover, Easterbrook reminds us that the journey from social science to law should be a process of conserving on the costs of error and information:

> we wish to hold to a minimum the sum of (a) the welfare losses from inefficient business arrangements; (b) the welfare losses from efficient business arrangements condemned or discouraged by legal rules; (c) the costs of operating the legal system. How? The judge must decide between approaches before the economics profession is confident which is best, and in the process increases all three of these kinds of cost. A century of antitrust law, and the profession is *still* debating the merits of almost every practice except cartels and mergers to monopoly — and dissenting voices are being heard even on those subjects.[60]

Accordingly, we are rather skeptical that the "surgical" approach to antitrust intervention confidently suggested by Deputy Assistant Attorney General Rubinfeld in his article in this issue of *The Antitrust Bulletin*, is in fact feasible. The agencies and the courts wield blunt axes, not surgeons' knives. While the agencies

---

[59] Frank Easterbrook, Ignorance and Antitrust in Thomas Jorde and David Teece (eds.), *Antitrust, Innovation and Competitiveness*, 1992, p. 119.
[60] *Id.* at 122.

and their advisors may be bright and well educated, the high-technology industries they seek to regulate have arguably attracted an even brighter and more hardworking cadre of top talent.

Moreover, the real world of high technology is extremely complex. The information requirements to determine when an action is likely to be anticompetitive in dynamic, high-tech industries are high. Assessing whether a firm has market power requires an understanding of the sources of its competitive advantages as well as customer preferences. Many actions that harm competitors have valid justifications or are strongly related to competitive motivations. Distinguishing between these effects is frequently very difficult, and the politics of the process gives considerable advantage to the complainers.

The problem of incomplete information escalates dramatically when the activity at issue involves issues about how firms design their products, and what firms decide to include as features in their products. Determining the right answer likely requires significant technological detail, and understanding of consumer preferences are inherently uncertain. Enforcement agency personnel are not likely to be capable of making the technical distinctions and would have to rely on industry personnel who may have divergent views and special agendas.

This indicates the need for extreme caution. Moreover, government antitrust investigations are typically long and costly procedures, particularly since nonmerger investigations do not face the constraints imposed by the Hart–Scott–Rodino Act.

Firms may even enter into consents to minimize litigation costs and negative public opinion, even if the conduct at issue is not anticompetitive. These consents can have two effects. If the agency has not made the right call, it will stop a behavior that is procompetitive. A secondary effect can occur with other firms that may be concerned that they could face investigation and potentially litigation for similar procompetitive behavior. For instance, a ruling that limits the design choices of firms can have far-reaching effects. In many high-technology markets, suppliers need to coordinate behavior with other vendors of complementary products to have their products be valuable to customers. However, it is not likely to be optimal to always insure compatibility with every potential complementary product. In addition, there may be times when it makes most sense to incorporate a complementary product into the platform. Any time a potential rival at one level is harmed by these decisions, the supplier could face investigation and potential litigation. This would likely affect the firm's strategies, and incentives, reducing innovation as it increases the cost of investment in innovation or reduces the benefits from innovation.

7. Conclusion

Despite the confidence displayed by some agency lawyers and economists, we do not believe the antitrust agencies anywhere in the world are at present well equipped to deal with competition policy in high-technology industries.[61] This is not because the agencies have failed to hire the requisite staff, but because the economic profession has for many years largely ignored the study of innovation. Belated attention to network effects and increasing returns, while admirable, is a sideshow. The very nature of competition, the definition of industries, the basis of competitive advantage, the effects of "restrictive" practices and the nature of economic rents are all different in the context of innovation. The costs of error are great. The agencies, whose reputations have improved considerably over the past two decades, run the risk of squandering their reputational capital and becoming viewed as clumsy-footed spoilers if they do not recognize that they are now on unchartered terrain.

The good news is that the cost of inaction is not high, and pales next to the costs and likelihood of error where innovation is rapid. In high technology, we observe competition orders of magnitude more fierce than in industries where the agencies have in the past found problems. We have little doubt in the eventual self-corrective capacities of markets in such contexts, even in the presence of networks.

In the U.S. the political economy of governmental antitrust action in high technology, we note that the activists seem to fall into two groups: the agencies themselves and former agency employees; and competitors who would benefit if leading firms were hobbled. Consumers themselves seem relatively silent and consumer surveys strongly disfavor agency intervention in high-technology situations.

The task ahead — learning how to apply competitive policy principles to high technology — is an important one to which we remain committed. This special issue of *The Antitrust Bulletin* is one small step. Fortunately, there is a large literature in "innovation studies" and "innovation management," but it is neither read nor cited by antitrust lawyers and economists. It is our belief that antitrust jurisprudence can be considerably enhanced by a deeper appreciation of the economics of technological innovation and the fragility of competitive advantage in the absence of continuous innovation.

---

[61] See also James Langenfeld and Mary Coleman, Antitrust Analysis and Remedies in High-Tech Industries, *Global Competitive Review,* June/July 1998, at 42.

Appendix A

Examples of Performance Competition

Diagnostic Imaging

In 1993, we studied the market for diagnostic imaging devices in some detail.[62] Diagnostic imaging devices are used by physicians and other health care professionals to obtain information about the internal condition of the body. Examples include x-ray machines, nuclear imaging devices, ultrasound machines, computer tomography (CT) scanners, magnetic resonance imaging (MRI), and digital radiography. The application of each is somewhat different but to varying degrees these devices provide, or could provide, alternative ways of getting the same or similar information. Each modality, however, has particular utility in certain applications; these applications overlap partially but not substantially.[63] Application of a small but significant and nontransitory increase in price (SSNIP) analysis would probably identify each modality as a separate market from the demand side. Since price is only one of three of more key demand attributes,[64] the SSNIP focus on price alone biases the assessment of competitive responses when the hypothetical monopolist raises prices. Narrow (and concentrated) markets necessarily follow, despite the strong qualitative evidence of competition between modalities.[65]

Microprocessors

The microprocessor industry has been characterized by an astounding rate of technological innovation. Competition is based not just on the speed of microprocessors (measured in millions of instructions per second, or MIPS), but on architecture, compatibility with hardware and software, reliability, power usage, and other factors. There is competition between architectures, manifesting itself primarily in competition between Motorola and Intel in earlier generations, and more recently between RISC and CISC-based architectures and between the Intel standard and the PowerPC. Intra-architectural competition has also been present, with AMD and Cyrix introducing clones of one of the dominant architectures (the Intel

---

[62] Raymond Hartman, David J. Teece, Will Mitchell and Thomas Jorde, Assessing Market Power in Regimes of Rapid Technological Change, *Industrial and Corporate Change* 2 (1993), 317.

[63] *Id.* at 329.

[64] *Id.* at 329.

[65] *Id.* at 325.

Log Performance

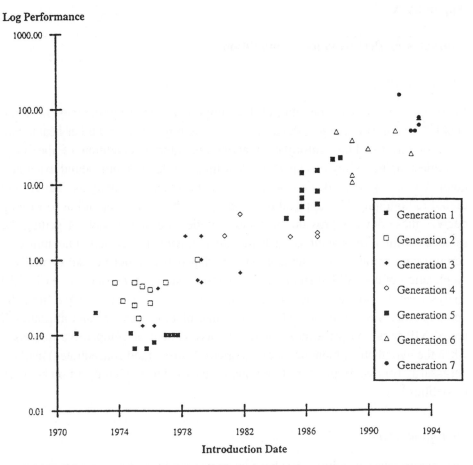

Source: Miriam Culjak and Jack Nickerson, Report on the History of Competition in the Microprocessor Industry (unpublished report). *EDN Annual μP/μC Directory*, 1974–1992: IC Masters (various years).

Fig. A.1. Generational performance of microprocessors million instructions per second (MIPS).

80×86 architecture). Competition is also intergenerational as well as intra-generational. New generations of microprocessors substitute for older generations, eventually replacing them entirely. This tends to occur rather quickly, as processing power has tended to double every 18 months to 3 years[66] (see Fig. A.1).

---

[66] Indeed, this rather astonishing (from a technological standpoint) tendency has become so engrained in the consciousness of the semiconductor industry that it is referred to as Moore's Law, after Intel founder Gordon Moore.

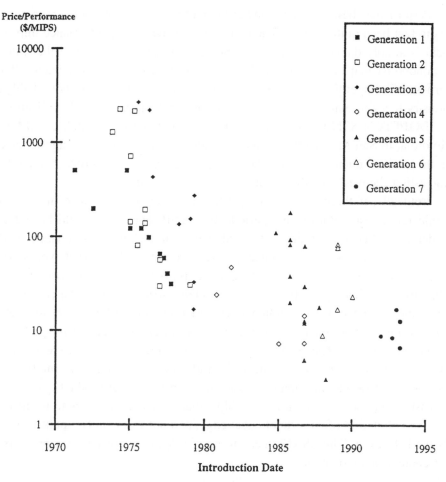

Source: Miriam Culjak and Jack Nickerson, Report on the History of Competition in the Microprocessor Industry (unpublished report). *EDN Annual μP/μC Directory*, 1974–1992: IC Masters (various years).

Fig. A.2. Generational price/performance of microprocessors.

Firms that fail to keep up with the pace of technological innovation in this industry will be left out.[67] Success in one generation does not guarantee success in the next, but merely offers the opportunity to compete in the next round of innovation and product launches.

---

[67] Figure A.2 shows the generational price/performance of microprocessors where performance is again measured in MIPS. The number of dollars per MIPS has declined from thousands of dollars per MIPS in the earlier generations to $10, or less per MIPS in the earlier generations.

Performance-based competition during multiple generations of microprocessors has in fact been quite intense. The magnitude of the price-performance improvement is simply dazzling — and is difficult to square with the idea that Intel is a monopolist that controls the industry and is free to do what it wants. If the purpose of competition is to bring benefits to the consumer, there is probably no industry that can match this one. Yet a mechanical and uniformed application of the DOJ/FTC's SSNIP might well impute market power to Intel, to AMD, to Motorola, to Sun Microsystems, and to others at certain times during the history of the semiconductor industry. These firms are clearly vigorous competitors, suggesting there is something quite wrong with the test.

Ironically, if there was anticompetitive conduct or dominance in the semiconductor industry during this period, the SSNIP approach would be unlikely to detect it. Because of the fast-paced nature of technological change in this industry, the only way one company might dominate the market would be to find a way of maintaining or leveraging its power from one generation to the next. But establishing such a leveraging claim would require the plaintiffs to prove the existence of two semiconductor markets that differed only in time — e.g., the market for generation 1 microprocessors and the market for generation 2 microprocessors. The SSNIP approach does not appear to leave room for such intertemporal market definition.[68] And while one company (Intel) has in fact managed to maintain market leadership across several product generations, at least among 80 × 86-architecture chips, that leadership appears to result from Intel's exploitation of its technological edge, and not from anticompetitive use of its market power. The SSNIP needs to be recast to have it perform properly in the context of innovation.

Appendix B

A Multi-Attribute Small but Significant and Nontransitory Increase in Price (SSNIPP)

When competition proceeds as much on the basis of features as price (as it does in regimes of rapid technological progress), an equally pertinent question

---

[68] A more likely leveraging claim in this industry is what one might call backward temporal leveraging — that (for a hypothetical example) Intel tied sales of its new 486 microprocessors to the purchase of its older 386 microprocessors, at a time when Intel was the only supplier of 486 chips but faced competition for 386 chips. This claim too would require that markets be defined intertemporally.

to ask is whether a change in the performance attributes of one product would induce substitution to or from another. If the answer is affirmative, then the differentiated products, even if based on alternative technologies, should probably be included in the relevant product market. Furthermore, when assessing such performance-induced substitutability, a 1-year or 2-year period is simply too short because enhancement of performance attributes may take a longer time to accomplish than price changes. While it is difficult to state precisely (and generally) the "right" length of time, it is clear that the time frame should be determined by technological concerns. As a result, it may be necessary to apply different time frames to different products and technologies. In the semiconductor industry, it might be tailored to each generation of the product (about 3 years for microprocessors).

When assessing performance-based competition among existing producers, the product changes to be included as a metric should include those available from the reengineering of existing products using technologies currently known to existing competitors.[69] Thus if firm A, by modifying its product X at a relatively modest cost using known product and process technology, could draw sales away from product Y of firm B, such that B would need to improve its products to avoid losing market share to A then X and Y are at least potential competitors in the same relevant market.

When assessing potential competition and entry barriers, a 1- or 2-year 5% price rule suggested by SSNIP must also be modified to include variations in performance attributes of existing and potentially new technologies. In high-technology innovative industries it is this potential competition that is often most threatening to a firm that attempts to dominate the market, and may be the most important from a welfare standpoint. Unfortunately, this potential competition also takes the longest time to play out and is the most difficult to fully anticipate. Antitrust regulators must determine a more realistic time frame over which the new products and technologies that may enter the market will be considered. The precise length of time allowed for the entry of potential competitors must reflect technological realities. Hence, it too may vary by product and technology.

To see how this approach would work, assume that several firms offer various products with different attributes. One producer improves the performance of a certain attribute, holding price and other attributes constant. If a shift in demand away from a similar product results, there exists a performance cross elasticity between the two products. If this cross elasticity is high enough, the products are

---

[69] Product changes that depend on anticipated technologies not currently commercially viable may also be relevant to future competition, depending on the circumstances.

in the same market. However, if the producer were to improve the performance of a certain attribute, while simultaneously raising the product's price such that no substitution occurs, this does not necessarily mean that the products are in different markets — merely that the price-performance ratio of the product had not in fact changed.

This framework requires one to analyze and quantify both price and performance (attribute) competition. For example, one can retain the 5% price guideline while extending the DOJ approach to incorporate performance competition, perhaps by assessing percentage changes in performance attributes. However, such an extension is far from straightforward. In general, performance changes are more difficult to quantify than price changes because performance is multidimensional. As a result, quantification requires measuring both the change in an individual attribute and the relative importance of that attribute. Unlike price changes, which involve altering the value of a common base unit (dollars), performance changes often involve changing the units by which performance is measured. Nonetheless, rough quantification is often possible, based on the pooled judgments on competent observers, particularly product users.

We suggest introducing a 25% rule for a change in any key performance attribute.[70] Assume that an existing manufacturer lowers the quality of a key performance attribute of an existing product by 25%, while the price of the product and all attributes of goods produced by other suppliers remain the same. If no substitution to other products occurs, then the original product constitutes a distinct antitrust market. If substitution to other product does occur, then those other products share the market with the original product. Conversely, assume that a new product is introduced that is identical to an existing product in all ways except that it offers a 25% improvement in a key performance attribute. If there is no substitution from the existing product to the new product, then the two products do not share the same antitrust market.

The criterion of 25% performance improvement for a single key performance attribute is conservative. Not only is a 25% improvement small compared with those that commonly occur in industries experiencing rapid technological change, but a 25% improvement in a single attribute is likely to imply an overall performance improvement of considerably less than 25%. Focusing on changes in a single attribute has the advantage of enhancing quantifiability. It avoids the need for determining the importance of the attribute itself in relation to the product as a whole as would be required in a general performance enhancement

---

[70] Raymond Hartman, David J. Teece, Will Mitchell and Thomas Jorde, Assessing Market Power in Regimes of Rapid Technological Change, *Industrial and Coroprate Change* 2 (1993), 317.

test. Further, single attributes may be more readily given to quantification in existing terms. For example, performance in microprocessors can be measured in MIPS (millions of instructions per second), or in clock speed, or in transistors per square millimeter, or in some other respect that consumers find relevant to their purchasing decisions.

While courts and regulators could rely on past market data regarding the effects of changes in performance on market demand they need not do so. Many product users are familiar with the key development programs of their suppliers and are able to assess the likelihood that a particular product change will emerge in the near future. One possible measurement procedure, therefore, would be to rely on the informed judgments of users of existing products. This procedure would involve identifying market experts, asking them to list key performance attributes, and then asking them to assess the substitutive effects of changes in the attributes. The sample of product users could be supplemented by a corresponding sample of commercial participants, although care would be required to avoid introducing competitive bias into the judgments. A sample of such participants could be asked whether a 25% change in the performance of any one attribute would lead to product substitution. While surveys are less exact than market data regarding past substitutions, they are forward- rather than backward-looking. In innovative industries, that tradeoff may be well worth making.[71]

Determining the value of an improvement may not always be so easy, of course. A percentage assessment requires both knowledge of market conditions and an accurate evaluation of the new product. Either one may be hard to come by when there is high uncertainty. The problem is most severe in the case of quantum changes, such as the introduction of a specific new application for a device. Entirely new products or applications have no background against which to benchmark the value of the new technology. Following introduction, however, most product changes take place along a relatively steady trajectory of technological improvement. Even performance improvements based on "unpredictable" problems like software bugs have this feature.

In addition to threshold rules regarding performance changes, market definition requires an identification of a time frame for the competitive product changes — that is, the definition of the "near future." Because there is significant variation

---

[71] A multiattribute SSNIP also has the virtue of effectively accounting for the level of appropriability in an industry. Industries in which intellectual property rights are particularly strong should be characterized by greater performance-based competition and low price competition, than industries without strong intellectual property protection. The flexibility of the multiattribute SSNIP allows it to account for competition in all sorts of appropriability regimes.

among products, no single number will be appropriate for all cases. We suggest that a 4-year period be established as a default time frame, with the option of adjusting the period if strong evidence suggests that it would be appropriate in an individual case.[72] Like the DOJ's old 1-year rule[73] or the patent law's traditional 17-year grant,[74] a fixed 4-year rule will not be optimal in all cases.[75] It could provide too broad a market definition in some cases and too narrow a definition for others; with the benefit of hindsight, it looks about right for the microprocessor industry.

---

[72] Teece *et al.*, *supra* note 2, at 341.

[73] The 1992 Merger Guidelines abolished the 1-year rule for testing the market efforts of a SSNIP (stated in the 1984 Merger Guidelines at Sec. 2.11), substituting instead market effects "for the foreseeable future." 1992 Merger Guidelines at Sec. 1.11.

[74] The term of patents beginning in 1995 was changed to run for 20 years from date the patent application is filed, with the actual term varying in practice depending on the length of time the patent spends in prosecution. For more detail on this point, see Mark A. Lemley, An Empirical Study of the Twenty Year Patent Term, *AIPLA Q. J.* 22 (1995), 369.

[75] This does not mean it is not optimal as a general rule. See Louis Kaplow, The Patent-Antitrust Intersection: A Reappraisal, *Harv. L. Rev.* 97 (1984), 1813.

The Analysis of Market Definition and Market Power in the Context of Rapid Innovation

Christopher Pleatsikas[a,1], David Teece[b,*,2]

[a]*LECG Inc., 2000 Powell St. No. 600, Emeryville, CA 94608, USA*

[b]*University of California, Institute of Management,*
Innovation and Orginization (IMIO), F402 Hass School of Business 930,
Berkeley, CA 94720-1930, USA

The basis for competition in many high technology industries is fundamentally different from that in more mature and stable industries. Most obviously, there is a much greater emphasis on performance-based, rather than price-based, competition. In addition, the competitive dynamic is different as well, with product often highly differentiated and periodic discontinuous paradigm shifts that can completely overwhelm per-existing market positions. The objective of this paper is to review and evaluate some of the traditional techniques used to define markets and measure market power in antitrust analysis. Most significantly, the limitations of these techniques when applied in high technology contexts are revealed, particular when inherently static analytical frameworks are employed. Often their use results in markets that are defined too narrowly, with the consequence that market power is overestimated. To rectify these problems, several alternative methods are suggested. Any method applied in a high technology context must have due regard for the dynamic nature of competition in such industries and must utilize an appropriate time horizon for analysis.

Reprinted from *International Journal of Industrial Organization* 19:5 (2001), 695–704.

* Corresponding author.
  E-mail address: Pleatsik@pacebell.net (C. Pleatsikas), teece@haas.berkeley (D. Teece).
[1] Also corresponding author. Current address: 6022 Rockwell Street, Oakland, California.
[2] Dr. Christopher Pleatsikas is a principal at LECG, Inc, an economics and financial consulting firm. He serves as a consultant and expert on antitrust and intellectual property litigation matters for clients in the US and Australasia. David Teece is Mitsubishi Bank Professor at the Haas School of Business at the University of California at Berkeley. He is also a founder and a Director of LECG, Inc.

Keywords: Market definition; Market power; Rapid innovation; High technology industries.

1. Introduction

Economic analysis has come to have strong influence on antitrust analysis. Frequently, however, the economist's vision of a "good" industry is animated by the vision of perfect competition, with its assumption of homogeneous products, identical technologies, and firms competing solely on the basis of price, with prices equal to marginal cost, and earning zero economic profits. However, the ideal of perfect competition is at odds with the reality of highly competitive, technology driven industries. In this paper, we indicate that competition policy and antitrust analysis must begin to think differently about certain "monopoly" issues. The nature of competition in market exposed to the effects of rapid technological innovation is quite different from competition in other markets. Market power is extremely difficult to measure, and the traditional models of competition may have limited utility. Accordingly, economists and antitrust lawyers must rethink some basic assumptions and revise their methods. Failure to do so may result in litigation outcomes and public policies that harm competition and consumers.

In many industries today new forms of competition dominate the landscape. In particular, innovation (both technical and organizational) animates the process in many sectors. Products are differentiated, often significantly so, due to differences in the technology employed. True high tech products are rarely commodities.

The introduction of new products and product differentiation accomplished by innovation is key to business success and customer satisfaction. In knowledge-based industries, performance features, quality, reliability, and service take on a special meaning. In the world of high technology, there is often high uncertainty and fierce competition. Waves of new product introductions are frequently accompanied by premium prices initially, followed by rapid price declines as imitative products emerge. Technology and features are as important to consumers as price, requiring consideration of price/performance competition rather than price competition alone.

Antitrust economics/industrial organization manifests a limited understanding of the nature of competition in high technology industries, where competition is driven by innovation. Among the public policy (and economic) issues that have not been well-explored are the evolutionary processes at work, the nature and sources of economic rents derived by participants, the degree of competition (or the lack thereof) in these industries, and the relevance of market structure as a proxy for market power. The recent decision in the *US vs. Microsoft* case has brought these issues (and the controversies they engender) into particularly sharp focus. Whatever one's views on the merits of that decision, it is clear that traditional antitrust analysis is inadequate to the task of defining markets and assessing market power in knowledge-intensive high technology industries.

This paper focuses on market definition and market power analysis. Our purpose is to demonstrate the inadequacies of the traditional structural indicia that have been used by economists and others to defines markets and assess market power in high technology industries and to suggest alternative approaches that are more appropriate for these industries. We do not consider conduct/ behavioral issues, except peripherally. We utilize examples from antitrust litigation and agency review that occurred in three industries to illustrate the shortcomings of traditional indicia.

The organization of this paper is as follows. Section 2 briefly discusses some features of competition in high technology industries. Section 3 describes the traditional indicia that have been applied to market definition and market power analyses. Section 4 demonstrates the problems that occur when these indicia are applied in high technology industries. Section 5 attempts to develop new indicia that are more appropriate for evaluating competition in high technology industries. Section 6 presents our conclusions.

2. Competition in High Technology Industries[3]

Competition in high technology industries can be fundamentally different from that in low technology and/or mature industries. Competition is often particularly fierce. There are periodic, unpredictable and discontinuous paradigm shifts[4] that can completely undermine incumbents using existing dominant technologies. Such shifts can and do often result in total change in the competitive positions in the

---

[3] For a more complete discussion of these issues, see Teece and Coleman (1998).

[4] Note that, for the purposes of this paper, the term 'paradigm shift' should be construed broadly. That is, it includes both fundamental changes in the character of the technology used in the marketplace (e.g., the shift from mainframe and mini computers to personal computers) and substantial improvements in technologies that do not represent such fundamental changes (e.g., the shift from 16-bit architecture in PCs to 32-bit architecture). The concept of "creative destruction", first advanced by Schumpeter (1942), is related to that of the "paradigm shift".

industry.[5] As a result, market shares can shift quite rapidly, and new leaders often emerge. Andy Grove, GEO of Intel, has referred to these as "major inflexion points" in the evolution of an industry. The existence, but unpredictable arrival, of inflexions underscores the high business risk that exists in these industries. Between inflexion points turmoil occurs as well, although the chances of survival are better.

Recognizing and then seizing the opportunities and threats afforded by major shifts is the essence of entrepreneurial leadership and is critical to business survival and prosperity. Indeed, entrepreneurial capabilities may be as or more important than technical capabilities. Established firms frequently have the most difficulties in adapting to paradigm shifts, often because they have too great a commitment to the existing technology or because decision-making is focused myopically on current problems.

Paradigm shifts open new opportunities for newcomers and/or other innovators, particularly when the underlying technology is competency destroying. The inability of incumbent firms in an industry to bridge a discontinuity is frequently observed, as in the semiconductor photolithographic alignment industry. In this industry, over five generations of products, no firm leading in one generation led in another generation.[6] Utterback (1996), in a more general analysis of discontinuous change, found that in only one-fourth of cases studied did existing competitors either initiate radical innovation or adapt quickly enough to remain among the market leaders once such innovation has occured.

Investors understand the implications of these paradigm shifts much better than economists do, recognizing that competition in such industries is often much more intense than in mature industries. Such intense competition generates high risk and requires higher than average returns to compensate. Yet high risk for the investor should translate to lower risk for the antitrust authorities, as incumbent positions may be fragile even in the short- to medium-term and, frequently, competitive forces are sufficiently powerful to undo monopoly power, should it arise.

3. Limitations of Traditional Indicia Used to Evaluate Market Definition and Market Power

The fundamental under pinning of all (non-collusive) competition policy issues is the analysis of market/monopoly power. In traditional antitrust economics and

---

[5] See Audretsch (1995).

[6] Henderson and Clark (1990).

jurisprudence, the starting point for competitive assessment is the concept of a (relevant) market. The presumption is that if a firm has a "high market share" coupled with high entry barriers, it has "monopoly" power. Thus, its conduct can be injurious to competition, and ought to be scrutinized most carefully.

Absent monopoly power, non-collusive business conduct never raises antitrust issues. In the presence of monopoly power, business conduct that would otherwise be unobjectionable may become problematic. This has traditionally been determined by defining the market in which a firm competes and then assessing the degree of control that a particular firm has over that market.

In US antitrust jurisprudence, there are two main categories of traditional indicia commonly used to define markets and derive measures of market power. These are (1) the methods contained in the *Horizontal Merger Guidelines* and (2) indicia that roughly correspond to those identified in *Brown Shoe*.[7] These have been utilized by the courts as if they are universally applicable, without regard to industry context.[8] Unfortunately, context is extremely important,[9] and these indicia, particularly the *Brown shoe* indicia, are not well-suited for analysis of high technology industries. In the following subsections, we describe the techniques of analysis that have been developed from these sources and the problems inherent in them for analysis of antitrust problems in high technology industries.

3.1. *The Horizontal Merver Guidelines*

The *Horizontal Merger Guidelines*, most recently revised in 1997, include several categories of analytical techniques or indicia that have been applied to mergers and, more generally, to the problem of market definition whether in a merger context or otherwise. These include the "hypothetical monopolist" test, the SSNIP (small but significant, non-transitory increase in price), HHIs (Herfindahl — Hirschman Index), and entry analysis.

---

[7] *Brown Shoe, Inc. v. United States,* 370 US 294 (1962).

[8] While both categories derive from market merger analysis, they have been widely applied by courts and analysts in circumstances where more general allegations of anticompetitive behavior have been made. It should be noted, however, that not all courts have accepted the use of these indicia for non-merger cases.

[9] By context, we mean not only the specific circumstances of the case — e.g., whether merger or allegations of anticompetitive behavior not related to a merger — but also the specific circumstances of the industry — most importantly the industry structure and nature of competitive activity in the industry (or industries) of interest.

The analytical techniques utilized in the *Merger Guidelines* have limitations for application in high technology industries — whether for mergers or other competition issues. For example, the hypothetical monopolist test relies implicitly on some measure of cross-elasticity of substitution because demand-side substitution possibilities are critical to assessing market boundaries under this approach. The central question involves identifying products that compete. All reasonable economic substitutes must be identified. Such identification may be relatively straightforward in many (though probably not all) mature industries. Even in the absence of definitive cross-elasticity data, it is sometimes relatively easy to identify substitutes in mature industries. There is a great deal of experience as to applications, and the criteria that are applied by users to decide among alternatives may be well understood and easy to express in economic terms. After all, different grades of steel may be good substitutes for one another in the manufacture of certain products, but it may be obvious that iron, aluminum or titanium are poor substitutes for steel in many uses.

With high technology products, substitution analysis becomes much more difficult. Most obviously, data for estimating cross-elasticities, which is often lacking even for products in mature industries, is seldom available at all for high technology industries.[10] In addition, it is often difficult for non-experts — including economists, lawyers, judges and juries — to determine whether and to what extent substitution is feasible between (or among) products that are highly differentiated and/or employ different technologies. The ability of customers to utilize specific high technology products in their businesses is often based on whether that product satisfies arcane technical and economic criteria, rendering even qualitative analysis of the substitution possibilities more difficult.[11]

For example, in the overcurrent protection market discussed in Section 4 below), devices employing several different technologies are feasible substitutes in many applications. However, the rationale for choosing a specific device and technology for use in a particular product is not often easy to quantify. There are performance tradeoffs among the different technologies on a number of dimensions. Given that there are multiple alternative technologies available (i.e., more than

---

[10] Even where such data are available, of course, they seldom provide definitive views as to the elasticity of substitution between two products.

[11] After all, auto makers needs for mature products, such as rolled steel from a specific producer may be relatively simple to understand (even by economists). However, their ability to utilize the electronic components produced by a specific manufacturer may not at all be obvious to non-technical analysts. Since, to a great extent, economic substitutability will depend on such assessments, this information is obviously relevant to an antitrust analyst.

two — often four or more), the assessment of substitution possibilities is even more problematical. This is particularly true because some technologies are clearly more expensive than other alternatives in terms of total costs. However, in terms of marginal costs and/or functionality, particular technologies may possess some key advantages in some circumstances.

This points to two quite different ways of viewing substitution in some circumstances. According to one view, it is the particular characteristics that are required for the end product that influence (or even determine) the choice of input technology that is incorporated. This requires that the manufacturer of the end product choose, say, the product's performance characteristics prior to designing the final product. According to the second view of substitution, makers of end products choose the input technology (or combination of input technologies) based on the functionality tradeoffs they present, and the manufacturer's views of the value of these tradeoffs. The resulting end products have features or characteristics that reflect these tradeoffs (that is, the features the product offers are not pre-determined but are an outcome of the engineering and design process).

While the differences between these views may appear to be rather subtle at first glance, the implications for market definition can be far-reaching. Under the first view — termed a "top-down" approach because it is the desired functionality in the end product that dictates choice of input technology — the scope for substitutability may be limited (or at least may appear so). The manufacturer chooses input technology based on pre-selected product attributes (e.g., the characteristics the end product must have to succeed in the marketplace) Substitution is then limited (or, perhaps, non-existent).

Under the second view — the "bottom-up" approach — the choice is more interactive, with costs and values for the various desired features assessed as a package rather than the desired value for each feature separately derived. The bottom-up approach allows for more freedom of choice among the technological alternatives available and therefore implies much more substitutability. However, the analysis required to establish the degree of substitutability requires a much more detailed (and micro) approach than is generally utilized in defining markets (and substitution possibilities) under the hypothetical monopolist framework employed under the *Merger Guidelines*.

The SSNIP test presents a separate set of challenges for analysis of high technology industries. Absent investigation of a merger or acquisition, when prevailing prices can usually be used as the basis for applying the SSNIP test, the most immediate problem that faces the analyst is the difficulty of identifying the competitive level of prices to be used as a benchmark to assess the impact of a SSNIP. This is much more difficult for highly differentiated products than for commodity or lightly differentiated products. With highly differentiated products, price and performance variations can be very substantial and markets may appear to be fragmented, with many customized products tailored to specific users and/or applications. In such circumstances, even assembling comparable price series for competing products may be difficult or impossible.

Another problem associated with attempts to apply the SSNIP test to high technology industries involves identifying the magnitude of "small, but significant" that should be used in this context. Earlier versions of the *Horizontal Merger Guidelines* specified 5% percent as the appropriate level for analysis. The 1992 and 1997 *Guidelines* were somewhat less prescriptive. As a practical matter, the agencies in the US use anything from 5 to 20%, and claim that the answers rarely differ whatever number between 5 and 20% is used.[12] In high technology industries, where non-price competition is often far more important than price competition, the appropriate price change for antitrust analysis will certainly be larger than five percent. Even at 20%, the SSNIP test may find a plethora of small "markets" involving new products.

Of course, this pints to an even more serious flaw in the use of SSNIP analyses for high technology industries. Because performance competition is usually the central focus of competitive efforts in these industries, the entire concept of SSNIP is awkward, for at least two fundamental reasons. First unlike more mature industries, where performance features often change in more incremental and predictable ways and, in shorthand terms, competitive efforts are focused on price changes, performance competition is at the heart of high technology competition. At times of paradigm shifts, and even in between, substantial performance increases are often achieved by manufacturers. For this reason, it might be more appropriate to focus on those dimensions of competition — i.e., specific measures of performance — that are the focus of competitive efforts.

Second, the entire concept of SSNIP is rather static. When technology, even during periods of incremental change, rather than revolutionary change, is advancing rapidly — with new product life cycles often only months in length — price/performance relationships change rapidly. It is the rate of change (i.e., improvment) in this relationship that is of interest to buyers. Thus, the ratio of price to performance measures over time may be more appropriate means of capturing the competitive dynamic.

---

[12] Based on a conversation with Director of Research, Department of Justice, Washington, DC, December 17, 1998.

Additional problems occur in the measurement and interpretation of market shares and market concentration. Unless, of course, the market is defined correctly, the HHI is meaningless. HHI analysis will overstate industry concentration levels, if markets are defined with reference to product differentiation. This could well lead competition in these industries and to policy errors concerning market definition and market power.

Finally, entry analysis must be reconsidered and substantially recast for application in high technology industries. The standards applied in the *Merger Guidelines* — entry within 1 year for uncommitted entrant and within 2 years for committed entrants — make little sense in many dynamic contexts. A more appropriate benchmark to assess entry is the duration of product or technology life cycles. It is not just immediate entry that tempers behavior in high technology industries; it is also the threat of the next generation of products and services that is of concerns to incumbents. Current leaders must succeed in each round of innovation or lose leadership. In such a dynamic environment, high market shares are fragile and may confer little, if any, future advantage.

Thus, it would be appropriate to view entry analysis more flexibly in high technology industries. While there is always some uncertainty as to the timing of paradigm shifts, it is not "speculative" to take the possibility of such shifts into account. Furthermore, the unpredictability of the timing of such shifts may help to constrain behavior, as current market leaders can never be sure that a shift will not occur tomorrow.

3.2. *Brown Shoe Factors*

While the agencies demonstrate increasing sophistication is dealing with market definition in the context of innovation, the courts are still burdened with case law which does not as yet connect with the realities of the new knowledge economy. In particular, *Brown Shoe* is still utilized from time to time, despite the fact that economic analysis and agency thinking has long eclipsed it. *Brown Shoe* enumerated a number of indicia for identifying markets and "submarkets"[13] (and, indirectly, for assessing market power within those markets). Without discussing the merits (or demerits) of the submarket concept, these indicia are particularly ill-suited to analyzing high technology markets. There are eight such factors set forth in *Brown Shoe* — one for markets and the others for submarkets. Although

---

[13] The assertion of relevant antitrust submarkets within relevant antitrust markets has justifiably been criticized as inherently contradictory and, thus, not at all useful because it requires the simultaneous existence of two types of economic substitutes. See, for example, Simons and Williams (1993).

seven of the eight factors were described by the Court as applying to analysis of submarkets, they have been more generally utilized in attempts to define markets by some economists. The eight factors are:

- interchangeability of use or cross-elasticity of demand;
- sensitivity (of sales) to price change;
- industry or public recognition of the submarket as a separate economic entity;
- the product's peculiar characteristics and uses;
- unique production facilities;
- distinct customers;
- distinct prices; and
- specialized vendors.

Of these factors, only elasticity and cross-elasticity of demand have a strong theoretical foundation as a basis on which to identify market boundaries and measure market power. Unfortunately, for most high technology markets insufficient data exist for estimating elasticities. As an alternative to rigorous estimation of elasticities, the *Brown Shoe* factors allow consideration of "interchangeability of use" and "sensitivity [of sales] to price changes". These suggest less rigorous tests, which consider substitutability more broadly in terms of economic and technical feasibility and, perhaps, in terms of marketplace evidence of actual instances of substitutability. If viewed in this manner, these factors can be of assistance in defining high technology (and other) markets and assessing market power. However, determinations of what constitutes sufficient evidence of economic or technical substitutability and/or of marketplace substitution would have to be matters of the weight and utility of the evidence, since no obvious and definitive economic test of sufficiency exists.

While the other six *Brown Shoe* factors may have some, limited applicability to defining markets and assessing market power in mature, relatively undifferentiated market, they present even greater difficulties in the context of high technology industries. In some cases these factors are entirely inappropriate

For example, "industry or public recognition of the submarket [or market] as a separate economic entity" is almost impossible to operationalize as a standard or test in an antitrust investigation. What constitutes "recognition"? Even if, in a business sense, a market is treated as separate in some manner, does this have any relevance to antitrust analysis?

A "product's peculiar characteristics and uses" are even less useful, since products (and services) in many high technology industries are highly differentiated. Subdividing the relevant market based on the very product differentiation that is one of the fundamental bases for competition risks defining markets much too narrowly and overstating market power, so that monopoly power is found where none, in fact, exists.

"Unique production facilities" are presumably an attempt to inject supply-side substitution effects into the analysis of competition analysis. However, in highly differentiated high technology industries, it is not uncommon for individual, but competing, products to require unique production facilities.[14] Thus, supply side substitution is sufficient, but not necessary, to integrate two otherwise separate "markets".

The "distinct customers" factor is particularly vague and difficult to put in practice. It could refer to either purchaser (users) or applications (uses). Of course, the key factor in defining relevant markets and assessing power in those relevant markets is substitutabilty, which is an empirical question. An *ad hoc* collection of identifiable or convenient groups of users or uses may not constitute a "market" at all.

The "distinct prices" factor also cannot be used for determining market boundaries. There are many reasons why products may compete but sustainable differences in prices may obtain.[15] These include, but are not limited to, differences in prices of complementary goods,[16] quality differences, branding and others. Economic theory, of course, provides some support for the notion that parallel movements in prices for two goods may indicate that they compete against one another in one relevant market. However, this condition may be neither necessary nor sufficient for two products to compete.[17]

The distinct prices factor has also been extended — erroneously in our view — to include "distinctive" — i.e., high — margins as an indicator of market boundaries (and market power). Under this view, producers that enjoy high margins are only able to do so because their prices are insulated from competition by

---

[14] For example, although inkjet and laser printers may compete closely (and indeed be nearly perfect substitutes) in many uses, one cannot produce engines for the former on a production line (or facility) designed to produce the latter.

[15] For example, for households, natural gas and electricity may complete for certain uses, but their energy prices are not the same, even on a heat equivalent (i.e., Btu) basis.

[16] For example, energy-using equipment, such as hot water heaters fueled by gas are generally more expensive than those fueled by electricity, but these differences are offset, to at least some extent, by the lower cost of gas as compared with electricity that pertains in most locales.

[17] Price correlation analyses may be relevant to defining the boundaries of relevant antitrust markets only where relatively low levels of product differentiation exist and where performance/quality differences are relatively stable over time.

substitutes. In some sense, this argument turns the cellophane trap,[18] as well as the problem of market definition, on their heads. That is, high margins are viewed an indicator, in and of themselves, of market power, which must, according to proponents of this view, in turn, be evidence of poor substitutability. To the contrary, particularly when applied in a high technology context, "distinctive" prices for individual products can persist in integrated relevant markets. For example, legal protection (e.g., from patents), the unique nature of the technology and/or the ability to protect proprietary information may affect the appropriability of the innovation by the wider market. In addition, product differentiation may affect margins.

More importantly, a focus on margins as an indicator of either market boundaries or market power is entirely inappropriate. Empirical research has not supported the position that market share or concentration is particularly correlated with accounting margins.[19] In addition, high net margins may merely be reflective of the high returns required on successful products, given the inherent uncertainty and riskiness of such investments.[20] High gross margins, which are even less appropriate in our view as an indicator of market definition or market power, merely reflect the division of costs between direct manufacturing costs and other costs. Research and development (R&D) costs, which may have to be maintained at relatively high levels to sustain market leadership (or even protect market share) are completely ignored when gross margins are used.

The final *Brown Shoe* factor is specialized vendors. This factor is particularly inappropriate for deriving market boundaries in high technology markets because specialized vendors are often utilized by producers in high technology industries for several reasons. These include situations where specialized knowledge is required to apply the technology (or utilize the product that incorporates it), where complementary assets are required that are more efficiently provided by vendors and/or where there may be free rider problems if a mix of specialized and non-specialized vendors are used.

Thus, the *Brown Shoe* factors are inappropriate bases for analysis of either market boundaries or market power in high technology industries. They do not

---

[18] *United States vs. E.I. duPont de Nemours and Co.* 351 US 377 (1956).

[19] For example, see Scherer and Ross (1990), pp. 422–423. Demsetz (1973) has also cast doubt on the relationship between industry concentration and efficiency.

[20] Note that most such investments do not produce positive returns. For example, see the work of Mansfield (1977). These observations he made about success rates remain valid as noted in several sources, both academic and popular (e.g., see *Marketing News* issues from February 1, 1993 and June 21, 1993).

reflect an appreciation either of the basis for competition in such industries or of specific nature of the innovative process.

4. Problems in Applying Traditional Indicia in High Technology Contexts

Technology-driven competition is frequently fierce. Standard ways of viewing competition and markets are usually inadequate. For example, the traditional indicia for defining relevant antitrust markets (and/or assessing market power in those markets) generally result in markets that are too narrow — because they exclude substitute products or services that should be included. As a consequence, market power would be overestimated. In the subsections that follow, we discuss three examples where traditional indicia have led to erroneous conclusions regarding market definition.

4.1. *The Legal System in Action.*
   Example 1: The Overcurrent Protection Market

Overcurrent protection devices (OCPD) are used in a wide variety of situations to protect electric and electronic circuits from the damage that would result if current flow to the product exceeded design tolerances. There are many applications for OCPD, ranging from the massive circuit protection devices used at high-voltage substations for electricity networks to circuit breakers used in homes, to fuses used in most automobiles to protect lighting, power windows, and other circuits.

PPTCs (polymeric positive temperature coefficient devices) are a newer class of high technology, low current, OCPD that were developed by Raychem Corporation, after substantial R&D investments, and were first marketed in the 1980s. PPTCs are essentially a resettable fuse.[21] Low-current OCPDs, such as PPTCs, are used in such applications as personal computer and other electronic devices (ranging from toys to medical diagnostic equipment), telecommunications equipment, batteries, and automobiles. Several other low current OCPD technologies have long been utilized. Subsequent to the introduction of PPTCs,

---

[21] PPTCs employ a low resistance conductive polymer that undergoes a phase change in electrical characteristics when its temperature increases (i.e., under higher current loads). When the temperature is reduced, it reverts to its low resistance state. As such, PPTCs work much like a conventional fuse, except that they can reset themselves automatically once an overcurrent situation is corrected.

integrated circuit overcurrent protection devices — sometimes referred to as "Smart Power" — have been introduced.

PPTCs have been a tremendous spur to competition for all type of low-current OCPDs in the last decade. For a lengthy period of time, the industry was characterized by a slow rate of technological change and displayed some of the characteristics of a mature industry. Technological competition was muted. However, with the introduction of more redical innovations — first PPTCs and then Smart Power — the industry has been transformed. As a consequence, R&D activity by developers of all technologies increased dramatically.[22]

Currently, the manufacturers of the different OCPD technologies are engaged in continuous innovation to develop new applications, improve performance and reduce costs. The rapid pace of innovation in the last decade in particular has often served to increase the degree of products that capitalize on the specific advantages of each of these technologies. These developments, in turn, have strengthened and accentuated the relative advantages and disadvantages of different overcurrent protection products and technologies. This has important implications for the specific OCPD purchase decisions made by individual buyers, who can choose from among several different technologies for most applications. Ultimately, the existence of unique sets of attributes for each technology implies that, for any specific user and application, a "best" choice will exist. This may not be the device or technology that unambiguously provides the best technical performance, but one that provides the best combination of technical features at a certain price point.

Recent litigation in federal court[23] concerned allegations that Raychem, the developer of PPTC overcurrent protection devices, had violated antitrust laws in alleged attempts to restrict the entry into the marketplace of a competitor, Bourns, Inc., that had introduced similar PPTC devices. Without discussing the merits of the case, the issues relating to market definition and assessment of market power aptly illustrate the problems of employing traditional indicia in a high technology context.

One problem encountered in the case was the lack of comprehensive data on prices and sales of OCPDs to allow estimation of the relevant elasticities. This situation is of course quite common in litigation. Thus, unless a special (and costly) survey is undertaken to collect appropriate data, economic experts must

---

[22] See, e.g., Arthur (1988) for discussion of competition among differentiated technologies.

[23] *Bourns, Inc. v. Raychem Corporation*, US District Court, Central District of California, Case No. CV 98-1765 CM.

rely on data that is anecdotal, incomplete (e.g., covering only a few firms or products), qualitative and/or only partly relevant because it was collected for a different purpose than for antitrust litigation. Furthermore, the analysis of these data must necessarily be framed within a methodology that is sensitive to the characteristics of the competition that has, is, and/or will be taking place.

This case was no different from the norm in this respect; the information available had obvious limitations, but did provide insight to help answer the relevant questions. But, despite the dynamic and innovative backdrop for the overcurrent protection marketplace, the economic expert for Bourns defined and analyzed the market using a variant of the *Brown Shoe* factors. The specific factors he used in his analysis were:

Customer perceptions: a variant of the "public recognition" factor from *Brown Shoe*. In this case, the Bourns' expert utilized mainly marketing materials developed by Raychem, which separated customers into the application categories that the Bourns' expert used as the basis for his market definitions.

Important characteristics, which is related to the "peculiar characteristics" *Brown Shoe* factor. Bourns' economic expert asserted that the particular performance advantages of PPTCs compared with other type of overcurrent protection devices indicated that these other types of devices must be poor substitutes for PPTCs and, therefore PPTCs must exist in a separate market.

Gross profit margins: Bourns' economic expert noted that Raychem's current gross profit margins for PPTCs were high in an absolute sense, as well as high when compared to certain broad industry averages. This index is particularly ill-suited to the definition of markets or the assessment of market power. Beyond the specific facts of this case — Raychem's cumulative internal rate of return over more than two decades on its PPTC overcurrent protection investment was well within industry norms — the use of gross margins for these antitrust purposes implies that short-run marginal costs are an appropriate measure of competitive market prices. This is clearly erroneous, since "imperfectly", but workably, competitive markets can sustain prices above even long-run marginal costs.

Pricing: Bourns' economic expert investigated several aspects of pricing behavior. For example, he utilized information on price levels (the "distinct" priced at a premium to other types of PPTCs). He also concluded that, because PPTC prices had declined faster than prices for most other overcurrent protection devices over a 5-year period, PPTC prices were "independent" of the pricing of other overcurrent protection devices (also related to he "distinct prices" factor). He stated that information that indicated that PPTCs gained share in terms of overall sales of overcurrent protection devices was not relevent to analysis of price independence.[24] He also used "standard" accounting margins as a basis for asserting that Raychem was able to price discriminate[25] and, thus, must have market power.[26]

Price elasticity: Bourns' economic expert also reviewed "findings" on the own-price elasticity of demand for PPTCs that were developed by Raychem's marketing employees. In fact, none of the information developed by Raychem qualified as an "elasticity" calculation, as economists understand the term. Rather, these calculations simply tracked changes in prices and quantities over time.

The Bourns' economic expert concluded that there were seven relevant antitrust "market" — each defined according to the broad application categories used for marketing analysis by Raychem. He maintained that these multiple and distinct markets existed despite the fact that many PPTC devices (as well as overcurrent protection devices that employed other technologies) could be and were in fact utilized in more than one (and sometimes several) applications categories. Furthermore, he maintained that these separate and distinct product markets existed even though the types of applications involved were exactly the same across at least some of the different markets. For example, the predominate OCPD application in the computer, general electronics and low- and high-voltage telecommunications market segments (which the Bourns' expert separated into four separate "markets") was precisely the same — i.e., printed circuit boards.

He further concluded that each of these relevant "markets" was a PPTC-only market because, for each purchaser of PPTCs, that device provided the best combination of technical features and prices — otherwise purchasers would have chosen another device. Not surprisingly, he found that Raychem, as virtually the only maker of PPTCs until very recently, had monopoly power in each of these "markets". He asserted, without supporting analysis, that technically feasible alternative existed, but they were not close enough substitutes to constrain Raychem's PPTC pricing. Thus, all alternative products employing other over current protection technologies existed in separate relevant "markets".

---

[24] In doing so, he rejected the possibility that increasing share during a period of declining declining relative prices (i.e., relative to alternative technologies and products) could be indicative of price responsiveness.

[25] He rejected, without any apparent analysis, the hypothesis that varying margins, by customer, could be the result of other factors. These factors couldinclude different product mixes, different levels of after-sale services provided and many other factors, even though he admitted that such differences did exist and would affect margins observed for sales to individual customers.

[26] He rejected the view that price discrimination could occur in a competitive market. Recent economic analysis, of course, contradicts his view. See, for example, Borenstein (1985).

In reaching this conclusion, Bourns' economic expert ignored ample empirical evidence of competitive behavior in the OCPD industry. He ignored much (admittedly anecdotal) evidence of switches from PPTCs to other technologies by customers, including a recent switch by the single largest consumer of PPTCs devices.[27] Further, he ignored evidence of technological competition such as form factor imitation (practiced by both Raychem and makers of competing devices), dynamic fluctuations in market share (particularly over the medium term — 2–5 years), and threats from entirely new technologies that had been developed and introduced into the marketplace. He even ignored several prominent examples where PPTCs and competing overcurrent protection devices were used interchangeably in the same manufacturer's product.

This case points to a fundamental flaw in the use of traditional market definition and market power assessment indicia — such as the *Brown Shoe* factors — when they are applied to high technology industries and any market with highly differentiated products. Most importantly, the traditional indicia fail to capture the full scope of competition in high technology markets. Market shares often shift markedly over time frames that, unfortunately, fall outside of the entry analysis specified in the *Merger Guidelines*. For example, external port applications for personal computers (e.g., printer ports, mouse ports and the new Universal Serial Bus — USB — ports) have been an evolving and dynamic battleground for overcurrent protection device makers. In the early 1990s, fuses predominated, but, by 1995, PPTCs held the largest share of sales. Even before this shift in sales, however, the threat from Smart Power solutions began to affect the market. Today, Smart Power and PPTCs have approximately equal shares. Entry analysis under the *Guidelines* approach — which focuses on 1–2-year time horizons — artificially narrows the analysis of competition in this and similar markets and masks the dynamic nature of competition and the constraints on the exercise of market power.

In fact, use of traditional indicia, such as the *Brown Shoe* factors, will inevitably favor a piecemeal, narrow approach that obscures the nature of competition and leads to findings of narrow, separate, and isolated markets. In high technology markets, products are often physically distinct. Entry with duplicate products is often difficult (because of trade secrets or intellectual property protections) or may even be competitively unwise (since product differentiation can be a source of competitive advantage under some circumstances). Competition is generally

---

[27] This customer alone accounted for nearly 10% of all PPTC sales. Further, the anecdotal evidence consisted of a large number (i.e., literally dozens) of examples of actual or threatened swithes by customers that represented a substantial fraction of Raychem's PPTC business.

based on performance (thereby leading to "distinct prices" for each product) and suppliers often utilize specialized vendors (who must develop specialized knowledge and specialized complementary assets to sell and service products). Narrow focus on such differences inevitably leads to the assertion of narrow markets.

In the Raychem case, given the overwhelming evidence on the fierce nature of inter-technology competition and the high level of innovative activity on the part of makers of the various technologies, both the judge and the jury came to the only reasonable conclusion. With one exception, PPTCs were seen to compete in a broad maket with other overcurrent protection devices. In fact, the judge labeled the Bourns' economic expert's market definitions a "tautology" based on his view that buyers entered and exited markets depending on which overcurrent protection technology they purchased. Unfortunately, the courts and even distinguished economists do not always recognize these fallacies.

4.2. The Legal System in Action.
Example 2: The Vascular Solutions Market

Vascular graft technologies are used to repair or replace diseased or damaged blood vessels. These technologies are but a subset of a wider range of treatments that are available for this purpose.

Many natural (e.g., human and animal) and synthetic (e.g., dacron and PTFE which is chemically related to Teflon) materials are utilized for grafts. Each of these graft materials has unique advantages and disadvantages in different situations. While each is used only for specific types of grafts, there is considerable overlap in applications, with the choice depending in part on each surgeon's preference and training. There are virtually no important applications where substitute materials are not commonly used.

Sales of graft materials are unusual in that the ultimate consumer — i.e., the person receiving the graft — has little or no input at all into the choice among competing products. Surgeons, sometimes with input from health plan administrators, have primary responsibility for the selection. Choices among the alternatives for any particular application in a specific patient are made based on peer choice, clinical trial results, experience (particularly during training), and patient health. Brand identification and customer loyalty are also significant factors in choice. Most surgeons utilize multiple materials in their practices. Cost of the material is not a significant factor because patients and physicians are focused on performance and because the cost of the procedure dwarfs the cost of the material. Thus, low sensitivity to price would be expected.

In addition to considerable demand-side substitutability among materials, there are three salient facts concerning market structure that indicate the competitive nature of the marketplace. First, there is considerable competition among suppliers of the basic synthetic materials, including PTFE. Second, while FDA approval represents a formidable entry barrier for innovators, many firms have undertaken research in vascular grafts and represent significant potential competition, not least because the possibility of a breakthrough technology (e.g., from biotechnology research) in such an innovative industry is so great. Third, excluding saphenous veins harvested from the patient's own body (an obvious substitute for synthetics), numerous manufacturers compete for share both in the US and worldwide, with no supplier having a dominant share.

In the early 1990s antitrust claims were filed against Gore, the leading maker of PTFE vascular grafts that, inter alia, alleged that Gore had monopolized and attempted to monopolized the market (and submarkets) for PTFE vascular grafts. The claims were filed by Impra, one of Gore's competitors.[28] The allegations concerned restraint of trade violations relating to PTFE resins — an essential input for the manufacture of PTFE vascular grafts — as well as other monopolization claims. As implied by the allegations, Impra defined the relevant antitrust market quite narrowly, confining it to PTFE vascular grafts. It also defined submarkets within this market based on the size (i.e., diameter) of these grafts.

The plaintiff attempted to utilize a static, narrow framework, centered on a mechanistic application of traditional market analysis. The plaintiff's expert did not consider that non-graft treatments might compete against grafts. He focused on the physical differences among the different vascular graft materials and the fact that the decision-makers who chose the graft materials were very insensitive to and often unaware of price and concluded that makers of PTFE grafts could profitably impose a SSNIP. This, he contended, indicated that PTFE grafts existed in a separate market.

However, the vascular solutions/treatment business cannot be appropriately analyzed using conventional tools. Orthodoxy is clearly at odds with reality when nearly all participants freely acknowledged that price was unimportant, yet fierce competition was readily apparent and widely recognized.

For example, there was strong evidence that vascular solutions — a much broader marketplace — was the relevant antitrust market in this instance. While

---

[28] As is common, these claims (like the antitrust claims raised by Bourns in *Bourns v. Raychem*) were advanced as counterclaims to an intellectual property suit.

not every treatment is appropriate in each individual case, advances in non-graft treatments have been providing and will continue to provide competing alternatives to grafts. This is particularly applicable in the long-run, since the need for grafts should decline as alternative treatments extent the "useful life" of tissue that might otherwise have to be replaced. In fact, several medical studies have noted the substitution effect of alternative — e.g., drug-based or other invasive procedures — treatments.[29] Since these treatments are so differentiated from vascular graft technologies, traditional relevant market definition methods are unlikely to define markets correctly.

As with overcurrent protection devices, there was no source of information readily available that provided data on the cost and number of treatments purchased. Thus, quantitative estimation of elasticities was virtually impossible. Instead, incomplete enecdotal information had to be used. Most importantly, the key to proper market definition is an appreciation of the nature and type of competition that takes place in this industry.

In fact, the basis for competition in this industry, as in most high technology industries undergoing rapid innovation, is performance. Performance criteria are most salient, particularly because the consequential benefits and detriments of performance are perceived as so substantial. Suppliers consistently strive to improve the performance characteristics of their products. These dimensions of competition are no less tangible and important than price. Ignoring them, in a single-minded and narrow focus on pricing, is inappropriate. This performance-based competition provides the basis for broadening the market definition beyond grafts to include at least some other types of treatment. Further, there are considerable R&D efforts on a wide range of fronts by a large number of companies to develop new treatments. Thus, potential competition is also likely to be a significant concern.

4.3. The Legal System in Action.
Example 3: The Medical Imaging Market[30]

Diagnostic imaging devices are used by physicians and other health care providers to view inside the human body without intervention. As with overcurrent protection devices and vascular solutions, medical imaging devices are highly differentiated on various dimensions. The different technologies employed include traditional

---

[29] Source: The Wilkerson Group, Inc., CV/MIS Profile #10-Vascular Grafts, July 1987, pp. 37–39.

[30] This section is drawn largely from Hartman et al. (1993).

X-ray instrumentation, nuclear imaging, ultrasound devices, CAT (or CT) scanners, magnetic resonance imaging (MRI) and digital radiography.

Each of these technologies has a unique set of characteristics that help determine when and under what circumstances they are employed as diagnostic tools, although there is considerable overlap in both capabilities and usage. Given the substantial performance variation among these technologies and the fact that large price differences persist both within and across these technologies, it is not surprising that performance attributes are of central importance in competition among these products and technologies.

In general, there is a rough trade-off between price and performance in this industry, but the trade-off is not and has not been stable. As with most high technology industries this instability is magnified by the coincident evolution of price and performance attributes. For example, early nuclear imaging devices could distinguish only between tissues that were centimeters apart, while more recent equipment can provide spatial resolution of a few millimeters or less.

Importantly, as the performance characteristics of the technology improved, often dramatically, prices did not necessarily follow a consistent path. Even within technologies, there has not been a monotonic movement of prices, as prices reflect capabilities. In fact, dramatic improvements in capabilities often are associated with substantial increases in price.

The industry began in the 1890s with the development of conventional X-ray devices. Nuclear imaging and ultrasound technology was first developed in the early 1940s, although commercialization of these technologies did not occur until the 1950s. CT scanners were first developed in the early 1960s and commercialized in the mid 1970s, at about the same time that MRI and digital radiography technologies were first developed. There was considerable lag between commercial introduction and commercial success for each of these technologies, although with more recent technologies this lag has decreased to a few years from a decade or more for some earlier technologies.

In terms of sales, X-ray devices dominated the industry until the latter 1970s. By the late 1980s, sales of X-ray devices constituted less than 30% of all medical imaging device sales, measured in dollar terms, although they still accounted for the largest share of sales of all medical diagnostic imaging devices.

The historical development of each of the technologies is even more interesting and manifests the dynamic nature of the industry. The competitive situation for CT scanners was typical. They were first developed as a practical medical diagnostic instrument by the British firm EMI. Initially, they were used in neurological imaging, at the time the primary application for nuclear imaging devices. CT scanners, although they were 4–5 times as expensive as nuclear imaging devices at the time, produced much clearer images.

EMI sold its first CT scanner unit in 1972. Competition quickly become vigorous, with the entry of several firms in 1974–75. During this period entrants improved upon the device. By 1977, there were 12 companies making CT scanners for sale in the US. The competition proved too much for EMI, which, under severe financial pressure, sold its scanner business to Thorn PLC in 1979. Subsequently this business was sold again — in the international operations to General Electric and the US operations to Omnimedical, Inc.[31] By the mid 1980s, most early entrants into the CT scanner business had exited, while more recent entrants dominated the sales of this device.

The attempted acquisition of Thorn EMI's CT scanner business by GE in 1980 brought the market definition question in this industry to the fore. The resolution of that case manifested the problems that persist in trying to identify markets in high technology industries. GE was ultimately frustrated in its efforts to acquire Thorn EMI's US scanner business because the Department of Justice was concerned that such an acquisition would increase GE's US share of the CT scanner business to levels that would raise competitive concerns in that narrow "market".

Subsequent developments have demonstrated that such concerns were misplaced. In fact, sales of CT scanners were already generally declining in 1980. While they temporarily increased again and reached a global peak in 1983, they never again attained those levels. The key to these sales trends was competition from other medical imaging technologies.

Indeed, the inter-technology competition in the medical imaging business is the key to understanding the competitive pressures and competitive strategies more broadly in this market. For example, in the early 1970s incumbent makers of nuclear imaging devices began to face competition on two fronts — from entrants that developed improved nuclear imaging equipment and from newly introduced CT scanners. However, although CT scanners were outselling nuclear imaging devices within 3 years (i.e., by 1975), CT scanners only partially supplanted them as diagnostic tools.

CT scanners were followed by MRI equipment. Introduced commercially in 1980, MRI devices produced even clearer images and with less invasiveness. Thus, although more expensive than CT scanners, MRI devices posed a formidable sales threat and, in turn, partially supplanted CT technology in the marketplace. Despite this technological success, however, the first three firms to introduce

---

[31] GE had wanted to purchase the entire scanner business of Thorn, but was deterred from doing so by a Justice Department investigation. Omnimedical's operations survived only into the early 1980s.

MRI technology has either exited the industry or were facing financial trouble by the late 1980s. Later entrants, which had introduced technically superior products and had provided better customer support, gained the major share of sales and enjoyed commercial success.

A review of the development of each of the new medical imaging technologies introduced in the past few decades actually manifests strikingly similar patterns. Each of the technologies has exhibited extremely high HHIs during the early period of commercial development. However, in a very short period of time, there had been substantial entry and very dynamic competition, driving down HHIs over periods of 5–10 years (see Table 1). In virtually all cases, the early pioneers in the industry did not even survive as leaders in the business through the first decade after market introduction.

Within each technology a snapshot HHI might lead one to conclude that market power existed. However, dynamic considerations would completely undermine such a conclusion. Even ignoring the impact of other technologies on competition, market leadership in any specific technology during these early years conferred no real market power. Early "monopolists" were generally and with alacrity displaced by competitors producing improved products employing the same basic technology or, even more significantly, producing differentiated, but highly efficacious products employing a totally different technology.

The tenuous character of technology leadership was often quite apparent contemporaneously with these market developments. This strongly suggests that static structural frameworks and techniques for defining markets and assessing market power are inappropriate and misleading in the context of industries undergoing rapid technological change. It would be far more useful in the medical diagnostic imaging industry, for example, to look at the combined impact of all relevant technologies when evaluating competition and market power (e.g., see the combined HHIs in Table 1). Among these technologies, performance competition was particularly fierce and concentration quite low throughout the period.

It is also significant that the competition that developed did not develop in a manner that may be familiar to those who study the long-term history of many industries that are now considered "mature". The technological competition in the medical imaging industry did not, as in railroad transportation or steel manufacturing, result in the complete replacement of older technologies by newer technologies (e.g., the replacement of the steam engine by the diesel electric engine). Competition in the medical imaging industry followed a path that is quite common in high technology industries (such as overcurrent protection) – makers of older technologies have been spurred to more vigorous technological

Table 1. Implied Hirschman–Herfindahl indices (HHI) 1961–1987.[a]

Year	X-ray	Nuclear imaging	Diagnostic ultrasound	CT scan	Magnetic resonance	Digital radiography	All modalities
1961	1469	5048	5000	—	—	—	1464
1962	1467	4718	4950	—	—	—	1461
1963	1548	4859	2904	—	—	—	1533
1964	1529	4719	3004	—	—	—	1494
1965	1326	4472	2293	—	—	—	1281
1966	1239	4582	2143	—	—	—	1173
1967	1158	4638	2152	—	—	—	1102
1968	1158	4715	2292	—	—	—	1060
1969	1268	4019	2363	—	—	—	1122
1970	1273	3089	1944	—	—	—	1089
1971	1284	3054	1353	—	—	—	1060
1972	1631	3894	1836	—	—	—	1297
1973	1578	2353	2293	10000	—	—	1253
1974	1507	2130	1190	9608	—	—	1133
1975	1527	1807	1141	5335	—	—	1005
1976	1556	1733	1073	3570	—	—	928
1977	1508	1648	1117	2468	—	—	961
1978	1675	1438	1072	2268	—	—	1033
1979	1813	1354	830	2428	—	—	1122
1980	1842	1319	822	3620	10000	—	1361
1981	1965	1424	860	3802	5000	3464	1418
1982	1965	1578	945	2992	3082	1404	1519
1983	1957	1450	942	2385	2794	1511	1408
1984	1948	1317	915	1848	2024	1220	1240
1985	1949	1426	772	1826	2489	1491	1341
1986	1949	1285	743	2212	1843	2403	1328
1987	2414	1794	1475	2576	2374	2222	1637

[a] Source: Mithcell (1988).

development by new technologies that have entered the marketplace. In this manner, the older technologies have been "renewed" and continue to enjoy market success. Such responses clearly indicate that different technologies compete. In addition, increasing specialization has occurred as competing technologies strive to serve niches with products optimized to perform certain tasks, but it is silly to characterize such niches as relevant markets.

In attempting to evaluate the level and nature of competition in the industry, traditional analytic tools are inadequate. For example, the *Merger Guidelines* framework, with its emphasis on small, but significant, price changes as the basis for market definition, seems particularly inappropriate in this context.[32] In fact, the competitive challenge delivered by new technologies in this industry had little to do with price (and certainly not price in isolation from other performance characteristics), as performance has been the focus of competitive efforts. Thus, the medical diagnostic imaging industry has, for decades, experienced numerous successful challenges to existing technology by more expensive technologies that possess improved performance.

In addition to ignoring the importance of performance competition in a high technology context, the analytical framework developed within the *Merger Guidelines* also implicitly undervalues the importance of potential competition, from vendors of both improvements in existing technologies and entirely new technologies. In particular, the short time horizon — 1 year for uncommitted entrants and 2 years for committed entrants — is biased against the reality of competition in high technology industries. For example, in the medical diagnostic imaging industry, the lead time from research and development to commercial success was much longer than 1–2 years, but vendors of existing technologies have had to respond to potential threats as a matter of course. Even after introduction of new technologies, the full extent of the threat to incumbent technologies was not manifest within a short time period, but, nevertheless, required vigorous competitive responses (i.e., both short-run and long-run strategic action) from manufacturers of existing technologies. This is consistent with the observation that in high technology industries it is potential and emerging competition that is often most threatening. Yet this aspect of the competitiv process is usually difficult or impossible to incorporate into static assessment methods.

5. New Indicia for Antitrust Analysis of High Technology Markets

As noted in Teece and Coleman (1998), defining markets from a static perspective when innovation is rapid will inevitably lead to the identification of markets that are too narrow.[33] This will, in turn, tend to overstate market power in many

---

[32] Even raising the "small but significant" threshold to 20% (which we understand the agencies do from time to time) may not cure the problem in part because price/performance relationships can change so dramatically over relatively short time periods.

[33] pp. 826–828.

circumstances. Thus, the emphasis in the *Guidelines* on short-term entry — 1–2 years — and price rather than performance competition will reinforce the bias toward findings of monopoly power in high technology markets. Put differently, a mechanical application of the *Guidelines* and *Brown Shoe* will find high technology industries riddled with monopolists, despite the obvious truth that high technology markets almost always present competitive circumstances which are far more vigorous than in many more mature markets. Because monopolies will be "found" when they do not exist, business practices will be scrutinized unnecessarily. In high technology markets, therefore, there is a substantial chance that traditional antitrust analysis and tools will result in findings that anticompetitive behavior exists when such behavior may well be pro-competitive.

What is needed is a set of tools and analytical techniques that would eliminate or, more likely, reduce the chance for such errors, to ensure that the incentives for innovation are not harmed. Others, such as Yao and deSanti (1993) and Ordover and Baumol (1988) have recognized some of the particular problems in assessing market definition and market power in high technology industries, but have proposed no real alternative analytical methods.

Hartman *et al.* (1993) have suggested a potential candidate technique for defining high technology markets that may be appropriate.[34] This was advanced again in Teece and Coleman (1998).[35] A hedonic framework was suggested to analyze the interaction of price and performance, including a tentative 25% threshold for performance parameters and four year entry horizon for analysis within the general framework set forth in the *Merger Guidelines*. Such a threshold would, in fact, generally be quite conservative, since multidimensional performance attributes are common in these markets. In such circumstances, a 25% change in one performance parameter would be equivalent to a small change in overall performance, particularly if interaction terms were important (i.e., customers were interested not only in single, stand-alone attributes but the interaction of those attributes on performance).

We recognize that the earlier proposal is not the only way to proceed. Here we suggest several alternative approaches. None of these, by itself, may be sufficient for defining markets and/or assessing market power, but in combination they should be more effective than the static-based analysis embodied in the *Guidelines*. In developing these measures we have tried to be pragmatic to assist the courts, as well as competition policy authorities.

---

[34] See pp. 855–856.

[35] See p. 69.

5.1. Defining High Technology Markets

First, as a very pragmatic and qualitative measure, a wide-angle lens is needed to assess competition. This is because, in high technology industries, there are often market niches where one differentiated product may gain an advantage — in some cases a substantial advantage — over the alternative solutions available to users. But common sense tells us that a myriad of such narrow niches cannot be relevant antitrust markets, in most cases because effective competition cuts across them.

Of particular importance in constructing a broad view of competitive activity is technology competition. If technology competition has "depth", with a number of firms' products and/or technologies advancing along a number of similar dimensions and applications, competition is likely to be very robust indeed. In fact, rapid innovation from a number of sources — even in dissimilar technologies (as long as they have similar applications) should be recognized as a hallmark of broad competitive activity and should shift the burden to those who argue for narrow markets. In such circumstances, price differences are sustainable because performance differences may be sustained. Importantly, participants in such a market are forced to continuously improve their products to maintain share.

In fact, an inquiry into the dimensions of competition would almost certainly be useful. Competition driven by new products and features is especially important. It may be useful to identify customer views about the extent of competition. In addition, such research may help to quantify the relative importance of various performance parameters, which may assist in developing a performance-based index akin to the one suggested in Hartman *et al.* (1993). Finally, by quantifying customer needs and customer response to product innovation by various suppliers, the information gained may help to determine whether the innovative and other "competitive" activity that has occurred (or is being alleged) constrains behavior sufficiently to support a specific market definition. In the example of overcurrent protection devices, because behavior by suppliers is directed mainly toward performance parameters that are very important to customers (i.e., that the customers value highly), the finding of broad markets can likely be sustained.

Another indicator of a broad competitive market in high technology markets would be substantial shifts in share over time — e.g., at least 4–5 years. Where this has occurred and, importantly, is (or has been) expected to occur, this should be viewed as definitive evidence of competitive forces and a broad market. In such circumstances, monotonic gains by one product or technology are not necessarily an indication that such a product or technology is insulated from competitive forces. If this gain is sustained only by out-innovating others in the market, competition may be broad and powerful.

For example, in 1992 Raychem viewed the threat from Smart Power as potentially powerful and likely emerge in the next 3–4 years (sooner in some cases). The fact that it had not yet emerged as powerfully as expected by 1997 should not be taken as an indication that potential competition from that source had not constrained Raychem's behavior, particularly given the advances in semiconductor technology that had occurred over the interim. It may only have been Raychem's ability to press on and succeed in its innovative activity for PPTCs that kept the threat of Smart Power at bat. Such market conditions do not indicate narrow markets or unconstrained monopolies.

Thus, indicia for defining high technology markets must focus on competitive conditions and competitive activity. There must be an investigation of behavior and actions and generally over a longer time horizon than the standard 1–2 years. Standard indicia, and particularly the hypothetical monopolist test, using the SSNIP (at or near a 5–10% level) will surely define markets too narrowly. If it is difficult to determine an appropriate SSNIP (whether the "P" is interpreted as "price" or "performance") so that markets can be confidently defined, then one can endeavor to assess whether monopoly power exists by assessing:

- Innovative activity (e.g., research and development expenditures and trends, product innovations and introductions, and performance enhancements);
- competitive activity (e.g., shifts in share, the impact of potential entry, shifts in customer purchases); and
- pricing responses and flexibility.

Where innovative activity is high, it is unlikely that monopoly power exists. High R&D spending relative to sales is generally an indication that participants view product performance as the ultimate arbiter of competitive strength. Furthermore, potential competition can also generally be assessed in such terms, as potential entrants attempt to match or even leapfrog existing technology to secure of foothold in the market. Unfortunately, particularly for potential entrants or even current participants with diversified activities (i.e., who participant in multiple relevant antitrust markets), assessing the magnitude and specific impact of R&D activities is usually problematic. However, this does not excuse the analyst from investigating such issue and attempting an evaluation of their impact on market definition — whether quantitative or, more likely, qualitative.

5.2. Evaluating Market Power

Of course, once the market is properly defined, there may be no need to proceed further to assessing market power. Where markets are broad, shares may be so small that there is little or no likelihood that anticompetitive behavior is possible. Where some question remains, however, there may be scope for developing/ specifying new indicia for such purposes.

If high profit margins are being advanced as indicia of monopoly power, the burden should fall upon the complainant to establish the extent and source of any rents being earned. As noted in Teece and Coleman (1998) the source of profits can generally be subdivided into three types — monopoly (Porterian), scarcity (Ricardian), and entrepreneurial (Schumpeterian). They are not always easy to distinguish. In high technology contexts, Ricardian and Schumpeterian rents will be common. The long-term economic consequences of discouraging the creation of scarcity and entrepreneurial rents could well be severe. Extreme care should therefore be used in making decisions about the existence of monopoly power.

Clearly, the use of high margins as an indicator either of market definition or market power is inappropriate in high technology contexts. Most obviously, many (some would say most) innovative efforts fail to result in a commercially successful product, even in firms that are well-known as successful innovators. Thus, successful products, in successful firms, require high returns to 'pay back' the most of unsuccessful R&D efforts. Absent the chance to earn high returns on research and development and innovative activities, firms would normally avoid such activities, given the high risk they entail. Certainly, a competition policy that simply (and rigidly) classified high returns as monopoly returns, with concordant antitrust liability, would only increase risk, thereby increasing further the returns that investors require.

Even more irrelevant to assessing monopoly power (or to defining markets) are indicators like gross margins. Gross margins do not include the R&D expenditures nor do they even include incremental selling costs. In competitive high technology markets, substantial, on-going R&D costs may be mandatory to increase or even maintain share, as competitors race to develop improved products or even to trigger the next paradigm shift. High incremental selling costs may also be incurred for innovative products as consumers may require educational services, value-added services or other specialized assistance to employ the product.

As an alternative, it is possible that an analysis of a firm's R&D portfolio may be of assistance in evaluating whether monopoly returns are being earned. Thus, even if high rates are being earned on one — or even a few — such projects, a competitive rate of return on the portfolio may be indicative — although not definitive — that monopoly returns are not present.

Finally, some analysis of the likely duration of the monopoly or monopoly power must be undertaken. Where power is relatively transient (or thought likely to be), it is generally (perhaps, always) innocuous. In such cases intervention may even be counterproductive, since it might disrupt the smooth functioning of the existing market.

Only if both market analysis and the analyses of rents and R&D portfolio returns indicate monopoly power should the inquiry pass to the next stage of the inquiry — specification and evaluation of alleged anticompetitive behavior.

Further, assessing the impact of R&D on market structure and behavior is as important to assessing market power as it is on market definition. The information that capable rivals are developing competitive (or, often, superior — in performance terms) products can be a powerful influence on the behavior of current market participants even if that R&D may not result in viable products within the 1–2-year framework identified in the *Merger Guidelines* analytical framework. Thus, a qualitative and, if possible, quantitative analysis of the likely impact of R&D activity on market power issues is critical for understanding the competitive dynamic in high technology/rapidly innovating industries and contexts.

6. Conclusions

There are no hard and fast indicia that lend themselves to precise definitions of markets in high technology contexts. However, the traditional indicia will typically define markets too narrowly and should not be used, at least not mechanically.

In their place, a qualitative analysis is likely to be less flawed. One should endeavor to address and analyze competitive circumstances rather broadly. Particularly if innovation competition across producers and/or technologies can be established on a wide front (i.e., beyond just isolated anecdotes), the burden should shift to the narrow market advocates to establish their case.

Survey research may be required and may be desirable to establish the most important dimensions of competitive efforts and the attitudes of customers. Such a survey might in fact help establish a performance-based SSNIP that could be used to define markets.

For assessing market power in such industries, the market definition exercise may provide obvious answers. If market power is provisionally identified, an analysis of rents would be useful to identify whether market power is in fact potentially troublesome or simply the outcome of innovation, entrepreneurial efforts, and /or natural scarcity.

We are disturbed by the low degree of attention to these issues in the literature. The agencies and the courts appear extremely reluctant to tackle the issues we have identified. Academic scholars have been quite slow to assist, perhaps because the issues seem so daunting and the ramifications too hostile to received wisdom. Whatever the reason, the imperative exists. Mainstream scholars will have much to answer for if they do not engage these issues vigorously. In our view, serious treatment of these issues is long overdue.

References

Arthur, B., 1988. Competing technologies: an overview. In: Dosi G. *et al.* (Ed.), Technical Change and Economic Theory. Printer, London, pp. 590–607.

Audretsch, D.B., 1995. In: Innovation and Industry Evolution. MIT Press, Cambridge, MA.

Borenstein, S., 1985. Price discrimination in free entry markets. Rand Journal of Economics 16, 380–397.

Demsetz, H., 1973. Industry structure, market rivalry, and public policy. Journal of Law and Economics 16, 1–10.

Hartman, R., Teece, D., Mitchell, W., Jorde, T., 1993. Assessing market power in regimes of rapid technological change. Industrial and Corporate Change. 2, 317–350.

Henderson, R.M., Clark, K.B., 1990. Architectural innovation: the reconfiguration of existing product technologies and the failure of established firms. Administrative Science Quarterly 35, 9–30.

Mansfield, E., 1977. In: The Production and Application of New Industrial Technology. Norton, New York.

Mitchell, W., 1988. Dynamic Commercialization: Innovation in the Medical Diagnostic Imaging Industry. Unpublished doctoral dissertation, School of Business, University of California, Berkeley.

Ordover, J., Baumol, W., 1988. Antitrust policy and high-technology industries. Oxford Review of Economic Policy 4, 13–34.

Scherer, F.M., Ross, J., 1990. In: Industrial Market Structure and Economic Performance, 3rd Edition. Houghton Mifflin, Boston.

Schumpeter, J.A., 1942. In: Capitalism, Socialism and Democracy. Harper and Row, New York.

Simons, J., Williams, M., 1993. The renaissance of market definition. The Antitrust Bulletin 38, 799–857.

Teece, D., Coleman, M., 1998. The meaning of monopoly: antitrust analysis in high technology industries. *Antitrust Bulletin* 43, 801–857.

US Department of Justice and Federal Trade Commission, Horizontal Merger Guidelines, revised 1992 and 1997.

Utterback, J., 1996. In: Mastering the Dynamics of Innovation. Harvard Business School Press, Harvard.

Yao, D., de Santi, S., 1993. Innovation issues under the 1992 Merger Guidelines. Antitrust Law Journal 61, 505–521.

V

Technological Innovation and the Theory of the Firm

Towards an Economic Theory of the Multiproduct Firm*

David J. Teece

University of California, Berkeley, CA 94720, U.S.A.

This paper outlines a theory of the multiproduct firm. Important building blocks include excess capacity and its creation, market imperfections, and the peculiarities of organizational knowledge, including its fungible and tacit character. A framework is adopted in which profit seeking firms are seen to diversify in order to avoid the high transactions costs associated with using various markets to trade the services of various specialized assets. Neoclassical explanations of the multiproduct firm are shown to be seriously deficient.

1. Introduction

"Of all outstanding characteristics of business firms, perhaps the most inadequately treated in economic analysis is the diversification of their activities" [Penrose (1959, p. 104)]. Little progress has been made since Penrose registered her dismay. Accordingly, the theory of the firm has yet to accommodate one of the principal features of the modern business enterprise — its multiproduct character. The mission of this paper is to outline how this deficiency might be rectified. To accomplish this objective it turns out to be necessary to modify the neoclassical theory of the firm to emphasize the distinctive properties of organizational knowledge and the transactions cost properties of market exchange. It is also necessary to make an analytical separation between a theory of diversification and a theory of growth since growth and diversification are not inextricably linked. A central issue for a theory of multiproduct organization is to explain

Reprinted from *Journal of Economic Behavior and Organization* 3 (1982), 39–63.

*I wish to thank Jay Bourgeois, John Cox, Victor Goldberg, Sir John Hicks, Richard Nelson, Jeffrey Pfeffer and Sidney Winter for helpful comments on an earlier draft.

why firms diversify into related and unrelated product lines rather than reinvesting in traditional lines of business or transferring assets directly to stockholders.

An earlier paper [Teece (1980)] argued that the multiproduct firm could not be explained by reference to neoclassical cost functions. Panzar and Willig (1975, p. 3) have argued that economies of scope explain multiproduct organization.[1] While economies of scope explain joint production, they do not explain why joint production must be organized within a single multiproduct enterprise. Joint production can proceed in the absence of multiproduct organization if contractual mechanisms can be devised to share the inputs which are yielding the scope economies. Whereas the earlier paper had the limited objective of exploring the relationship between economies of scope and the scope of the enterprise, the objective here is more ambitious — to outline a theory of multiproduct enterprise.

As mentioned earlier, the existing literature has failed to grapple successfully with the multiproduct firm. Some theories depict the multiproduct firm, particularly when created by mergers and acquisitions, as a manifestation of managerial discretion. Other explanations emphasize how taxes and regulations provide the driving force for diversification. Managers and business policy researchers often explain that value maximization through the capturing of "synergies" lie at the heart of the incentive to diversify. (Rarely, however, are the nature of the efficiencies generating "synergies" spelled out in a convincing fashion.) All of these factors undoubtedly help explain in part the ubiquity of multiproduct firms. The purpose here, however, is to focus on those incentives most likely to be operative in an economy which is dynamically competitive in the Schumpetarian sense, and which are consistent with profit seeking behavior by business firms. This focus is chosen partly because it traverses an essentially unexplored theoretical niche, but also because the perspective holds promise of explaining a good deal of observed behavior in modern industrial economies, a mission which orthodox theorizing has failed to accomplish.

2. Some Traditional Perspectives

2.1. *The Neoclassical Firm and Multiproduct Organization*

The neoclassical theory of the firm generally assumes profit maximizing entities operating in competitive product and capital markets exhibiting zero

---

[1] Economies of scope exist when for all outputs y_1 and y_2, the cost of joint production is less than the cost or producing each output separately [Panzar and Willig (1975)]. That is, it is the condition, for all y_1 and y_2: $C(y_1, y_2) < C(y_1, 0) + C(0, y_2)$.

transactions costs and competitive equilibrium. Under these assumptions, it is virtually impossible to erect a theory of the multiproduct firm. For instance, consider a cost function displaying scope economies (operating "synergies"). Irrespective of the source of these economies, there is no compelling reason for firms to adopt multiproduct structures since in a zero transactions cost world, scope economies can be captured using market contracts to share the services of the inputs providing the foundations for scope economies [Teece (1980)].

Nor are "financial synergy" arguments compelling within the classical framework. Thus, define for a firm both a mean return μ, and a probability distribution of returns described entirely by the variance σ^2. Statistical theory establishes that if the returns to independent firms are non-correlated, the creation of a single diversified firm leads to a reduction in the variance of total cash flow.[2] But within the context of the capital asset pricing model (CAPM), this need not reduce stockholder risk since all gains from this kind of amalgamation should have already been achieved by stockholders, all of whom are able to diversify away unsystematic risk. The argument clearly only has merit if the stock market is imperfect in some way, or if all stockholders are not following the precepts of the CAPM.

Nor does multiproduct organization increase the value of the firm by reducing default risks. While bondholders risk — and hence the costs of debt — can be reduced through diversification, Galai and Masulis (1976) point out that

---

[2] This can be most easily illustrated by considering the merger of two firms with identical premerger μ and σ^2. The expected return, μ_m, of the merged firm is, of course, 2μ. The variance of these returns is given by $\sigma_m^2 = \sigma_i^2 + \sigma_j^3 + 2r\sigma_i\sigma_j$, where i and j refer to the pre-merger firms and m to the merged firm. r is the coefficient of correlation between the two profit streams, and can take values between $+1$ and -1. If $r = 1$, then a positive or negative deviation in firm i returns is paralleled by an identical variation in the profits of firm j. In this case $\sigma_m^2 = 4\sigma^2$. This means that the expected returns to the merged firm are exactly the sum of the expected returns of the constituent firms, and the spread of returns (measured by the standard deviation σ_m) has also doubled. There has been no reduction in the variability of the earnings stream expressed as a ratio of the average return. (This measure is the coefficient of variation, a normalized measure of variability.) However, for $r < 1$, it is clear that $\sigma_m^2 < 4\sigma^2$. Specifically when $r = 0$, i.e., the two profit streams are completely independent of each other, $\sigma_m^2 = 2\sigma^2$. So the return has doubled, but the standard deviation increases by only $\sqrt{2}$, so the coefficient of variation diminishes by a factor of $1/\sqrt{2}$. Finally if $r = -1$, the two streams move in precisely opposite directions: a positive deviation in firm i is exactly offset by a negative deviation in firm j. In this unlikely case, the variance of the returns falls to zero. Obviously in all cases where $r < 1$, a merger reduces the variability of profits.

since the value of the firm is simply the sum of the constituent parts, the value of the equity of the merged firm will be less than the sum of the constituent equity values and the value of debt will be higher. Options pricing theory indicates that increased variability increases the value of options and conversely. Since equity is an option on the face value of debt outstanding, its value will fall with a decrease in volatility [Black and Scholes (1973)]. "What is taking place ... is that the bondholders receive more protection since the stockholders of each firm have to back the claims of bondholders of both companies. The stockholders are hurt since their limited liability is weakened" [Galai and Masulis (1976, p. 68)]. Hence a pure diversification rationale for the multiproduct firm is not valid within the context of orthodox theories of financial markets. Reducing the risk to bondholders represents a redistribution of value from shareholders, leaving the total value of the firm unchanged.

Thus multiproduct firms can emerge within an economy operating under neoclassical competitive assumptions, but they must do so only by accident. Whether firms are organized along specialized or multiproduct lines is economically irrelevant since market arrangements and internal organization are perfect substitutes. Thus divesting multiproduct firms or diversifying specialized ones is a transformation lacking economic significance in the context of a neoclassical economy.

2.2. Managerial Explanation

Another class of theories used to explain diversification are based on managerialism. Marris (1966) and Mueller (1969) have made important contributions which are illustrative of this literature. In Marris's growth maximizing managerial enterprise, managers not only bring the existing supply of resources and the demands upon them into line, but also their future rates of growth. Thus the equating of the growth of supply of resources and growth of demand upon them is an equilibrium condition. In identifying the main determinants of the growth of demand, Marris recognizes that firms are usually multiproduct and that diversification into new products is the main engine of corporate growth. Thus in order to grow any faster than the rate of growth of the markets in which the firm establishes itself, it must carry out further successful diversification.[3] However, there are significant costs attached to successful diversification and these costs of diversification all reduce the firms' rate of return on capital.

---

[3] Thus $g_D = f_1(\hat{d})$, where g_D is growth of demand and $\hat{d}$ is the rate of successful diversification.

The growth of demand is thus an inverse function of the rate of return on capital because faster growth of demand via more rapid diversification either requires a lower profit margin, which lowers the return on capital, or leads to a higher capital — output ratio, which also lowers the return on capital, or both.

The core of Muellers (1969) theory is that managers are motivated to increase the size of their firms further. He assumes that the compensation to managers is a function of the size of the firm and he argues therefore that managers adopt a lower investment hurdle rate. The lower investment hurdle rate prompts the managers of older, larger, mature firms to invest more heavily than they would if they were confronted with a higher hurdle, and represents a basic motivation for diversification.[4] However, the basic premise of the theory — that compensation is a function of the size of the firm — is problematic. In a study critical of earlier evidence, Lewellen and Huntsman (1970) present findings that managers' compensation is significantly correlated with the firms profit rate, not its level of sales. Thus Muellers theory has to fall back on the non-pecuniary benefits — such as status and visibility in the business community — which managers may obtain from managing larger enterprises. Nor are the basic facts of diversification via merger supportive of Mueller's theory. The larger acquirers during the 1954–1968 period were about 1/10 the average size of the larger, more mature non-acquirers [Bock (1970)]. Thus the initial size of the active conglomerate acquirers was small, not large as Mueller's theory suggests.

This is not to say that managerialist theories are entirely without merit. Managerial motives may well explain a portion of observed diversification activity. However, diversification can also be efficiency driven, as this paper will seek to demonstrate. The nature of possible efficiencies are delineated, thereby providing the foundations for an efficiency-based theory of the multiproduct firm. This theoretical exploration is of relevance to managers and policy analysts since a framework is developed within which it is possible to assess the likelihood that economies can be captured through corporate diversification strategies. Within this framework the firm is conceptualized as a structure designed

---

[4] The Mueller theory must also confront efficient market theory. If managers are making investment decisions using a hurdle rate below the market equilibrium rate and therefore below the alternative returns available to stockholders, stockholders will shift their investment to firms offering higher rates of return. Capital market forces will not permit different firms to follow a "two-tier" investment hurdle rate policy, at least not in the long run.

to organize the employment of various assets which have greater value when employed under the internal control apparatus of a firm than under the external control apparatus of a market.

3. Nature of the Firm

In microtheory textbooks, and in much contemporary research, it is accepted practice "to represent the business enterprise abstractly by the productive transformations of which it is capable, and to characterize these productive transformations by a production function or production set regarded as a datum" [Winter (1982, p. 58)].[5] Furthermore, production functions and hence firms can be eliminated or replicated with amazing alacrity, as when prices a whisker above competitive levels attract new entrants. New entry in turn drives profits back down to equilibrium levels. Embedded in this conceptualization is the notion that a firms' know-how is stored in symbolic form in a "book of blueprints". Implicit in this commonly used metaphor is the view that knowledge can be and is articulated. Following Winter (1982), and Nelson and Winter (1980, 1982), the appropriateness of this abstraction is examined below, and the implications for multiproduct organization explored.

3.1. Individual and Organizational Knowledge

Polanyi has stressed, in obvious contradiction to the book of blueprints metaphor, that individual knowledge has an important tacit dimension, in that very often know-how and skills cannot be articulated. It is a "well known fact that the aim of a skillful performance is achieved by the observance of a set of rules which are not known as such to the person following them"[6] [Polanyi (1958, p. 49)]. In the exercise of individual skill, many actions are taken that

---

[5] In modern general equilibrium theory [Arrow (1951), Arrow and Debreu (1954), Debreu (1959)] "commodity outputs in amounts represented by $q = (q_1,...,q_m)$ may or may not be producible from input commodities in amounts represented by $X = (\chi_1,...,\chi_n)$. If q is producible from x, then the input/output pair (χ,q) is 'in the production set'. Whatever is known or considered plausible as a property of the structure of technical knowledge is treated as a postulate about the properties of the production set" [Winter (1982, p. 63)].

[6] "The premises of a skill cannot be discovered focally prior to its performance, not even understood if explicitly stated by others, before we ourselves have experienced its performance, whether by watching it or engaging in it ourselves" [Polanyi (1958, p. 1962)].

are not the result of considered choices but rather are automatic responses that constitute aspects of the skill.[7]

Similarly, in the routine operation of an organization such as a business firm, much that could in principle be deliberated is instead done automatically in response to signals arising from the organization or its environment. Articulation of the knowledge underlying organizational capabilities is limited in the same respects and for the same reasons as in the case of individual capabilities though for other reasons as well, and to a greater extent. This routinization of activity in an organization itself constitutes the most important form of storage of the organization's specific operational knowledge. In a sense, organizations "remember by doing". Routine operation is the organizational counterpart of the exercise of skills by an individual. [Nelson and Winter (1982, quoted in part from an earlier draft).]

Thus, routines function as the basis of organizational memory. To utilize organizational knowledge, it is necessary not only that all members know their routines, but also that all members know when it is appropriate to perform certain routines. This implies that the individual must have the ability to interpret a stream of incoming messages from other organizational members and from the environment. Once received and interpreted, the member utilizes the information contained in a message in the selection and performance of an appropriate routine from his own repertoire.[8] Thus to view organizational memory as reducible to individual member memories is to overlook, or undervalue, the linking of those individual memories by shared experiences in the past, experiences that have established the extremely detailed and specific communication system that underlies routine performance. [Nelson and Winter (1982, p. 105).]

---

[7] Polanyi illustrates this point by discussing how a bicyclists keeps his balance: "I have come to the conclusion that the principle by which the cyclist keeps his balance is not generally known. The rule observed by the cyclist is this. When he starts falling to the right he turns the handlebars to the right, so that the course of the bicycle is deflected along a curve towards the right. This results in a centrifugal force pushing the cyclist to the left and offsets the gravitational force dragging him down to the right. This maneuver presently throws the cyclist out of balance to the left which he counteracts by turning the handlebars to the left; and so he continues to keep himself in balance by winding along a series of appropriate curvatures. A simple analysis shows that for a given angle of unbalance the curvature of each winding is inversely proportional to the square of the speed at which the cyclist is proceeding. But does this tell us exactly how to ride a bicycle? No. You obviously cannot adjust the curvature of your bicylcle's path in proportion to the ratio of your unbalance over the square of your speed; and if you could you would fall off the machine, for there are a number of other factors to be taken into account in practice which are left out in the formulation of this rule" [Polanyi (1958, pp. 49–50)].

[8] An organizational member's repetoire is the set of routines that could be performed in some appropriate environment [Nelson and Winter (1982)].

While there is abundant reason to believe that remembering-by-doing may in a wide range of circumstances surpass symbolic storage in cost effectiveness, one circumstance where complications arise is where the knowledge is to enter market exchange for subsequent transfer to a different organizational context. The transfer of key individuals may suffice when the knowledge to be transferred relates to the particulars of a separable routine. The individual in such cases becomes a consultant or a teacher with respect to that routine. However, only a limited range of capabilities can be transferred if a transfer activity is focused in this fashion. More often than not, the transfer of productive expertise requires the transfer of organizational as well as individual knowledge.[9] In such cases, external transfer beyond an organization's boundary may be difficult if not impossible, since taken out of context, an individual's knowledge of a routine may be quite useless.

3.2. *Fungible Knowledge*

Another characteristic of organizational knowledge is that it is often fungible to an important degree. That is, the human capital inputs employed by the firm are not always entirely specialized to the particular products and services which the enterprise is currently producing. This is particularly true of managerial talent, but it is also true for various items of physical equipment and for other kinds of human skills as well. Of course, various items of capital may have to be scrapped or converted if an organization's product mix is changed but these costs may in fact be quite low if the opportunity cost of withdrawing the equipment from its current use is minimal.

Accordingly, the final products produced by a firm at any given time merely represent one of several ways in which the organization could be using its internal resources. [Penrose (1959).] As wartime experience demonstrated, automobile manufacturers suddenly began making tanks, chemical companies began making explosives, and radio manufacturers began making radar. In short, a firm's capability lies upstream from the end product — it lies in a generalizable capability which might well find a variety of final product applications. Economies of specialization assume a different significance when viewed from this conceptual vantage point, as specialization is referenced not to a single product but to a generalized capability. (It might be "information processing" rather than computers, "dairy products" rather than butter and cheese, "farm machinery" rather than

---

[9] "Over the years an individual may learn a piece of the company puzzle exceptionally well and he may even understand how the piece fits into the entire puzzle. But he may not know enough about the other pieces to reproduce the entire puzzle" [Lieberstein (1979)].

tractors and harvestors, and "time measurement" rather than clocks and watches.) The firm can therefore be considered to have a variety of end products which it can produce with its organizational technology. Some of these possibilities may be known to it and some may not. What needs to be explained is the particular end product or configuration of end products which the firm chooses to produce.

This view of the nature of the firm turns the neoclassical conceptualization on its head. Whereas the neoclassical firm selects, according to factor prices, technologies off the shelf to manufacture a given end product, the organization theoretic firm depicted here selects an end product configuration, consistent with its organizational technology, which is defined yet fungible over certain arrays of final products. In short, the firm has end product as well as technological choices to confront.

4. Dynamic Considerations

4.1. *General*

Whether the firm's know-how is embedded in a book of blueprints or in individual and organizational routines will not explain its multiproduct scope unless other dimensions of the neoclassical model of firms and markets are modified. Thus following Schumpeter (1950) and others, the competitive process is viewed as dynamic, involving uncertainty, struggle, and disequilibrium. In particular, two fundamental characteristics of a dynamic competitive system are recognized: (a) firms accummulate knowledge through R&D and learning, some of it incidental to the production process, (b) the market conditions facing the firm are constantly changing, creating profit opportunities in different markets at different times. Furthermore, the demand curve facing a specialized firm is rarely infinitely elastic, as is assumed in the perfectly competitive model.

4.2. *Learning, Teaching, and "Penrose-Effects"*

Edith Penrose (1959) has described the growth processes of the firm in a way that is both unconventional and convincing. According to Penrose, at any time a firm has certain productive resources, the services of which are used to exploit the production opportunities facing the firm. Opportunities for growth exist because there are always unused productive services which can be placed into employment — presumably in new as well as existing lines of business. Unused resources exist not only because of indivisibilities, but also because of the learning which occurs in the normal process of operating a business. Thus, even with a constant managerial workforce, managerial services are released for expansion without any reduction in the efficiency with which existing operations are run. Not only is there continuous learning, but also as each project becomes established so its running becomes more routine and less demanding on managerial resources. The managerial workface can also be expanded, at least within limits. Existing managers can teach new managers. However, the increment to total managerial services provided by each additional manager is assumed to decrease the faster the rate at which they are reoriented. (The "Penrose-effect".)

A specialized firm's generation of excess resources, both managerial and technical, and their fungible character is critical to the theory of diversification advanced here. What has to be explained, however, is (1) why diversification is likely to lead to the productive utilization of "excess" resources, and (2) the sequence in which this assignment is likely to occur.

4.3. Demand Conditions

A specialized firm's excess resources can of course be reinvested in the firm's traditional business. Indeed, if the firm confronts a perfectly elastic demand curve, has a distinctive capability (lower costs) in its traditional business, and markets elsewhere are competitive, it has incentives to reinvest in its traditional line of business, both at home and abroad. Assume, however, that at some point competitive returns can no longer be obtained through reinvestment at home or abroad, either because of a secular decline of demand due to life cycle considerations [Grabowski and Mueller (1975), Mueller (1972)], or because the firm is facing a finite degree of elasticity to its demand curve, in which case reinvestment and expansion will serve to lower prices and profits. Confronted with this predicament, a profit seeking firm confronts three fundamental choices:

(1) It can seek to sell the services of its unused assets to other firms in other markets.
(2) It can diversify into other markets, either through acquisition or de novo entry.
(3) If the unused resource is cash, it can be returned to stockholders through higher dividends or stock repurchase.

A theory of diversification for a profit seeking enterprise emerges when conditions are established under which the second option appears the more profitable. The first option involves the use of markets for capturing the employment value of the unused assets. Multiproduct diversification (option 2) will be selected by profit seeking firms over the market alternative (option 1) when transactions cost problem are likely to confound efficient transfer. Accordingly, an assessment of the efficiency properties of factor and financial markets is warranted.

4.4. *Market Failure Considerations: Physical and Human Capital*

If excess resources are possessed by a single product firm, there is the possibility of disposal in factor markets, i.e. sale and transfer to other specialized firms. This strategy permits standard specialization economies to be obtained, and if transaction costs are zero, ought to usurp incentives for diversification. Consider, therefore, whether efficient employment of these resources is likely to involve multiproduct organization. Assume, furthermore, that the excess resources are either indivisible or fungible, so that scope economies exist.[10] Four classes of scope economies are identified and analyzed.

Class I. Indivisible but non-specialized physical capital as a common input into two or more products:

Scope economies may arise because some fixed item of capital equipment is indivisible. It may be a machine — such as heavy gauge sheet metal shears — which is needed occasionally in the production process for product A but is otherwise idle. Assume that the machine could be used to manufacture both products A and B. Even if this is the case it need not indicate that an efficient solution is for the manufacture of A to diversify into the manufacture of B. There are at least two other options. The manufacturer of A could rent the services of another firm's machine, or it could acquire its own machine and lease access to it when it would otherwise remain idle.

To the extent that there is not a thin market for the services of the machinery in question — which will often be the case — there does not appear to be a compelling reason for diversification on account of the hazards of exposure to opportunism. [Williamson (1975), Klein, Crawford and Alchian (1978).] Market solutions would appear to be superior.[11]

---

[10] As a general matter, "economies of scope arise from inputs that are shared, or utilized jointly without complete congestion. The shared factor may be imperfectly divisible, so that the manufacture of a subset of the goods leaves excess capability in some stage of production, or some human or physical capital may be a public input which, when purchased for use in one production process, is then freely available to another" [Willing (1979, p. 346)].

[11] A related example would be the provision of air services between points A and B. An airport will be needed at both A and B and in the absence of complete congestion, service can also be provided from both points to C (which has an airport) once airport terminals A and B are constructed. Hence $C(AB, C, AC) < C(AB,0,0) + C(0,BC,0) + C(0,0,AC)$. While economies of scope exist, it need not imply that one airline ought provide services AB, BC, and CA. Individual airlines could specialize on each route and access to terminals (the source of the assumed indivisibility) could be shared via contracts. Only in the extent to which transactional difficulties can be expected in writing, executing, and enforcing contracts will common ownership be necessary to capture the scope economies.

Class II. Indivisible specialized physical capital as a common input to two or more products:

Assume that the piece of equipment is specialized but not entirely so. Assume specifically that it can only be used for making products A and B, that there is some idle capacity if it is only used to manufacture A, and that the market for A and B will only support a small number of producers. In these circumstances there may be incentives for the manufacturer of A to also manufacture B because of the transactional difficulties which might otherwise be encountered in the small numbers markets assumed. Since the fixed asset is highly specialized, and the number of potential leasees is assumed to be quite small, markets for the services of the fixed assets will be thin. Bilateral monopoly situations can then arise in which leasees may attempt to extract the quasi-rents associated with the utilization of the leasor's fixed and specialized asset.[12] [Williamson (1975, 1979), Klein, Crawford and Alchian (1978), Monteverde and Teece (1982a, b).] In order to avoid these hazards, intrafirm trading — that is, multiproduct diversification — can be substituted for market exchange. Internal trading changes the incentives of the parties and enables the firm to bring managerial control devices to bear on the transaction, thereby attenuating costly haggling and other manifestations of non-cooperative behavior. Exchange can then proceed more efficiently because of lower transactions costs.

Class III. Human capital as a common input to two or more products:

To the extent that know-how has fungible attributes, it can represent a common input into a variety of products. Know-how may also display some of the characteristics of a public good in that it may be used in many different non-competing applications without its value in any one application being substantially impaired. Furthermore, the marginal cost of employing know-how in a different endeavor is likely to be much less than the average cost of production and dissemination (transfer). Accordingly, the transfer and application of proprietary information to alternative production activities is likely to generate important economies.

However, internal organization (multiproduct enterprise) is generally needed for these economies to be realized. Markets do not work well as the institutional mode for trading know-how. One reason is that an important component of organizational knowledge is tacit. As discussed above, the transfer of tacit knowledge from one enterprise to another is likely to be difficult and costly. A

---

[12] The quasi-rents will be the difference between the asset value if the equipment is used to produce multiple products and its value when it is used to produce the single product.

temporary if not permanent transfer of employees may be needed, especially if the technology involved is state of the art and has not as yet been stabilized and formalized. If this is the case, multiproduct organization is likely to have appeal because it provides a more efficient technology transfer mode.

Besides the logistical problems surrounding the transfer of tacit knowledge, technology transfer must confront an important class of transactions cost problems. These can be summarized in terms of (1) recognition, (2) disclosure, and (3) team organization [Teece (1980), Williamson and Teece (1982)]. Thus consider a firm which has accumulated know-how which can potentially find application in the fields of industrial activity beyond its existing product line(s). If there are other firms in the economy which can apply this know-how with profit, then according to received microtheory, trading will ensue until Pareto Optimality conditions are satisfied. Or, as Calabresi has put it, "if one assumes rationality, no transactions costs, and no legal impediments to bargaining, all misallocations of resources would be fully cured in the market by bargains" [Calabresi (1968)]. However, one cannot in general expect this result in the market for proprietary know-how. Not only are there high costs associated with obtaining the requisite information but there are also organizational and strategic impediments associated with using the market to effectuate transfer.

Consider, to begin with, the information requirements associated with using markets. In order to carry out a market transaction it is necessary to discover who it is that one wishes to deal with, to inform people that one wishes to deal and on what terms, to conduct negotiations leading up to the bargain, to draw up the contract, to undertake the inspection needed to make sure that the terms of the contract are being observed, and so on [Coase (1960, p. 15)]. Furthermore, the opportunity for trading must be identified. As Kirzner (1973, pp. 215–216) has explained:

> "...for an exchange transaction to be completed it is not sufficient merely that the conditons for exchange which prospectively will be mutually beneficial be present; it is necessary also that each participant be aware of his opportunity to gain through exchange ... It is usually assumed ... that where scope for (mutually beneficial) exchange is present, exchange will in fact occur ... In fact of course exchange may fail to occur because knowledge is imperfect, in spite of conditions for mutually profitable exchange."

The transactional difficulties identified by Kirzner are especially compelling when the commodity in question is proprietary information, be it of a technological or managerial kind. This is because the protection of the ownership of technological know-how often requires suppressing information on exchange possibilities. For instance, by its very nature industrial R&D requires disguising and concealing the activities and outcomes of R&D establishment. As Marquis and Allen (1966, p. 1055) point out, industrial laboratories, with their strong mission orientation, must

> "... cut themselves off from interaction beyond the organizational perimeter. This is to a large degree intentional. The competitive environment in which they operate necessitates control over the outflow of messages. The industrial technologist or scientist is thereby essentially cut off from free interaction with his colleagues outside of the organization."

Except as production or marketing specialists within the firm perceive the transfer opportunity, transfer may fail by reason of non-recognition.

Even where the possessor of the technology recognizes the opportunity, market exchange may break down because of the problems of disclosing value to buyers in a way that is both convincing and does not destroy the basis for exchange. A very severe information impactedness problem exists, on which account the less informed party (in this instance the buyer) must be wary of opportunistic representations by the seller. If, moreover, there is insufficient disclosure, including veracity checks thereon, to assure the buyer that the information possesses great value, the "fundamental paradox" of information arises: "its value for the purchaser is not known until he has the information, but then he has in effect acquired it without cost" [Arrow (1971, p. 152)].

Suppose that recognition is no problem, that buyers concede value, and are prepared to pay for information in the seller's possession. Occasionally that may suffice. The formula for a chemical compound or the blueprints for a special device may be all that is needed to effect the transfer. However, more is frequently needed. As discussed above, know-how has a strong tacit and learning-by-doing character, and it may be essential that human capital in an effective team configuration accompany the transfer. Sometimes this can be effected through a one-time contract (a know-how agreement) to provide a "consulting team" to assist start-up. Although such contracts will be highly incomplete, and the failure to reach a comprehensive agreement may give rise to dissatisfaction during execution, this may be an unavoidable, which is to say irremediable, result. Plainly, multiproduct organization is an extreme response to the needs of a one-time exchange. In the absence of a superior organizational alternative, reliance on market mechanisms is thus likely to prevail.

Where a succession of proprietary exchanges seems desirable, reliance on repeated contracting is less clearly warranted. Unfettered two-way communication is needed not only to promote the recognition and disclosure of opportunities for information transfer but also to facilitate the execution of the actual transfer itself. The parties in these circumstances are joined in a small numbers trading relation and as discussed by Williamson, such contracting may be shot through with hazards for both parties [Williamson (1975, 1979)]. The seller is exposed to hazards such as the possibility that the buyer will employ the know-how in subtle ways not covered by the contract, or the buyer might "leap frog" the licensor's technology and become an unexpected competitive threat. The buyer is exposed to hazards such as the seller asserting that the technology has better performance or cost reducing characteristics than is actually the case; or the seller might render promised transfer assistance in a perfunctory fashion. While bonding or the execution of performance guarantees can minimize these hazards, they need not be eliminated since costly haggling might ensue when measurement of the performance characteristics of the technology is open to some ambiguity. Furthermore, when a lateral transfer is contemplated and the technology has not therefore been previously commercialized by either party in the new application, the execution of performance guarantees is likely to be especially hazardous to the seller because of the uncertainties involved [Teece (1977)]. In addition, if a new application of a generic technology is contemplated, recurrent exchange and continuous contact between buyer and seller will be needed. These requirements will be extremely difficult to specify ex ante. Hence, when the continuous exchange of proprietary know-how between the transferor and transferee is needed, and where the end use application of the know-how is idiosyncratic in the sense that it has not been accomplished previously by the transferor, it appears that something more than a classical market contracting structure is required. As Williamson notes "The nonstandardized nature of (these) transactions makes primary reliance on market governance hazardous, while their recurrent nature permits the cost of the specialized governance structure to be recovered" [Williamson (1979, p. 250)]. What Williamson refers to as "relational contracting" is the solution; this can take the form of bilateral governance, where the autonomy of the parties is maintained; or unified structures, where the transaction is removed from the market and organized within the firm subject to an authority relation [Williamson (1979, p. 250)]. Bilateral governance involves the use of "obligational contracting" [Wachter and Williamson (1978), Williamson (1979)]. Exchange is conducted between independent firms under obligational arrangements, where both parties realize the paramount importance of maintaining an amicable relationship as overriding any possible short-run gains either might be able to achieve. But as transactions become progressively more idiosyncratic, obligational contracting may also fail, and internal organization (intrafirm transfer) is the more efficient organizational mode. The intrafirm transfer of knowhow avoids the need for repeated negotiations and ameliorates the hazards of opportunism. Better disclosure, easier agreement, better governance, and therefore more effective execution of know-how transfer are likely to result. Here lies an incentive for multiproduct organization.

The above arguments are quite general and extend to the transfer of many different kinds of proprietary know-how. Besides technological know-how, the transfer of managerial (including organizational) know-how, and goodwill (including brand loyalty) represent types of assets for which market transfer mechanisms may falter, and for which the relative efficiency of intrafirm as against interfirm trading is indicated.

Class IV. External economies:

George Stigler has cast the coase theorem [Coase (1960)] in the following form: "Under perfect competition and any assignment of property rights, market transactions between a firm producing a nuisance and one consuming it will bring about the same composition of output as would have been determined by a single firm engaged in both activities. That is, market transactions will have the same consequences as internal management no matter what the property structure, *provided transactions costs are negligible.*" [Stigler (1966, p. 113, emphasis added).] The converse of this is that external economies — which can generate economies of scope — will dictate multiproduct organization when there are significant transaction costs.

External economies in the production of various goods are quite common. For instance, there are locational externalities if a new airport opens up a previously remote area and stimulates tourism.[13] There are also externalities if a cost saving innovation in one industry lowers costs in another. If these externalities can be captured at low cost by common ownership, then multiproduct organization is suggested.

Of course there are limits to the economies which can be captured through diversification. If diversification is based on scope economies, then there will

---

[13] Common ownership may also be needed if the external economies are in the form of skills. Suppose firm X_1 is a monopolist in industry A. A new industry Y emerges which requires labor skills developed in industry X. Because of the transactional difficulties which confront X_1 in appropriating the skills with which it has imbued its employees, X_1 may generate an externality in industry Y. Diversification of X_1 into Y enable the externality to be internalized.

eventually be a problem of congestion associated with accessing the common input. For instance, if the common input is know-how, then while the value of the know-how may not be impaired by repeated transfer, the costs of accessing it may increase if the simultaneous transfer of the information to a number of different applications is attempted. This is because know-how is generally not embodied in blueprints alone; the human factor is critically important in technology transfer. Accordingly, as the demands for sharing know-how increase, bottlenecks in the form of over-extended scientists, engineers, and managers can be anticipated.[14] Congestion associated with accessing common inputs will thus clearly limit the amount of diversification which can be profitably engaged. However, if the transfers are arranged so that they occur in a sequential fashion, then the limits imposed by congestion are relieved, at least in part [Teece (1977)].

Control loss considerations may also come into play. However, the establishment of a decentralized divisionalized "M-Form" [Williamson (1975)] structure is likely to minimize control loss problems. In fact Chandler argues that the M-Form innovation made diversification a viable strategy [Chandler (1969)]. It is also important to note that diversification need not represent abandonment of specialization. It is simply that a firm's particular advantage is defined not in terms of products but in terms of capabilities. The firm is seen as possessing a specialized know-how or asset base from which it extends its operations in response to competitive conditions. This element of commonality simplifies the control problem, at least compared to other forms of diversification.

4.5. *Market Failure Considerations and Financial Capital*

Suppose that cash is the only excess capacity possessed by a specialized firm. Assuming, for the moment, that taxation of dividends and capital gains is unimportant, I wish to investigate whether allocative efficiency and/or a firm's market value can possibly be improved by diversification if financial markets are "efficient". Oliver Williamson, among others, has postulated that multidivisional firms can establish internal capital markets with resource allocation properties superior to those obtained by the (external) capital market. In particular, he postulates "a tradeoff between breadth of information, in which respect the banking system may be presumed to have the advantage, and depth of information, which is the advantage of the specialized firm". [Williamson (1975, p. 162).] Inferior access to inside information and the weak control instruments exercised by

---

[14] The 'Penrose-Effect' discussed earlier focuses on this problem with respect to managerial resources.

financial intermediaries and the stock market provides the foundation for Williamson's assertion that the "miniature capital market" within the firm has distinctive efficiency properties.

Financial theoreists, however, are often quick to reply that since the financial markets have been shown to be "efficient", no improvement in allocative efficiency or market value can possibly derive from managers usurping the role of financial markets. Myers (1968), Schall (1972), and Mossin (1973) have all argued that value is conserved (value additivity obtains) under the addition of income streams, as would occur with diversification by merger. However, the notions of "efficiency" as used by financial theorists is highly specialized and do not accord with the concept of allocative efficiency used in welfare economics. Nor does it deny that stockholder wealth can be improved through the operations of the firm's internal capital markets. These issues are critical to the analysis of follow and so are examined below.

In the finance literature, the term "efficient markets" has taken on a specialized and misleading meaning. One widely employed definition refers to informational efficiency. For example, according to Fama (1970, p. 383) "A market in which prices fully reflect available information is called 'efficient'",[15] and according to Jensen (1978), "A market is efficient with respect to information set Θ_t if it is impossible to make economic profits by trading on the basis of information set Θ_t." The other widely employed definition is what can be called

---

[15] Fama (1970, 1976) actually defines three types of efficiency, each of which is based on a different notion of the type of information understood to be relevant in the phrase "prices fully reflect available information". Specifically, he recognizes:

(1) *Weak-form efficiency.* No investor can earn excess returns if he develops trading rules based on historical price or return information. In other words, the information in past prices or returns is not useful or relevant in achieving excess returns.

(2) *Semistrong-form efficiency.* No investor can earn excess returns from trading rules based on any publicly available information. Examples of publicly available information are: annual reports of companies, investment advisory data such as "Heard on the Street" in *The Wall Street Journal*, or ticker tape information.

(3) *Strong-form efficiency.* No investor can earn excess returns using any information, whether publicly available or not.

Obviously, the last type of market efficiency is very strong indeed. If markets were efficient in their strong form, prices would fully reflect all information even though it might be held exclusively by a corporate insider. Suppose, for example, he knows that his company has just discovered how to control nuclear fusion. Even before he has a chance to trade based on the news, the strong form of market efficiency predicts that prices will have adjusted so that he cannot profit.

mean-variance efficiency. The market is mean-variance efficient if capital market prices correspond to an equilibrium in which all individuals evaluate portfolios in terms of their means and variances, about which they all have identical beliefs. Unfortunately, these concepts have nothing to do with allocative efficiency. As Stiglitz (1981) has shown, neither informational efficiency or mean variance efficiency are necessary or sufficient conditions for the Pareto optimality of the economy. In short, "there is no theoretical presumption simply because the financial markets appear to be competitive, or 'pass' the standard finance literature tests concerning efficiency, that they are efficient" [Stiglitz (1981, p. 237)].

One reason for this result is that it is costly to obtain and transmit information about investment opportunities. Since managers are obviously more informed about investment opportunities available to the firm, they must somehow convey this information to potential investors if efficient outcomes are to be obtained solely through utilization of the (external) capital market. However, capital markets in which it is costly to obtain and transmit information look substantially different from those in which information is assumed to be perfect, and they fail to possess the standard optimality properties' [Stiglitz (1981, p. 244)].

The capital market clearly does not fully reflect all information — which is what is necessary for Pareto optimality to obtain.[16] If markets were perfectly efficient in transmitting information from the informed to the uninformed, informed individuals wouldn't obtain a return on their investment in information; thus, the only information which can, in equilibrium, be efficiently transmitted is costless information. With costly information, markets cannot be fully arbitraged [Grossman and Stiglitz (1976, 1980)].

The above considerations indicate why a useful economic function can be performed by the internal allocation of capital within the firm. If managers have access to an information set which is different from investors, and if it is difficult and costly to transmit the content of this information set to investors, then managers may be able to increase stockholder wealth by making investment decisions on behalf of the stockholders. In the process, resource allocation is likely to be improved over a situation in which all earnings are returned to stockholders who then make all reinvestment decisions. The transactions cost properties of such an arrangement render it absurd in most circumstances. Accordingly, the existence of internal capital markets and the (partial) internalization of the capital allocation process within the firm appear to possess a compelling rationale — both in terms of stockholder wealth enhancement and allocative efficiency.

---

[16] Strong form efficiency, defined in the previous footnote, would be necessary for Pareto optimality to hold.

In this context it is possible to recognize that if a specialized firm possesses financial resources beyond reinvestment opportunities in its traditional business, there are circumstances under which both stockholder wealth and allocative efficiency can be served if managers allocate funds to new products. However, the domain within which an efficiency gain is likely swings on empirical factors, and is likely to be quite narrow, given the relative efficiencies within which managers and stockholders can scan investment opportunities. It is generally only with respect to related businesses — businesses related functionally, technologically and geographically — that a relative advantage seems likely. It is for those investment opportunities in which the firm has a decided information advantage that managers are likely to possess such an advantage. Broader investment opportunities are better assessed by mutual funds which specialize in that function and can make portfolio investments at low transactions costs.

Nevertheless, financial theory provides insights into other ways by which stockholder wealth might be changed through diversification. In particular, the Capital Asset Pricing Model (CAPM)[17] provides a framework for assessing the rate of return the capital market expects an individual asset to earn. According to the CAPM, this rate of return is a function of the asset's level of systematic risk, the on the market portfolio rate of return, and the risk-free rate of return. A security's systematic risk, measured in the marketplace, depends on the degree of correlation between its return and the market's return. Defined as cash income plus capital appreciation over one time period, these "returns" are equivalent to a security's cash flow over its lifetime. Focusing on cash flow allows systematic risk to be decomposed into the systematic risk of the current-period cash flow, and the systematic risk arising from future cash flows. Whereas current cash flow is fixed in timing and size, the future cash flow component of systematic risk if not fixed. It has a variable time horizon and the possibility of growth, and its estimated size is affected by changing investor expectations. The effect of varying the time horizon and growth of cash flow on present value is obvious; an increase in either results in more cash in absolute terms at some future date, and consequently a greater present value.

In the context of the CAPM, multiproduct organization can increase stockholder wealth by (1) increasing the income stream, (2) improving forecast reliability, or (3) decreasing the systematic risk by an amount greater than could be obtained by creating a portfolio investment in specialized firms. Economies of scope, where the economies would not be captured by a set of contracts amongst

---

[17] The CAPM was developed almost simultaneously by Sharpe (1963, 1964), and Treynor (1961), while Mossin (1966), Lintner (1965, 1969) and Black (1972) made important extensions.

specialized firms, is a case in point. In addition, stockholder wealth could be increased if diversification assists the creation of free cash flows that have a negligible relationship to the level of activity of the economy, or improved investor confidence about future cash flows, since these developments would lead to reduced systematic risk. Outcomes of this kind seem possible, in that a distinctive attribute of internal organization is that it enables physical and human resources to be transferred, using powers of fiat, from one kind of business to the other, at low cost and with considerable speed. This flexibility, if exploited, might in fact provide the foundation for enhanced stockholder wealth. Businesses could be assembled in a fashion which enables the low cost and timely transfer of resources from one to another.

5. Related Issues

5.1. *Slack and Managerial Discretion*

The concept of excess resources used here and in Penrose (1959) bears certain similarities with the concept of slack found in the organization theory literature, excellently summarized by Bougeois (1981). For instance, slack has been variously defined as: "(The) disparity between the resources available to the organization and the payments required to maintain the coalition" [Cyert and March (1963, p. 36)]; the "supply of uncommitted resources" [Cyert and March (1963, p. 54)]; "The margin or surplus (performance exceeding 'satisficing' levels) which permits an organization's dominant coalition to adopt structural arrangements which accord with their own preferences" [Child (1972, p. 11)]; "The difference between existing resources and activated demand" [March and Olsen (1976, p. 87)]; "... since organizations do not always optimize, they accumulate spare resources and unexploited opportunities which then become a buffer against bad times." Although the buffer is not necessarily intended, slack produces performance smoothing, reducing performance during good times and improving it during bad times [March (1979, p. 17)]; "organizational slack is that cushion of actual or potential resources which allows an organization to adapt successfully to internal pressures for adjustment or to external pressures for change in policy, as well as to initiate changes in strategy vis à vis the external environment." [Bourgeois (1981).] While definitions abound, the concept of slack has, unfortunately, never been successfully operationalized. Part of the problem is that it can perform many functions; it can be a technical buffer, an inducement mechanism to attract and sustain organizational numbers [Barnard (1938)] a resource for conflict resolution, or a facilitator of strategic behavior [Bourgeois (1981)].

As used here, the concept of excess resources refers to the services of factor inputs available once managerial goals and the requirements for the long-run profitable operation of a production process have been met. In short, it refers to excess factor services over and above what is needed to meet managers requirements for organizational slack. As such, the concept is consistent with both satisficing and maximizing theories of the firm, as excess resources, as defined, can emerge in business firms no matter the behavioral rules it is following. Thus, if the desired level of organizational slack is zero, all redundant factor services become excess resources.

5.2. *De Novo Entry versus Acquisition or Merger*

The appropriate vehicle for diversification is an issue upon which the theory is not silent. If an enterprise has excess or slack internal resources, and market failure considerations dictate internal utilization, then the choice of de novo entry or acquisition will depend upon the amount of slack, the time period over which it is available, and the complementary resources which can be accessed through acquisition. Thus, if the slack appears gradually over a long period of time, de novo entry is likely to provide an effective entry vehicle. This is because de novo entry can be tailored as an incremental approach to diversification. If, on the other hand, slack resources are expected to emerge suddenly — due, for instance, to a sudden surge in technological innovation or due to an adverse change in demand which suddenly throws internal resources into unemployment — then merger or acquisition is likely to be the most favored route. Merger or acquisition will also be preferred if complementary resources can thereby be acquired.

Another consideration will be the relationship between the firm's internal valuation and the market value of the takeover candidate. Since the acquired firm possesses, by assumption, complementary resources which will work with the acquiring firm's slack resources, then the lower the price of the acquired firm relative to the market price of the individual resources which it possesses, then the greater the attractiveness of the takeover alternative. Hence, a depression in the stock market coupled with buoyant factor markets may change the relationship between the market value of the complementary resources purchased as a "team" and their value if purchased in factor markets. This differential — which reflects the difference between the value of a firm as a "going concern" and the value of its underlying assets when disaggregated — will help determine whether acquisition or de novo entry is the preferred route. Thus, as firm specific or economy wide factors depress the market value of a firm, the firm will appear more attractive as a takeover target to other firms which wish to diversify into its product line(s). Furthermore, the faster internal resources are released, the more attractive does the acquisition strategy become.

A curious implication of this analysis is that viewed on this framework, an active takeover market not only provides discipline for the acquired firm, thereby serving to minimize managerial discretion [Williamson (1975, Ch. 9)], but it may also function as a vehicle for channelling the internal resources of the acquiring firm into productive use. Hence, it appears that mergers and acquisitions may serve to minimize slack in both the acquiring and acquired firms, thereby generating a positive contribution to economic efficiency.

5.3. *Lateral versus Conglomerate Diversification*

A robust theory of the multiproduct enterprise should ideally be able to explain the richness of diversified enterprises existing on the industrial landscape. At least two different types of diversification can be identified: lateral or "related" diversification in which the different physical capital and technical skills of business or products bear an important element of commonality; and conglomerate diversification, where the physical capital and technical skills requirements are quite disparate.

The above analysis supports an efficiency rationale for the lateral integrated (diversified) enterprise. The efficiency rationale for the conglomerate is much more circumscribed. The only skill likely to be common to "unrelated" businesses is management, but except in those circumstances where the market for managerial services is subject to high transactions costs, it is doubtful whether the scope economies arising from transferring managerial resources are large enough to provide compelling efficiencies.

A firmer foundation for conglomerates can be built by examining the operation of the internal capital market. Conglomerate firms may be able to develop distinctive capabilities in assessing investment opportunities in disparate businesses. As compared to banks, operating companies can often bring industrial experience to the assessment of acquisition candidates. Furthermore, with the appropriate internal governance structure, disparate businesses can be managed efficiently. For these and other reasons, Williamson concludes "a transactional interpretation of the conglomerate, in which the limitations of capital markets in corporate control respects are emphasized, reveals that conglomerate firms (of the appropriate kind) are not altogether lacking in social purpose" [Williamson (1975, p. 175)]. The Williamson conglomerate with its own internal capital market is superior to the unassisted capital market in its ability to identify and direct cash to high yield investment.

5.4. *Some Historical Observations*

The economic theory of the multiproduct firm outlined above has firms adopting multiproduct features due to the coupling of market failures and the emergence of excess capacity. Implicit in the analysis is a conviction that this model explains a substantial portion of the diversification activity which has occurred in the American economy. To demonstrate this convincingly would involve a major empirical effort. I settle here for a more limited objective — to establish that the historical trends appear broadly consistent with the theory.

Diversification has unquestionably made for great changes in the profile of American industry during the last half century [Chandler (1969, p. 247)]. Furthermore, the Depression apparently triggered the trend towards diversification. Historians point out that the purpose of diversification was not to reduce portfolio risk or to pursue managerial motives, but rather to put slack resources to work. Furthermore, it was the technologically sophisticated firms which led the way. As Chandler (1969, p. 275) observed:

> "Precisely because these firms had accumulated vast resources in skilled manpower, facilities, and equipment, their executives were under even greater pressure than those of smaller firms to find new markets as the old ones ceased to grow. In the 1920s, the chemical companies, each starting from a somewhat different technological base, began to widen their product lines into new industries. In the same decade, the great electrical manufacturers — General Electric and Westinghouse — which had concentrated primarily on the manufacture of light and power equipment, diversified into production of a wide variety of household appliances. They also entered electronics with radios and X-ray equipment. During the Depression, General Motors (and to a lesser extent other firms in the auto industry) moved into diesels, appliances, tractors, and airplanes. Some makers of primary metals, particularly aluminum and copper, turned to consumer products like kitchenware and household fittings, while rubber firms developed the possibilities of rubber chemistry to compensate for declining tire sales. In the same period food companies employed their existing distribution organizations to market an increasing variety of products."

Whereas the Depression triggered diversification by generating excess capacity, the Second World War stimulated the demand for new products because the world market for many raw materials was severely disrupted while the war effort generated demand for a wide range of military products. The synthetic rubber program caused both rubber and petroleum firms to make far greater use of chemical technologies than they had even done before. Similarly, the demand for radar and other electronic equipment carried the electrical, radio, and machinery firms farther into this new field, and the production of tanks, high-speed aircraft, and new drugs all created skills and resources [Chandler (1969, p. 275)]. Once these capabilities were created, they were applied, where possible, in the production of civilian goods for the peace time economy. Thus, "the modern diversified enterprise represents a calculated rational response of technically trained professional managers to the needs and opportunities of changing technologies and markets" [Chandler (1969, p. 279)].[18]

6. Implications and Conclusions

Recent contributions to the transactions costs and market failures literature [Williamson (1975, 1979), Klein, Crawford and Alchian (1978), Teece (1980)], and to the literature on the nature of the firm [Nelson and Winter (1982)] have made it possible to outline a theory of the multiproduct firm. Important building blocks include excess capacity and its creation, market imperfections, and the peculiarities of organizational knowledge, particularly its fungibility and tacit character. Further research on each of these elements, and how they relate to incentives for diversification, is likely to assist in the construction of a robust theory of the multiproduct firm. The successful completion of this mission could provide the foundation for a discriminating approach towards mergers and acquisitions.

References

K.J. Arrow, An Extension of the Basic Theorms of Classical Welfare Economics, in J. Neyman (ed.), *Proceedings of the Second Berkely Symposium on Mathematical Statistics and Probability* (University of California Press, Berkeley, CA, 1951), pp. 507–532.

---

[18] While Chandler's original focus was on managerial and technological considerations, his more recent writings indicate that he has been able to identify additional sources of underutilized resources — such as marketing and purchasing know-how — which could also provide the foundation for an efficient diversification strategy. In the years after the First World War, "many American companies ... added lines that permitted them to make more effective use of their marketing and purchasing organizations and to exploit the by-products of their manufacturing and processing operations" [Chandler (1977, p. 473)].

K.J. Arrow, *Essays in the Theory of Risk Bearing* (Chicago, IL, 1971).

K.J. Arrow and G. Debreu, Existence of Equilibrium for a Competitive Economy, *Econometrica* 22 (July 1954), 265–290.

C.I. Barnard, *Functions of the Executive* (Harvard University Press, Cambridge, MA, 1938).

F. Black, Capital Market Equilibrium with Restricted Borrowing, *Journal of Business*, July 1972, pp. 444–455.

F. Black and M. Scholes, The Pricing of Options and Corporate Liabilities, *Journal of Political Economy*, May/June 1973, pp. 657–659.

B. Bock, *Statistical Games and the "2000 Largest" Industrials: 1954 and 1968* (The Conference Board, New York, 1970).

L.J. Bourgeois, On the Measurement of Organizational Slack, *Academy of Management Review* 6(1) (January 1981).

G. Calabresi, Transactions Costs, Resource Allocation and Liability Rules: A Comment, *Journal of Law and Economics*, April 1968.

A. Chandler, The Structure of American Industry in the Twentieth Century: A Historical Review, *Business History Review* (Autumn 1969).

A. Chandler, *The Visible Hand* (Harvard University Press, Cambridge, MA, 1977).

J. Child, Organizational Structure, Environment and Performance: The Role of Strategic Choice, *Sociology* 6(1) (1972), 2–22.

R.H. Coase, The Problem of Social Cost, *Journal of Law and Economics*, October 1960, pp. 1–44.

R. Cyert and J.E. March, *A Behavioral Theory of the Firm* (Prentice Hall, Englewood Cliffs, NJ, 1963).

G. Debreu, *Theory of Value* (Wiley, New York, 1959).

E.F. Fama, Efficient Capital Markets: A Review of Theory and Empirical Work, *The Journal of Finance*, May 1970, pp. 383–417.

E.F. Fama, *Foundations of Finance* (Basic Books, New York, 1976).

D. Galai and R.W. Masulis, The Option Pricing Model and the Risk Factor of Stock, *Journal of Financial Economics*, January/March 1976, pp. 53–82.

H. Grabowski and D. Mueller, Life Cycle Effects of Corporate Returns of Retentions, *Review of Economics and Statistics*, November 1975.

S.J. Grossman and J.E. Stiglitz, Information and Competitive Price Systems, *American Economic Review* 66 (May 1976), 246–253.

Jensen, M.C., Some Anomalous Evidence Regarding Market Efficiency, *Journal of Financial Economics* 6 (June/September 1978), 95–101.

I. Kirzner, *Competition and Entrepreneurship* (University of Chicago Press, Chicago, IL, 1973).

B. Klein, R.G. Crawford and A.A. Alchian, Vertical Intergration Appropriable Rents and the Competitive Contracting Process, *Journal of Law and Economics* XXI (2) (October 1978), 297–326.

W.G. Lewellen and B. Huntsman, Managerial Pay and Corporate Performance, *American Economic Review*, September 1970, pp. 710–720.

S.H. Lieberstein, *1979, Who Owns What is in your Head* (Hawthorn Publishers, New York, 1979).

J. Lintner, The Valuation of Risk Assets and the Selection of Risky Investments in Stock Portfolios and Capital Budgets, *The Review of Economics and Statistics*, Febuary 1965, pp. 13–37.

J. Lintner, The Aggregation of Investor's Diverse Judgments and Preferences in Purely Competitive Security Markets, *Journal of Financial and Quantitative Analysis*, December 1969, pp. 347–400.

J. March, *Interview in Stanford GSB* (Graduate School of Business, Stanford University, Stanford, CA, 1979).

J. March and J. Olsen, *Ambiguity and Choice in Organisations* (Universitets-forlaget, Bergen, 1976).

D. Marquis and T. Allen, Communication Patterns in Applied Technology, *American Psychologist* 21 (1966).

R. Marris, *The Economic Theory of Managerial Capitalism* (London, 1966).

K.M. Monteverde and D.J. Teece, Supplier Switching Costs and Vertical Integration, *Bell Journal of Economics* (Spring 1982).

K.M. Monteverde and D.J. Teece, Appropriable Rents and Quasi Vertical Integration, *Journal of Law and Economics*, October 1982.

J. Mossin, Equilibrium in Capital Assets Market, *Econometrica*, October 1966, pp. 768–783.

J. Mossin, *Theory of Financial Markets* (Prentice-Hall, Englewood Cliffs, NJ, 1973).

D.C. Mueller, A Theory of Conglomerate Mergers, *Quarterly Journal of Economics*, November 1969, pp. 643–659. (See also comment by D.E. Logue and P.A. Naert, November 1970, pp. 663–667; comment by D.R. Kanerschen, pp. 668–673, and reply by D.C. Mueller, pp. 674–679.)

D.C. Mueller, A Life Cycle Theory of the Firm, *Journal of Industrial Economics*, July 1972.

S.C. Myers, Procedures for Capital Budgeting Under Uncertainly, *Industrial Management Review* (Spring 1968), 1–19.

R.R. Nelson and S.G. Winter, Firm and Industry Response to Changed Market Conditions: An Evolutionary Approach, *Economic Inquiry*, April 1980.

R.R. Nelson and S.G. Winter, *An Economic Theory of Evolutionary Capabilities and Behavior* (Harvard University Press, Cambridge, MA).

J. Panzar and R. Willig, Economics of Scale and Economies of Scope in Multioutput Production, unpublished working paper (Bell Laboratories, Murray Hill, NJ, 1975).

E.T. Penrose, *Theory of the Growth of the Firm* (Blackwell, Oxford, 1959).

M. Polanyi, *Personal Knowledge: Towards a Post-Critical Philosophy* (University of Chicago Press, Chicago, IL, 1958).

L.D. Schall, Asset Valuation, Firm Investment, and Firm Diversification, *Journal of Business*, January 1972, pp. 11–28.

J.A. Schumpeter, *Capitalism, Socialism, and Democracy* (Harper and Brothers, New York, 1950).

W.F. Sharpe, A Simplified Model for Portfolio Analysis, *Management Science*, January 1963, pp. 277–293.

W.F. Sharpe, Capital Assets Prices: A Theory of Market Equilibrium Under Conditions of Risk, *Journal of Finance*, September 1964, pp. 425–442.

G. Stigler, *The Theory of Price* (Macmillan, New York, 1966).

J.E. Stiglitz, The Allocation Role of the Stock Market, *Journal of Finance* (2) (May 1981).

D.J. Teece, Technology Transfer by Multinational Firms: The Resource Cost of Transferring Technological Knowhow, *Economic Journal* 87, June.

D.J. Teece, Economies of Scope and the Scope of the Enterprise, *Journal of Economic Behavior and Organization* 1(3) (1980), 223–247.

J. Treynor, Towards a Theory of the Market Value of Risky Assets, unpublished manuscript, 1961.

M. Wachter and O. Williamson, Obligational Markets and the Mechanics of Inflation, *Bell Journal of Economics* (Autumn 1978).

O.E. Williamson, *Markets and Hierarchies* (Free Press, New York, 1975).

O.E. Williamson, Transactions Costs Economics: The Governance of Contractual Relations, *Journal of Law Economics*, 1979.

O.E. Williamson and D.J. Teece, European Economic and Political Integration: The Markets and Hierarchies Approach, in P. Salmon (ed.), *New Approaches to European Integration* (1982), forthcoming.

R. Willig, Multiproduct Technology and Market Structure, *American Economic Review*, May 1979.

S.G. Winter, An Essay on the Theory of Production, in S.H. Hymans (ed.), *Economics and the World Around it* (The University of Michigan Press, Ann Arbor, MI, 1982).

Competition, Cooperation, and Innovation Organizational Arrangements for Regimes of Rapid Technological Progress

David J. Teece*

Walter A. Haas School of Business, University of California at Berkeley, Berkeley, CA 94720, U.S.A.

Received September 1989
Final version received May 1990

Discussions of the link between firm size and innovation are outmoded because the boundaries of the firm have become fuzzy in recent decades. Strategic alliances — constellations of bilateral agreements among firms — are increasingly necessary to support innovative activities. Such alliances can facilitate complex coordination beyond what the price system can accomplish, while avoiding the dysfunctional properties sometimes associated with hierarchy. Antitrust law and competition policy need to recognize that these new organizational forms are often the functional antithesis of cartels, though they may have certain structural similarities. A more complete understanding of bilateral contracts and agreements ought to reveal when and how cooperation can support rather than impede innovation and competition.

1. Introduction

Competition is essential to the innovation process and to capitalist economic development more generally. But so is cooperation. The challenge to policy

Reprinted from *Journal of Economic Behavior and Organization* 18 (1992), 1–25.

*I am grateful to Thomas Jorde and two anonymous referees for their helpful insights. I am also indebted to Michael Gerlach for assistance in understanding the differences in industrial organization between the United States and Japan. Patrizia Zagnoli and Oliver Williamson provided insights into the theory and practice of strategic alliances. An earlier version of this paper was published in Japanese in *Business Review*, Hitotsubashi University, March 1989.

analysts and to managers is to find the right balance of competition and cooperation, and the appropriate institutional structures within which competition and cooperation ought to take place.

Unfortunately, the economics textbooks tell us virtually nothing about these issues. While there is usually some consideration given to the import of monopoly and competition on incentives to innovate, it is almost always implicitly assumed that the price mechanism can effect whatever coordination the economic system requires for rapid technological progress. Typically there is no discussion of how interfirm agreements, vertical and horizontal, can help the process. If interfirm agreements are discussed, it is almost always in the context of cartel theory. It is not surprising, therefore, that the economics textbooks, at least those used in the United States, do not convey a sense that interfirm cooperation is either desirable or a subject worthy of study.

This is despite the fact that economists have always recognized the central importance of technological innovation to economic growth and welfare, and to capitalism. Adam Smith's *Wealth of Nations* plunges immediately into discussions of "improvements in machinery," and Karl Marx's model of the capitalist economy ascribes a central role to technological innovation in capital goods. Nor did Alfred Marshall hesitate to describe knowledge as the chief engine of progress in the economy. Paul Samuelson, in his principals text, has always acknowledged the importance of technological change, but then proceeded like all the other leading texts to largely ignore it, causing Stiglitz (1987) in the *Brookings Papers* to recently lament that "while it is the dynamic properties of capitalism ... that constitute the basis of our confidence in its superiority to other forms of economic organization, the theory — at least the version we teach our students — is based on a model that assumes an unchanging technology." When technology is taken into account, the profession at large, according to Rosenberg (1982), has treated it as events transpiring inside a black box, and has "adhered rather strictly to a self-imposed ordinance not to inquire too seriously into what transpires inside that box."

Therefore, it is not surprising that the economics profession is relatively silent on matters of innovation policy and technology strategy, and on matters of economic organization and innovation more generally.[1] A large but unsatisfactory

---

[1] In a recent paper, Dasgupta (1988) set out "to study the sorts of social institutions which can, at least in principle, sustain an efficient level of inventive and innovative activity" (p. 2). This led him to consider what he called the Samuelsonian contrivance, Pigovian subsidies, and Lindahl property rights. The operationality of these mechanisms is remarkably obscure. Dasgupta's gallant efforts notwithstanding, it would appear that there is ample room in the literature for new approaches. More compelling treatments of other relevant organizational issues can be found in the economic and business history literature. See, for instance, Mowery and Rosenberg (1989).

literature exists in industrial organization on the relationship between market structure and innovation, and between firm size and innovation, but both the theoretical and empirical literature are almost completely silent on interfirm and intrafirm organizational issues.[2] When these issues have been addressed, it is without much of a theoretical foundation. Analysts and policy makers have tended to stress the values of pluralism and rivalry as the best organizational arrangement to promote innovation. While these are important values, they are not the only ones. Moreover, with increased global competition, such values are now adequately represented in the global system, and in national economies open to international trade and investment.

This paper does not question the value of rivalry and pluralism; rather, it asks whether in the United States such values ought to be balanced at the margin by a recognition of the importance of coordination, accomplished via non-market forms of cooperation, to a well-functioning national system of innovation. In what follows, the relationship between technical innovation and aspects of industrial organization other than market structure and firm size are examined. In particular, in Sec. 3, the role of cooperative agreements (national and international) among firms are examined for their impact on innovation. Implications for business organization, for corporate strategy, and for public policy are derived.

The basic conclusion of the paper is that complex forms of cooperation are usually necessary to promote competition, particularly when industries are fragmented. Very few firms can successfully "go it alone" any more. Co-operation in turn frequently requires interfirm agreements and alliances. In this regard, the Japanese form of industrial organization, with complex interfirm relationships, may have distinct advantages. European and American firms are now only beginning to learn how to effectively cooperate in order to compete. Antitrust authorities in Europe appear increasingly willing to let them try;[3] unfortunately, antitrust policy in the United States remains uncertain and ambiguous.[4]

---

[2] For an excellent survey, see F.M. Scherer (1970).

3 European companies, and particularly German companies, have a long tradition of cooperation in innovation from the beginning of the development of modern science-based industries in the early years of the 20th century. Europe had no antitrust tradition, not even the common law tenets concerning combinations in restraint of trade. Antitrust came only after World War II. Accordingly, Europe has had little difficulty in creating close interfirm cooperative agreements.

[4] For a discussion of the antitrust treatment of cooperative agreements in Japan, Europe, and the United States, see Jorde and Teece (1989, 1990).

2. Innovation and Competition

Ever since Schumpeter (1942, p. 106) advanced the hypothesis that "the large scale establishment or unit of control ... has come to be the most powerful engine of ... progress," and that "perfect competition looks inferior, and has no title to being set up as a model of ideal efficiency", economists have been ambivalent as to what role market structure and competition play in the innovation process. This ambivalence is particularly pronounced with respect to theoretical discussions. Tensions in the theoretical literature are very briefly noted below. It is also contended that Schumpeter and others did not frame the debate very well for today's circumstances, as the unit of analysis Schumpeter used — the firm — is an increasingly fuzzy concept. One reason is that cooperative interfirm agreements are so pervasive among firms in advanced industrial countries that firm boundaries are often very difficult to define in a meaningful way. Accordingly, Sec. 3 will discuss the coordination requirements of innovation and outline the various organizational alternatives by which they can be achieved. Implications for corporate strategy and public policy are then derived.

Schumpeter's claim that large firms were necessary to promote innovation has fostered exploration of the links between innovative performance and market structure. Schumpeter linked firm size and innovation for three distinct reasons. First, he contended that only large firms could afford the cost of R&D programs. Second, large, diversified firms could absorb failures by innovating across broad broad technological fronts. Third, firms needed some element of market control to reap the rewards of innovation.

The Schumpeterian legacy has spurred discussion of the link between firm size and innovation, and between market structure and innovation. Section 2.1 suggests that this discussion is inconclusive; Sec. 2.2 indicates that it is also outmoded. Schumpeter did not frame the firm size hypothesis in a way that is particularly relevant today, as the boundaries of the firm can no longer be assessed independent of the cooperative relationships which particular innovating firms may have forged. Indeed, this paper posits that firm's ability to forge cooperative relationships can in many instances substitute for more comprehensive forms of integration. Put differently, in some circumstances cooperative agreements can enable smaller firms to emulate many of the functional aspects of large integrated enterprises, without suffering possible dysfunctional sometimes associated with large size. These points are now briefly explored.

2.1. *Firm Size, Market Concentration and Innovation*

As a theoretical matter, economic models of the innovation process are decidedly non-robust, showing that competition can lead to too much or too little R&D investment.[5] In fragmented market structures, several kinds of market failures are commonly recognized. First, if firms are unable to exclude other firms from using technology they have developed, there is the classic "free rider" problem. Even if patents prevent direct mimicking, there is likely to be a technological "neighborhood" illuminated by the innovation that is not foreclosed by the patent, so the externality problem remains, though in a different form. The second problem is what is sometimes referred to as "overbidding". This arises in the early development phase as competitors are stimulated to invest for the potential rewards that will go to the patent winner. Incentives to be the first to invent, or to be first to get to the patent office, may induce too many firms to try to invest early. In such a competitive race, too many resources may get applied too early. One consequence may be that firms drop out of the industry after the patent race is over but before the serious development work begins. A misallocation of resources is the unfortunate consequence.

A monopolized industry avoids both the free rider and the patent race problem. Moreover, the knowledge externalities that come from successful exploration of uncharted technological areas are internalized. Economies of scale and scope may also be available. But the cost is the output restriction that the monopolist will supposedly engineer. This in turn cuts R&D investments. The results, as Nelson and Winter (1982, p. 289) explain, is that "it is hard to say whether there would be more or less R&D undertaken in the monopolized case than in the competitive case". However, Nelson and Winter surmise that the balance probably tips against the monopolist, because in a centralized R&D regime which monopoly would entail, the diversity of approaches characteristic of competition would probably fall, as managers adopt simplified decision making styles. In short, the theoretical literature identifies a wide range of possible outcomes, and accordingly provides little guide to policy.

2.2. *Defining the Firms' Boundaries*

As a practical matter, the economists' debate seems highly stylized and out of touch with global realities. Neither perfect competition nor complete monopoly is observable or realistically attainable in any industry today. Moreover, to abstract

---

[5] For a useful survey, see Baldwin and Scott (1987).

from industrial structure in such narrow terms is to miss key elements of industrial organization.

First, the boundaries of the firm are extremely difficult to delineate, particularly when there are complex alliance structures in place. In Japan, for instance, Gerlach (1988) notes that alliances are "neither formal organizations with clearly defined, hierarchical structures, nor impersonal, decentralized markets. Business alliances operate instead in extended networks of relationships between companies, organized around identifiable groups, and bound together in durable relationships which are based on long-term reciprocity". Much of the complexity and subtlety of these arrangements is missed by analysts who narrowly focus on legal titles and the structure of property rights, narrowly defined. Even worse, since the most familiar model that economists have of cooperative behavior is that of the cartel, many scholars have missed the efficiency inducing characteristics of alliance structures in Japan and elsewhere. Indeed, Caves and Uekusa (1976, p. 158) appear to push alliances into the straightjacket of cartel theory when they contend that "Japanese industries are prone to collusive arrangements but are also rich in structural incentives for the conspirators to cheat. The net outcome for the gap between actual and ideal industrial output is thus hard to predict, but we do expect increased distortions from sporadic price discrimination, reciprocity, and the diversion of rivalry into uncontrolled nonprice forms".

Alliances are a form of contractual relationship, but they are much more than a legal contract. Alliance partners are not faceless entities operating at arms-length in Walrasian markets. Rather, exchange among alliance partners (at least in Japan) can be characterized, according to Gerlach (1988), by: (1) an emphasis on relational rather than transactional exchange, wherein the focus is toward the actors participating in rather than being the objects of exchange; (2) a state of continuous indebtedness and mutual obligation between the parties; and (3) the implicit negotiations of a socially significant order through symbolic activities and ceremonies. Alliances are defined by interests among specific subsets of firms that are familiar with each other through historical association, rather than immediate task requirements.

The alliance structure in Japan appears to have enabled smaller Japanese firms to attain the degree of functional integration found within some large integrated American enterprises, but with less in the way of common ownership of the parts. Subcontractors, trading companies, and distributors take on for the firm functions often done internally in the United States. While many American firms, particularly those in high technology industries, rely on outside suppliers and distributors to a similar degree, the level of functional integration attained with these relationships in the United States is markedly lower. In Japan, the appropriate Western image is perhaps neither that of the "visible hand" nor the "invisible hand" but of the continuous handshake.[6] Japaneses corporate strategy is therefore formulated to a considerable extent by maneuvering within alliance relationships, by industrial visions worked out among firms, and also by the broader industrial policies set by government.

Where the law permits, alliance and consortia structures are increasingly coming to characterize aspects of European and American business. Though more transactional and less relational than alliances in Japan, these structures nevertheless involve high levels of cooperation, particularly for new product development and commercialization. So pervasive have these relationships become that one can no longer fruitfully explore industrial organization questions in the neoclassical tradition. Discussions of firm size which do not take cooperative agreements into account seriously mischaracterize the nature of the business firm. Discussions of product market structure that do not take the market for know-how into account are also likely to mischaracterize the nature of competition faced by a firm in a fast-paced industry. In the remainder of this paper, cooperative agreements are explored more fully. The next section discusses both the importance of coordination for the innovation process and the organizational mechanisms available to effect it.

3. Innovation, Coordination and Cooperation

The contention advanced in this paper is that the intensely competitive environment in which high-tech firms find themselves, coupled with the global dispersion of productive-technical competence, often requires complex forms of cooperation among competing firms. This paper stresses the need for both "operational" and "strategic" coordination to develop and profitably commercialize new technology.

3.1. *The Global Dispersion of Competence*

Global industrial competence became widely dispersed within a century of the industrial revolution. The predominant method of organizing these competences was first the factory. As Chandler (1977) so ably describes, the transportation and telecommunications revolution facilitated the rise of the modern (vertically) integrated corporation. The vertically integrated enterprise, beginning around 1900, internalized R&D activities [Mowery and Rosenberg (1989)]. U.S. industrial

---

[6] See Gerlach (1992, p. 2).

R&D emerged a private-sector affair, with R&D closely tied to the large enterprise through in-house labs. By 1945, the United States had an industrial structure dominated by large industrial enterprises, with a research system appended to it. American firms became dominant across a broad front of technologies.

The decades of the 1970s and 1980s saw the manifestation of three trends, two of which have been in progress since 1945: (1) a catching up of Europe and Japan with the United States, and the greater dispersion of technological and organizational resources which has accompanied it; (2) enhanced global competition through a gradual liberalization of trading and investment regimes; and (3) the growth in venture capital, from the late 1960s in the United States, and in Europe and Japan in the 1980s. The growth of venture capital has provided, at least in the United States, a second avenue for developing new technologies — namely, the "start-up" firm.

A consequence of these trends is that industrial competence is now more widely dispersed, both organizationally and geographically. Couple this with the generic nature of many new technologies — like microelectronics and biotechnology — and one recognizes that the competitive challenges associated with developing and commercializing innovation are very considerable. That is not to say that in earlier periods — such as the second half of the 19th century — technology capacity was not geographically dispersed. However, global communications were such that the distinction between local and global was economically much sharper than it is today; the ability of firms to quickly assemble and efficiently operate complex forms of interfirm agreements was severely limited. The capacity to organize and operate complex and geographically dispersed organizational forms is now widely available; with enhanced competition, the need to select efficient structures is even more pressing.

3.2. *The Need for Operational Coordination*

Innovation is a special kind of economic activity, with very special kinds of informational and coordination requirements. This subsection examines these requirements, without addressing the question of whether they are organized most appropriately by markets, hierarchies, alliances or other organizational forms.

1. *Accessing complementary assets.* Innovative new products and processes will not yield value unless they are commercialized. It is during commercialization that the greatest organizational challenges arise and where the bulk of the resource commitment occurs. The profitable commercialization of technology requires timely access to complementary assets on competitive terms. Thus an innovating firm or consortium that has developed the core technology needed for a new

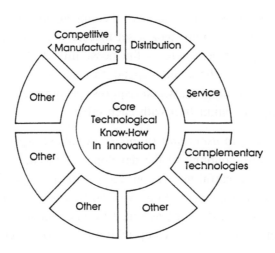

Fig. 1. Representative complementary assets needed to commercialize technological know-how.

product or process with good commercialization prospects has taken only the first step. It must then secure access to complementary technologies and complementary assets on favorable terms in order to successfully commercialize the product or process.[7]

Assets such as marketing, competitive manufacturing, reputation, and after-sales support are almost always needed. The range of complementary assets that are necessary is indicated in Fig. 1. These assets need not bear a relationship to the innovating unit that is either strictly vertical or horizontal.[8] Moreover, these assets will often need to be specialized to the innovation. For example, the commercialization of a new drug is likely to require the dissemination of information over a specialized information channel. In some cases, the complementary assets may be the other parts of a system. For instance, computer hardware may require the development of specialized software both for the operating system and for applications.

The interdependence between the innovation and the relevant complementary assets can, of course, vary tremendously. At one extreme, the complementary assets may be virtually generic, have many potential suppliers, and be relatively unimportant when compared with the technological breakthrough represented

---

[7] See Teece (1986).

[8] Vertical relations are upstream or downstream. Horizontal relationships involve firms competing for the same customers in the same market.

by the innovation. At the other end, successful commercialization of the innovation may depend critically on a bottleneck asset that has only one possible supplier. Between these two extremes there is the possibility of "cospecialization" — where the innovation and the assets depend on each other. An example of this would be containerized shipping, which requires specialized trucks and terminals that can work only in conjunction with each other.

2. *Coupling developer to users and suppliers*. A salient aspect of innovation is that it requires a close coupling of the developer of the new technology to the user. Commercially successful innovations require linking scientific, engineering, entrepreneurial and management skills with an intimate understanding of user needs. Indeed, in some fields, such as scientific instruments, it is often the user that stimulates innovation and comes up with a new product concept or product

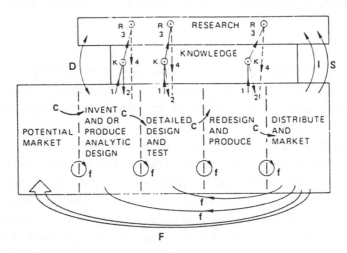

Symbols used on arrows:
 C = central-chain-of-innovation
 f = feedback loops
 F = particularly important feedback

K-R: Links through knowledge to research and return paths. If problem solved at node K, link 3 to R not activated. Return from research (link 4) is problematic — therefore dashed line.
 D: Direct link to and from research from problems in invention and design.
 I: Support of scientific research by instruments, machines, tools, and procedures of technology.
 S: Support of research in sciences underlying product area to gain information directly and by monitoring outside work. The information obtained may apply anywhere along the chain.
Source: Kline and Rosenberg (1986).

Fig. 2. Model showing flow paths of information and cooperation.

prototype which is passed back upstream for further development work. Hence, innovation requires considerable vertical interaction and communication flows. Moreover, these flows must occur expeditiously. With uncertainty, learning, and short product life cycles, there must be organizational systems in place to facilitate timely feedback, midcourse correction, redesign, and rapid commercialization. The necessary linkages and feedbacks are summarized in Fig. 2.

Kline and Rosenberg (1986) have described the process as "chain linked". Their characterization recognizes aspects of a linear model — such as a flow of activity through design to development production and marketing — but also recognizes constant feedback between and among "stages". Moreover, "the linkage from science to innovation is not solely or even preponderantly at the beginning of typical innovations, but rather extends all through the process ... science can visualized as lying alongside development processes, to be used when needed".

The correct identification of needs is critical to the profitable expenditure of R&D dollars. R&D personnel must thus be closely connected to the market and to marketing personnel. R&D managers must have one foot in the lab and one in the marketplace. Knowing *what* to develop and design, rather than just how to do it, is absolutely essential for commercial success. Developing this understanding involves a complex interplay between science and engineering, manufacturing, and marketing in order to specify product functions and features. It is not just a matter of identifying user needs and assessing engineering feasibility. One must also separate those user needs which are being met by competition and those which are not. This may not become clear until the product is introduced, in which case the ability to redesign quickly and efficiently may be of the utmost importance. In short, commercialization is an extremely important ingredient to successful innovation.

This model recognizes the existence and exercise of tight linkages and feedback mechanisms which must operate quickly and efficiently. These linkages must exist within the firm, among firms, and between firms and other organizations, such as universities. Of course, the positioning of the firm's boundaries, for example, its level of vertical integration, determines in part whether the required interactions are intrafirm or interfirm.

Thus no matter how innovation proceeds, it is likely to require access to capabilities which lie beyond the initiating or driving entity. These capabilities may lie in universities, other parts of the enterprise, or in other unaffiliated enterprises. The role of some of these key organizational units is now explored. We will examine both the development and the commercialization of new technology.

In a series of important pieces, von Hippel (1977, 1988) has presented evidence that, in some industries in the United States, industrial products judged by users to offer them a significant performance improvement are usually conceived and prototyped by users, not by the manufacturers. The manufacturers' role in the innovation process in these industries is to become aware of the user innovation and its value, and then to manufacture a commercial version of the device for sale to user firms. This pattern of innovation involving vertical cooperation is contrary to the usual assumption that product manufacturers are responsible for the innovation process from finding to filling the need. Successful management of the process requires that product engineering skills (rather than R&D skills) be resident in the manufacturer, and that manufacturers search to identify user solutions rather than user needs.[9] A further implication is that there may be a symbiotic vertical relationship between users and equipment manufacturers that depends upon social and geographical proximity.

Balancing the role that users play in stimulating innovation upstream is the role that suppliers play in stimulating downstream innovation. A good deal of the innovation in the automobile industry, including fuel injection, alternators, and power steering, has its origins in upstream component suppliers.[10] The challenge then becomes how to "design in" the new components, and possibly how to avoid sole source dependency on the part of the automotive companies. As discussed below, deep and enduring relationships need to be established between component developer-manufacturer and supplier to ensure adoption and diffusion of the technology.

A related set of vertical relationships involving innovation has been remarked upon by Rosenberg (1972) in his treatise on technology and American economic growth. The machine tool industry in the 19th century played a unique role both in the initial solution of technical problems in user industries, such as railroad locomotive manufacture. Rosenberg's description seems to suggest that the users played some role in the development of new equipment. He notes that before 1820 in the United States, one could not identify a distinct set of firms who were specialists in the design and manufacturer of machinery. Machines were either produced by users or by firms engaged in the production of metal or wooden products.[11] Machinery-producing firms were thus first observed as adjuncts to textile factories. However, once established, these firms

---

[9] Note that user innovation requires two kinds of technology transfer: first from user to manufacturer, and then from manufacturer to the developer-user and other users.

[10] For example, Bendix and Bosch developed fuel injection and Motorola the alternator.

[11] See Rosenberg (1972, p. 98–99).

played an important role as the transmission center in the diffusion of new technology.[12]

3. *Coupling to competitors*. Successful new product and new process development innovation often requires horizontal as well as vertical cooperation. Horizontal linkages can assist in the definition of technical standards for systemic innovation. Horizontal linkages can also assist firms to overcome the appropriability (spillover) problems because the set of firms receiving the benefits is likely to include a greater portion of firms which have incurred R&D costs. The effect of greater appropriability is to encourage greater investment in new technology.[13] In addition, collaborative research reduces needless duplication of effort.[14] Independent research activities often proceed down identical or near-identical technological paths. This is often wasteful and can be minimized if research plans are coordinated.[15]

Furthermore, innovation and commercialization of new products and processes are often high cost activities. The scale and scope of assets needed will often lie beyond the capabilities of a single firm. Thus, cooperation — both horizontal and vertical — may be the only viable means for moving forward. In addition, cooperation will also reduce wasteful duplicate expenditures on research and development. Innovation also entails significant risk. While successful innovation and its financial rewards are often highly visible, behind the scenes there are usually many failed efforts and unproductive paths. "Dry holes" and "blind alleys" are commonplace. Risk can be diversified and spread through cooperation. Indeed, when risk is particularly high because the technology being pursued is both expensive and undeveloped, cooperation may be the only way that firms will undertake the needed effort.

Until very recently, it has been fashionable in the United States to argue that diversity is the leitmotif of successful innovation. Unquestionably, a system of innovation that converges on just one view of possibilities is likely to close off productive avenues of inquiry. However, in a private enterprise economy without some horizontal coordination and communication, there is no guarantee that the level of diversity obtained is ideal. If firms are able to coordinate their research programs to some degree, uneconomic duplication in some instances

---

[12] *Ibid.*, p. 102.

[13] This has been shown empirically by Levin and Reiss (1984).

[14] See David (1985, p. 42).

[15] Needless to say, uncertainty often requires that multiple (but not identical) technological paths be pursued simultaneously. See, for example, Nelson (1984, chapter 2).

can be minimized without the industry converging on a single technological approach.

4. *Connections among technologies.*[16] Another dimension of coordination is that which must take place among various technologies. Particular technological advances seldom stand alone. They usually are connected both to (a) prior developments in the same technology, and (b) to complementary or facilitating advances in related technologies. In addition, a generic technology may be capable of (c) a wide variety of end-product applications. Each is discussed in turn, along with related reasons for cooperation.[17]

a. *Connections to prior technologies.* Many technologies evolve in an evolutionary fashion, with today's round of R&D activities building on yesterday's, which in turn builds on the day before's. Thus, with respect to memory devices, advance is cumulative along a particular technological trajectory, from 1 K to 4 K to 64 K to 256 K to 1 megabyte and so on, up to the theoretical limits of a particular technology. Similarly, in the aircraft industry, the DC-3 improved upon the DC-2, and subsequent aircraft built on what was learned with the DC-3. Hence, whether an enterprise is able to participate in one technology often depends on whether it participated in the earlier generation. If it did not, and the technologies in questions have path dependencies, then in order to enter at a subsequent stage the enterprise in question will have to link up, in some fashion, with enterprises familiar with the prior art. Relatedly, experience and competence in a particular technological regime may count for little, and may in fact be a handicap, when a significant shift in technological regime occurs. A regime shift signals opportunities for new entrants; but to engage these opportunities, new entrants may need to link up with incumbent firms who may not have the relevant new technology, but do in fact have complementary capacities, such as marketing and distribution.

b. *Connections to complementary technologies.* Technological advances are often linked together because of systems interdependencies. Thus, the electric lighting system — dynamos, distribution system, and incandescent bulbs — was severely limited by nondurable bulb filaments that existed until Edison and his associates invented a high resistance filament. Artificial intelligence technologies depend

---

[16] This treatment is based in part on Nelson (1984, pp. 8–10).

[17] It is obvious that the treatment here breaks with the traditional "book of blueprints" approach to technology often embedded in economic models of the innovation process. We implicitly postulate market failure in the market for know-how. For a more extensive treatment, see Teece (1980).

both on the availability of computer software and hardware. Containerization of ocean shipping could not move forward until new facilities to handle containers had been put in place in ports, in distribution centers, and in railroads and trucking. The innovation, of course, also required the construction of ships with the requisite capacities. In a system technology, an advance in one part of the system may not only permit but require changes in other parts. The tightness of interdependence and the requirements for organizational connectedness are discussed later. Suffice to say here that tight interdependencies require interaction and information and materials flows among organizations. Whether the appropriate governance mechanism is a contract, a joint venture, equity cross-holdings, or merger is a matter we consider in Sec. 4.

b. *Connections to enabling technologies.* New technologies may simultaneously affect several different activities, typically because they provide a common core technology to several businesses (e.g., microelectronics, composites, biotechnology). Thus advances in semiconductors increase the technical capabilities of industries that use chips, from computers to telecommunications. Advances in semiconductors also facilitate more powerful computer-aided engineering and design and computer-integrated manufacturing.[18] Organizations must be designed in order to facilitate the complex cooperation which utilization of the enabling technology requires. Without the appropriate organizational mechanism, the full potential of the enabling technology will not be realized.

3.3. *Strategic Coordination*

In Sec. 3.2, the operational dimensions of coordination were sketched. These activities must take place if *any* system is to be innovative. Strategic coordination refers to coordination of a different type. It refers to activities which affect the distribution of returns to innovation through impacts on prices and competitive entry.

Because of fundamental weaknesses in the system of intellectual property law,[19] leakage and free riding are commonplace. Moreover, because of the use of strategic trade and industrial policies by some nation states, strategic coordination either by firms or governments is often necessary if innovating firms are to capture value from technology. Strategic coordination can thus enhance the public as well as private interests.

---

[18] See National Advisory Committee on Semiconductors Report (1989).

[19] See Levin, Klevorick, Nelson and Winter (1987, p. 3).

Strategic coordination is often desirable to ensure that capacity levels at various stages in an industry are matched to the level of residual demand, to ensure that beneficial standards are adopted, and to ensure that strategic moves of competitors are blunted if not deterred, and to ensure that economies and advantages associated with increasing returns are attained. Unfortunately, in the United States, strategic behavior is often uncritically viewed as anticompetitive, with negative effects on economic welfare assumed. While such behavior may be "anticompetitive" in the sense that it limits the entry of competitors, strategic behavior can sometimes enhance national if not global economic welfare.[20] This is because it can help innovators capture enough of the return from innovation to keep them in the business of innovation, thereby invigorating competition. There is no opportunity in this paper to document all the various forms of strategic coordination. Suffice to point out that the timely assembly of complementary assets may well have both a strategic and an operational dimension, as is discussed more fully elsewhere [Teece (1986)].

4. Governance Structures to Facilitate Innovation

4.1. *The Organizational Menu*

There are of course a wide variety of organizational mechanisms that can be used to effectuate the coordination which successful innovation requires. Economists at some level have been aware of this for decades. Thus, "Marshall introduces organization as a fourth factor of production; J.B. Clark gives the coordinating function to the entrepreneur; Knight introduces managers who coordinate" [Coase (1937)]. But it is only recently that significant progress has been made.[21] Unfortunately, the emerging literature on the economics of organization has yet to deal with matters of innovation.

The state of the art is such that many economists are still in the un-comfortable position of claiming that the price mechanism achieves the necessary coordination while at other times entrepreneurs and managers do the

---

[20] Jacquemin and Slade (1989) single out two areas where governments can usefully encourage cooperative behavior; R&D-intensive industries, and declining industries. The work of Brian Arthur (1988) also points out the critical role of increasing returns and lock-in by small chance events. Government policy obviously can be of great importance, positively and negatively, in such environments.

[21] Oliver Williamson (1975, 1985) has pioneered the economic analysis of organizations building on fundamental insights presented by Coase (1937).

coordination.[22] While Williamson (1975, 1985) has elaborated the distinctive merits of markets and certain hierarchical forms, alternative organizational arrangements until recently have received relatively short shrift in the literature. But interfirm agreements and alliances must clearly be among the alternatives considered. The following subsections will explore each of the various options in more detail.

4.2. *The Price System*

The invisible hand is one of the oldest notions in economic science. Prices are considered sufficient statistics; sufficient that is to guide resource allocations toward Pareto optimal outcomes. The invisible hand theorems require, it would seem, that economic agents know not only today's supply and demand but supply and demand for all future periods. Otherwise, we cannot be confident that the market outcomes generated will be optimal. In particular, investment levels will be incorrect unless we know about future market demand and the future investment plans of competitors and suppliers. Any single investment will, in general, only be profitable provided first that the volume of *competitive* investment does not exceed a limit set by demand, and second, that the volume of *complementary* investment reaches the correct level.[23]

However, there is no special machinery in a private enterprise, market economy to ensure that investment programs are made known to all concerned at the time of their inception. Price movements, by themselves, do not generally form an adequate system of signalling. Indeed, Koopmans (1957) has been rather critical of what he calls the "overextended belief" of certain economists in the efficiency of competitive markets as a means of allocating resources in a world characterized by ubiquitous uncertainty. The main source of this uncertainty, according to Koopmans, is the ignorance which firms have with respect to their competitors' future actions, preferences, and states of technological information. In the absence of a complete set of forward markets in which anticipation and intentions

---

[22] As Coase (1937) notes, "it is surely important to enquire why coordination is the work of the price mechanism in one case and of the entrepreneur in another." Coase went on to develop an approach to economic organization that saw the firm as suppressing the price mechanism in circumstances where transaction costs were high. Hayek (1945) saw the situation somewhat similarly, there being three fundamental choices: central planning, competition (decentralized planning), and monopoly — the latter he refers to as the "half-way house" about which many people talk but which few like. Despite recent progress, the economic literature has not gone much beyond Hayek and Coase.

[23] See Richardson (1960, p. 31).

could be tested and adjusted, there is no reason to believe that with uncertainty competitive markets of the kind described in the textbooks produce efficient outcomes.[24] The information-circulating function which economic theory attributes to competitive markets is quite simply not discharged by any existing arrangements with the detail and forward extension necessary to support efficient outcomes.[25] Ancillary organizational mechanisms are needed.

Arrow (1959) suggests that the firm performs the dual role of entrepreneur and auctioneer when the system is out of equilibrium. Richardson (1960) argues that some form of market imperfection is essential to the process of economic adjustment. Telser (1985) has articulated the case for efficient cartels where firms discuss new investment decisions and share capacity in order to overcome the shortcomings of the price system.

There is no arena in which uncertainty is higher and the need to coordinate greater than in the development and commercialization of new technology. Moreover, there are no theoretical grounds for believing that an economy that is all tooth and claw will out perform one that involves a judicious mix of tooth, claw, and intramarket and intermarket cooperation. Adam Smith's[26] warning — that "people of the same trade seldom meet together, even for merriment and diversion, but the conversation ends in a conspiracy against the public, or in some contrivance to raise prices" — needs to be tempered with the recognition that in global markets the difficulty of assembling all the relevant parties to effectuate an international conspiracy is an insurmountable challenge in industries' experiencing rapid technological change. It also needs to be tempered with a recognition that the exchange of information on common values such as future demand is often socially desirable. This is because prices clearly are not sufficient signals in all cases. The price mechanism does not always find prices efficiently, and it may fail to elicit those responses from economic agents that will maintain an optimal allocation of resources. The presence of scale economics or collective goods are just two considerations which upset the invisible hand theorems.

Yet in the traditional textbook, the price system magically allows all of the necessary coordination to occur smoothly and efficiently. In the Walrasian system, which is implicit in textbook thinking about equilibrium price determination, profits

---

[24] Koopmans (1957, p. 146) points out that because of this deficiency economic theorists are not able to speak with anything approaching scientific authority on matters relating to individual versus collective enterprise.

[25] *Ibid.*, p. 163.

[26] This did not appear to be an important part of Smith's (1976) overall thesis.

cause output expansion, losses contraction.[27] In equilibrium, firms make neither profits nor losses. In this system, entrepreneurs, together with the auctioneer, act as coordinators to bring harmony to the competitive pursuit of self-interest. In this simple view, the only information firms need to develop and commercialize innovation is provided by the auctioneer in terms of price.

A pure unassisted Walrasian-type market system is clearly inadequate to effectuate most types of innovation. Yet many economists cling to the belief that it is adequate, or very nearly so. This would appear to stem from what Koopmans calls an overextended belief in the efficiency of competitive markets, coupled with a lack of understanding of the nature of the innovation process.

3.3. *Internal Organization*

Coase (1937) saw the costs of using the price system, and in particular the costs of discovering the relevant prices, as the fundamental reason why it is profitable to establish firms. Williamson (1975) took several cues from this thesis and has developed a more sophisticated contractual variant of the Coase thesis. He shows that it is not so much the difficulty of establishing prices as the difficulty of regulating economic activity with incomplete contracts that provides the reason to abandon markets in favor of internal organization. Unless safeguards can be provided against opportunistic recontracting, transactions must be brought inside the firm where a managerial hierarchy and appropriate incentives can ameliorate the consequences of opportunism.

But the full integration solution has liabilities, not least of which is that it can impair the autonomy so necessary for aspects of the innovation process to proceed. Still, it has obvious advantages for effectuating strategic coordination. For example, Michael Borrus (1988, p. 231) recognized that new institutional forms are needed in U.S. microelectronics if the industry is to compete effectively in the future and

---

[27] As Aoki (1984) explains, the prices of goods and services are set by the auctioneer, who adjusts them according to the law of supply and demand. Given a system of prices, the excess of sales price of entrepreneurial output over the cost of production may be either positive, null, or negative. This excess is termed *benefice de l'enterprise* by Walras (1954). A positive or negative *benefice* is a sign of disequilibrium, and entrepreneurs respond to this signal according to the law of cost price; that is, they increase their scale of production when the *benefice* is positive and reduce it when the *benefice* is negative. The presumption that firms strive for higher incomes and lower losses through entry and exit is implicit. However, entrepreneurs in their purely functional roles are only catalytic agents who accelerate combinations of atomistic factors of production only when the *benefice* is positive. Thus, in a state of equilibrium, entrepreneurs make neither profit nor loss. 'Profit in the sense of *benefice de l'enterprise* ... depends upon exceptional and not upon normal circumstances.'

at the same time avoid antitrust problems.[28] However, his solution — the establishment of a number of holding companies for Silicon Valley firms — implicitly endorses internal organization (accomplished via merger) as the solution to the problem.[29] While it may be better than the current fragmented structure, there are many reasons why one should be skeptical of its viability. Many of these relate to the change in incentives and compensation structures which the arrangements would imply.[30] As explained below, when high technology activities are at issue, contractual agreements, alliances, and joint ventures are likely to be superior to full-scale internal organization.

4.4. Strategic Alliances and Interfirm Agreements

There are a wide range of contractual agreements between and among firms to facilitate the development and commercialization of new technologies. Strategic alliances are constellations of bilateral and possibly multilateral contracts and understandings among firms, typically to develop and commercialize new technology. These may well constitute a new organizational form.

---

[28] Borrus (1988) comments:

Almost a decade ago it was clear that Japanese producers would emerge as enduring players in the semiconductor industry, and would, as a consequence, radically alter the industry's terms of competition. Yet it has taken almost that long for U.S. firms to cooperate sufficiently to begin to devise appropriate responses. It is almost a truism that had the industry been able to coordinate its actions strategically a decade ago, an adequate response would have been far less costly and far more likely to succeed. To accomplish such strategic coordination, the U.S. chip industry needs an ongoing analytic capacity, embedded in an electronics industry-wide institution, with the ability to carry on competitive analysis of foreign market and technology strategies, and with sufficient prestige to offer strategic direction on which planning can occur.

There is, of course, a substantial problem associated with industry-strategic planning. To assure its health, the industry needs strategic coordination short of market sharing. All U.S. industries facing international competition ought to be permitted to develop industry-wide competitive assessment capability, at least whenever the industry can demonstrate substantial involvement of foreign governments in assisting foreign competitors.

[29] Borrus (1988, p. 233) remarked:

[I]t is possible to envision chip-firm holding companies built around common manufacturing facilities ... R&D resources shared among the holding company's chip firms would eliminate the problem of duplication of R&D among smaller companies. The high capital costs of staying in the technology race could be shared among firms in the form of shared flexible fabrication facilities ... Shared facilities would permit high usage of capacity ... In essence, the holding company structure would gain the advantages associated with consolidation without the disadvantages associated with integration.

[30] See, in particular, Williamson (1985).

Agreements are bilateral when A agrees to secure *Y* from B as a condition for making *X* available, and both parties understood that agreement will be continued only if reciprocity is observed.[31] When constellations of these agreements exist between or among firms, they can be considered to constitute alliances. While the term is often used rather loosely, a *strategic* alliance is defined here as a constellation of agreements characterized by the commitment of two or more partner firms to reach a common goal, entailing the pooling of their resources and activities. A strategic alliance might include the following: (i) an exclusive purchase agreement; (ii) exclusionary market or manufacturing rights; (iii) technology swaps; (iv) joint R&D or co-development agreements; (v) co-marketing arrangements. A strategic alliance denotes some degree of strategic as well as operational coordination.

Alliances can be differentiated from exchange transactions, such as a simple licensing agreement with specified royalties, because with an exchange transaction the object of the transaction is supplied by the selling firm to the buying firm in exchange for cash. An alliance by definition can never have one side receiving only cash; moreover, it consists of a constellation of bilateral agreements. Alliances need not involve equity swaps or equity investments, though they often do. Equity alliances can take many forms, including minority equity holdings, consortia, and joint ventures.

Strategic alliances are capable of achieving the various forms of operational and strategic coordination described in Secs. 3.2 and 3.3. Complementary assets, user know-how, complementary technologies and enabling technologies can all be accessed in this way, though the terms are likely to be different from what could be obtained through a intrafirm agreement were it feasible since the costs and risks of innovation can be lowered through such arrangements.

Strategic alliances have increased in frequency in recent years, and are particularly characteristic of high technology industries. Joint R&D, know-how, manufacturing, and marketing agreements go well beyond exchange agreements because they can be used to access complementary technologies and complementary assets. The object of the transactions, such as the development and launch of a new product, usually does not exist at the time the contracts are inked. Whether equity or nonequity forms of alliances are the most desirable governance structures depends on a variety of circumstances.[32]

Equity stakes provide a mechanism for distributing residuals when ex ante contractual agreements cannot be written to specify or enforce a division of

---

[31] *Ibid.*, p. 191.

[32] For a fuller treatment, see Pisano and Teece (1989).

	Nonequity	Equity
Exchange	short-medium term cash-based contracts	passive stock holdings for portfolio diversification
Alliance	mid-long-term bilateral contracts (non-cash based), non-operating joint ventures and consortia	operating joint ventures and consortia, minority equity holdings, and cross-holdings
Cartel	price fixing and/or output restricting agreements	price fixing and/or output restricting agreements

Fig. 3. Taxonomy of interfirm arrangements.

returns. If equity membership also provides board membership, higher level strategic coordination is also possible in some cases. These governance structures are summarized in Fig. 3.

Strategic alliances appear to be an attractive organizational form for an environment characterized by rapid innovation and geographical and organizational dispersion in the sources of know-how. As compared to the price system, they enable investment plans for complementary assets to be coordinated more concisely than the price system would allow; as compared to hierarchy, incentives are not dulled through bureaucratic decision making. In short, the strategic alliance appears to be a hybrid structure well suited to today's global realities in industries experiencing rapid technological change. Such industries frequently require operational and strategic coordination. Alliances facilitate reciprocal specialization among firms, such as when one firm does development and its partner manufacturing. But as suggested elsewhere [Teece (1986)], market failures are such that the distribution of the profits that may follow need not be equally distributed among alliance partners.

5. Strategic Alliances and the Logic of Managerial Capitalism

The above analysis might appear, at first glance, to be at odds with Chandler's recent claim (1990) that firms that deny what he calls 'the logic of managerial enterprise' will not survive. Chandler's historical analysis suggests that innovating firms that fail to invest in facilities of sufficient scale will lose market share and technological leadership to competitors. Thus, according to Chandler the early lead which the British had in dyestuffs was lost to the Germans because British firms failed to make the necessary investments to capture economies of scale and scope. This is the principal reason why German firms outcompeted the British; vertical integration is thus essential to managerial capitalism according to the Chandler argument.

The thesis in this paper is that the logic of managerial capitalism may well be eroding, although not as fast as the growth of strategic alliances involving U.S.-based firms might suggest.

The "logic" of managerial capitalism is being tempered in some industries because of the heightened importance of generic enabling technologies and time to market. Both favor small autonomous organization units that can avoid the complex decision-making complexities usually, though not always, associated with large integrated hierarchies. Large amounts of information critical to innovation must move horizontally; if forced to move vertically before it can move horizontally, its timeliness as well as its value will erode dramatically. A valued price system has no advantage in this regard; small autonomous organizational units communicating and interacting directly with each other are likely to develop and implement an action plan faster and more efficiently than if they were responding just to price signals. When product life cycles are short, the ability to quickly and effectively coordinate business units into a coherent operation often assumes great significance.

One additional reason for the frequency of strategic alliances involving U.S. high-tech firms, however, is the decline in U.S. manufacturing skills, particularly in relation to Japan and Germany. U.S. firms still seem to possess a strong advantage in early-stage technological activity, but their advantage at commercialization has eroded markedly in recent decades. It is therefore advantageous for innovative firms which are unable to build and operate world-class manufacturing facilities to team up with those that can. Unfortunately for U.S. firms, the market for know-how is riddled with imperfections, and the ability of innovators to capture a significant share of the rents through alliances is highly attenuated — except in unusual circumstances where the innovator has a strong worldwide patent position. When intellectual property protection is weak, strategic alliances — implying a constellation of interfirm agreements and the ability to temper opportunistic behavior — are likely to be more effective than a pure licensing arrangement. But an alliance is likely to be inferior to vertical integration if the innovator is in the position to integrate at low cost. In the United States one can perhaps agree with Chandler that there aren't intrinsic theoretical disabilities associated with vertical integration; but there may be disabilities associated with an integration strategy built on decaying U.S. manufacturing skills. Hence, strategic alliances may often be the best alternative available to U.S. firms, though that alternative may well be inferior to an integration strategy based on world-class manufacturing. Hence while strategic alliances may be the best that many U.S. firms can do, it may not be enough, as Chandler suggests, to survive in today's highly-competitive global environment.

6. Conclusion

Successful technological innovation requires complex forms of business organization. To be successful, innovating organizations must form linkages, upstream and downstream, lateral and horizontal. Advanced technological systems do not and cannot get created in splendid isolation. The communication and coordination requirements are often quite stupendous, and in practice the price system alone does not suffice to achieve the necessary coordination.

A variety of organizational arrangements exist to bring about the necessary coordination. The price system described in the textbooks provides only a useful backdrop in market-oriented economies. By itself it is not up to the task because investments required to effectuate innovation cannot be appropriately coordinated by price signals alone. Fully integrated companies, on the other hand, must be careful not to suffocate creativity and to dampen incentives. Strategic alliances constitute viable alternatives in many instances. Alliance structures can facilitate innovation, and are increasingly necessary as the sources of innovation and the capacities necessary to effectuate commercialization become increasingly dispersed.

A variety of implications follow for management and public policy. Managers must become adept at managing not just their own organization, but also their relationships and alliances with other firms. Very often difference skills are required for each, which makes management tasks more complex and challenging. Strategic alliances also must be designed to be self-reinforcing. There is the danger that changing circumstances can upset delicate balances, thereby causing relationships and agreements to unravel. Equity can be judiciously used to anchor alliances, but it may not suffice as a safeguard if inadequate in amount, and if not bolstered by other mechanisms. At present there is considerable organizational learning occurring with respect to such matters, both nationally and internationally, and new arrangements which are balanced and durable will undoubtedly be crafted.

The greatest challenge probably goes to public policy, particularly in the United States, where there has been a failure to recognize the importance of cooperation. This has manifested itself in the absence of inter-agency coordination in the federal government, with science and technology policy appearing to be weak and uncoordinated, and a reluctance in some quarters to permit and encourage the private sector to forge the interfirm agreements, alliances and consortia necessary to develop and commercialize new technologies like high-density television or superconductors. A key reason for this is the shadow that neoclassical thinking casts over antitrust policy. It renders antitrust policy hostile to many forms of beneficial collaboration, because of fear that such arrangements are a subterfuge for cartelization and other forms of anticompetitive behavior. Until a greater understanding emerges as to the organizational requirements of the innovation process and antitrust uncertainties are removed, antitrust policy in the United States is likely to remain a barrier to innovation because it has the capacity to stifle beneficial forms of interfirm cooperation. Antitrust policy, which has always been rather hostile to horizontal agreements, must accommodate this feature of capitalist economies if it is to promote enterprise performance and economic welfare.[33]

The framework also has strong implications for business history. It suggests the viability in some instances of new hybrid organizational arrangements, such as strategic alliances, linking firms with complementary capabilities and capacities, over both the integrated alternatives and stand-alone firms coordinating their activities exclusively via the price mechanism.[34] These organizational forms may well represent a new and dramatic organizational innovation in American business history. In retrospect, the emergence and proliferation of alliances, dating from about 1970, may turn out to be as significant an organizational innovation as the moving assembly line and the multidivisional structure. This trend does not deny what Chandler calls the logic of managerial enterprise; it may simply suggests its declining attainability for U.S. companies.

References

M. Aoki, *The Cooperative Game Theory of the Firm* (Clarendon Press, London, 1984).

Kenneth J. Arrow, Toward a Theory of Price Adjustment, in Moses Abramovitz *et al.* (eds.), *The Allocation of Resources* (Stanford University Press, Stanford, CA, 1959), pp. 41–51.

---

[33] For fuller elaboration, see Jorde and Teece (1989, 1990).

[34] These instances are more clearly delineated in Dosi, Teese and Winter (1990).

W. Brian Arthur, Competing Technologies: An Overview, in Giovanni Dosi *et al.* (eds.), *Technical Change and Economic Theory* (Pinter Publishers, London, 1988), pp. 590–607.

W. Baldwin and J.T. Scott, *Market Structure and Technological Change* (Harwood Publishers, Chur, 1987).

Michael, Borrus, *Competing for Control: America's Stake in Micro Electronics* (Ballinger, Cambridge, MA, 1988).

R. Caves and M. Uekusa, *Industrial Organization in Japan* (The Brookings Institute, Washington, DC, 1976).

Alfred D. Chandler, *The Visible Hand* (Harvard University Press, Cambridge, MA, 1977).

Alfred D. Chandler, The Enduring Logic of Industrial Success, *Harvard Business Review*, March-April 1990, pp. 434–444.

Richard Coase, The Nature of the Firm, *Economica* 4 (1937), 386–405.

D. David, R&D Consortia, *High Technology*, October 1985.

Partha D. Dasgupta, The Welfare Economics of Knowledge Production, *Oxford Review of Economic Policy* 4(4) (Winter 1988).

Giovanni Dosi, David J. Teece and Sidney Winter, Toward a Theory of Corporate Coherence: Preliminary Remarks. Unpublished manuscript (University of California at Berkeley, Berkeley, CA, 1990).

Michael Gerlach, *Alliance Capitalism* (University of California Press, Berkeley, CA, 1992), forthcoming.

F. Hayek, The Use of Knowledge in Society, *American Economic Review* 35 (1945), 519–530.

A. Jacquemin and M.E. Slade, Cartels, Collusion and Horizontal Merger, in R. Schmalensee and R.D. Willig (eds.), *Handbook of Industrial Organization* (Elsevier, Amsterdam, 1989), p. 1.

Thomas M. Jorde and David J. Teece, Innovation, Cooperation and Antitrust, *High Technology Law Journal* 4(1) (Spring 1989), 1–113.

Thomas M. Jorde and David J. Teece, Innovation and Cooperation: Implications for Competition and Antitrust, *Journal of Economic Perspectives* 4(3) (1990), 75–96.

S.J. Kline and Nathan Rosenberg, An Overview of Innovation, in R. Landau and N. Rosenberg (eds.), *The Positive Sum Strategy* (National Academy Press, Washington, DC, 1986), pp. 275–305.

Tjalling, Koopmans, *Three Essays in the State of Economic Science* (McGraw-Hill, New York, 1957).

R. Levin and P. Reiss, Tests of a Schumpeterian Model of R&D and Market Structure, in Z. Griliches (eds.), *R&D, Patents and Productivity* (University of Chicago Press, Chicago, IL, 1984).

R. Levin, R. Klevorick and Sidney Winter, Appropriating the Returns from Individual Research and Development, Brookings Papers on Economic Activity, 1987.

David C. Mowery and Nathan Rosenberg, *Technology and the Pursuit of Economic Growth* (Cambridge University Press, New York, 1989).

National Advisory Committee on Semiconductors, *A Strategic Industry at Risk, Report to the President and the Congress* (U.S. Government Printing Office, Washington, DC, 1989).

Richard Nelson, *High Technology Policies* (American Enterprise Institute, Washington, DC, 1984).

Richard Nelson and Sidney Winter, *An Evolutionary Theory of Economic Change* (Harvard University Press, Cambridge, MA, 1982).

Gary Psiano and David J. Teece, Collaborative Arrangements and Global Technology Strategy: Some Evidence from the Telecommunication Equipment Industry, in R.A. Burgelman and R.S. Rosenbloom (eds.), *Research on Technological Innovation, Management and Policy* 4 (JAI Press, Greenwich, CT, 1989), pp. 227–256.

George Richardson, *Information and Investment: A Study in the Working of a Competitive Economy* (Oxford University Press, London, 1960).

Nathan Rosenberg, *Technology and American Economic Growth* (Harper and Row, New York, 1972).

Nathan Rosenberg, *Inside the Black Box: Technology and Economics*, Vol. 7 (Cambridge University Press, New York, 1982).

F.M. Scherer, *Industrial Market Structure and Economic Performance* (Rand-McNally, Chicago, IL, 1970).

J.A. Schumpeter, *Capitalism, Socialism and Democracy* (Harper, New York, 1942).

Adam Smith, *Wealth of Nations, Book 1*, Chapter X, Part II (University of Chicago Press edition, Chicago, IL, 1976).

Joseph Stiglitz, *Technical Change, Sunk Costs and Competition, Brookings Papers on Economic Activity*, Vol. 3 (Special Issue on Microeconomics), (The Brookings Institution, Washington, DC, 1987), pp. 883–937.

David J. Teece, Economics of Scope and the Scope of Enterprise, *Journal of Economic Behavior and Organization* 1(3) (1980), 223–247.

David J. Teece, Profiting from Technological Innovation, *Research Policy* 15(6) (1986), 286–305.

L. Telser, Cooperation, Competition and Efficiency, *Journal of Law and Economics* 28 (1985), 271.

Eric von Hippel, The Dominant Role of the User in Semiconductor and Electronic Subassembly Process Innovation, *IEEE Transactions on Engineering Management EM-24* (2) (May 1977).

Eric von Hippel, *The Sources of Innovation* (Oxford University Press, New York, 1988).

Leon Walras, Elements of Pure Economics (translated by William Jaffe from the original French version, 1874), (Kelley, New York, 1969).

Oliver E. Williamson, *Markets and Hierarchies* (Free Press, New York, 1975).

Oliver E. Williamson, *The Economic Institutions of Capitalism*, Chapter 6 (Free Press, New York, 1985).

The Dynamics of Industrial Capitalism: Perspectives on Alfred Chandler's *Scale and Scope* (1990)*

David J. Teece

University of California at Berkeley

Financial support from the Sloan Foundation to the Consortium on Competitiveness and Cooperation at the University of California at Berkeley is gratefully acknowledged. Helpful comments were received from Richard Nelson, Peter Grindley, David Mowery, F.M. Scherer, Oliver Williamson, and Klaus Zimmer, as well as from the reviewers and editors of the Journal.

1. Introduction

This review essay is about a major treatise on modern capitalism by Alfred D. Chandler, one of the great authorities on business history. *Scale and Scope: The Dynamics of Industrial Capitalism* (1990) is a monumental work that answers important questions about managerial behavior and business institutions — the heart of the capitalist system of organization. The book ought to influence, if not shape, the research agenda for work in business history, industrial organization, the theory of the firm, and economic change for decades to come. In one powerful sweep it has also helped rebalance the literature on processes of wealth generation in capitalist society by displaying how the competitiveness of nations has depended in an important way upon the organizational and financial capabilities of firms, and their supporting institutions.

Reprinted from *Journal of Economic Literature* XXXI (March 1993), 207–234.

Scale and Scope: The Dynamics of Industrial Capitalism. By Alfred D. Chandler, Jr. with the assistance of Takashi Hikino. Cambridge, Mass. and London: Harvard U. Press, Belknap Press, 1990, pp. xviii, 860. $35.00. IBNS 00-674–78994–6, 1990.

Professor Chandler recounts the history of how managers in the United States, Britain, and Germany built the organizations and took the risks of investment necessary to capture the economies of scale and scope opened up by the technological innovations of the second industrial revolution. His thesis is not that markets shape business organization as is commonly supposed in economic theorizing; rather it is that business organizations shape markets. The implication of this tour de force is that much of what is in the textbooks in mainstream microeconomics, industrial organization, and possibly growth and development ought to be revised, in some cases relegated to the appendices, if economic analysis is to come to grips with the essence of productivity improvement and wealth generation in advanced industrial economies. It challenges much current economic orthodoxy enough so that most will choose to sidestep rather than deal with the ramifications.

The structure of this essay is as follows. I will first try to summarize in a few pages what is contained in 850. My treatment is accordingly incomplete and selective. I have focused on aspects of the work which I believe are of greatest interest and relevance to industrial organization economists and to those economists interested in productivity improvement and wealth generation in modern industrial economies. My main purpose is to help distill the implications of Chandler's findings for economic thought and for business policy — two areas which Chandler has wisely not addressed. In identifying the broader implications of Chandler's work I try to link his analysis with a rapidly expanding heterodox literature in organizational economics, business strategy, and "competitiveness" which is grappling with fundamental questions highlighted by Chandler's comparative historical analysis. I conclude by suggesting that Chandler has grasped some fundamental facets of enterprise performance largely neglected by economic theory — facets which must come into sharper focus if economists are to understand the new forms of business organizations, financial institutions, governance systems, and policies needed to develop and exploit the wave of new industrial technologies which are now upon as.

2. Major Themes and Propositions in Scale and Scope

In *Scale and Scope* Chandler examines the beginnings and subsequent growth of managerial capitalism in the United States, Germany, and Great Britain through the lens of what he considers then and now to be its basic institution, the modern industrial enterprise (p. 3). The period covered is from the 1870s through the 1960s, with brief references to the 1970s and 1980s. The individual companies studied were the 200 largest manufacturing firms in each of the three countries, using the sources familiar to business historians — company and individual histories, monographs, investment directories, published company and government reports, secondary sources, and archival records (p. 10). Chandler uses these sources in each country to examine what in the United States he labels *competitive managerial capitalism*, in Britain *personal capitalism*, and in Germany, *cooperative managerial capitalism* (pp. 11–12). What we receive is numerous case studies woven together into an insightful comparative study of the development of industrial capitalism with the firm put center stage. Various charts and statistical tables help track the firms that are the main actors during the periods studied.

Chandler's implicit thesis is that firms and markets evolve together to shape industrial outcomes. A perspective that relies on markets only as the lens through which to understand industrial development is likely to be seriously flawed. Rather, the strategic and organizational choices made by managers — choices not necessarily dictated by markets and technologies — shape if not determine both firm level and national economic performance.

The framework Chandler advances to interpret the beginnings and the evolutionary paths of each form of capitalism is his own unique blend of organizational economics. He recognizes that the modern industrial firm is basically an organization that has developed the capacity, through complex hierarchy, to make the activities and operations of the whole enterprise more than the sum of the parts (p. 15). The purpose of managerial hierarchy is to capture scale and scope economies within and among functions through planning and coordination (p. 17). Some systems and structures accomplish this better than others.

During the last quarter of the 19th century, major innovations made in the processes of production created many new industries and transformed old ones. Technological advances during this period were scale dependent and capital dependent and organizational innovations (as described by Chandler) were needed to exploit these scale-dependent advances (p. 21). Many older labor-intensive industries, including textiles, lumber, furniture, printing, and publishing were largely affected. Capturing the economies available in new industries was not an automatic process. It came by

> improving and rearranging inputs; by using new or greatly improved machinery, furnaces, stills, and other equipment; by reorienting the processes of production within the plant; by placing the several inter-mediary processes employed in making a final product within a single

works; and by increasing the applications of energy (particularly that generated by fossil fuel). (p. 22)[1]

It required coordination and control, exercised through organizational structures and systems designed by management.[2]

Indeed, Chandler argues that it required new forms of industrial enterprise — organizational innovation — to take advantage of the opportunities which were afforded by new technologies. In Chandler's framework, *investment* in capital intensive production facilities of sufficient size to capture scale and scope economies and in supporting managerial systems was key to the creation of the modern industrial enterprise.

> The critical entrepreneurial act was not the invention — or even the commercialization — of a new or greatly improved product or process. Instead it was the construction of a plant of the optimal size required to exploit fully the economies of scale or those of scope, or both. (p. 26)

To Chandler, marketplace success involved three essential steps by top management: (1) the investment in production facilities large enough to achieve the cost advantages of scale and scope; (2) investment in product-specific marketing, distribution, and purchasing networks; (3) recruiting and organizing of the managers needed to supervise and coordinate functional activities and allocate

---

[1] The new processes which emerged in the final quarter of the 19th century were applicable to the refining and distilling of sugar, petroleum, animal and vegetable oil, whiskey and other liquids; the refining and smelting of iron, copper, aluminum; the mechanical processing and packaging of grains, tobacco, and other agricultural products; to the manufacturing of complex, light standardized machinery through the fabrication and assembly of interchangeable parts; the production of technologically advanced industrial machinery and chemicals by a series of interrelated mechanical and chemical processes (p. 23). These technologies, Chandler asserts, were characterized by economies of scale and scope (p. 24).

[2] The observation that 19th century technological progress was scale-intensive, requiring large scale to exploit fully its potential is not original to Chandler. It was the staple of all the great 19th century and early 20th century economists in a line *stemming* from Smith and *stretching* to Mill, Bohm Bawerk, Sidgwick, and Allyn Young. In economic history, it is almost a cliché that technological progress has been scale intensive and that one of America's advantages, which helped bring the United States to a position of technological and productivity leadership was that the U.S. early enjoyed a relatively large, unified, and homogeneous market. Chandler's contribution here is not his perception of the scale-intensivity of the dominant path of technological progress, but rather his understanding that to exploit it required managerial structures and systems, and investment in manufacturing and distribution.

resources for future production and distribution. The entrepreneurs first to perform these three critical steps "acquired powerful competitive advantages" — what Chandler defines as first-mover advantages associated with learning and incumbency effects (p. 34). Latecomers had to make larger investments to compete, and they also had to deal with the added risk flowing from the competitive strengths and moves of the incumbents.[3]

3. Competitive Managerial Capitalism in the United States

Chandler sets out to explain why the modern, integrated, multi-unit enterprise appeared in greater numbers and attained a greater size in a shorter period of time in the United States than in Europe. He finds the answer related in part to the large size of the U.S. market, integrated by the railroad and the telegraph, a story told in more detail in the *Visible Hand* (1977), and partly due to its competitive characteristics. The railroads pioneered modern management in the 1850s and later, through bills of lading, intercompany billing, equipment identification and management, cost accounting, pricing, and so forth. But in *Scale and Scope* the essential thesis is that

> between the 1850s and the 1880s the transportation and communica-
> tions networks established the technological and organizational base
> for the exploitation of economies of scale and scope in the processes
> of production and distribution. (p. 58)

The entrepreneurial response in distribution preceded that in production because innovation in distribution was primarily organizational, not technological. The reasons for the decline of commission agents and the growth of full line, full service wholesalers and mass retailers is not entirely clear from Chandler's analysis.[4] Many of the names of the mass retailers that emerged after the Civil War are still familiar today and include Macy's, Lord & Taylor, Strawbridge & Clothier, John Wanamaker, Marshall Field, and Emporium. Montgomery Ward and Sears Roebuck came to dominate the rural market, relying heavily on

---

[3] In Chandler's taxonomy, it is important to recognize that the first movers are not the inventors. "The first movers were pioneers or other entrepreneurs who made the three interrelated sets of investments in production, distribution, and management required to achieve the competitive advantages of scale, scope, or both".

[4] It probably had something to do with the superior control and incentives that flowed from ownership, coupled with scale and scope opportunities generated by the railroad and telegraph.

mail-order operations. These houses built administrative systems to handle more transactions in a day than most traditional merchants could handle in a lifetime.

The new forms of transportation and communication eventually created an even greater revolution in production, stimulating impressive technological as well as organizational changes.

> The laying down of railroad and telegraph systems precipitated a wave of industrial innovation in Western Europe and the United States far move wide ranging than that which had occurred in Britain at the end of the eighteenth century. This wave has been properly termed by historians the Second Industrial Revolution ... (p. 62)

and involved systemic innovations in oil refining, steel, machinery, glass, artificial dyes, fibers, fertilizers, and food processing. But for the potential of these innovations to be realized, entrepreneurs had to make the three pronged investment.[5]

In industries where only one or two pioneering enterprises made the three pronged investment, these enterprises quickly dominated the market. More often, however, the modern industrial enterprise in the United States appeared after merger or acquisition (p. 71). This is turn was often preceded by efforts to manage capacity utilization by fixing prices and output. Cartel agreements in the United States were, however, extremely unstable because, as in Britain, contractural agreements in restraint of trade could not be enforced in courts of law. Moreover, after 1980 and the passage of the Sherman Act made what was previously unenforceable quite illegal. The Sherman Act "was to have a profound impact on the evolution of modern industrial enterprises in the U.S." (p. 72). Shortly after its passage and subsequent amplification by a number of Supreme Court decisions, there began

> the largest and certainly most significant merger movement in American history. It came partly because of continuing antitrust legislation and activities by the states, partly because of the increasing difficulty of enforcing contractural agreements by trade associations during the depression of the mid-1890s, and partly because the return of prosperity and the buoyant stock market that accompanied it

---

[5] "It was the investment in the new and improved processes of production — not the innovation — that initially lowered costs and increased productivity. It was the investment, not the innovation, that transformed the structure of industries and affected the performance to national economies". (p. 63)

facilitated the exchange of shares and encouraged bankers and other financiers to promote mergers.[6]

However, Chandler cautions that market control was not the only reason for mergers at the turn of the century, as

> a number of merger-makers saw such combinations as the legal prerequisites to administrative centralization and rationalization. DuPont, for instance, did not seek to gain a complete monopoly through consolidation. Rather, it saw advantages associated with being the low cost provider with a dominant market share, able to maintain high capacity utilization by expanding share in recession and reducing it during periods of expansion. (p. 76)

While some mergers initially created little more than federations out of previously independent companies, Chandler asserts that "nearly all the mergers that lasted did so only if they successfully exploited the economics of scale and (to a much lesser extent) those of scope" (p. 78).

The merger movement is to Chandler the most important single episode in the evolution of the modern industrial enterprise in the United States from the 1880s to the 1940s as it permitted the rationalization of American industries in a way that did not begin in Britain and Germany until the 1920s. Moreover, nationwide consolidation tended to reduce family control, which in turn facilitated putting representatives of investment banks and other financial institutions, often important in arranging financing for mergers and acquisitions, on the boards of American industrial enterprises for the first time. However, the influence of the financiers waned as the companies were able to finance long-term investment as well as current operations from retained earnings, and the influence of management correspondingly increased.[7]

---

[6] The merger boom reached its climax between 1899 and 1902, after the Supreme Court had indicated by its rulings in the Trans-Missouri Freight Rate Association case (1897), the Joint Traffic Association case (1898), and the Addyston Pipe and Steel case (1899) that cartels carried on through trade associations were vulnerable under the Sherman Act. (p. 75)

[7] The challenge of managing large, complex hierarchies increased the demand for trained executives, and U.S. colleges and universities responded quickly by expanding the training of engineers and managers. Early providers of business education were the Wharton School at the University of Pennsylvania, founded in 1881, the University of Chicago, and the University of California at Berkeley which set up business schools and colleges in 1898. Harvard followed in 1908 with its Graduate School of Business Administration.

By World War I managerial capitalism had taken root in America, and the companies that were "the first to make the essential, interrelated, three pronged investments in production, distribution, and management remained the leaders from the 1880s to the 1940s" (p. 91), not only in the United States but also Chandler argues in Britain and Germany. To support this proposition for the United States, Chandler provides industry-by-industry reviews in Chapters 4 through 6. He shows how the Standard Oil Company came to lead, not just domestically, but in Europe where it obtained an early and significant advantage through exports of kerosene from the U.S. (strong demand for gasoline came only after 1900). Standard's unprecedented throughputs provided the foundation for its low cost position, as the railroads offered lower rates to J.D. Rockefeller to get Standard's business than they did to Rockefeller's competitors. The favorable transportation rates in turn helped Rockefeller form the Standard Oil Alliance, which attempted to set price and output levels in the industry. The coming of oil pipelines, a technological innovation in transportation which the Alliance first saw as a threat, required massive investment but by dramatically lowering transportation costs, helped provide the foundation for transforming the Alliance into a trust because it supported larger scale refineries which in turn required consolidation of refining capacity.[8] But the enterprise was so successful that it was able to create "several of the world's largest industrial fortunes, not only for the Rockefellers but also for their close associates, including the Harknesses. Payne, Henry Flagler, and others" (p. 94).

The Standard Oil breakup of 1911 split the company along functional lines, with only Standard of New Jersey and Standard of California remaining vertically

---

[8] At the turn of the century the competitive significance of oil pipelines, and oil transportation more generally, was considerable. As the *Report of the Commissioner of Corporations on the Transportation of Petroleum*, U.S. House of Representatives, May 2, 1906, p. 33, makes apparent, "The cost of transportation is an exceedingly large factor in the cost of oil to the consumer. Consequently, any difference in transportation costs, as between different procedures and refiners of oil, has a powerful influence upon their respective positions in competition." These concerns were raised in a context in which the Standard Oil Trust owned most of the pipeline mileage in the United States. While the Standard lines were common carriers in many oil-producing states, they were not common carriers in interstate commerce. They thereby provided Standard with a considerable cost advantage over competitors, and outsiders allegedly paid fees which exceeded "cost of service." In its May 2, 1906 Letter of Submittal accompanying its Report on the Transportation of Petroleum, the Bureau of Corporations argued that the "natural advantages" of the Standard Oil Company stemming from its pipelines "have been and are greatly increased by discrimination in freight rates … which gives … Standard monopolistic control in the greater portion of the country." Nevertheless, observers at the time did seem to recognize the tremendous cost saving that pipelines afforded when significant volumes of crude oil or refined products needed to be moved.

integrated structure set about trying to create one. "Successful challengers were those that made the interrelated three-pronged investments" (p. 104) and included Sun, Philips, Sinclair, and Gulf. Meanwhile, long before World War II, salaried managers, not the founders or the founders' families, were in control of the Standard Oil companies — members of the Rockefeller family were generally not involved, even on the board of directors. In contrast to the history on the European continent, "no investment banker ever played a significant, on-going role as a decision maker in a major American oil company" (p. 104).

Chandler describes the evolution of many other important industries, including machinery, electrical equipment, industrial chemicals, rubber, paper, cement, and steel. Steel is of particular interest, not just because of its overall importance to the economy in this period, but because, as Chandler puts it, "the most effective first mover sold out." The first mover was Andrew Carnegie who understood, as did Henry Ford and John D. Rockefeller, the significance of high capacity utilization — " 'hard driving'[9] as Carnegie termed it" (p. 128). The successor company to Carnegie, U.S. Steel, was run by lawyers and financiers and was less committed to the principle and "dissipated Carnegie's first-mover advantages and thus permitted the rapid growth of challengers" (p. 128). In steel a near monopoly was translated into an oligopoly, not by changing markets and technologies, but through the unfortunate decisions of one or two senior executives whose focus was on controlling the market through collusion rather than through being more efficient, which they were not.

Carnegie, while not the first to install new technologies like the Bessemer converter, was the first to build a large, vertically integrated facility, the Edgar Thomson Works in Pittsburgh, which remained for decades the largest steel works in the world. The large investments made by Carnegie and Illinois Steel enabled unit costs and prices to fall dramatically.[10] Carnegie also pursued an integration strategy, first backwards into iron ore and coke. He then threatened a forward integration strategy into fabricated products like wire, rail, tubes, and hoops. The investment banker J. Pierpont Morgan, who had extensive ties to the fabricators, including Federal Steel, who would be threatened by this move, offered to buy Carnegie Steel at Carnegie's price. In 1900 he merged Carnegie Steel and Federal Steel, the two leaders in the steel industry, and then in the

---

[9] Hard driving refers to the practice followed in the U.S. steel industry of driving blast furnaces at pressures of 9 psi, as compared with the British practice of 5 psi. Hard driving required frequent rebricking but permitted higher throughput.

[10] The price of steel rails at Pittsburgh plummeted from $67.50 a ton in 1880 to $29.95 in 1889, to $17.63 a ton in 1898, yet profits soared.

following year negotiated to merge or acquire secondary producers, thereby establishing the world's largest industrial corporation, U.S. Steel.[11]

The new company was initially set up as merely a holding company, with the existing enterprises retaining both legal and administrative autonomy and headquarter's functions being performed by investment bankers and lawyers, among them Elbert Gary. Gary saw the function of the corporate office to be much like that of a federation or cartel office to set prices rather than to allocate resources. This created a tension with the inherited Carnegie Steel managers who wanted to continue the policy of "exploiting the competitive advantages of low costs by maintaining throughput, even though this mean reducing prices" (p. 34). Gary's policies delighted U.S. Steel's competitors, and when competitors reduced prices

> Gary instituted his famous dinners of 1907 and 1908 to urge them to support the prices that he had done so much to stabilize …. A decade of Gary's policies permitted his competitors to overcome the first mover advantages Carnegie had achieved in the production and distribution of steel. (p. 135)
>
> In steel, as in rubber goods, paper, window glass and tin cans, the failure of the new industry-wide merger to take steps to exploit fully the potential economies of scale made possible the rise of challengers and enlarged the size of the oligopoly. And these challengers were not, it must be strongly emphasized, new entrants but established firms. (p. 136)[12]

U.S. industrial firms, once they had honed their organizational capabilities and begun generating significant cash flow, continued to expand through investment abroad and through diversification. Where the dynamics of growth rested on scale economies, firms grew more by direct investment abroad (e.g., machinery and transport equipment); where economies of scope were available, growth was through diversification (p. 147). The latter strategy was supported in part by organized research which expanded significantly as firms built R&D facilities in

---

[11] "In arranging this huge merger the house of Morgan did not carry out the normal, time-consuming procedures of investigating potential cost advantages of rationalization, appraising the properties of the firms coming into the merger" (p. 32). Chandler leaves no doubt that the strategy was to earn promoters profits and effectuate market control.

[12] U.S. Steel provides one of the very few examples of banker control in American industry, and Chandler leaves little doubt that he believes that the financiers and lawyers running U.S. Steel made serious mistakes.

the 1920s first to improve products and processes, and subsequently to develop new ones. The producers, of industrial chemicals, along with electrical equipment manufacturers, used R&D to develop new products. DuPont was an early leader, developing several new products from its core capabilities in the nitrocellulose technology that it used to produce explosives and propellants.[13] The increased complexities of the products and the managerial challenge associated with running multiple businesses increased the role of professional managers at DuPont and elsewhere in the chemical and machinery industries, and further separated management from ownership.

Chandler concludes his review of the American experience (pp. 224–233) with a frontal attack on what he refers to as "orthodox economics" (p. 227) which views large hierarchies and oligopolistic market structures suspiciously. Chandler points out that at least during the time period studied it was the modern, hierarchical industrial firm that was responsible for America's economic growth. The firms that obtained market power rarely got it through "artificial barriers" or anticompetitive conduct. Nor did it come in the main from the technical efforts of inventors alone, though Thomas Edison, George Westinghouse, Cyrus McCormick, and George Eastman made important organizational contributions as well. Rather, it came from the ability to develop and commercialize the new technologies through the three pronged strategy of investing in manufacturing, distribution, and management systems and people."[14]

---

[13] While most of the new industrial departments continued to build on this base, developments in dyestuffs and ammonia came from technologies first developed by German entrepreneurs and scientists. Even though the war removed German dye makers from American markets and made available German patents to American manufacturers, DuPont faced stiff competition form Germany even in the interwar years. Research at both DuPont and General Motors in the 1920s produced tetraethyllead, a gasoline additive that increased horsepower and reduced engine knock. In 1924 General Motors and Standard Oil of New Jersey formed the Ethyl Corporation to manufacture and market the product. (p. 183) Freon, neoprene (synthetic rubber), and polytetrafluoroethylene (Teflon) were also developed in the interwar years, although Teflon did not go into volume manufacture until the post-World War II period.

[14] Thus it was the integrated capacities, physical capital and human skills of firms (p. 230) that were critical. The "dynamics came from the organizational capabilities developed after the three pronged investment and enhanced by continuing functional and strategic competition with other first movers and with challengers who made comparable investments" (p. 231). To underscore the importance of organizational capabilities, Chandler points out that it was the new branded, packaged goods with the lowest technology and scale requirements where the large firms had a competitive advantage over small firms (p. 63). Chandler suggests that differential competitive advantage lies not in technology, which is often available to all, but in the firm's capacity to find markets and coordinate production, distribution, and marketing.

4. Personal Capitalism in Great Britain

Chandler's thesis is that few large industrial firms appeared in Great Britain —
and British economic development during the second industrial revolution suffered
as a consequence — because British entrepreneurs frequently failed to make the
essential three pronged investment in manufacturing, marketing and distribution,
and management. Most importantly, "the pioneers recruited smaller managerial
teams, and the founders and their families continued to dominate the management
of the enterprise" (p. 235) until well after World War II, to the considerable
detriment of the British economy.[15] Boards of directors were restricted to family
and those with family connections or social position, with little place for senior
managers.

Thus Cadbury Brothers, Ltd., Britain's leading maker of cocoa and chocolate
which began making chocolate in the middle of the 19th century, provides a
good example. Cadbury's built a substantial plant in 1879 and had nearly 3,000
workers by 1900. However, its investment in marketing and distribution was
limited.[16] The Cadbury family — the sons, daughters, and grand-children —
continued to manage the production, marketing, and sales functions as well
as the enterprise as a whole. The senior Cadburys were completely absorbed
in day-to-day operational activities. Whether the comparison is German or
American, Chandler finds the management structure of Cadbury at the outbreak
of World War II to be quite limited (p. 246). Moreover, after the merger with
J.S. Fry and Sons in 1919, there was cross membership on each other's
boards,

> but the activities of the two operating companies remained
> separate . . . . Until the 1930s the two firms, Cadbury and Fry,
> remained little more than allies using the holding company board
> to supervise their overseas marketing and their jointly owned and
> operated overseas factories, and to continue to purchase supplies
> for both firms. (p. 246)

---

[15] In most British enterprises senior executives worked closely in the same office building, located in
or near the largest plant, having almost daily personal contact with, and thus directly supervising,
middle and often lower-level managers. Such organizations had no need for the detailed organization
charts and manuals that had come into common use in large American and German firms before 1914.
(p. 242)

[16] Cadbury's had its own sales force, and in the 1920s set up depot distribution in major cities and had
a small fleet of trucks to supply them.

The Cadbury–Fry arrangement was typical of mergers carried out in Britain during the interwar years.[17]

Chandler attributes the smaller size, family ownership, and less professional management of British firms to the smaller size of the British economy, the greater importance of foreign trade to the British companies, and the historical fact that Britain had industrialized and urbanized before the coming of the transportation revolution. The smaller geographic size of the island nation and the relative excellence of its pre-rail transportation system, meant that the railroad and telegraph were less watershed factors in Britain. The British railway companies were smaller and did not provide the same organizational challenges as the much larger American ones; accordingly, it is not surprising that they were not pioneers in modern management, accounting, and finance.

While British firms did respond to the opportunities in distribution that appeared, British entrepreneurs too often failed to make an investment in production large enough to utilize fully the economies of scale and scope, to build a product-specific marketing and distribution networks, and to recruit a team of salaried managers. So they continued to rely on older forms of industrial enterprise — firms that were personally managed, usually family managed. In many of these new industries substantial tripartite investments were, indeed, made in Britain; but foreign, not British, enterprises made the investment. Foreign firms reaped the profits (pp. 261–262).

However, the British did have some success in branded packaged goods. The new production technologies for refining, distilling, milling, and processing food, drink, tobacco, and consumer chemicals were not complex, and product-specific distribution facilities or specialized marketing services were not required. By the turn of the century many producers of branded consumer goods — names like Cadbury, Huntley & Palmer, and Peak Frean — were among Britain's largest and most successful industrial enterprises (p. 262). Until after World War I, however, the companies producing foods and consumer chemicals rarely operated more than one major factory within Britain (p. 265). Such firms operated much like

---

[17] Mergers of much more significance had occurred earlier in Britain. Chandler describes the birth of Imperial Tobacco in 1919 which, instigated by W.D. and H.O. Wills, organized a small number of family-controlled firms into an industry-wide holding company. Imperial was organized as a federation, through an executive committee consisting of members of the families operating the largest constituent companies. The subsidiaries produced and distributed their products independently, even after the merger. In contrast, in the United States, American Tobacco had a large hierarchy of middle and top management that had developed procedures to produce and distribute large volumes of cigarettes a year.

Cadbury, through functionally departmentalized organization, with department heads who were apt to be family members.[18] Thus

> in branded, packaged products British entrepreneurs created national and international organizations that could still be personally managed by an extended family with a very few close associates. Such family management was much more difficult to maintain in the more technologically complex new industries. (p. 268)

However,

> in industries in Britain where owners made the investments in production and distribution that were needed to exploit new technologies, and where they recruited even relatively small managerial hierarchies, their enterprises competed effectively in global oligopolies. (p. 273)

Examples included Dunlop in rubber and Courtaulds in synthetic fibers. But there were more failures than successes in Great Britain (p. 274). While in oil and meat packing the lack of supplies and natural resources limited opportunities for British firms at home, in light machinery (sewing machines, typewriters, etc.), electrical equipment, chemicals, and metals, the foundations of domestic demand and a domestic supply infrastructure (skills, finance, etc.) were in place. Here

> British entrepreneurs failed to grasp the opportunities the new technologies had opened up, precisely because they failed to make the necessary, interrelated, three-pronged investment in production, marketing, and management. These opportunities within Britain were seized instead by Germans and Americans. (p. 275)[19]

The British failure in organic chemicals ("dyestuffs") is especially striking because in 1870 Britain held a commanding technological lead. In 1856 William Perkin, a Britisher, had invented the first process for making dyes by chemical synthesis. Britain had plenty of the basic raw material (coal) and had domestic

---

[18] There were a few exceptions, most notably the brewers such as Bass, Worthington, and Watney.

[19] Thus while British inventors such as Joseph Swan and Sebastian Ferranti were as able technologically as Thomas Edison and George Westinghouse in the United States, or Werner Siemens in Germany, failures in entrepreneurship prevented the British from building industrial empires around the new developments in electricity.

demand as well. Indeed, the British textile industry remained the single biggest market for dyes until World War II. But despite these advantages, Britain lost to Germany, as it was the German entrepreneurs who made investments in giant plants, recruited managerial teams, built the worldwide marketing organizations, and educated the users (p. 278).

In Steel, the British pioneered in both the invention and early adoption of the Bessemer and open-hearth processes, but quickly fell behind. Here Chandler seems to attribute the failure to the absence of demand. The British rail network was already in place before the great expansion of the American and continental systems, thereby providing less incentive for British entrepreneurs to construct new, integrated facilities. In any case, the British did not do so, and by 1915 American and German steelmakers had taken the lead in all major markets except the British Empire and Britain itself. In aluminum and copper, British firms did adopt the revolutionary electrolytic techniques but failed to utilize them effectively.

Chandler recognizes that the reasons why British entrepreneurs, "hiers of the First Industrial Revolution," did not take full advantage of the opportunities of the new technologies of the second industrial revolution are complex. In some industries like steel,

> British entrepreneurs may have been paying the price of having been pioneers before the opportunities to fully exploit the new technology appeared .... On the other hand, in chemicals, electrical equipment, and copper, British (and French) entrepreneurs had almost the same opportunities as the Americans and Germans. In dyes and pharmaceuticals British entrepreneurs had even greater opportunities and incentives than German industrialists. (p. 185)

Whatever the exact reasons for entrepreneurial failures were, it was the failure to make in a timely fashion the three pronged investment in production, distribution, and management needed to exploit economies of scale and scope which was the essential failure. The window of opportunity was short; having missed it, continuing innovation by incumbents made it hard for later entrants to catch up. The British bias for small-scale operation and personal management was a significant handicap.[20]

---

[20] [In] personally managed firms, growth was not a primary objective ... profits made by the enterprise went to the owners. Many preferred current income ... . This view made it easy ... to hold back on expanding investment in production, distribution, research, and development, and on the recruitment, training, and promotion of salaried managers — all of which were fundamental to the continuing, successful exploitation of new technologies. (p. 292)

In general, however, Chandler argues that British failures were more often than not a consequence of the basic goals and governance of the enterprise. Whereas in "American managerial firms the basic goals appear to have been long-term profit and growth ... in Britain the goal for family firms appears to have been to provide a steady flow of cash to owners — owners who were also managers" (p. 390).[21] For the relatively few British firms run by professional managers — ICI, Unilever, and British Petroleum — success was noteworthy, but the general failure to develop organizational capability weakened British industry and with it the British economy (p. 392).

5. Cooperative Managerial Capitalism in Germany

While in Germany the modern industrial enterprise appeared soon after the completion of the transportation and communication networks, as it did in the United States, German industrial enterprises acquired distinctive features because of differences in markets, sources of supply, methods of finance, the antitrust environment, and the educational system. In particular, the enforceability of contracts in restraint of trade meant that "German industrials had much less incentive to merge into industry wide holding companies" (p. 298). German universities and institutes were ahead of the United States in providing industrial enterprises with scientific knowledge and skilled technicians and managers and, unlike the United States and Britain, the banks played a major role in providing the finance necessary to facilitate the investment needed to capture the economies of scale and scope inherent in the new technologies. Only in Germany among the three did the bankers play this role; it entitled them to positions on the board of directors of industrial companies, from which they sometimes helped shape critical resource allocation decisions.

A truly distinctive dimension of the German industrial system was the banks. The demand for capital to finance the railroads led in the United States to the centralization and institutionalization of the nation's money and capital market in New York; in Germany, it encouraged the creation of a wholly new financial intermediary — the Kreditbank — which became central to the later financing of large-scale industrial enterprise. "A handful of the largest Kreditbanken, termed Grossbanken, have dominated German finance ever since" (p. 145). The Grossbanken, like the Credit Mobilier in France, developed as diversified

---

[21] The implication is that the cash was needed to maintain expensive lifestyles of the English upper class.

financial institutions simultaneously providing the services of commercial bank, investment bank, development bank, and investment trust. The Creditbanken, and particularly the Grossbanken, "were the instrument[s] that made possible the rapid accumulation of capital on a scale vast enough to finance the building of the new continental transportation and communications infrastructure" (p. 416). As the Grossbanken moved into industrial finance, their extensive staffs developed in-depth knowledge of specific industries and companies. Senior bankers sat on the supervisory boards of the industrial companies the banks financed. The banks provided venture capital as well as the financing needed to exploit the economies of scale and scope so important in the capital intensive industries in which German enterprises clustered.

Besides the role of financial institution, another key differentiating factor was the legal structure. In Germany the common law did not prohibit cartels, nor was there any antitrust legislation. In 1897, one year before the enactment of the Sherman Act, the German High Court held that cartel agreements were not only enforceable but were also in the public interest (p. 423). As investment in capital-intensive technologies increased, so did the number of cartels, going from four in 1875 to 106 in 1890, then to 385 in 1905 (p. 423). Conventions, consortiums, formal associations, and profit pools were formed in the quest for arrangements with some durability, for even with legal sanction "contractural arrangements remained difficult to negotiate and even more difficult to enforce" (p. 423). However, because cooperation was legal, there was less incentive for industry-wide mergers to restrict competition. Given Chandler's view that industry-wide mergers were a prerequisite to industry-wide reorganization and rationalization, he concludes that "far fewer such rationalizations occurred before World War I in Germany than in the U.S." (p. 424).

The dual board structure that emerged in Germany was another significant difference with the United States and Great Britain. An 1884 law required joint stock companies (AG) to have both a management board for the routine running of the business and a supervisory board for long-term guidance and policy. The functions of the two boards became deeply intertwined. However, as the majority stockholders and the banks, which usually occupied the seats on the supervisory board, were mandated to do little more than monitor, the full-time company executives on the management board often "made long term policy as well as short term operating decisions. Nevertheless, representatives of the banks on which companies still relied for funding and the parent companies continued to influence policy making" (p. 425). Moreover, the supervisory board, by including bankers and officers from other companies, could assist interfirm cooperation.

German institutions of higher education also affected the beginning and the continued growth of the large German industrial enterprise. "They led the way in the development of the disciplines of physics and chemistry and their application to medicine and industrial technology" (p. 425). Technical universities were specifically created to train men for industrial appointments. German universities, like the American, but unlike the British, established graduate programs in engineering. Business education was also provided around the same time as it was in the United States. Indeed, Chandler suggests that the linkage between the sources of technical knowledge in the universities and institutes and industrial enterprises "was much closer in Germany than in Britain, where it rarely existed at all, and even in the United States, where at the turn of the century the process was just beginning" (p. 426).[22]

Cooperation was thus a hallmark of the German industrial system, as viewed by Chandler (pp. 498–499).[23] The legal and cultural environment fostered cooperation, and the challenge of meeting the needs of a fragmented European market encouraged cooperation at home.[24] The banks preferred cooperation as a way to protect profits and enable debt to be serviced.

The German system was managerial capitalism that involved extensive hierarchies — a concept not at all foreign in Germany with its long tradition of bureaucratic management. In essence, the growth of German industrial power and the weakening of British industrial power resulted from the differential capacities of German and British entrepreneurs and managers. "German industrial growth and the concomitant British industrial decline emphasize the importance of organizational capabilities in providing the underlying dynamics for modern industrial capitalism" (p. 500). Government played only a minor role — financial

---

[22] See also Ralph Landau (1991) for an excellent treatment of the links between MIT and industry involving chemical engineering. Chemical engineering is especially interesting because it shows how German knowledge in chemistry was transferred to the United States through the university connection, where it was coupled with understanding of large-scale production processes. In this manner U.S. universities and business firms rapidly developed global preeminence in chemical engineering.

[23] However, the weakness in the system of cooperation was, in Chandler's view, that it forestalled the industry-wide rationalization of facilities and personnel that merger would have facilitated. In short, in some industries, including chemicals, cooperation "forestalled the creation of an effective corporate office comparable to that of Siemens in Germany, ICI in Britain, and the leading chemical and food firms in the U.S." Despite these disabilities, German firms still outcompeted British firms because whether a small cartel office or a large headquarters office ran the business, at least salaried professionals were in charge, as was also the case in the United States (pp. 590–591).

[24] Chandler does not explain (p. 427) why the need to serve a fragmented European market fostered co-operation at home. Presumably it was because information about foreign market opportunities could be shared across industries to mutual benefit.

and educational institutions (many publicly funded) played a more important role that the government.

6. The Logic of Managerial Capitalism

6.1. *The Business Enterprise (and its Management) as the Central Actor*

Lest the reader not be fully aware of the import of what I believe Chandler has to say, let me reiterate that Chandler sees the historical record as indicating that the business enterprise, through the development of organizational capabilities, played the central role in industrial development in the United States, Britain, and Germany. Organizational capabilities once created had to be maintained for the leading enterprises and nations to stay ahead. Changing technologies and markets constantly make existing facilities and skills obsolete; industrial firms accordingly need to be in a process of constant organizational renewal. While new technologies provided opportunities, it was the business enterprises and their managers that determined whether those opportunities would be converted into sustainable advantages.

Needless to say, this view is not the dominant view reflected in most history books[25] or in the economic literature on growth and development.[26] Certainly those literatures stress the importance of investment, but Chandler's thesis is that the discriminating factor in the advance of the United States and Germany over Britain was not the rate of investment in conventional tangible capital alone. Nor was it government, the personalities of the entrepreneurs, culture, or ideology, though each are of some importance. Rather, it was the development of effective professional management and organizational systems to support the development of vertically integrated business enterprises.

The significance of these conclusions can perhaps be better assessed by what Chandler relegates to subsidiary importance. Already mentioned is the relatively insignificant role of direct government policies and programs. Technology is

---

[25] David Landes in his monumental work *The Unbound Prometheus* devotes at most only a few pages to the role of firms in industrial development in Western Europe from 1750–1950.

[26] As Moses Abramovitz (1991, p. 3) points out, the view that still shapes the modern economic approach to the economics of growth was laid out by John Stuart Mill in the *Principles of Political Economy* (1848). Mill's view was the simple production function approach, that sees increases in output as stemming from increases in labor, capital, and land, "or of their productiveness." Both Chandler and Abramovitz would undoubtedly argue that the standard approach fails to see organizational innovation as part of "technological" progress and investments in managerial systems and structures in production, distribution, and marketing as part of aggregate capital formation.

another factor relegated to a subsidiary role,[27] at least with respect to any particular nation. Chandler is not saying that technology or "preconditions" or government policy is not important to industrial success. Rather, he seems to be saying that the new technologies in question were in the main open to all; accordingly it is understandable, though perhaps surprising to some, that technological pioneering did not lead inexorably to industrial dominance. Unless supported by the three pronged investments, technological success did not translate through to marketplace or national dominance. It was a necessary but not a sufficient condition for industrial development.

Without Britain, Chandler's thesis would be difficult to advance at the national level, as both American and German firms often did make the critical three pronged investment. But British firms did not, and the consequences are clear. Chandler claims that it is equally clear that the reason was the system of ownership and governance that existed in Britain — what he calls personal capitalism. Needless to say, his thesis here is controversial, as there are numerous competing hypotheses including a failure in entrepreneurship, the preoccupation of British investment banking with oversees investments, and the handicaps that some associate with Britain's early lead.[28] Whatever the cause, the failures of British firms to adequately respond to the opportunities afforded by the new technologies impaired Britain's growth and development.

6.2. Determinants of the Scale and Scope of the Enterprise

Scale and Scope ought to do a great deal to combat a rather traditional literature in economics, following Jacob Viner's (1932) classic investigation of cost curves,

---

[27] However, technological change provided the opportunities and the requirement for organizational responses in the capital intensive industries. If pressed, Chandler would undoubtedly agree that technologies and organizations coevolve, and he would also recognize, along with Nelson and Winter (1982), Teece (1977), and others, that at minimum there are often significant costs of imitation, technology transfer, and adaptation so that technology was not quite freely transferable among firms.

[28] Most persuasive is a thesis, closely aligned with Chandler's, that institutional rigidities were Britain's fundamental problem. As Bernard Elbaum was William Lazonick explain, "what British industry in general required was the visible hand of coordinated control, not the invisible hand of the self-regulating market" (1986, p. 10). The fragmented industrial structure of many industries like cotton, coupled with reliance on unassisted market adjustment processes, was often the source of the problem, as Lazonick (1983) has shown. This is not the place for a recitation of all the competing hypotheses. Thorstein Veblen's (1915) is an early statement of disadvantages of being the pioneer, while Donald McCloskey (1981) is an excellent treatment of the failure in entrepreneurship thesis. The essential point which Chandler makes is that the system of business organization in Great Britain, whatever its foundation, was the source of the failure. For further discussion, see Roy Church (1990).

which posits a rather tight relationship between scale and scope economies, the optimum size of the enterprise, the optimum size of the enterprise, and market structure. As Jean Tirole (1988, p. 18) puts it, "one of the main determinants of the size of a firm is the extent to which it can exploit economies of scale or scope." Thus in searching for explanations for optimal firm size and market concentration, many economic theorists still confine their inquiry to the basic technological conditions of production.[29] Chandler's analysis would seem to suggest that explanations for the scale and scope of particular firms and of industry structure lie not so much with the technology-based economies of production or distribution, but with organizational factors, especially the ability of firms to make the investment in plant management and distribution systems necessary to garner competitive advantage. Perhaps this explains why Chandler has not tried all that hard to measure scale and scope economies. His argument seems to be that because the technologies in question are basically available to all, the more interesting question for economists interested in explaining firm size and market structure is how and why different industrial firms respond to and manage the opportunities afforded by new technology.

This is not to suggest that the international technology transfer process is costless. Teece (1977), Nelson and Winter (1982), and others have established that transfer costs are often significant, particularly if the competence level of the transferor and transferee are disparate. Moreover, knowledge at the level of existing best practice is not equally relevant to all industries everywhere. It depends on the availability of materials, supplies of labor of the requisite qualities, and the character and size of markets. Furthermore, much industrial knowledge can only be acquired through practice.

Yet Chandler seems to suggest that the key inventions quickly become public knowledge, leaving commercial success to depend upon the rapidity and completeness with which the invention is exploited. As W. Arthur Lewis has stated of Britain's lackluster performance:

> It is not necessary to be a pioneer in order to have a large export trade.
> It is sufficient to be a quick imitator. Britain would have done well
> enough if she merely imitated German and American innovations.

---

[29] As one text points out, "many of the predictions of economic theory, such as those involving price and firm size, revolve around concepts like marginal costs .... [Moreover] knowing the cost function of a firm and knowing its technology are equivalent" (Dennis Carlton and Jeffrey Perloff 1990, p. 35). The traditional approach is devoid of any consideration of organization and management (Teece 1980, 1982).

Japan, Belgium, and Switzerland owe more of their success as exporters of manufactures to imitation than they do to innovation. (Lewis 1957, pp. 00)

Chandler's is a study of entrepreneurship and how different forms of capitalism — competitive, personal, or cooperative — shape the response of firms. It is also a study of the incumbency effects created by the first movers; and what it suggests is that governance structures, managerial systems, and the institutional-legal contexts are critical to understanding industrial outcomes. If taken seriously, Chandler's thesis requires a rewrite of industrial organization textbooks, both the traditional and the new.

Missing from Chandler, however, is the systematic comparison of contracting alternatives (Williamson 1975, 1985; Teece 1980, 1982).[30] Certainly, Chandler describes how contracting modes gave way to integrated modes as scale economies in production drove unprecedented manufacturing volumes, which in turn required forward integration; but he simply does not probe very deeply into scale and scope economies and their relationship to the boundaries of the firm. Chandler's failure to develop an analytic framework for doing so may turn out to handicap his subsequent work aimed at coming to grips with the proliferation of strategic alliances and joint ventures exhibited in the post 1975 period, a topic taken up in Sec. 6.5 below.

6.3. *The Sustainability and Sources of Differential Competitive Advantages*

While never stated directly, possibly because he considers the point so obvious it does not warrant special comment, Chandler clearly subscribes to the premise that firms competing in the same markets have differential competitive advantages — advantages that can be sustained over long periods. Implicit in Chandler's argument is that just how and when the three pronged investments are made establishes different organizational capabilities among firms. This would not be remarkable but for what Nelson (1991) has referred to as

the strong tide in economics, particularly in theoretical economics, that downplays or even denies the importance of such differences.

---

[30] There is now an extensive literature which looks at alternative organizational forms and explicitly compares vertical integration to less hierarchical forms of organizations. Because Chandler does not analyze firms which failed, the reader receives scant advice as to what is wrong with many of these alternatives.

The argument in economics is not that firms are all alike ... rather the position is that the differences are not discretionary, but rather reflect differences in the contexts in which firms operate. (p. 61)

The main thrust of much economic theorizing is that what firms do is determined by the conditions they face, and possibly by certain unique attributes such as possession of a patent or ownership of a choice location. While firms facing different markets will behave and perform differently, if market conditions were reversed, firm behavior would be too. Different firms can produce different products but any firm can choose any niche. As Nelson (1991) puts it, "the theoretical preconceptions shared by most economists lead them to ignore firm differences, unless compelled to attend to them" (p. 65).

Chandler's histories compel us to attend to firm differences, because they provide numerous illustrations that advantages are created and sustained over long periods.[31] Thus DuPont grew faster and more profitably than its competitors due to first mover advantages as well as far-sighted and insightful strategic and organizational decisions.[32] Firms declined if they were unable to create and maintain key organizational capabilities. However, Chandler's data on rankings of the largest industrial firms by assets (for 1917, 1930, 1948 for Great Britain; 1913, 1928, 1953 for Germany) indicate considerable stability in asset rankings — at least as compared to what economic theory would predict.[33] The firms that were the leaders (as measured by asset size) in their industrial groupings often remained there over long periods. Indeed, using Chandler's data, across all groupings the probability that a firm ranked 1 or 2 before the outbreak of the World War I would still be first or second in the early post World War II

---

[31] As Chandler states, in industries where innovations were particularly revolutionary, first movers had significant competitive advantages that as a general rule allowed them to remain dominant for decades. The first movers in industrial chemicals remained leaders for decades and nearly all of the top firms in 1948 had been long established since 1900 (pp. 171–172).

[32] David Hounshell (1992) supports this contention and notes Dupont's abiding "faith and commitment" to R&D during the eight decades of this century. Its strong R&D orientation distinguished it from its competitors, and was a direct consequence of its strategy.

[33] Economic theory predicts a wide range of outcomes, but absent strategic behavior, the predilections of economists are to see entry and exit and changing market shares as occurring with alarcrity. This stems from a faith in the workings of adjustment processes and implicit assumptions about the tradability of assets. Certainly, leading firms are viewed as being always vulnerable, and they often are. As one text put it, "Generally, a dominant firm's share of an industry's sales shrinks over time" (Carlton and Perloff 1990, p. 201). In neoclassical theory, as compared to evolutionary theory (Nelson and Winter 1982), the long run is rather short.

Table 1. Survival Probabilities of Leading Industrial Firms (Leading Two Firms Only)*

Country (Period)	Number of Leading Firms Selected	Displaced from 1st or 2nd Position Over Period	"Survival" Probabilities
U.S. (1917–1948)	33	14	.57
U.K. (1919–1948)	30	13	.56
Germany (1913–1953)	29	20	.31

*Number of firms in first or second place (measured by assets).
Source: Derived from Chandler, Appendices A, B and C, which provide tabulations of the 200 largest industrial enterprises in the United States, Great Britain, and Germany for the time periods indicated. "Survival" is used here to indicate the likelihood that a firm that was ranked first or second at the beginning of the period would be so ranked at the end.

period was .57 in the United States, .56 in Great Britain, and .31 in Germany (Table 1). This would appear to be strong evidence that differential competitive advantages are sustained over long periods of time,[34] and that within industry groupings it is more difficult than economic theory would suggest for challengers to develop superior organizational capabilities to displace first movers.

In Chandler's framework, differential advantages are often path dependent. First movers developed advantages through a variety of mechanisms: (1) *preemption*: in industries with significant scale economies, a large initial investment would entrench the incumbent; (2) *learning*: Chandler frequently notes that first movers gain substantial experience over followers in key functional areas such as sales and marketing as well as in production; (3) *cheaper capital*: Chandler claims that capital is more expensive for challengers than first movers because challengers must confront the behavioral uncertainty stemming from the competitive moves of the incumbent. However, from time to time challengers did succeed due to mistakes by first movers (as with Ford Motor and U.S. Steel), government action (e.g., Britain's support of oil, Germany's support of aluminum, and antitrust action in the United States), and changing technology and markets. Thus oil discoveries in Texas and California gave opportunities to new entrants, and the advent of refrigeration enabled Swift to reconfigure the meat packing industry by using refrigeration cars to distribute dressed meat from central slaughterhouses to East Coast markets.

---

[34] Wartime dislocation probably helps explain the lower survival rate in Germany.

6.4. *Technology Strategy*

In addition to implications for economic theory, Chandler's work continues to have profound implications for the literature in business strategy. In both *Strategy and Structure* (1962) and now in *Scale and Scope* (1990), Chandler has shown how *different* enterprises carried out the *same* activity and how decentralized structures were invented and then implemented in the interwar years by companies including DuPont, General Motors, Standard Oil of New Jersey, and Sears Roebuck. This highlights the topic of differential competitive advantage already discussed. Chandler also crafted one of the most widely accepted definitions of strategy — the determination of the basic long-term goals and objectives of an enterprise, and the adoption of courses of action and the allocation of resources necessary for achieving these goals.[35]

As indicated, Chandler has already done much to contribute to and indeed mold the business strategy literature.[36] *Scale and Scope* will continue that tradition. Quite remarkably, Chandler's thinking is meshing with recent thinking on technology strategy. For instance, "Profiting from Technological Innovation," Teece (1986) outlines a parallel thesis in which the marketplace success of innovators depends upon several elements: (1) the intellectual property regime — which will determine whether competitors can gain access to the basic enabling technology; and (2) the competitive positioning of the firm in complementary assets — manufacturing, distribution, complementary technologies, sales and service, etc. Put differently, my thesis is that innovators need to have an n-pronged strategy, where n is the number of specialized complementary assets needed for the user to capture value from the technology. I submit that my discussion of complementary assets is somewhat more general than Chandler's in that I explicitly recognize the circumstances where contracting-out may be a valid competitive strategy. Chandler's thesis does not leave much room for such circumstances as being historically valid or conceptually viable.

The point of possible departure with the recent work in technology strategy is Chandler's emphasis on the need to build managerial hierarchies. At a superficial level, this may seem quite at odds with much of the recent literature on innovation which stresses the advantages of shallow hierarchies and decentralized decision making as a means to ensure the responsiveness needed to compete in today's

---

[35] Adhering to these definitions would make for clearer discussion. In the modern literature and in business discussion, choices on practically any decision variable are too frequently referred to as "strategy."

[36] For a discussion of Chandler's contribution, see Richard Rumelt, Dan Schendel and Teece (1991).

fast-changing markets (Thomas Peters and Robert Waterman 1982; James Womack, Daniel Jones, and Daniel Roos 1990). However, a deeper reading of the innovation literature would appear to provide considerable support for the key aspect of hierarchy that Chandler recognizes, namely coordinating the internal allocation of resources quickly and efficiently so as to capture economies of scale and scope.[37] Chandler repeatedly argues that the absence of such coordination will lead to fragmented efforts that will prevent these economies from being realized. Interpreted as the recognition by Chandler of the need to coordinate and integrate resource allocation within the firm, there may be much in common between Chandler's historical observation and the thrust of the modern literature on management, which stresses the need to closely couple activities (as with "concurrent engineering") and integrate functions.

It is important to recognize, however, that the emphasis in Chandler is on how to harness the capital intensive technologies in chemicals, steel, autos, etc. of the second industrial revolution. This was a somewhat different managerial challenge than is confronted by firms today as they deal with what might be called the third industrial revolution, driven by remarkable breakthroughs in microelectronics, biotechnology, and materials. The challenges are somewhat different, and the organizational forms suited to each may vary to some degree, and may also differ from those that were effective in the second revolution. Nevertheless, it is Chandler's thesis that the logic of managerial capitalism is timeless.

6.5. *Limits to the Logic of Managerial Capitalism*

A key question for all but business historians is whether this logic is now obsolete. In the final chapter of *Scale and Scope*, Chandler suggests that it is not, and in a related publication is quite explicit that "The passage of time has not made the logic of managerial enterprise obsolete" (p. 136). In the post World War II environment, Xerox is advanced as an example of a company that obtained its early dominance in copiers "through its massive investment in production, distribution, and management" (p. 610).[38] Similarly for IBM in mainframe computers. It was its massive investment in the IBM System 360 which enabled it to eclipse Sperry Rand, the industry's most successful

---

[37] Cooperation induced and facilitated by administrative processes and formal organization has received less theoretical attention than it deserves. Contributors include Chester Barnard (1938), Herbert Simon (1947), and Williamson (1990).

[38] Further hints as to where he might be going can be found in Chandler (1992a and b).

pioneer.[39] Likewise in personal computers, the first entrepreneurial firms to make substantial investments — Apple, Tandy (Radio Shack), and Commodore — by 1980 accounted for 68 percent of the dollar sales in the United States, a percentage which dropped dramatically lower a decade later.

The historical examples which Chandler advances to support his thesis are indeed compelling. He constantly reminds us that while the Englishman Perkin invented the first man-made dyes in the 1850s, 1860s, and 1870s, and British companies seemed to have all the raw materials at hand, it was German companies like Bayer, BASF, and Hoechst that took the lead because they were willing to invest big. Likewise in electrical equipment where the inventions of Thomas Edison spawned a new industry, one in which British firms like Mather and Platt were active early; it was nonetheless AEG and Siemens in Germany and G.E. and Westinghouse in the United States that captured the market. They made large-scale investments that brought them dominance by the end of the century — a dominance that proved durable for at least another half century.

But as Chandler recognizes, from about the 1960s on a new era of managerial capitalism may have been launched — a topic which he hints will be "the subject of another study" (p. 621). The changes Chandler identifies include proliferation of unrelated diversification strategies,[40] the isolation of top management, the opening up of the market for corporate control, and the expanded roles of pension funds in stock ownership. A key question that affects the utility of Chandler's work for observers of the contemporary scene is whether these and other changes suggest that the strategy Chandler advances — the three pronged investment — is simply a useful generalization about the past or whether it also holds for the present and the future.

In essence, Chandler's thesis is that large integrated enterprises, where free cash flows are carefully invested and coordinated to reduce price and assure

---

[39] Remington/Sperry Rand failed to make the financial commitment that was necessary and failed to commit the time of senior management to solve the problems that were involved in designing and manufacturing and marketing computer systems at that time. Moreover, Remington Rand's failure to support its computer business did not stem from a lack of available resources (Franklin Fisher, James McKie, and Richard Mancke 1983, p. 39).

[40] In Teece *et al.* (forthcoming) it is shown, using 1987 data on U.S. business establishments, that as U.S. firms grow more diverse, they maintain a constant level of coherence (relatedness) between neighboring activities. This finding runs counter to the idea that firms with many activities are generally more diversified. It suggests that, in general, as firms grow more diverse, they add activities that relate to some portion of existing activities. This is consistent with Chandler's notion of how firms generate scope economies. However, variability in the data suggests that at a point in time some firms may stray from the Chandler dicta. We predict that when they do, they are unlikely to be profitable and will eventually abandon unrelated diversification.

quality, are necessary to build and hold market share.[41] Taken literally and projected forward, it would suggest that "computerless" computer companies like Sun Microsystems and Dell Computer which outsource much of their manufacturing must have uncertain futures, unless they integrate, because their strategy has at most two of the necessary three prongs.[42] Certainly such firms have invested in product design, management control system, and in limited circumstances distribution; but generally they have only a modicum of manufacturing capabilities, outsourcing many components and subsystems. These companies have undoubtedly been successful, but it is also true that many have been around for barely a decade.

If the Chandler thesis is a little at odds with what seems to work for many U.S. companies today, perhaps it is in part because of the erosion in the relative skill base of the U.S. economy,[43] leaving U.S. firms from Apple (its Notebook computer is made by Sony) to Boeing (the 767 is co-produced with Aeritalia, Shorts, Kawasaki, I.H.I., ad Mitsubishi Heavy Industries) to Hewlett Packard (the engine in the Laserjet printer is made by Canon) little choice but to use components manufactured abroad. Perhaps it is because classical economies of scale and the unit price advantages can be accessed contractually in today's markets. Flexible specialization (Michael Piore and Charles Sable 1984) and contracting may today yield greater advantages than economies of scale and scope generated internally.

Indeed, it is arguably the case that firms that do not make the three pronged investment but instead simply build a capacity to manage a customer responsive network (e.g., Nike) can constitute a viable organizational form in today's global economy, with rapid diffusion of know-how and global dispersion of industrial competences. Raymond Miles has called such firms "network firms" and suggests that they may constitute a new organizational form.[44] If they are,

---

[41] Chandler's thesis would also appear to be somewhat at odds with his Harvard colleague Michael Jensen (1989) who argues that, at least in mature industries where long-term growth is slow and cash flow outstrips investment opportunities in traditional markets, the public corporation is an anachronism because discretion is capable of being misused by the managerial group Chandler sees as critical to economic development.

[42] This debate has been entered in a series of articles in the *Harvard Business Review*. See Anatol Rappaport and S. Halevi (1991).

[43] Certainly relative to other countries; possibly relative to its own recent past.

[44] See Miles and Charles Snow (1986). Several other writers have suggested that there may be a "post modern" successor to the modern corporation, one formulated partly in reaction to the ideal type of integrated Chandleresque corporation (see Thomas and Hughes 1990) and partly to adapt it to the realities of today's global marketplace (Gary Pisano and Teece 1988; Teece 1992). That marketplace would appear to require firms to master both information technologies and relationships with supplier networks seamlessly integrated with their customers networks so that the corporation would look almost boundaryless.

they are distinctly non-Chandleresque. Perhaps Chandler will address this and related phenomena by suggesting that professional managers today need to develop the information technologies and organizational systems to enable companies to achieve responsiveness and efficiency through seamless interaction with peers in different companies.

The logic of managerial enterprise that Chandler advances is also limited in that it is insensitive to the need to differentiate between the success of firms and the success of nation states.[45] Chandler implicitly correlates the two; this may in fact be more appropriate for the time period he has studied than it is today. But American firms in particular have in many instances unshackled themselves from their home base to quite significant degrees. It is not clear anymore whether IBM or Motorola ought be thought of as American companies, given the significant global dispersion in production, stock ownership, and the international composition of their professional managers. Such firms may to some degree be able to uncouple their success from that of the nation state in which they were once incubated. Companies that originated in Europe like Asea–Brown–Boveri (ABB), and in Japan like Honda, are likewise disconnected to varying degrees from their home base(s).

While further study is obviously required, the development of industrial capitalism in Japan — an unfortunate omission from *Scale and Scope* — would appear to support the Chandler thesis.[46] Industrial development in Japan began later than in Europe, but the form of industrial capitalism established there had much in common with what Chandler has called cooperative capitalism in Germany.[47] Unquestionably the Japanese companies have pursued the three pronged investments, with the only possible exception being domestic distribution, where fragmented systems are only now beginning to be displaced, sometimes by foreign firms like Toys-"Я" Us. Many Japanese companies, especially those

---

[45] Chandler seems to imply that the success of national enterprises and nation states are closely coupled. This has recently been challenged by many writers, most notably Robert Reich (1992, ch. 12).

[46] While cooperative elements were undoubtedly present in the prewar zaibatsu, it is also worthy of note that the Japanese zaibatsu were family-owned enterprise groups. In this sense,

> the personal management style unique to British companies cannot be explained solely on the basis of family structure. Family-run businesses in Britain produced personal management that obstructed the development of organizational capabilities, whereas in Japan the leadership of salaried managers checked family control and personal management, encouraging the growth of organizational capabilities. (Hidemasa Morikawa 1990, p. 722).

[47] Jurgen Kocka (1990, p. 715) believes that Japanese managerial capitalism was more cooperative than that of Germany.

manufacturing commodities, have relied on the trading companies to help them establish overseas markets. But integration, especially vertical integration, and the development of extensive managerial hierarchies is unquestionably a hallmark of Japanese capitalism which my colleague Michael Gerlack (1992) has labelled "Alliance Capitalism."

6.6. *Implications for the Theory of the Firm and Industrial Organization*

The logic of managerial capitalism Chandler identifies suggests a theory of firm and markets which is quite different from the standard textbook approaches. Although Chandler appears, until quite recently, to have been unaware of the importance of his work for industrial organization theory, the selection of the title *Scale and Scope*, employing words with loaded economic content, coupled with his recent self-conscious commentary on the subject in the *Journal of Economic Perspectives* (1992b), has thrust the issue center stage. Chandler (1992) identifies four different classes of theories of the firm — neoclassical principal agent, transaction cost, and evolutionary theory — and slots himself in the fourth category with dynamic capabilities lying at the heart of the theory. Chandler nowhere outlines a formal theory of the firm. Accordingly, this section merely identifies aspects of a theory of the firm and markets which *Scale and Scope* eschews, and that which it supports.[48]

With respect to markets, Chandler does not see adjustment processes working automatically; not does he see market structure being the determinant of economic performance as in the structure-conduct-performance paradigm (Scherer and Ross 1990, Fig. 1.1, p. 5). Rather managerial decisions and the style of capitalism (cooperative, personal, competitive) shape market outcomes. Firms on occasion, but not continuously, are seen as having choices; how those choices are made, moreover, may affect matters for decades. There is a strong path-dependent tone to many of Chandler's hypotheses and to his reported findings.

However, there is one area, the emphasis on scale and scope, where Chandler may appear conventional, but closer investigation indicates that he is definitely not. Chandler clearly recognizes the potential for scale and scope economies afforded by the second industrial revolution. But whereas neoclassical theory presents these economies as immediately available to all (absent intellectual

---

[48] A virtue of much of Chandler's historical analysis is that it is blissfully ignorant of many of the theoretical debates which exercise economists. But there is little doubt that Chandler's findings are cold water to neoclassical conceptualizations of firms and markets.

property protection) and attainable by all (absent government interference), Chandler sees the availability and attainability of these economies constrained not by the size of the market (the usual explanation) but by the nature of managerial structures and systems and the investment capabilities represented by the three pronged investment. Put starkly, Chandler appears to view the cost curves suggested by the technology as figments of the economist's mind, as their realization requires a set of supporting infrastructures, organizations, and firm-level strategies.[49] Economies of scale and scope requires *coordination* and *control* of complex production and distribution activities. Contemporary advocates of "lean" production systems (Womack, Jones, and Roos 1990) echo much Chandleresque language when they suggest that efficiency requires control of throughputs.

Chandler stresses that it was the differential ability of firms to integrate and coordinate through the three pronged investment which defined their competitive advantage.

> The potential economies of scale and scope, as measured by rated capacity, are the physical characteristics of the production facilities. The actual economies of scale or scope, as determined by throughput, are organizational. Such economies depend on knowledge, skill, experience, and teamwork. (p. 24)

In this passage Chandler sounds more like Chester Barnard than Alfred Marshall; his analysis suggests that the apparatus of conventional micro theory is seriously wanting if one is to address issues of competitiveness in the global economy then or now. It is for these reasons that there is little merit in challenging Chandler with respect to the exact shape and position of the cost curves which the second industrial revolution afforded (see Scherer 1990).[50] Chandler's response would undoubtedly be that a firm's costs, then and now, depend on much more than the available technology.[51] Contemporary evidence (Womack, Jones, and Roos 1990;

---

[49] Put differently, absent well functioning managerial systems and structures, one should not have confidence that firms operate on or near the least cost position which the available technology permits.

[50] Scherer's arguments may be somewhat more correct for petroleum than for other industries. But the two-thirds rule he refers to is an engineering rule and Chandler explicitly disavows engineering relationships as being determinative of the scope and scale economies actually achieved (p. 24). Scherer's (p. 696) diagrammatic representation of the Chandler thesis is simply incorrect as Chandler's main point about organizations is omitted.

[51] It also depends on forms of organization that require invention or discovery and on investment to put the organization in place.

David Garvin 1988; Kim Clark and Takahiro Fujimoto 1991) would seem to support this position.[52]

If the conventional production function view of the firm embedded in microeconomic theory is unsatisfactory, what does *Scale and Scope* suggest might be more helpful? As mentioned above, Chandler has no formal theory of the firm to offer as an alternative. However, he has recently suggested the relevance of preliminary work in business strategy, organization theory, and industrial organization which is attempting to grapple with the concept of dynamic capabilities. Bits and pieces of an alternative theory can be found in Penrose (1959), Nelson and Winter (1982), Teece (1980, 1982, 1992), Teece, Pisano, and Shuen (1992), and Teece *et al.* (forthcoming). In essence, firms are seen as organizations that are quite distinct from markets, where administrative processes displace market processes, and where both formal and informal organizational structures guide resource allocation and organizational behavior. Firms consist of bundles of generally nontradable firm-specific assets. Firms are heterogeneous with respect to these assets; asset endowments are specific and hence sticky, at least in the short run if not much longer. Firms also lack the organizational capacity to develop new assets quickly; tradability is limited by tacitness. The profitable expansion of firms is both a process of exploiting firm-specific capabilities and developing new ones.

The essence of differences between firms are their differential abilities to achieve organizational coordination (Masahiko Aoki 1990). The essential question is "why the costs of organizing particular activities differs among firms" (Ronald Coase 1988, p. 47). The answers depend on (1) how the firm learns new

---

[52] There is considerable field-based empirical research which provides support for the notion that coordinative capabilities are the source of differences in firms' economies and competences in various domains. Garvin's (1988) study of 18 room air conditioning plants reveals that quality performance was not related to either capital investment or the degree of automation of the facilities. Instead, quality performance was driven by organizational routines that influenced coordination in some way. These included routines for gathering and processing information, for linking customer, experiences with engineering design choices, and for coordinating factories and component suppliers. The work of Clark and Fujimoto (1991) on project development in the automobile industry also illustrates the role played by coordinative routines. Their study reveals a significant degree of variation in how different firms coordinate the various activities required to bring a new model from concept to market. These differences in coordinative routines and capabilities seem to have a significant impact on such performance variables as development cost, development lead times, and quality. Furthermore, they tended to find significant firm-level differences in coordination routines, and these differences seemed to have persisted for a long time. This suggest that routines related to coordination are firm specific in nature, and that technological relationships are not at all determinative of competitive position.

skills; (2) the forces, both internal and external, to the firm which constrain and focus the learning process; and (3) the selection environment in which the firm competes for resources as well as customers. Elaboration of these factors can be found elsewhere (see Teece *et al.* forthcoming). Developments in the evolutionary theory of the firm and what Williamson (1990b) calls the "incipient science of organizations" will, as we learn more, enable new intellectual structures to be shaped that will permit a more robust understanding of firms to evolve. Chandler's *Scale and Scope* suggest the directions of profitable lines of inquiry.

7. Parallels and Contrasts with Gerschenkron and Schumpeter

The history Chandler has to tell carries forward in some places and challenges in others the theories of economic development put forward by Alexander Gerschenkron and Joseph Schumpeter. Identifying the parallels and contrasts with these authors also enable one to question whether Chandler's thesis is truly original, whether he has gotten mileage out of his comparative approach, and whether his focus on firms provides new insights.

Gerschenkron's "main proposition" is that industrialization processes, when launched in backward countries, showed considerable differences, as compared with more advanced countries, not only with regard to the speed of development but also with regard to the productive and organizational and financial structures of industry by means of which the development took place. Furthermore, these differences in the speed and character of industrial development were to a considerable extent the result of application of institutional instruments for which there was little or no counterpart in countries that began their industrialization earlier (Gerschenkron 1962, p. 7).[53]

A subsidiary proposition in Gerschenkron is that economic development is often triggered by discontinuities and indivisibilities. In characterizing nineteenth century Europe, Gerschenkron (p. 11) claims

---

[53] Thus Gerschenkron notes that the industrailization of England has proceeded without any substantial utilization of banking for long-term investment purposes because the more gradual accumulation of capital from trade and agriculture obviated the need for the creation of special institutional devices for provision of long-term capital to industry. In contrast, continental Europe, including Germany, which entered the process of modern industralization later, when the prevailing technology had become more scale-intensive and capital-intensive, required banks to amass the necessary capital. The banks in turn helped shape the structure of industry and, in the case of Germany, gave momentum to the cartel movement (pp. 14–15), thereby causing the German industrial economy to develop along lines different from England's.

that only when industrial development could commence on a large scale did the tension between pre-industrialization conditions and the benefits expected from industrialization become sufficiently strong to overcome the existing obstacles and to liberate the forces that made for industrial progress.

A corollary is that, as with Russia, significant state involvement may be necessary in countries which have remained especially backward.

There is no doubt that Chandler's treatment of industrial development in the United States, Great Britain, and Germany is sympathetic to the Gerschenkronian metaphor.[54] Certainly he documents significant differences both in the styles of capitalism that emerged, and in the preconditions which characterized each economy. Business was molded differently by differing prevailing structures and prevailing conditions in each economy. Personal capitalism in Britain, in Chandler's view, was a natural consequence of the existing class structure and the distribution of wealth and favor which characterized British society. The tight geography and limited population of the British Isles limited the scope for multiplant firms. The fact that the railways were already built attenuated the need to adopt the Bessemer open hearth processes in the steel industry. In Germany, the banks played a larger role than in the United States and Britain because of the absence of organized capital markets and the much larger scale required for efficient operation by the time industrialization got underway in Germany.[55] The absence of antitrust law and the legality of contracts to restrict commerce attentuated the need for merger, which in turn reduced opportunities for industry wide reorganizations.

While recognizing these differences, Chandler nevertheless implies that they mattered little as compared to the willingness and ability of managers to pursue the three pronged strategy. Indeed, in Britain success was attainted by firms like ICI, Unilever, and British Petroleum when they pursued this strategy. Likewise in Germany and the United States.

The key point that needs to be made is that the Chandler thesis, while having Gerschenkronian overtones, is quite distinct from it, and an advance over it. Chandler points out that the success of firms is often substantially disconnected from the home base; moreover, the development of firms is not simply a microcosm

---

[54] Yet there are points of difference. Gerschenkron emphasized social background, political tradition, and a sense of temporal characteristics of technology at various periods of industrailization; he had basically nothing to say about the role of management and business organization.

[55] For a discussion of finance and the development of firms, see Mowery (1992) and Bruce Greenwald and Joseph Stiglitz (1992).

of the development of the nation state. In Chandler's view, the wealth of nations depends on the development of organizational capabilities. Gerschenkron and other historians rarely looked at organizational capabilities and the successes and failures of national firms; Chandler suggests they should have done, because it would have brought into focus the development of organizational capabilities essential for business development, and for industrial development more generally. If Gerschenkron has provided the covers and the preface for a book on the organizational aspect of economic development, Chandler has begun to write the chapters.

There is also much in common with the Schumpeter of *Capitalism, Socialism, and Democracy* (1942). There are also important points of departure. Like Schumpeter, Chandler sees large industrial firms as being important to the industrial development from the late 19th century onward. While they both have in common a managerially administered view of industrial development in which large hierarchial organizations are innovative and efficient, Schumpeter's concept of a competitive economy where new combinations mean the "competitive elimination of the old" receives little attention in Chandler (see Schumpeter 1934, pp. 66–67). This may stem in part from Chandler's focus on intraindustry rather than interindustry competition; the incumbency effects Chandler documents and which provide his backdrop are softened when one recognizes that the industrial categories he examines are expanding (and sometimes shrinking) at rates that are impacted considerably by differences between groupings in rates of innovation and concomitant cost reduction and demand growth. However, Chandler's main contribution to the Schumpeterian literature is his development of the distinction between a firm's capacity to "innovate," which includes a capacity to build an organization appropriate to the new product or process and a capacity to build market share.[56] Chandler's thesis, while also advanced elsewhere,[57] is an important elaboration of the Schumpeterian framework, and one which will require subsequent researchers to take a much more microanalytic approach to questions of industrial success. In a sense, Chandler has perhaps begun to give a substance to what Schumpeter had in mind when he referred to innovation as involving "new combinations."

---

[56] One interpretation of Chandler is that he is exploring the firm level analogue of what Abramovitz has referred to as "social capability," by which he seems to mean the intangible infrastructure necessary to support the adoption of advanced technology (Abramovitz 1991).

[57] See Teece (1986) where a framework is outlined which shows how ownership of complementary assets, standards, and the intellectual property condition work together to determine whether innovators or followers are more likely to end up with the largest market share.

8. Conclusion

Scale and Scope, together with Chandler's earlier writings, gives us the best single consistent set of accounts we have of the business organization side of the development of industrial capitalism, and in particular the rise of large firms. These materials, based on careful archival research as well as secondary sources, have to be studied seriously by all interested in industrial organization, economic growth, and development. In *Scale and Scope* Chandler has for the first time focused on the comparative histories of firms in the three most significant countries leading the second industrial revolution. While much business history is arid, Chandler's is not only easy reading but provocative to economists because it is clear that Chandler is writing rather self-consciously about the wealth of nations. His analysis is rich in institutional detail, but shaped by a commanding thesis that the business firm and its managers are not merely reacting to broader technological and market forces; rather they are shaping technological development and market outcomes. Firms are not simply agents of the market; rather, markets are also agents of the firm. Markets simply cannot be understood without an understanding of firm's strategies and structures. This is Chandler's argument.

While Chandler does not set out to be provocative to economists — indeed, he is quite oblivious to most of the tenets of the discipline — he has provided a fundamental challenge to the modes of analysis and implicit assumptions that economists commonly employ. Chandler can be challenged but he cannot be ignored by economists and others concerned with economic growth and industrial organization. Unlike many institution-free studies of industrial organization and

---

[58] Many macroeconomists are of the view that the problems of U.S. competitiveness are essentially problems of macro policy. Robert Lawrence (1984) is a good example of the mainstream belief that if the United States gets its macro policy right, competitiveness will automatically be restored, since the erosion of U.S. competitiveness is simply misdirected market forces. *Scale and Scope* suggests that while macro policy matters, it is the building of organizational capabilities that are essential. Traditional macro policy remedies focusing on monetary and fiscal policy do not suffice. Industrial development requires the long-term commitment of resources, coordination of interdependent activities, education of the labor force, and enhanced rates of organizational learning. Whether private enterprise alone can create these organizational conditions is not addressed by Chandler. Clearly, cooperative strategies can assist Thomas Jorde and Teece 1992). However, as Mancur Olson (1982) suggests, an "upheaval" may be necessary to break the intellectual, social, and political rigidities that impede the organizational transformation necessary for the United States to regain its competitiveness. Chandler's sagacious comparative business history can be seen as an important contribution toward building a better understanding of the wealth of nations.

economic growth, *Scale and Scope* argues that firm-level strategies and structures are of great importance. Economists and historians must take this work seriously; it is trenchant scholarship which challenges much of the orthodox diagnosis of the fundamental economic questions of our time.[58]

References

Moses Abramovitz, The Elements of Social Capability, unpublished manuscript, Department of Economics, Stanford University, 1991.

Masahiko Aoki, Rents and the Theory of the Firm, in Aoki Masahiko, Bo Gustafsson and Oliver E. Williamson (eds.), *The Firm as a Nexus of Treaties* (Sage, London, 1990).

Chester I. Barnard, *The Functions of the Executive* (Harvard University Press, Cambridge, 1938).

_____, *The Functions of the Executive* (Harvard University Press, Cambridge, 1962).

Dennis W. Carlton and Jeffery M. Perloff, *Modern Industrial Organization* (Scott, Foresman, Glenview, IL, 1990).

Alfred D. Chandler, *Strategy and Structure: Chapters in the History of the Industrial Enterprise* (MIT Press, Cambridge, MA, 1962).

_____, The Enduring Logic of Industrial Success, *Harvard Business Review* 90(2) (March–April 1990a), 130–140.

_____, Corporate Strategy, Structure and Control Methods in the United States During the 20th Century, *Industrial and Corporate Change* 1(2) (1992a), 263–284.

_____, Organizational Capabilities and the Economic History of the Industrial Enterprise, *Journal of Economic Perspectives* 6(3) (Summer 1992b), 79–100.

Roy Church, The Limitations of the Personal Capitalism Paradigm, *Business History Review* 64(4) (Winter 1990), 703–710.

Kim B. Clark and Takahiro Fujimoto, *Product Development Performance: Strategy, Organization, and Management in the World Auto Industries* (Harvard Business School Press, Cambridge, 1991).

Ronald H. Coase, The Nature of the Firm: Influence, *Journal of Law, Economics and Organization* 4(1) (Spring 1988), 33–47.

Bernard Elbaum and William Lazonick (eds.), *The Decline of the British Economy* (Clarendon Press, Oxford, 1986).

Franklin M. Fisher, James W. McKie and Richard B. Mancke, *IBM and the U.S. Data Processing Industry: An Economic History* (Praeger, New York, 1983).

David A. Garvin, *Managing Quality* (Free Press, New York, 1988).

Michael Gerlach, *Alliance Capitalism: The Social Organization of Japanese Business* (University of California Press, Berkeley, 1992).

Alexander Gerschenkron, *Economic Backwardness in Historical Perspective* (Harvard University Press, Cambridge, 1962).

Bruce Greenwald and Joseph E. Stiglitz, Information, Finance, and Markets: The Architecture of Allocative Mechanisms, *Industrial and Corporate Change* 1 (1992), 37–65.

David A. Hounshell, Continuity and Change in the Management of Industrial Research: The DuPont Company 1902–1980, in Giovanni Dose, Renato Glanetti and Pier Angelo Toninelli (eds.), *Technology and Enterprise in a Historical Perspective* (Clarendon Press, Oxford, 1992).

Thomas Hughes, Managerial Capitalism Beyond the Firm, *Business History Review* 64(4) (Winter 1990), 698–703.

Michael C. Jensen, Eclipse of the Public Corporation, *Harvard Business Review* 89(5) (September–October 1989), 61–74.

Thomas M. Jorde and David J. Teece, *Antitrust, Innovation, and Competitiveness* (Oxford University Press, New York, 1992).

Jurgen Kocka, Germany: Cooperation and Competition, *Business History Review* 64(4) (Winter 1990), 711–716.

Ralph Landau, Academic Industrial Interaction in the Early Development of Chemical Engineering at MIT, *Advances in Chemical Engineering* 16 (1991), 41–49.

David S. Landes, *The Unbound Prometheus: Technological Change and Industrial Development in Western Europe from 1750 to the Present* (Cambridge University Press, Cambridge, 1969).

Robert Z. Lawrence, *Can America Compete?* (Brookings Institution, Washington, DC, 1984).

William Lazonick, Industrail Organization and Technological Change: The Decline of the British Cotton Industry, *Business History Review* 57(2) (Summer 1983), 195–236.

W. Arthur Lewis, International Competition in Manufactures, *American Economic Review* 47(2) (May 1957), 578–587.

Donald N. McCloskey, *Enterprise and Trade in Victorian Britain: Essays in Historical Economics* (Allen and Unwin, London, 1981).

Raymond E. Miles and Charles C. Snow, Organizations: New Concepts for New Forms, *California Management Review* 28(3) (Spring 1986), 62–73.

John Stuart Mill, Principles of Political Economy, in John N. Robson (ed.), *The Collected Works of John Stuart Mill*, Vols. 2 & 3 (University of Toronto Press, Toronto, 1965).

Hidemasa Morikawa, The View from Japan, *Business History Review* 64(4) (Winter 1990), 716–725.

David C. Mowery, Finance and Corporate Evolution in Five Industrial Economies, 1990–1950, *Industrial and Corporate Change* 1 (1992), 1–36.

Richard R. Nelson, Why do Firms Differ, and How does it Matter? *Strategic Management Journal*, Special Issue, 12 (1991), 61–74.

Richard R. Nelson and Sidney G. Winter, *An Evolutionary Theory of Economic Change* (Harvard University Press, Cambridge, 1982).

Mancur Olson, *The Rise and Decline of Nations* (Yale University Press, New Haven, CT, 1982).

Edith Penrose, *The Theory of the Growth of the Firm* (John Wiley, New York, 1959).

Thomas J. Peters and Robert H. Waterman, *In Search of Excellence* (Harper and Row, New York, 1982).

Gary Pisano and David J. Teece, Collaborative Arrangements and Global Technology Transfer, in Robert A. Burgelman and Richard S. Rosenbloom (eds.), *Technology, Competitive, and Organization Theory* (MIT Press, Cambridge, MA, 1988).

Anatol S. Rappaport and S. Halevi, The Computerless Computer Company, *Harvard Business Review* 69 (July–August 1991), 69–81.

Robert B. Reich, *The Work of Nations* (Vintage Books, New York, 1992).

Richard P. Rumelt, Dan E. Schendel and David J. Teece, Strategic Management and Economics, *Strategic Management Journal*, Special Issue, 12 (1991), 5–29.

Frederic M. Scherer, *Industrial Market Structure and Economic Performance*, 2nd ed. (Rand-McNally, Chicago, 1980).

Frederic M. Scherer and David Ross, *Industrial Market Structure and Economic Performance*, 3rd ed. (Houghton Mifflin, Boston, 1990).

Joseph A. Schumpeter, *The Theory of Economic Development* (Harvard University Press, Cambridge, MA, 1934).

_____, *Capitalism, Socialism, and Democracy* (Harper and Row, New York, 1942).

Herbert Simon, *Administrative Behavior*, 2nd ed. (Macmillan, New York [1947], 1961).

David J. Teece, Technology Transfer by Multinational Firms: The Resource Cost of Transferring Technological Know-How, *Economic Journal* 87(346) (June 1977), 242–261.

_____, Economies of Scope and the Scope of an Enterprise, *Journal of Economic Behavior and Organization* 1(3) (September 1980), 233–247.

_____, Towards an Economic Theory of the Multiproduct Firm, *Journal of Economic Behavior Organization* 3(1) (March 1982), 39–63.

_____, Profiting from Technological Innovation, *Research Policy* 15 (1986), 286–305.

_____, Competition, Cooperation, and Innovation: Organizational Arrangements for Regimes of Rapid Technological Progress, *Journal of Economic Behavior Organization* 18(1) (June 1992), 1–25.

David J. Teece *et al.*, Understanding Corporate Coherence: Theory and Evidence, *Journal of Economic Behavior Organization*, forthcoming.

David J. Teece *et al.*, Dynamic Capabilities and Strategic Management, *Strategic Management Journal*, forthcoming.

Jean Tirole, *The Theory of Industrial Organization* (MIT Press, Cambridge, MA, 1988).

Thorstein Veblen, *Imperial Germany and the Industrial Revolution* (Macmillan, New York, 1915).

Jacob Viner, Cost Curves and Supply Curves, *Z. Nationalökon.* 3 (September 1931), 23–46; in George J. Stigler and Kenneth Boulding (eds.), *Readings in Price Theory* (Irwin, Homewood, IL, 1952).

Oliver E. Williamson, *Markets and Hierarchies* (Free Press, New York, 1975).

_____, *The Economic Institutions of Capitalism* (Free Press, New York, 1985).

_____, *Organization Theory* (Oxford University Press, New York, 1990a).

_____, Chester Barnard and the Incipient Science of Organization, in Oliver E. Williamson (ed.), *Organization Theory* (Oxford University Press, New York, 1990b).

James P. Womack, Daniel T. Jones and Daniel Roos, *The Machine that Changed the World* (Macmillan, New York, 1990).